3

ALSO BY RM JOHNSON

The Harris Men

FATHER FOUND

RM JOHNSON

Simon & Schuster

New York   London   Toronto   Sydney   Singapore

SIMON & SCHUSTER
Rockefeller Center
1230 Avenue of the Americas
New York, NY 10020

SIMON & SCHUSTER and colophon are registered trademarks
of Simon & Schuster, Inc.

Designed by Jeanette Olender
Manufactured in the United States of America

10 9 8 7 6 5 4 3 2 1

Library of Congress Cataloging-in-Publication Data
Johnson, R. M. (Rodney Marcus)
Father found / R.M. Johnson.
p. cm.
1. Birthfathers—Identification—Fiction. 2. Fathers and sons—Fiction.
I. Title.
PS3560.O3834 F38 2000
813'.54—dc21   99-055720
ISBN 0-684-84471-0

ACKNOWLEDGMENTS

First I must continue to thank my friend, colleague, and mentor, E. Lynn Harris, and his Better Days Foundation, for his undying support and interest in my work. Thanks go to my agent, J. Warren Frazier, for his care and attention. I hope this is the beginning of a lifelong relationship. You're a great agent! Thanks to my editor, Geoff Kloske, and his assistant editor, Nicole Graev. Your contributions have been invaluable to the betterment of this work. To Sybil Wilks and Yolanda Starks, two wonderful women whom I can't thank enough for taking an interest in my last novel. To Darryl Roberts, writer, director, and good friend: I see great things ahead for us. To Randy Crumpton: Much success in the future, and whoever gets there first, bring the other along. To all the other industry people and booksellers, thanks go to you as well.

Thanks to all my friends for your support and kindness.

And to my family, the bottomless well from which I draw my strength, courage, and perseverance: I am forever grateful to all of you.

For the children
whose innocence
has been stolen

FATHER FOUND

CHAPTER ONE

It was dark and late, and Zale's body was telling him to go home, but his mind, his heart was telling him to continue the walk through this poor, run-down neighborhood. He would continue the walk, at least a little farther, and if he didn't find what he was looking for, he would turn around and go home.

One block to go, he told himself as he passed under a dim circle of light from a streetlamp above. He stopped, pulled the collar of his trench up around his ears in a weak attempt to defend against the soft rain that started to fall on his head. He began walking again, then halted, seeing something, not twenty feet ahead, and he already knew what it was without taking another step. He walked up to it, standing just over it, shaking his head sympathetically. It was a body lying across a soggy cardboard box, rolled up in a blanket. Zale knelt down over the end that he figured to be the head.

"Excuse me," Zale said softly. There was no response, just the faint sound of unrestful sleeping.

"You awake?" Zale said, then gave the lump a finger stick in the area where he thought his ribs would be.

There was a stir under the blanket for a moment, then nothing.

"Hey, you awake under there?" Zale put his hand on what he assumed was the shoulder and gave the person a shake.

Immediately, the body under the cover sprang up, whipping the blanket from over his head, his body retreating backward, sliding across the ground on hands and feet, like a human crab. He was shocked to have been awakened like that. He looked as though he thought he would be shot.

"Who are you? What you messin' with me for?" It was a boy, like Zale hoped it wouldn't have been, but expected it to be. A boy of maybe fifteen, if he was lucky, and Zale only gave him that much age because of the dirt that was smeared across his face, resembling facial hair.

"No, no, don't," Zale said, both his arms out, his palms showing, an attempt to show the boy he had no weapon. "I don't want to hurt you. I was just walking by."

"Then why did you wake me up?" the boy said. He was pushed up against the wall of a building now, his blanket up over his chin, a protective shield against evil.

"Did you know it's raining, you shouldn't be—"

"I know it's raining," the boy said sharply. "What am I supposed to do, make it stop so I can go to sleep?"

"No. I know you can't do that, but you'll catch pneumonia out here."

"Aw, man," the boy said sarcastically, the blanket lowering. "What was I thinking about. Let me go up to my hotel suite where it's nice and dry, so I won't get sick."

"That's not what I'm saying," Zale said, almost apologetically.

"Then what are you saying? What do you want?"

"Look, you shouldn't sleep out here. Have you eaten? Let me take you somewhere to eat, and then you bunk out at my place tonight."

"I'm not doing you," the boy said.

"What?"

"I don't do that. I ain't no punk pleaser, you fucking pervert!" The boy started to roll his blanket up in a ball, getting up as he did.

"What?" Zale said, then finally understanding what he meant, said, "No! No! I'm not like that. I just want you out of the cold. I'm trying to help you." Zale reached into his trench. The boy jumped.

"I'm just getting my card." He pulled out his card and reached out for the boy to take it. The boy hesitated a moment, then plucked the card from the man's hand.

It was one of Zale's business cards. It read "Zaleford Rowen, President, Father Found."

"And, so what? Who are you supposed to be?" the boy said, pulling his eyes away from the card.

"Zale Rowen, like the card says. Where is your father?" Zale asked without explanation.

The boy looked thrown by the question.

"Where is your father? Does he live with your mother? Do you live with her? Do you live at home?" Zale stopped to slow things down, reading the lost look on the boy's face. "First, what is your name?"

"Billy."

"Well, Billy, I have an organization, and we try to find fathers that have abandoned their children and reunite them with those children."

Zale tried to read the boy's eyes, tried to decipher his expression to see if he was following along, and if Billy even believed what Zale was saying, but he saw nothing but dirt and shadows on the boy's young, white face.

"Does your father live with you?"

"Look around, do you see him?" Billy said, examining the ground around him.

"I mean, did he live at the home you left?"

"My old man left a long time ago. Ten years maybe, I forget. But it doesn't make a difference. I'm out here now, and this is where I'm going to stay, so if you'd just leave me alone so I can get back to sleep," Billy said, offering the card back to Zale.

"Come with me so we can at least get you something to eat." Zale extended his hand. "I'm buying, and I don't want anything from you. I promise."

It looked as though Billy was giving it some serious thought, but then he declined. "Naw, I don't want to. I'm fine right here. I'm fine."

Zale slid a ten and a five-dollar bill out of his wallet and held them out to Billy. The boy snatched the money out of Zale's hand like a wild dog snapping up a piece of meat from a stranger. Billy held out the card again.

"Keep it, please. I want you to call me sometime. Will you do that?"

Billy stood there watching Zale, the blanket balled up in his arms, the pestering drizzle still falling on both their heads.

Billy nodded his head.

"Will you promise me?"

"Yeah, I promise."

Zale gave the boy a long look, worried about what he would do for the rest of the night, for the rest of his life, for that matter. He wanted to get him home, get him some warm food, and find this man-child's father so someone could start taking responsibility for him. But he knew Billy wouldn't let him. The boy had either seen or heard too many horror stories to walk anywhere with a perfect stranger at past one o'clock in the morning, and Zale couldn't really blame him.

Zale turned around and headed back for home. After a number of paces, Zale heard the boy calling him.

"Mr. Rowen!" Zale turned around, barely seeing the figure in the darkness and mist.

"Thanks for the money. I really need it," Zale heard him call.

"Don't mention it," Zale called back, feeling a pang of sadness in his heart. "But I want to hear from you," he called in a louder voice, but something told him that that was the last he would ever see of Billy.

Zale planned on heading home, planned on finally crawling through the door of his house, lumbering up his stairs and falling into his bed without even first taking off his clothes or his coat, just letting himself drop, a small border of moisture forming around his body, the sheets and blankets absorbing the rain from his damp clothes. But he didn't do that, even though he was so tired that he could barely keep his eyes open or the car from swerving now and then on the slick street. He guided the automobile toward the building where he worked, and parked on a slant. He was led there almost subconsciously, like a lost dog finding its way home on senses alone.

He opened the door of his car, almost tripped up the high curb of the street, and stood in front of the building that housed the Father Found organization.

It was an old two-story building that used to be a store of some sort but had gone out of business, boarded up like so many of the other buildings that lined the streets of the South Side of Chicago. These were businesses opened up by African Americans, but without the support of African Americans, so they ultimately failed.

After the owners no longer wanted to invest in it, the building was bought by a real estate company, refurbished, and put up for sale. It wasn't that much money, so Zale decided to start his organization there. It was actually the perfect place, in the heart of the city, where many of the people were deprived of the opportunity to work, to earn

money, to live a decent life. Because of that, this was where a high oc-
currence of child abandonment took place.

Zale entered the building, exhausted, and walked the creaking steps
to the second floor where his office was located. He went in, spun his
chair around and sat behind his desk. It was dark, for he had not bothered turning on the lights. Splotches of light came in through the windows of his office from the streetlights outside. He stretched his arms
out on the desk, placed his head on top of them, and blew out a long,
exhausting breath. Finally, rest of some sort. He could not remember
the last time that he had relaxed. It seemed like days, and he knew for
sure that it had been at least one full day and a half since he closed his
eyes. Thirty-six hours he had been running and working, trying to accomplish this and find out that, and his body was weary, his muscles
weak, and his mind seemed to be fraying at the edges. He realized he
should've just taken himself home and gone to sleep, but he didn't.

He wanted to, but he couldn't. His conscience wouldn't let him.
Billy was still on his mind, and he looked over at the phone that sat not
six inches from his elbow. He hoped it would ring, that Billy would tell
him he wanted shelter for the night, that he was tired of being on the
street, but Zale knew that wouldn't happen. He knew it wouldn't because that wasn't how things happened in his business.

Zale kept telling himself that he had to get up, he had to work, do
something, and there were so many things: cross-check the list of fathers Father Found had contacted who had gone home and stayed
there against the list that had gone home and left already, or had not
gone home at all. There were fathers who were in trouble with the law,
on the verge of going to jail, and there were people Zale could talk to
to try and keep these men out of the system under the condition their
offense wasn't too bad and they promised to remain with the child and
its mother. At this moment, Zale could be pulling those names. There
were also jobs Zale needed to locate for the men who used unemploy-
ment as an excuse for not being responsible. He needed to get on the
Net and do that, and while he was there, get the names and requirements for a number of the drug abuse houses, for every now and then
drug addiction was a problem he would encounter with these men.
The monthly national list of "deadbeat dads" had just arrived at his office, and he hadn't scanned across it yet to find out how many of these

men were local, so he could start their files, and get the ball rolling on them. There were so many things he could be doing, should be doing, because even though it was after two in the morning, that didn't mean kids who should've been with their families weren't walking the streets. He had to work.

"But I'll just sleep for five minutes," he said to himself, his voice filled with exhaustion, barely able to complete the sentence before falling off into a deep, much needed slumber.

Seven hours later, Zale sat bolt upright in his chair, his eyes bulging, sweat covering his face, breathing as though he had just run up several flights of stairs. He looked quickly around the office, orienting himself. It was another nightmare, he told himself, angry that he was still having them. Still, after so many years.

The sun was shining through his windows, and he winced against the light as he looked down at his watch. It read 9:30.

He wiped the sleep from his eyes, then reached for his phone and checked his voice mail, hoping that maybe Billy had called, and that he had just slept through the ringing, since he was so tired. But the boy hadn't—there were no messages.

When Zale got home half an hour later, he bent down and picked up the thick Sunday paper, then slid his key into the door, stepping into his house. He dropped his things on a nearby table and climbed the stairs to his bedroom, taking off his shirt and tie. He went into the bathroom, clicked on the light, and stared at himself in the mirror. He didn't like what he saw. He looked bad. Dark circles hung under his eyes, as if he had been socked repeatedly by a large man with big fists. His face was getting thin, his body deteriorating as if he was on some sort of hunger strike, and he knew his awful appearance could be attributed to the fact that he had not been sleeping or eating properly.

He slid his medicine cabinet open and reached for the short, fat, round prescription bottle with the childproof cap. He remembered his doctor giving him the prescription for the blood pressure medication, just after he founded his organization and started experiencing minor health problems: headaches, nausea, stress, and tension-filled muscles.

"I want you to take these, one every day, and take them religiously," the older woman had said, looking over her glasses like a schoolteacher addressing her third-grader. "Unless there is a major change in your lifestyle, these are going to be a permanent addition to your life."

But he wasn't going to live like that, Zale thought, as he looked down at the bottle in his hand. He considered not taking the pill, then after some thought, decided he would, popping one in his mouth, and swallowing it with water that he cupped in his hands from the running faucet. He'd take it this time, only because he hadn't taken one in two days and it'd probably be another two or three till he saw the bottle again. He wouldn't carry bottles of pills around everywhere he went, his pockets rattling with the things as if he were seventy-five years old when he was forty years from that. Besides, his problems, his stress, his fears, he'd have to eventually solve himself. No drug would do it for him.

He walked back downstairs to the kitchen and made himself a cup of coffee, black, no sugar, no cream. He sat down, opened up the Sunday paper and thumbed through the sections, occasionally taking a sip of the coffee, wincing a little at its bitter taste.

Zale avoided most of the paper, not wanting to read about all the violence, the stores that got robbed, the baby that got thrown out of a window, or the kid that was found in the alley, a long, bloody smile carved in his neck. He especially didn't want to hear about that, because every time it happened, he felt responsible. Even if only a little bit, he still felt as though he were to blame. If he had only done more, he would tell himself, or done just that one thing that would've made a difference, could've gotten that child off the street, like maybe finding the child's father faster, and convincing him that his kid would be next on the butcher's list. But it seemed he was always too late, and all Zale could do was turn a deaf ear to the news, mourn for a brief moment, and try to convince himself that it was not his fault.

He pulled the brightly colored comics out of the fat of the paper and looked them over. A couple of them were clever enough to get a chuckle out of Zale, but for the most part, they were corny, and dry.

He thumbed further through the paper, bypassing the coupons, the sales inserts, and the theater section. Then he stopped, his attention grabbed. He went back and pulled out the Sunday magazine. He held it in front of his face with both hands, staring at it, and what stared back was an image of himself. He was on the cover. He had forgotten that the interview he gave would be in this week's paper. As a matter of fact, he had forgotten all about the interview the moment it was over.

He brought the magazine closer to him. The photo was a close-up, and how he hated close-ups. He hated photos of himself period. They never got the color right, always making him look a shade or two lighter than he was, as if he didn't have enough problems just being a light-skinned black man. He was only thirty-five, but these photos always made him look older. The makeup they used was supposed to make his skin look flawless, but it just made him look as if he were ready for viewing by family and loved ones. But what was worse was the look in his eyes. There was an intensity in them, a purpose that a blind man could see. A look of unswerving direction and suppressed anger that would probably scare most people into thinking that he was some sort of fanatic who stayed awake around the clock and infused coffee into his veins, just to afford himself the time to search for abandoning fathers. Zale glanced down at his coffee mug and pushed it aside with a nudge of his elbow.

The truth was, he was just dedicated, but no one understood that, so he never tried explaining it.

Across the top of the magazine, just under the title, he read, "Zaleford Rowen—Friend or Foe?" As if he were a politician running for office, kissing babies, yet possessing the potential to turn around and stab the infants with the same hand he used to shake the parents' hands.

Zale opened up the thin sheets of the magazine and examined them. He took his usual no-nonsense, nonsympathetic "I don't want to hear any excuses" standpoint on the issue of fathers leaving their children to suffer and grow up alone. "There are no excuses!" Zale remembered saying to the young man who interviewed him. "These men thought enough to lay down and have sex, then they should think enough to care for the child they helped bring into this world. Their financial situations, their feelings as to whether or not they'd make an adequate father, or how they feel about having to raise a child when they'd rather be doing so many other things has nothing to do with that child. To put it plainly, the child is innocent, and the father is guilty. So guilty that he should be jailed. Jailed for as long as it takes for that child to grow up and be able to provide for himself."

The interviewer stopped writing and looked up at Zale. "So you're saying these fathers should be punished somehow for abandoning their children?"

"No, not somehow. They should be jailed, just like criminals, because leaving your child is a crime beyond explanation, and beyond forgiveness. And if that does not stop the rash of fathers leaving their children, then the men considered at risk of having children just to leave them should be castrated! That should put an end to this. Have I made myself clear?" Zale said, leaning back in the large chair, his fingers intertwined, resting on his crossed knees.

"Very," the interviewer said, smiling mischievously. "I love this!" he said, tightening his grip on the stub of a pencil and jotting everything down verbatim.

Zale would get calls about this one, just like all the other interviews he'd done in the past where he stated his uncensored opinion. He would get calls, and have letters waiting for him at his office from angry men who felt that he was just some overcrusading radical who had no idea what he was talking about because he had no children, and hadn't had to suffer all their pains. He would hear from them, and probably one or two of them would drive by his building at night and throw bricks through the windows, or spray-paint filth of some sort across the door. And even though he went to great extremes to keep where he lived a secret, one of these men might find out, and . . . Zale crumpled the magazine into a ball and tossed it aside, where it fell off the table to the floor.

It had happened before. It was only a year after he started Father Found, and he was so full of energy, so ready to fight against these fathers who left their children, that he said and did things without thought of how some of these men would respond. "Heartless coward" was one of the expressions he often used to describe them. But it wasn't enough that he demoralized them in the papers and on television, after all, they might not have been listening. Whenever he got a call from a mother looking for the father of her child, Zale would go after them with the eagerness of a bloodhound. He would go to the man's place of business and inform his employer that he was looking for this man because he had left his child. Zale would stick flyers on the windshields of the cars in the parking lot, a black-and-white mug shot of the man on the center of the page, the words "Wanted for Child Abandonment!" in big bold letters across the top, as if he were actually a criminal wanted by the FBI.

If the man didn't respond to those tactics, Zale would hit him where it really counted, and that was in the pocket. He would arrange to have the child support that the man owed taken directly out of his check. That usually got his attention, had him calling the woman to find out exactly what was happening, at the very least.

But for one man the scheme backfired. Instead of calling the mother of his children, he called Zale. But he didn't call him for help, or even for answers. He called Zale telling him that he wanted him dead, and that he'd be the one to kill him. The phone dropped from Zale's hand. He could still hear the man's voice cursing from the receiver that lay on the floor like some vile living creature with the ability to talk.

"You hear me, motherfucker! Dead! You're gonna be dead, mother-fucker!"

Zale picked up the phone, put it to his ear, but the caller hung up. The caller—that was the only way Zale could identify him because it could have been one of at least twenty different men he was pursuing at that time, and he went after them all with the same intensity.

He convinced himself to let it pass, it wasn't the first time he had received a crank call, and it wouldn't be the last. But when he got the same call at his home, waking him out of his sleep at four in the morning, he began to worry. He called the police, but they said they couldn't do anything about crank calls, so Zale went down to the station the following morning, angry and upset. He was directed to the desk of a Detective Rames, a tall, athletic, clean-cut white man, who looked about forty.

"Are you Detective Rames?" Zale said, anger still coursing through his body at the indifference he had sensed from the police officers.

"Yeah, I'm Frank Rames, and you're that guy, the Father Found guy, right?" the detective said, waving a finger at Zale. "You're the guy giving all those dads a hard way to go."

Zale stood, looking down at the man, unamused by his remark.

Detective Rames stood and offered Zale a seat. He wore a gun holster across his back and shoulder, a huge handgun sitting snugly in the shiny leather pouch. He pulled out the seat for Zale. When Zale sat, Rames took his seat again.

"Now what can I do you for?"

"I've been receiving threatening phone calls, death threats, and I want someone to do something about it!"

Detective Rames leaned back in his swivel chair. "What are we supposed to do about that, Mr. . . ."

"Mr. Rowen!" Zale said, becoming more upset by the lousy treatment he was receiving.

"What are we supposed to do about that, Mr. Rowen?"

"I don't know. You're the police! You're supposed to do whatever it is you normally do when someone receives death threats!" Zale said, raising his voice.

"We don't do anything right away, Mr. Rowen, so calm down."

"Listen, someone is calling me telling me that he wants to kill me. I'm not going to calm down," Zale said, standing. "Now, I don't care what it takes, but you need to get someone on this. Tap my phones, stake out my home, I don't care, but this needs to be taken care of before I end up dead." Zale was breathing heavily, standing over the detective's desk. He felt the sweat from his anger accumulating around his tight collar, and in his clenched fists. Rames was still sitting in his swivel chair, the butts of his hands on the edge of his desk, tilting himself back and forth, almost playfully, as if not affected at all by what Zale said.

"Are you calm now, Mr. Rowen?"

Zale said nothing.

"Two crank calls, then a phone tap, only happens in the movies, so you might as well stop looking for it here. To tell you the truth, we're going to almost need to see someone grabbing you by the throat, yelling at the top of his lungs that he wants to kill you, before we take the action that you're looking for. But I will do this much." Rames went into his shirt pocket, pulled out his business card, and placed it on the desk. "That's me," he said, stabbing it with his index finger. "There's the office number, and my pager, and . . ." He flipped it over and wrote on it. "And that's my home number. If you really think you're in serious shit, if you really think someone is about to kill you, give me a call and I'll rush right over." He picked up the card and held it out for Zale to take.

Zale looked at the man for a moment, wondering if this was just some line of bull he was giving him, but he took the card.

"It's the best I can do, Mr. Rowen, and I'm only doing it because I think what you're trying to do making these fathers own up to their responsibilities is really commendable. I have two of my own. They're the world to me, and I would never leave them. Never," Rames said with stern commitment. "Want to see a picture?"

"No, thank you."

Zale left the police station feeling no better than he had when he entered. He made a beeline straight for a gun shop and bought himself some protection, since the police felt they didn't have to do their job.

A week passed, and Zale had received only one crank call, and that had just been a hang-up at the office. It was late, he was at home, and he was about to go to bed when the phone rang. He picked it up without second thought.

"Hello?"

There was no answer, but Zale could hear someone on the line.

"Hello!" he said again.

Then Zale got a dial tone. He placed the phone slowly back in its cradle and thought about calling that detective. It just would've taken the push of just one button, because Zale had entered his number in his speed dial just in case he really did need him. Instead, he walked to the closet and looked to the top shelf to make sure he saw the .22 he had bought a week ago. If something were to happen, and he had to take care of it himself, he would be ready.

Zale went back to bed, and was lying down for only minutes when he heard a noise. He sprang up in his bed, his eyes wide, his fist clutching his sheets. His breathing was coming hard and fast, but he tried with everything inside him to suppress it. He listened intently, hearing nothing but the pounding of his heart. Then the noise came again, but this time he knew what it was. It was someone trying the front door. Zale's entire body stiffened, unable to move. He was wondering whether he had locked the front door before going to bed. He knew he had, but his mind could see a dark figure walking through his hallway, filling the space of his doorway, a refraction of light dancing across the sharp blade of the huge knife he was holding. Then, all of a sudden, as if the man could fly, he was on Zale, in his bed with him, the blur of his shiny blade speeding down toward Zale's bare chest.

Stop it! Zale thought to himself, and told himself to move. Move!

He tumbled over in bed, grasping for the phone, then punched the button for Detective Rames.

Two rings that took two decades. Then he answered, his voice groggy.

"Rames."

"Detective Rames, it's Zale Rowen," Zale whispered loudly, as his eyes jetted back and forth in his head, looking for danger. He was pushed back in a corner of his bedroom, the phone cradled within the space of his folded knees and stomach.

"You have to come. You have to come now! He's here! Do you hear me? He's here!" Zale gave Rames the address. "I'm going to grab my gun, but hurry," Zale said.

"Mr. Rowen," Rames said, already out of bed, slipping on his shirt. "I'll be right over, but don't you go shooting the neighbor's kid, all right?"

"Just hurry!"

Zale scurried across the carpet on all fours, making his way to the closet. He stood up, blindly reached for the gun, then huddled within the tight confines of the closet, the gun in his hand, looking out into the darkness, listening for the intruder.

Zale didn't know how much time had passed, but it seemed like an eternity. Rames should've been there by now, or whoever it was that was trying to enter his home should've been in his bedroom by now, standing over him. But nothing had happened, and it was driving Zale close to insanity. He still sat in the closet, his pajamas soaking wet from sweat, both his hands cramping from holding the small gun so tightly for what seemed so long.

Zale decided to leave the safety of the closet, telling himself that nothing had happened so nothing was going to happen. The noise at the front door had probably been Ted, Zale's next-door neighbor who sometimes drank a little more than he should've and somehow managed to get his car home without plowing it into a tree, and oftentimes tried entering Zale's front door, thinking it was his own. That's what had happened, plain and simple, Zale told himself. Believing that, Zale stood, although very slowly, the gun still glued to his hand. He walked cautiously through the house, light from the streetlamps entering the partially curtained windows, casting strange shadows across the living room. Zale tried the door, and it was locked. He searched the rest of the house, checking all the windows and doors, and all was well. Feeling more comfortable, he placed the gun back on the shelf, thinking that it was a good thing that his life wasn't in danger, because that lazy bastard of a cop hadn't shown up. But Zale never really thought he would to begin with.

Zale pulled back the blankets of his bed, and was about to climb in when he looked toward the bedroom window and decided he should check that as well. He knew it was locked, but better safe than sorry. He walked through the dark room over to the window, fidgeted with the already secure lock, then took a peek out the window. He looked left, and then he looked right, and then his eardrums seemed to have exploded, and the skin of his face felt as though it was being ripped from his skull. It was because of the loud crash of the window glass shattering, the razor-sharp shards flying everywhere, some hitting him in the face. Zale fell back on the bed, covering his eyes. He had seen the brief glimpse of a body before the glass was broken, enabling him to cover his eyes before the glass started flying toward him.

Zale heard the man unlocking the window, sliding it up. He heard his grunts as he hoisted himself up through the opening in Zale's once-secure home, then he felt the stranger's presence, heard him trampling the already broken glass into glass dust, smelled him—he was a smoker—felt the cold he brought into the house with him.

"Come here, you motherfucker!" the voice commanded. The intruder wrapped his arm around Zale's neck, yanking Zale into him, placing a gun to his temple.

"You want to fuck with me, hunh! You wanted to fuck with me, because you just can't leave business that don't belong to you alone!" Toward the end of each sentence, the man tightened the grip on Zale's neck to make his point. Zale was choking. He could barely breathe. His head was swimming, he was about to pass out, and he wondered why the man even had the gun to his head, because it seemed he planned on strangling him to death.

"Do you know what you did? Hunh! Hunh!" he yelled, jerking Zale, his arm tightening around his neck with each jerk. Zale tried to loosen the grip, but he had no strength, no oxygen, and almost no sense of where he was any longer. He was going to die, was going to be killed for what he believed most in, Zale told himself, and he was trying to prepare himself, trying to accept it when . . .

"Freeze. Police, you sack of shit!"

The stranger's arm loosened some, and Zale choked and gasped on the air that was almost foreign to him. He looked up and saw Rames standing in his doorway, his gun drawn, aiming at the man that held him.

"Now you just put that gun down and let that man go, you hear me."

"I'm not putting shit down, and you need to turn your ass around and walk back to wherever you came from unless you want to be a part of this," the man said, calming. Then when he saw Rames not moving, he screamed, "This is between me and this motherfucker!"

"I'm a part of this now," Rames said, taking a step forward into the dark room. "The minute I entered this house I—"

"Don't you take one step closer, you fuck, or you're dead!" the man yelled, pointing the gun at Rames, then sticking it back at Zale's head.

"All right, all right, I'm stopping. But let me tell you something. You point that gun at me like that again, I'm going to assume you're gonna shoot me, and then I'll have to kill you. You got that?"

"Fuck you! I told you to get the hell out of here!"

"I can't do that," Rames said calmly.

"I'm going to do this bastard!" the man yelled, pulling Zale closer.

"You're not going to do that."

"I'm going to kill him, right here!"

"Put the gun down," Rames said, raising his voice.

"Fuck you!"

"Put the goddamn gun down!" Rames yelled.

"Get out of here, or I swear I'll kill you too." He pointed the gun at Rames again, then back at Zale, then back at Rames, then let it rest on Zale.

Rames took two steps closer, his arms outstretched, the gun dead on the stranger.

"You point that gun at me one more time, I swear, you're going to make me shoot you."

"Fuck you!" the man yelled, as he raised the gun to Rames.

"POW! POW! POW!" The dark room lit up with three explosions of orange flames. Then the man that was holding Zale by the neck flew backward, his upper body flying out the window, his arms dangling out over his head, his legs remaining within the room. Zale fell to the floor, wrapping both his hands around his throat, still choking, his face bleeding from the cuts of broken glass.

Rames approached the man's body, grabbed him by the scruff of his jacket, not seeming to mind the blood that was there, and hoisted him into the room.

"Mr. Rowen."

Zale got to his knees, then laboriously stood to his feet.

"Mr. Rowen, you know this guy?" Rames said, holding the man up like a puppet. His head rolled limply on his neck; a thin stream of blood crawled down his chin from the corner of his mouth.

Zale had not seen the man's face the entire time the man was behind him, choking him, bringing him near death, but now, upon looking at it, he knew who it was. It didn't even take a moment. He was Calvin Thompson, Case Number 106. Left his three kids two years ago, had a drug problem, spent time in jail, never once tried to get help from Zale, which was all Zale was trying to get him to ask for.

"Yeah, I know him," Zale said. He watched Rames hang him back out the window, as he had found him, and wipe the blood he had gotten on him off on the man's clothes. Zale stood there, fear still holding a firm grip on him, but his heart started to slow. He had a dumbfounded look on his face as he stared at Rames.

"What?" Rames said.

"Why'd you kill him?"

Rames looked shocked by the question, then looked over at the man hanging out the window. He cracked a smile, chuckled a little, ran a hand through his cropped hair, then looked down at the floor, as if he were trying to elude the question, embarrassed by what he had done.

"I told him if he pointed that gun at me again, I'd have to kill him." Rames slipped his gun back in his holster, then walked very close to Zale. The smile disappeared from his face, replaced with something much more solemn, a mask carved from granite.

"I wasn't taking any chances," he said, spite creeping in his voice. "You'd at least think that some people would be grateful." He turned and walked out of the room.

■ ■ ■

That was two years ago and nothing had happened since, and Zale hoped nothing would as he looked over at the crumpled Sunday magazine. But if it does, then it just does, he thought. He couldn't stop what he was doing, stop trying to save all those children just because every now and then some lunatic didn't like the way the truth sounded, couldn't stand to have someone hold a mirror up to him and show him that he was really a coward. Zale wouldn't stop, and he wouldn't shy away. He wouldn't allow himself to be bullied, or slowed down. He couldn't let himself or his work be affected by such men. He had to meet them head-on, match them, show no fear, and prove to them that if they had no reservations about taking his life, then, for this cause, he had no reservations about losing it.

Zale eyed the crumpled magazine sitting on the floor, again seeing his face distorted on the cover, twisted like a weird fun-house mirror reflection. He thought to himself, If there are calls, then there'll be calls, and if people don't like what I have to say, then tough!

CHAPTER TWO

"Is that her, Daddy?" Renee said, running to the window in her pajamas. Martin Carter's seven-year-old daughter moved into the space between her father and the curtain to look out at the driveway.

"No, baby. It was just a car turning around, that's all," Martin said, disappointed himself. "But she should be home any minute." Rebecca, Renee's little sister, came running up to her father, the top of her head barely reaching his waist.

"Was it Mommy?"

Martin bent down and picked Rebecca up and grabbed Renee's hand, walking them into the kitchen.

"No, sweetheart, but she should be home soon, okay?"

"But didn't you beep her?" Renee said.

Martin looked down at his watch. It read 9:30.

"Yeah, but she's probably on her way home right now. That's why she probably hasn't bothered to call back." Martin said that for their benefit, not believing his own words.

Martin let Rebecca down in the kitchen. "Anybody need water before bed?"

"I'll take some, Daddy," Renee said. Rebecca just nodded her head.

He gave the children water from a small plastic cup, allowing them only two swallows apiece. Then he walked them upstairs and put them to bed.

"Will you wake me up when she gets home?" Rebecca said, her covers pulled up to just below her chin.

"And why would I do that?" Martin was sitting on the side of her bed, rubbing his hand gently over her hair.

"Because I want to ask her how her day was."

"I'm sure her day went fine. But I'll ask her for you, because five-year-old kids need all the sleep they can get. How does that sound?"

Rebecca nodded her head and turned her face slightly to accept the kiss her father placed on her cheek. He stood and bent over Renee's bed, preparing to kiss her good night. "And, no, I'm not going to wake you just because you're two years older than your sister. You'll see Mommy in the morning, too. Okay?"

Renee smiled, accepted her father's kiss, rolled on her side, and pulled her blankets over her shoulder.

Martin walked through the dark room and stood at the door for a moment, admiring his daughters. "Good night," he said softly, then closed the door.

Martin went straight for the phone, punched in his wife's pager number, then hung up, trying to convince himself that the first page hadn't gone through. He sat down on the living room sofa, then he stretched out, kicking his feet up. He remained like that for only a moment, not able to control the urge to get up and walk back to the window and look out for his wife's Saab rolling into the driveway.

His actions made him angry. Standing there, leaning on the windowsill like some frantic puppy, waiting for Master to come home. He was behaving foolishly, he told himself, his reflection showing the proof in the window in front of him. He stood there, holding the curtains aside with one hand, staring at himself.

He wanted to walk away from the window, forget about the time it took his wife to come home, forget about the image in front of him, the reflection that stared back at him that he was never really satisfied with, but he couldn't. He just continued to stand there and stare, his self-confidence dropping a notch as each minute passed.

How did he end up with his wife in the first place? That was the question that popped into his mind whenever she would come home late, and she'd been coming home late a lot lately.

Why was such a beautiful woman with *him?* Long black hair, caramel complexion, and the biggest, darkest eyes imaginable; she was stunning. Every time he looked in her eyes, he felt like a child, wanted to confess how he could never get her out of his mind, even when she was just in the next room.

He, on the other hand, was plain, simply plain. Martin was not hideous by any stretch, but he was not handsome either. He landed smack-dab in the middle of the physical-appearance scale, having a face that people neither ignored nor admired. His body was the same. He was six feet even, a little taller than average, but of average build, not too large, not too small, and even though he worked up an intense sweat at the gym every day, and got stronger doing it, his body never appeared more than the average body that the average guy who never worked out walked around with.

Because of this, Martin tried to better everything within his power, things that he had some control over. He got his hair cut once a week, keeping it neat and close. It made a difference, he told himself each time the barber handed him the mirror for him to check his haircut, the man's other hand extended, waiting for the fifteen dollars Martin owed him. It made a difference.

The clothes he bought were the nicest he could afford. He often stopped off at the mall after work to pick up a shirt or a pair of pants even if he didn't need them, just wanting to add them to his collection so he could put something new on the following day. New clothes always made him feel better-looking, more confident than he actually was. And as he stood at the mirror those mornings, the tags still dangling from the new clothes, he would sometimes stare at himself, trying to find that something that his wife had seen in him, saw in him. He knew it was there, but he could never find it. He would straighten the new tie, or adjust a cuff link, taking pride in these things as opposed to himself. All of this he did for his wife, the beautiful woman that he loved so much. Even though he knew it was a failing attempt, he did all this to at least equal her appearance, because he knew on every other level she was above him. Her level of education far exceeded his. She seemed more confident, more outgoing, and she even brought home something like three times what he made.

So how did he get her, he asked himself again. He was always unsure of the answer, and even when he was standing next to her at the altar, all done up in his tuxedo, his soon-to-be wife appearing like a vision in her beautiful white gown, the preacher asking her, "Do you take this man, Martin Alexander Carter, to be your lawfully wedded husband?" He remembered holding his breath, and closing his eyes hoping that she wouldn't come to her senses all of a sudden and embarrass him in front of all his family and friends. But she said yes, and she made him the happiest man in the world, and he knew he always would be, till recently.

Martin shook the thoughts out of his head, angered by the fact that she had not driven up yet. He looked down at his watch; it read 10:25. He moved from the curtain, grabbed the phone again, and prepared to dial his wife's pager, but decided against it and hung up the phone forcefully.

If she hadn't called him back yet, what made him think she'd call him back at all, he thought as he took the stairs two at a time, rushing toward their bedroom. He stood in the center of the room, his arms at his sides, his chest heaving from the quick climb, looking bewildered, as if he had been suddenly transported there and had no idea where he was. He walked quickly to their closet, yanked the sliding doors to one side, then tugged at the string to turn on the light. It was a large walk-in closet, his clothes lining one side of the small area, his shoes filed neatly under his garments, her clothes and shoes lining the other side. That was where he found himself standing, his fists clenched at his sides, his willpower being tested as he looked at her garments.

Don't do it, he told himself, begged himself, and the command was made to stop himself from forcing his hands into her coat pockets, or patting down the fronts of her business suits, looking for things that shouldn't be there, things that proved she was doing things that he didn't want to think that she was doing. He didn't want to check up on her like that, like some fanatical wife, checking her husband's shirt collar for lipstick stains. He didn't want to do that, because it would make him feel like far less than the man he was, and considering his already low opinion of himself, he couldn't afford to sink any lower. But more important, he didn't want to wrongly stop trusting his wife. If he did what he was about to do, went through her pockets, or went to her dresser to go through her undergarment drawer, bringing her panties to his nose, sniffing them for the scent of sex, or some other man's fragrance, and found nothing, he would never be able to forgive himself. And then every time she came in late, or didn't call him back after a page, his mind would race to the place where she was lying in some man's arms, holding some man the way she should've been holding him, giving some man the attention she should've been giving to her children.

He couldn't do that to himself, he thought, as he yanked the string on the closet light and closed the doors. It would be far better to trust his wife and have her cheating on him than to distrust her and find out that she wasn't. Besides, he knew her better than that. She loved him, and he told himself it was just his insecurities talking and nothing else. He sat on the edge of the bed, placed his flattened hands between his knees, and told himself to wait, wait until his wife came home.

When Martin heard a car pull into the driveway, he knew that it was his wife, but he didn't bother getting up or rushing to the window to see her step out of the car and make her way to the front door. He knew it would happen, and he saw the actions happening in his head when he heard the car door slam. He imagined and counted her paces as she walked to the front door, saw her setting her coat down on the sofa, saw her kicking her high heels off, one of them sitting upright, one of them falling to a side. There was silence for a moment, but he knew she was walking to the kitchen. She was probably opening the refrigerator door, peeking inside for no other reason than just to reaffirm the fact that she wasn't hungry, then she'd make her way upstairs.

Martin still didn't move. He heard her climbing the stairs, even though her movements were muffled by the thick carpeting. Martin canted his head just a little and looked down at the watch on his wrist. It was 12:45 A.M. He had been sitting on the edge of that bed, his hands folded between his knees, waiting like a patient little schoolboy, for more than two hours.

He felt her presence as she stood in the doorway. He didn't have to turn to look at her to see how she appeared there. She would be wearing the same pale pink business jacket and skirt she was wearing when she walked out of the house that morning, a time that seemed like an entire day ago, twenty-four hours, to Martin. She would be standing there, probably a huge run up her stockings from all the walking she had done back and forth through the hospital, her hair slightly mussed about her head, her makeup faded, but still somehow looking stunningly attractive.

"You didn't have to wait up," Debra said.

She didn't sound exhausted the way Martin thought she would. She sounded as refreshed as she was when she walked out of the house earlier that morning, and he could not help turning to take a quick look at her to see if her appearance matched the voice, and it did. She looked as though she had just stepped out of a shower, had just torn the dry-cleaning plastic away from her suit and had some stylist do her hair and makeup. She had a smile on her face, and that made Martin crazy, made him so angry he wanted to yell at her, wanted to grab her by the ear and drag her over to their daughters' room and tell her how she neglected seeing them before they went to bed. But he didn't do that. He just answered her in as plain and as calm a voice as he could find within him without staring at her.

"I didn't wait up. I just sat down here after I put the girls to bed, and before I knew it, it was almost one." He put emphasis on the time.

"Yeah, right," Debra said, walking over toward him, resting a hand on his shoulder, and kissing him on the cheek. "You were waiting up for me and you know it." She was smiling as she balanced herself on him, allowing herself not to fall as she stood on one foot, taking off her stockings.

Martin looked up at her as she did this, smelled her perfume, and a hint of her perspiration as she took off her jacket, a scent that always drove him crazy. He felt the anger start to dissipate, and if he really tried, he could forget about the late hour, forget about the unanswered pages, and just go to bed with his wife, but if he did that, then the problem would never be resolved.

"So how was your day, anyway?" Martin said.

Debra paused, unbuttoning one of her blouse buttons, and looked down at him, as if trying to decipher what may have been a coded question.

"It was fine." Martin sensed apprehension in her voice.

"That was it? Fine. Can you give me a little more than that? It's almost one in the morning, and you're just walking in the house, and all you can say was that your day was fine."

"I worked in the clinic until about five, treating a lot of sick babies like I do every day. Some had the flu, some had fevers, a couple were just teething. Then I went over to the hospital, like I do every day, and I saw some patients over there. You know, the routine doctor stuff," she said, taking off her shirt, and tossing it on the dresser, a suggestion of resentment in her voice.

"Does it take you sixteen hours to see patients, Debra? You work in a hospital, not a coal mine. You're a damn pediatric doctor, not a sweatshop worker. Can't you get home at a decent hour?"

"I really don't feel like going into this, Martin."

"Fine. Fine!" Martin said sarcastically. "Come in at midnight, come in at four in the morning, for all I care." Martin got up from the bed and walked over to his wife. She was standing in front of him, stripped down to her skirt and her bra. He wanted to touch her, and he moved to place his hand on her soft, smooth shoulder but stopped himself. "What's going on? Can you tell me that?"

"Nothing."

"I can't believe that," Martin said, trying to sound sympathetic. "You come in here at this time of night, and you say nothing is happening."

"So what are you saying, Martin?" Debra raised her voice, stepping back from him. "I say that nothing is happening, but you say there is. What do you think is happening, Martin? Please tell me."

He didn't want an argument. He didn't want them to sling hateful words at each other just to prove who could yell the loudest, all he wanted to know was the truth.

"Did you know that Renee and Rebecca wanted me to wake them up when you got home? They wanted to see you before they went to bed."

The angry look on his wife's face softened some, but she didn't say a word.

"I told them that they'd see you in the morning, but I was even be-ginning to doubt that."

"And what the hell is that supposed to mean?"

"I tried paging you twice, and you didn't even call back here. I just wanted to know how late you were going to be, just wanted to let you talk to the girls before they went to bed, but you couldn't even call back. It's like you don't even care."

"I didn't get the pages, okay? Maybe there was something wrong with my beeper."

That was a lie, and Martin knew it. He could tell the way his wife was looking at him, that same look, as though she were waiting for something ridiculously terrible to happen, like a car falling from the sky and flattening her for the fib she told. He walked over to her bag, picked it up, stuck an arm in it down to his elbow and started search-ing through the bag.

"What are you doing?" Debra asked, shocked by what she saw.

Martin still tore through the bag, tossing papers and other belong-ings to the floor until he pulled out his wife's pager. He looked down at it, pressing the little button that displayed saved pages, bypassing a number of pages till he saw their home phone number, once at 8:35 P.M. and again some hour and a half later.

He walked over to his wife and stood directly in front of her, sticking the pager in her face, holding it so the tiny green display window was in her sight. "So maybe your beeper's not working, hunh! It looks like it works just fine to me, Debra. Now can you tell me what's going on?"

"Nothing," she said, turning to walk away, but Martin caught her by the arm and spun her back to face him.

"Bullshit!" he said, his arm raised, pointing in the direction of the children's room. "Your daughters are wondering why they haven't seen their mother before they went to bed. I've been sitting in this room wondering the same thing, waiting till one in the morning, and you tell me nothing is going on. That's bullshit! I don't believe it, and you bet-ter come up with something better than that!" Martin said, his big hand still around his wife's small arm.

"Can you let me go, please." The expression on his wife's face led Martin to believe he was hurting her.

Martin released her. He never wanted to grab her like that to begin with, but his emotions got away from him.

"I finished around nine. I had a long day, had an infant die that I was treating in the NICU for two months now. I needed to get out. Me and some colleagues went out and had some drinks, released some stress, that's all. And when I looked up, it was after midnight."

"And why didn't you answer my pages?"

Debra hung her head, smoothing a hand over her face, her long hair falling about her arm. Then she lifted her head, looking Martin in the eyes.

"Because I just didn't want to, okay?" It was a statement filled with emotion, her face contoured as though she were about to break down and start bawling out loud. Then, almost immediately, she straightened up in order to speak.

"I just didn't want to answer your page. I told you what happened. All I wanted to do was sit there and drown my problems in that damn alcohol, and I didn't feel like being bothered with anything."

"Not even your husband, or your daughters?"

"What is it, Martin?" Debra said, exasperated. "What is it you want to know?"

Martin stared at his beautiful wife; his jaws tightened. He swallowed hard.

"Are you seeing someone else?" he asked, almost regretting the fact that he had, because if he hadn't, the possibility of the answer being yes would've never been known to him.

Debra laughed, but it was a sad, sarcastic, and somehow sympathetic laugh. But not the sympathy one feels for the dying or the needy, but the sympathy felt for the the pathetic. And that's how his wife looked at him at that moment, as if he were pathetic.

She shook her head. "That's what this is all about? This has nothing to do with me staying out late, and it probably has nothing to do with me not seeing the girls to bed, does it?"

"It does have something to do with that," Martin interjected.

"It's about you putting yourself down, about you questioning yourself, and when I'm not there exactly when I should be, when I'm not there to tell you that you have no reason to treat yourself like that, you just automatically think it's because I'm out sleeping around." Debra turned her back on him to walk away. Then she stopped and faced him again, giving him that sad, pathetic look. "Martin, it was cute when I first met you, but it's really starting to get old now. You need to give it up."

Then, without another word, she turned and headed for the bathroom, reaching behind her, undoing the clasp on her bra and letting it fall just outside the bathroom door as she disappeared into the small room.

Martin stood there feeling stupid, insecure, and immature, but he was not totally convinced by a long shot. Just because she says she's fed up doesn't mean she's faithful, he thought, and the little scene she made may have been the best way to squirm her way out of a conversation she never wanted to be having in the first place, a discussion she felt she was losing. Then again, if she was telling the truth, Martin didn't want to continue to beat her up, question her every move just because he was lacking terribly in self-confidence. He didn't know what to do.

Martin walked slowly to the door and placed a soft, flat hand on its surface, and then put his ear to it. He heard the shower water running, and under that, faintly, he could hear his wife singing. True, she always sang in the shower, but after the argument they just had, he would've thought, or would've hoped to think, that she would've been too distraught to follow her normal bathing routines, and if she did, he didn't think that she should've sounded so cheerful.

He turned his back on the door, leaned against it, realizing how tired he was, not just physically, but mentally, emotionally. If she only knew what she meant to him, how much of his life was just her, and only her, she would stop doing whatever it was she was doing. She would allow him to trust her implicitly, and allow him to stop trying to find some hidden lie in each word she spoke, because it was beginning to take its toll on him. But he wouldn't stop, he told himself. Yes, he did love her, almost more than anything else known to him, but he would not allow himself to be used or played like some fool—he just wouldn't. And whatever it took to avoid that, he would do. Whatever it took.

CHAPTER THREE

It was 2:00 A.M., and Zale sat in his pajamas, slouched in his chair, exhausted, staring at his bed. His body needed sleep desperately, and he knew that because he felt as though he could barely move, as though he had been shot with some type of paralyzing drug. He needed sleep, but his mind would not let him drift off, and despite how weary his body felt, his mind was wide awake, and he knew it was due to the thoughts that raced throughout his head.

He needed to control those thoughts, switch them to something peaceful, something that he could take to his pillow and would not torment him through the night. But he knew he couldn't do that. He had to let the thoughts run their course, run out, and only then he could sleep.

He looked over at the clock again. It read three minutes after the last time he checked. He thought about jumping in bed, saying hell with everything. If he dreamed, then he did, and that was the end of it. But he was scared, and he hated to admit that to himself, and if he had to stay up long enough to get the thoughts out of his head so he wouldn't dream about them, it'd be worth it. He slouched deeper into the chair, crossed his arms over his chest, and let his head fall back against the chair as he looked up at the ceiling, allowing the thoughts to have their way with him.

His mother was so thin. Maybe if she would've eaten something herself sometimes instead of coming in the house, opening a can of the first thing she blindly put her hand on from the cabinet, dumping it in a bowl without even heating it, and sliding it to her child, she wouldn't have been so skinny.

She'd give little Zale a spoon and ask him in a hurry, "We all right?," holding her breath, as if she could not breathe till he answered. When he nodded his head, she'd take off to the other room, slamming and locking the door as if that was the only place she could've actually breathed out the air she was holding.

Zale would sit there in his chair, the bowl in between his legs like a drum, and eat his SpaghettiOs or his pork and beans, always taking out the little piece of fatty pork, and when he was done, he would set the bowl on top of the table and climb down out of the chair and walk to the door and knock on it.

"Mama, you in there?" he'd ask. And it would take a while for her to answer, but when she did, she would always clear her voice as if she was about to give a speech and say, "Yes, boy, Mama just fine. Go play now, you hear."

"Can I come in, Mama?" Zale would ask, standing right up against the door, one hand flat against the wood, caressing it, as if it were his mother's smooth skin.

"No, boy. Run along and play," she'd say, then he would hear her cough, and he wanted to go in there more.

"Mama!" he'd call out.

"You heard me, boy!" she'd say more forcefully. "Go along and play!"

But Zale wouldn't leave, just sit outside the door, pushed right up against it.

When she finally came out, Zale was usually in the front room watching cartoons. His mother would saunter into the room, a huge smile on her face, her eyes half open, her forehead clear of wrinkles and whatever tension she was experiencing when she walked in from work so frantically.

She would come in the room and fold her thin body down on the floor around her son, hugging him from behind and ask in a soft, tired voice, "We all right?"

"Yeah," Zale would say, and nod his head without bothering to look back into his mother's face, because he knew she was all right, now. Most times she would stay awake for only five or ten minutes, laughing strangely at the cartoon people getting their heads flattened by falling safes, or getting cut into a million pieces by a giant cheese grater, then she'd be out. On her side at times, but mostly flat on her back, one arm stretched out to her side, the other on her belly, like she was doing a dance in her sleep. Zale would sometimes lie beside her, or just sit cross-legged near her head and look at her. How beautiful she was.

Her skin so fair, her dark, straight hair, always pulled back in a ball, contrasting starkly with her skin. Her nose was small, her lips thin, her eyes the most intense black imaginable, and Zale could see all the love his mother had for him reflect from those eyes when she looked at him.

Zale lowered his head and kissed her softly on the cheek, then began to stretch out to lie next to her, when all of a sudden, she began to cough. Softly at first, two times. Zale waited till she stopped, looking at her, concern in his eyes. When she stopped, he laid his head down in the space between her neck and shoulder, but she started coughing again, forcing him up. It was more violent this time, and when she didn't stop, wouldn't seem like she would ever stop, he grabbed her by the shoulder and started to shake her.

"Mama!" Zale cried. "Mama!" But she wouldn't wake up, just continued to cough, her face turning a pale shade of pink, spittle flying from her lips onto Zale's face. He didn't know what to do, but he had to do something. He got to his feet and started to run around the house. He would've called 911, but their phone had been disconnected long ago. He thought about running to one of the neighbors in the building, but he didn't want to leave his mother writhing on the floor like that. He ran through the front room, into the kitchen, terrified. "Mama, Mama!" he cried as he ran, tears streaming from his eyes. He could still hear her coughing even more violently. He stood in the kitchen for a moment, spun around, looking, for what he didn't know. Then he ran into her bedroom, looked all around the room, his mother still coughing. Quickly, he searched for something, something to make her stop, not having any clue to what that would be. He looked frantically through her drawers, then under the bed, then . . . Then there was silence. Zale noticed it right away. His body was halfway under the bed, his arm reaching, when he heard his mother stop coughing. He waited another moment, waited to see if the silence was really true, almost hoping that it wasn't, because he knew that she might be dead.

He pulled himself out from under the bed and walked slowly into the front room. His mother was there, curled up on her side, her arms folded, her hands disappearing into the curve of her stomach. She did not move, just lay still, deathly still. Zale approached her, filled with fear and anguish. He sat down next to her and put his hand on her forehead. She was damp with sweat. Then he put his cheek next to hers. Faintly he felt her body moving. She was alive.

Zale got a damp washcloth from the bathroom and blotted her forehead and face dry. He covered her with a blanket, then walked out of the room. Zale slid under his mother's bed again and reached out for what had caught his eye before, what he had been reaching out to grab when his mother stopped coughing.

He took it in his hand, slid out from under the bed and looked down at it. What it was he wasn't sure, but it looked like some kind of pipe. It was glass, though. Something that he had never seen before. It was odd-looking, and it was burned on one end. With the pipe, there was a cigarette lighter, and a small plastic bag. In the bag were little white pebbles or rocks of some sort. Zale held them up to his face very closely, and moved them around in there. He didn't know what they were, but for some reason, he felt they were why his mother was in the condition she was in.

Zale took what he had found, stuffed it in his pockets and ran outside. He ran till he got to the bridge, the bridge that crossed the railroad yard where all the trains stopped. He walked out on that bridge and looked down. It was a long way down, such a long way. He pulled the contents of his pockets out, held them in his hands a moment, then let them fall. They fell and fell and fell. The little glass pipe exploded as it hit the ground, the lighter landed with a "clack," and the little plastic bag floated down, landing softly as though it had a parachute attached. Zale pulled himself off the rail, for he had been leaning almost all the way over to see the fate of the things he had found. He stood there for a moment, feeling better for what he'd just done. Everything would be better now, he told himself. Everything would be better.

Zale raised his head and sat up in the chair. A tear was lodged in the corner of his eye, threatening to fall, but he wiped it away before it had the chance. Something told him that if it made its way down the length of his face, more would fall, and he didn't need to go walking down that path again. He could feel sad without crying, and he could miss his mother without becoming so hopeless that he didn't know what to do with himself.

It was an hour later than the last time he looked at the clock, and his mind was idle. He would be able to rest now. He slowly pulled himself from the chair, his pajamas wrinkled from the long period of rest, and reached for his alarm clock. He set it for 6:30 A.M., the way like he always did. He quickly added the hours he had to sleep in his head, and told himself they wouldn't be enough. But something had to be sacrificed, his sleep or all the children he was trying to help. He set the alarm clock back down, grateful for the three and a half hours of sleep he would get, turned out the lights, fell into bed on his stomach, his arms down beside him, his face on its side, his eyes still open, staring at nothing, waiting for sleep to take him.

Zale was in his office by 7:00 A.M., before anyone else got there. He was reviewing and updating files of abandoning fathers. The one he was looking at belonged to a man by the name of André Hinton. He was thirty-two and had a daughter with a woman by the name of Kayla Pope, and who knew how many other children walking the street. Ms. Pope called almost nine months ago looking for the man, saying that he'd left shortly after the child was born, and hadn't seen her or the child since, and had not offered support of any kind.

Zale made attempts to reach out to this man many times, had his investigator give him notices that he wanted to meet with him, that he would try to avoid any legal action, but the man never responded, never called the office, never thought to visit his daughter, even though he knew the child needed him, and was probably going without because he wasn't there, and that angered Zale. It really pissed him off.

He would have that problem addressed and hopefully resolved today. The man's child could wait no longer. Zale wrote "Urgent" on a small stick-it pad, peeled off the page, affixed it to the file and placed it to a side. He was preparing to review the next file when there was a knock on his door.

"Come in," he said.

The door opened and Martin Carter stood just inside the doorway. "Can I come in?" he said.

"Of course," Zale said, closing the file and placing it aside.

Martin came in and sat down in the chair in front of Zale's desk. He had something folded in his hand, resting on his lap, and immediately Zale knew what it was and what trouble it would bring. "Good morning," Martin said plainly, looking very uncomfortable in the chair.

"Good morning to you," Zale said, staring at the item. "And how are you? You look tired."

"I had a long night. I don't want to talk about it," Martin said.

"Is everything all right at home?"

"Everything is fine," Martin said, a chill in his voice. "I don't want to talk about me," he said curtly. "You read Sunday's magazine in the *Tribune*, I'm sure."

Zale looked down at the next file in front of him, opened it up, peeked inside it briefly, then closed it. "Yes, I read it, so what?"

"I thought we had an agreement. I thought you said you would tone down."

"We're not going to get into this again, Martin," Zale said, standing from his desk, and walking to the window, where he turned his back on his friend to look out on the street.

"I was hoping that we wouldn't have to talk about this again, but did you read what you said? Do you remember what's in here?" Martin said. He was standing now and had tossed the magazine over to Zale's desk. It landed faceup, and when Zale turned around, the picture he disliked so much was staring up at him.

"Of course I remember. I said it!"

"And why did you have to say it?"

"What do you mean, why did I have to say it? Because that's how I feel. And if I feel a certain way about something, I'm going to say it, especially in this case."

Martin shook his head, grabbing the magazine off the desk, an exasperated look on his face. He sat down in the chair again, looking beaten. "You just don't get it, do you?" he said, waving the magazine in front of him. "You've managed, again, to further alienate every single father out there who has abandoned, or has plans to abandon, their children."

"And what do I care about that?" Zale said.

"Well, you should care something about that, because it's not just them that you alienate, Zale. Not just those men, but people who understand that sometimes things go wrong. Sometimes there are situations that make men leave their children, even though they don't want to, and when you go after them the way you have in this article, when you call them every name that you can think of, from irresponsible parent to coward, other people start to feel that you're too hard, that you aren't trying to understand, that you have no soul. It's bad for us, Zale."

"I'm trying to get my point across. I'm not trying to fool these people into thinking that I'm someone they want to invite to Sunday dinner, someone they want to date their daughter. I don't have to make myself look good in their eyes. That's not my job. It's yours."

"And you're making it damn hard to do. Did you know I heard the phones ringing in my office before I even walked in the building, but I didn't rush, because what's the bother in running to catch that phone call? There'll be plenty others. The phone will be ringing all day with infuriated people wanting to bitch and scream at me for shit you said. For most of them, that's all they'll want to do. But some of these people won't feel as though a phone call will convey the same message a brick through the window will, or they may go as far as going after you again." Martin leaned forward in the chair. "Those remarks you said, getting your point across, is it worth going through that again?"

Zale remembered back to when the man had him by the neck, had the gun pressed to his head. Zale knew he was dead, he knew it, and at that moment, he told himself he would never do anything to put himself in harm's way like that again. But when he thought about it later, he realized that the experience almost didn't make a damn bit of difference to him, because he couldn't let fear stand in the way of what he had to do. He just couldn't.

"It's worth it," Zale said softly, almost to himself.

"What did you say?"

"I said, it's worth it! Martin, I don't care what they think about me, or about what I have to say. I'm not running for office; this is not a popularity contest, I'm trying to get these cowards—"

"There you go again with the coward business," Martin said, throwing his hands up in disgust.

"I'm trying to get these *fathers* to recognize what they're doing to their children when they leave them, what position they're putting them in, and what they are in turn saying to these kids. They're saying that they don't love them and they never will. They're saying don't try and find me, because if I thought enough about you to care what you thought, how you feel, I would make myself available. Bottom line, they're saying that they don't care if their children live or die. They don't give a damn." Zale was silent for a moment, his mind racing over unwanted memories.

"How do you think that makes them feel!" Zale said, his voice filled with emotion, the expression on his face unsteady. "How are you expected to go through life feeling like you're worth something, when one of the two most important people in your life tells you, screams to you, that you aren't worth a damn moment of their time. Do you know how that makes a child feel?"

Martin sat in the chair, still clutching the paper, expressionless.

"Do you, Martin!"

"I can't say that I do," he said plainly, his tone even.

"Then don't tell me what's worth what! Don't tell me about public opinion, and the things I should or shouldn't say." Zale walked back over to the window, placed his hands high on the window frame above his head and looked out. "Is that all?" Zale said, his back still turned.

Martin took a moment to answer him. "No, that's not all. This is a business, right?"

Zale didn't turn around, nor did he answer the question.

"I said, this is a business, right?" Martin said again.

Zale slowly turned around to look at Martin, still not answering.

"Yes, it's not-for-profit, but it's still a business," Zale answered reluctantly.

"That's right," Martin said. "And I'm sure you're aware of this, but we depend on the public for most of our money to keep this business running. Do you see what I'm saying? I know you're trying to deal with this huge problem that's affecting our community in so many ways. I'm trying to deal with it, too. But if you alienate the people out there that we depend on for funds to keep this boat floating, then they won't donate, and we have no boat, and if we have no boat, all those kids out there we're trying to save—they drown."

"We get money from the government," Zale said.

"It's not enough. Don't you see, Zale. We're barely making it. Every time I open up the books, it gets more depressing. Now I know this hits very close to home for you. We've known each other for five or six years now, and you're my best friend, there's nothing I wouldn't do for you, but you still haven't told me why this is like life and death for you. Do you think one day you'll let me in on that?"

Zale was leaning with his back against the window, his arms crossed over his chest. His stance was defiant but the look on his face was very subtle, almost vulnerable.

"Do you think you'll tell me, Zale?"

Still no answer.

"It might be wrong for me to say this, Zale, because, like I said, I really don't know how deep this is, but you have to learn to separate the emotions from business. It will tear this organization down, and it will eat you up inside. Now we need every dollar we can get our hands on, so I'm asking you, not just as your partner, but your best friend. Tone down your comments, your opinions, whatever they are, and not just for the sake of the money that's at stake. I don't want you getting your head blown off. Can you do that?"

Zale looked around the room, his eyes resting on nothing in particular. Then he looked at Martin and blew out a frustrated sigh. "Yeah, I can do that, I guess."

"Good," Martin said, standing from the chair. "And that speaking engagement you have tonight, I'm going to call and cancel."

Zale snapped out of the melancholy mood he was in. "Why are you going to do that?"

"After this article, you don't need to be speaking to these people. This will be a room full of men who are being forced by the courts to listen to you speak. After what you said, do you think they'll stand and clap when you enter the room?"

"That doesn't matter to me. Like you said, they're being forced, so they have to listen, and the things I have to say are very important. I'm going to speak tonight."

"Zale, there's no telling what could happen. I'll call and postpone till after this article is forgotten."

"I'm going. You're not canceling."

"But—"

"I'm going!"

"Fine, have it your way," Martin said, raising his palms in surrender.

Zale reached over to his desk and grabbed the file marked "Urgent." "Remember this guy?"

Martin took the folder and opened it to see André Hinton's photo staring back at him. "Yeah, I remember him. Tried a million times, but never was able to get in touch with him."

"Well, the mother of his child has been calling a lot lately, and I want to try reaching Mr. Hinton again."

"Do you want me to get Rames on it?" Martin said, moving toward the phone. "I can page him right now."

"No, he's not scheduled to come in till this afternoon."

"I see," Martin said, placing the phone down. "But this folder says 'Urgent.' Urgent does mean now, doesn't it? Not this afternoon."

"He's not scheduled to come in till noon," Zale said again. "What do you have against Rames?"

"I have nothing against him, and outside the fact that I think he's lazy, can't be trusted, and not worth the price of the shoelaces he has in his shoes, I think he's a pretty decent guy. So I'll page him. It's eight A.M., he should be out of bed anyway."

"Don't page him, Martin. Wait till he comes in. I may not have a life outside of this place, but I'm sure he does. Besides, I'm sure there will be phone calls directed your way all day today in regard to that article, so you should have enough on your plate without having to rattle Frank's cage."

"And what about this?" Martin was holding the folded magazine out to Zale. "Are we okay with this, we have an agreement?"

Zale took the magazine and slapped it on his open hand a couple of times. "Yeah," he said softly, as if unsure of himself.

Martin smiled, turned, and left the office.

Zale walked back behind his desk and sat down. He slouched down in the leather executive chair, unfolded the magazine, and stared at it again.

"'Zaleford Rowen—Friend or Foe?'" he read aloud. "As if you don't know."

Zale grabbed either side of the magazine in his fists and ripped the thin book down the middle, the tearing sound filling the office. His face was torn in half, a representation of how he was feeling, torn between what was supposedly best for the organization and what he truly believed in. But regardless of what Martin said, Zale was sure what he had to do, and as he watched those torn pages fall into the trash can, he realized that the harsh words he had spoken in the past had to be spoken for the sake of the children, and he decided that no man or amount of money would stop him from saying or doing what needed to be done.

CHAPTER FOUR

Frank Rames sat on the edge of his bed, his elbows on his knees, his face in his hands, wearing his underwear: white briefs, and matching white T-shirt. He had been there like that, staring at the phone, for almost half an hour. He wanted to call his ex-wife and ask for permission to see his daughter, his only child—his only remaining child.

Ask for permission, he thought. Ask for permission like a child wanting a cookie. The thought angered him, but he squelched the growing anger, telling himself it would do no good, because it hadn't done any good in all the times that the rage had gotten out of control in the past. All it had done was screw things up, and that's why he was in the situation he was in right now.

He reached over to the phone and rested a hand on the receiver. His hand was shaking, but he held tight to the phone to make it stop. He was scared that his ex-wife wouldn't allow him to see his daughter, that she would turn him down like she had done all the previous times he had asked to see her. If she did it again, it would make three months since he had seen his child. No man deserved to go through that, he thought, no matter what he did, no matter how bad, no man deserved to have his child stripped from him.

The phone was ringing, and Frank held the receiver nervously up to his ear, waiting for his ex-wife to pick up. He looked over at the clock, and it read 8:19. Wendy wouldn't have to go to work today because she was a teacher, and it was one of those little-known holidays that only schools observed.

"Hello," his ex-wife's soft voice said. Frank's heart almost stopped beating, he missed her so much.

"Hello," she called again. Frank wanted to speak, but couldn't. Something wouldn't allow him to, and all he could do was clear his throat.

"Frank!" Wendy said, obviously recognizing the sound of his voice even though he had not spoken.

"Yeah, it's me."

"What do you want, Frank? You know you aren't supposed to be calling here." The tone of her voice was that of a disciplinarian.

Frank looked at his nightstand. Movement caught his eye. It was a roach, and it was crawling on the fast-food trash that was last night's dinner.

"I know that, but I had to," Frank said, turning his head away from the filth that lay so close to his bed. "I had to because I have to see—"

"Frank, don't even say it. Because I'm not going to let you see Bianca. How many times have I told you that."

"Why can't I see her!" Frank raised his voice, standing from the bed, the phone held tightly to his head. "Why!"

"Because the courts say you can't, that's why." Wendy blew a sigh. "Frank, we've been through this already, and I really don't feel like continuing this conversation."

"What do the courts have to do with me wanting to see my child? With her wanting to see me? Tell me that."

Wendy didn't answer right away, pausing for a moment. "What makes you think she wants to see you?"

Frank was taken aback by what she just said, thinking about the possibility that his daughter no longer wanted anything to do with him. He seriously thought about it for a moment, feeling saddened by the thought, then blanked it out of his mind.

"Let me talk to her! I want to talk to my daughter."

Wendy paused again. "Uh . . . she's not here. She spent the night at one of her friends' house last night."

"Wendy, that's bullshit and you know it! Put her on the phone, all I want to do is speak to my child, that won't be doing anyone any harm."

"And all you wanted to do was take William for a drive. That wasn't supposed to do anyone any harm either, remember!" she spat.

"This has nothing to do with him!" Frank yelled. Why did she always have to bring that up, revisit it, as if he had to be reminded of the terrible thing he did, as if he didn't see the boy's face every time he saw himself in the mirror. He was angry now, past anger, infuriated to the point where he could barely stand there and hold the phone.

"I just want to see Bianca. Just let me see her, just for a moment," he begged.

"No, Frank! I said no!" Wendy said, then Frank heard a voice in the background.

"Is that Daddy?" It was his daughter, and there was urgency in her voice. An urgency that matched her father's.

"No, you can't talk to him," Frank heard his ex-wife's muffled voice tell his daughter, and he could envision her pulling the phone from her ear, cupping her hand over the mouthpiece so he couldn't hear what was going on as she pushed her daughter away.

"Let me speak to her!" Frank yelled.

"For the last time . . ."

Frank couldn't stand it anymore, hearing his daughter, knowing that she wanted to see him regardless of what Wendy said, regardless of how much she tried to stop her. "I'm coming over there," Frank said, already looking around the floor for his pants.

"No, don't you dare, Frank."

"I'm coming over there to see my daughter. I just want to talk to her. I swear I won't do anything."

"Frank, we won't be here," his ex-wife warned.

"Don't you leave that house! Don't you take her anywhere!" Frank yelled into the phone, sliding his pants on. "I'm going to be—"

She hung up before Frank could finish the sentence.

That bitch, Frank thought, as he ran through the filthy, run-down, one-bedroom apartment looking for a shirt to put on. She was probably doing the same thing, dragging his daughter about the house, forcing her to put some clothes on so they could get out of there before he arrived. It was a race, but Frank would win this one, he told himself as he slipped his pager on his belt, and fastened his gun holster across his back. He threw on a short leather jacket and raced out of the apartment.

He took the stairs at a blinding pace, almost falling down them. He jumped in his late-model Chevy Impala, threw the car in gear and sped off. Why does she have to make things so difficult? Frank thought, as he eyed the speedometer. He was doing fifty miles an hour down a side street, and he just hoped no kids would pop out from between any parked cars, because if they did, he would make a child-size speed bump out of them and keep on going. He took a hard right turn, going almost thirty-five miles an hour, feeling as though the car was riding up on two wheels. Then he blew past a streetlight that had just turned red. He looked over his shoulder, hoping no cops were around, but it probably wouldn't make any difference anyway. He knew all of them from when he was a cop, and unless a couple of rookies stopped him, he had nothing to worry about.

Frank raced down a three-lane street, ducking in and out of traffic, his eyes darting from one side of the car to the other, looking in the rearview, over his shoulder, gripping the steering wheel tight enough to almost break it, yanking it this way and that, as he cut cars off, jumping ahead of them, trying to make a light that was less than a block ahead of him. It had been green for some time, and he knew it would turn yellow in a second, so he punched the gas, hunched his shoulders up over the steering wheel, and flew toward the intersection, trying to use whatever mind power he had to force the slow-driving car in front of him to drive through the now-yellow streetlight. "Go, go, you bastard!" Frank yelled at the car, but it slowed down at the intersection, allowing the light to go from yellow to red. Frank's car squealed to a halt, the back end hiking up from the force of halted momentum.

"Fuck!" He banged the steering wheel, considered jumping out of the car and beating the old lady in front of him as he caught her eyes glancing at him in the rearview.

Wendy was probably walking out of the house, grabbing Bianca by the hand, forcing her into the car right now, Frank thought, but he was only five minutes away. He could make it, if he could just get out of this traffic. Then he felt something moving on his waist. He almost flew through the roof of the car, he was so shocked, throwing his jacket back to reveal his pager. He was so involved with getting to his ex-wife's house that he forgot he was wearing it. He pulled it off his belt and flipped it from vibrate to alarm, not knowing how it got on the other setting in the first place. He looked down to see who was paging him, then cursed when he saw that it was his asshole of an employer.

"What is he doing paging me now! I'm not due in till noon." He tossed the pager aside and punched the pedal again, driving through the green light.

Not three minutes later, the pager went off again. Frank ignored it. Then after what seemed two minutes had passed, it sounded again. Frank picked it up, stared evilly at it, and saw that all three pages were from Martin Carter.

"Why the hell is he fucking with me!" Frank yelled, as he reached into his glove box, pulled out his cell phone and jabbed the connector into the cigarette lighter.

As he dialed the office, he realized that he was only a couple of minutes from Wendy's house.

"Why are you paging me, Martin?" Frank asked, trying to suppress his anger as much as possible.

"Because I need you to find this guy André Hinton. Do you remember him?"

"Yes, I remember him," still speeding, holding the phone in one hand, the steering wheel in the other. "But what has that got to do with right now? I'm not in till noon."

"Hinton's file is marked 'Urgent,' so I need you in now."

Frank bit the inside of his mouth, trying to hold back what he truly wanted to say to Martin. "What do you mean, now? I have business I need to take care of."

"Does that business have anything to do with Father Found?"

"No."

"Then it's going to have to wait. Like I said, this is urgent."

Frank made a wild turn, catching the corner of the sidewalk, not three blocks from the house. "Look, I'm not coming in. I'm not due in till noon, and if you have a problem with that, you need to talk to Rowen."

"Zale's not here, and it wouldn't matter if he was, you report to me. Now you're our investigator, and we need something investigated, so I'm calling you. And the business about not being available till noon, you know what you can do with it, because you're on call—all the time. That's why you carry a pager. Now, I need you to come in now and get this file, got that?" Martin hung up the phone before Frank could answer.

"Yeah, I got it, asshole," Frank said, pulling up in front of his ex-wife's house. Her Toyota wasn't parked in front, and the garage door was up, no car inside, as if they had just backed out two seconds ago. He threw his head in his hands and sighed in frustration.

One hour later, Frank had the file of André Hinton, and was sitting outside a run-down bar in one of the neighborhoods of the West Side of Chicago, known for violence and gang fights and all the things that kept people like Frank, white people, out of those parts. But there he was, sitting in his Impala, the car that looked like an unmarked cop car, outside of this hole-in-the-wall. He figured that Martin, knowing where this André Hinton usually hung out, probably couldn't wait to send Frank out after him, hoping that he would get his ass kicked, or his head blown off. But he had some very well-chosen words for Martin next time he saw him, that was for sure.

Frank opened up the file, and took a look at Hinton's mug shot. He is an ugly bastard, Frank thought, it's a wonder that some woman let him slide up in her long enough to get her pregnant. He pulled the picture from the file, slipped it in his jacket pocket, pulled out his .44 and made sure that it was loaded. He had no plans to shoot anyone, but if it came down to it, he would have no second thoughts about emptying both his magazines into any fuck face that moved against his instruction.

Frank stepped up to the building and waited as two men walked out the door. They gave Frank strange looks as they passed, letting the door slam behind them, not bothering to hold it open for the white guy that looked like a cop. Frank watched as they walked away, watched as they eyed him for a while as they walked down the street. They want to kick my ass, Frank thought to himself, and for a moment, reconsidered walking in the place.

He pulled the door open, and his eyes were met with darkness, his ears introduced to funk music that they had never heard before, James Brown screaming, "Please, please, please!" as a number of black men sat at tables, a couple at the bar, hunched over tiny shot glasses of alcohol, puffing cigarettes and cigars out of the corners of their mouths.

Obviously, these men had nothing better to do, considering it wasn't even 11:00 A.M. yet, and they were already hitting the sauce, but, then again, who was he to criticize? He had known the routine once, had known it quite well.

When Frank walked in, he tried to seem unassuming, inconspicuous, but was eyed by every man in the bar. He walked straight over to the bar, leaned an elbow on it casually, and waited for the bartender to approach. The bartender was a huge man, fat and muscle, and Frank couldn't tell of which he had more of. He stepped in front of Frank and didn't say a word, just gave him an inquisitive look.

"I need some help," Frank said, his voice low.

The bartender still said nothing.

"I'm looking for this man." Frank pulled out the picture and placed it on the bar. "His name is Hinton, André Hinton. He hangs out in here. You seen him lately?"

The bartender didn't look down at the picture, just stared at Frank, no expression on his face. "You a cop?"

"No. An investigator."

"Ain't never seen him."

Frank pulled a twenty-dollar bill from his pocket and slapped it on the bar. "How about now?"

The bartender's big hand reached for the bill. Frank slid it back. "You got to look at the picture first, big man."

The man's eyes moved from the bill to Frank, to the photo. "He was in here earlier this morning, left a little while ago."

"Do you know where he is now?"

"Don't know, but he might be down the street. There's an old building down there where drug heads smoke and shoot up. He ain't down there, I don't know where he is."

"Thanks," Frank said, leaving the twenty, and got out of there.

Frank walked up the street, even though common sense told him better, but he didn't want to miss the chance of bumping into Mr. André Hinton, if he had passed out on the way to this building, or if he had stopped to take a leak in a corner. Frank wanted to find this guy, make sure that he went to see Rowen over at Father Found, so he wouldn't have to deal with him again. He had spent too much time doing the legwork on this Hinton fellow, dropping notices at the places he was supposed to be staying, leaving business cards with his relatives and supposed friends, telling him to call Rowen at the office. All of that work, and the guy never called, and Frank took that as being given the big fat middle finger, and he didn't like that, couldn't stand it, as a matter of fact. Because if the jerk had done what he was supposed to, had at least made an effort to see his child or talk to the mother, Frank wouldn't have been called in this morning, and he could've spent more time tracking down his ex-wife instead of this asshole.

Frank approached the old building. The windows were all busted out and boarded up. Bricks were falling from the structure as if they were held in place by good intentions and not cement, and the entire thing looked as though it would tumble to the ground during the next heavy gust of wind, which seemed to have been coming in Frank's direction by the way the clouds rushed overhead, darkening the once-blue sky with gray.

A few people sat outside in clusters, one of them smoking a pipe, the others huddled around him, thirst in their eyes, waiting their turn for a hit, as if it were the last canteen in the middle of a scorching desert.

Frank took a look at all their faces as he stepped into the old building. None of them matched the photo that hid in his back pocket. It was his bad luck that the sky was overcast, and it was darkening now, because when he stepped in, it felt as if he had walked into a cave. He could barely see a thing, and he waited a moment for his eyes to adjust, holding his arms out to the side so he would not fall. He stepped slowly, cautiously, through the place, hearing what sounded like scores of people, talking, some laughing, most inhaling or exhaling. He could smell the smoke, and it reminded him of walking into a movie theater long after the film started, but instead of having the illumination from the screen, all he had was the every-so-often flicker of a cigarette lighter, or the tips of reefer joints, and cigarettes floating around in the darkness like fireflies; he couldn't see a damn thing.

Telling himself that this would take all day, Frank yelled out, not very loud at first, "André Hinton! Is André Hinton in here?"

There was no answer, forcing him to yell louder, his hands cupped around his mouth.

"Is André Hinton in here?"

"Who wants to know?" a voice called back. Frank tried to note where it came from so he could follow it, but it got lost in the darkness.

"It's your old buddy, André. It's Frank."

"I ain't got no old buddies named Frank, but if you got a rock that you willing to share, you can be my new buddy." He laughed out loud at his joke, and the people around him laughed, too, and the noise they made was like someone taking Frank by the hand and leading him directly to him. André flicked his lighter, preparing to smoke his pipe, when he saw Frank's shadow-covered face dip into the circle of light.

André's eyes bulged from surprise. He fell backward off the crate he was sitting on, dropping the lighter and the pipe. He scrambled around on the floor long enough to regain the pipe, got to his feet, and took off through the building.

Frank went after him, following the man's footsteps and heavy panting, tripping over people, then actually falling as they made their way outside. Frank saw André getting away, the long trench coat flapping behind him like a cape as he fled, but Frank was able to get back to his feet and run him down, grabbing him by that coat and slamming him against a brick wall.

"What the fuck was that all about!" Frank said, panting.

"I ain't done nothing," André said, his hands up before him, the pipe still clutched in his right hand.

"Then why did you run?"

"Because you white. Ain't no white people coming up in here unless they the po-leese. And like I said before, I ain't done nothing."

Frank didn't say anything.

"You is the police, ain't you?" André said, slowly lowering his hands.

"No, I'm an investigator for Father Found."

André's hands dropped all the way down to his sides. He slipped his pipe into one of the big pockets of his coat, and what fear had remained in his face left. "You mean, you the one that was leaving all that crap with my people, talking about you wanted me to meet with some man about my kid. That was you, and you ain't no cop?"

"That's right," Frank said, feeling far less important than the days when he was a detective.

"Well, you know what . . . Frank. Frank, right? You can take your notices and your business cards and shove them up your white ass. Fuck you!" André said, pointing a finger at Frank, then turning and casually walking away.

Frank couldn't believe what this lowlife had said to him. He had to stop and let it sink in for a moment before he realized he'd actually said it. Before Frank even knew it, he had André by the collar of his coat, railroading him backward, the man tripping over his heels till he slammed up against another brick wall, Frank's forearm buried in his chest. Frank grabbed the man's cheeks in his other hand, and held his face firmly, as if he were scolding a child.

"What is your fucking problem! You don't say those things to me. That was rude and I didn't like it. Was I rude to you, André? Was I!" He squeezed André's face tighter in his hands, making the man's mouth form an *O*.

André shook his head.

"You're André Hinton, right? Isn't that right?" Frank questioned him, his arm still in the man's chest.

André shook his head and grunted a yes.

Frank reached into his back pocket, pulling out the photo, sticking it in André's face.

"This you?"

André was staring angrily in Frank's face, looking as if he wanted nothing more than to see the white man dead.

"Look at the fucking mug shot. Is this your ugly ass?" Frank shifted André's attention to the photo for him.

André nodded his head.

"That means I got the right man, like I thought. You're the mother-fucker I've been chasing all over town, leaving shit for, but you never responded like it didn't make any difference, like I don't have anything better to do. There are people out there who actually want to be helped, you know that?"

"Well, go help them," André warbled, his cheeks still being held.

"Don't you smart off with me! Don't you fucking do it! I'm trying to help you. I'm trying to help that kid of yours who had no choice whether or not he wanted your sorry sick ass for his father. Now if you just let me, I can help you. Now, I'm going to pull my arm out of your chest here so we can talk like a couple of men, all right?"

The look in André's eyes said he agreed, but when Frank released him, he said, "Fuck you!" And took a swing at him. Frank blocked the punch and delivered a hard shot to his gut, doubling him over to his knees.

"Why did you have to do that?" Frank said, becoming angry, but still maintaining composure. "All I wanted to do was talk, but—"

"Fuck your talking. You ain't trying to talk," André said, rising slowly to his feet, holding his gut. "You trying to come up in here and beat my ass. What you care about my kid? All you want . . . all you want is . . ."

Frank noticed how he stopped talking for a moment, noticed the switch of attention in his eyes, from staring Frank in the face to something just over Frank's shoulder. That prompted Frank to turn, and when he did, he met a man in full momentum, charging toward him, a bottle clutched in both hands, lunging down at him. Frank was almost too late, but he sidestepped the man, kicking out his foot, tripping him up, sending him sprawling to the pavement. The bottle flew out of his hands, bouncing away from him, shattering. But before he was able to turn and get to his feet, Frank beat him down with the heel of his shoe, kicking him in the jaw. There was a dull "pop," like smashing a pumpkin with a baseball bat, and the man fell unconscious.

Frank turned around and was swept off his feet, held tightly around the waist by a huge man. He was forced backward through the air, slamming into the wall of a surrounding building. Frank hit hard, most of his wind being knocked from him, but he remained conscious. The huge man wrapped his giant hands around Frank's neck and started to squeeze. "What you coming around here for, boy?" the man mumbled, craziness in his eyes, as he continued to choke Frank.

Frank could feel himself becoming light-headed, could see everything becoming distorted before him, as he beat at the huge man's arms, and he knew if he didn't act now, the man would probably kill him. He reared back and sent the butt of his hand into the man's nose. The man wailed in pain, and a stream of blood shot from out of his nostrils, and though this didn't stop him from strangling Frank, it loosened his grip enough for Frank to act. With all his might, he kicked the man in the groin, and the man dropped to one knee, crying out, holding himself. Then Frank whipped his knee around, like a half kick, hitting the man against the side of the face. The man spun on his knees, his face crashing into the ground, his arms limp, falling to his side, unable to break his fall.

Frank looked up quickly and caught sight of André. He took off after him, but saw another man running straight toward him from another direction. Frank tried to dodge him, but the man ran right into him and grabbed him. They both rolled across the pavement, their arms and legs locked within each other's, vying for position. When they stopped rolling, Frank found the man straddled across his chest, a brick in his hand, preparing to club Frank. Before he could, Frank struck him in the sternum with his fist. The man froze, gasping for air, grabbing at his chest. The brick dropped from his hand, falling just to the side of Frank's head. Frank grabbed the man by his collar and yanked him off, rolling on top of him. Frank was infuriated by that time. The man grabbed Frank's jacket, but Frank still had ahold of his, and he raised the man's head off the ground and slammed it against the fallen brick. But the man didn't let go, just held on tighter. So Frank slammed his head again.

"Let go, you fuck! Let the fuck go!" Frank yelled from between clenched teeth each time the man's head struck the brick, until his arms finally fell limp to his side. Frank let him go. He saw a thick stream of crimson crawl from out behind the man's head, and wondered if he had killed him. He placed his palm under the man's coat and felt for his heart; it was still beating. "Lucky bastard," Frank said, at that point not caring if the man was dead or alive.

Frank heard a noise, and he whipped his head and saw André running. Frank chased him down and tackled him, both men falling to the ground in a cloud of dirt.

"What the fuck was all that! I ought to kill your ass right here, I swear I ought to!" Frank said, standing up, out of breath again.

"I ain't tell them to jump you," André said. "They see a white boy in the hood beating up a brother, who side you think they going to take?"

Frank clenched his jaws, trying to suppress the anger he was feeling for fear it would take him over, and someone would eventually find old André Hinton's body decaying in an alley somewhere.

"I'm not trying to hurt you. I told you that. I'm trying to help you!"

"How you going to help me?" André said, pointing at Frank, the black man's face showing all the hate in the world. "You ain't got shit to do with this! You ain't got to be out here, you don't deal with not having no job, trying to take care of some kid you don't even know is yours for sure. Having to have to rob folks just for a little pocket change so you can feel like you ain't no worthless piece of shit with no money in your pocket and nothing to live for. All you got to do is get back in your car and roll back to the damn suburbs, 'cause the only reason you out here is 'cause you gotta be. Fuck you trying to help," André said, his face starting to soften, as if he were on the brink of crying. "If they weren't paying you to do this shit, you wouldn't give a damn about my black ass."

Frank looked at the man and actually felt sorry for him. He didn't know if the statement that André just made was true or not, but he wanted to think that it wasn't, that he was doing this for more than the pennies that Rowen tossed his way. But something told him that that wasn't actually the case. He did care about what was going on with this guy. Maybe because he could sympathize with him, being at the end of his rope, knowing no one to turn to, figuring no one really gave a damn. He knew exactly how he felt, and the funny thing was, he wanted to tell André that. He wanted to tell this man that he'd never met before, that had almost got him killed, that he understood the pain he felt. And what was even more strange was that Frank wanted to confide in him, tell him his problems, let him know that he wasn't the only one who thought his life was shit.

"I care," Frank said slowly, testing the water. "And I know what you're going through, but your situation ain't that bad. At least if you want to see your child, all you have to do is go there. That's it. Let me tell you something, I can't do that. I try to see my child every day, but the damn courts say I can't. They took my rights away. They said I can't step near her without the permission of her mother, and she refuses to let me. Do you believe that? She refuses to let me see my own daughter," Frank said, looking down. When he looked back at André, he saw that he still had the man's attention. He didn't know what was going through his head, but Frank continued on anyway.

"So your situation isn't that bad, but you have to take advantage of it, André. You can't let problems stand in the way of seeing your child. Problems don't mean anything to them, all they know is they aren't seeing their father, and it hurts them, do you know what I mean?"

André didn't say anything, just looked up at Frank from the ground.

Frank squatted down so that he could look directly into André's eyes. "I want you to promise me something. I want you to promise me that you'll go see the mother of your child, and do what you can for them, because that child needs you, his mother needs you, and children only grow up once. You understand? Let me help you up."

Frank extended his hand. "Will you do that for me?"

André grabbed Frank's hand, pulled himself closer to the white man, face to face, then André spat a mouthful of saliva and mucus into Frank's face. "Fuck no, I won't do that for you!" André said, releasing Frank's hand and falling back to the ground. "You don't know nothing about me, motherfucker!" André spat. "Talking that nonsense, like we got things in common. We ain't got jack shit in common, so you can take that white-bread child-psychology shit back to your local library, prick!"

While André was telling Frank off, the saliva was slowly crawling down Frank's face as he stood there still, like a park statue just blasted by a mess of bird droppings. He didn't move an inch, just stood there, not even looking down at the man in front of him, but over his head, letting the anger build in him till he could contain it no more, till his blood boiled and felt as if it would spew out of his ears like molten lava from a volcano. He didn't try to control the anger, but he welcomed it, because there were some times when suppression did nothing but stop things that were supposed to happen.

Frank directed his stare at André. There was enough hate in Frank's eyes to kill the man without ever touching him, but Frank had different intentions.

"I tried to help you, you bastard," Frank said softly, his anger building, his body becoming hotter with each word he spoke. "I tried to help you, and I told you about my problems, thinking that we could relate, and you spit in my face like it doesn't mean anything, like what I'm going through, or what I'm trying to do here isn't worth a damn! Isn't worth a goddamn!" he said, raising his voice. "Well, fine. I tried to do it their way, I tried, but now I'm going to do it mine."

Frank went inside his jacket, into the secret pocket, and pulled out two twin objects, slipping them onto his fist. They were brass knuckles. It had been years since he'd used them, since he'd had to, but they felt good on his hands, like an old pair of favorite gloves he'd lost and found again. He struck his fists together, the brass striking, making a metal clanking sound. He looked down at André, barely able to see him through the rage that was blinding him. The man was cowering beneath him, a look of stark fear on his face, and as Frank approached him, he remembered a pertinent expression that Rowen always said to the groups of worthless fathers he spoke to, and Frank spoke those words.

"Your child can't wait any longer, shit bag!" he said, as he charged at the man, his fists flying in a blind flurry.

CHAPTER FIVE

Zale looked down at his watch, finished some paperwork, grabbed his things, and went to Martin's office. When he poked his head through the door, Martin was on the phone, no doubt still cleaning up the mess from the interview.

"I'm on my way out," Zale said, mouthing the words more than speaking them.

Martin excused himself from the phone call. He pulled the phone from his head, and cupped his hand over the mouthpiece.

"What would you say if I told you I still think you shouldn't go. Wait till this thing blows over."

"I would say that you've already told me that today, and telling me again really won't serve any purpose," Zale said. "But thanks for the concern. Is Frank back yet?"

"No. I sent him with a number of files today, he shouldn't be in till late."

"All right, I'm gone, then."

"Good luck," Martin said, and Zale knew, even though that was something that never seemed to brush up against him, he needed it, especially tonight. He stepped out of the building, and although the sun was not down, the evening sky had already begun to darken. With his briefcase in hand and his jacket over his arm, he walked briskly toward his Volvo. He wasn't late, but he always preferred to arrive sometime earlier than he was scheduled. As he walked closer to his car, he noticed that something didn't seem quite right about the way it was sitting, and it sparked fear in him that made him start to run toward the car. When he got there, he stopped just in front of it, examined it briefly, dropped his head down, and let his briefcase and jacket fall to the ground.

All four tires of his car had been knifed, and from the front of the hood, across the front windshield, over the roof of the car, stretching to the back windshield and on down the trunk, the words "Father Fool" were spray-painted in big, white, dripping letters. Zale walked slowly around the car, not believing what he was seeing. He spun around, looking up and down the street, as if the person who had done this terrible thing had just fled and could be caught running frantically down the sidewalk, looking over his shoulder, or hiding behind a nearby tree, hoping he wouldn't be spotted. But Zale knew this could've been done any time that he was in his office, and that had been hours.

He kicked the car's wheel as hard as he could, as cars drove by him, their occupants craning their necks to get a look at the defaced car and the pissed-off owner. Zale walked around to the street side of the car, and as he was unlocking the door to see if any damage was done to the inside, a car pulled up next to him. It was a big car, a huge Lexus with tinted black windows, fat tires, and rims so shiny that they reflected each smashed cigarette butt and wad of chewed bubble gum that stuck to the filthy street. Zale's back was facing the car that was so quiet he didn't even hear its exhaust or realize that it had pulled right up beside him. The darkly tinted passenger window slid down; a wisp of cigar smoke escaped from the opening.

"Mr. Rowen!" a voice yelled from the car, shocking Zale so much that he spun around, rolled on his back, and quickly slid as far under the dash as he could, fearing an attack. In that brief moment, Zale waited to hear shots ring out, feel shattered glass rain on his arms and head, but nothing happened.

Zale sat up cautiously, looking over the dashboard to see the 400 series Lexus pulling forward a few feet. Its hazards came on, and the driver stepped out, walking toward Zale. Zale's heart was still pounding in his chest, but it started to slow when he realized whom the car belonged to, and who the man was that was walking toward him.

It was Mace, a friend from a long time back, a very long time back, who on occasion would come by to see Zale. He felt he had an obligation to protect Zale from all the evil in the world. He felt that Zale knew nothing about the streets, nothing about the people that he was dealing with on a day-to-day, and if he wasn't watched over, protected, he would eventually end up dead.

Mace knew that he was the man to do this for Zale, since he had power on the street, he liked to say. That power came from the product he sold. It made him "the man," it gave him strength and authority. People wouldn't cross him because he was Mace, the big drug kingpin, and the penalty for doing anything foul to, or against, him would be, at the very least, no more drugs, and at the extreme, something Mace described without words, but with a gesture: dragging his index finger across his throat, a tortured look on his face, representing someone getting their throat slit.

Every time Mace did that, Zale thought he looked pretty foolish, like a boy threatening his sister if she told their mother about the vase he broke and glued back together. But Zale knew the gesture was nothing to take lightly. He knew where it came from, saw how it originated.

Zale stood and stepped out of his car to see Mace walking toward him wearing a matching gray-and-black-striped linen shirt-and-pants outfit. It was very loose-fitting, flowing as he walked, the gold rings that covered four of the five fingers on each hand sparkling in the late-afternoon sun, as did his brilliantly polished Italian shoes clip-clopping across the pavement. His face was barely visible due to the wide gray derby he wore, and the dark shades, but Zale could see the smile that was emerging on the man's face as he came closer.

"Man, you sure ducked your ass for cover. You would've thought someone yelled grenade around this bitch."

Zale didn't respond to the comment, just shook Mace's hand when it was offered to him.

"You shoved your foot way down your throat this time, didn't you,

Ro," he said, pulling a smoking stogie from between his teeth, looking down at the vandalized car, shaking his head. "They jacked your ass pretty bad."

"I know," Zale said, slamming the door, and grabbing his jacket and briefcase. "I have someplace I have to be. Can you take me there?"

"Now that wouldn't have happened if you'd let me put a couple of my guys on you like I asked you to," Mace said, wheeling the big car slowly through the evening traffic. He was leaning far to the window side of the car, slumped way down in his seat, a limp wrist dangling over the steering wheel. He had taken off his hat. His hair was naturally straight and thin, and it was pulled to the back of his head, held together by a tiny red rubber band.

"Like I said before, I don't need any of your guys on me," Zale said, sitting in the huge leather seat, his briefcase in his lap, staring out the window through the dark tint.

"You don't? Why, because you have that white boy Rames taking care of matters? I don't like him, Ro. Something's wrong about him, and you letting him work for you is like letting the wolf in the henhouse just because he promises to be good."

"The man saved my life."

"And what does that mean?" Mace said, cutting ahead of a slow-moving driver. "When hasn't 'Thank you' been enough to express your gratitude?"

"I don't need your help, Mace. I told you that," Zale said, turning to look at him. "And I don't need any drugs either."

"Oh, so why we got to go there?" Mace said, halting at a light, looking over at Zale.

"We didn't go anywhere, I'm not the one who's selling."

"And what the fuck is that supposed to mean!"

"I'm just letting you know why I don't want your help. I can't have that type of business mixing with my business. I have enough negativity around me without any help from you."

"I see," Mace said, taking a slow, wide turn onto a busy street. "Let me tell you something about this negativity, Mr. Rowen." He said the name as if it were royalty. "I do good things with the money I make from selling, all right? I put a lot of it right back in this fucked-up community."

"How much is a lot?" Zale asked. "Seventy-five, eighty percent?"

"A lot, all right, and leave it at that. See that supermarket right there?" Mace stabbed a finger at the window in the direction of a grocery store. "I donated a bunch of cash to have that built, and if I had time, I could drive you around this neighborhood and show you all kinds of things I had some play in."

"So that makes the drugs you sell okay? A small portion of the money goes back into the community and everything is just fine, right? Folks aren't knocking people over the head and robbing people just for the money to pay for a five-dollar hit, all because Mace is building supermarts. Forgive me for saying so, but I think that's bullshit, and I don't think you're looking at the whole picture."

"Well, I don't think you're looking at the whole goddamn picture, either!" Mace raised his voice, then reached over and clicked off the radio with enough force to almost pull off the tiny knob. "You need to understand that drugs going to be sold out here, 'cause that's how it is. Life out here is fucked-up, and it demands drugs to be sold just to make it bearable. And let me tell you, it's better I sell them, someone who cares about these people, and puts the money back, than someone else who don't even live here, someone who can give less than a damn about these folks, takes his money and goes back to the fuckin' burbs."

"You do really care about these people, don't you," Zale said sarcastically. "How many of your *clients* are children?" Zale said, looking hard at the side of Mace's face.

"I don't do that, man! I don't do that! All I do is provide. I don't have no promotional shit going on. I ain't trying to lure people to get on the wagon so I can increase my take. The ones who are already hooked, I give to, that's it, and none of them is kids."

"You must feel pretty good about yourself, Mace."

"I don't have to answer to you, Ro. I don't, and the only reason I'm explaining this to your high, mighty ass is because we go back. I know who the hell you are. I know you like nobody else knows you. I see those articles in the magazine, 'Who the fuck is Zaleford Rowen, and what drives him?' And I think to myself, I know who he is, and I know what drives him. It's the same thing that drives me, Ro. The exact same thing, and you know what the hell I'm talking about. We went through it, and we went through it together, and we came out not bad considering, but we battle those ghosts, in different ways, that's all. We go back, Ro, too far back, that's why I'm trying to help you here, because you swimming down the wrong lane. It shouldn't take me to tell you that. Just take a look at your car."

Zale sighed, slumped in his seat, and turned his attention out the window at the street passing quickly by. "I'll deal with that."

"You're a fucking fool! How, Ro, how are you going to deal with it? When a mob of angry men charge your building with knives and bats, what are you going to do, climb to the top with a bullhorn and tell them to settle down? They'll throw rocks up there till they knock you off, then they'll take turns smashing you with their heels till you're dead."

"Thanks for telling me my future."

"Ro," Mace said, pulling over to the curb just before the building he was to let Zale off at. He turned to Zale and looked at him very seriously. "Have you ever killed anyone before?"

Zale returned the look of seriousness, but didn't have to think about the answer. "No, I can't say that I have."

"It's not something you ever want to do. It's not a pretty sight, and sometimes it can be damn messy, but, then again, you know a little about that," Mace said, his voice lowering in volume but becoming more intense. "People get dead for a lot of reasons. Sometimes for messing with the wrong man's woman. Sometimes it's for selling in the wrong hood, or sometimes it's for nothing at all. Some people will kill for nothing at all, just for the hell of it, and that's bad. But what's worse is a man who feels he has a reason. What you've been saying about some of these men, what you've been doing, fucking with their money, making them lose their jobs, that'll give a motherfucker a reason. And there ain't nothing worse than a man on a mission, with a purpose." Mace placed a hand on Zale's shoulder. "I'm only trying to help you because I believe in what you're doing. I was there, remember. But don't let the past get you so screwed up in the head that it takes away your future. This fucked-up world can't afford to lose one Zaleford Rowen. Don't sleep on this, you hear me."

"Don't worry, I haven't been sleeping on much lately," Zale said, stepping out of the car, slamming the door.

He walked around to the other side and shook Mace's hand. "Thanks for the ride, and the offer for your help, all right? I hope you understand why I can't take you up on it."

"Don't worry about it, you'll need it one of these days, but then I might make you pay," Mace said, giving Zale a half smile. "What time is this over? I'll have a car and a couple of my boys waiting on you, just in case you say the wrong thing in there."

Zale looked over his shoulder at the building. "That's okay. I'll call Regina and have her pick me up."

Mace gave him a look as if he was again making the wrong decision. "Whatever you say, Ro." He clicked his radio back on full blast, threw on his sunglasses even though the sun was down and the streetlights had already started to flicker on.

"Remember what I said. Don't sleep. I like you living." The black window of his car raised back up, and he sped off, his brake lights flashing only briefly at a stoplight. Then the car continued on through the red light, speeding down the street.

Zale walked up the stairs into the building. It was an old state building, somehow linked to the courts. He was late, but only by five minutes. He walked down the long corridor until he was greeted by a woman in a blue blazer and skirt.

"Mr. Rowen, how are you? The lecture hall is this way."

She guided Zale to a door with a small window in it. "This is it, Mr. Rowen. Will you be needing anything else?" she said, smiling.

"No," he said. "Nothing."

She walked off, leaving him standing there, just outside the door. He peeked in through the small window, making sure not to be seen. The room was filled to capacity, as he knew it would be. Filled with men of all races and social classes, wearing everything from work boots to ties and business suits. Men that had no choice but to attend this lecture, or else pay a fine of $500. Some of them were looking down at their watches impatiently, as if they had other places to go, better things to do. Zale would make them wait. They had no better place to go, he told himself, but to see their children, but since he knew they weren't going there, he would just make them wait.

He had no lecture prepared for these men, because the one he was going to use was far too brash and he'd tossed it, since he'd told Martin he would tone down. But then he thought about what happened to his car and realized nothing was too harsh for these men. Yes, he knew what he told Martin, but Martin didn't really know what was going on, wasn't out dealing with these men as he was every day, and Zale was sure Martin's car looked as nice at it had when he drove it to work this morning. So his promise to Martin was voided. And as far as fearing for his life, he had all the time in the world to do that, but right now he was too angry.

Zale walked in the room, a stern look on his face, his teeth clenched, his fist folded into a hard knot at his side, wishing that he could hit someone with it. The air in there was thick, and as soon as he was seen by the group of fifty or so men, their low chatter of conversation silenced. Zale put his briefcase down and stood behind the podium. He didn't look out into the audience, but he could feel the combined stare of all those men burning on him, trying to make him turn and walk away, but there was no way he would do that. The truth was, he was right where he wanted to be, would've rather been nowhere else. These men were his for as long as he wanted them to be, and they *had* to sit and listen.

When he finally looked up at them, all their faces seemed to be reading the same thing—anger. It looked as though every single one of those men blamed Zale for whatever wrong was going on in his life. He recognized quite a few of them, had files on them, and he even remembered speaking to some of them on the phone, getting an earful of curse words and foul suggestions while they ranted in anger. He also saw several reporters from local newspapers, both small and large.

The room was very quiet, and Zale let it remain that way for almost a full five minutes. He saw the men start to fidget, look at him as though he should start speaking or get his ass off the podium, but it made no difference to Zale. He wasn't trying to find something to say because he already knew the first words that would come out of his mouth. They would be the exact words he felt, and after five minutes of complete silence, he spoke.

"I hate you men!" he said, feeling and meaning every single one of the words, and although he spoke in a very calm voice, his hand was wrapped so tightly around a pencil that he was on the verge of snapping it in half. "I thought I'd say that first, get it out of the way so you'd know right up front that I'm not trying to befriend any of you. So when you give me the evil stares, thinking that they will hurt my feelings, make me feel uncomfortable, or drive me away, you'll know that that won't happen, and that I really don't give a damn. I don't give a damn that you don't like me, because I don't like you men either." He paused for a minute, giving someone an opportunity to stand and say something, almost hoping that someone would, so he could chop him down at the knees, sending him back to his seat, but no one said a thing, so Zale continued.

He continued on about how he hated them, not for who they were, but for what they were doing, depriving their children of one of the most important things they would ever need—a father. He spoke very directly to them, telling them of their extreme importance, how much they were needed, and telling them how wrong they were for shucking their responsibilities, and when some of the men became outraged and tried to reply to the things Zale was saying, Zale yelled at them to sit down. He took no question, heard no man's opinion, and made them feel like dirt, like men afraid to take responsibility for the decisions they made.

"When someone asks you men if you have any children, I wonder what you say. I'm sure most of you just lie and say no. And although you don't realize it, that's the proper response. The men in this room who do claim their children are wrong, because they are not yours to claim if you aren't there for them. If you hoard your money like it's doing more good in your damn pockets than it would buying the things needed for your child, that child is not yours, and you men aren't their fathers. And I hope none of you cowards call yourselves a part of your children's lives when you stop by on Christmas and drop off some cheap trinket you bought at the last minute, expecting a warm hug and gratitude from that child. Or my favorite is when some of you men swing around on some Saturday evening just because you were in the neighborhood, saying that you came to see your child when all you were actually doing is trying to fuck the child's mother! And you know you can, because you know all she wants is to have you back in her life, in her child's life! And she would be willing to do almost anything. Including fucking you limp-dick bastards."

There was a huge uproar from the men, some of them standing, some jabbing fingers and fists in Zale's direction, all of them shouting loudly as they could to be heard over all the other enraged fathers.

Zale allowed them to lose their minds for only a moment, then yelled at the top of his voice, "Sit your sorry asses down!"

The men were still arguing and yelling, squirming around like a mob of crazed fans trying to rush to the stage to engulf their favorite singer.

"I said, sit down!" Zale yelled again, this time, much louder, as loud as he could, but they still didn't respond. Zale looked to the side of the podium, and picked up the heavy crystal pitcher he had been drinking water from during the speech. He lifted it up high above his head and flung it to the floor. The heavy pitcher crashed into a million pieces, causing a deafening sound that silenced the entire room.

The men were still. Some men sat, some stood in the aisles, all looking at Zale with dumbfounded expressions on their faces.

Zale paused a moment, looking at them, disdain in his eyes, frustration in his heart.

"You just don't get it, do you?" he said, his voice lowered, but holding just as much rage. Zale looked back and forth over the crowd of men, shaking his head with pity.

"You're like a bunch of damn kids. Someone tells you what you don't like to hear and some of you pout and cry, and some of you stomp your feet and poke your lips out, and then some of the brave ones raise their fists like they're going to do something. What big men you are," Zale said sarcastically. "But the truth is, you aren't going to do shit! You're going to raise your voices, and complain, and then a couple of you may muster up the courage to vandalize my building or my car, like someone did this afternoon. That's a cowardly move, but what should I have expected from a room full of . . . cowardly children."

The men said nothing to Zale's words this time. No one sat up, not a single man stirred. They just took what was dished out to them, as if they were numbed by the previous insults.

"You men must not know what you're doing. You can't know. You just can't, because if you did, you wouldn't be doing this!" Zale squeezed the space in between his eyes with his thumb and forefinger, telling himself to relax, begging himself to gain control so he could reason with these men, so he could give them something that they would be willing to take with them.

"Let me tell you something. Your children you left, a lot of them are still asking, Where is Daddy, when is he coming back? They're staying awake at night, lying in their beds, because they can't sleep. They're hoping to hear the doorbell ring, hoping that it's their father, but when you don't show night after night, and when every time the phone rings, you're not on it, your children are going to stop asking about you. And when they're lying in bed at night, and the only thing they feel is loneliness, eventually they're going to replace that with hate and resentment. And they're going to get to the point where they can't stand you, where they would rather not see you ever again, and would prefer that they never had met you."

Zale looked out upon the men's faces, and their eyes were glued on him. There was not a single movement among the men, but if they were actually believing him, if this was hitting home, he could not be sure.

"I know what I'm talking about. I'm speaking from experience. Do something now," Zale said, looking sternly out into the men's faces. "Your children can't wait any longer."

Zale didn't announce that he was finished, just stopped speaking and started to gather up his things as if he were in his home alone, getting ready to leave for work. He assumed the men would realize that they had been dismissed and start to leave themselves; they would have to, because he was still too bitter to say another word to them.

They slowly began standing, filing out quietly and peacefully, not one man glancing at or saying a word to Zale. He didn't know if that was good or bad, but it didn't really matter, because he felt he had gotten his point across, and maybe even reached a few of them.

When the last man filed out the door, Zale was surprised to see one man remaining in the room. It was a man in the front row. He was wearing an expensive suit, his legs crossed and his hands folded in his lap the entire length of the speech. When all the other men were in an uproar, he sat there as if patiently waiting for the noon bus to arrive. He was still sitting there as he had been throughout the entire lecture, not seeming to move an inch. He stood, walked over to Zale, and extended his hand. Zale shook it.

"Very inspiring speech, Mr. Rowen, but you were quite hard on those men," the fortyish-looking man said.

"I was quite hard on you, too, unless you just sat in to check my technique," Zale said, pulling his hand from the man.

"No, I wasn't, but I didn't take what you were saying as being directed toward me."

"Well, you had to come here just like the rest of the men, didn't you?"

"Yes, but I am taking care of my children, and I give all that I can give without taking the shirt off my back and pawning it for a dollar." The man spoke slowly, articulating each word, almost elegantly.

"Judging by the look of your shirt, I'd believe you could get more than a dollar."

"That is beside the point, Mr. Rowen. I give what I can, in time, money, and effort, and that is because I love my children. But 'child support' is not a term that is meant to be interchanged with 'mother-of-child support,' because this woman is not my wife, and just because she feels I owe more and has somehow persuaded the courts into believing that, I am sent here and referred to as a coward. You are wrong, Mr. Rowen. To cover such a wide group of men, with such differing circumstances, with so wide a blanket statement is wrong, dead wrong. And if you knew what was best for you, you would withhold your opinions for the men they properly suit. Good night, Mr. Rowen." The man turned and walked toward the door.

"And what is that supposed to mean? Is that a threat of some kind?" Zale said.

The man turned back to face Zale. "I don't need to make threats, Mr. Rowen. You have more than enough rope to do the job yourself. Good night."

Zale studied the man as he walked out the door. It was one more man that wouldn't listen, one more man that thought Zale had no idea what he was talking about, and, unfortunately, one more man that Zale had to keep his eye open for. But he would have to step in line, because there were many, and after tonight, Zale was sure there would probably be many more.

Zale went to the pay phone and called Regina. She was home, as he knew she would be, and when he asked her to pick him up, she said she would be right over. Zale walked outside and stood on the curb of the dark street. Everyone had gone by now, leaving him out there by himself, just him, his briefcase, silence, and his thoughts. And this is how he felt almost all the time, when someone was staring him in the face, having a conversation with him, or when surrounded by a room full of people: alone. He wondered, was this his fault, or was it meant to be that way? He didn't know and didn't feel like trying to figure it out. He was too tired, so what he did was stand out on that dark, lonely street, watching the occasional car go by, and wait. He would wait for Regina to pick him up, and wait for whatever other problems he would encounter.

CHAPTER SIX

Martin held himself over his wife, and it was the only place on earth he wanted to be. His arms were beginning to tremble from holding himself elevated above her, but he paid them no mind, lowering his face just a little to kiss her on the forehead. His bare body touched hers, his legs upon her legs, his chest smashing her breast, his body playfully threatening to slide into hers at the slightest turn, and it seemed like an eternity since he had felt his body against hers like that.

Earlier that evening, on the ride home from work, he was dreading returning home. He was hating the idea of walking into that house, dismissing the babysitter, and having to tell his children some lie, make another excuse for their mother. As he wheeled his car home, he told himself that he would have to be firm with her, tell her that there would be no more staying out late, no more denying him for a damn job, paying more attention to ailing children in the hospital than her well children at home.

Martin slid the key into the front door, expecting to open it and see the babysitter standing there, her book bag on her shoulder, waiting to be freed so that she could bolt out of there quickly. But when he opened the door, there was no babysitter; there was no Renee or Rebecca complaining about going to bed; there was nothing but quiet, and it made Martin feel uncomfortable, as if he had walked into someone else's home by mistake.

He looked around a moment, then saw his wife's shoes near the door. He wandered into the kitchen and saw her keys on the hook and realized that she was home early. He stopped there in the kitchen, staring at the keys, not able to remember the last time that she beat him home. It had to be the talk he had with her last night. Even though it seemed she was apathetic to what he was saying, she must have really taken note of the words he spoke and realized that he was dead serious. And if that was the case, he wouldn't have to reiterate. He wasn't looking forward to it anyway.

Excited, he took the stairs, smiling like a child with a surprise gift waiting atop his bed. He stopped into the girls' room and kissed them both good night. Then he went into his bedroom, where his wife was lying on the bed watching television.

"I'm glad you made it home early tonight," Martin said, taking off his jacket and tie, then cuddling up next to her.

"Well, we weren't that busy tonight," Debra said, her attention on the TV. "Besides, you act like every single night of the week I stay out late. It only happens sometimes, so I don't see why you always make such a big deal out of it."

Martin just looked at her, a love-struck haze over his eyes. "Let's not talk about that right now, all right? I have you here and I don't want to spend this time arguing. We do enough of that, don't you think?"

Debra nodded, her arms crossed over her chest, her attention still directed toward the TV.

"Can I at least have a kiss hello?" Martin asked.

Debra didn't move immediately, but waited a moment, as if she would miss something crucial on television if she moved too soon. Then she turned and gave Martin a quick, dry kiss on the lips. "Hello, baby," she said, then went back to her program.

Martin sat there and chuckled. "You don't really call that a kiss, do you?"

"I don't know what else to call it."

"Well, let me show you what a kiss really is." Martin grabbed the remote, clicked off the television, scooted over on top of his wife, and began to kiss her passionately. He felt resistance at first, but then she started to relax. He smoothed his hands over her long, black hair. His hands caressed her beautiful face, her soft skin, roamed about her body. Then he started to undo the buttons on her blouse. When it was all the way open, he tried to slip his hands behind her back to undo her bra, but it didn't seem as if she was trying to help him.

"Martin, wait," she said, her words muffled by Martin's lips.

"What, baby?" Martin said, continuing to kiss her, still fumbling with the clips on the back of her bra.

"I said, wait!" she said, pushing her hands into his chest, trying to push him off her.

Martin realized what was going on, realized that she was serious, and pulled himself off from on top of her. "What's the problem?"

She lay there, her shirt open, her arms down at her sides, breathing harder than normal, as if she had just survived an attack of some kind. Seeing her like that made Martin feel like a molester or a pervert for wanting to make love to his own wife, and that wasn't right.

"I just don't feel like it tonight, all right?" Debra said, running her hand through her frenzied hair, attempting to straighten it after Martin's assault.

By that point, Martin was frustrated, mind and body.

"When was the last time you did feel like it, Debra? When was the last time we made love? Do you remember?"

Debra covered herself with the halves of her shirt and crossed her arms over her chest again. "I don't know," she said, looking toward the ceiling. "I think it's been almost a week."

"Try almost three. Almost three weeks since I made love to my wife, because every time I try, she turns me down. You're tired, you say. Why have you been so tired lately?"

"Because I work," Debra said sharply, as if angered by his not remembering the reason.

"And you can't do both? Your work is so involved, it demands that much of you physically, that you can't even come home to your husband and fuck him once every couple of weeks!"

Debra looked hurt by the remark. "So what do you think, I'm lying again?" she said, getting up from the bed, walking around it and making her way toward the bathroom. Martin cut her off, stood in front of her and grabbed her by the shoulders.

"I don't think you're lying, because I don't think you'd lie to me," he said. "I just know how much I love you, how much I need you. There are times when I'm at work and all I do is think about you, think about getting home to be with you, and it's like torture, but I think about it anyway, because I can't get my head to stop. That's how I feel about you, that's how I love you, and when I get home, and you tell me you're tired, it says to me that you don't feel the same, and it makes me wonder what the hell is going on." Martin placed a gentle hand on her face, looked into her beautiful brown eyes, nothing giving him any insight to what she was thinking. Then he kissed her softly on her lips.

"All I want to do is love you."

"Okay," she said, and it sounded more as if she were complying with some form of instruction than agreeing to make love to her husband. But Martin paid no attention to that, didn't even catch how much it lacked emotion, just began to undress her, as she let him, not fighting him, nor helping. When all her clothes lay at her feet, he lowered her in the bed, between the sheets, and undressed himself, an intense desire coursing through him, making it hard to concentrate on the small buttons of his shirt and the clip on his trousers.

He took his underwear off, and slid between the sheets of the bed. He climbed on top of his wife, stabbing her a number of times with his overexcited organ. He elevated himself over her and just stared at her for a moment, then lowered his face and kissed her on the forehead. He felt his arms start to weaken, so he lowered his entire body on top of hers, and he felt himself coming close to losing it all right there, before it even started.

Martin kissed her neck and her shoulders, smoothing his hands excitedly all about her body as he maneuvered between her legs. He looked up to see the expression on his wife's face, but there wasn't one. She was staring up at the ceiling, but when she noticed his stare, her expression changed quickly to something between mild pain and extreme pleasure.

"It feels good, baby," she said, in an overly sexy, 1-900 voice. "I want you now." Her hands were on his bottom, forcing him into her, and those were the words Martin had been waiting so long to hear.

He slid into her, feeling only mild resistance, but once he was in, it felt like pleasure he had never experienced in life. It was as if he were a virgin once again, and he knew he would have to be careful, take his time, because it had been so long since their last encounter.

But as soon as he was entirely within her, before he even had an opportunity to get his bearings, her arms wrapped around his body, her legs clamped around his back, urging him deeper into her. Then she started to roll her body this way and that, gyrate her hips, while forcing him in and out of her by pushing him off with her arms and pulling him back in with her legs. Already he could start to feel his head spinning, start to feel himself losing control, his body no longer listening to him but listening to her, as she whispered in his ear, "Come on, Martin. Come on, baby." She said it rhythmically, each time she pulled him in, urging him to abandon his will to maintain. "Come on, baby. Come on."

Martin spread his arms out wide above her head, grabbing on to the sheets, trying to hold on. But it was no good, and it seemed that Debra knew it. She sensed it like a shark smells blood, and she attacked, doing everything she was doing before, but twice as hard, twice as fast, pushing him out, pulling him in, and somehow lifting herself off the bed and throwing herself into him. "Come on, baby. Come on!"

"No. No!" Martin said, in a last attempt to fight the unavoidable.

"Come on!" she said more forcefully, her nails digging into his back, as if her life depended on him ejaculating. Then she stuck her hot, moist tongue into his ear and it was all over.

"No!" he cried out, as every muscle in his body contracted, and something inside him seemed to rupture in an explosion of extreme pleasure. It was over, all three minutes of it, and his body settled upon her like a ton of cement. Martin turned his head to slowly look up at his wife. She was sweating profusely, as he was, strands of her hair pasted to her face. She looked at him and smiled, but it was an uneasy smile. Then again it should've been, he told himself, because he had known what she was trying to do, what she had done.

He pulled himself up from her without saying a word and went into the bathroom to take a shower. When he came back out, a towel wrapped around his waist, the first thing out of his mouth was "What was that?"

Debra had been lying on her side, facing away from him. She turned. "What was what?"

"What we just did, or should I say, what you just did?"

"We made love. I thought that's what you wanted."

"It was what I wanted, but what was the rush? You got somewhere to be tonight?" Martin said, his arms crossed.

Debra looked at him for a moment, quizzically. "There was no rush," she said innocently. "It's just that it had been so long, like you said. I was excited. I guess too excited."

"Nonsense!" Martin raised his voice. "It's not that you were so excited or too excited. It was that you wanted it over, wanted it over as soon as possible, because you never wanted to do it in the first place. What you did was not making love to me, it was giving me charity, because you felt sorry for me. I begged you for sex, and you felt obligated, so you gave me some, and I want to know why it takes that, why you can't want me just because you do?"

"What are you talking about, Martin?" Debra said in a voice that trivialized his question.

"You know what I'm talking about. Are you seeing someone else?"

"Why do we always have to come back to this? I told you before."

"Answer the question," Martin insisted.

"Martin . . ."

"I said, answer the question."

Debra got out of bed and fished her blouse off the floor, wrapping it around her, as though what she was about to say could not be said in the nude.

She looked at him sternly, and something seemed to drain from her face, something that always made her recognizable to him in a way other than just her physical features, but she looked almost like a stranger the way she was looking at him now.

"Do you want the truth, or do you want what you want to hear?"

Martin knew what he wanted to hear, but he wanted that to be the truth, oh how he wanted it to be, but for some reason he felt it wasn't one and the same, and it made him fearful of answering the question.

"You know I want the truth," he said, trying to steady himself, for he was rattling inside.

Debra came around the bed facing him, sat down on it, her bare legs crossed, looking like a very well-endowed third-grader.

"Martin, you know I love you, and I'd never do something like that to you."

Martin just looked at her for a moment. "Do I know that?"

"Of course you do. You should know nothing different. From the beginning, I've never given you any reason to doubt how I feel about you, and just because I take my job seriously, and I come home tired sometimes, I'd like to think that wouldn't be enough to have you doubting my love for you. Does it, Martin?"

Martin looked away from her, toward the floor, because he couldn't continue to look in her eyes, look at her on that bed like that, half her body exposed, because she was melting his resistance, destroying his ability to think about this objectively. He wanted to tell her that there was no doubt that he was acting foolish, that it was just his self-confidence hitting rock bottom again when it came to her, but he couldn't just discount his feelings so easily. What he felt was real, and she made it that way.

Debra called his name again. Martin mumbled something, acknowledging the fact that he heard her, but he didn't look up.

"Martin," Debra called again, and then Martin saw her feet standing just in front of his, felt her hands on his chest, smelled her scent all about him.

"You don't believe I still love you?" she asked.

Martin looked up, stared her straight into her eyes, and for some reason he couldn't read her the way he always could. It was as if he were talking to a stranger.

"I think you still love me. What I'm unsure about is if you're cheating on me."

Debra blew out a long sigh of frustration. Her hands fell from his chest, and she turned her back on him, walked to the other side of the room. "This is becoming too much, Martin," she said, her back still facing him. "How am I expected to be trusted by you when it's not just you I'm dealing with? I also have to deal with your damn low self-esteem, the constant questioning of yourself. Asking, are you good enough to be with me? Do I really love you?" she said, spinning around. "Martin, I love you! I wouldn't be here if I didn't. I just wish you'd get past that, so you can stop with all your ridiculous suspicions."

"They aren't ridiculous, and it's not my self-esteem that has me questioning you this time. Believe it or not, I've learned to deal with that, or at least I'm trying. What I can't deal with is you traipsing in here after midnight, as if you live alone and have no one else to consider. Of course I'm going to be suspicious of you, and when you don't call me back when I page you, it's going to take more than just you telling me how you feel about me to trust in you. When I page you, you page me back, period. I don't care how you feel. I don't care if the entire hospital died, and the building crumbled to the ground. When you hear that beeper going off, you rush through the smoke, the rubble, and all the dying people, and find a phone that's working and call me back. Because what happens there has nothing to do with what happens here. Do you understand that?"

"I don't think so," Debra said under her breath, looking to the floor.

"What did you say?" Martin said, all of a sudden feeling rage.

Debra looked at him, surprised, as if she had not realized she spoke a word.

"I said, what did you say?"

"I said, I don't think so," Debra said, not backing down. "There are times when—"

"You don't think so, hunh," Martin said, rushing over right up in her face. "You don't think so! There's no such thing as an emergency at home? Or it really doesn't even have to be an emergency. Whenever you page me, I call you right back. Right back! That is me being considerate of you, caring about you. But forget about me for a moment. You've been neglecting me, but that's okay. I've almost gotten used to it, but what about those girls, your daughters. How are they supposed to feel when you come in hours after they go to bed and leave before they wake up? They don't see you for days sometimes, and I guess that's all right with you?"

Debra didn't say anything, just looked up into Martin's eyes.

"I asked you a question. Is that all right with you?" Martin barked, and it made his wife jump. She looked saddened by what he was saying, how he was saying it, and he wanted her to be saddened. He wanted her to feel hurt and low for neglecting the people whom she was supposed to love, and at this point, his anger went far beyond the question of her cheating on him.

"You still didn't answer my question."

Debra looked up at him, on the verge of tears, but her face remained dry.

"You know all I wanted to be was a doctor. That's all I ever wanted to be. Take care of sick children."

And at those words, Martin blew up. "And what about your own! You would neglect your own children for some other people's?"

"It's not like that, Martin," Debra said.

"What is it like? You're either there taking care of some other people's children, or you're here taking care of ours."

"Why are you saying that to me!" Debra said, the tears starting to fall.

"Are those children more important than ours!"

"Of course they aren't," Debra answered through her tears.

"Is that job more important than your family!"

"No!"

"Well, you're sure acting like it! You spend more time there than you ever did at home. More time with those children than your own. What kind of mother do you think that makes you!"

"Stop!" Debra screamed, her fists wrapped around the roots of her hair. "How dare you say those things to me. Those girls in there aren't even my own daughters!"

Martin had to stop, freeze, for he couldn't believe what he just heard from his wife. He couldn't speak for a long moment, just stood there, slack-jawed, for he never heard Debra say that before about his daughters. Not that it wasn't the truth, but the way she said it made his beautiful daughters seem like some horrible, dirty secret that she was ashamed of.

"Does that mean you shouldn't be expected to be a good mother to them?" Martin said, the volume and intensity in his voice now knocked down to that of a normal conversation.

"I didn't say that. I just don't feel I should be treated like some criminal just because I can't be around them every waking moment of their lives."

"Then who should be treated like a criminal? Their teacher, the babysitter? Are they supposed to be mother to my daughters since you can't?"

"I'm not saying I can't," Debra said, frustration in her voice. "Just maybe not as much as you would like. They would understand, considering the circumstances. Wouldn't they?"

Martin stood there not saying a word.

"I think it's time that we tell them the truth, Martin," Debra said, canting her head so she could look into her husband's downturned face.

"Martin, look at me."

Martin reluctantly pulled his head up to look at his wife.

"Oh, is that what you think? And when are we supposed to tell them that? At breakfast, while walking them to school, or maybe before putting them to bed, while kissing them on the cheek. 'Good night, and one more thing before you fall peacefully off to dreamland. That woman who you've known all your life as Mommy, ain't! Nighty-night.' How are we to tell them that?"

"I don't know!" Debra said frantically. "But how can we keep that from them? We need to tell those girls. They have the right to know!" Debra shook her head, as though there was something she was trying to shake from her brain. "No, no! If we can't agree to tell them, I will!"

Martin grabbed his wife by the arm, shaking her out of whatever frenzy she seemed to have had fallen in. "It's not time yet. They aren't ready! And maybe if you weren't crawling in here at all hours of the night, being a half-assed mother, you could see that."

Before Martin could tense up, close his eyes, he was met with a hard slap across the face. Debra stood there in front of him in no way looking remorseful for what she had just done, looking as if she would hit him a second time if he spoke like that to her again.

"Those girls have to know," Debra said.

Martin stood there in front of her, a blank look on his face, wondering how they got to where they were.

He remembered the first time he saw Debra. She was standing next to him in surgical scrubs, as he was, looking down at his wife. But he really didn't notice the nurse with the beautiful eyes, because at that moment, there was no other female living in the world that mattered but Martin's wife, his two-year-old, Renee, and the little girl that his wife was about to deliver.

Martin held his wife's hand, rubbing it with the other, telling her it would be all right, and trying to make himself believe the same. He told himself not to think about the first delivery, not to think about how both she and the baby came close to dying. After that, Martin told her that they would never have another child, that it was too dangerous, but his wife became pregnant not long after, as he knew she would.

"I'm sorry," she said, smiling, holding the little wand from the home pregnancy kit over the toilet. "But Renee's going to need someone to play with. I don't want her to be lonely. Please don't be mad."

But anger was the farthest thing from Martin's mind. He was overjoyed, but the joy was overshadowed by fear.

In the delivery room, he held her hand, bearing the force his wife put on it as her labor pains became worse. The doctor yelled instructions for her to breathe, breathe! But she yelled back that she wanted to push, she wanted to push so bad. Then all of a sudden, all the monitoring machines in the room started to scream. Lights began to flash all over, lines on the monitoring screens skipped and jumped as if they were reading an oncoming earthquake, and the doctor started barking out orders as the nurses ran around the small room carrying them out.

Martin looked around, his wife's hand still in his grasp. He looked down at her, and her head was lying to the side, her eyes closed.

"What's going on!" he yelled.

Then he heard someone say, "Get the husband out of here. Get him out!"

Before he knew it, he was being forced backward out of the room, through a number of sets of double doors.

"But my wife? What's wrong with my wife!"

"We don't know yet, Mr. Carter, but we're trying to find out, and we will. But we need you to stay out here," the nurse said, staring intently at him from over the surgical mask. "Can you do that?"

Martin nodded his head, and watched as she disappeared back through the doors.

"God help her," he said, ripping the mask from his face and falling to a chair. "God help her!"

An hour later, Martin was still sitting in the waiting room chair. He had not moved, and his body was as rigid as stone. He heard the doors behind him open, and whipped his head around to see the doctor and the nurse coming through the door. He got to his feet, and waited for them to approach him.

The doctor stopped and pulled the paper cap from his head.

"We saved your child, Mr. Carter. You have a beautiful baby girl," he said, but he didn't sound excited, and the dark look in his eyes foretold his news.

"But there were complications. We did everything in our power, used every resource we had available, but your wife didn't make it. I'm sorry."

Martin's breathing stopped. He couldn't move and he couldn't breathe. He couldn't even see, but there was this man standing in front of him, like something unreal, telling him his wife was dead, his life, his future, all that he cared about was gone.

"Mr. Carter? Mr. Carter?" He heard the doctor's voice echo around him, but Martin didn't respond, couldn't.

Martin saw the doctor look into his eyes to make sure he was all right.

"Debra, stay with him. I have to get back." It the doctor's voice again. Then he was gone, leaving the nurse out there alone.

"Mr. Carter. Mr. Carter," he now heard the nurse's voice call in a soft, soothing voice. He still could not move, but he saw her eyes, focused on them, and from one of them a tear fell, and then another, and as if he needed first to see someone else cry to know that it was okay, tears began to stream from his eyes. The nurse moved into him and wrapped her arms around him as he wept aloud, his body shaking from the realization that he would never see his wife again.

"It's okay, Mr. Carter, everything will be all right. Everything will be all right."

Martin's eyes focused on his wife standing before him, her hair mussed about her face, the blouse hanging open to display her nakedness.

"I'll tell the girls," he said. "In my own way. I'll tell them."

CHAPTER SEVEN

Frank sat on a stool in a bar owned by a few detectives he used to work with when he was on the force. The walls were covered with black-and-white pictures of policemen and police cars from years and years ago, and the ceiling fans spun at a lazy pace, not doing much for the mugginess and smoke that filled the room, but lending to atmosphere.

Cops lined the bar standing over their mixed drinks and mugs of beer. Some that Frank knew, a lot that he didn't. But that didn't matter, because he wasn't in a talking mood anyway. He sat at the corner of the bar, half sitting on his stool, half standing off it, one foot on the floor, as if he were about to leave. He was turned so that he was looking at no one, and no one was looking at him. He was in his own world, in conversation with himself, and the only reason he was even at the bar was that it was somewhere familiar to him, something that linked him to his past when things were good, or at least acceptable.

But things weren't even acceptable anymore. They were the pits, they were for shit, and he could barely stand crawling out of bed in the morning and going to that garbage-picking job. Frank slid his glass closer to himself. It was half empty, like his life, never half full, and it was warm, and the ice had melted, and the drink had probably gone all the way flat because it was halfway there when the fat bastard behind the bar gave it to him in the first place.

He pulled it up to his lips and the ginger ale slid into his mouth, warm, flat, and watered-down. He pursed his lips at the bad taste, slammed the glass to the bar and asked for another.

He was a human garbage picker, running around after trash that no one gave a damn about, not even the trash itself. So why should he give a damn? Why should he spend his time running around asking people questions about a man that they could care less whether he was living or dead? Why did he have to run these fools down, and on so many occasions, like today, risk his life, for nothing, for the little bit of pay that Rowen gave him? Why? He yelled at himself, picking up the fresh glass of ginger ale, and taking a sip.

Because he needed the job, he answered, lowering the glass. He needed the job, not just to survive, but to prove to his wife that he was still a man worth being with, worth taking back even though he did the terrible things he did. So that's why he was chained to this job he hated so much, but to get back to his wife and child was worth the sacrifice, and he told himself that every time a situation got stressful. Or every time Martin started messing with him for no reason, and he felt like taking those files and throwing them back in Martin's face and telling him where he could shove them, Frank told himself that all the hell that he had been enduring would be worth it.

He reached for the glass again, but not to drink from it, just to hold it in his hand, to look busy, so as not to seem like he was just sitting there, zoning out like some fuck face, space case.

A little while ago, things started to get particularly rough for Frank. Between handing out business cards and notices like some glorified paper boy, trying to track these men down, asking questions all around town, showing up at the places they used to live at, or the place they just left an hour ago, he started to feel as if he were just spinning his wheels. He was doing all the damn work, but getting nothing accomplished, and when he finally did catch up to these bastards, they looked at him with less respect than they would give a night watchman or a damn dogcatcher, all because he was no longer a "real cop," and that pissed him off no end.

They would damn near laugh in his face and spit on his feet, telling him to beat it, and all he could do was try to reason with them, tell them why they should try to see their children, the difference it would make in the long run for all parties, and so on, and so on. But they wouldn't hear Frank. He wouldn't have even made the effort if he didn't believe in what Rowen was trying to do. He would've dumped all the pamphlets and cards and everything else upon stepping out of the office in the morning, but he did believe. So he went through the motions. If they don't seem interested, tell them anyway, Rowen said. Leave them the notice letting them know someone is looking for them, and that if they don't act soon, the situation will be turned over to the government, and they may even have to go to jail.

Oooooooo! That was supposed to be the big threat, Frank thought. That was supposed to bug their eyes and get their attention, but it didn't do shit. They laughed and walked away, leaving Frank standing there with the notice in his hand, feeling like some supermarket-coupon lady handing out discounts on some worthless crap that nobody would be interested in if it was free. And then, a week later, the same file would land in his lap because the guy had never contacted the mother or Father Found, so Frank would be running the same circles again. For what?

But not anymore. Frank thought that Rowen was a good man, and he firmly believed in what he was trying to do, and when it came to organizing and giving speeches and doing paperwork, he was fine. But he knew nothing about policing, nothing about discipline, so there was no way that he could possibly tell Frank how to manage those fools out there. So Frank had to do it his way. And it was surprising how few repeat files he got when he initiated his own strategy. Grabbing these guys and slamming them up against the wall when they looked at him as though he were joking, or giving them a knee to the groin when they blurted something disrespectful, or just beating the hell out of them when they said they just wouldn't see their kids anymore. It was amazing what a little physical contact could achieve.

But, like today, sometimes it got out of hand, and his fists alone couldn't properly convey the message he intended for them. That's when he had to use his special tools. That's when they had to know that he meant business, and know that this wasn't some fucking game that they were playing. He hated to do that, see them lying out, bruised, oftentimes unconscious and bleeding. He would just stand over them, shaking his head, their blood dripping from the metal loop around his knuckles, hoping no one would find out about the measures he had to take. But he didn't think they would, because it only happened three times, and after each time, he told himself it would never happen again, but he meant it this time.

Frank took another sip of his ginger ale. When he brought the glass down, a man was standing in front of him. He was a big, well-built black man, wearing a suit jacket and slacks, his gun holster slightly visible.

"Frank, what are you doing here?" he said. It was Frank's old partner, Harper.

"What does it look like I'm doing here? I'm unwinding like the rest of these guys. I just happen to be doing it with ginger ale." He lifted the glass.

Harper looked around for a bar stool, placed it next to Frank, and had a seat.

"Why did you come *here* to wind down?"

"What, I'm not a cop anymore, so I can't come here?"

"You know that's not what I'm talking about. Being around all this liquor, didn't they tell you that would make you want to drink?" Harper said, his voice lowering on the second sentence.

"Yeah, so what? That's what they said, but I'm not tempted. I know what it did to me, what it did to my family. You think I'd be ready to crawl back into a bottle after that?"

"Not that I'm not happy to see you, but if you aren't here to drink, why are you here?"

Frank looked at him, shaking his head. "I've known you ten years, and you've always been a dumb son of a bitch. I don't have to come in here to drink myself into oblivion. I could get a bottle and get torn down in the privacy of my crappy one-bedroom apartment, or get trashed doing seventy-five down I-Ninety-four if I wanted to. I'm just here because I miss this place. Am I supposed to drop off the face of the earth just because I'm not a cop anymore?"

"I'm not saying that, Frank. I just know you had a rough time, *we* had a rough time, and I don't care if you're picking trash for a living, you're still my partner, and I don't want you to go through that again." Harper rested a hand on Frank's shoulder.

Frank appreciated what he said, but didn't like the example he used.

"Don't worry about me, Harp. I'm trying to get my life back together here, and I'm not going to let a drink ruin that."

"That's the way I want to hear you talkin'," Harper said, slapping him on the side of the shoulder. "I got to get out of here. Old man's got a hot date, and those been coming too far and in between for me to miss. But you ought to stop by sometime. I'll make us dinner, we'll talk about old times. What do you say?" Harper smiled.

Frank forced the muscles in his face into a smile. "That'd be fine." He watched his friend leave. Frank missed him, missed his companionship, and would never be able to thank him enough for how he helped him through all the hell he went through, but more than anything, how he stood up for Frank, how he lied for him.

Frank remembered crouching down behind one of the shelves of the convenience store, his gun drawn. There was a black man, no older than eighteen, with a gun behind the glass counter. He had the storekeeper around the neck, threatening to blow his head off if Frank and Harper didn't leave the store and let the boy get out of there.

Frank kept his head as low as possible. The boy had already shot at Harp once, Frank twice, one bullet going into the wall, the other shattering bottles of grape juice, the contents spilling to the floor just behind Frank, giving off a nauseously sweet smell.

Frank wanted to put a bullet right between the bastard's eyes, but he was holding the old storekeeper so close that Frank might possibly hit him. It was a chance that Frank was willing to take, but there would be consequences if he missed, so he waited.

Frank looked across the store where Harper was crouched down behind a shelf. Harper waved his finger, signaling that he was going to race over to the refrigerator, where he would be closer to the guy and possibly get a shot at him. Harper darted out from behind the cover of the shelf, his head and back lowered. The boy saw him, whipped the gun in his direction and squeezed off a shot, then another. Frank heard Harper crash into the wall where the refrigerator was standing, heard boxes and cans fall to the floor around him.

"I'll kill you, motherfucker!" the boy yelled, his face balled up, making him appear much older than his age.

Frank looked frantically in Harper's direction. "Harp, you all right!"
Harper poked his head from around the fridge and gave him the
thumbs-up.

Frank signaled that he would move now.

"If you were smart, you'd put down the gun now, asshole!" Frank
heard Harper say. He was trying to draw the boy's attention from
Frank while he made his move.

"I don't give a . . ." Frank heard the boy begin to answer, and that's
when he darted out. Frank heard the gun go off. As he darted through
the small store, his head down, keeping an eye on the area of cover he
was trying to get to, glass shattered just in front of him, spraying him.
He squinted his eyes, still running, hearing shots coming closer to him,
hearing objects explode just behind him. He left his feet, diving for the
small corner of cover behind the flat freezer. Frank heard the boy
screaming, heard another shot go off, and a second later, Frank felt as
though something had taken hold of his arm and ripped it from its
socket. He screamed out in agony, falling down an aisle of frozen food,
his gun jumping from his hand, skidding farther down the aisle. He
landed on his back, seeing bright fiery orange in front of his eyes, feeling scorching pain in his shoulder. He reached for his arm, clutching
it, feeling the damp stickiness of his blood. It felt as if someone had
hammered a railroad stake into his arm. He pulled his hand away and
it was dripping with his blood. His stomach flipped, and he felt as if he
was going to vomit, but he held back his gorge.

"Frank! Frank!" He heard Harper calling him. "You all right?"

"Fuck! Fuck!" Frank threw his hand back on his shoulder. "That
son of a bitch!" he cried out, flat on his back, staring up at the brilliant
ceiling lights, feeling as though they were about to blind him.

"Frank! You all right?" Harper called again, more frantic this time.

"That bastard shot me! That motherfucker shot me!"

"I didn't mean to shoot you," the boy yelled, remorse in his voice,
grabbing the old storekeeper and yanking him closer to himself. "But I
told you to get the fuck out of here!"

Frank got to his feet, still holding his shoulder. "You're a dead
man!"

"Fuck you! You just let me out of here!" There was definite fear in
the boy's voice now.

"You aren't going no damn where. I told you, you're a dead man," Frank said, wincing in pain, his head bobbing up from the aisle.

"Get down, Frank!" Harper yelled.

"No, I want this fuck to shoot me again. C'mon, shoot me!"

The boy waved the gun wildly. Obvious fear was in his eyes. He squeezed off two shots, and they hit targets nowhere near Frank.

"Frank, get your ass down!"

"Come on, you can do better than that, fuck face!" Frank yelled, getting to his knees, picking up a can of dog food and whipping it at the boy. The boy shot at the noise near him three times, the third was an empty "click," and it alerted Frank like a dog whistle only canines can hear. Frank sprang to his feet and saw the boy staring dead at him. He pointed the gun at Frank and fired. When nothing but an empty click emitted from the gun, Frank was after him, forgetting the pain in his shoulder, only remembering the anger that accompanied it.

The boy threw the storekeeper to the floor like dead weight. The storekeeper quickly got to his feet and ran out of the store. The boy was right behind him, but Frank caught him by the collar and yanked him back.

"You want to shoot me, you fuck!" Frank yelled, and with both arms, the good one and the bloodstained, injured one, held him by the scruff of the shirt and threw him backward. He went sailing back, tripping over his own feet, his arms flailing in wild circles, the useless gun still in hand. He flew into the huge glass counter, the gun swinging into it, shattering it into a million pieces. Small shards littered the floor, and huge jagged razor-sharp teeth jutted up from the base of the counter.

Frank ran over to the boy, feeling all the hate inside him coming to a head, his arm still bleeding profusely. Amazingly, he felt no pain now. He yanked the boy up and kneed him in the gut. The boy doubled over, and then Frank came down with an elbow to his back, sending him flat to the floor, swimming in tiny pieces of glass.

"Frank, stop! He doesn't have a gun," Frank heard Harper yelling at him. He felt his partner grab him from behind, but Frank was so angry that nothing he said registered. Frank swung his good arm behind him, catching his partner in the face. He heard Harper tumble backward, but he wasn't thinking about him. He was consumed with the boy that lay on the ground in front of him, how he tried to take his life for some damn pocket change. How he tried to steal him from his wife and two kids.

Frank's rage was boiling, threatening to erupt, and what Frank thought was, fuck if he doesn't have a gun, he has to pay, and he has to pay dearly! Frank yanked him off the floor again, the boy offering no resistance but allowing himself to be flung around. Frank held him by the neck with his bad arm and punched him repeatedly with his fist until the boy looked like he could no longer stand. Then, with all the force and strength he could muster, Frank swung his elbow into the boy's face. The boy's head snapped back, and he tripped and stumbled back toward the glass case again, and that's when Frank came out of his raged stupor, realizing that there was no longer any glass case, just the jagged teeth of broken glass that looked like overturned icicles.

Frank's eyes ballooned in their sockets, and he ran toward the boy, reached out with both arms, lunging for him, the pain finding its way back to his injured shoulder, shooting through his entire body. With everything he had, Frank reached for this boy, clawed for a thread that he could hang on to to stop him from falling, and he came so close that he felt the boy's warm breath from his mouth on his outstretched fingers. But Frank wasn't fast enough. The boy landed backward on one of the large shards of glass, and it split through him, perforating him. The bloodstained glass shot out of his chest like some weird, gory jack-in-the-box.

Frank couldn't bear the sight. He whipped his head around and violently vomited his guts out on the floor. Harper was standing behind him, witnessing the horror of what just happened. He had just awakened from the blow that Frank dealt to him, and sirens could be heard in the background.

Frank went to court, and although there was an investigation, which resulted in his dismissal from the force, Frank was amazingly found not guilty of murder. Most likely that was because Harper had lied for him, telling the jury it was self-defense, even though he was out cold when the actual killing took place. The entire hellish event took a little more than a year, and if it wasn't for the bottle, Frank didn't think he would've gotten through it. Then again, if it wasn't for the bottle, he would still be with his family, his entire family.

Frank tipped back the glass of ginger ale, sucking the last of it down. He fingered a few dollars out of his wallet, set them on the bar, then left.

Frank pulled up in front of his ex-wife's house. It was late, after 11:00 P.M., but the house looked just the same as it had this morning, the garage door hanging open as if she had just made her getaway with his daughter. She stayed away this long because she knew him, knew his persistence and knew that he'd be back around this time to see his child.

Frank threw his head in his hands, the dim green illumination of the dashboard lights coloring his pathetic figure, the gentle drone of the car's engine in no way soothing him. He wanted to cry, but what good would it do him? It wouldn't make his wife see him as human again, it wouldn't make her realize that seeing his daughter was something that he needed to survive, and it wouldn't bring his son back.

"William," he said, shaking his head, pain striking his heart. He had to get back to where he was before all this started, he told himself. He had to.

As if it weighed a ton, he lifted his head, looked once again at the emptiness of the garage, feeling the same void in his heart, in his soul. Then he put the car in gear and headed home.

CHAPTER EIGHT

When Zale's mother found that her belongings where missing, she stormed into little Zale's room and yanked him out of his bed, held him right up to her face by the scruff of his pajama top.

"Where is it?" she questioned, fire in her eyes. Zale's eyes were still opening, he was still coming out of whatever dream he was in, but he could see that his mother looked strange, looked tortured, and looked like she had exerted herself. Like she had run around the house searching for whatever it was Zale took from her and tossed down onto the railroad tracks. There was a thin coat of sweat covering her face, and a look so severe that Zale wanted to cry.

"Where is it!" she demanded again, yanking Zale, trying to waken him more so he would come out with the answer.

"Where is what?" Zale asked, even though he knew what she was talking about, exactly what she was talking about.

His mother reached back and slapped him hard across the face. It burned as if he were scorched by a hot steam iron. The shock of the slap shook a single tear loose from Zale's eye; it ran down his face.

"Don't go crying, boy. I said where is my shit!" his mother said, both hands now grabbing him around his collar. He could feel that her hands were trembling, and she looked scared, and that made him scared. "You tell me now, or I'll beat you, I swear I will."

"I . . . I threw it away," Zale said in the tiniest voice.

"You threw it away! Go to the goddamn trash and get it. Get it now!"

Zale lowered his head. "I threw it down to the railroad tracks."

There was silence from his mother, but her eyes widened, and her chest started to heave. "You did what!" she said in shock, as if he said that he just killed a man.

"Do you know what that was! Do you know?" she said, becoming more frenzied. She started to rake her hands through her hair, and over her sweat-dripping face.

"I need that, Zale, and I need it now, and you fucking threw it over the bridge!" She was up pacing the small space in front of his bed.

"I'm sorry, Mama," Zale cried.

His mother didn't acknowledge his apology, just continued pacing back and forth, mumbling to herself. "I can't get no more. That was my last, and I don't get paid for another two weeks. I can't get no more, and this foolish boy goes and throws my shit down to the tracks."

"I'm sorry, Mama," Zale said again. "But it was hurting you!"

His mother stopped right in front of him, stuck her face in his. "It was hurting me? And how did you know that? Who made you a damn doctor? Who!" She grabbed him by the hair on the back of his head, wrenched his head back until he was looking straight up at the ceiling.

"That was my last, boy! My last!" she screamed at him. Then she threw him aside and disappeared without saying a word. But Zale knew that she would back. He sat there kneeling on his bed, terrified. He heard his mother approaching the room again, saw her step in with the broom.

"Take off your shirt!" she ordered.

"No, Mama!"

"Take off your shirt, boy, and get on your stomach!" his mother said, sticking both her hands into the straw of the broom, clutching handfuls of the thin sticks.

Zale slowly pulled off his shirt, crying as he did. He lay on his stomach, spreading out his arms and legs to the four corners of the bed. He knew what was going to happen, for she had done it before, and it had taken him a week to recover. He tried not to think about it, tried to concentrate on something else, told himself to relax, because if he tensed up, braced himself for it, it would hurt so much more. But he felt his fists clutching the sheets, felt the muscles in his back tightening in anticipation of the torture he was to receive. He couldn't help it, but he knew that there was no way to prepare for—

Zale cried out when the broom handle cut across the center of his back. It was like no other pain that he had ever encountered before, and he thought that he was about to die right there, wished that he would, because he knew that his mother had planned on teaching him a lesson that he'd never forget.

"You go in my room taking my shit!" And she swung the broom down on the boy's bare back again. "And it wasn't yours to take, so now you have to learn." And Zale's mother brought the broom high over her head again, then swung it down on the small boy's back. And she raised it again, and again, beating him, grunting like some insane animal, the tip of the broom handle hitting the ceiling each time she raised it overhead.

And each time his mother struck him, Zale cried out, hoping that the sound of his agony would reach her, that his tortured moans would appeal to the humane side of her and she would stop. But she was unaffected, and she continued to swing, bloody cuts opening up on her young son's back, splotches of black and blue raising to the surface of his skin. She swung the broom down on him countless times with all her might, like a lumberjack cutting tree trunks into firewood, but with more determination, her strength being supplied by her anger.

Zale couldn't take it anymore. The pain was almost indescribable. The thin broom cut into his back with the sharpness of a razor, but the force of the wood made him feel as if he were being beaten with a club. He writhed about the bed, contorting his body, trying to shield his back with his hands and arms, but his mother continued beating him, coming down on his delicate fingers with the stick. He felt as if his fingers were going to break if she hit them again, and she said, "If you do that one more time, I'm going to beat you twice as long!"

Zale quickly stretched his arms back out, clutching the corners of his bed, wincing every time the broom handle struck him. But it wasn't as painful anymore. That was because his back was becoming numb, and his head was starting to float away. Zale still heard his mother screaming as if she were going mad, but she sounded far away. She would hit him a few more times and he would black out, and that's when she would stop. So Zale turned his tear-covered face to the side and waited for the darkness to steal him from the pain.

"No! No!" Zale woke up shaking, his body covered in sweat, his arms crossed and locked against his chest, as though he were trying to protect himself from something dreadful nearing him. He was turned over on his side, his face buried into his pillow. When he rolled over and started to awake, he saw his girlfriend Regina's face come into focus. She was looking down at him, deep concern in her eyes as she held a folded washcloth to his forehead.

Zale's eyes opened fully, then he smiled, as if the dream had never taken place.

"Good morning," he said, sleep still in his voice, stretching, lying on his back.

"It was another bad dream, wasn't it?" Regina said, pulling the cloth away.

Zale looked up at her but didn't say a word, as if the question would go away if he didn't answer it.

"Wasn't it, Zale?"

"If I told you it wasn't, you wouldn't believe me anyway."

"What was it about?"

Zale looked frustrated. "It was about the same thing it always is about, nothing. It was about nothing."

"Why don't you tell me," Regina said, sliding closer to him in bed. "Obviously there's something that's really bothering you if you're having nightmares about it almost four times a week. Maybe if you tell me it'd help, it'd be out in the open."

Zale turned his head away from Regina, thinking that it had to be the hundredth time he dealt with this problem.

"It won't do any good, getting it out in the open. It does enough harm being locked inside where I want it. Why would I want to let something like that out, so we can have long talks about it, so whenever I start to act a little funny, you can say, 'Maybe it's because of those terrible dreams you're having' and go into detail, having me relive every moment of those dreams? No, I think what's in my head is best where it is, in my head, and if you needed to know about it, trust me, I would tell you."

"Maybe you should see somebody," Regina offered in a timid voice.

"What do you mean, see somebody?"

"A psychiatrist, or something. Maybe he could help you deal with why you're having those dreams since you don't want to talk to me."

Zale couldn't believe what he was hearing. The person that was closest to him, the woman who said she loved him, was calling him crazy and telling him to seek help. She seemed reluctant to say anything, but obviously she had to have been thinking about it for a while, and felt that he really did need professional help.

"Well?" Regina asked.

"I'm not even going to begin to get into this conversation."

Regina gave Zale a disappointed look. She was hurt because of how he had spoken to her, but he had to make it clear that he didn't want to speak about it again.

She got up from the bed and went into the bathroom. Zale heard the cabinet open and close, heard the water run for a brief moment, and knew she was coming back in the bedroom with his medication.

"And what's that?" Zale said, staring at the little pill in her hand.

"You know what it is," she said, extending the pill out to him. "You haven't been taking it every day, have you?"

"I've been taking it when I need it," Zale said, still lying on his back. "And that hasn't been every day, no."

"Zale," Regina said, shaking her head. "Is it a joke to you? Do you think your doctor prescribed this medication for you just because it makes her feel more like a doctor? You need these pills, and you need to take them every day. Something is going on with you more than just a little stress and some high blood pressure, and if you don't want to tell me just yet, I guess that's your business. But when you're doing something that directly threatens your health, and I can do something about it, best believe I will, every time. Now take your pill, Zale," she said, her hand still extended out to him.

He gave her no further discussion, figuring it wasn't worth the argument. He sat up in bed, took the pill, took the water from her, and swallowed it down.

He had to get to work anyway. He hadn't heard his alarm go off, so he figured he woke up early. That was good, he would be able to spend a little more time with Regina before he started getting ready. He reached over to check the time, and cut his alarm off before it sounded. That's when he caught sight of the time. The clock read 9:32 A.M. He looked at it as if his mind was playing tricks on him. He blinked his eyes slowly and looked again. It couldn't have been right, because his alarm usually went off at 6:30 A.M.

"What time is it, Regina?" Zale said, his body still turned, looking over at the clock on his nightstand.

"That clock is right."

"Then how come . . ."

"Because I turned your alarm off."

Zale quickly got out of bed, unbuttoning his pajama top. "What did you do that for! I set the alarm clock because I wanted it to wake me up, not so you could just turn it off! Would you do me a favor next time and just leave things the way they are!" He threw his pajama top into the hamper and went into the bathroom. He looked in the mirror, and he looked bad. But not as bad as most mornings. The extra sleep must have done him some good, but it made him late, so it hampered him more than it helped. He slid the medicine cabinet open, grabbed for his toothbrush, sloppily squirted some paste on it, and jabbed it in his mouth. He considered shaving, but it would take too long, and he decided to skip his shower as well. He worked the toothbrush around in his mouth a few times, spit the foamy white stuff into the sink, and put the brush back in the cabinet, without first rinsing it, or his mouth, leaving toothpaste on both.

Zale raced out into the bedroom, darted into his walk-in closet, and started to sift through the shirts hanging in there. He yanked one from the rack, tore the plastic from it, and threw it on, trying to button it as he pulled off his pajama bottoms.

"What time is it, Regina?" Zale called from inside the closet.

There was no answer.

Zale came out of the closet, hopping as he tried to put his other sock on.

"I said, what time is it? You know I'm late for—" Then he stopped. He stopped and stood in the center of his bedroom, dried toothpaste on his mouth, his shirt buttoned in the wrong holes, making one half longer than the other, a sock on one foot, the other dangling from his hand. Regina sat there in front of him, her face in her hands.

"Do I even matter to you anymore?"

Of course she did, but for some reason, Zale didn't know how to say it.

"I'm sorry for turning off your alarm," Regina said. Her words were slow, and carried the same tone. "But you were tired, and I thought . . . I knew you needed your sleep. Do you remember last night?"

Zale thought for a moment. He remembered calling her from his lecture, waiting outside for her, and jumping in the car, but outside of that, he couldn't remember, and it reflected on his face.

"That's because you fell asleep as soon as you got in the car," Regina said. "Just like a child, you fell asleep midsentence, and when we got home, I tried waking you up, but you wouldn't wake up all the way. I thought it was so cute." Regina smiled sadly.

"So I walked you up here. You were hanging on my shoulder, your eyes weren't even open. I don't even think you were awake, but I walked you up here, took off your clothes, washed your face, put your pajamas on, and put you to bed. I held your head in my arms, looking down at you, realizing how much I love you, until you fell asleep. Then before I went to sleep, I reached over and turned off your alarm. And you know what the funny thing is? I stopped myself for a moment from reaching over there, knowing that you'd be angry if I turned your clock off. But I thought about it again, and I said, He'll just have to be mad, because he needs his sleep.

"But my question to you is, does this job mean so much that you will ignore your body when it tells you to slow down, when it tells you that it can't take any more. This job means so much to you that you're willing to just overlook your health, ignore it like it's an annoying itch and not your body actually breaking down.

"And about me," Regina said, shaking her head, laughing a short, pathetic laugh. "I've almost come to the realization that this job means more to you than I ever will, but I keep telling myself that's not true, and I'm waiting for you to prove it to me. Does that job mean more to you than I do?"

Zale stood there feeling trapped, between the two things that he loved most, his cause and his woman, and feeling as though he had to choose one and only one. He couldn't do that. He glanced over at the clock and hoped that Regina didn't notice. For every moment that he stood there trying to explain himself, another child was being sacrificed. Those are the sacrifices he cared about, to hell with his body, and her feelings would always mend themselves and be as good as new. They always had.

"It's not a job," Zale said. "It's not something that I go to. Punch a clock, put in my hours and leave at the end of the day, leaving the stress and the worries at work till the next day, weekends and vacations off, things like that—it's not like that for me. This is not a job, this is my life, and the stress I go through, and the things I worry about, aren't exclusive to a location. They follow me around every moment of the day. This is so important to me that if my body starts to ache, sometimes I don't even notice it, because my mind is elsewhere. Sometimes my body will be so sleepy that I can barely stand, but my mind is still working out problems, trying to bring me closer to accomplishing my goals. It won't let me go to sleep, and I would almost feel bad if I were able to go to sleep. These children can't wait any longer for people to get sleep."

Regina looked down at her hands, then raised her face to look at Zale. "Then what about me?"

Zale walked over to her, knelt down before her, placing his hands on her waist.

"I love you. I love you so much, there is no question, but I have to keep my priorities in order."

"I don't know how I should feel about that. I don't know if I should be offended or not," Regina said, placing her hand on Zale's shoulder. "Has it always been like that? Have you always put the woman you loved below what you were trying to accomplish?"

He looked at her, wondering if she were asking the question because she was really interested in the truth, or if she was trying to grade herself by how he treated others.

"It's always been this way," Zale lied, trying to appear as sincere as possible. "It's just the way I am. I mean, what is the problem?" Zale said, standing. "Am I not treating you right?"

"No, no. I love the way you treat me, and I know how you feel about me, but sometimes a woman wants to know, or at least think, that she's the most important thing in her man's life, that's all. I don't know." Regina lowered her head for a moment, then looked back up at Zale, her face looking as though something heavy was weighing on her mind.

"Will you stay home from work today? I don't have to go in, and we could do something together."

Zale shook his head. "I don't think that would be a good idea."

"When was the last time we did something together? Has to be at least two weeks ago. What harm will one day do?" she pleaded.

"More than you could ever know. Look, I've already missed almost half the day, so I might as well go on in, but we can do something soon. We'll do a show and dinner. Tomorrow night. I'll meet you at your place at eight, all right? But I have to go."

Zale walked over to her, bent down, and kissed her on her lips. To his surprise, she returned it, then lowered her head again as if something was still on her mind. Zale continued getting ready, washing his face, combing his hair, and throwing on a blue suit.

He walked back over to Regina, who had not moved during the entire time he was getting dressed.

"I'm going to go now," Zale said, briefcase in his hand. He bent down to kiss her again. "You have a good day off."

She nodded, and he was turning to head downstairs when she stopped him.

"Zale?"

Zale turned back around.

"What if I told you that I had to come first? What if I said that I had to be your first priority?"

Zale slightly canted his head to the side, a look of mild sadness appearing on his face. "You wouldn't want to do that."

"But what if I did? What if I said that you had to choose between me and your job?"

"Then you'd be hurt," Zale said solemnly. He turned and left her sitting there.

Zale sat on the semicrowded bus surrounded by early-afternoon travelers. Because of the late hour, he assumed that none of these people were on their way to work, unless they worked odd jobs flipping burgers or scrubbing up scuff marks on hallway floors. No one who had serious work to do went in this late, and that thought made Zale think of Regina and how she made him late by turning off his alarm clock. She was trying to help him, she had said, but that's the type of help that knocks you down, not lifts you up, and he had no problem messing up by himself.

He lied to her about putting his work before every woman that he had seen. But he had to. She didn't really want to hear the truth; besides, he didn't want to go into it. There are so many things better off left buried inside one's mind than let out to be scrutinized by everyone with a two-bit opinion. If he'd told Regina about Cassaundra, she would've wondered why she wasn't placed above what he was trying to accomplish. She would've almost demanded him to change his priorities, instead of asking the question hypothetically. Then he would've surely had to leave her, and he didn't want that, because he loved Regina, loved her and needed her, almost as much as he had Cassaundra.

Cassaundra, he mouthed the name without actually speaking it, as the bus rolled and leaned clumsily over the dips and curves of the downtown streets, his body swaying gently with the motion.

■ ■ ■

He had been out of school only a year and had not yet even come up with the idea of Father Found, but had begun to feel some type of calling. For a long time, he closed his mind to it, trying to dismiss everything about his past, for fear that it would consume his life again. In an attempt to keep his mind clear, he made Cassaundra the most important thing in his life.

They had loved each other for five years, and one day he intended on marrying her. But she had a slight problem with his way of thinking. She wanted children. At least three of them, and Zale was firmly against the thought of even one.

"I want you to at least think about it, okay?" she said so many times, laying her hand on his face.

And Zale would do that. He took her advice because he loved her so, and he thought about it. Many hours some days, alone in his room, staring at the walls, trying to make himself see the advantages of bringing children into this hateful, godforsaken world, but all he could see was the disadvantages. He could only see through his eyes, the terrible things he had seen and experienced, and sometimes he thought that if there were a humane way of doing it, he would lay to rest all the children of the world to make sure they would never feel his pain. He knew then that having a child of his own was out of the question. Of course he never told her that, for fear of losing her.

"We'll see when we come to that bridge," Zale always said when she asked about it, but he was sure Cassaundra had her doubts about him.

He remembered the night she left. She stood before him, not the most beautiful girl physically, but her personality made Zale blind to every woman that stood beside her. She had just graduated from school and had a job offer in Washington, D.C. It was an opportunity that she couldn't pass up, she said.

"I'll call you as soon as I get settled," she said, standing before Zale in the dim light of his apartment.

He tried to remain strong, tried to seem indifferent to the fact that she was going away, but he couldn't for two reasons. One was that she was leaving him, and he knew in his heart that she had no intention of seeing him again. The other was that with her gone, the dark void she filled would open up again, and it would overcome him, and he feared that more than anything. He stood there fighting back, with everything he had, tears that threatened to fall. He felt like a child in bed who was scared of his mother leaving the room, fearful of the darkness, of what it would do to him all alone.

"I'll be waiting for your call," he said softly.

Cassaundra stepped close to him and brought him into her arms. He lay his head against her breast.

They made love that night, and afterward they fell asleep in each other's arms. Hours later, when he heard her stirring about the room, gathering her things to leave, he pretended not to hear her. He knew it was the way she would've preferred it. She leaned over him and kissed him softly on the lips.

"I will always love you," she said.

And I will have to stop loving you, Zale thought, saddened beyond comprehension, as he felt her move away from him and watched as she walked out of his life.

That was six years ago, and ever since then, his life had been devoted to the children, the way it should be. He even came to appreciate Cassaundra leaving as the catalyst for his starting his organization. If she hadn't left, he probably would've still been running from his life's calling, in a dream of marriage and family-minded ideas and plans for the future. His mind would've been filled with the gabble of what color to paint the nursery, or which barbecue pit is better, gas or charcoal? But would that have been so bad? He often thought of how his life would've been had Cassaundra not gone, had he not allowed her to go. They would've been happy, he knew that, and every time Zale felt himself ready to entertain those thoughts, to create images in his mind of them smiling, walking hand in hand, sharing their love, he shut down his mind, telling himself he didn't need that. If he allowed himself to go there frequently, think those thoughts, he would realize that maybe his present life truly couldn't compare to that which he could've had.

He might have realized that he was in pain, he had lost the woman he loved beyond all others and could lose another. He could realize that his goals might be more than lofty, but ridiculous, unattainable by any stretch, and that could make him consider giving it all up. But he would never do that. Regardless of how much pain he was in, how much he had to sacrifice, those children suffered and were sacrificed more. Zale thought about that, as he found himself staring at a little girl of maybe seven years old, swallowed up by one of the bus seats.

He fixed his eyes on her, smiled at her, and she smiled back. Her clothes weren't tattered, but they were dirty. Not fresh dirt, like the spill of grape jelly from lunch, but week-old dirt that was pressed into the clothes by a steam iron to make the clothes look more presentable, even though they hadn't been washed in so long. Her hair was parted down the middle, a braid sticking out either side of her head, one starting to unravel.

Zale walked over to her, and sat down beside her.

"What's your name?" he asked, in his small-person's voice, leaning toward her.

"Olivia," she said.

"You going to school, Olivia?"

The little girl nodded her head. A couple of food crumbs fell from the corner of her mouth.

"How long have you been taking the bus by yourself?"

"Three months," she said. She held up three little fingers to further express her answer.

Zale wondered if her being on this bus by herself or her looking the way she did had anything to do with her parents just being poor, or her father abandoning her mother and her, making her mother unable to get her child to school a safer way.

"Daddy's car is broken?" Zale carefully phrased the pointed question. He went into his briefcase and reached for one of his business cards, expecting to hear that the father wasn't there.

"Daddy don't have a car. Mommy don't neither. But Daddy said we going to get one real soon, 'cause he saving up."

Zale paused, his hand still in the briefcase, holding a stack of his cards. Then he shut the briefcase, and slid the cards in his pocket, making sure the little girl didn't get a glimpse of them, as if she could read the small print from her seat and know why he was about to offer her one.

"Well, that's good," Zale said, and patted her on the head. "I hope your daddy gets it real soon. I hope he does," he said sincerely.

Zale stood up from the seat, thought for a moment, then reached in his suit pocket, took out the business cards, and started passing them out to all the women on the bus, whether they were old or young, six years old or sixty. Some of them looked up at him as if he was trying to take something from them, rather than giving something. But it made no difference to him. If one person was able to use that card, if one person needed him, needed his services, then he would've taken one more step toward accomplishing his life's goal.

Zale got off the bus and walked down half a block to a car rental shop. He rented what they had available, which was a blue Pontiac Sunbird, and he was thankful the shop he called to tow his car said he would have it back soon.

It was 11:30, and he figured he wouldn't make it back to the office until a little after noon, so instead he decided to head in the opposite direction. He drove toward Chicago's West Side, and twenty minutes later parked the car in to the faculty parking lot of an aging elementary school. He walked into the building, the sound of his shoes hitting the floor and echoing off the walls and high ceiling of the hallway. He made his way farther down the corridor until he came to an office door.

"Elizabeth Miller, Principal" was stenciled on the glass of the door. Zale knocked three times, waited for a reply, then stuck his head in.

"Are there any principals in the house?" Zale said, seeing Mrs. Miller sitting behind her desk, her reading glasses sitting on the tip of her nose. She peered over them and smiled. She stood up from behind her desk, opened her arms, and moved to hug Zale. Zale walked into the office and they embraced.

"How's my favorite second-grade teacher?" Zale asked, feeling as though he was still in grammar school by the hug he received.

"Wishing I were still teaching second grade, that's how I am," Mrs. Miller said, pulling away from him to look him over.

"It's almost been six months since I've seen you last. What's kept you away? I was starting to worry about my favorite student." She walked back behind her desk, wearing a smart gray suit. A white shirt with ruffles down the front stuck out from under the jacket, making her look like some sort of English judge. Her silver hair was rolled up and pinned in the back with what looked like a crocheting needle. She extended her hand out toward the chair in front of her desk. Zale sat in it.

"What's kept me away so long?" Zale repeated the question.

Mrs. Miller nodded and removed her glasses, letting them hang on the silver chain around her neck.

"You, Mrs. Miller. After I gave my last speaking engagement here, you never called me back. And when I tried to contact you, it seemed you were always out, and you never returned my calls."

Mrs. Miller lowered her head for a moment, then looked up at Zale. "I'm sorry, Zale, but the way you talked about those men, in such an unforgiving manner, I could barely stand to listen. Yes, to abandon a child may be a horrible, unforgivable thing, but these men are still these children's fathers. To put them down, to make them seem like criminals in the eyes of their sons and daughters, is wrong. Regardless of what they may have done, a lot of these men are still heroes in their children's minds, and if they wish to believe that, I can't let you change their thinking. They're just children, Zale."

"And what was I?" Zale said, leaning forward in his chair. "I was a child growing up without a father, but there was no one there to tell me why he wasn't there. There was no one there to try and find him, bring him back so that I could have a father. So, it's wrong for me to tell why their fathers may have left them. Should I let them figure it out on their own? Let them find these men on their own, maybe when they're thirty-five, and all the damage has been done?"

"What about their mothers, Zale? They have more than one parent."

"And what about my mother!" Zale said, banging his fist on the desk, shooting up from his seat. "My mother didn't tell me a thing. What makes you think theirs will do anything different?"

"What makes you think they won't? Why do you think you know exactly what's going on with these children, in their households, in their minds?"

"Because I'm the example!" Zale shouted, jabbing himself in the chest with his finger. "I didn't grow up with a father. Hell, I didn't have a mother for very long. Anything bad that could've happened to a child happened to me. When I look down at these kids, I see myself, and you know what else I see? I see the possibility of the same thing happening to them. Do you know what I went through?" Zale said, leaning over Mrs. Miller's desk, his voice full with emotion.

"I was told, remember, Zale," she said, her voice soothing.

"But do you know how it felt? Do you know! It was hell, and it shouldn't have happened. I know that now. But the entire time, I blamed myself. Me! And you tell me that I'm wrong for trying to stop that from happening here." Zale shook his head, a disbelieving, disappointed look on his face. "Well, I know what I'm doing is right. And it doesn't matter what you—"

"Zale, sit down," Mrs. Miller said, her voice cutting into his.

"If what I'm trying—" Zale continued.

"Mr. Rowen, I said sit down!" Mrs. Miller said again, her voice more commanding, making Zale forget their relationship as friends and remember his place as her student.

He looked at her for a moment, and more out of respect than fear, he slowly lowered himself into his seat.

Principal Miller looked at Zale, a slight smile appearing on her face.

"Zale, you haven't changed. You haven't changed one bit," she said sweetly. "You see that look on your face? The way your eyebrows are furrowed, your forehead wrinkled up like a bedspread after it's been slept on. That's the same expression you wore on your face as a child. And I would often ask myself, what's wrong with that little boy? He is so young, but looks to be carrying the weight of the world on his shoulders."

Mrs. Miller extended her open hand out across the desk, bidding Zale to place his in hers. He did, and she caressed it with her other hand.

"That's how you look now, Zale. Like you're balancing the weight of the world on your shoulders, and it's looking like it's quite a heavy load, almost too heavy. I commend you for what you're trying to do. There should be more men like you. But you can't do it all yourself," Mrs. Miller said, the intensity of her gaze increasing as the grip of her hand tightened. "You can't do it all yourself. You have to have faith that some of these men will realize that they've taken the wrong steps away from their family, and they will retrace those steps on the path back to them, sooner or later. You have to have faith that some of these mothers will be mother enough, and father, too, like so many have, and provide for their children, and have faith that every child won't experience what it was you went through. Do you think you can do that?"

Zale heard the question, but did not look up at his old friend, just stared down at her wrinkled hands. Those hands that he had held on more than one extreme occasion.

"Zale, can you do that?" he heard the principal ask him again.

"I need a favor of you, Mrs. Miller."

The older woman looked at him for a moment, her expression changing as if abandoning the idea of getting an answer to her question. She raised her eyebrows, a gesture inviting him to ask his question.

Zale looked down at his watch. "It's almost lunchtime. I need you to let me go out into the courtyard and talk to the children."

A look of concern quickly covered Mrs. Miller's face again. She brought her interlaced fingers up to her lips, and thought for a moment.

"Zale, you asked me this before. I can't let you go out there and—"

"I just want to talk to them, be around them. I don't know why, let's call it the first step toward having faith. Seeing these kids will remind me of the resilience they have, the strength to overcome situations they may be faced with."

"That's a steaming pot full of bull, Mr. Rowen, and you know it. But I'll let you go out there under the conditions that you don't speak of missing fathers, and don't you dare pass out one of those business cards to any of those children."

Zale smiled. "I left them all at home."

Zale got out to the playground a few minutes before the bell rang. He stood where he figured the middle of it was and just waited. All by himself, he stood there, a single figure wearing a suit, holding a briefcase, waiting as if a train would rip through the middle of the lot.

The bell rang, and the kids came busting out the door, yelling and screaming, smiling and laughing. Some of them carrying lunch boxes, a paper bag swinging from the hands of the other children. They looked so happy, so carefree, as they rushed to the outdoor tables, or grabbed the swings and jumped in them.

It almost made Zale question himself why he was there in the first place. If he were to go on what was on those children's faces, he should have no concern, but he knew that that wasn't the reality. They were children, and unlike him when he was a child, they stopped thinking about their problems the moment they were separated from them. If they had been beaten or bruised, the second they were taken from under the cord or belt and sent to school, the pain would no longer be in their thoughts, even if the wound was still stinging.

So as the kids blew by him as if he were no more than a tree that looked strangely like a man, Zale realized he was needed. If not just to help them, also to remind them of what they were going through. Remind them that their fathers' responsibilities shouldn't be based on the "out of sight, out of mind" principle, but that he was obligated, by what should be more than legal authority. Obligated by more than the idea of being a father or the shame that he would feel if word got out that he abandoned his kids. A father was obligated by blood, by the fact that his children came from him, and denying them would be like denying himself, and he should rather die than do that.

Zale turned toward the group of children, and went over some of the questions that he would ask the kids, questions that didn't make it seem as if he was inquiring about the status of their fathers. He dipped his hand into his briefcase, grabbed another stack of his business cards, and walked toward the crowded cluster of eating children.

CHAPTER NINE

Martin sat at his desk, staring at the picture of his daughters. They had their arms around each other's shoulders, smiling wide, looking like the happiest children in the world. They looked that way because they knew all was well in their little world, or at least it had been before Debra decided she no longer wanted to be their mother.

Martin reached across the desk, picked up the framed photo delicately, and stared at it for a moment, then placed it back as gently as he had picked it up. He hated himself, and he didn't know if it was because he considered himself a coward for not telling his daughters about Debra's secret when he should've, or for fearing telling them now.

He slammed his hand against the desk, feeling the sting that covered the surface of his palm, wishing he could hurt himself more. He deserved it.

"How am I going to tell them?" he said aloud. But what also weighed on his mind was whether his wife was telling him the truth about being faithful to him. He wanted to believe her more than anything in the world, but there was this suspicion that lurked over his shoulder, this voice in his head that whispered to him not to trust her. He didn't know if his intuition was right, but he would follow it, and he would find out for sure whether the woman could be trusted.

He shouldn't have to go through this, he thought. Shouldn't have to question her devotion to him, wonder whether he could trust her, because he gave her no reason to question his fidelity. He never had, not from the day he accepted her into his life. It was soon after his wife died, and now he wondered if it was too soon.

At first, the young nurse seemed to only want to comfort him through the tough period he was experiencing, then Debra started to help him care for Renee and the newborn. She said that she didn't mind at all, as she cradled Rebecca in her arms, feeding her a bottle. She said she loved it, and someday she would be a doctor, maybe specialize in pediatrics. After a while, Debra started coming to the house every day to check on the children, see how they were doing. She would come at all times of the day, for her schedule was constantly changing.

Martin remembered one night, he was sleeping soundly, when the newborn started to cry. He thought it was in his dream—the sound of his wife crying just before she died on that table, her stomach still round with their unborn child, her body covered in blood-saturated sheets, droplets of red forming puddles on the delivery room floor. Then he sprang out of bed when he realized that it was Rebecca. He stumbled into her room, still shaken by the dream, scooped her up and started to rock her, sing to her. But she was crying loudly, incessantly, and she would not stop. Martin placed the infant on her back, undid her diaper and checked it, but she was clean and dry. He warmed a bottle, and placed it to the tip of her lips, but she would not take it. He even tried burping her, even though she had not eaten, but that didn't work either. He walked back and forth across the living room, the baby in his arms, crying at the top of her lungs. He was trying to decide if he should pack up Renee so he could take Rebecca to see a doctor when the doorbell rang.

Martin paused for a moment, the baby's crying stopping for the same split second, then beginning again as he stepped slowly to the door. Who could be at my door this late at night? he thought. He pulled back the curtain near the door, and saw that it was Debra. She was standing there, looking down at her watch, her nursing uniform still on.

Martin opened the door, a smile on his face, happy to see her.

"I'm sorry I'm coming by this late, but when I drove by your house, I saw the light on, and I just wanted to . . ." Then before she could even finish her sentence, she noticed the baby crying. "Awwww," she cooed, taking the baby gently from her father's arms.

"She won't stop crying for anything," Martin said. "I checked her diaper. I tried feeding her. I even tried burping her, but nothing worked."

Debra took the baby and adjusted her in her arms, her tiny head lying against Debra's bosom. She lay there quiet, not making a sound.

"She stopped crying!" Martin said, astonished. He looked down at the baby, and her eyes were closed, half her fist was in her mouth.

"Sometimes it's just a particular touch, or a scent that makes the baby feel comfortable, that's all," Debra said, smiling, walking over to the couch, sitting.

"Do you want something?" Martin asked, ready to bring her the world if she desired it. He sat down next to her, admiring his child and the woman holding her.

"I don't want anything else," she said, looking at Martin, then her eyes moving down to the child. "I don't know what made me drive by here tonight. It's not the way I normally take home, but something told me, just go by, just go by. I'm glad I did," she said, softly, sweetly.

And he was glad she did, too. He continued looking at her, the way she held his child, cared for his child, and was able to sense in her a need to see the child. It was as if she had given birth to Rebecca. It was as if there was something as strong as a mother-and-daughter bond there, when technically there was no relation whatsoever. On the other hand, poor Rebecca was never held by her natural mother, and the first woman she probably came in contact with was the woman holding her right now.

Martin watched as Debra bent down and kissed the child lightly on her face, and something went through his head, a feeling. It was love. He wasn't sure if it was love for the fact that she was able to do for his child what he couldn't do, or if he was just so grateful that someone was there, or if he was already trying to fill the void his wife left. He didn't know, and it didn't matter, because he felt it, sure as anything, and to be so soon, it was very strong, very very strong.

Martin was staring at her, and when she pulled her eyes up from the child, she stared back at Martin, holding his gaze, until he started to move near her. She did not move, just continued to look at him, her eyes closing, the closer he came to her. Then his lips were on hers. He was kissing her, and to his surprise, she was kissing him back as she was holding his child, what felt like their child, and at that moment, he knew this woman would be his wife someday.

A loud knock on Martin's door yanked him out of his thinking. He didn't respond right away, just looked down at the picture of his daughters, then over to the other side of his desk at the picture of Debra.

The knock again, and this time it was even louder and more forceful.

"Who is it!"

The door opened, and it was Frank Rames holding the knob, a thin stack of files in his opposite hand.

"I asked, who is it? I didn't say open the door," Martin said, still angry at himself.

"Well, you found out who it was, didn't you," Frank said with attitude.

"Come in and sit."

Frank walked over to the chair in front of Martin's desk and sat down.

"You take care of those cases I assigned to you yesterday?"

Frank tossed the files over to Martin's desk. They landed with a slapping sound.

Martin looked at Frank for a long moment, a look of dislike on his face. Frank returned his stare, as if he had eaten something that he was ready to spit out.

Martin reached for the files and opened the first one, looked over it, then looked briefly through the others.

"Any of these guys give you trouble?" Martin said, not taking his eyes off the file.

"Not a bit," Frank said, slumped some in the chair, his tie loosened at the neck of his shirt.

"Not even André Hinton?"

"Specially not André Hinton."

Martin continued to look though the files, flipping through each of them to the second page, paying particular attention to line two.

"So what's the status on these men? You marked on all of them: 'Father will return home immediately.'" Martin looked up at him suspiciously.

"That's the status. I spoke to them, and for some reason, this time we seemed to hit it off particularly well. They all seemed very receptive, and we were able to come to an understanding without many words. They realized it was just best for them to go on home," Frank said, his elbows on the arms of the chair, his fingers laced, his arms forming a bridge across his body.

"You're sure about this?"

"Positive."

Martin closed the files and tossed them back in Frank's direction. One of them slid off the desk and hit the floor. Martin made no attempt to apologize.

"You're going to follow up on all these men no later than early next week, you got that?"

Frank slowly bent down, retrieved the fallen file, and placed it on the desk.

"Yeah, I got that," he said, a smug look on his face.

"Good," Martin said, turning his attention to something else. "You can get out of my office now, but keep your pager on because I might need you for something else."

Frank didn't move from his seat, didn't reach for the files off Martin's desk, just sat there staring at the man in front of him.

"Is there a problem? I said you were dismissed."

"Yeah, there's a problem. I wasn't scheduled to come in yesterday till noon, but you go paging me at eight-thirty. I had important business to take care of."

"We went over that yesterday, Rames," Martin said, his eyes still on something else. "Now if you don't mind, I have more important things to take care of right now."

"No you don't!" Rames said, standing up.

Martin's attention was snatched from what he was doing and focused on Frank standing there in front of his desk, looking as though he were ready for a street brawl.

"You have to take care of this business with me, that's what's important!"

Martin looked at him, astonished. "Have you lost your mind?"

"No. I want to know what your fucking problem is with me!"

"What did you say!" Martin said, standing, equaling Frank's intense stare.

"You heard me. I want to know what your fucking problem is with me. You treat me like shit in here. Like you can just walk all over me, say whatever the hell you want to and not expect me to say or do shit about it. I had important things to take care of yesterday, family things. And I was trying to do it on my time. My time!" Frank said, poking himself in the chest with his thumb. "And you go calling me in for some shit that could've waited. What is it? You don't like me? Is that it?"

"No, I wouldn't say that. Besides, I never gave it enough thought to determine what I thought about you."

"Bullshit! Then why do you treat me like this? Why do you go out of the way to make my life hard? I don't got to take this shit. You aren't the boss here, Rowen is."

Martin casually walked around his desk, and stood just before Frank. They were of almost equal build and stood just about the same height, staring each other in the eyes.

"Let's get something straight," Martin said. "I'm not the boss, but I'm your boss. And everything that goes on between you and me, Zale knows about. His chief concern is that the job gets done. And the job is getting done, thanks to you, Frank," Martin said sarcastically. "And I like that in you, I really do. Tell you the truth, you're doing a fine job, almost bordering outstanding. And I will gladly write that in a recommendation for you for another job if it gets so bad around here that you consider leaving. You know what I mean, Frank." Martin slapped a hand on Frank's shoulder. He didn't move in response, but Martin could almost feel the extreme hate coursing through the man's body. But this made no difference to Martin. He stepped even closer to him, close enough that he knew Frank could feel his breath on his face. Martin spoke to Frank in words just above a whisper.

"And about your time, let's come to an understanding. You report to me, and like I said before, if I need you, I need you. I don't care what time it is. I don't care if you're grilling hot dogs with the kids, and you got your cute little 'Kiss the Cook' apron on. When I need you, I need you. I don't care if you're taking a dump, washing your dog, I don't even care if you're in the middle of ballin' your wife, and you're about to get off the best nut of all time, if I page you, you suppress that shit until you find out what I want. But, then again, I forgot, you're divorced. So you shouldn't have to worry about fucking your wife, hunh. Someone else has probably gotten that assignment by now."

At that remark, Frank snatched Martin by the collar of his shirt, pulled his fist back, ready to beat Martin's face unrecognizable. But he held his blow, not because he didn't want to pummel Martin, but because Martin didn't flinch. He didn't try to fight back or defend himself; he stood, as if posing, wanting to get hit, and that was the trap, Frank knew. Frank released Martin, although it took everything within him.

"Fucking asshole. You're just a coward hiding behind that position," Frank said, his eyes not on Martin, but staring straight ahead. "If you weren't . . ."

"If I wasn't what! What would you do, Rames?"

Frank continued to look straight ahead, the muscles in his jaws dancing about.

"Let's get something straight, if there's something that you feel we need to take care of, something that we can't handle in this office by pen and paper, I have no problem taking it to the alley. Do you get what I'm saying?" Martin hissed in Frank's ear.

"I read you loud and clear," Frank sneered.

Martin stayed there, almost threatening Rames to make a move, their bodies glued together by the hate they both felt.

"If there's nothing else, you can remove yourself," Martin said, stepping away from Rames.

Frank gave Martin a hard stare, then turned to leave the office.

"Uh, don't forget these," Martin said, holding the files out to Frank. Frank snatched the folders and left the office.

"Prick!" Martin said, as Frank closed the door. He was hard on him, but he didn't care. Everything that was said to him he deserved, except maybe the divorce thing. That probably came from the anger he was feeling for his own situation. Martin sat back at his desk and massaged his temples with his fingers. Bottom line, the man didn't belong there. Martin knew it, and what was worse, Frank himself knew it. Martin could see it on his face every morning when he came in to work. Money alone was not enough to motivate a man to do a good job, especially when it was as little as they were getting paid.

There was a knock on Martin's door. Who is it now? he said to himself. "Come in."

It was his secretary, Mrs. Owen. An older, gray-haired, block-shaped woman, who had an affinity for flower-print dresses.

"I got the mail, Mr. Carter," she said. "And I separated them. These are the donations for today." She placed a stack of three letters on one side of his desk. "And these are the bills." The second stack was composed of so many letters that it took a fat rubber band to hold them together.

Martin looked at the mail, disgust written all over his face.

"I'm sorry, Mr. Carter," Mrs. Owen said. "Do you need anything else?"

"No, thank you." She left the office and closed the door. Martin reached for the thin pile of donations. He opened the first letter. It was from Mrs. Martin. Little old lady of no relation, but had the same name as his. She got a kick out of that, and always referred to him as her grandson. He knew the amount the check would be made out for before he even looked at it. He turned over the envelope and the check floated to his desk blotter: "*Make payable to:* Father Found. *Amount:* Five dollars and zero cents."

Martin couldn't help but smile. She had been sending the same check every six months since they started. He opened the other two envelopes, and they were people who never donated before, which was a good thing, but their donations didn't amount to more than fifty dollars.

He opened all the bills except one, the mortgage for the place, and

totaled them, writing down the amount of money taken in from donations beside the money that was owed. It figured $53.45 received;
$729.34 owed. Martin brought his hand up to his mouth, and shook
his head. More money that would be coming out of Zale's personal account, and he wondered just how much money Zale had saved, and
how much he made from investments before he started this thing.

He felt sorry for him a bit, but only a little. What was happening
here was a reflection of Zale's behavior. If the man only listened to him
and toned down some, the figures sitting before Martin wouldn't be so
lopsided. But blaming Zale for the situation still wouldn't make it go
away. It was his responsibility. His job was to find the money to run
this place, and he had to do that, because if they kept on receiving figures like the ones they got today, they wouldn't be able to stay afloat
much longer, and that meant, among so many other important things,
that he'd be out of a job. But it wasn't just that. Martin wouldn't let
Zale down. He couldn't, considering that if it wasn't for Zale, Martin
would probably be a nobody right now, nothing. With Martin's low
opinion of himself, his lack of confidence, he was oftentimes his worst
enemy, but Zale saw something in him, knew he could do it, and gave
him more responsibility, more authority, than anyone had in Martin's
life. From doing this job, he developed a self-confidence that he never
felt before. He was a part of something, something good, something he
believed in, headed by a man he not only trusted, but who trusted him.
He would not let him down.

Martin pushed the bills and donations aside, and slid the final bill in
front of him. This was the most important bill—the money owed on
the building that housed their organization. He opened it up and
looked it over. He looked to the right of the statement in the box labeled Amount Due: $2,745. Then he looked to the box labeled
Amount Past Due: $1,830. He drummed his fingers against the letter
as he thought. Their note was $915, and somehow they had managed
to fall back three months. Normally, there wouldn't have been a need
to worry. Martin always seemed to have been a month behind on the
note, and the people at the bank understood, letting him double up on
the payment at the last minute. But this was something different. That
grace period had already passed, and he had since received a phone
call from one of the Weinman brothers, the owners of the bank, which

Martin didn't take, because he had no idea of what to tell the man. Martin took a red pen, circled that large figure of money that he owed, and stood the bill on his desk between his pencil holder and a large paperweight. He had to get this thing paid. Their entire organization relied on it, but the only problem was, where would he get the money?

CHAPTER TEN

Frank stood over the woman lying on the filthy motel bed of the filthy motel room. He was buttoning his shirt, looking down on her. She was stark naked, her knees bent, her legs cocked open, waving slowly from side to side, as if she were trying to hypnotize him with the fleshy orifice, enticing him to crawl back on top of her for another $100 ride. Frank looked at her as if she were vermin, wondering why he ever slid up in the whore in the first place, but it's not like he had anyone else to release his tension into, and for a man forty years old, it was as much a habit as going to the bathroom.

"You wanna ride again?" the woman said, smiling, a thick coat of bright red lipstick covering her lips. She looked to be in her midtwenties, but Frank knew the girl had just turned nineteen.

Where the fuck was her father, Frank thought. He would sure like to find that guy's file in his stack one day. Frank sifted out five twenties and tossed them to the bed without answering her. He couldn't even look at her, feeling ashamed for what he had done.

He threw on his jacket and walked toward the door. He had the doorknob in his hand when the girl spoke to him.

"Mister," she said, her voice almost childlike now, sitting up in bed, looking more like her young nineteen years. "It ain't really no big thing. I been called a little bit of everything, but why were you calling me Wendy all night?"

Frank stared at her for a long moment, then opened the door. "I like the sound of the name, that's all. I just like the sound of the name."

Frank was driving, switching the knob on his radio back and forth, trying to find something halfway decent to listen to, but there was nothing, so he snapped the thing off. He was angry again, and it seemed that was a feeling he was experiencing far too often nowadays. He was angry for fucking the girl, angry for having to, and that made him angry at his wife. And he was angry for calling the girl by his wife's name, and, again, that made him angry at his wife. For some damn reason, he hadn't been able to get her out of his head, and it had been over a year since their divorce. It was because he still loved her. No matter how many times he tried to tell himself that wasn't the truth, no matter how many prostitutes he screwed to try and relieve himself of the lust he felt for her, he could not wash his mind clean of it.

Frank looked down at his watch, and it read 10:35. He was on his way home, but what would be there for him? The answer was nothing. He spun the Impala around, making a wild U-turn across a busy intersection, and headed for his ex-wife's house.

Frank switched off his headlights when he turned down the block that the house was on. It wasn't necessary, and he didn't think that it would make a difference, but he just didn't want to take any chances. He shut off the car three houses down from his ex-wife's house and sat there for a moment. She won't want to see me, he told himself, so why the hell am I here? The question saddened him, made him want to turn around, but to go where? He was there because his body, his mind, wouldn't allow him to go anywhere else. He had to be with her and his child, plain and simple, and he wouldn't stop trying until they were back with him.

He got out of the car, closed the door as quietly as possible, even though he was almost a half block from the house. He walked down the dark, quiet street, feeling his gun against his ribs, feeling like a criminal with intentions of committing a crime. When he neared the house, he slowed his pace, seeing that there were lights on in the front room. She was home, there was no question, because he saw someone through the sheer curtains, moving across the room. He wanted to hide, dive in some bushes for fear she would look out the window and see him, but he just stood there, frozen for a moment until the figure passed.

He stepped up to the door, thinking of what he would say to his wife, of what she would say to him, how she would look. He knew she would still be as beautiful as when they were married. Frank took in a deep breath, blew it out, then knocked on the door. Only a moment passed, but out of anxiousness, he knocked again. His hands were shaking and starting to perspire. He jabbed them into his pockets for lack of anything better to do with them.

He heard the door locks being undone on the other side, then heard the doorknob turn, and Frank tried to prepare himself to look into his ex-wife's eyes. But when the door opened, it wasn't his wife that stood there, but a man. A dark-haired, handsome man, around the same age as Frank, but dressed as if he were five or even ten years younger.

Frank looked at him, shocked at first, then saddened, then indifferent, figuring that he should've known that his wife would have some hard leg in the house, and he remembered what Carter said about someone else banging the woman he still loved. It angered him beyond belief. Frank walked in the house, brushing by the astonished man.

"Who the fuck are you?" Frank said, standing in the center of the living room, his arms crossed against his chest, looking prepared to beat the man if the wrong answer was given.

"Who am I? Who are you?" the man with the colorful collarless shirt and baggy blue jeans said.

Frank walked up to him, stood in his face. "Wrong answer, Boy Scout, and I'm the one asking the questions around here. Now let's try this again. Who are—"

"Frank!" Wendy said, coming out of the kitchen, holding two glasses of wine.

Frank looked over at her. She was still very beautiful. Her hair was done in a way that he had not seen in all the years that they were married, and her face was fixed so that she even appeared younger than she was over a year ago. Frank saw the wine in her hands, and not until that moment did he notice how the lights were dimmed or hear the soft music playing in the background.

"What are you doing here?"

"What is he doing here?" Frank said, stabbing a finger in the stranger's direction.

"That's none of your business," Wendy said, setting the glasses down, moving toward her ex-husband. "You know what the judge said. You're not supposed to be here."

"I don't care what the judge said. I came to see my daughter."

"She's not here," Wendy said, crossing her arms as if to say that Frank would have to go through her in order to find out if that was the truth or not.

"Is there a problem, baby?" Wendy's guest said, stepping into the area of confrontation that circled Frank and Wendy. Frank turned on the man.

"Baby? Baby! And if there was a problem, what the fuck would you do?" Frank said, stabbing a stiff finger into the man's colorful shirt. "Call your designer to beat me with a roll of fabric? 'Cause *you* sure ain't going to do a damn thing."

Wendy stepped between the two men, pushing Frank away.

"Frank, stop it. I'm tired of this. If you don't believe that your daughter isn't here, take a look around. But when you're done, get the hell out, so we can have some privacy. Or I swear I'll call the police."

"I'll do that," Frank said, turning slowly away from the other man, but giving him a deathly stare. "Bianca," Frank called, walking through the living room, taking the stairs to the second level. He stopped in front of his daughter's room, stood there a moment, thinking back to the last time he was in this place. It had been too long, seemed like another lifetime. Finally opening the door to Bianca's room, Frank was immediately hit in the face by a hard gust of memories. He had to just stand there, bracing himself against the door for fear of stumbling, waiting for the emotional wave to pass over him. He slowly stepped into her room, gazing around it as though it were the first time.

He looked at the walls, covered with posters of teenage dream boys, posters of Michael Jordan dunking on cowering defenders. He walked over to her dresser, stopped in front of the portable stereo there, remembering when he bought it for her, how happy she was. He smoothed a finger across the length of it, then walked slowly over to her bed, sat on the edge. He scooted over all the stuffed animals that covered half her bed, then pushed himself back till his back was against the wall, his legs hanging off the edge of the bed. Frank just sat there for a moment, looking about him, taking in the soft pink of the painted room. Smelling the scent of his daughter, feeling her presence as if she were there next to him. He closed his eyes, trying to see a picture of her, then he reached over blindly, grabbed her pillow, and wrapped his arms around it, as if it were her.

"I'm sorry, Binky," he said, feeling responsible for their separation. "I miss you so much."

He sat on that bed, his arms wrapped tightly around his daughter's pillow, his face pushed into the top of it, for almost ten minutes. He tried to drum up every memory he could of her, and being in her room like that, so close to her, allowed him to do that, so much more easily than when he was so far away from her.

"We're going to be back together," he said, his words muffled by the pillow that his face was sunk into. "We'll be back together, and it will be soon, sweetheart. It'll be soon."

Frank placed the pillow gently back on the head of her bed, lifted himself up and scooted all the stuffed animals back to where they were originally. He walked around the room, looking for something that he could take of his daughter's that would remind him of her all the time, for he had nothing. He looked over everything, becoming anxious when he was unable to find what he was looking for. Then he saw it. It was a key chain. A little pink dinosaur with green spots. It was something that Bianca always carried with her when she was younger. The two keys that belonged to nothing at all swinging from the chain made her feel as important as her father, with his fat loop of keys. He wondered why it was there on her dresser instead of with her, and he imagined that at age eight, she felt that she had outgrown it. Or maybe, just maybe, she sensed he would be coming one day, and pulled it off her keys and set it there for him. That's how Frank wanted to see it, and it was how he did, as he picked the little pink rubber dinosaur key chain up, fished in his pockets for his keys, then slid the thing around the thick loop of his own key chain.

He looked down at it in his hand and smiled. It was his daughter's, and it was like having a little bit of her with him till he came back. He walked out of the room, taking a last look before closing the door and walking back down the stairs.

When Frank descended the final stair, he noticed his wife sitting on the living room sofa with her back to him. She was alone.

"Where is that guy?" Frank said, looking around.

"I told him to leave," Wendy said, without turning around. She paused for a long moment, then said, "I told you Bianca wasn't here."

Frank walked around so that he could see her face. "Why won't you let me see my daughter?"

"Because the courts said I don't have to."

"Bullshit!" Frank yelled, then took a deep breath in and exhaled, trying to control his temper. "Bullshit," he said again, in a much calmer voice. "I asked you, why won't you let me see my daughter. This has nothing to do with the courts, or any damn restraining order. Why?" he asked, walking over to her.

Wendy stood and walked away from him, her arms crossed, hugging herself. She stopped and turned to face him again. She sighed. "I told you why."

She was lying, and Frank could see it, feel it. It was all over her face. He bit his lip, trying to suppress his anger, then walked over to her again.

"Don't you know that not seeing me is bad for her?"

"I'm thinking that *seeing* you would be worse."

Frank grabbed Wendy by her shoulders. "Don't you think she misses me?"

"I don't know."

"Don't you miss me?" Frank said, tightening his grip on his wife's arms.

Wendy didn't speak, just stared into his eyes, as if it were a trick question she was asked.

"What does that have to do with Bianca?"

"Everything," Frank said, his heart pounding, his eyes filled with determination. "Because I still love you, Wendy. I love you so much. Look, I want you to take me back. Take me back so we can be together again, so I can be with my child. Things can be the way they used to be."

Wendy looked at him strangely. "That's what you want, for things to be the way they used to be?"

"Yeah, baby, that's what I want," Frank said, almost desperately.

"The way they used to be. Uhm, let me see," Wendy said, tilting her eyes to the ceiling as if trying to remember back. "You mean back to the way they used to be when you used to drink so much that you were barely able to make it home. And when you did, you couldn't even make it up the stairs. You'd pass out on the sofa, or on the floor. Remember the first time Bianca came downstairs and saw you like that, she ran to my room, waking me up, shouting that you were dead on the couch. Then every time since then, whenever she'd find you there, she'd just say, 'Daddy's downstairs dead on the couch again.' You want to go back to those days?

"Or are you talking about the good ole days when I used to step out of line by telling you that I didn't want you drinking anymore, and you'd curse at me like I was some street whore in front of the children, or you'd come up to my job, stumbling, reeking of alcohol, telling me you needed money for food when it was more booze you were trying to buy. Are those the days? Or could you be referring to the best time of our lives when you were so fed up with being out of work, and most of the time so juiced up off alcohol, that the slightest thing set you off.

"Like the time you came in and dinner wasn't cooked. You started yelling and losing your mind. Bianca started crying, and William stood in front of me, as if he was going to stop you from hurting me. But I told them I'd be all right, told the kids to go into the other room, and told you I'd start dinner for you right away. But that wasn't good enough for you, Frank. Even though I was rushing around that kitchen, pulling shit out the fridge, setting the table and arranging pots and pans, that wasn't good enough. You had to teach me a lesson. And remember how you did that, Frank?" Wendy said, staring directly in his eyes.

"I wasn't myself then, you know that!" Frank passionately tried to defend himself. "I didn't mean for that to happen."

"I see. You didn't mean for it to happen, that's why you yanked that pan out of my hand and started to beat me with it. In the face, on top of my head, across my back. And these weren't love taps, Frank. You were bringing it from all the way back, giving it all you had. And even after I was lying across that cold kitchen floor, half unconscious, my face covered with blood, you continued to beat me. I can remember looking up at you through the blood and tears, seeing that monstrous mask on your face, asking myself, trying to understand, how a man who said he loved me could do this to me. But you continued hitting me, and hitting me. You wanted to kill me."

"I didn't."

"You did! You did!" Wendy yelled. "And I thought I'd never see my children again. But I thought if I survived that beating, the worst beating, there would never be another. Never. And there never will be."

Wendy paused, resting her eyes sternly on Frank, making sure he understood the last thing that was said.

"Is that the way you want things to be again? Like that?"

Frank's hands slowly slid off her shoulders. His head lowered in front of her.

"I never meant to hurt you," he said softly.

"But you did, Frank. You did, and how long do you think it would've taken before you started beating Bianca like that, and William, if he had lived?"

"I wouldn't have touched those kids! I loved them!"

"And you claimed you loved me, too."

"I did love you. I do love you!" Frank said, looking confused. "Things were different then. You know that. I was under investigation. Things were crazy, and I started drinking. I'm not drinking anymore. I've been through a program, and you know I'd never do that to you again."

"Do I, Frank? How do I know that? How?"

"Because I'm telling you I wouldn't. I'm giving you my word."

"Frank, your word doesn't mean much anymore. To tell you the truth, it means just about nothing."

"I do still love you. Will you believe that, Wendy?"

"If you say so, but I don't think it means anything."

Frank pulled his head up, and straightened himself so he wouldn't look so pathetic in the eyes of his wife. "I understand," he said. "But will you do me this favor. You don't have to answer me now. Think about it and tell me later. But will you please let me see Bianca. Please, I don't care under what conditions. You can chaperon, you can even sit us on either sides of a chain-link fence, but I have to talk to her, see her. What do you say?"

Wendy didn't look as if she was giving it much thought. Frank thought she looked as though she was able to give him his answer right then, and if that was the case, he knew it would be no.

"I don't know, Frank, but I'll give it some thought."

"That's all I want you to do."

CHAPTER ELEVEN

Zale sat in his office, a number of files spread out in front of him, the photos of so many fathers staring up at him. Amazingly enough, today had been a very good day. For some reason, three of the men that Father Found had been trying to contact for so long had actually contacted him, and that included André Hinton.

Zale couldn't believe that he was talking to him. It was the first time, and Zale became very excited.

"Mr. Hinton, I'm very glad that you called. I've been looking forward to talking to you for quite some time."

Mr. Hinton didn't say anything, just grunted in response, his voice low and raspy.

"I was wondering if you could come in, maybe tomorrow, and we could maybe sit down and talk things over. See what's been going on, and how we can change things to benefit everyone involved."

"No, no. I can't do that."

"Well, give me a time, and I'll be glad to come out and see you."

"No! That's no good," Mr. Hinton said, more adamantly.

There was silence for a moment, then Hinton's voice came off the phone, low and unsure. "I have things that I got to take care of for about the next week, then I'll come in to see you. But I'm at home, with my baby's mother, so everything is all right."

"But Mr. Hinton—" Zale said.

"Look, I got to go. I'll get back with you later." He hung up the phone.

Zale told himself that the phone calls he received over the course of that day were good news. Four men called that day by their own will, looking for help, and Zale couldn't remember the last time that actually happened, if it ever had.

He wasn't sure what Frank was doing. If he was just happening to catch these men at the right time, while they were feeling guilty about leaving their children, or if he appealed to the man's family or friends, telling them to pass on what he said. Or if Frank just found a new way, a better way, of communicating with them. Maybe sitting down and having a long discussion with them, going over the literature that he was supposed to give them, and laying things out in such a comfortable, nonthreatening manner that the men felt almost obligated to call, if for no other reason than just to see if the white man from Father Found was actually telling the truth about how the organization could help them.

Zale figured that to be the case and he was glad, and he got a good feeling, knowing that he was right when he hired Frank on. And the way Mace felt about Zale trusting the man was wrong. If Zale was able to trust Frank to save his life, he could trust him with anything. But there was one thing that hung in the back of Zale's mind. Yes, all of these men called, and all of them seemed willing to discuss their situation, but not one of them wanted to come in and do it tomorrow. And when Zale offered to come to them, they all quickly turned him down as if they were terrified of the man.

The peculiar thing was that they all gave the same excuse, almost word for word. "There's a situation I have to take care of for the next week, then I'll come in to see you." And then they all continued to offer that they were at home with their child's mother, and everything was all right.

Zale thought about it for a moment and then realized that the main objective had been reached, at least for right now. They were at home, and if it took them a week or two before he spoke to them, then it just did. It would be more time that they'd spend with their family.

Zale closed the file he had open, a slight smile on his face and a content feeling in his heart. It was a feeling that he didn't experience very often in his work, but when he did, it made everything, from the sleepless nights to the occasional death threats, worth the trouble.

It seemed as though he was hitting an upswing, and he believed in riding the wave as far and as high as it would take him. Zale reached for his briefcase, opened it up, and pulled out a pad. On it, he had names and phone numbers, almost a dozen of them. They were the names of the mothers of the children he had spoken to from the school courtyard yesterday. These were the children whose fathers weren't at home.

He didn't know what the legal situations for all of them were, so he asked questions like:

"Does your mother ever get mail from your father?"

The little boy he asked nodded his head, as he took a bite out of his peanut butter and jelly.

"How often does she get it? Once a year? Once every six months? Once a month or per week?"

"Every month," the boy answered, his head turned toward some friends who were calling him.

Zale assumed that those were payments, and allowed the boy to take off into the crowd of children, but he put the mother's name and telephone number down anyway, just to confirm what he thought. One could never be too sure.

Zale asked a number of questions. Direct, but disguised very well so as not to alert them to what he was doing. He didn't think that any of these children would suspect what they were doing was wrong, answering questions about their parents, but some parents make a point to tell their children not to talk to strangers, and a stranger was what Zale was from head to toe. So he kept the questions conversational, speaking to them as a teacher would, or an uncle that they never met before.

He made it a point to find out what the mother did for a living.

"What does your mom wear to work? Does she ever bring you home any goodies from her job, and if so, what is it? When you call her job, what does the person say when they pick up the phone?"

He needed to find out if the mother was on welfare.

"I can remember when I was little, my mother used to send me to the store with food stamps. I hated that," he said, smiling in the face of a young girl. "Does your mother make you use them? Or when your mother takes you to the doctor, do you have to wait for a long time, in a room crowded with a lot of people?"

The girl shook her head to all the questions, which left Zale nowhere. He knew he had to be more direct, more specific.

"Does your father live at home with you?"

"No," the little girl said, looking away, her attention taken by some of her friends playing.

"Did he leave you and your mother?"

"No, my mother kicked him out."

"Then how are you and your mother making it?" Zale asked, coming a little closer to the girl, crouching lower, more concern on his face.

The girl turned and looked at Zale as if he was speaking another language.

"How are we making it?"

"Living. Buying food. Paying rent. How do you get from place to place? Do you walk, take the bus?" Zale asked sadly.

"My mom drives a Jaguar. She's a lawyer. We live in a condo in a tall building downtown."

"I see," Zale said, and what a fool he felt like, as he stood up and slowly started to walk away.

"I can see the Sears Tower from my bedroom," she called to Zale.

That's wonderful, Zale thought to himself. This was obviously a woman who had no problems taking care of her family without a man, probably preferred it that way. Zale realized there were many women who successfully raised their children without the aid of the father, but he could not concern himself with them right now.

He questioned a few more of the kids, constructing fairly decent profiles of the home situations, determining if the father was taking care of his children or not. He put an asterisk by the names of the children he felt weren't being provided for.

Those were the names that he was looking at while sitting at his desk. He looked down at his watch and it read 6:30 P.M. Feeling comfortable that most of the mothers of these children were home from work, if they worked at all, he was about to call the first of those names and see if he could build on his luck when someone knocked on his door.

"Come in," Zale said.

The door opened and Martin walked in, something behind his back, and he did that so often that Zale would be shocked if ever he entered his office empty-handed. Martin kicked the door closed with his foot and stood in the center of the room, just before Zale's desk, a melancholy expression on his face.

"How goes it?" Zale said, feeling quite chipper, regardless of how his best friend looked.

Martin still didn't say a word, just looked at Zale, shaking his head slightly from side to side.

"Well?" Zale said.

"I don't like to say this, but we're going to need more money from your account."

"Hmmm," Zale said, pushing himself away from his desk, rolling an inch or two back, then crossing his hands behind his head, trying to appear more unaffected by the news than he was. "And how much is that?"

"Not much. The usual amount," Martin said, sounding ashamed of what he was saying. He didn't even mention the amount owed for the mortgage. "Do you want to see the book?" he said, bringing the over-sized book from behind his back and preparing to lay it out for examination in front of Zale.

"No, no, no!" Zale said, waving the book away. "You don't have to do that. I believe what you say. I mean, you're the man I trust with all the money. If anyone should know that we need more, it should be you, right?"

"Right," Martin said, lowering his eyes for a moment. "You do have more, don't you? In your account, that is."

"Sure, sure!" Zale said, sitting up in his chair, trying to sound more enthusiastic, as if this presented no problem at all. Then he looked away from Martin, withdrawing, reflecting on the situation. "Everything will be fine. I'll write a check and leave it for you. It won't be a problem," he said, as if he were trying to convince himself of that fact. "Is there anything else, because I was about to . . ." Zale held the pad of numbers up for Martin to see.

"No, no!" Martin said, as if he was imposing on Zale's time. He turned to leave, going as far as reaching for the door, then he stopped and walked back to Zale's desk.

"Why do you do it?"

"Do what?"

Martin sighed, and shook his head in frustration. "I saw one of to-day's papers. They had an article about your speaking engagement the other night. We sat and talked it that that day, and I deliberately asked you, damn near begged you, to tone it down, and what did you go and do? You said things to those men more hateful than you did in your last interview, and that's just what they were able to print.

"I called the guy who did the story, and he let me listen to his tape."

Martin set the account book down on a chair, walked up to Zale's desk, leaned over it and got right up in Zale's face.

"Zale, do you even care anymore? I looked at our donations yesterday and we received fifty-three dollars. Fifty-three lousy dollars. What are we supposed to do with that? We can't even go out and get dinner with that, Zale. How are we supposed to fight this epidemic in our community? Do you want us to fail? Do you want us to go so far in debt that we lose this place, and then where will we be? Can you tell me that?"

"You know what happened to my car? You know how—"

"Awwww!" Martin said, throwing his hands up, turning his back on Zale. "Can you get past that? I know you were mad as hell. I would've been, too, but the engagements you speak at are not the places to release your personal frustrations. You can't jeopardize this organization just because someone does something to you that pisses you off!"

"Well, they shouldn't do things to piss me off," Zale said.

"I see, I see," Martin said sarcastically, bobbing his head up and down. "But have you ever thought of it this way? They wouldn't do things to piss you off if you didn't say things to piss them off first?"

"They made the first assault by leaving their children. That's what pisses me—"

"Zale, I'm not going to argue with you anymore! We can go back and forth with this. But answer three questions for me. One—if they continue to piss you off, what will they lose? Two—if you continue to piss them off, what will we lose? And three—who do you think stands to lose more?"

Zale sat there at his desk, rubbing his chin with his hand, giving the questions serious thought.

"Well!" Martin said, exasperated.

"It's more than that. It's not that cut and dried. I know. I'm aware of what's going on."

"No, what you are is pigheaded!" Martin grabbed the book. "We're going to lose this, and when we do, don't blame it on me. It won't be my fault." He went for the door, then halted and turned.

"Oh, yeah. I'm going to need tomorrow off, if that's all right with you. I have some very important personal business to take care of."

"Sure," Zale said.

"I don't think we have to worry about me being here, just in case the mail box overflows with donations," Martin said before he left.

Zale sat there and just stared at the door for a long while. Was Martin right? Did he do the wrong thing? Was he directly jeopardizing Father Found, the organization that he had built from the ground up? Was he tearing the place down, brick by brick, just because he had to let people know how angry he was at the fathers who left their children?

He didn't know, he just didn't know. He threw his face in his hands and squeezed. He couldn't lose Father Found. It would almost be like committing suicide, for there would be nothing else worth living for, nothing else to look forward to.

He pulled his face from his hands, and looked around his office. It was spinning, slowly, everything appearing with a soft, blurred haze around it. It was the stress, the anger, the anxiety that he was feeling.

He had to get out of there, had to get away from that desk, his office, the questions that were plaguing him. He had to clear his head of the accusations that Martin threw at him, the doubt that he was starting to feel in himself.

He had to stop thinking about everything, and just clear his mind before it got so overcrowded that it would pound with pain until he feared it might explode.

He had felt like that before, had migraines that wrapped themselves around his brain like a vise, had him blind with pain, where all he was able to do was fall to his bed to suffer through the pain that was too intense to sleep through. He didn't want to encounter that again.

He stepped out the back door of the building, and a cool evening breeze hit him in the face. Already he began to feel a little better, felt he could breathe some. He loosened the tie around his neck and took steps toward his car. He parked it in the back of the building now, within a gated area. He didn't know why he didn't do that before. It had to be trust in the men that he was dealing with. Trust that they would handle their business with him, the way Zale handled his, honestly and straightforwardly. What he did and said was right out in the open, and trusting them to confront him the same way was foolish of him, he now knew. He would never trust them again.

To his satisfaction, the car was just as clean as when he picked it up from the auto body shop. Still feeling burdened by the trouble in his mind, Zale walked out onto the street.

Trash littered the area. Empty cups and fast-food containers sat on the ground not five feet from an empty trash can. Garbage of all sorts lined the gutters of the streets, and people walked by boxes of this and bottles of that as though they were something that enhanced the streets as opposed to diminishing their appearance.

Little dirty kids with torn dirty clothing dodged in and out of traffic, as if the cars were their friends, trying to tag them like in a friendly game of It. This was where they played, for there were no backyards for a lot of them whose apartments sat bordering a busy street. This was their backyard.

Zale wanted to run out there, grab them, yank them in by the collars of their shirts and give them a good lesson on why children shouldn't play in the damn street, but he couldn't. He couldn't move from the spot he stood in. All he could do was look and hope the kids didn't get hit by a bus or speeding car. He couldn't save them all, not every single one of them, not every minute of the day. It was a realization that pained him to think about. He turned and continued trudging down the street, every so often looking over his shoulder to see if the kids were still running around in traffic.

He walked around for almost an hour, his head lowered, his shoulders slumped, his hands in his pockets, a general feeling of failure in his heart, when just a short time earlier, he felt he was nearing the top of the world. What a difference an hour makes.

After his long walk, Zale was on his way back to Father Found, when he stopped just one building away. He didn't know why he did, but he felt compelled to. He looked up, and it was a building almost identical to the one that he was in. The sign bolted to the old structure read South Side Community Center. He had always known that it was there, but never really paid much attention to it. He was about to turn, head back to work, but he wasn't ready for that. He needed more time away, even if it was just to wander through the halls of an old community center. It would keep his mind off all his problems for just a little longer.

He looked over both shoulders, then walked up to the door, cupped his hands around his eyes and looked in through the glass window.

There was no one he could see inside. Chipping paint on the glass door read "Weekdays: 9:00 A.M.–9:00 P.M." Zale looked at his watch, and it was a little after 8:30 P.M.

He walked into a large room with a number of empty chairs lined up in rows, a single large wooden desk sitting in the front of the room.

"Hello," Zale called, and didn't know exactly why he was calling. If someone popped out from behind a door, Zale would've probably looked at them, a stupid expression on his face, and said nothing, but he called again anyway.

"Is anybody here?"

There was a long corridor, doors lining each side. Zale walked down the hallway slowly, looking at the doors, peeking into some of the rooms. "Game Room" was stenciled on one of the doors. "Reading Room" on another. "Substance Rehabilitation," "Planned Parenting," and a door that read "Family Disorders." Zale stopped and walked up to that door and tried the doorknob. It was locked. He looked in through the window, but the room was dark. All he could make out were some chairs that were arranged in a huge circle.

I wonder if those people have any stories that could beat mine, Zale thought. Then he heard a noise coming from the other side of the hall. He spun around, thinking that someone was behind him, but all he saw was an open door, light coming from the room. He slowly walked in that direction, feeling drawn by something.

He approached the door and read what was printed there. "Psychiatric Counseling" the door read, and he thought about what Regina had told him the other day, about seeing someone for help. He would never, he told himself, standing there in front of that door. It would never get so bad that he would trust some stranger with all the secrets of his life. He could handle it by himself, just fine, like he had always done.

Curious, he stepped into the doorway of the room. It looked just like the "Family Disorders" room, with chairs in a circle. He guessed that was where people spilled their guts right out in the open, hoping to receive pity and pats on the back. "Aww"s and "Poor baby"s given to them by perfect strangers who could really give a damn about all the shit that person went through, but hoping for the same shallow sympathy when it was their turn to air their old memories. No way, Zale thought. That would never be him, and he could feel himself becoming angrier at Regina for even mentioning it.

There was a woman in the back of the room, and she was pinning construction-paper cutouts to a board, just like the teachers did in kindergarten. How sweet, Zale thought sarcastically. She was probably the counselor, or psychiatrist, or whatever, and Zale was curious, wanted to ask her what she got out of digging through people's personal memories? What good did she actually think would come from dredging up those old experiences? He considered it for a long moment, looking at her as she pinned up the cutouts as if she were preparing for an open house.

Zale looked down at his watch for a moment, and when he looked back up, the woman had turned around and was staring him in the eyes from the back of the room. He felt like an animal sitting in the middle of a rural highway, caught in the bright lights of an oncoming car. Almost against his will, he held her stare for what seemed a lifetime, then he turned away, quickly headed down the long corridor, trying to get out of there. He walked briskly, as if he feared something coming after him. And as he walked, he could almost feel that the woman from the back of the room, the woman who looked into people's past for a living, reacquainting them with the most painful parts of their lives, was standing at that door, watching Zale retreat, and for some reason, he was scared to look back to see if she was actually there.

He blew out the door of the South Side Community Center and leaned up against the wall of the building, feeling a chill running through his body, his heart beating a lot faster than it should've been.

Back in his office, he took off his jacket and tie and unbuttoned his shirt. It had been a long day, a forgettable day, and all he wanted to do was put it behind him.

There were the phone numbers that he was supposed to call earlier, but it was too late now.

Besides, there was too much going on his head, and the thought of sorting through it only made him feel worse. He would try and go to sleep, not because he was necessarily in desperate need of it, but to try and forget, or at least suspend, all the questions and problems that filled his head at that moment.

He opened a door in the back of his office that led into a large storage place. He rolled out a small folding bed, opened it up, and spread the sheets and blanket about it. He would sleep there tonight, as he did so many nights when he just didn't feel like going home, or when he felt that he had work to do at five or six in the morning.

Besides, he didn't want to take another chance at Regina being there and turning off his alarm clock again.

Regina, Zale thought. Damn! And he remembered that he was supposed to have picked her up at her place to take her out. He had promised her dinner and a movie, but he had forgotten.

Zale went to the phone and called her number, checking the time, seeing that it was almost two hours since he was supposed to have picked her up. The phone rang several times, and her machine answered. Zale was prepared to say something, tell her how sorry he was, that things got terribly busy, but he knew she had heard all that from him before, and saying it again would probably do more harm than good.

When her message ended, Zale simply said, "It's me. I'm sorry."

He hung up the phone, pulled his slacks off, cut out the lights, and slid into the portable bed. He pulled the covers up to his chest and crossed his hands behind his head, looking up into the darkness. She'll be mad at me, he told himself. She'll be mad, and she'll have every right to be, and he felt that he should've actually made more of an attempt to contact her, paged her, but he just didn't feel like dealing with any of that right now. He didn't feel like dealing with anything.

CHAPTER TWELVE

Martin lay in bed on his stomach, his wife beside him. He had awakened fifteen minutes or so ago and had been staring at her through partially closed eyes. He looked at her right up close, her face not even two inches from his, and he could feel the soft wisps of air as she breathed through her nose. She was beautiful even as she slept, if not more beautiful, but that could not keep Martin from feeling skeptical and suspicious toward her. He had not forgotten about the other night, and he had come up with an almost surefire plan that would let him know what his wife was really up to.

When Debra finally got up, Martin didn't move, just pretended to still be asleep, watching her as she moved about the room, going in and out of the bathroom, brushing her hair, spraying herself with perfume, the room smelling of chemically enhanced flowers for a moment. She sat on the edge of the bed, pulling her stockings on. Martin cautiously watched her legs, how smooth and firm they were as she rolled the stockings up the thickness of her thighs. She stopped abruptly for a moment and turned to look at him, probably feeling that he was awake. Martin quickly closed his eyes and exaggerated his breathing to pretend he was still sleeping.

Debra went back to getting dressed, putting on an attractive suit, as always. She went back into the bathroom, and Martin knew it was to do her makeup. She always did that last, and not long ago, she would come out and nudge him, waking him up just long enough to say goodbye and kiss him on the cheek, leaving an imprint of her shapely lips, the freshly applied lipstick still clinging to his face when he finally got up and prepared to go to work.

But over the last few weeks, she would come out of the bathroom, grab her briefcase, and walk out the bedroom door, not even nearing Martin. And as he faked sleeping, still peeking at her through the slits of his eyelids, he saw her as she came out of the bathroom and stopped, just outside the door, looking over at him. Martin closed his eyes even tighter, but still allowing space to see her. It looked as though she were questioning approaching her husband, questioning performing what used to be a ritual in their house. Martin hoped that she would do it. Hoped that she would forget everything that was said the last night they argued, or at least put it aside, and kiss him goodbye. It would let him know that she still loved him, that no matter what they argued about the night before, it would never affect how she felt about him in the morning.

She continued to look at him, seeming torn, and in his mind, his heart, Martin begged her to approach, feeling that this was the mo-

ment of truth, that everything hinged on this. He even told himself that
if she walked over and kissed him, did something as small as that, he
would forget about what he had planned for today, and try to start on
a new page.

But after just another moment of debating, Debra bent down,
picked up her briefcase, and walked out of the room, closing the door
behind her. Martin's heart sank.

An hour later, Martin got up and got the girls ready for school. He
fixed their breakfast, Trix for Renee and Fruity Pebbles for Rebecca,
like there was actually a difference between the two colorful sugar-
coated cereals. He got them into their clothes as he always did, and
stood them at the front door, kneeling down in front of them.

"We aren't forgetting anything, are we?"

Both girls shook their heads.

"Okay, wait right here, Daddy has to do something." Martin went
into the kitchen, picked up the telephone, and punched in the code to
have the phone calls that were meant for his home directed to his cell
phone.

"Okay, we're all set." He took the girls, helped them into the car,
buckling them both into the back seat.

"You guys aren't going to come home right after school today, all
right?" he said, looking at them through the rearview mirror. "You're
going to stay at the babysitter's house until tonight."

"Why, Daddy?" Renee asked.

"Yeah, why, Daddy?" Rebecca repeated.

"Because Daddy has something very important to do today."

"You aren't going to work?"

"No, I took the day off, but don't you tell Mommy about it, okay?"

"But why not?" Rebecca asked.

"Because it will be a surprise to Mommy, and if she knows about it,
it won't work right," Martin said.

Martin pulled up across the street from the building that housed his
wife's small medical practice. He pulled in between a truck and a large
car, making it almost impossible for his wife to see his car if she came
out unexpectedly, but still giving him clearance to see her.

He pulled the plastic lid off a cup of McDonald's coffee and took a sip of the steaming liquid. He had stopped at the restaurant and got himself the coffee, a breakfast sandwich, and some potatoes, because he knew that it would be a long morning, a long day, for that matter, and he was prepared to sit out there until he saw his wife leave the building. He was going to shadow her, tagging behind her to lunch, then to the hospital, and wherever else she would go.

Martin had been sitting in the car for over two hours, trying to amuse himself with whatever he could to take his mind off the time crawling by. The radio played softly, music from a contemporary jazz station, and the dial would stay there until they started with the long stream of mindless, useless commercials. Then Martin would turn the dial, as he had been doing all morning.

He wished he had brought something to read, and he was looking in the back seat, under the front seats, and through the glove box for anything to keep him occupied when, out of the corner of his eye, he saw Debra step out of the building, her purse on her shoulder and a wide smile on her face as she waved goodbye to someone.

She looked happy, very happy, and Martin couldn't remember the last time he saw her appearing so carefree. His eyes followed her till he lost her around the back of the building. He waited a moment, then he saw her beige Saab pull out on the street and head north.

Martin had already started his car, and after waiting for a clearing, pulled out to follow her. He was four or five car lengths behind her, moving along slowly in the lunchtime traffic. He wasn't terribly worried about his wife spotting him, because he was sure that she wasn't expecting something like this to be happening. Besides, when she drove, she always had her music cranked up full blast, one of her favorite CDs blasting out the windows and sunroof, loud enough for the pedestrians she passed on the street to sample her taste in music. Her head would be bobbing, and she would be drumming her fingers on the steering wheel, thinking only about how snappy the beat was she was listening to.

She drove rather fast, as she always did, dodging in and out of traffic, taking turns as if she were actually in a Porsche rather than the family vehicle she drove. All her maneuvering made it hard for Martin to keep up with her. He sped up, cutting the distance between them down to two cars, making it very easy for her to see him. All she had to do was lift her eyes, look through the rearview for longer than the usual glance, and she would've seen him, weaving through traffic as she was, hunching down behind his wheel, trying not to be seen.

Debra made a quick turn without signaling, and Martin almost flipped his Ford Taurus trying to duplicate the action. She sped down a single-lane street, almost losing Martin when she made another turn onto a wide four-lane street.

He had to stay with her, he told himself, and he felt as if he were participating in some weird race for his life.

Debra was now three car lengths ahead of him. She was cruising at about fifty miles an hour down a street displaying speed-limit signs of thirty-five miles an hour, and Martin clutched his steering wheel and yelled out, "Why the hell are you driving so fast!"

There was a major intersection up ahead, and the light above it was green, had been green since Martin saw it from far down the street. He knew what was going to happen, and he couldn't let it. As his wife sped toward the intersection, the light turned yellow, then red, and she blew through the light, as if red not only meant "Go" but "Go as fast as you can." The car behind her skidded to a stop, forcing the other two to do the same, but Martin couldn't stop. He would lose her for sure and he couldn't allow himself to do that. He didn't know where the hell she was going, what she was about to do, and he had to know it. He had to!

Martin yanked the steering wheel hard to the right, and slammed down on the gas. He cut the car into the far lane, and ran through the red light just before the crossing traffic started to proceed. He cut back into the center lane and he could see his wife's car. He couldn't afford to lose her. Yes, he almost killed himself, but it was a necessary move, and he would've done it over again if he had to. Then he heard the siren behind him, looked up, and saw the blue lights flashing in his rearview. Martin was hoping the policemen weren't following him, hoping that they were just trying to get by him, but then he heard, "Pull over to the curb." Martin took one last look down the street and saw the Saab disappear around a corner.

■ ■ ■

Martin sat back in the spot he had held earlier that morning, in front of his wife's practice. He had been sitting there for over an hour, steaming at the fact he had lost his wife, the orange moving-violation ticket sitting on the dashboard. All he could do was come back here and hope that she showed up after lunch.

After another half hour, he saw his wife enter the building, looking just as bubbly as she had when she left. Something happened over lunch, and he was angry at himself because he wasn't there to see what that was. And he knew that smile wasn't there because the food at lunch was just so tasty.

Martin waited until his wife got off work at the office, then he followed her to the hospital. He stopped outside the parking garage and settled in, expecting to wait until very near midnight if what she said to him about her having to work late was true.

It was starting to get dark—7:30 P.M. was approaching, and Martin realized that he had been in that car for ten hours. He was starting to get hungry again, felt his stomach growling, and he wanted to go and get something quick to eat, even if it was just a hot dog or a bag of chips from a convenience store. But he didn't want to leave his perch. He knew that his wife could leave at any moment while he was gone, and if that happened, the entire day would've been a complete waste.

But the question was, had he wasted the day already? Did he waste the day when he first had the idea of following her? Debra had done nothing so far today to warrant suspicion. Yes, she had left this afternoon, and had taken a long lunch, but Martin had no proof of just where she went. And outside of that lunch, she was following her routine just as she had detailed it to him time after time.

Martin decided he would go and grab something, his stomach demanded it, and so did his mind. He needed a change of scenery, even if it was just the parking lot of a fast-food spot. And even if his wife had some sort of agenda this evening, he was sure it would wait until she got off work. It seemed nothing came before that.

Martin sat in the parking lot of a convenience store, not five minutes away from the hospital. He had bought two hot dogs, with some chips and a drink. He had finished the first dog and was about to take a bite of the second, when the phone rang.

Martin pulled a sip from his soda first, then grabbed his cell phone.

"Carter here," he said, a business tone about his voice.

"When did you start answering the phone like that while you're at home?" Martin's wife asked, and he had to think a moment about the question, quickly remembering that before he left the house he had transferred the calls to his cell phone.

"Oh, well, you know. Work is always on my mind," he said, recognizing the close call.

"How was it today?" she asked.

"Just fine. Kind of long and boring, but it wasn't bad. How is work going for you?"

"Fine here, too. Can't complain, I guess."

"What did you do for lunch?" Martin asked, listening very intently for her reply.

His wife paused before answering. "Nothing, just ate another one of those delicious low-fat, microwavable lunches."

"You didn't go out to eat?" Martin said, the statement sounding less like a question and more like a correction. He cringed, hoping his wife didn't catch on.

She paused again, as if thinking about the way he said what he did. "No. Like I said, I stayed in and ate."

"Okay."

"Well, the reason why I'm calling is to tell you that I'm going to be late again, and I didn't want you to get mad."

"What's going on?"

"One of the babies in intensive care is having some serious difficulties. We don't think she's going to make it, but we're going to try and do everything we can."

Martin didn't respond to what she said because he was busy clearing the food out of his lap, starting the car and heading back toward the hospital. He didn't know why, but something told him to get over there. Something in his wife's voice didn't sound just right, didn't sound honest, and he drove as fast as he could to get back to the entrance of the parking garage.

"Martin?" his wife called.

"Yeah, I'm still here," he said, seeing parts of the hospital come into view.

"What's that noise over the phone?" she asked, obviously referring to the static and the traffic noise.

"Oh, I'm on the cordless, and I walked out front. It's a nice night out," he said, pulling up at the intersection just adjacent to the entrance to the parking garage.

"Yeah, it was nice this afternoon. I wish I wasn't trapped in here, so I could feel a little bit of it."

And then, Martin couldn't believe what he saw. It was his wife's Saab, his wife behind the wheel, her head canted, the cell phone to her ear, rolling out of the garage and through the intersection. She drove right by Martin. And he was shocked that she didn't see him, for he looked right in her face, saw her lip movement correspond to the words he heard over the phone. The light turned green and he followed her, very carefully this time.

"So there's no way that you'll be able to get out of there, hunh?" Martin said.

"No. I'm here till midnight, if not later. But I really have to go, someone's calling me. I just wanted to let you know in light of what's been happening with us. Just wanted to start on a clean slate."

"Yeah, me too," Martin forced himself to say, trying with everything within him to stop the hate from appearing in his voice.

But as he followed his wife, made the turns she made, sped when she sped, he realized that it wasn't mostly anger that he was feeling. What he was feeling was excitement, but not the type you feel when you ride a roller coaster, but how you feel when you know something big is about to happen, something life-altering. He felt very nervous, not because he wanted to see what he thought he would see, but because he was finally going to know, one way or the other, what had been going on, and then he could get past it, be done with it once and for all.

He slowed down when he saw his wife pull into the drive of a hotel. She got out, went into the trunk, pulled a bag from it, and allowed the valet to take her car. She looked over her shoulder briefly, causing Martin to duck quickly behind the wheel, but he was not spotted. He watched as his wife entered the hotel through the revolving door, and that's when the excitement he was just feeling a minute ago turned to fear, anger, and pain. It was as if it was all now coming true. Everything that he suspected, but never really believed that she could do. All the pieces of the sordid puzzle were pretty much in front of him. All he had to do now was see, see with his own eyes as the pieces came together so there could not be the slightest bit of doubt.

Martin pulled into the drive of the hotel, angrily flipped on his hazards and got out of the car, leaving it running. The valet grabbed the door and was about to enter.

"Don't you get in that fucking car, and it better not move an inch. Do you read me!" Martin barked at the middle-aged Hispanic man in the marching-band outfit. "This won't take but a minute," Martin said, more to himself than to anyone.

He pushed his way through the revolving door and approached the counter. A young man, tall and thin, his hair cut neatly, a feminine look about him, was at the desk.

"May I help you, sir," he said with a sincere smile.

"That woman that just left this counter, what room did she go to?" Martin asked, seriousness on his face and in his voice.

"Excuse me," the young man asked politely.

"You heard what I said. What room did she go to?"

"I can't give out that kind of information. It's personal."

"I know it's personal," Martin said, behind clenched teeth. "But I don't care! What room did she go to?"

"Sir, maybe if you'd like to talk to a—"

Martin grabbed the boy by the collar and yanked him right up to his face. The boy was on his tippy-toes, his entire upper body over the counter.

"Listen, you little shit! That woman you just gave a key to is my fucking wife. Now if you don't tell me what room she went to, I swear you'll regret it for the rest of your short life!"

"Fourteen-fifteen! Fourteen-fifteen!" the boy cried out. Martin released him. "Elevators!" Martin ordered.

"Right there, sir," the boy pointed with a trembling finger.

Martin jumped on the elevator, jabbed a finger into the 14 button, and waited, seething, as the motors began to lift the carriage up to the fourteenth floor.

I'm going to kill her. I'm going to kill her! is what ran through Martin's head, over and over again, as he saw himself in the mirrors that covered the elevator's walls. He was enraged, and the anger that boiled in him made him look like a different person. He could barely recognize himself, and maybe that was because he felt this was not his life he was living. Something like this was not supposed to be happening to someone like him. But he would find out why. If he had to strangle his wife to get the words out of her, he would find out why.

The elevator hit the fourteenth floor with a "ding" of the bell, and when the doors slid open, it was as if they stripped something from Martin. The anger was still there, but the willingness to do something with it was gone. The burning desire to go in there and see with his own eyes what his wife was up to was no longer there, and again he felt more scared than anything.

He took slow steps down the hall, looking for 1415. He stopped when he saw it and almost wanted to turn around, as if he had no business being there, as if he may have been intruding on something that was meant to take place without him. He wanted to slap himself. Where was this hesitation coming from? And he knew it had something to do with his feelings of inadequacy. But that should have nothing to do with this, he told himself. She was his wife, and he was her husband, and this should not have been happening, regardless of how inferior he felt compared to her.

Martin walked up to the door and placed his ear to it. He heard very little, but what he could make out was muffled talking and giggling by two people. He recognized his wife's voice, and heard that the other voice was that of a man. A man who had somehow taken his wife from him, convinced her that he was a better man, that her time would be better spent away from her husband and her kids, and spent with him.

Martin never felt lower or more hurt in his life, and he questioned himself. Maybe Debra was right to be with this man. He had to be more than Martin was, considering he couldn't even find enough within himself to intervene on the worst sin possible.

He lowered his head, and walked back to the elevator, telling himself it was best not to make a scene anyway. The problem could just as easily be addressed at home, and that's when he would do it. When she got home, he would let her have it, he thought, trying to make himself feel better. The doors opened and he walked into the elevator, stepping to the side of a couple who were already on. By the way they were staring at each other, petting, and pecking each other on the cheeks and lips, they must have been newlyweds.

Martin stood there watching them, staring at them, not caring if they noticed, but they didn't because they started to kiss passionately, probably not caring if *he* noticed. That's the way he and Debra were when they first got married. The man caressed the woman's back, his hand sliding down to her behind, cupping it, squeezing it, as if they were in the privacy of their room.

To be so excited about one another, they had to be newlyweds, Martin thought. The only other explanation could be that they were . . . Martin looked at the way their heads rotated about the axis of their lips, the way the man's hand rubbed and squeezed the hell out of the woman's bottom.

. . . The only other explanation was that they were having an affair. And that man upstairs with his wife was probably pawing at Debra the way this man was pawing on whosever wife that was. The man upstairs was probably watching as Debra undressed for him, sensually, a smile on her face, not having to convince her, or take off her clothes for her, like Martin had to.

Debra was probably laughing and smiling with that man. Engaging in foreplay, getting him to the point where he was so excited that he was about to bust, but Debra continuing to play with him, wanting him to want her more, so unlike the way she was with Martin. Then Debra would climb on top of him, instead of suffering through Martin being on top of her. And she would pleasure that man every way she could without letting him inside her, and then when she felt that both of them could no longer take it, she'd guide the bastard into her and they would make love. Hot, animalistic love, the kind that's made only by strangers who have met moments ago, or by porno film stars, or by couples who cheat on their spouses.

She stopped making love to Martin like that years ago, and stopped making love to him almost altogether recently, and this man was the reason why. And while Martin played the devoted husband, the loving father, and protector of the home, this man played gigolo with no attachments or responsibilities outside of not being late for the rendezvous and making sure he bought the condoms, if they even used any.

And that thought was the one that broke the fucking camel's back. The idea of some strange man feeling his wife raw! Martin snapped, and started punching the 14 button like crazy, even though the elevator was on its way down, and two of its occupants were headed in that direction.

The couple pulled from their embrace and looked over at Martin. He continued punching the button, even after the elevator hit the ground floor and the doors opened.

There were people waiting to get on, but Martin gave them a death stare, warning them not to take a single step forward. He rode back up to 14, busting out of the elevator, racing down to room 1415. He didn't knock on the door, but started to kick at it with the sole of his shoe, as if his intentions were to break the thing down.

He kicked at it numerous times, neighboring doors started to open, people peeked out to discover what was going on. Martin continued to kick the door, until he heard a man's voice from behind the door.

"Okay, okay, okay." The door opened, and a man stood there with a bath towel wrapped around his waist. Martin looked at the man for a moment. He was a better-looking man than Martin. He was in better shape, droplets of water glistening off his well-defined body, but that didn't make a shit's bit of difference at that point to Martin.

Martin forced the door open, pushed past the man, and walked straight into the large room.

"What the fuck do you—"

"Where is she?" Martin said, pointing his finger an inch from the man's nose, as if it were a gun. Then Martin heard the shower water running, and looked toward the bathroom.

He stepped in that direction, but stopped when he saw his wife step out of the bathroom, stark naked, her body still wet, toweling the narrow space between her large breasts.

"Who was that at the door?" she asked. Then she looked up, and her eyes went wide with shock, and her face paled as much as her brown complexion would let it.

Martin just stood there in shock as well, watching as she quickly wrapped her towel around her body, as if it was all right for the man to see her nakedness, but not her own husband.

Martin walked toward her. She shielded herself as if she were going to get hit, but Martin walked right by her.

"Martin, it's not what you think."

Martin went into the bathroom, looked around and grabbed a hotel bathrobe.

He stuck it in her face. "Put this on," he said, suppressing his anger as much as he could.

"I said, I can explain." Martin said nothing. He didn't want to hear it.

She held tight to her bath towel and looked at him as if *he* were the stranger.

Martin ripped the towel from around her, threw it to the bed, and yelled, "Put this on!"

She reached out with a trembling hand, took the robe and put it on. Martin grabbed her just below her shoulder, and started to force her about the room.

"Grab your shit." She bent down, grabbing her clothes, shoes, and purse, rolling them into a ball in her arms.

"Don't you think you can take it a little easier on her?" the man said. He was blocking the doorway, looking as though he was trying not to let Martin pass.

"I take it any way I please with her. I am her husband. Now get out of the way!" Martin said, feeling as though he were trying to hold in the force of an erupting volcano.

The man looked to Debra for verification, not seeming as if he was going to move until he heard from her. But she wasn't saying a word.

"Look," Martin said, softly, almost respectfully. "At this point, I hold nothing against you. I know that it is a man's natural instinct to try and conquer any woman that he can. And just because this one here is so much of a slut that she would allow you to do that, that is not your fault. But I swear, if you do not move yourself and allow me to take my wife from here, I will kill you where you stand."

The man looked into Martin's eyes, at first seeming he would need proof of that. But as Martin continued to stare back at him, not moving an inch, not seeming to breathe, the grip around his wife's arm like stone, the man slowly moved away. Martin yanked his wife, pushing her through the door.

On the way home Martin drove like a madman, but displaying none of the anger or pain he was feeling. He just sat stiffly as a crash test dummy holding the wheel, saying nothing, but pushing the gas pedal damn near through the floor, racing the car up to seventy-five miles an hour.

When they got home, Martin dragged his wife out of the car by the arm and pushed her into the house as forcefully as he had taken her from the hotel. She was still wearing the fuzzy white bathrobe and nothing else. She walked cautiously over the pavement, trying not to step on anything that would cut her bare feet.

Once inside the house, Martin started to pace the living room floor, occasionally taking a look at his wife, her head down, her arms crossed, looking ashamed of what she had done. And it's how she should have looked, Martin thought, as he angrily walked past her, brushing against her intentionally. What was theirs and only theirs, she gave away to someone else. The woman that he saw in his eyes as pure was no longer, because she let some man contaminate her, and things would never be the same for them, they couldn't be, and that angered Martin to no end.

At that point, Martin didn't know what to do. Yes, he was angry as hell for what she had done, so much so that he could see his hands around her neck, strangling the life out of her, but there was one thing that was stopping him, and that was the fact that he still loved her, didn't love her any less, not one bit, and that was the thing that made him most angry.

Martin paced the floor away from her, then turned around, walked directly over to her, pulled her off the couch by the arm, reared back and slapped her across the face. Debra spun, her hair flipped to a side, her body leaned toward the floor, but she didn't fall. Her head remained lowered as Martin stood in front of her, waiting for her to face him.

"Look at me!" he commanded of his wife.

Her hair was down covering her face, making it hard for Martin to see what she was thinking, how she was feeling.

"I said, look at me, dammit!"

Debra looked up, her hand resting on the side of her face where her husband had slapped her. She wasn't crying as Martin expected her to be. She didn't look sorry, or regretful, and the look in her eyes seemed to read anger, as if she felt she didn't deserve the slap given her, but she said nothing, just continued staring in her husband's eyes.

"Why did you do it?"

It took a moment for her to answer; she was still rubbing her face.

"I didn't mean for it to happen. It just did, Martin," she said. "I was feeling a lot of stress, and he's a doctor. He was able to relate with what I was going through, the stress from working long hours, the pain and guilt I felt when I lost a baby, and there have been so many lately. We would go out for coffee or drinks after work sometimes, and talk about it, try to make some sense of it all, and it just happened, Martin," Debra said. The side of her face was starting to redden now. She touched it gently with the tips of her fingers.

"I didn't mean for it to happen. He was just there, and he understood."

"And that's all it takes, for someone to just be there, and you fuck them! I was here, I would've understood!"

"No, you wouldn't have, Martin. You were always so caught up in that Father Found business."

"You didn't give me a chance."

"Martin, you didn't want a chance. Whenever I brought up what I was doing, what was bothering me at work, you would act as though it wasn't important, and switch the subject to something about Father Found, or something about the all-mighty Zaleford Rowen. Nothing was more important than that, than him. You look up to him as if he's some sort of God, and he probably only sees you as a glorified gofer. A lapdog that he has jump through hoops on occasion and toss a bone to make you feel good about it."

Martin looked at his wife, shock in his eyes. He couldn't believe the words she was speaking, the things she was saying. How hateful they were, how filled with bitterness and intent to hurt. He had to ask himself again, make sure that it was her that was in trouble, her that was caught buck-ass naked in a hotel room, and not him.

"So it's not good enough that you run the streets, screwing some man like a common street hoe, but you have to try and belittle me. It's not enough that you take what I've given you, all my trust, all my love, trust you with the lives of my daughters, make everything that I own available to you, but you have to try and deny the fact that you were wrong. Try and shift the blame, like it was my fault that you were fucking this man. Like I suggested to you that you play games, duck and dodge, call me at home and tell me lies about how late you're going to be working so you can meet him and screw his brains out and whatever else you did to him.

"I'm not wrong in this, and this has nothing to do with what I do for a living, and what I think about Father Found. This is about you not giving a damn about me, about my daughters, your daughters, not giving a damn about this family!"

Martin stood in front of her, waiting for her to say something in her own defense. It took her a while, and that just further demonstrated to Martin that she really didn't care.

"I do care about you, about your daughters, our daughters," Debra said, in the same conversational voice.

"Then why were you willing to throw everything you had away? Was he that good, Debra? Was there something you found so much more of in him than in me?"

"It was nothing like that."

"Then what was it? What was it! Make me understand!"

Debra's eyes glazed over for a moment as if she were trying to retrieve something deep in her mind. "I don't know," she said simply.

That was it, Martin thought, as he stood staring at her, finding it hard to believe that she could be so cool about this. Considering how he found her, she had to know that she was on the verge of losing everything she had. Him, the place where she lived, the girls she called her daughters, everything, yet there was no emotion on her face, no tears in her eyes, not even a hint of regret in her voice. She stood barefoot, in that fuzzy white hotel bathrobe, her arms crossed over her chest, almost defiantly, as if nothing could harm her. As if she was fully aware of everything she had done wrong, and was willing to accept it regardless of the punishment.

Martin couldn't believe it. It infuriated him, but it also perplexed him. If she was crying, begging for his forgiveness, it would've been easier to tell her to go to hell, for it would've seemed that she was admitting guilt, taking the responsibility for her wrongs. But this, this was something Martin wasn't ready for, and all he could think about was if he told her to beat it, get the hell out of his life, he would be losing the woman that he loved. He would be losing that, but not just that. It would be another wife gone, just like when he lost his first wife. After four years of marriage to someone he thought he would've been loving for the rest of his life, she ups and dies, and she's gone. And where does that leave Martin? Alone, beaten down by guilt and fear, questioning whether he is able to take care of his two young daughters —hell, questioning whether he can even continue living from day to day.

It was something he wasn't sure that he was going to make it through, and oftentimes, upon reflecting, he believed the only reason he did was because of the woman standing in front of him. He didn't want to go through all that again. Didn't want to lose another one, didn't want to lose her.

Martin gave his wife a most serious look, cleared his throat, and prepared himself for the answer to the question he was about to ask.

"Do you love him?"

Again, Debra took her time in answering. "No, Martin, I don't," and she said it as if he was a fool for asking the question in the first place.

Martin looked deep into Debra's eyes, and he believed what she said. But was it enough? He thought for a moment, and tried to stop himself from saying what he was about to say because he needed to give it more thought, make sure he was doing the right thing. But he knew how he felt about his wife, so he said it.

"I'm willing to forgive this. I want you back," Martin said. "We can move past this."

Debra showed an expression of mild shock, which seemed to read, "We can?"

"That is, if you want to."

"Yes, I want to," she said, not sounding one hundred percent sure about her answer. "I never meant you any harm to begin with."

"I know you didn't," Martin said, holding his arms out, bidding his wife to come into them. She walked hesitantly into Martin's arms and he closed them around her.

He didn't notice that she wasn't hugging him back, all he knew was that he wouldn't be alone, that his children wouldn't be alone, and that he still had the woman he loved so much. He would get past it, they would, just like he said, and everything would be fine. He would make sure of that.

CHAPTER THIRTEEN

Zale sat on the edge of the portable bed in the dark. He was staring out the windows of his office, catching the streetlamps and the faint lights of downtown Chicago as they speckled the slowly lightening early-morning sky.

It was sometime after 5:00 A.M. and Zale was in deep thought. His face in his hands, thinking about the dream that tortured him, making him toss and turn, and then woke him up, leaving him feeling that life was no longer worth living.

He remembered the day as if it were yesterday. He was sitting in class, looking up at the clock like most of the other children who had finished their test, waiting for the bell to ring so they could rip out of there for recess. The second hand made its final revolution around the clock, and when it hit the twelve, the bell rang and all the kids sprang from their seats as if the building were on fire. They grabbed their papers and pencils off their desks and handed them to the teacher as they passed her desk, the line slowly inching out the classroom door toward the freedom of the playground.

It seemed like such a wonderful day, Zale thought that morning. The sky was blue, the sun was shining brightly, and he had finished his test early, because he knew everything on it and that was because he studied really hard the night before, as he always did.

The line continued past the teacher's desk, Mrs. Miller standing beside it, smiling down at her students as they filed past her for recess. Zale stared up at her as he approached her desk. What a wonderful teacher she was. He loved her, but not the way a student normally loves his teacher. He had a huge crush on her, having some farfetched fantasies that someday he would marry her. Zale just thought she was the best woman in the world outside of his mother, and he thought that she thought he was the best little boy in the world, considering she hadn't had one of her own.

Zale placed his test sheet, work side down, on the desk, along with his pencil, and smiled at the teacher.

"Hi, Mrs. Miller," Zale said, happier than he could remember being in a long time.

"Don't play too rough out there," the teacher said, laying a hand on his shoulder.

And when she did that, Zale felt a pain as if someone stabbed him in the back. He winced, almost crumpling to the floor, trying to release himself from whatever was causing him that pain. And when he looked over his shoulder, Mrs. Miller was recoiling back from him as if she *could've* stabbed him and didn't know it.

Zale fell out of line, and the children stopped to see what was going on. He was on the other side of the children, cowering near a desk, staring at his teacher as if she wanted to kill him. He had forgotten all about his back.

"Move on, children, or recess will be over before you know it. Zale, you wait for a moment."

The children all left the room, and Mrs. Miller closed the door behind them, leaving her and Zale alone in the second-grade classroom.

"Zale, come here," she said, a look of concern on her face.

Zale shook his head and continued to stand behind the desk.

"I want to see something, Zale," the teacher insisted.

"There ain't nothing wrong with me."

"Yes, there is. I saw blood coming through the back of your T-shirt."

Zale whipped his head around, as if it were possible to actually see his back.

"There ain't no blood back there. I had . . . got some ketchup on it last night when I ate dinner," Zale lied.

Mrs. Miller appeared angered by his fib, and she approached him, grabbed him by his arm and spun him around so his back was facing her. Zale felt ashamed and embarrassed as she started to slowly raise his shirt, and when she pulled it up to expose his entire back, all he heard from Mrs. Miller was "Oh my God!"

She sounded shocked, and in disbelief at what she saw. She knelt there, looking for another few moments, and when she spun him back around, it looked as though she wanted to cry.

"Who did this to you!" she said, and Zale could hear the extreme emotion in her voice, as if he told her, she would hunt down that person and do the same to them.

Zale didn't say a word.

"I said, who did this!" Mrs. Miller said.

"I . . . I slid and fell on my back and . . ."

"Zale," she said, and she grabbed his face in both her hands, and he could see the liquid form in the corner of her left eye, preparing to fall at any moment.

"Who did this to you, because you didn't do this falling. You couldn't have done this falling." He had looked at it last night with his back to the big mirror, looking through the smaller mirror in his hand.

His back was scarred with long, wide welts. Some light red, some darker, for they had healed sooner and crusted over with scabs. Some of the cuts leaked blood, probably because of a scab that cracked open in retaliation for the way he was playing outside earlier that day, and one of the wounds oozed a clear pus. It was infected, he knew, and that night he told his mother, and she put some ointment on it, dressed it, and gave him some ice cream in a bowl. She told him how much of a big boy he was and how much she loved him, and he believed her. She wouldn't have beat him like that if she didn't love him, she told him. Zale had to sleep on his stomach at night, even though he normally slept the opposite way, and when he subconsciously turned on his back in his sleep, he would wake almost in tears, but he still loved his mother more than anything in the world.

The tear had fallen down Mrs. Miller's cheek and she was begging Zale to tell her who had done this to him.

"Zale, please."

But he was reluctant and he knew it showed on his face. He knew if he told her, they would take his mother away, and probably put her in jail, and leave him to live in their apartment all alone, and he couldn't do that, because he would be afraid, and he would miss his mother too much. He couldn't tell his teacher. He wouldn't.

Zale shook his head.

"Zale," his teacher spoke again, desperately. He felt her grip tighten around his small shoulders.

"Was it your mother? Was it her, Zale?"

He wasn't going to say, he told himself.

"Zale, if it's her, nothing will happen to her, no one will hurt her, I promise."

"How do you know?" The words slipped from Zale's mouth, and he knew asking that question was just like admitting that it was actually her.

Mrs. Miller closed her eyes for a moment, shaking her head in disgust. Another tear squeezed its way from the other closed eye, and she pulled Zale into her, hugging him, her hands on the back of his head, making sure not to further injure him.

Not two weeks after Mrs. Miller had found out about Zale's back, the world seemed to come to an end. Zale was sitting at the kitchen table as he watched his mother cook. She had the day off, so she had time, and she was stirring a small pot of grits. It was all that was in the cabinet. As she stirred the pot, she looked lovingly over at Zale now and then as he played with a spoon, as if it were some expensive toy he dreamed night and day of having.

There was a knock on the door, and Zale's mother walked by him to answer it. Zale paid her no mind, just continued on with the adventures of his spoon. He heard his mother talking, but Zale still didn't feel there was cause for concern. He heard some papers rustling, then he heard the volume and intensity of the voices heighten.

"You're not taking him!" he heard his mother yell, and Zale spun around in his seat to see his mother trying to close the door on the people on the other side. Zale jumped out of his seat to help his mother, but the two men and one woman on the other side easily pushed it open and walked into the apartment.

They stood there, just inside the small apartment, in dark clothes and long coats, the two men behind the woman, the woman holding some papers in her hand.

"This is a court order saying that we can take the boy. We know that someone spoke to you about this."

Zale didn't know what was going on, but saw the people in front of him start to advance. Zale's mother yanked him by his arm, and pulled him toward the back of the kitchen.

"You ain't taking my boy!" she screamed, tears falling from her face. And it didn't hit Zale till then, but they were really coming for him. They were really trying to take him from his mother.

"No!" Zale screamed, in his high-pitched voice.

The people didn't acknowledge Zale's outbreak, just continued to slowly move closer to him and his mother.

"Don't take me!" Zale cried again, but still they ignored him, moving in closer, reaching for him. Zale kicked at them, trying to beat them away, trying to kill them somehow so they would leave him alone, but they wouldn't go. His mother was still screaming at them, telling them to get out, as she pulled Zale farther away from them, her arm around his neck.

His mother and Zale ended up pushed back in a corner of the kitchen, and she was crying harder now, Zale feeling as her tears landed on his bare arms. She was clutching him as though she needed him for survival. He screamed and cursed at them, telling them not to come any closer, but they continued to come.

Zale was folded up in his mother's defenses, his body almost within hers, and he clung to her, as if trying to become one with her, and he could feel her heart racing, pounding against her chest. He could feel the fear coming from her, and it made him frightened. It was nothing like he had ever felt before. He had never seen his mother so scared, and he thought it was a dream, a nightmare, because there was no way that this could actually be happening.

One of the men reached in and took hold of Zale's arm, and the cold clamminess of his hand almost sent Zale into shock. It was the first time a white man ever touched him, and the vision of that huge white hand on his light-brown skin he knew would forever be burned into his memory.

Zale shook wildly, trying to free himself, but the man was too strong. He was being pulled away from his mother, while his mother still had her arms around him, and she was screaming out "No! No! Don't take my baby! Please don't take my baby!" And the way she cried, the way her shrieks tore through the tiny one-bedroom apartment, sounded as if they were trying to rip his unborn body from her womb, rather than prying him out of her trembling arms.

They continued to pull, the other man grabbing onto Zale's arm, and they were stronger, Zale thought. They were stronger than his mother, and he could feel it in his own body as he was being pulled in both directions. But he willed his mother to keep pulling, prayed that she keep fighting, but he began to feel her hands slip. He could feel her grip loosening, the perspiration that coated her palms allowing her child to slip away from her. And the farther her child was pulled away from her, the more she screamed, the more intense the cries became, and the harder she fought, but she could not hold on.

They had him entirely, and they were rushing to the door, about to open it, but before they could, they were hit with the scorching grits that Zale's mother threw at them. The men screamed out in pain, swatting at the thick grits that clung to their faces. The woman barely got hit at all, but Zale got hit on the arm, and it burned, it stung like hell, and as Zale was being pushed out the door, looking back to see his mother collapse to the floor in anguish, he told himself that burn would forever be a reminder of what happened that day.

Zale looked down at his right forearm, gently smoothing his hand over the place where he was burned, a slight tinge of red appearing in that area, the picture of his beaten mother in his mind. He shook the thought clear, knowing that it had no place with him now, in this time, in his office. He diverted his attention to the window, and saw that the darkness was now entirely gone, and it looked as though it was going to be a fairly nice day outside.

By the time people started coming into work, Zale was up, dressed, and already working on some business he had to take care of.

"Come in," Zale said, responding to a knock on the door.

Martin walked in casually, closed the door, and stood in front of it.

"What, nothing behind your back this morning?" Zale joked.

"I just wanted to apologize for some of the things I said over the past few days."

"There's nothing to apologize for. All you were doing was speaking your mind. Just because you see things somewhat differently than I do doesn't mean you're wrong and I'm right. You feel just as passionately about all of this as I do, and I expect you to. That's why you're my partner." Zale knew his best friend was feeling down, so he got up from behind his desk and walked over to him, extending his hand.

"So, everything is square?"

Martin extended a weak hand, grasped Zale's, and allowed it to be shaken.

"I am sorry, and I think I was only acting that way because I had a lot on my mind over the last week or so."

"Like what?" Zale asked.

Martin looked up at Zale, a disgusted look on his face. "I suspected Debra of having an affair, and yesterday I followed her and verified it. Caught her in a hotel room with some man."

"Debra? Your wife? You sure?" Zale asked, shocked.

"I said I caught her in a hotel room with him. They weren't there for business, because if they were, I think they would've had their clothes on."

"I'm sorry, man," Zale said, coming from around the desk to offer his friend more support. Martin waved him off.

"You give everything to a woman, and this is what happens," Zale mused. "Must have been a pretty bad breakup."

"There was no breakup," Martin said, lowering his head. "I forgave her."

Zale didn't speak a word, didn't know if he should. He just shook his head.

"What?" Martin said, looking curiously into Zale's eyes.

"Nothing. I'm just listening to you."

"You have something to say. Say it!"

"It's your business," Zale said, turning and putting some distance between the two of them. He leaned on the front of his desk. "My opinion doesn't make a difference either way."

"I want to hear it anyway. If you don't mind."

"If you say so." Zale clasped his hands together and started to speak from his heart as if he were giving a lecture to a room full of fathers.

"You say you took her back. You found her in a hotel room with a man. Were they . . . you know?"

"No, they weren't," Martin said, a painful look on his face.

"Well, it doesn't take a genius to know that's what they were going to do, or what they had just done. And knowing that, you took her back!"

"You know I love her," Martin said.

"This woman cheated on you. This woman that is supposed to be your wife, and you say you love her so much. And how much do you think she loves you? Ask yourself that. And for her to go out there and do what she did, she must have believed that there would be no consequences for her actions if she was caught, and you know what? All you did was prove her right. If that were me, all it would've taken was for me to see her there in that room, forget being naked, she could've had the top button on her blouse undone, or a shoe untied, and I would've told her to have a good life, and she didn't have to worry about being home at any certain hour, because all her things would be on the curb," Zale said, so much spite in his voice, and anger on his face, that it looked as though he was the one that had been cheated on. "We would've never spoken again, I would've never looked in her direction, and she would've never crossed my mind. Never. Ever, again."

Martin stared at Zale, shaking his head, a pathetic, unbelieving look on his face.

"I'm glad it would be so easy for the confident, self-reliant Zaleford Rowen. But considering you've never been married before, and don't want to ever be, and considering you don't have any children to think about, I imagine it would be easy for you. And the entire love issue, that would be the slightest of your worries considering you love no one more than yourself."

"And what the hell is that supposed to mean?" Zale said, standing up from his leaning position.

"You're standing there talking down to me like I'm less than half a man because I can't just forget the fact that this woman raised both my children, that I've been with her for the past six years, and that I've grown to love her more than myself. You speak as though I'm not a man if I don't just kick her to the curb and never look back."

"I didn't say that you weren't a man if you didn't get rid of her for what she did," Zale said, walking closer to his partner. "What I'm saying is that you're a fool."

Martin stood from his chair, eye to eye with Zale. "Oh, I'm a fool, hunh?"

"Yeah, and not just a fool, but a fucking fool! You ever talk back to your mother?"

Martin looked thrown by the question. "What?"

"You ever talk back to your mother?"

"Yeah, but what does that—"

"Did she ever hurt you, beat you?"

"No."

"And you kept on talking back, didn't you."

Martin didn't answer, leading Zale to believe that was the case.

"Well, I talked back to my mother one time. One time!" Zale said, holding a single finger up before Martin. "And I never did it again. Because she slapped the hell out of me. I did something wrong, and she made me pay. She made me realize that she wasn't going to tolerate that from me. And I never did it again. You, on the other hand, did it, knew you could get away with it, so you did it again, and again, and again. Just like Debra is going to cheat on you again, and again, and again, and don't tell me you don't realize that. You really would be a fool if you don't."

"So I'm supposed to leave this woman, who I, and my children, love because she made one mistake?"

"Yes," Zale said, without hesitation.

Martin turned his back on Zale. "Well, I'm not going—"

"Well, she's going to go on fucking him, and if not him, someone else."

Martin turned back around. "Don't say that! She's not going to do that!" Martin yelled, as if he was attempting to defended his wife's already wounded honor.

"And why wouldn't she?" Zale persisted. "You're not going to do anything to stop her, Martin! You aren't going to do a damn thing but tell her how much you love her and ask her to please not do it again. That's what you're going to do, isn't it. Isn't it!" Zale said, raising his voice, poking Martin in the chest with his finger.

"I don't know what to do!" Martin cried out, falling back into his chair, his face dropping into his hands.

Zale stood there, looking down at his partner, his best friend, and he had no sympathy for him, not the slightest bit. He thought, How pathetic for a man to allow himself to be so affected by a woman, by anything, for that matter. Zale knew this was one of the reasons he was still single.

"I'll tell you what to do," Zale offered.

Martin's face slowly emerged from the cover of his hands, a quizzical look on his face.

CHAPTER FOURTEEN

Frank sat nervously in the police station. He was sitting in the office of his old lieutenant, waiting for the man to return from wherever it was he went. Frank had been sitting there for almost half an hour, and that was far too long for him to think about the mistakes he made, the mistakes that got him tossed off the job that he thought so much of.

Just sitting in that office, seeing the pictures on the wall of other police officers, posters and papers listing standard operating procedures for this and that, made him long to be a part of it all again. The office was glass-enclosed, and Frank could see out into the main working area where all the other detectives worked, running back and forth, escorting suspects to the interrogation room, tracking down leads, putting together cases. God, he missed that. It was what he was born to do. He had to find a way back on the force.

But his attempt to get back on the force wasn't the only thing on his mind. He was thinking about Wendy, thinking about Bianca. After seeing Wendy the last time, Frank figured that there might be a chance for them to get back together. She hadn't kicked him out of the house when she saw him standing in her living room as he had expected, and when he asked her about them reconciling, she said no, but she paused for a long moment before she said it, and Frank could've sworn that he saw her actually giving it some thought, as if the possibility wasn't too far out of the realm of reality. That night he hugged her before he left, and she allowed him to, allowed him to put his arms around her, touch his cheek to hers, and smell the sweet scent of freshly shampooed hair. And if he wasn't mistaken, he could feel her body start to relax in his arms, like the space was familiar, and she longed to be there, safe again.

He left there that night, feeling overjoyed, knowing that he had to do everything within his power to get her back, and getting his old job back would make it seem as if he was getting his life together. As if he was the old Frank that she had loved so much in the past.

A detective that Frank knew when he was on the force walked by the office, looking in as he passed, then did a double take. Frank quickly ran to the window and closed the blinds, not wanting anyone else that he knew to see him there. They would assume that he was coming back on hands and knees, groveling for his job, which in essence was exactly what he was doing, but he didn't need anyone in his business. It was bad enough that he lay awake all night trying to get his courage up to come in here and talk to his lieutenant about it.

The door to the office opened, and the man that Frank had been waiting for entered, walking past Frank as if he were nothing more than a week's worth of dust that had accumulated in the chair in front of his desk.

The lieutenant was a trim white man, well dressed, wearing stylish glasses, graying around the temples. He was a meticulous man, and it was apparent in the way he kept his office, the way he walked, the way he organized his already neat desk. Even the air around him seemed cleaner than it was around everyone else, if that was possible.

The lieutenant's name was Crain, and he spoke no word to Frank as he shifted pencils from the surface of his desk into a drawer, and Frank didn't try to start conversation, because he knew what type of man this was. He knew that Lieutenant Crain wasn't happy to see him, and had actually told Frank a million times not to come there, to stay away, because Frank had asked for appointments countless times in the past.

Lieutenant Crain took off his jacket, hung it on a hanger, and neatly placed the hanger on a hook behind his desk. He sat down, adjusted the cuffs of his shirt, then said, in an emotionless tone, "What are you doing here, Mr. Rames?"

Frank sat up in his chair, and tried to appear as neat and crisp as his onetime lieutenant.

"I want to know if there is any way that I can get my job back. Get back on the—"

"Can't do that, Rames, and you know it," Crain said curtly.

"Why not? I was a damn good cop," Frank said, leaning forward in his chair.

Crain didn't respond to Frank, just sat behind his desk, a blank expression on his face as if he didn't give a damn about what Frank was saying.

"I think I deserve another chance. I've changed."

"You don't deserve jack shit on a stick, Rames. We don't owe you nothing, don't owe anyone anything. It is, or was, your job to prove to us that you were a valuable asset to the force. You didn't do that. You fucked up on a consistent basis, so your ass was fired. You had your chance. There are no seconds, so I don't even know why you're sitting here in front of me."

"Because I need it back," Frank appealed to the man. He was a hard-ass, seemed to care about nothing or no one, but he had to listen to Frank. If at no other time, he had to listen now. And if Frank could just make him understand, make him see things his way, maybe he would consider letting Frank back on.

"Lieutenant," Frank began. "You know that my wife divorced me, and that I can no longer see my child."

"Rames, I don't care about any of that," Crain said, eyeing his wrist-watch. "That's not important to me. Do you think I have time to get involved with every sob story of every swinging dick that works for me? No. I don't have time for them, and they *still* work for me, so I sure as hell don't have time for you. So if you'd just leave."

Frank stood from his chair, walked right up to Crain's desk. "But I've changed," he begged. "I've learned my lesson. I'm ready to do better. Just give me another chance. I promise I won't let you down."

Crain looked up at Frank, slightly adjusting the glasses on his nose, still no expression on his face.

"You've changed, have you, Rames? What do you mean by that? That you won't beat the hell out of people for crossing against the light anymore? That you won't muscle people around just because they don't move along when you tell them to, or use your authority to break what everyone else considers the law, just because you're a cop? Or do you just mean that you won't murder anyone else like you did that boy in the store that night."

"I didn't murder him!" Frank yelled. "The courts proved that!"

"The courts, Rames. You know what cops think about the courts, and shifty defense lawyers, and plea bargaining for this, and making a deal for that. It's all bullshit, you know it. So the courts can't prove shit to me. You and I know the truth. You can say that you didn't kill that boy in cold blood, but I don't believe you. I don't believe you as far as I can toss you. And for you to come in here asking me to give you your job back is the most insane crap you could've imagined.

"Let me tell you something, Rames. Even if I wanted you back on the force, I don't have that type of authority. But the truth is, I was glad that we got rid of you. But I wasn't as happy as I wanted to be. I would've been truly happy if they would've put you away like you should've been. You should be in a cell right now for what you've done. And if I had my way, you would be, because I pushed for it. But I guess you had a few more friends here than I thought.

"So knowing all of that, I hope you realize now that if there is any way in hell you're going to get your job back, it won't be through me."

Crain went into his desk, pulled out a single fresh sheet of white paper, and a fresh pencil with a lead on it as sharp as a needle, and looked as though he was about to write, but before he did, he said to Frank, without looking up, "Now get your sorry ass out of my office. And don't ever let me see you in here again, or I'll personally drag your ass off to the joint."

Frank ended up at a bar. He had never been there before, just picked the first one that came up on the street. It was crowded as hell, people talking and laughing, holding drinks in their hands, cigarettes hanging out the sides of their mouths. It was dark, and the few candles that sat in the center of tables, and the couple of dim hanging lamps, didn't do much to brighten up the place any. It was a dump, plain and simple, and Frank thought that he really didn't deserve much better. Besides, he wasn't there for dinner and dancing, he was there to make everything go away. To blot out his recent past, make his mind numb like he used to do.

He pushed his way through the crowd, bumping into a few people, shaking the drinks in their hands, but offering no apologies. He stepped up to the bar, took a seat, and ordered a shot of whisky, and after a brief moment of thought, he ordered a glass of ginger ale as well.

The bartender sat Frank's drinks on the bar and disappeared. Frank could smell the pungent odor of the liquor before he even handled the glass, but he raised it to his nose and inhaled deeply. The scent brought back so many memories, so many horrible memories, and after another moment of holding the glass to his nose, the smell almost made Frank heave, but that would pass. He knew it was only because it had been a year since he'd had a drink. But that didn't mean he hadn't been longing for one. Every time he saw a damn beer commercial on TV, or heard someone mention going for a drink, Frank felt the desire in the pit of his stomach. But he always held out, telling himself that it would make a difference, that folks would see that he was the same person that he was before the incident took place, and his employers would realize that they made a mistake, and they would take him back, and after that, naturally, he would get his wife and child back. But that didn't happen, regardless of the fact that he stayed off the sauce. It didn't make any difference, so why should he continue? Why?

Frank lifted the drink to his nose again, and the smell didn't bother him that much this time. As a matter of fact, it smelled appetizing, and it tempted him to taste it. He lowered it just an inch, and prepared to knock it back, feel it burn the insides of his throat as it rushed its way into his stomach, but he held back for a moment, thinking about his wife.

No, he hadn't gotten his job back, but that didn't mean that reconciling with his wife was out of the question. She knew him for who he really was, and just because he wasn't a cop didn't mean that she didn't still love him, or wouldn't love him again.

He thought about it for another brief moment, then set the glass down, and picked up the glass of ginger ale he had ordered with the drink. He took a sip from it, and was immediately annoyed. Did all the local bars buy the same shitty brand of ginger ale and intentionally leave it sitting somewhere with the cap off so it could get warm and stale?

Frank frowned at the taste of the stuff, realizing how sick he was of it, how sick he was of sitting in bars and not getting drunk. It was like ordering food and not eating, or like rolling on a condom and not fucking! Frank was tired of not fucking, damn tired of it! He was tired of being abstinent, or celibate, or whatever the hell they called it, and he told himself it was time to strip down, get buck naked, and roll around in what he had been keeping himself from for so long. What the hell, his life was shit anyway.

Frank picked up the small glass of light-brown fluid with just his thumb and forefinger and brought it slowly up to his lips. He held it there for a moment, still having second thoughts, frightened, his lips quivering just a little on the rim of the glass. Then he tipped it back, and the warm liquor filled his mouth, and it was like breathing after being dead for a year. The liquid was hot, as he knew it would be going down his throat. It felt good. It tasted good.

Frank lowered the glass from his lips, the taste still in his mouth. He looked out into the space in front of him, the space that the bartender occupied, but Frank was not looking at him, but through him.

"Give me another," Frank said, as if in a trance. The bartender reached for Frank's glass, but Frank covered it with his hand before the bartender could grab it.

"No. On second thought, bring me the bottle."

Frank got out of his car and stumbled up the stairs. He didn't know what time it was, but the last time he checked, it was after midnight, and that was a while ago. He stood there in front of the door, his head spinning lightly, the taste of alcohol still in his mouth regardless of the fact that a bottle of Fresh Burst Listerine lay in the seat of his car, half empty. It was what he used to do back when he drank heavily. He cupped his hand over his mouth and blew. His breath smelled of whisky and Listerine. Who would he fool with that? Not his wife, but at that moment, he didn't care, and whether it was the fact that it was long overdue, or just the alcohol making everything seem so much more urgent, he had to see his wife and little girl again.

His wife would be the only person that would understand what he was going through. And she would help him shed light on why Crain wouldn't allow him back, why he thought Frank wasn't worth taking another chance on, and why that, in turn, made Frank feel like he wasn't worth spit on the streets. His wife would explain all that to him. She would have to, because he was at his wit's end, had tied the last fucking knot at the end of his rope, and if she didn't let him in, tell him something to make sense of it all, Frank felt that he would just drive to some alley, pull out his gun and blast his brains all over the ceiling of his car.

As he stared at the doorbell, it split in three. "Always shoot for the middle," Frank said softly to himself, following an old drunkard's rule. He rang the doorbell, and straightened up, trying to look presentable, as if he hadn't been drinking.

There was no answer, so he rang again and waited. There was still no answer, and Frank began to worry that she wasn't home. But she had to be home, he told himself. Of all nights, she had to be home on this one. He pressed his face up against the window beside the door and looked in.

Where the hell is she? he thought, his hands cupped around his eyes.

He felt his pulse quickening. Frank rang the doorbell three or four more times, then he started to tap on the door, and after no immediate response, he used his fist and started to bang. He started to bang on it as if there was something out there that would kill him if he didn't get in, and he realized that person may have been himself.

"Who is it!" Frank heard a groggy voice call through the door, but he banged again, one last time just for the hell of it.

The door opened, and his wife looked both shocked and disappointed. Shocked by the hour, and disappointed because it appeared that she knew he had been drinking.

"Frank," she said sympathetically.

Frank's heart dropped at the sight of her. How he loved her.

"I tried, baby, but they didn't want me back. They didn't want me back, and I didn't know of anywhere else to go."

Frank saw that his wife was looking at him sadly. Then she opened her arms and motioned him forward. Frank lowered his head and moved into the soft, warm, safe place she provided for him.

■ ■ ■

"I'm sorry I'm here," Frank said to Wendy, who was holding his head in her lap, gently smoothing her hand over his hair. They were in the dark, lying in Wendy's bed. "I know that you told me that you'd think about it, but I had to see Bianca. I just had to. I'm sorry for coming by so late."

"It's okay, Frank."

"No, it's not okay. I'm sorry. I'm sorry and not just for coming over here, but for the way I treated you," he said, his head still on his wife's knees, his words slurred. "I'm sorry for yelling at you all the times I did. Sorry for hitting you. I'm sorry for not trusting that you'd be enough to get me through all the hell I was going through, and turning to the bottle for help. I'm sorry for ruining our marriage, and most of all . . . and most of all . . ." Frank couldn't continue. A large lump the size of an egg sat in his throat, and painful memories already began to rush into his head.

"And most of all, I'm sorry for killing our son." He had never said that before, and the words were almost too much for him to bear. He pulled his hands up and covered his face, his eyes closed tight, trying to block out the images that invaded his mind.

"I'm just going to have one more," Frank told his son, William. The boy was only fourteen, but the owner allowed him in the bar anyway because Frank was a cop.

"Dad, I really don't think you should drink that. Don't you think you already had too much," and William reached over to stop Frank from bringing the drink up to his mouth, but all the boy managed to do was spill half the drink on the table. Frank looked down at the spill, looked at his glass half empty, then downed what little drink he had left. Then without losing a step, Frank reached across the table and slapped his son with the back of his hand, tossing William from the high bar stool onto the floor.

Frank slowly moved from his seat and stood over him, his legs weak and unsure from all the alcohol he had ingested.

"Don't you ever do that again!" he said. "I'll drink till I stop! Till I'm good and damn ready to stop! You hear me!"

And if the boy didn't, the rest of the bar did, because they were all

staring at Frank and his son, the boy slowly getting up off the floor.
The bartender walked up behind Frank.

"You're gonna have to get out of here now."

"Aw, c'mon, Jerry, I just started," Frank pleaded.

"No. You just finished." He looked down at William, grabbing him,
helping the boy up, sympathy on his face. "I don't know what you do
at home, but around here you ain't hitting this kid, now get the hell
out, now. Or next time you ain't gettin' back in."

Frank gave the bartender an evil look, made his way around the
small table, snatched his son, and dragged him out of the bar by the
arm. Frank walked around to the driver's side of the car, got in, then
jumped back out when he saw that his son was still standing beside the
passenger's door, as if he were waiting for the door to automatically
open and allow him to get in.

"Get in the car, son," Frank said, over the roof.

William looked scared standing there, and Frank didn't know what
his son was more scared of, getting in the car after his father had been
drinking so much, or how angry his father would be if he didn't get in,
and Frank told himself that it had better be the latter.

"I said, get in the car, William. We're going home. Your mother is
expecting us for dinner."

"I'm not getting in, Dad," William said softly, timidly, looking at the
ground.

"What did you say to me, son?"

William raised his face and looked over the roof of the car at his father, not saying a word. But he didn't have to, because the horrified
look on his face only restated what he had said a moment ago. He
wasn't getting in the car.

Frank rushed around the car, grabbed his son by the shirt and
yanked him up into his face.

"Look, son. You disrespected me in that bar and had us thrown out.
You disrespected me again by telling me that I'm not fit to drive when
I know damn well that I am. And now you're telling me what you
won't do. Wrong, son! Wrong. You're going to get your little ass in that
car, right now, or I'll take off my belt, right here. I don't give a shit if
you're fourteen or not. I'll whip your ass like I used to when you were
eight. Got that? Now get in that damn car."

William reluctantly got in the car, immediately buckling his seat belt, looking back at his father as if Frank was making him drink a cup of something that had been poisoned, or walk the plank into shark-infested waters. Frank slammed the door for his son, fed up and angry with him for giving him so much shit. Frank walked around to the front of the car, giving his son the evil eye, jumped in, started the car, and sped off.

As Frank drove, he held tightly to the steering wheel because the car seemed to be swerving a little more than usual, and he told himself that he would have to get the alignment checked one day next week.

He made a point to pay close attention to the road ahead, fix in on an object or a sign or something, because he realized that maybe he was a bit more tipsy than he thought, he had just one too many, and was now actually thankful that his son made him spill half of his last drink. But he wasn't going to pull over and prove his son right. The boy already thought he knew too much anyway, and, besides, Wendy was expecting them home.

Frank fixed in on the gas station sign about three blocks ahead, locked his eyes on it, paying close attention. Then something happened, and it was no longer there. What the hell is going on, Frank thought, gripping the steering wheel tighter. He looked over at his son, and the boy sat with his arms crossed, staring straight out at the road.

Frank tried it again, focusing on the traffic light about half a mile ahead of them. He zoned in on it, would not take his eyes off it, but then there was a second that passed unaccounted for, and all of a sudden, it was gone. Frank looked up, shocked, and it was shrinking behind him in the rearview mirror as they sped forward, and he realized that he was drifting off at the wheel. He briefly thought about pulling over, but they were only five minutes from the house. Just five minutes and he would be home, and he could get a hot shower, some food, and he would be a lot better. It just didn't make sense to stop, Frank told himself, as he sat up in the seat of the car, rolled down his window, letting the wind hit his face, opening his eyes wide as he possibly could.

"We'll be home in a second, William. And you don't have to tell your mother what happened, all right?"

William didn't say a word or make a gesture to say he understood, just continued looking forward.

Frank gripped his hands even tighter around the steering wheel and thought about home. Thought about going upstairs and having a shower. Thought about toweling himself off, not having dinner, just jumping in bed, and relaxing. Relaxing, relaxing, relaxing. Lying across his bed, letting his mind clear of everything, letting his body surrender to the drug that was coursing through his bloodstream. Close his eyes and then just fall off into a deep sleep, and that's exactly what Frank did.

He wasn't awake to feel the steering wheel spin out of his hands and the car swerve into the other lane. He wasn't awake to see his son's eyes practically pop from his skull when he saw that his father had passed out behind the wheel of a car going almost fifty miles per hour. And Frank didn't feel as his son reached across his body, grabbed the steering wheel, and jerked it hard to the left, whipping the car out of the opposite lane to avoid a speeding eighteen-wheeler that was bearing down on them. The car swerved from one lane of the street to the other, rolling off the road, ripping through the mud and grass on the side of the pavement. William held tight to the steering wheel, trying to stop the car from swerving, but he couldn't, because he couldn't reach the brakes. He undid his seat belt, sliding over closer to his father, trying to move his foot over to that side. The car just seemed to go faster, and the awkward way that he was stretched across the driver's seat made the thing harder to control. But William tried, pulling the wheel in whatever direction he could to keep the car on the road while he tried to move his foot to the brake. The car continued to swerve and careen, jumping on and off the curb of the dark, rural road, and when William finally got his foot over toward the driver's side, finally felt that he had control of the thing and was prepared to stop it, he saw a huge tree, the size of small building, racing closer to him, as if not only the car was moving, but also as if the tree had grown legs and was running toward them just as fast, filling the entire view of the windshield. William closed his eyes tight and threw his arms over his face, screaming for dear life as the car raced, head-on, into the trunk of the huge tree.

There was smoke and steam, and burning juices from the car's engine blowing up from under the crumpled hood, and this was what Frank smelled as he began to wake. Frank found himself folded over to the left side of the steering wheel, the deflated air bag draped over his head, a path of dried blood running from the side of his mouth and both nostrils. He started to awaken more, not moving, his eyes still closed, not realizing where he was, but trying to remember what happened just before he fell off to sleep.

Frank remembered being mad at William, remembered he was driving home, and remembered falling asleep at the . . . he was in the—!

Frank jerked up, his memory coming back to him, a sharp pain hitting him in the back. He tried to sit up, but there was something over his head. He wrestled with it for a moment; it was tangled about him like a huge spiderweb. Frank yanked the thing off his head quickly, for his son's life may have depended on it. Then he stopped. He stopped and sat there frozen, seeing the devastation before him, knowing that it was too late.

There was shattered glass all over the front seat, and his son wasn't there beside him, because although Frank had an air bag on his side of the car, there wasn't one on the passenger side. There was a huge hole in the windshield of the car, and the edges of that glass hole were rimmed with blood. Frank didn't come to this conclusion through deductive reasoning. He saw his son's body, mangled, crumpled, torn, and bloody, there on the top of the hood.

Agonizing grief filled Frank's entire being, transforming his face as he stared at his son's body.

"William," Frank whined.

Frank tried to open his door, pushed at it, kicked at it, but it wouldn't budge, so he pushed his body out of the window and fell to the ground. He pulled himself up, and slowly stumbled around to the front of the car, fearful of seeing this grotesque scene up close.

The car was smashed up against the tree, and Frank could see dried blood on the bark of the tree. His son's arms were wrapped behind his back as if he had been cuffed, and judging by the way his son's head was almost spun around facing the back of his body, Frank figured he broke his neck, either going through the windshield, or hitting the tree, and he hoped, prayed, he had felt no pain.

"Oh, God, William," Frank whined again, stepping slowly toward his son, wanting to touch him, but not knowing where or how. "I killed you. I killed my son," he cried, and he took his son's hand and fell down to the side of the car, crying, waiting for the sirens he heard in the far distance to come.

The detectives that came were all men that Frank worked with or knew well. Everyone knew he had been drinking, could smell the alcohol on his breath, in his clothes, but no one bothered to have him tested. They didn't try to convict him either, just wrote it off as being an accident caused by a truck that swerved into the wrong lane. They knew all the pain Frank was going through with the grand jury indictment he was facing, and there could be no greater punishment than losing one's only son.

The next morning, Frank was up cooking breakfast for his daughter. She was sitting at the kitchen table, beaming up at her father as he scooped the eggs from the skillet to their plates.

"I hope you still like 'em hard."

"Yeah, Daddy, I do," Bianca said, smiling wide.

There was no place that Frank would've rather been than where he was, no moment that he would've rather been living than that one, and if he could relive it over and over again for the rest of his life, he seriously thought he would.

He sat down, stuffed a napkin in his shirt, and was preparing to eat, when he saw his wife standing in the kitchen doorway. The look on her face was serious.

"Can I talk to you a moment, Frank?"

"We're about to eat," Frank said, feeling that what she was about to say wasn't going to be good news.

"Good morning, Mommy."

"Good morning, baby," Wendy said to her daughter, then turned her attention back to her ex-husband. "Frank, please."

Frank met her in the living room.

"I want you to go now," Wendy said.

Frank looked at her, not believing what she had said.

"I just sat down. Me and Bianca were about to have breakfast. What are you talking about?"

"I'm talking about, I want you to leave. I want you out of this house, Frank," her voice becoming more firm on the second demand.

"I haven't seen her in almost a year. What about last night? I thought there was a chance in us getting back together."

"I thought maybe, too, Frank. But you came in here drunk. You came in here drunk last night, and we were right back where we were more than a year ago. As I was holding you, I was wondering if all of a sudden were you going to snap and just start beating me for no reason. I'm not going through that again. I'm not."

"I would never do that again. I told you I was sorry."

"You don't know that, Frank. When you drink that stuff, it has control of you. How would I know that I could trust you with Bianca."

"What are you talking about?" Frank said, becoming more upset.

"How do I know that you won't be out driving her around and the same thing that happened to our son won't happen to her. How, Frank! How!" Wendy said, her lips starting to quiver. Frank stood there wanting to answer her question, wanting to tell her something that would ease her, ease himself, but there was nothing.

"Are you coming back to breakfast, Daddy?" Bianca said, standing in the doorway.

"Baby, Daddy won't—" Wendy started, but Frank held up a hand, stopping her.

He walked over to his daughter and squatted down in front of her, placing his hands on her shoulders.

"Daddy can't finish breakfast, sweetheart."

"Why not?"

"Because Daddy has to go. And I really don't know when Daddy's going to see you again. I know it doesn't make sense now, but one day it all will. I promise. And until then, I want you to know that I will always love you. Do you hear me?"

Bianca looked at him like she had no idea of what was going on, but she nodded her head anyway.

"I will always love you," he said again, fighting back the tears. Then he reached in his pocket and pulled out his keys. "And I have this." The pink dragon with the green spots was hanging from his key ring.

"Did you leave it for me? Did you leave it for me on your dresser?" Bianca nodded her head.

Frank grabbed his daughter, pulled her in and held her tight. He loved her so much, but something told him that this would be the last time he would see her. He held her back to take one last look at her, kissed her on the cheek, and stood to his feet. He turned to his wife, who showed no tears, no emotion.

"Goodbye," he said.

"Good luck, Frank," and she started to open her arms as if to extend him a hug, but he walked right past her, because it would've done him no good. It would've been fake, just as he learned everything he received from everyone else was.

CHAPTER FIFTEEN

A week had passed and Martin had done exactly what Zale told him. He had waited till his wife had left for work, then woken the girls and ushered them into the shower. While they were bathing, he dumped their drawers out on their beds and started to fill their suitcases with their clothes.

When Renee came out of the shower, a huge towel wrapped around her body like a cotton ball gown, she said, "What are you doing, Daddy?"

Martin turned around, shocked, as if caught robbing the neighbor's house.

"You're not going to school today, baby. We're going to go to Grandma's, and that's where you and your little sister will stay for a while, okay?"

"But why?"

"Because there's some business that has to be taken care of here." He looked down at his daughter, and she looked up at him, bewildered, as if trying to make sense out of the meaningless explanation he just gave her.

"Is Mommy going to stay with us?"

"No. Mommy's not coming."

"Then I don't want to go," and that was Rebecca talking. She was standing in the doorway of the bathroom, her towel around her as well, and she had heard everything that Martin had told Renee.

"Daddy, I don't want to go either," Renee said.

Martin stopped packing, sat on the edge of the bed, and opened his arms, gesturing for his daughters to come near.

"Look, I know you don't want to go, but there are some things that have to be taken care of. Now, it won't be for long, and your grandmother can't wait to see you two. You'll have a lot of fun over there, and I'll come and visit you every day."

"What about Mommy?"

Martin didn't want Debra to see them. That was all part of the plan, Zale told him. Martin would tell his wife where the kids were, but he would tell her that it would be best if she didn't see them. He would say that it had something to do with him telling them that she wasn't really their natural mother, even though he was nowhere near telling them about that and didn't know when he would be.

Martin would tell Debra to stay away, and just in case she acted as if she didn't understand those instructions, he would tell his mother not to let the woman step foot in that house, not to let her talk to the kids through the backyard fence, and if she tried, sic the dog on her. She was not even to speak to them over the phone.

"I'm not going," Renee said. Her little sister agreed, and they both broke away from their father's hug. They crossed their arms over their chests and poked their bottom lips out.

Martin tried to reason with them. "Ladies, please don't do this. I wouldn't be asking you to do this if it wasn't very, very important. Now, I told—"

"We don't want to go!" his daughters protested again in unison, turned, and started to make their way back toward the bathroom.

"Hold it!" Martin said, his voice strong and authoritative. "This is not a vote. Now, I told you what's going to happen. I'm going to finish packing your things, you two will get dressed, and we are going to your grandmother's house, where you will stay for a little while, and be very happy about it—tickled pink. Is that understood!"

The two girls nodded their heads quietly, sadly.

Martin hated to be so hard on them, and as they stood there looking up at him with their huge sad eyes, he wanted to grab them up and tell them that he was sorry, give them a full and detailed explanation as to why this was happening, but he couldn't do that. He had to be strong and follow this plan to the letter if he wanted it to work.

He dropped the girls off, gave his mother her instructions, then made his way to work.

When Martin got home that night it seemed strange to open the door and not hear the girl's voices, not have them run up to him and give him a hug and tell him about their day.

Martin looked at his watch. It was 7:30 P.M. and he figured that he had more than enough time to get all his things together before his wife got home. He took the stairs up to their room, took out two suitcases and a garment bag and started to fill them with his clothes.

It was for the best, he told himself. This was something that he had to continue telling himself, or he wouldn't have been able to go through with it. He didn't want to ship his kids off the way he did this morning, he didn't want to leave his wife, but Zale told him that if he wanted to keep the woman, it was the only thing he could do. But, for some reason, this didn't make a whole hell of a lot of sense to Martin. As a matter of fact, it made no sense at all. He complains that his wife is staying out too late, finds her practically in bed with another man, then what does he do? Gives her space! Moves out so she can do whatever the hell she wants? Stay out till the next morning, invite the man over to stay with her if she wants. Screw her in the comfort of his bed, in his house!

It didn't make sense at all, but he believed in his friend, and, besides, he had no other idea of what to do, and his actions proved just how desperate he was to keep her.

"If she really loves you, if she ever really has, she'll look around and realize that she made a mistake. She'll realize what you and the kids really meant to her, and she'll value you all the more for what you did. This way, she'll ask for you back, instead of you accepting her back," Zale said, and it was easy as hell for him to speak of everything so absolutely, Martin thought, standing there in front of his friend.

What was he risking, except being wrong for once in his life. How many children did he have to raise without a mother if this plan didn't work? When would he have to muster the courage to go out in the streets again, visiting singles bars to try to enchant some middle-aged divorcée with some one-liner. Zale didn't have to worry about any of that, and Martin resented him, was almost angry at him for his unencumbered position, and his crackerjack scheme that he believed would make everything better if all the directions were followed by the numbers.

When Martin was done packing his clothes, he took the bags down to his car and put them into his trunk. It was getting late, and he expected his wife to arrive home soon. He went up to the girls' room, dragged a chair in between their beds and sat there, missing their presence, waiting for his wife to arrive.

Some thirty-five minutes later, Martin heard the downstairs door close, and his heart skipped a beat. He felt nervous, wondering if he could tell this woman what he had to say. Look in her eyes, tell her that he was leaving, pretend that he meant it for good, and not break down or give in if the news was something that seemed to please her. She could hear the words come out of his mouth, and a smile might stretch across her face, and she might view his news as her way out. And then what would he do? He would have to hold his ground, act as though it made no difference to him. That's what Zale said, and Martin found himself resenting his friend a little more because of those instructions.

Martin heard his wife climbing the stairs, heard her standing just outside the door, and his heart felt as if it were going to pop right out of his throat into his mouth. Then Martin saw the doorknob turn. His wife poked her head in, and he saw the shock register on her face when she saw him and not the two children lying peacefully asleep in bed.

Debra opened the door more, walked in, and dropped her bag.

"Where are the girls?"

It took Martin a moment to answer.

"They're at my mother's house."

"And why is that?" Debra's voice was already filled with suspicion.

"They're going to stay there for a while. I think it's best they be away from this house for a little bit."

"This house, or me?"

"Both. And I won't be here either." Martin pulled his head up to see how his wife was reacting to the news. She was standing there in high heels and a cool baby-blue business suit, her arms crossed, but her facial expression gave her away. She didn't look as confident as she normally did, and it seemed as if this news threw her.

"So where will you stay?"

"At Zale's. He has a guest room."

Debra accepted the answer without saying anything, just looked around the room as if it would never again be the place it always had been.

"So what, is this what you call teaching me a lesson? Is that what this is all about?"

"Yes, no—maybe. I don't know."

"Give me a straight goddamn answer for once, Martin!" she said loudly.

"What if I am? What if I am trying to teach you a lesson?" Martin said, starting to anger. "You don't think you should have a lesson taught to you? Do you remember the way I found you? Do you remember what the hell you were doing! And I took you back, but did you think that would be the end of it! Go out there, fuck whoever you want, get busted by your husband and live happily ever after. I don't think so. Yes, let's say I'm teaching you a lesson. Is there a problem? You don't like it?"

She was quiet, and Martin could tell by the way her head lowered, her arms hanging to her side, that she had backed off her aggressive approach.

"So you're taking away the children, and I imagine that you told your mother not to let me see or talk to them."

Martin didn't answer the question.

"How can you do that?" Debra said. "How can you use them as leverage against me. Not allow me to see them when you know how much they mean to me."

"What was that?" Martin said, shaking his head, as if his ears were playing tricks on him. "One minute you're telling me that you don't have time for them, that they aren't your responsibility, and now it's the opposite. I don't think they are all that important to you. It seems to me that that dick you were getting is more important to you than my children. Is that right? Because that's how you were spending all your time. Am I right about that, Debra?"

Martin could tell that she took the remark hard, but that was exactly how it was intended.

"Debra, is that right? I'm asking you a question," Martin persisted.

"I see. I understand completely now," Debra said, shouldering her bag, not bothering to answer him. "If you don't want to give me anything to come home to, then I guess I don't have to make a big deal about coming home anymore, now do I." And before he had a chance to answer, she was out the door. He heard her descend the stairs, and walk out of the house. And, at that moment, even though he loved her, he couldn't have cared less what she did.

"You never did make a big deal about coming home!" Martin yelled, leaning back in the chair, folding his arms angrily.

That was a week ago, and all the way up until that point, Martin was trying to figure out just what she meant by her last statement. Did she mean that she would start back up with the man he caught her with, or did it mean that she would never return to the house? On many occasions, Martin wanted to call her, wanted to drive by, see if she was home, if her car was out front, or another car parked behind it, maybe that man's car, but he didn't dare. He couldn't start down that path, because it was one greased with suspicion and jealousy and he knew he would only slip and fall faster and faster, till he was going back on everything he said, and begging her to come back to him.

She had called him once at work, a couple of days ago. The message was written on a stick-it pad, and taped to his desk lamp, and there it remained. Martin just looked at it on occasion, and a couple of times had the phone in his hand and was reaching to dial Debra's number, but he stopped himself. It was torture, but he had to stay strong.

Martin was pulling a few things out of his desk to try and get some work done when the phone rang.

"This is Martin Carter," he said, snapping the phone up quicker than he normally did.

There was a pause, and Martin knew it was his wife. He could feel it, was almost hoping that it was her before he picked up the phone.

"Martin," the soft voice said, and she sounded timid, unsure, so unlike her normal self.

"Yeah."

"How are you doing?"

"Fine." Martin intentionally kept his answers short, not encouraging long conversation.

"How are the girls?"

"They're fine, too."

"Well, I was wondering. The weather is supposed to be nice this weekend and—"

"Debra," Martin interrupted. "That's my other line. I'm going to have to call you back, all right?"

"Oh, okay. Yeah, just call me back," Debra said self-consciously. "Bye, Martin."

Martin slowly hung up the phone, there being no other phone call waiting. He hated to lie to her like that. He hated everything that was going on right now, but it had to happen for her to understand. He couldn't let her call when she wanted to, talk to him as if they were still husband and wife, or even friends for that matter. She had to feel what it was like to be without him entirely, to sit in that house and have nothing to do with her time but dwell on the foolish mistake she made.

The phone rang again a moment later, but Martin didn't pick it up for fear it would be Debra again. He let his secretary get it, and her voice came through the little speaker of the desk intercom.

"It's a Tim Kirkland on the phone. He says he's from the Government Grants and Loans Agency."

"Yeah, yeah, put him through," Martin said, sitting up in his chair. This was a phone call that Martin had actually been expecting, but in light of everything that was going on at home, he had forgotten about it. After Martin realized how much in debt Father Found was in, and that they risked losing the building to the bank, he had to look for alternative sources to finance them. He was told by a friend that a department of the government was dedicated to awarding grants to agencies and organizations in dire need, just like Father Found. Martin called that same day, spoke with a Mr. Kirkland, and was told where he could pick up an application. The man told Martin to address it directly to him, and send it overnight mail, and he would call him back within a week. Now the call had finally come, and for the sake of Father Found, Martin was praying that he had good news.

"Mr. Kirkland, this is Martin Carter. Did you get my application?"

"Yes, we got it, and it looks pretty good."

"So that means you can let us have the money!" Martin said excitedly.

"Now hold on just a moment, not so fast," Mr. Kirkland said, laughing. "There are a couple of things I want to go over. Have you been in business at least five years?"

"No. Not quite."

"How long?"

"Three, maybe a little longer."

"Well, we might be able to work around that. . . . Is your business recognized by the state, federal government, or any accrediting organization?"

"No, I can't say that we are," Martin said, despair starting to fill his voice. "I didn't know that we had to be."

"Well, that would normally make you ineligible for a grant, but don't worry about that, Mr. Carter. It's just a minor formality. I'll send a packet to you. You fill it out, stick all your records in there, and send it to the address stated and we'll be all set."

"But how long will that take?"

"Considering that everyone under the sun is starting a not-for-profit organization nowadays, and you know how long it takes the government to do things, I figure three or four months, six at the latest."

"We can't wait that long. We need this money now. We have to have it right now, or we risking losing this place!"

"Maybe you need to try a private lending institution, like a bank or a credit union."

"We can't afford a loan, Mr. Kirkland. We are up to our necks in debt as it is. That's not an option. Is there any way that we can get around this!"

There was a period of silence, then Mr. Kirkland said, "Take down this information." He rattled off a series of numbers, and some other instructions.

"Now someone is going to call you back, and when they do, you give them that number. I'm going to Fed-Ex this application back to you, and you just change the things I tell you to, sign it, and send it back to me. We're just going to say that your business is already recognized and start the paperwork now. By the time they bring up your folder to verify, the accreditation and licenses should be in your possession, making everything fair and square. How does that sound?"

"It sounds great, like a lifesaver. But one thing. This is not illegal, is it? I'm not putting your job in jeopardy or anything like that, am I?"

There was another short stretch of silence, then Mr. Kirkland spoke again.

"Your organization—Father Found, right?"

"Yeah," Martin said, not knowing what he was getting at.

"My mother died when I was a boy. Died in a car accident. My father decided that he didn't want the responsibility of raising me, so he gave me to my grandparents to raise, and I never saw him after that. I had a wonderful childhood, loved my grandparents, and to this day I look at them as if they were my parents. But that doesn't mean I wouldn't have loved to see my old man on occasion. I understood he obviously had things he had to do, possibly better things, maybe not, but a visit on a sunny Sunday afternoon once a month, I didn't think would've been too much to ask.

"So about this being illegal, not really. But let's put it like this, Mr. Carter. There's risk involved in everything, but if I feel it's worth it, then that risk I'll take. You have a good day, Mr. Carter."

"You too, Mr. Kirkland. You too." Martin hung up the phone, feeling relieved, feeling that the future of Father Found was no longer black and without hope. But he wasn't going to sit there and trust that Mr. Kirkland would actually take care of all their problems for them. He would be trusting someone else to take care of his business, and he learned long ago never to do that. He would trust the man to do what he said he would do and hope that it would solve their problems, but Martin would also try to do what he could on his end. Because he had no other alternative than the one he just exhausted, short of grabbing a paper cup and begging for change on the corner, he would have to talk to the Weinmans over at the bank. He may have been more behind than they were accustomed to, but he had to try to get an extension of some sort just in case this Mr. Kirkland didn't come through.

Martin walked into Zale's office to tell him the news.

"I just got off the phone with a Mr. Kirkland, down at the Government Grants and Loans. We had a slight problem with the paperwork, but he feels that he can work something out, so I'm pretty sure we'll be all right," Martin said, standing over the corner of Zale's desk.

"You think so, hunh?" Zale said, his face expressionless. "So I can continue to go out there and stick my foot in my mouth with your permission without worrying about the financial repercussions, is that right?"

"No. I know you'll continue to do that. But not with my permission. No way, with my permission." Martin laughed, feeling somewhat relieved that their financial problems might be behind them.

"So how is the situation with Debra and the kids?" Zale asked, and immediately Martin's laughter stopped. He looked over at Zale, a grave look on his face.

How do you think the situation is? I seem to have lost my wife, and my kids, and I feel like hell, and you told me that all this is for the best, Martin wanted to say to Zale as he looked down at him. But then again, he continued to think, You shouldn't have to ask me how things are going. You see me every night, closing myself off in your small guest bedroom, as if I'm a nineteen-year-old living in a college dorm. It's no way for a man to live. Away from his family, squeezed in the confines of four walls that seem to be closing in tighter each night. It's no way for a man to live, Zale.

That is what Martin wanted to say to Zale, but what he said was, "It's hard. Hard as hell."

A hard knock came at the door, then it flung open, the doorknob hitting the wall behind it. Frank Rames walked in and threw some files to Zale's desk.

"I'm done with these guys. I need some more," he said, standing in front of the desk, very close to Martin, looking rumpled and haggard as if he had just pulled himself out of the dirty laundry basket.

Martin gave him a hard look, staring at the side of his face. But when Frank didn't respond, Martin spoke. "Don't you know how to knock?"

"I did knock," Frank said, not backing down from Martin. "It's not my fault if you didn't hear me." He turned away, ignoring Martin to speak to Zale. "You got any more files?" He was spinning his ring of keys in his hand, over and over, almost frantically.

The noise bothered Martin, but more than that, Frank's attitude angered him to the point where he could no longer contain himself.

Martin grabbed Frank by the arm, and spun him back to face him.

"You don't enter until you're told. Do you understand that?"

Frank slapped Martin's arm off him, then grabbed him by the lapels of his jacket. "You got a fucking problem?" Frank hissed, pushing Martin up against the desk.

Martin was caught off guard, but quickly threw both his arms over Frank's, wrapped both his hands around Frank's neck, and squeezed.

He felt Frank struggle to get out of his hold, but Martin wasn't letting go. It was as if he couldn't let go. For some reason, he'd been dying to have this man's throat in his grip as long as he could remember. He wanted to strangle him till his eyes popped, till his veins swelled up and exploded, spilling blood all over the place, and then he would shrivel up and dissolve into nothing.

Martin didn't realize how hard he was squeezing, but got some indication by the bright red color Frank's face was turning. He struggled some more, gasping for air, then he pulled Martin into him, somehow positioned his legs between Martin's, and pushed. Martin felt himself losing his balance, beginning to fall, but he held tight to Frank, bringing the man with him. The two of them fell over Zale's desk, scrapping and punching at each other the moment they hit the floor.

"What the hell are you two doing!" Zale said, grabbing Frank off Martin.

"He started the shit!" Frank yelled, his hair and clothes in disorder, his face still bright red, darker red rings around his neck from where Martin was squeezing. Frank struggled, trying to pull away from Zale like a chained animal to get at Martin, but Zale had him around both arms.

"He's been treating me like shit ever since I can remember, and I'm not taking it anymore! All I'm trying to do is my job, and I'm getting shit from him for no reason! No reason at all!"

"What is he talking about, Martin?" Zale asked, still holding a firm grip on the struggling man.

"I don't know what he's talking about," Martin said, pulling himself off the floor, straightening his clothes.

When Frank heard that, he exploded, flailing his arms, thrashing about, trying to get at Martin again.

"Let him go, Zale. Let him go, if he really wants me so bad," Martin said, not impressed by Frank's slight display of insanity.

"Frank! Frank!" Zale yelled, pulling at Frank until he calmed down. "This is not going to get resolved with you acting like some wild animal, you got that?"

Frank struggled just a bit more, then calmed down considerably. His face was still beet red and his chest was heaving up and down, but he was in control.

"You all right?" Zale asked.

Frank just nodded his head, still breathing hard.

"So you say none of what Frank is saying is true?"

Martin looked at Frank. "I don't know what he's talking about."

"You fucking liar," Frank spat between clenched teeth. "You're just a coward hiding—"

"Frank! That's enough! Maybe you should go, so I can talk to Mr. Carter and find out what's going on here."

"But what about my side?" Frank said.

"I'll hear your side later, now go!"

Frank didn't move, just stood there staring at Martin with hate in his eyes. "I came here for more files. I need more files," he said, his eyes not moving from Martin.

"Forget about the files. You have the rest of the day off, now get out of here!"

Frank walked out the door.

"What the hell was all that about?" Zale asked Martin.

"What are you talking about, Zale? He grabbed me by the collar first."

"Nonsense. You grabbed him by the arm, but that doesn't even make a difference. He said you're giving him a hard way to go, and if that's the truth, I want to know why that is."

"Why did you ever hire him?"

"Because we need an investigator, and that's what he is, and considering what we pay him, we're lucky to have someone of his caliber."

"But he killed that boy," Martin said, sitting down on the edge of the chair in front of Zale's desk.

"The boy died," Zale said. "It was speculated that Frank killed him, but that was never proven."

"And all the newspaper clippings I have on him, all the charges brought against him . . ."

"Like I said before, I don't want to see that," Zale said, leaning back in his chair, as though that would be the last word of the discussion.

"You're willing to overlook all of that because he saved your life?"

Zale slowly sat up, folded his hands on his desk, and with a wry smile said, "And isn't that enough?" Martin didn't say a word. "But it's not just that," Zale continued. "He's good at what he does, and we need him. It's that simple."

"There's something about him," Martin said, shaking his head. "I don't like his attitude, I don't like the way he treats this job as if he's cleaning up dog shit for a living."

"It's a shit job, Martin. He runs around chasing delinquent fathers all day. Trying to reason with people who have nothing to say to him, and getting paid little of anything to do it, and you think he should greet you with a smile every morning."

"Sounds like you're sticking up for the man," Martin said, crossing his arms over his chest.

"You got something on him then, something hard, relating to Father Found?" Martin didn't say anything, because he didn't have a shred of evidence more than what Zale had already rejected. But he would find some, all he needed was a little time.

"Good, so you'll stop giving him a hard time," Zale said. "Because he doesn't deserve it. He has enough problems of his own. Besides, he's been doing some serious work for us lately." Zale scooped up the files that Frank had thrown to his desk.

"The reason why he asked for more files is because every file that I recently gave him he returned marked, 'Father will return home.' And I imagine if I look at these, they will say the same thing."

"Do that," Martin said, leaning forward in his chair to get a look at the files.

"Do what?"

"Check the files."

Zale walked around the desk, placed the files down and opened one after the other. There were four of them, and all were marked as Zale said they would be. Zale looked up at Martin, a confident smile on his face. "What did I tell you."

"That doesn't seem strange to you? Over the past two weeks, every file he walks out with, he brings back with the father returning. He's probably out sitting somewhere drinking coffee, laughing at us, marking the folders without even looking at them."

"I've called their homes, Martin. They are there. I've spoken to them."

Martin looked down at his hands. That couldn't be right, he thought. But Zale wouldn't lie about something like that. But, then again, Martin wasn't wrong about that man, he knew he wasn't. Frank didn't belong there, and Martin wouldn't feel that way if it wasn't true.

"I still say there's something not right about him, but I'll back off till I get what I'm looking for."

"You have no choice," Zale said, stacking the files on his desk.

CHAPTER SIXTEEN

Zale pushed himself away from his desk, and was preparing to grab his briefcase when the phone rang. He reached over and picked it up.

"This is Zaleford Rowen."

There was no answer.

"Hello, this is Mr. Rowen speaking, may I help you?" There was still nothing.

Zale waited another moment, then hung up the phone, thinking nothing more of the call. He had to get out of there. It was the end of another long, exhausting day. He was beat, and his mind was overrun with problems, from how long the money in his personal account was going to last if he had to continue dipping into it to finance Father Found, to what he was going to do about Frank and Martin not being able to get along.

The incident today was nothing, just a spark compared to the explosion he figured the two of them were capable of creating if their situation wasn't resolved. Martin was being overcautious of Frank, or at least Zale hoped that he was. His investigator was doing fine work, better than he had ever done before, and now, for some reason, Martin seemed to have a problem with him. If it was up to Martin, Frank would be put on the streets next time he looked at Martin crooked or spoke out of turn. Martin would toss him out, and throw all his belongings out on the street after the man, but Zale couldn't allow that to happen.

Frank had problems, has problems, and they can affect the way a man thinks, and feels. Problems can affect the way he sees his future, make him lose sight of where he belongs or what he should be doing with his life, if he feels it's worth doing anything with at all. Zale knew about all of that firsthand, and he wasn't about to suspect Frank just because Martin didn't like the way the man looked, or spoke to him, or feel he didn't love his job enough. He wasn't going to put this man out on the street, just on Martin's suspicions alone. Besides, the man saved Zale's life. He could never forget that, and it would take a whole hell of a lot for him to overlook it and fire Frank.

Zale walked past his secretary, not saying anything to her. He felt her looking at him, stopping what she was doing, a surprised stare on her face because he was leaving at such an early hour. He had enough problems stored up in his mind to have him sitting up in bed, thinking well past midnight, never finding an answer to any of them, so he had to escape while he still had the strength to walk.

Zale opened his car door, threw his briefcase in the back seat, and was about to jump in, but he stopped midway into the car, one leg in, one leg out. He thought for a moment, visualizing the face of the woman from the community center. He didn't know why she popped into his head, but she did. He shook his head clear of the thought, replaced it with one of the many problems he was thinking about a moment ago, then sat down in his car and closed the door.

He held the key in his hand, inches from the ignition, poised to put it in, but didn't. He stared out the front window for a moment, thinking. Then he jumped from the car, closed the door, and started in the direction of the community center. He walked briskly down the street, as if he was late for an appointment, asking himself why he was going there, but nothing came, other than this urge compelling him to go.

He stopped just outside the old building, hesitated for a moment, asking himself if he really wanted to go in. His mind was telling him not to, but something forced Zale to push open the doors and walk through the lobby. There was a girl at the reception desk, not a day older than nineteen. She looked up at Zale as if he was going to stop and ask for information, but he walked right past her, his heels clip-clopping quickly against the dirty tile floor.

It was the fifth or sixth door on the right, Zale told himself, as he counted, stopping at the door that read "Psychiatric Counseling." He stood right up against the door and looked in, both his hands flat on the wood just below the window.

There was a group of people sitting in the chairs that formed a cir-cle. These were troubled-looking people, expressions of pain and de-spair on their faces. One person was speaking—a middle-aged white man with long facial hair, and a ponytail tied with a rubber band. He wore tattered blue jeans, a T-shirt, and a matching denim jacket, equally as torn as the jeans. He looked as if he was homeless, and as he spoke of whatever problems he had, the entire circle of people grabbed their chins, or hugged themselves, and nodded their heads, looks of sympathy and understanding on their faces.

Obviously, they had problems similar, some probably worse, and they took turns speaking. A thin young man next, then a heavy woman, clutching a handkerchief that she dabbed against her pink cheeks a million times, then a kindly-looking older woman with round granny glasses balanced on her nose. They spoke, and Zale stood there, looking in through the window at them for a long time. Then someone else spoke, and Zale recognized her. It was the woman from the last time he was there. The woman that was pinning pictures to the board, the woman who looked up at him and held him frozen by her stare alone.

She was talking, sitting in her chair, a pad of paper over her crossed legs, and then she stopped for a moment, midsentence, as if something was wrong. Zale felt a moment of tension, expecting that the woman would look up at him, and she did. She stared directly at him, the way she had before, but Zale didn't fear her stare this time. She looked at him, and Zale stared back, and although there was no movement, or gesture from her to ask Zale in, he felt that she was inviting him, just from the look that she was giving him. Zale slowly lowered his hand to-ward the doorknob, moving to turn it, as if he had no control, then he stopped. He looked back at the woman, a more intense stare this time.

She continued looking up at him, but a faint smile lengthened across her face. At that, Zale pulled himself away from the door and quickly walked away.

When Zale neared his home, he saw that Regina's car was sitting out in front of his house. He saw that she was in it, sitting up straight, as if she was waiting for something to happen at any moment.

"Damn," Zale said to himself. "I don't need this right now. Not now." He pulled his car up behind Regina's, got out, then walked over to it.

"This is a surprise. What are you doing here?" Zale said, trying to sound cheerful, bending over, speaking into the driver-side window.

There was a look of disgust on Regina's face, and when she spoke, she didn't face him, but addressed the front windshield.

"I'm sure this is a surprise, just like it was for me when you didn't come and pick me up after saying we'd do dinner and catch a movie. That all came as a shock to me, but, then again, I don't know why it continues to be, I should be used to this by now."

"I'm sorry," Zale said sincerely, knowing that he would have to confront this situation sooner or later, wishing it was later, much later. "It must have slipped my mind. I've got a lot going on and I must have forgotten, but I promise it will—"

"Don't say that. Don't say that it will never happen again, because it will, Zale. It will and you know it!" Regina said, raising her voice, looking at him now. "I'm tired of this! I'm tired of always being second! I'm sick and tired of this!"

Zale didn't say a word, just stood there, leaning over the car, watching her rant, hoping that she would stop, because he wouldn't be able to take much more of it before his head exploded from the pressure.

Regina looked at him, flustered. "Well, aren't you going to say something!"

Zale looked at her, his body drained. "Not out here, and not with you yelling like that," Zale said, not wanting the neighbors to start peering out at them between parted curtains.

Zale and Regina went into the house. Zale walked into the kitchen and Regina followed, standing by the doorway.

"Do you want anything?" Zale said, his hand on the refrigerator door handle.

Regina just shook her head, a perturbed look on her face, her arms crossed.

"When is this going to stop, Zale?" she finally said.

Zale pulled out the chair nearest her from under the table. "Can you sit down, or do you have someplace to go?"

Regina sat down, and Zale took the chair opposite her.

"Now, I said that I was sorry. I know you've heard that before, but that doesn't change the fact that I am."

"And what is that supposed to do for me, Zale? Does that make everything better? Does that replace the times that I wanted to see you, should've seen you? Does it even make me feel better? No, Zale. It doesn't do a damn thing, so why do you keep saying it?"

"Because it's how I feel," Zale said, under his breath.

"But it's not good enough!" Regina said, pushing away from the table, standing, and walking through the small kitchen, her back toward Zale. "I don't want a whole hell of a lot from you. All I want is to love you, know that you love me, and see you some of the damn time. But I don't get any of that."

"You don't know that I love you?"

"You tell me that, Zale. And I accept it like it's really the truth, but I don't know for sure, and to tell the truth, I really wonder sometimes. I never see you because you're always out running around with this Father Found business. It's always the same thing. Father Found this, Father Found that. When will it be about me, about us?"

"I've told you that I've been busy. I have a lot going on right now, and I am sorry, but it's not like I haven't told you what my priorities are."

"Yes, I know what they are. They're fucked up, is what they are! I know that your organization is the most important thing in the world to you, and will probably always be. But the least you can do is try to trick me. Try to fool me into believing that I'm just as important. Do crazy things like keep a damn date when you make one, or return my phone calls after the first message, not wait until the light on your machine is blinking a million times a second. Or here's something really over the top, tell me that I mean just as much to you as your job. Fuck-

ing lie to me! Have you ever thought to do that? I'd know you were lying through your teeth, but at least it would sound good, and you never
know, I might even try believing it.

"But you don't even do that. You make sure it's loud and clear that
I'm second. You grab a bullhorn, stick it up to my ear and scream, 'You
know what my priorities are! You know what comes first!' Yes, I know,
Zale. But I'm tired of hearing it, and tired of knowing it." Regina
quickly lowered her head, turning away from Zale for a moment, not
wanting him to see the tears that threatened to run down her face.

"How long have we been together?" Regina said, smoothing her
face, turning back to face him.

Zale didn't answer.

"That has a little squiggly thing after it called a question mark,"
Regina said sarcastically. "That means it's a question, Zale."

"Five years," he answered.

"Five years, and I haven't given you a hard time, have I? I've stuck
by you, and when there were things that I wanted to do, engagements
that I had to attend that you couldn't make, because you were busy
saving the world, I didn't complain. I just sat there beside that empty
seat, and while everyone else was busy conversing with their partner, I
was thinking, I'm so proud of Zale, and I can't wait till things get better for him so we can have more time together. And when I'm out
somewhere, somewhere where I should have a date, and guys are hitting on me left and right, asking me, where is my man? I tell them it's
none of their business, and get pretty pissed off that they even have the
nerve to ask. But the more I'm out by myself, the more I find myself
out late at night driving home from somewhere, worrying if the car behind me is trying to follow me home, knowing that you should be beside me to stop that fear from entering my mind, the more I start to get
angry. But I still try to tell myself that things will get better, that we'll
spend more time together.

"But things never do get better; they seem to get worse. And the
worse they get, the less time we seem to spend together, and the more
you seem to pull away from me, miss dates, and not return my phone
calls. It's like I don't even know you anymore, like I never really have.
You have this shit going on with these dreams that you won't tell me

about. How do you think that makes me feel?" she said, sitting down, pushing her chair very close to Zale's.

"You're supposed to be the man I love, the man I'm going to marry one day, and I don't even know what pains you. That kills me, Zale," she said, grabbing his hand, her face filled with extreme emotion, bordering on what resembled physical pain. "And when you wake up from one of those dreams, I want to help you so bad, but there's nothing I can do, not a thing. And it's not because I'm powerless, it's because you won't tell me what's wrong. I can't live the rest of my life like this, Zale. But I guess the real question is, would you even want me to?"

Zale sat there in his chair, not looking at Regina, and not bothering to answer her question.

"Nothing to say to that, hunh? Are we ever going to get married, Zale?"

"I told you we would. I put that ring on your finger, didn't I?"

Regina stuck her hand out in front of her to look at the ring, a fake look of surprise on her face. "Oh, that! I get a lot of compliments on it, and it's a good thing that people notice it, because I would've forgotten it was there."

The remark was harsh, and Zale didn't like it. If he still had the receipt, he would've ripped the ring right off her finger and returned it.

"We were engaged years ago, and you haven't spoken about it since. How does that work? Is it like layaway? You put down a deposit on something you like at the time, and you don't have to worry about anyone else buying it."

"And what the hell is that supposed to mean?"

"That means just how long am I supposed to wait for you? I'm thirty-two years old, not getting a day younger, and I would like to have children before my teeth fall out. That is, if you're willing to get me pregnant, but that's another argument altogether. I just want to know that I'm not making a mistake, and I want to know it from you."

"And what am I supposed to do to make you know that? What am I supposed to say?"

"Say that I'm just as important to you as Father Found."

Zale lowered his head for a moment. She seemed to have a million questions and a billion complaints all of a sudden, and she was throwing them all at Zale as though he was supposed to answer all of them, resolve all of her insecurities right that moment. He couldn't do that, and why in the hell was she asking him to. He had far too much on his mind to deal with this right now, and what she was talking about could wait. It could always wait. They could talk about it later. At least she had always made him believe they could, and that was one of the things that kept him with her, that she never pressured him about how he handled their relationship. But this! Didn't she know what she was risking by displaying this behavior? Zale thought.

"Am I just as important as Father Found?" Regina asked again, yanking Zale from his inner thoughts.

"You're important," Zale said plainly, knowing the effect it would have.

"I see," Regina said. "But not as important. Tell me that when we get married we'll have children."

"That's a possibility."

"Tell me that you'll trust in me enough to let me know what continues to torture you in your dreams."

"I can't do that."

"At least tell me that when you make a date with me, you will keep it from now on."

Zale interlaced his fingers on the table, and closed his eyes.

"I'll try, but I never know what will come up with Father Found until it happens."

Zale didn't open his eyes until he heard the sound of Regina's voice again, and that was for quite a long moment. He heard her sigh, then heard her say, "I see. That's pretty much what I figured. At least you didn't surprise me. . . . Whatever I had here, I packed it up already. It's in my car, so I won't need to come back for anything."

How he didn't want her to go. But when she gave him the opportunity to keep her there with him, when she gave him the right to make the decision, he told her exactly what he knew she didn't want to hear. For what? For this damn job? For this damn cause?

Zale didn't look up at her standing directly above him, just nodded his head.

"Do you want your ring back?" Regina said, reaching to pull it off.

"No, no. You keep it," Zale said, glancing up to see her looking as if she was about to cry.

"Good, because it probably wouldn't come off anyway," and she laughed sadly.

She moved closer to Zale, leaned over and kissed him on the cheek. "I love you."

"I love you," he returned, feeling as though his heart was shattering.

Regina walked slowly toward the front door, then stopped, and turned. "You're really going to let me go?" she called back to Zale.

Zale turned around in his chair. "I'm not letting go," he said. "You're leaving me."

He watched until she was out the door. Then he heard the faint sound of her car door slam closed and her engine start. He jumped from the chair and hurried to the front window, pulling back the curtains a bit to see her pulling away. He wanted to run out there. Jump in front of her car and tell her not to leave, beg her not to leave. Promise her, give her whatever it was she wanted, just as long as she would stay, but he knew he couldn't do that. Again, she was asking him to make a decision between her and all the children in jeopardy. Making her happy, or saving them from what he went through.

It was a decision that she would lose every time, that's why he always avoided the conversation when it came up. Because he was afraid of the answer, afraid of the result. It would be him alone again with his problems, and his ghosts, and the darkness that seemed to be on all sides of him. And even though Regina never cured him of what ailed him, she made the pain more bearable. But now she was gone, and the mere thought of living, coping, without her seemed like a mountain a million stories high that he had to climb, and he told himself there was no way that he could do that.

The sharp edges of everything around him started to soften, started to blur, and he felt his head begin to spin slightly, felt his legs getting weak. He reached his hand out, finding the wall, steadying himself, before he stumbled to the ground. He had to get out of there, had to go somewhere to try and get away from the emotional chaos that was taking place in his head. He ran back into the kitchen, grabbed his keys off the table, and bolted out of the house.

CHAPTER SEVENTEEN

Martin Carter rustled the papers on his desk together in an attempt to get out of the office quickly. He looked down at his watch and it read 5:35. He had to get over to the bank, and talk to one of the Weinman brothers. He knew they left no later than 6:00 P.M. They had called him and stated how imperative it was that he remit the payment for the chunk of money that he owed them. Martin didn't get into the details, didn't tell them that the organization just didn't have that kind of money, and that the $3,000 they owed might as well have been $1,000,000.

Zale didn't have it either, Martin was almost sure just by the way the man looked when he asked him to cover their usual expenses. And if he did have it stashed away, Martin was sure that it was to take care of his own living expenses. Martin couldn't let this problem get to Zale. He had to take care of it himself, because knowing Zaleford Rowen, he would take that money and sacrifice food and shelter just for Father Found.

Martin cleared his desk and walked out of his office.

"I'm taking off," he said to his secretary. "Is Mr. Rowen still in his office?"

"No, he left almost three hours ago," she said.

Something must have been happening with him to drive him out of here this early, Martin thought. "Well, switch my calls to my voice mail, and if anything serious happens, it can wait till tomorrow, all right?"

Martin made his way downstairs and out the front door. He approached his car, opened the passenger-side door and was placing his briefcase on the seat when he was startled by a hand on his shoulder. He jumped and spun around to see a man standing behind him, wearing an orange suit jacket and pants, dark glasses, his hair slicked back in a ponytail. The man was laughing a bit as Martin caught his breath.

"Damn, man, you almost as jumpy as Ro. Where he at?"

"Who the hell are you?" Martin said, then, before the man could answer him, Martin recognized him. It was Mace, that drug-dealing bastard that through some strange association, Zale knew and seemed to befriend.

"I'm your boss's friend," Mace said, casually looking up and down the street, as if he was being hunted. "Where he at anyway? He still in his office, tracking down those bastards that don't want to come off they child support?"

Martin just looked at the man, not saying a word, as if whatever he had to say, whatever questions he asked, were not worth Martin's time to answer. He didn't know him, but he knew of him, and his reputation was more than enough to make Martin think that he hated this man. The way he looked, the way he stood in front of Martin talking to him as if they were old pals that hung out and did drugs in his basement, only made Martin sure of his dislike for him.

"Yo, he in his office or what?" Mace asked, lowering his glasses to look into Martin's eyes.

Martin felt the muscles of his face freeze into a frown.

"No. He's gone for the day," Martin hissed.

Mace continued to hold his glasses just below his eyes, giving Martin a long stare, then he slipped them back, and cracked a simple smile.

"Well, tell him I stopped by to see him." Then Mace turned and pimped off down the street.

Martin stood there against his car, for some strange reason feeling victimized. He closed his door, then briskly walked to catch up to Mace, and grabbed him by the arm, spinning him around.

Before Mace was completely spun about to face Martin, his hand was already in his jacket, his elbow pointed upward as if he was about to whip something out. But when the two men were face-to-face, his hand relaxed and a cautionary look covered his face.

"What the fuck's wrong with you! Don't go grabbing me like that. I almost put a hole in your ass. You was almost blown away," he said, and then laughed a little as if him killing Martin on the street, in broad daylight, would've been nothing he'd have a single regret or second thought about.

Martin looked at the man's hand disappearing into his jacket, and knew that he was holding a gun. Knew that, indeed, Mace was intending to shoot him if he was someone else, or if he just didn't recognize him in time, but that did not intimidate Martin, it just made him angrier.

"Why do you come around here?" Martin said, his jaws tightly clenched together, trying to suppress his hate.

"What the fuck you talking about, man?" Mace said, what little bit of a smile he had on his face disappearing, as if he was insulted by the question.

"I said, why are you here? Why do you come around here? There's nothing here for you, and no one wants what you have to offer. So why don't you just take yourself and your *product* back to the ghettos, or wherever you sell your death." The look of extreme hate on Martin's face made it seem like the words he spoke were poison, and he was spraying them at Mace, hoping they would kill him.

Mace looked to his left, then to his right again, and then stepped closer to Martin, looking as though he had possibly been hurt by Martin's remarks.

"Oh, I can't come around here no more?" Mace spoke softly.

"Nobody wants you around here."

Mace strained a smile at Martin's remark, smoothed a hand over his slick hair, removed his sunglasses and stuck them into his pocket.

"And this is your street, now. Is that it?" Mace said without emotion, stepping right up in Martin's face, looking coldly, deeply, into his eyes. "Is that what you saying? That this is your street, and I can't come around here, because nobody wants me and my *product*. That's what you saying?"

Martin looked back, square into Mace's eyes, not backing down.

"Yeah, if that's what you're hearing, if that's what you make of it, then that's what I'm saying. And I'll go as far to say this. That if I ever see you around here again, I'll call the police. I'll tell them what you're doing, and they'll arrest you, and hopefully throw you in jail for all the lives you've ruined. Do you understand that?"

Mace didn't speak, didn't say a word, just stood there, a look of mild surprise on his face as if someone told him it was Thursday, and not Friday, like he had thought. He slowly turned his head to look down both sides of the street again, and before Martin could even comprehend what was going on, Mace had him by the shirt, yanked him a few steps off the main street, and threw him into an alley. Martin was taken off guard, and he tripped and spun, and when he finally caught his bearings and turned to rush back at Mace, he was met by the barrels of Mace's huge gun.

"Where the fuck you going, motherfucker? You comin' at me! You comin' at me to kick me off your motherfuckin' street!" Mace said, racing to Martin, placing the barrels of his gun right up against the side of Martin's head. Martin froze, slowly raising his hands above his head.

"Tell me something," Mace said, his arm extended straight out, the gun still pressed against Martin's head. "How you know who wants me here? You take a poll? You hand out questionnaires, motherfucker? You tell me that no one wants me here, that I'm selling death. You think I want to do this? You think this is shit that I dreamed about doing coming up? Well, it ain't. But if it was, who in the hell you think you are telling me that you going to call the cops. That you going to have them put me away. I been there, and I ain't going back. That's why I'm doing this," Mace said, emotion starting to fill his voice. "I'm doing this because I got to! I'm doing this to survive, motherfucker! You understand?" he said, nudging the gun against Martin's head. Martin nodded his head, trembling, sweat rolling down his face.

"You do?" Mace asked. "You do?" Martin nodded his head again, quickly.

"You don't understand shit. You privileged motherfuckers coming up with everything you want. Everything you need is right there for you. All you got to do is ask Mom or Dad. Your life is made for you from the time that you're born, right up to this minute, and you got the nerve to pass judgment on me. Well, I'm going to flip it this time. Get on your knees," Mace said.

Martin turned to him, shock in his eyes, his hands still over his head.

"What did you say?"

"I said, get on your fucking knees!" Mace yelled.

"I'm not going to do it," Martin found the courage to say, his voice trembling terribly, for if he did, he knew he would surely die.

"You're not going to do it. Oh, okay," Mace said, then reared back and whacked Martin on the side of the head with the butt of the gun, dropping him to his hands and knees. When Martin tried to get up, he felt the gun placed back to his head, Mace standing over him, shouting.

"Give me one reason why I shouldn't kill you, punk ass, bitch!"

Martin didn't say a word, couldn't say a word, for his head was still spinning from the blow delivered, and he feared any word spoken could set Mace off, could trip his wire and make him pull the trigger, emptying Martin's brains all over the alley Dumpsters. By the way Mace was jumping around, yelling emotionally, coming very near to tears, Martin knew that he was unstable, and he knew the man could kill him, could kill him and not think anything of it. The only thing for Martin to do was to remain there on his hands and knees and pray to God that this man would spare his life.

"Do you know what I've been through? Do you know what I've seen, the shit I did, had to do! It was fucked up, and it fucks with me every day, every night, in my dreams and shit! I'm trying to deal with that, trying to make some way in this world for me so I don't have to go back to that shit, and you're telling me that I don't deserve to be away from that. That I don't deserve to be here, because people don't want me!"

"I didn't say that," Martin felt brave enough to say.

"Shut the fuck up! Just shut the fuck up!" Mace yelled at the top of his voice, nudging the gun harder into Martin's head, as if he was trying to push the thing through his skull.

"I didn't ask you for shit, and I'm still trying to decide if I'm going to kill you or not."

Mace stood there over Martin, holding the gun to his head for a full minute, which to Martin seemed as long as the entire length of his life. And at the end of that minute, Mace said, "Close your eyes."

Martin's heart immediately started beating wildly, as if it were going to rip itself from between his lungs, and tear through his chest. No! Martin thought. No! Not like this! Not in an alley, not before he could say goodbye to his children—to his wife. He raced through his brain, trying to find something that would stop this man from stealing his life, but everything was jumbled, scrambled, and nothing that would save his life made itself available to him. He heard Mace tell him to close his eyes again. Martin shook his head defiantly.

"Close your fucking eyes, or I'll kill you right now!" Mace yelled.

Martin closed his eyes tight, tears squeezing out from the corners. He was preparing himself to die, waiting to hear the gunshot, the explosion that would halt his life, pull him from this world, from everyone he loved, everything he knew. He was preparing himself, then . . .

"I'm not going to kill you," Mace said softly, the gun still to Martin's head. "But that's only because you're Ro's right hand. Killing you would hurt him, and I would never do that, because I love that man, and he's the only one that can relate to how I feel. The only one." Mace removed the gun from Martin's head and looked down at him for a long moment, as if rethinking his decision.

"Tell him that I'm looking for him," Mace said, then took slow, casual steps out of the alley, as if he had entered it just to relieve his bladder.

After a moment, Martin looked up to see that Mace was gone. He brushed the tears from the corners of his eyes, and thanked God to still be alive. He would forget this. He would never tell Zale about it, and he would forget it, because he had to. There were too many other things to worry about, and Mace didn't kill him, and he wouldn't for the single reason he stated, Zale needed him, and Mace loved Zale for some reason that Martin didn't know of, and probably never would. But it kept Martin alive and always would and that's all he was concerned about.

Martin looked down at his watch. It was 5:50 P.M., and although he was pretty badly shaken, he had to get to the bank and speak to Weinman, because Martin knew that he was on the verge of starting the foreclosure procedure, if he hadn't started already.

By the time Martin got to the bank, the lights were off in the building, and Anster Weinman was just about to slide his key in the door to lock the place up for the evening.

"Mr. Weinman," Martin said, rushing from his car. "I'm sorry I'm late, but I had a very serious engagement I couldn't possibly get away from."

Mr. Weinman slowly looked over his shoulder. He was a dark, wavy-haired man, roughly around the same age as Martin. He wore a dark-brown, expensive-looking suit and he looked at Martin through small, round, studious-looking eyeglass frames.

Mr. Weinman looked down at his watch and a gold Rolex peeked out from under the cuff of his shirt.

"I leave at six. This place closes at six," he said, offering nothing else.

"I know that," Martin said.

"If you know that, why are you here now?" The man talked to Martin as if he were a child.

"Do you know who I am, Mr. Weinman?"

The man turned to face Martin. Studied him briefly from head to toe, then said without regret, "I can't say that I do."

"I didn't think so. But I owe you almost three thousand dollars, so I thought it was something that you'd want to take care of as soon as possible, but if you have other things to do, I understand. Goodbye." Martin turned and started toward his car.

"Um, excuse me. Your name again?"

Martin sat in the office of Mr. Anster Weinman while the man looked through a drawer of files.

"You said Father Found, is that correct?" Mr. Weinman asked.

"Yes."

He pulled a file from the drawer, placed it on the desk beside his jacket and briefcase, then opened it up and took a look.

"That's right, Mr. Carter, we called your office today. You owe us two thousand seven hundred and forty-five dollars," Mr. Weinman said, looking down at the papers. "And because you came all the way out here to take care of that, I'll let you pay by check, even though you're three months late."

"I don't have it," Martin said bluntly.

Mr. Weinman quickly looked up. "What do you mean, you don't have it?"

"I'm going to be perfectly frank with you. Father Found is in a situation right now. We're experiencing some hardships, and we just don't have it right now, and to tell the truth, I don't know when we will, but I do have something going right now, and it might show promise."

"Something going, and it *might* show promise." Mr. Weinman said the words as if they were personal insults. "Mr. Carter, I'm sure you're aware of this, but promise doesn't pay your bills."

"Yes, I am aware of that, but I was hoping that we could arrange some sort of extension, or payment plan."

"What do you think a mortgage is? You pay your mortgage once a month, or at least you're supposed to. A mortgage is a payment plan. The plan we agreed to, the plan you and your partner signed your names to. Would you like to see that?" Mr. Weinman said, starting to lift the folder.

"That won't be necessary." Martin waved him away.

"And as far as an extension goes, we've already granted you one, for approximately three months, and, by these records, have always allowed for you to be at least one month late without giving you any problems or fining you any penalties. But Mr. Carter. This is different," Mr. Weinman said, sitting in his leather executive chair. He began playing with a gold ring on one of his hands, twisting it around his finger.

"You're three months behind, and say you have no way of paying. What am I supposed to do here? What would you do?"

"That's not important," Martin said, sitting tensely in an upholstered chair. "I'm not the one that has to make the decision. I'm more interested in what you're going to do."

Mr. Weinman sat straight up in his chair, stopped spinning the ring on his finger, and folded his hands together in front of him.

"I'm going to do the only thing I can do. I'm going to put in paperwork to get my property back." He spoke very casually, as if the repercussion of his actions would have no effect on anything other than his bottom line.

"You can't do that!" Martin said, pushing forward in his chair. "That building houses our organization, Father Found! Do you know what we do? We find fathers—"

"I know, I know. Who have abandoned their children, and try to reunite them. I've seen some stuff on TV about it, and it is a noble idea, it really is, but good intentions don't pay the bills, Mr. Carter."

Martin couldn't believe what he was hearing. He looked at the man, his expensive clothes, fine jewelry, the professional manicure. Martin looked around the office at the huge oak desk, the expensive paintings on the walls, the sculptures that stood on tables and in corners, and Martin knew that $3,000 was change to this man, something that he would probably spend on a gift for his mother, or wife. But to Martin, to Zale, and to all the children that they were trying to help, it was the future. It was their lives on the line.

"Mr. Weinman, if you knew how important this building was to the people in our community, you wouldn't be trying to take it from us."

"I'm not trying to take it. It's mine, Mr. Carter. I was just loaning it to you for a cost, but you stopped paying. By the tone of your voice, I think you're trying to make me out as a tyrant. I'm only handling my business. I assume you're an educated man, Mr. Carter, so you know that I cannot extend you any more favors than I already have. Your promises or heartfelt attempts don't feed my family, don't pay my mortgage, or car notes. Money does."

"What if those were your children out there? What if it was your community that was suffering with this illness," Martin said, trying to find some level on which he could appeal to this man.

"As cold as this my sound, those aren't my children, it's not my community, so it's not my concern, Mr. Carter," Mr. Weinman said, leaning forward on his desk, as if he was about to impart some treasured secret information handed down over the generations. "Let me tell you something, and see if this rings true for you. If *some* people stopped exerting so much energy begging for things, and put forth some effort to acquire them honestly, maybe your community would be in a better situation."

Martin sat there, in no way confused about what the man in front of him just said, and who he said it about. But Martin did not spring from his chair, leap over the man's desk, and beat him in the face till his little eyeglasses shattered against Martin's knuckles, even though he should have.

Martin just sat there, trying to absorb all the pain, absorb the shame he was feeling by being in that situation at that moment, like so many times before when all he could do was listen. Listen to a man who thought he was above him, thought he was above Martin's intelligence, and therefore above Martin's problems. A man who felt he had done his homework while everybody who wasn't as fortunate as he was were outside playing in the street, and doing things to toss their futures out the window, and not giving a damn about it. Martin just sat there, hating the man just for living, and then Mr. Weinman said, "I'll give you a week," as if he were sacrificing his left arm or something. "But if I don't receive my payment in full, I'll draw up the papers to take back my property."

When he said that, Martin rose from his seat, and without saying a word, turned and walked out of the man's office.

Martin sat in his car wondering what he would do—he could do nothing but wait, and hope that this Mr. Kirkland would come through as he said he would. It was imperative. He started his car and headed toward home. Debra had called him earlier today, and asked if she could see him. Martin told her no, that he was very busy, that he had too many things to do to make time for her, but she persisted, and Martin couldn't stand to lie to her any longer. He heard the emotion in her voice, felt the sincerity of her requests to see him, so he agreed that he would come by the house after work.

When Martin arrived home, he rang the doorbell as if he were approaching a stranger's house. He had the key right on his ring, but for some reason, he didn't feel right using it. He waited for a moment, then his wife opened the door and waited for him to come in.

She smiled, but it was an uneasy smile, and Martin could tell that she was uncomfortable, unsure of herself. It was the first time.

"I'm glad to see you," Debra said, and Martin couldn't remember the last time he heard those words come out of her mouth.

Martin stepped in, noticing what she was wearing. A lavender nightgown, with a matching sheer robe over it. She was beautiful, but at that moment, her beauty made no difference to him.

"Yeah, good to see you too," he said. "What did you want to see me about?"

"Can't I at least get a kiss?" Debra walked up to Martin and placed her hands on his face and kissed him on the lips. Martin made no attempt to return the kiss, just stood there.

Debra pulled her hands away and stopped kissing him.

"I see," she said. She seemed disappointed. "You haven't forgiven me."

"What did you want to see me about, Debra?" Martin said, ignoring the comment. "I really have a lot on my mind."

"What's going on?" Debra asked, taking a seat on the sofa, crossing

her legs, her tone and demeanor changing to something very busi-
nesslike.

"I don't understand the question."

"I assume you're trying to teach me a lesson. Okay, it's been more
than a week that you've been gone. More than a week since I've seen
the girls. Hasn't that been enough? I'm tired of walking into this house
at night and no one being here."

"So you've been coming home at night now," Martin said coldly.

Debra shook her head, as if not surprised to hear such hard words
from her husband.

"What point am I supposed to get? What lesson am I supposed to
learn, Martin, and when will all this be over?" She spoke of their separation, not sounding like a loving wife, but like someone suspended
from her job for unbecoming behavior, and in a hurry to get back because of lost income.

Martin shook his head at her approach. "What lesson, hunh? Have
you forgotten what you did? Did it slip your mind, and do I constantly
have to keep reminding you, because if I do, just let me know, because
I keep it right up front in my memory," he said, poking himself in the
forehead with his pointer finger. "It sounds to me like you think you've
been punished enough, like maybe I'm going overboard with this."

"I think that you are," Debra said.

"Let me tell you something." Anger was starting to fill Martin's
voice. "Considering what you did to me, if I took the kids and left
for five years, I wouldn't be going overboard. A million damn years
wouldn't be going too far considering how I found you, and to tell you
the truth, if I never came back, if you never spoke to those girls again
in your life, the punishment still wouldn't be too harsh for the crime."

Martin stared at Debra with eyes that could kill. She turned away,
looked down at the floor, her hair falling over, obscuring her face.

"So is that what you're going to do?" she asked, her voice not as
harsh, almost timid with uncertainty, looking up at him with saddened
eyes.

It's what he wanted to consider, he thought to himself, and God
knows, she deserved to be without them, but he didn't think that he
could really find it in himself to do that to her, and to his children. He

just loved her too much, needed her, and regardless of how hard he tried, he could not deny that fact.

"Why did you do it, Debra?" Martin asked, instead of dealing with her question. "Why did you have to put me in this position?" And as the words came out, he realized that it was something that he had never asked her. Maybe because he didn't want to know the answer, just wanted to get past the incident as quickly as possible, without looking at it too harshly, examining it under a microscope, thinking it would go away quicker that way.

Debra didn't answer the question, just continued sitting on the edge of the sofa, her chin in her hands.

"I asked you a question, Debra. I'd appreciate an answer."

"I don't know," she said softly.

And that was the worst answer that she could've ever given Martin. It was like she hadn't even thought about the question, and just offered up any excuse to shut him up. Like he didn't deserve a real answer, or would be satisfied with whatever she offered him. That was wrong. That was the wrong damn answer, he thought angrily, as he raced over to her, grabbed her by her shoulders, pulled her off the couch, and shook her with all the force he dared summon.

"Do you know what this is doing to me?" he yelled at her, her head flying back and forth. "Do you know how this is tearing me apart! I can't eat, I can barely sleep, for the goddamn image of you in that hotel room naked with that man. And when I do finally sleep, it's you I see. You on top of that man, having sex with that man, making love to that man, telling him how you'd rather be with him than your husband. I think about that and I don't know what to do with myself. I think about how much I love you, and how because of some shit you did, I have to pull myself and our children away from you. Punish myself, punish those kids, for some stupid shit that you did. And when I ask you why you did it, you tell me you don't know. You don't know!" Martin tightened his grip on her shoulders, could feel his fingers digging deeper into her soft flesh, could see the increasing expression of pain on her face, but he didn't care if he hurt her at that moment.

"What am I, some fool? Am I your flunky, or some lapdog that you think you can just do anything you want to with? You don't think that I can walk out of here right now and never come back? You don't think I can do that? Answer me!" he yelled, shaking her more violently than before. She was crying now. Her face was covered with tears, strands of her fine hair stuck to her wet cheeks. But she still didn't answer.

"I don't need this," Martin said, pushing her away from him in the direction of the couch, not caring if she landed on it, or fell to the floor and banged her skull. He was going for the door.

"Martin!" Debra called. His hand was on the doorknob, but he turned back to look at her. She was a pathetic sight, lying on her side, her hair wild about her head.

"I thought about it so much, so many times, but I don't know why I did it. I don't know. I tried to think of something that gave me the reason, but there was nothing, and it doesn't make any sense to me," Debra said through her crying. "I knew we would have this talk. I knew you would finally ask me why, and I tried to think of things, tried to find some way to blame it on you, to blame it on the kids, anybody but myself, but there is no one. It's my fault, I did it. But I don't know why, and now I risk losing you and the children. I was a fool, Martin. A fool!" she said, banging her fist into the couch repeatedly. "And now I'm going to lose the man I love so much, and the kids that mean more to me than anything else in the world.

"I don't know why I did it. But, Martin," she said looking up at him with puffy, tear-filled eyes, "you have to understand, I never meant to hurt you, or the kids. I never meant to hurt you."

Martin stood there at the door just looking at her, telling himself not to run to her, not to pick her off that couch and throw his arms around her, but he couldn't help himself. He went to her and embraced her tightly.

"I'm so sorry, Martin. I'm so sorry," she cried into his shoulder.

"*Shhhhh, shhhhh.* Everything will be all right," he said, kissing her on top of her head.

"Do you forgive me, Martin? Do you forgive me?"

He continued to hold her, continued to kiss her head, but he could not answer the question. He wanted to forgive her, but that didn't mean that he would. He wanted to forget the images in his head, wanted to stop feeling the pain, feeling betrayed, but that didn't mean that he could. Did he forgive her? He very seriously asked himself the question, and decided that he did. But he would not tell her that now, and he didn't know if it was because he wasn't really sure, or if he just wanted her to suffer more.

CHAPTER EIGHTEEN

Zale pushed through the door of the community center, ran down the hall, looking for the psychiatric counseling classroom. When he spotted it, he ducked into the classroom, expecting, praying to see the woman that he had seen before, the woman that was asking him into the class with her eyes, but when he saw no one, he just stood in the middle of the classroom, greatly disappointed, huffing and puffing, winded by the run.

He turned in a circle, still to find no one in the class but himself. She was gone, he told himself, and Zale felt as though he was going to collapse to his knees right there, fall to the ground because he was no longer able to hold himself up against the anxiety he was facing. The weight of his problems, the adversity he faced at every turn, the realization of losing Regina. It was all too heavy for him to continue to bear. He had to get all of it out of his system, because it all felt like venom, deadly poison, racing through his veins, and if he didn't get it out of his body soon, he felt he would die.

That is why he stood there in that classroom. That was why he grabbed his keys off the kitchen table after Regina left him, and recklessly drove his car down here, because there was no place else to turn. And now that he was finally ready to speak about all that had been plaguing him—to some stranger, no less—the woman was gone. But why was he surprised. He should've expected just that. For all his life, the people nearest to him had been leaving him. His mother, his old girlfriend, Cassaundra, and Regina. Why would he expect someone he didn't even know to be around at his time of need? He wasn't supposed to have someone to listen to his problems, to help alleviate his pain. It was meant for him to carry all the weight himself, for him to suffer.

Zale felt his knees getting weak, his legs trying to give from under him. He would have to sit. He reached for one of the chairs arranged in the counseling group circle, and sat down. He threw his face in his hands, telling himself that he had to go, but dreading the fact that there was no place to go. This was it. And as he pulled his weary body up from the chair and turned around, there standing in the doorway was the woman he'd seen twice before.

He was shocked to see her there, and for some reason he was scared; his pulse quickened and whatever controlled his speech froze, because he could not say a word. He stared at her, and now, again, he asked himself why he was here. He had driven twenty miles an hour over the speed limit to get here, thinking that speaking to this woman would solve all his problems. Now, upon seeing her, he couldn't say a word, and all he could think about was leaving.

"Hello," the woman said, smiling as if they were friends.

Zale didn't respond, just looked at the dark-haired woman, who didn't appear any older than twenty-five or twenty-six years old. Her body was thin, and she wore a plain, dark-colored dress that hung off her body as if it was a size or two too big.

She smiled and took a step forward into the room, and in response Zale took a step back.

"I'm not going to bite," she said, walking toward him, her hand extended. "I'm Laura, the counselor here."

Zale took her hand in his, relaxing some. "I'm Zale—"

"I know who you are. How could I not? You work right next door. You're Zaleford Rowen." She spoke his name as if he was a legend. "Founder of Father Found. The man who sacrifices all he has for the children. The man that all abandoning fathers fear, and the man they also hate." Her voice lowered on the second half of her statement.

That's me, all right, Zale thought. "I'm sorry that I'm bothering you. I really just came to—"

"I know why you're here, Mr. Rowen," Laura interrupted again. "As you can tell, I keep up-to-date with what you do. Anytime you're in the papers, I'm reading it, anytime you're on television, I'm sitting right up on the tube like a six-year-old watching cartoons."

Laura dropped her head toward the floor, blushing slightly. "I don't mean to sound fanatical, Mr. Rowen, but you intrigue me. Why would a man single-handedly try to solve such a huge problem that faces so many people? But the more important question is, what would make him think he could?"

Zale looked at this woman oddly, not knowing whether or not he should feel insulted.

"I don't mean to offend you, Mr. Rowen. I envy what it is you are doing, and I stand behind you in your beliefs, but this is an issue that has been around since the beginning of time. As long as there have been fathers and children, there have been fathers abandoning their children. And I imagine when a man leaves his child, he believes that he is doing it for the right reasons, or he feels he has no other alternatives, and I suppose that for some of them, it's the last thing in the world they want to do. So what I often wonder is, what makes a man think that he can influence another man about his own decisions pertaining to his own children?"

When Laura was finished talking, she stood in front of Zale, an inquisitive look on her face, as if waiting for him to spill his guts and answer all her questions.

Zale looked at her, and although no less weary than he was when he came in, his dislike for this woman made him feel that he was strong enough to leave.

"Obviously, you *don't* know why I'm here. I came here because I needed help, and I thought, I wrongly thought, that I could get it here. The last thing I need is someone else trying to tell me that what I'm doing is foolish. So if you will excuse me." Zale walked past her, making his way toward the door, when she grabbed him by the arm, then quickly released him, seeming embarrassed by her irrational behavior.

"Mr. Rowen. I don't think what you're doing is foolish. I'm just letting you know that I am aware of what obstacles you face. Of what it must be like trying to tell someone that has never seen you in all his life, who may be years older than you, and may have endured many more hardships than you, that *you* know what's best for *him*. That you know what's best for his life, even though that means maintaining more responsibility, continuing to take care of another life, or two or three, when he can barely take care of himself.

"So when I saw you the other night standing in my doorway, this lost, beaten look on your face, Mr. Rowen, I knew right then what was bothering you. And for some reason, I knew you would be back. And when I saw you earlier this evening, that same look on your face, but this time more intense, I wanted to invite you in. I wanted to talk to you, but you left. And, again, I told myself that you'd be back, and here you are."

Zale didn't know what to say. All he knew was that this woman sized him up fairly accurately, and to a degree that scared him. She was probably choosing out which chair she wanted him to take in the circle of manic-depressives and schizophrenics, deciding on what additional drugs she would put him on. He was hurting, but he was not that far gone, not yet.

"You know, I thought that I needed help, but I'm feeling much better now, and I think that I'm just going to go on home and get some sleep."

Laura stood there looking disappointed in what he was saying. "And which home are you going to get some sleep at, your house or your office?"

Zale was shocked by the question, and it showed on his face.

"You're wondering how I know that," Laura said, smiling shyly. "There was one evening when I left this building, and I saw your car parked out front. And under the front tire of your car there was a crushed box of KFC, and under the back tire was a crushed pop cup from the same restaurant, and I remember chuckling, joking, saying to myself, the least he could do when he's done eating is put his trash in its place. But the next morning, when I came to work, I noticed the same trash under your tires, exactly the way it was when I left. Since then, I've paid particular attention to your car, and it's apparent that you've been sleeping in your office at least twice a week, sometimes for a couple of days straight. I can imagine that it's because you're putting in overtime, trying to make things work when they don't seem to be going just right. And let me tell you, Mr. Rowen, it's taking its toll on you, and it will continue to until—"

"Hold it!" Zale said, raising his voice. "What are you doing? Are you spying on me or something?" Zale looked around the room, as if he would see tools of the trade lying out, a huge magnifying glass like that of Sherlock Holmes, or a two-way radio. "Is that what you do with your time when you're not counseling people, checking the trash under my tires to see if my car has moved an inch in the past eight hours, or looking to see if there's a light on in my office, so you know if I'm sleeping there?" He was at the windows now, pulling back the curtains to see if she had a view of his office window. She did not, so he let the curtains fall back and turned to face Laura.

"Maybe it's not me who needs help, or maybe it's not even that group of people who sit around in these chairs like kindergartners and cry about their problems. Maybe it's you, Ms. . . . ."

"Eckert," Laura said, appearing disappointed by Zale's accusations.

"Well, Ms. Eckert, maybe you should retire your license in psychology and pull yourself up a chair."

Zale looked at her, waiting for her response, but she didn't say anything. She was looking away from him, still appearing hurt by what he had said.

"Well, thank you for what you *tried* to do, Ms. Eckert." Zale turned to leave.

"Mr. Rowen," Laura said, and her voice was pleading, almost desperate, and it was the only reason why Zale stopped and turned around.

"You shouldn't go. You came here for a reason, I know you did. You felt it was your only hope. You're here right now because you had nowhere else to turn, isn't that the truth?"

How did she know that? Zale thought, and then realized that she didn't know. He didn't know why she was trying to find out everything about him, trying to dissect his mind as if he were some frog split down the middle, an assignment for a sixth-grade science class. He was tired of hearing what she had to say, and tired of being there. He turned to go but Laura said, "Mr. Rowen, don't leave. I know what you're going through."

And those words made Zale stop dead in his tracks. He halted for a moment, going over what she said in his head to make sure he got it right before he retaliated. How could this cute little white girl, who most likely grew up with both her parents in a suburban home, white picket fence, dog named Sparky, squeaky swing set in the backyard, and sleepovers in the tree house, know what the fuck he was going through.

Even if she was actually, certifiably crazy and had been smoking weed, laced with heroin, sniffing coke, and sipping on a bottle of gin, could she actually think that someone like her could understand him? Someone who he was sure was sheltered all her life, never saw people with dark skin outside of the pages of *National Geographic* until she left home for college, had her way paid through the finest of universities, and decided to work somewhere like this only because she had some Jane Goodall black-folk-in-the-inner-city-mist thing going on. Could she actually believe that just because she has had some occasion to sit and listen while some people spoke of their unfortunate times, cried on her shoulder, and smiled in her face, after she smoothed her hand across their backs as if they were her children, telling them, "Aw, let it all out, everything will be okay," did she think that opened up the doors to Zale's mind, to people like Zale, and made her privy to what he was actually feeling? Did she think this allowed her to feel his pain, his hunger, his loneliness, his desperation? There was no way, and for saying such words, Zale thought, as punishment, she should experience one tenth of what he had gone through. If she had, she wouldn't be able to take it. She would die.

Her hands probably had never seen a day of hard honest work, her stomach had probably never felt the dull nagging pain of hunger, and her ears had probably never heard a single negative word about herself. How in the hell could she say those words to him! By this point, Zale was so angry that his body was rattling. His jaws were clamped tight, his hands locked into fists to try to control the anger that was shaking him. Ms. Laura Eckert looked at him, this pitiful sympathetic stare on her face, and Zale knew she probably thought that she was showing him something. Making him feel as if she cared with the showing of her sad eyes and all. That little display of sympathy, Zale thought, maybe enough for a child who fell and skinned his knee on the sidewalk, but for all the shit he had been through, she would have to slit her wrists, cut her throat, and impale herself for her to feel what he had been through.

"You know what I'm going through," Zale said angrily, slowly walking back toward her.

Laura nodded her head, the same sympathetic look in her eyes one would show to a caged puppy.

"You really think you know what I'm going through, what the fuck I been through!" Zale said, yelling loud enough to startle Laura.

She stood there, shock in her eyes, shaking. Zale could see her hands trembling.

"If I don't know everything, Mr. Rowen, why don't you tell me."

Zale looked at her, then looked away, almost ashamed of all the horrible things his memory held. "You wouldn't understand. You couldn't understand."

"Then make me. Make me, Zale." She had called him Zale. That caught him off guard, and for some reason that made him relax some, made him trust her more than anything she had said that entire evening. She placed a soft hand on his back and guided him to a chair, where he sat down.

The chair was huge, or he so small that it swallowed him up. "She'll be here in a minute," the white woman said, then disappeared. Little Zale looked over his shoulder, watching her till she was gone. It was the same woman that came to take him away from his mother, and since he had been here at the orphanage, she had been the closest person to him.

Zale turned back around in the chair, and focused his eyes on the door in front of him. It was where his mother would come through, and it had been almost a month since he had seen her. He sat there in that chair, his hands crossed on the table in front of him, his feet swinging just above the floor below him, the last few scars on his back finally healing from the last beating he took at the hands of his mother. He sat there, and for some reason, he felt nothing. A blank expression covered his face as he waited patiently, watching the door his mother was going to come through as he would've watched the toaster, waiting for the toast to pop up. It was something that he knew was about to happen, but was nothing to get terribly excited about.

And then the door opened, and he saw the white woman again, and she was holding his mother by the arms as his mother was trying to break free of her, tears of joy streaming down her cheeks, and all that Zale thought a moment ago was erased. As much as she was trying to make her way toward Zale, he wanted her to be next to him.

Zale jumped from the chair, ran around the table, and threw himself into his mother's arms. She wrapped herself around him and held him

so tight that he could barely breathe, but he didn't mind. She was crying, her body shaking from her emotion, and Zale had to ask her,
pulling away from her so he could look into her eyes.

"Why are you crying, Mommy?"

And at that question, his mother's crying slowed. She looked at him,
then smiled and started to laugh. "Because I'm happy to see you, baby.
Because I'm so happy to see you." And then she gave him a big kiss on
the cheek, her tears wiping off on the side of his face.

That day, they talked for hours, more than they ever had when Zale
was at home. His mother told him how sorry she was about everything
she had done to him, and that the last thing she wanted was for someone to take him away from her, because he was all she had.

"Will you forgive me, Zale?" she asked him, sweetly, rubbing his
hand in hers.

Zale looked in her face. It was the same face that had been balled up
into a horrifying mask, swinging that broom down on him till he
blacked out. Would he forgive her?

Her face was the same face that he would see stepping outside the
apartment, then closing the door, saying, "Now lock the big lock, and
don't let anybody in here till I get back. Be back in a couple of hours,"
which always ended up being a couple of days. Would he forgive her?
Her face was the same face that he would see coming out of her bedroom behind some man, any man, black or white, tall or short, handsome or ugly. And they would be buckling their pants, or buttoning
their shirts, and they'd hand her some money right there in front of
Zale, after which they'd kiss her on the lips, pinch her ass, then disappear. Could he forgive her? That was the question, and Zale took another look, a deeper look. This was his mother, and he loved her more
than he could understand. Of course he would forgive her.

At the end of their visit, his mother kept telling him how she was doing everything she could to get him back home. That she was talking to
"some people" and that they were working on it. "I'll never rest until I
get you back," she said, teary-eyed, and Zale knew she wouldn't. She
said she would see him in a week, then left. When she came back, it
was two weeks later, but he was overjoyed to see her.

She told him the same thing. "I'm still trying, and I won't stop till I
get you back." It took her a month to come back and see him the next

time. Then another month, then two, then she stopped altogether. Zale never saw his mother again.

Soon after, Zale was placed in a foster home. It was supposed to be temporary, until someone decided they wanted to adopt him, but he knew that no one would want an eight-year-old black child.

When he walked into the huge old wood-frame house, he was greeted by a middle-aged fat white woman with curly red hair sitting upon her head like a round hat, and red freckles across her nose and cheeks. Her name was Mrs. Connors, and she seemed nice enough, for when she saw Zale for the first time, she bent down and gave him a big hug, as if this boy was her own. She held him in that embrace a little longer than Zale would've wanted, then she gave him a wet kiss on his cheek, very near the corner of his mouth.

"Welcome, young man," she said, still holding him, but loosening her hug. Zale looked over the big woman's shoulder to the back of the room, and in that doorway he saw four boys. Two of them were white, one black, and the other one—Zale couldn't make out what he was— had hair that was black and straight and his skin was dark. They all appeared a bit younger than Zale. The closest one to his age seemed to be the other black boy.

Three of the boys peered out from the side of the doorway, seeming as though they didn't want themselves to be seen, but the black boy stood right there in the middle of the doorway, a strange look on his face. A look of sadness, of sympathy, and he was directing it right at Zale, right into Zale's eyes, as he was still being hugged by the big red-headed woman, and Zale wondered what was going through this boy's mind.

Mrs. Connors released Zale and asked him a question, but Zale didn't hear her. And when she turned around to see what was holding Zale's attention, she saw the boys in the doorway. They all scattered like mice, except the black boy. He gave Zale that stare a moment longer, then turned and walked away.

The room the boys slept in was a big bay area, bunk beds lining the walls like those in a military barracks. Zale was given the bunk next to the black boy that he had seen earlier. When it was time for the boys to get dressed for bed, all of them except that black boy dressed behind the cover of their dressers, or knelt down beside their bed to take their underwear off, hiding their nakedness, even though there was no one else in the room but boys. It all seemed very strange to Zale as he changed his clothes right out in the open, wondering if he was breaking some kind of rule.

Zale and this boy had been introduced and they had been exchanging looks all day. The boy hadn't bothered to say a word to him, so Zale didn't speak either, although he was dying to find out what that look was all about that he was given when he first arrived.

Mrs. Connors came in the room, and it was like the boys went into shock, freezing with their clothes in their hands, fear in their eyes.

"All right, lights out," she said, smiling. "Time for you boys to get in bed."

The boys climbed in bed quickly, their little bodies disappearing under their covers. The boy next to Zale just stared at the woman until she left the room, deep hate in his eyes, then he got in bed himself. Zale didn't know what was going on, and if he waited for this boy to say something, he would never know.

Zale crawled in bed, turning his back to the boy, then after a moment, he rolled over to face him. The boy had the covers pulled up over his shoulders, his head tucked down into the blankets, but Zale could still see his forehead, and the space above his eyes, and it was wrinkled with lines of anger, and Zale wondered why a boy of seven or eight years old would be so angry.

"*Spppppp!*" Zale whispered. "What's your name again?"

The boy peeked up over his cover. "Derek," he said, his voice muffled by the blanket.

"What's happening? Why is everybody—"

"Go back to sleep. You don't want to know."

"Why were you looking at me like that today? Why do you look at Mrs. Connors the way you do? Why were these boys hiding while they were getting dressed like they were girls, and why do they seem so scared whenever they see Mrs. Connors?"

Derek lowered his blanket. There was a solemn look on his face.

"It's better if I don't tell you," he said, his voice lowered.

"Why not? I want to know. Just tell me! Everybody's acting crazy and I don't know why."

Derek seemed to be thinking it over a moment.

"Look, I can only tell you this much." And the boy pulled the blankets off of him, and was preparing to climb out of the bed when there was a noise at the door, and Derek quickly slid his legs back into the bed and whipped the covers up over him.

"What!" Zale asked, shocked, looking at the boy for some form of answer.

"Just close your eyes and act like you're sleeping, now!" Derek hissed.

Zale did as he was told. He was scared, and he was trembling under his blankets, but he didn't know why. He looked over his covers at Derek, and he was sunken into his blankets like a turtle in his shell. Zale closed his eyes again, and mimicked the boy's actions, when he heard another noise. It was the door. Zale wanted to look to see who it was entering their room, but something told him that he dare not.

He listened, and heard the sound of slippers dragging across the bare wood floor.

"*Sssssssppppppp, sssssspppppppp!*" It sounded like someone slowly sanding a piece of wood. Then the sound would stop. Then Zale would hear it again, louder, nearer, and it would stop, and he figured that it was Mrs. Connors checking up to see if the boys were asleep.

Then he heard her again, this time nearer to his bed. She was at the bed next to his. Not at Derek's bed, but the one on the other side of him. She was there, very near to Zale, and he could feel her presence almost over him, could smell her cheap-smelling perfume. Then he heard the springs of the bed squeal softly, and he heard Mrs. Connors speak.

"Wake up, Tony. You know it's your turn," she said, happiness in her voice. "It's time for another encounter with Mommy."

Zale heard the boy squirm about in bed.

Zale heard the boy getting up from his bed. Then he heard the slippers again, and the boy's bare feet, softly slapping against the bare floor as they made their way toward the door. Zale turned around and caught a glimpse of them, Mrs. Connors in a big white nightgown, holding the hand of the little boy just before they stepped out of the room.

Zale spun around in bed, flipped his legs over the edge, sitting up, facing Derek's bunk.

"Where are they going? Where is she taking him?" Zale asked, wanting answers.

Derek threw the covers off him again, but just lay there in bed, not saying anything.

"Well!" Zale said. Then there was a scream. It was a high-pitched, bloodcurdling scream, and Zale knew it came from the boy. Then, after that, there was the sound of laughing. A loud, hard cackling, and Zale knew that belonged to Mrs. Connors.

"What is she doing to him!" Zale said frantically.

Derek was sitting up in bed now, his legs over the edge like Zale's, and then Zale noticed that all the other boys were sitting up in bed as well.

"What is she doing!"

Derek shook his head. "I told you, you don't want to know."

"Why?" Zale said, becoming aggravated.

"Because that will be you tomorrow night."

The first thing Zale did that morning was to find the boy who slept next to him. When Zale pulled himself out of bed that morning, the boy wasn't there, just the bed made neatly as if it hadn't been slept in the night before, or never before, for that matter. When Zale finally found the boy, he was in the playroom by himself, at a desk, assembling a puzzle with little enthusiasm.

"Hi," Zale said, walking up behind him.

The boy turned a little, looked over his shoulder, then nodded his head casually at Zale without saying a word, going back to the puzzle.

"What happened to you last night?" Zale asked.

The boy looked at Zale again, this time devoting more attention to the stare.

"What are you talking about?" he said, as if he had no idea.

"Mrs. Connors came and got you out of bed last night. Then we heard you screaming. That was you screaming we heard, wasn't it?"

The boy turned around in his chair, facing Zale straight on.

"You ain't heard nobody screaming. And if you did, it wasn't me because I was right there in bed. Mrs. Connors never came to get me. You must have been dreaming."

"I wasn't dreaming," Zale said, angered that the boy was lying to him.

"You must've been, because I was asleep in my bed all night." The boy looked at Zale for a long moment, and it looked as if he was trying to see if Zale believed the lie. The boy turned back around, but Zale didn't leave just yet. He just stood there, still angry that the boy was trying to hide what was going on. Then the boy looked over his shoulder again, probably to see if Zale was still there, and when he saw that he was, he quickly turned his attention back to what he was doing.

That night, Zale lay in his bed, his covers pulled up to his chin, his fists wrapped around the blanket. It was a warm night, and he was sweating like crazy, but the blankets seemed to be his only protection against whatever it was that was supposed to happen to him.

"Just go to sleep," Derek told Zale right after they got in bed, which was an hour ago, but Zale couldn't go to sleep. He lay awake, his eyes wide open, jumping and twitching at every noise he heard in the darkness. Zale got to the point where he didn't think he could take the waiting anymore. It was almost driving him crazy, and he thought of stepping out of bed, walking out of that room and finding Mrs. Connors, and asking her what in the hell was supposed to happen. It was the question that he had suppressed asking her a thousand times today.

Zale moved slightly within the warm sheets and blankets that were making him sweat, trying to find a position that he could fall asleep in.

"You still awake," a voice came from the bunk next to Zale's. It was Derek.

"I can't go to sleep. I'm scared."

Derek blew out a long sigh. "Don't be scared, man."

"Why not?" Zale said, his fists still wrapped around the top of the blanket.

"I don't know, just don't be. But let me tell you this . . . you listening?"

"Yeah."

"Think about something else," Derek said. "I always think I'm out fishing with my daddy. We used to go out to the lake early in the morning when it was still dark, and we used to light a lantern till the sun came up."

A bit of light came in the window from the moon, lighting a corner of Derek's face. Zale saw a smile lengthen across his face, a distant look appearing in his eyes.

"That was before he got shot," Derek said, his eyes clearing, snapping back to reality. "But that's what I do. I just think I'm somewhere else, and it helps. At least a little."

"What do you mean, think I'm somewhere else? Why? When?" Zale said, becoming frustrated. "Derek!" Zale whispered, but there came a noise, and Derek quickly burrowed under his blankets, like a rabbit going underground, fleeing an enemy.

Zale froze, and although his body was wet with sweat, he felt cold chills race through it. He lay there, not making a move, or a sound, his eyes shut so tightly that they started to ache. He heard the sound of Mrs. Connors's slippers against the bare floor, and each time he heard them, the sound become louder and louder, till it was right upon him. Then it stopped.

Zale lay as still as he could, trying to breathe normally, as if he were actually in a sound sleep, praying that she walk past him, leave him be, but he felt a cold hand on his forehead. It smoothed some of the sweat away that had accumulated there.

"You're sweating," Zale heard Mrs. Connors's voice say. "You have too many clothes on."

Zale didn't say a word, just remained there still as a corpse.

"I know you're not sleeping, Mr. Rowen. I'm sure you heard what goes on here, and you would be far too nervous to sleep. But everything will be fine," she said, pulling the covers down from on top of Zale's small body. "It's just time for you to have your first encounter with Mommy."

Zale abandoned the sleeping act, and he was looking at her now. Her face was all done up like she was going on a date. Eyeliner, blush, a mouth full of bright red lipstick, and when she smiled, Zale could see the paint smeared across the front of her teeth.

She wore a huge white gown, like the one she wore last night, and her hair was done up in huge curls, cemented in place by cans of holding spray.

Mrs. Connors grabbed Zale's hand and tried pulling him out of bed.

"I don't want to go," Zale resisted, pulling back weakly.

Mrs. Connors smiled, canting her head to one side. "Awww, that's so sweet. Little man doesn't want to go. But everything will be just fine. Trust me," she said, pulling at Zale again.

But Zale yanked his hand from out of Mrs. Connors's grasp, recoiling back into what little safety the bed provided.

Mrs. Connors looked down on Zale, shaking her head as if she had gone through this a million times before. The smile she wore remained on her mouth, but her eyes were filled with anger. She bent down over Zale and said in a hushed, threatening tone, "You will come with me, little man, or the next place you'll go is on the street. This is all you have, because no one wants a grown little black boy like you. Nobody. Not even your drugged-out, prostituting mother. Now, come on!"

She grabbed Zale tightly by the wrist and walked him toward the door. Before leaving the room, Zale looked back at Derek, and saw the same sympathetic expression on his face as the first time Zale saw him.

Mrs. Connors pushed Zale into a small bedroom and closed the door behind them. The first thing that Zale noticed was how bright the light was. He looked up to see three high-wattage bulbs shining down on the room like an electric sun, casting hard, dark shadows on everything, and illuminating every crevice and corner of the room.

There was a huge bed in the room, the corners seeming to stretch out and touch each of the four walls, allowing only enough room for a chair, placed against one of the walls, and a small nightstand, on which a number of bottles of oils and lubricants sat.

Mrs. Connors sat down in the chair like a man, her knees spread apart, her nightgown hiked up, staring at Zale.

Zale had no idea why she pulled him out of bed, why he was there, and why she was just staring at him, and those questions reflected on his face.

"Don't act like you don't know what's going on. Take off your clothes!" Mrs. Connors ordered.

Zale looked at her like she was crazy, or like he didn't trust his ears in properly relaying to his brain what was actually said.

"You heard what I said." Mrs. Connors leaned forward in her chair, reached behind her back and pulled a leather belt from off the back of the chair, and slapped the folded belt against her hand. "Now we can make this easy, or we can make it hard. It doesn't matter to me, because either way, I'm going to get mine," and the look she gave Zale made his skin crawl. He unbuttoned his pajama top and let it fall to the floor.

"The stylish trousers, too, little man. And don't forget the undies."

Zale let his pajama pants fall to the floor, stepped out of them, then hesitantly slid his underpants off. He stood there, his thin boyish frame shaking, his arms wrapped around himself, his body hunched over trying to hide as much of his nakedness as possible.

"Now get on the bed and lie on your back," she said.

"But why?" Zale asked in a barely audible voice.

"Just do what I said!" Mrs. Connors yelled.

Zale crawled to the bed and lay on his back. He still didn't know what was happening, and he didn't want to know. He turned his head away from the woman, and closed his eyes against the bright light that was coming from the three bare bulbs overhead. He was pleading, begging God that this was all just a dream, that he would wake up in his bed in the morning. Then he heard Mrs. Connors moving, the fabric of her gown moving about. Zale didn't want to know what was going on, but he felt compelled to turn his head and look, and what he saw was Mrs. Connors pulling the gown over her head. Zale saw her standing there naked. He saw her large, pink, inflated body, saw the green veins traveling up through her huge misshapen breasts. He saw the orange patch of pubic hair that grew out of control in between her legs, and he saw the long Frankenstein monster–looking scar that ran up the center of her round belly.

Zale quickly whipped his head back around, wishing he could blank the image out of his mind.

"That's right. It's all yours tonight," Mrs. Connors said. "And you don't know it now, but you're going to be thanking me for what I'm going to give to your young ass."

Mrs. Connors grabbed Zale's right hand and directed it in between her legs, and started to jab herself there.

Zale felt the coarseness of her hair brush across his hand, through his fingers. He felt the heat and stickiness of her feminine anatomy, and then he felt his stomach begin to turn.

"Yeah, you see what you're getting. A real woman. You don't know that yet, but you will see, little man. Oh, you will see."

And then Zale felt the bed give greatly on one end, and he felt a part of her cold body touch his, and he wanted to scoot away, but he told himself he dare not move.

He smelled her awful perfume again, mixed with the sweat coming from under her arms, and the odor from in between her legs. Then Zale felt her breath on the side of his face. Mrs. Connors kissed him on the cheek, then baby-kissed him all over his face, working her way to his lips. She kissed him on the mouth, and when he turned his head away, she grabbed his chin with one of her huge hands and held his face straight up. She continued kissing him on the mouth, and tried to pry his mouth open with her tongue, but when he wouldn't let her, she abandoned her attempts and started to kiss him on the neck. Then she kissed him on the collarbone, on his chest, circling his nipples with her tongue. She kissed him on his stomach, steadily working her way down, and all the while, Zale felt himself becoming increasingly more sick.

Mrs. Connors grabbed Zale in between his legs. "You're going to like this, little man," she said, then took him into her mouth.

"You like that, don't you. Say you like that!" she warbled up to him, but the chaos in Zale's head would not allow him to understand the question, let alone answer it.

She continued what she was doing, grabbing him, sucking him, and he realized what she was doing, but he told himself that he wouldn't allow her to ready him, would not allow her to get him there, because he knew what she would do with him next. But she continued working on him, and he begged his body not to react. Then Zale felt his sickness getting worse. He felt his stomach flip in retaliation to what she was doing. But she kept on, and his stomach turned again, and he felt his insides, boiling, rumbling, like a pot of nauseating stew on a high flame. Then he felt the fluids start to race around in his belly, trying to find the opening in which they could free themselves, and at the last moment, when he felt he could no longer hold it, Zale turned his head to the side and spewed his insides out all over the side of the bed and floor.

"You nasty little bastard!" Mrs. Connors said, looking up at him angrily, but then she looked down at her hands, and within a second her expression changed to one of happiness.

"Well, look what we have here. Mission accomplished," she said, getting to all fours, working her way back up toward Zale.

"About that mess you made, I'll beat your ass later, and make you clean that up, but now I'm about to make a man out of you."

Mrs. Connors straddled Zale's small body with her large legs, grabbed behind her, and tried to guide Zale into her.

"No! No!" Zale screamed, beating at her, wriggling around, trying to topple her off him. "Why are you doing this! Why?"

She looked down at him, with bulging, rage-filled eyes. "You want to play hard! Is that what you want!" Then she stuck one of her huge hands into Zale's neck, and clamped it around his throat, cutting off his air, and casually went back to trying to insert Zale into her.

"I try and do you a favor, try to make a man out of you, and look what thanks you give me." Zale felt her wetness against his organ, felt himself penetrate her. Then he felt her let herself all the way down on him.

Mrs. Connors gritted her teeth, shut her eyes, and let out a grumbling moan, then started to gyrate around on top of him.

Zale still couldn't breathe, for the big woman's hand remained on his throat. He was feeling light-headed, and his vision was becoming hazy, but he saw this big, sweat-covered woman, strands of red hair plastered to her face, moaning and moving around on top of him.

Zale felt hot tears stream from the corners of his eyes, race down the sides of his face, and again he asked himself, Why? Why is she doing this to me? What have I done wrong to deserve this? And just before he blacked out, before he felt he would die, he heard her voice.

"I'm going to let you breathe, but when I do, there ain't going to be no more fighting. We're going to fuck like grown-ups, and if I get any more shit out of you, I swear, I'll kill you next time," and she tightened her grip around his neck, just before letting go, to prove it.

■ ■ ■

Tears came to Zale's eyes and dropped to the table. He quickly brushed the tracks away from his face, then looked up at Laura for only a moment, then looked down at his hands.

"I'm sorry," he said. "I have to deal with that enough in my dreams. I don't like to go back there voluntarily."

Laura gave Zale a moment to compose himself, then she asked him, "How long did that continue to go on?"

"Once a week," Zale said, still smoothing the tears away. "There were some nights when it was quick, when it didn't take much to please her. Then there were nights when the torture lasted for hours and hours. It continued like that for almost six years, then it lessened, then it stopped altogether when I was sixteen."

"What made her stop?"

Zale dug his thumb and forefinger into the inner corners of his eyes.

"I really don't want to talk about that right now."

"Why didn't you or any of the other boys say anything to anybody about it?" Laura said.

Zale looked across the table at her sternly. "We had a home! Someplace warm, clean, and dry we could lay our heads at night. Yes, we were getting abused, but if we said something, we feared we would've ended up on the street. On the street, kids got abused just like we were, but they had nothing."

Laura shook her head, making no comment. "Have you ever received any help for what you went through? Counseling, or advisement of any kind?"

"My work is my help. Call it self-help," Zale said, staring Laura straight in the eyes.

"It helps you cope with the dreams, the memories?"

"Yes."

"How does it do that?"

"If nothing else, it keeps me busy, so I don't have time to think about it."

"And how often do those thoughts bother you?"

"Almost all the time."

"So is that the real reason you work so hard, work so many hours, and go after these men so relentlessly? So you have something to occupy your mind with other than the horrible memories from your childhood?"

Zale looked at her oddly, and wondered what she was trying to get at. He thought her purpose here was to try to help him, but for some reason he was feeling as though he was being attacked.

"No," Zale said, an edge to his voice. "I go after these men, and work as hard as I do, because that's what's required. That's what it takes."

"But you said it was therapy. You're telling me those events that took place in your childhood don't serve as any form of motivation?"

Of course they did, Zale thought. He remembered during the first days of Father Found, the paint had not completely dried on the door of their building when a young boy stood outside of it, looking in. He appeared lost. Zale went to the door, opened it.

"Can I help you with something?"

The boy, he looked nine or ten, glanced up shyly at Zale, then back to the paint on the glass door.

"You look for people's fathers?" The boy said it in a way that suggested he was hoping the answer would be yes, but knew it would be no.

The boy's name was Taylor. His father had left a month ago, but before that, he would beat Taylor once, twice a week. The boy said it was the drugs. Said he didn't know why it made his father do those things to him, but he knew for sure that it was definitely the drugs and not his father.

His mother told him to forget about the man. That he wasn't worth thinking about. But Taylor came to Father Found without even letting her know. During the time he was gone, sometimes Taylor would see his father on the street, sometimes lucid, behaving normally, but most times he was strung out, lying against some building, passing a crack pipe between so-called friends.

Taylor would go to his father, try to pull him up, drag him away from those people, that place. But the man would just smack his son's hands away, yell obscenities at him, tell him to forget about him, just like the boy's mother had told him.

One night, late, Zale, the boy, and Frank rolled up on him. Taylor Sr. was sitting out on the stairs of an abandoned building by himself.

Frank parked the car, and Zale and Frank got out. They walked up to the man, stood in front of him. It took a moment for him to lift his head, and another for his eyes to find their way to the faces of the men standing before him. He was gaunt, his eyes cloudy, his face dark and dirty, and his clothes were past the point where they should've been burned.

"Excuse me, sir," Zale said. "Are you Taylor Jenkins, Sr.?"

The man's eyes seemed to focus more intensely on Zale, then he nodded.

"Yeah, that's me. Who's askin'?"

And before Zale could respond, Frank was behind Taylor, wrestling his arms behind his back.

"Don't be so hard on him," Zale said, trying to protect the man from harm while trying to stay out of Frank's way.

"He's the one being hard on me," Frank said, still fighting with the man, ducking a lazy swing Taylor Sr. threw at him. Frank bent his arms back and cuffed them.

"What are you doing to me!" Taylor screamed as Frank dragged him toward the car.

"I'm sorry, sir, but we need for you to come with us," Zale said, yelling into the man's face, over his ranting. "Right now you don't see it, but this is the best thing for you."

"Let me the fuck go!" Taylor yelled, kicking his foot out against the car, trying not to be thrown into it. He fought like an animal. Zale opened the backseat door. Taylor struggled some more, trying to kick Frank to free himself, trying to bite Frank's hands, his arms. But Frank had him from behind, forced him to double over, and in the direction of the open door, and that's when Taylor saw his son. Taylor Jr. looked frightened, as if the man that was before him was not his father, never could've been. Taylor Sr. must have read that look, for he calmed some, allowed himself to be handled, placed in the car quietly, next to his son. Frank and Zale got in the car and drove off.

It took a painful month of long nights, yelling, cursing, and talking to get the man through his addiction.

"Cold turkey" is what Frank said was the best approach, and that's the method they used. Zale knew it wasn't humane, and probably even against the law, but he locked Taylor Sr. in his office for the duration.

There they would take shifts, helping him through the fits, through the bouts of throwing up, the high fevers, night sweats, and the many threats he would make of killing Martin, Zale, and Frank if they didn't let him out of "this goddamn tiny-ass room!"

His son would come by every day to see him, and would have to be told to leave at night so his mother would not become suspicious of what he was doing. She couldn't know about this till the man was over it, clean, because if she did, she would pull her son away from him, and his presence was vital.

It took a month, but at the end of that month, Taylor Sr. was clean and thankful for what Father Found had done for him. Zale was able to find him a job at a tool-casting factory. That was two years ago, and now, every month, the Jenkins family invites Zale to their home for dinner. They are happy. Taylor still holds his job, the beatings of the boy have stopped, and now there is an obvious appreciation for his son, his family, his job, and the fact that he was so close to losing them.

"Mr. Rowen"—Zale heard Laura's voice finding its way into his mind—"did the events that took place in your childhood serve as motivation for you to go after these fathers?"

"No!" Zale said, slapping his hand down on the desk. "The motivation comes from the desire to get these fathers back with their damn children. The motivation comes from seeing the good it does a child when he sees his father after a number of months or years and finds out that the man still cares for him, loves him. And the motivation comes from knowing that there are two parents now, so if, God forbid, something happens to one of them, these kids won't be bounced around to relatives' houses, live in the street, or be shipped off to some foster home and have to—"

"Go through what you went through, Mr. Rowen?"

Zale didn't answer the question, just sat there, a hand to his chin, thinking, resenting the questions she was firing at him.

Laura returned his stare for a moment, then asked him another question. "When you think about these men you deal with, is there a negative feeling you get?"

"What are you getting at, Ms. Eckert?" Zale asked, looking at her suspiciously.

"I'm just asking questions," Laura said, sidestepping the real question. "Do you get a negative feeling—"

"I tell you how I feel about this," Zale interrupted, "why I'm doing what I'm doing, and you turn my words all around like I'm lying or something. I have no reason to lie about this."

"Well, answer the question I just asked you," Laura instructed him.

"No, I won't!" Zale said, springing from his chair, leaning over the desk. "I came to you looking for help. I spill my guts about things I've never told anyone else, shed tears in front of you like some grown-ass baby, and now you're talking to me like I'm on trial for murder. What are you trying to get at!" Zale asked forcefully.

"What's bothering you!" Laura said, still sitting in her chair, almost equaling his emotion.

Zale heard what she said, but didn't know if it was a statement or a question.

"What is bothering you, Mr. Rowen?" Laura asked this time.

Zale looked at her, then around the room, as if he were in third grade, clueless about the answer to a tough history question.

"These thoughts, these dreams, everything that happened . . . why are they still bothering you? Why do they plague you, making your life almost unbearable, and don't ever seem to stop even though these things happened to you twenty years ago?"

"I don't know," Zale said, feeling defeated.

"That's what I'm getting at." She gave Zale a long, concerned look. "Please sit down."

Zale slowly lowered himself into his seat, folded his hands on the desk, and waited for the next question, deciding he would trust whatever route she was taking in trying to help him, if only for a moment.

"I get the impression that you don't think very much of men who leave their children," Laura said.

"That's the right impression."

"And the man that left you and your mother, I'd assume you don't think very much of him either."

Zale readjusted himself in his seat. "No, I don't think very much of him. I'm sure I wouldn't like the man, and I think he was a coward for what he did."

"Is that because you think his leaving put you in the position that you were in? Was that the main reason you had to go to the foster home, went through the hell you went through? Do you hold him responsible for that?"

"I can't deny the fact that if he was there, my mother wouldn't have had to raise me by herself. Be the father and the mother. Work for every single dollar that came into the house, solve every problem, and handle every chore. If he was there, she wouldn't have succumbed like she did, and she would've never lost me."

"And that makes you angry at him, yes?"

"Of course it does," Zale said, without hesitation.

"It makes you angry with him for what he did, and it makes you angry when you think about all the other men who are doing exactly what your father did, and you see all those children moving into the same dark tunnel because of them. Because of these men, those children's lives are doomed. That's how you see it, right?"

She wasn't exactly right, but she was close enough, so Zale nodded his head.

Laura paused for a long moment, and just stared into Zale's eyes. He didn't know what that was about, but he just returned her stare till she spoke again.

"You said, your father left when you were just a baby, right?"

"That's right."

"So you didn't even know him, or what kind of man he was."

Zale didn't answer verbally, and the shaking of his head indicating no was barely noticeable.

"Now, I'm about to say some things, and ask you a few more questions," Laura said, and she extended her flattened hand out on the desk near Zale as if she were making an attempt to touch him, comfort him. "I don't want you to get angry, because this is still all in the attempt to find out what's wrong. Okay?"

Zale didn't say anything, just pulled his hands off the desk and crossed his arms over his chest, leaning back in his chair.

"Mr. Rowen, I know a lot of people who have been raised by just one parent, just their mother, and they are happy, well-rounded, level-headed, and, in one way or another, successful people.

"You say your mother had to work for every dollar. That's nothing new to the world. There are single mothers out there caring for two, three, even four children, and somehow they manage to do it. You say she succumbed to the pressures of life. What made her succumb? Was it your father leaving, or was it something that she did? Did your father make her turn to drugs? Did your father make her start beating you? Did your father tell her to sell her body, lock you up in the house alone for days?"

"But if he hadn't left, she wouldn't have had to resort to that," Zale defended.

"Are you saying those were the only choices? They were her choices. She chose them. After the people came and took you away, did your father stop your mother from visiting you? Did he tell her to stop coming altogether?"

"He wasn't there to tell her to stop coming," Zale said, frustrated with the woman's line of questioning.

"It seems to me that you're blaming everything you went through on your father, and in turn directing those feelings toward other men who leave their children. You look at them and you see your father's face, and you don't consider what their reasons or intentions are for leaving, just that they are leaving. So you go after them, not just trying to reunite them with their children, not just with the notion that you're trying to save these children from what they may go through, but you go after these fathers with this undying fire, this blood-boiling passion, as if somehow, maybe, possibly, you can save your life, too. That if you can get these men back with their children, you can somehow undo all the wrongs that were done to you, make the pain of your father leaving you disappear. Is that true, Mr. Rowen?"

Zale said nothing.

"But therein lies the problem. I don't think it's your father you're truly angry at. I think it's your mother. But because she did her best, tried all she could, but failed, you don't believe that anger should be directed toward her. I'm thinking this is the issue that has to be re-solved. I'm thinking this is the link that every other problem you're having is attaching itself to, and if we can rid you of this problem, then we will put ourselves firmly on the road to recovery." Laura leaned forward on the desk, and looked intently into Zale's eyes.

"What do you think about that?"

Zale just stared at her through eyes red with rage. He tried to continue to control himself, as he had been doing while she was tearing down the one person in this world that he loved unconditionally, and that he knew loved him equally as much. This woman before him, who didn't know him from one of the derelicts off the streets whom she counseled, was trying to tell *him* how he feels about his family, when all she heard of them is what he told her. She was trying to tell him what was causing his problems, when she had no idea of what it feels like to suffer through a migraine so strong that it makes you feel you want to slam your head in the door of a car. Or feel so fatigued that you fall asleep standing in the shower, regardless of how cold the water is beating you in the face. She'd never felt so troubled, and so lonely, felt such a huge emptiness living in the pit of her stomach, and growing throughout her entire body, that she just walked the dark, damp streets late at night, like Zale had, his collar up around his ears, his face buried in his chest, not looking at anyone in the face as he passes them, and not allowing anyone to see him, but concentrating on what little he has, what few people he knew, and how he seemed to be failing terribly at what he considered the true definition of his life. She has never felt any of that, Zale thought. Yet she sits here in front of me, suggesting how *we* can get on to the road of recovery!

There was a metallic taste in Zale's mouth, and it made him realize that he was biting down so hard on the inside of his cheek that blood was oozing from the wound onto his tongue.

"What do you think, Mr. Rowen?" Zale heard Laura's voice again.

Zale pulled himself out of his fury-filled thoughts and refocused on her.

"You want to know what I think?" he said through clenched teeth, standing from his chair.

Laura looked up at Zale, a subtle smile on her face, as though he was about to speak words of enlightenment in agreement with her assessment of him.

But what Zale did was reach down, grab the back of his chair with both hands, hoist it up, rear back, and fling the thing over Laura's head toward the far end of the room, where it crashed into a water cooler, shattering the glass bowl with a deafening crash, sending tiny shards of glass, carried by a wave of water, across the floor.

Laura was bent over, almost completely under the table, both hands covering her head, because the chair seemed to have missed her head by only inches.

Zale stood there in front of the desk, breathing hard, more from his anger than the energy exerted.

"You don't know what the hell you're talking about!" Zale yelled, when he saw Laura slowly rising up from under the desk. "My mother loved me, and she did all she could for us!" He was pointing at her, his finger shaking violently as he spoke.

"What I went through was not her fault. It was not her fault!" Then he looked over at the broken glass on the floor, the stream of water running from it, the chair sitting on its end, and the woman that tried to help him cowering, her eyes round with horror, as if she feared for her life. Zale was somewhat sorry for what he had just done. He thought about apologizing, but what difference would it make? What difference did anything make?

CHAPTER NINETEEN

Frank sat, parked in a desolate lot near a shipping yard. It was a hot, hazy morning, and the sun poked through the clouds, beaming down on Frank's car, baking him in it like a metal oven.

Frank wrapped his hand around another can of beer, pulled it from the plastic ring, and popped it open with his other hand. Manipulating the tab on the beer can hurt, and Frank had to think a moment why that was.

He realized that the pain in his hands was a result of the beating he had given the last guy he tried to convince to return to his family.

Frank took a swig from the beer that had now turned warm from sitting in the warm car, then looked at the back of his hand. His knuckles were still slightly swollen and scarred. He had misplaced his brass knuckles that day, but on occasion there was nothing like the bare feeling of a man's facial bones shattering under the force of a good punch.

Frank took another swig of his beer, and opened and closed his hand before him, feeling the soreness throughout his fingers and hands. He really didn't have to hit him. Frank tried to remember his name, but it escaped him. Jackson, or Johnson, or maybe Meyers. The names all started to blend together in a long list of faceless individuals, and that could've been because he was racing through so many of their files lately, or it could've had something to do with the fact that lately he had been drinking as if his body needed it to function, like a car needed gasoline.

Frank remembered going through the doors of a large bank and walking toward the back offices. A tall, thin woman jumped from her desk and stood in front of him.

"I'm sorry, sir. Can I help you?"

Frank looked her up and down, entertaining the idea that she may have made a decent lay, then pushed her aside with one hand, and said, "No, sweetheart, I know exactly where I'm going."

Frank saw the wide door, "Peter Mason" on the nameplate. He grabbed the doorknob and flung the door open.

"How ya doin', Pete?" Frank said to the well-dressed man behind the huge oak desk.

Mr. Mason stood from his desk, shocked, and gave his secretary an angry stare. She was standing at the door behind Frank, an apologetic look on her face.

"Don't blame her, Pete," Frank said, slowly walking toward the desk. "She can't handle all your business. There's some things that you have to take care of yourself, and let me tell you, this is one of them. This is definitely one of them," Frank said, chuckling, a sly smile on his face.

"Should I call Security?" the secretary squealed.

Frank gave Mr. Mason a hard look, shaking his head no.

"No, just leave," Mr. Mason said.

"And tell her to close the door behind her," Frank instructed.

Mr. Mason did so.

Frank took a seat in front of the desk, and told Mr. Mason to sit. The man did as he was told.

"I can't count how many times I've come by here and left you flyers and notices, left my fucking card with your long-legged secretary, and told her to tell you to call me back. I can't count the times, but guess what, you never called. Now that has to be because when you got the messages and notices, you looked at them, laughed, and said, to hell with all that. That dumb fuck can kiss my ass. Or it was because your secretary out there just forgot to pass all that along to you, and I'm hoping for your sake it was the latter. Which was it, Pete?" Frank asked, leaning back comfortably in the leather chair.

"I got the messages," Mr. Mason said, and he was holding up fairly well, Frank thought, but he saw his cheek quivering a little, like he had a nervous twitch, and Frank liked to see that. It made him feel in control, like he had power over the poor man.

"Then why didn't you call Father Found?"

Mr. Mason looked at him, like the question was delivered to him in a foreign language.

"What the hell are you looking at?" Frank said, raising his voice, leaning forward in the chair. "I asked you why didn't you call Father Found?"

"Because I didn't have time," Mr. Mason said, then he looked at Frank, as if waiting to see if the answer was approved or rejected.

"That's not good enough. You make freakin' phone calls all day back here. You didn't have time to make one more? Now I'm going to ask you again, and this time I want to tell you that things are a little different now down at old FF. I have a little more authority, and if this doesn't work the way it should, I'm going to leave you with more than my card."

Frank scooted forward in his chair and stacked his forearms on the desk, and stared square into Mr. Mason's eyes.

"Now, why didn't you phone Father Found?"

Mr. Mason swallowed hard. The muscles tightened in his jaws, and he lifted his head up as if to take a stand.

"Because I didn't want to," he said, courage in his voice.

Frank leaned over the desk, and with his right fist, casually punched the man in the mouth. Mr. Mason fell back into his chair, and threw both hands over his face.

"Wrong answer," Frank said plainly, shaking that right hand, feeling as though he may have cut his knuckles against the man's teeth.

"You don't go making decisions like that for yourself, not when you have kids, you don't. They depend on—"

"Who do you think you are?" Mr. Mason said, his voice muffled, yelling from behind the hands that covered his face.

"What?"

"Who in the hell do you think you are?" Mr. Mason dropped his hand. His lip was split and blood oozed from the wound. Blood was smeared about his lips and chin; he looked like an infant who rejected the taste of his strained tomatoes.

"I'm Father Found," Frank said, standing from his chair. "That's who the hell I am."

"You just can't come in this office and think you can bully me into doing whatever you want by—"

And before he could finish his sentence, Frank reached over his desk, grabbed him by the lapel of his suit, and hit him again. But this time, Frank did not connect cleanly, because the man was trying to fight Frank off, throwing up his arms over his face, trying to bat punches away with his hands, and that just angered Frank more.

Frank pulled the fighting man closer to him. All the papers, pens, photos, and other objects that covered the desk went spinning to the floor as Mr. Mason fought, and Frank tried to beat the man into submission.

Frank swung again, this time connecting with the man's right eye. Mr. Mason cried out, and threw both hands over that eye, which left the rest of his face open, and Frank pummeled it with four more blows. When Frank was done with him, Mr. Mason no longer fought, nor did he cover his wounds, trying to defend himself against another assault. His arms fell to his sides, his face was a bloody mess, as was his shirt and suit jacket, as were Frank's fists.

Frank pushed the man backward, and he landed in his chair with a grunt.

"You lay down and have kids, and you don't want to see them, or take care of them. You don't know how lucky you are to even have that choice."

Of all the debris that was knocked to the floor from Mason's desk, a photo caught Frank's eye. It was a picture of two little girls smiling. Their faces were freckled, the two front teeth missing from each of their mouths.

Frank shook his head in disgust.

"They're good enough to display, but not good enough to spend time with."

Frank leaned over the desk and placed the picture gently on the man's bloodstained shirt.

"Father Found's not going to allow this shit from folks like you anymore. We just aren't. So unless you want more of the same, I would do the right thing and take your ass home. Your children won't wait any longer, and, more important, neither will I."

Frank opened the door a crack.

"And one more thing, don't think about going to the police about this. I was a cop, and I'm connected, so let's just keep this between us. See you around, Pete."

That same day, he opened Peter Mason's file and checked the box "Father will return home," confident that when Mr. Mason was called there, he would be the one answering the phone, or the wife would inform Father Found that Mr. Mason intended to start making child-support payments pronto, and happily at that.

Again Frank was almost amazed at how a little force could get men to act right, and make his job a whole hell of a lot easier. He realized it the first time he was forced to use his hands, and the few times after that. But then Martin called Frank in his office, asking him all sorts of questions about the files and the return rate that he was achieving. Frank thought that Martin was either just trying to find another way of messing with his head, or that he may have actually been on to something.

On that day, he decided that he would stop with the beatings, and the only time he would use force was when his life was in direct jeopardy. But two weeks ago, Rowen himself pulled Frank into his office. He told Frank to have a seat. The first thing that Frank noticed was how bad the man looked, worse than Frank had ever seen him.

Zale Rowen looked as though he had not slept in three or four days, and when he had rested, it looked as though the wrinkled, dirty clothes he was wearing were the ones he tossed about in during his sleep. His hair was barely combed and the stubble on his face made it look as though he had shaved that morning with a dull butter knife.

Zale was sitting behind his desk, his hands crossed on top of it, just staring at Frank, looking as if he was using all his strength just to keep his head from dropping to the surface of his desk.

Frank didn't know why Zale had brought him in to see him. He rarely did that—Martin Carter usually handled whatever business there was concerning Frank—and it led him to believe that maybe one of the men he worked over may have squealed. He may have run to Carter, or Carter may have found him, gotten him to tell them the entire story, and now Zale was about to give him his walking papers.

But Frank couldn't lose his job. Yes, he accepted the fact that he didn't have another chance with his wife, and to save himself the never-ending agony of thinking about his daughter, in his mind, he disowned her. He told himself that as long as his ex-wife was still living, he would probably never see Bianca again. So instead of putting a bullet in Wendy, he told himself he would never think of the little girl again, never see her face in his head, never recall the memories they both shared. He would file that part of his life with Bianca far away in the recesses of his mind. A place where he could never find them, and would never want to. And right after that, he pulled the little pink dragon from his key chain, raised the window of his apartment, and flung the plastic trinket somewhere out into the street. Frank cried that night, but he got it all out.

So now, while he sat in front of a very weary-looking Zale Rowen, Frank feared losing his job, not because of what his wife would think, but because he needed to survive. He needed his job to survive, to put food on the table, to keep his ass out of the cold at night, and give him something to occupy his mind with, so he wouldn't sit on the stoop of some abandoned apartment building with a number of other losers and drink himself into an alcohol-induced coma.

Frank started to think about what he would do with himself if he lost his job, and there was nothing he could do. Could he find another job? Sure, but it wouldn't be on the street, where he was free to do what he wanted, when he wanted. He would probably end up being a security doorman for some ritzy condo building, or a security guard at a bank, fixed up in some blue and gray Barney Fife getup. He would kill himself first.

Frank told himself to deny it. Deny whatever Rowen accused him of. But then he remembered that Rowen had always been straight with him, had always considered his side. Frank decided to tell him, if not everything, something. Tell him that it was life and death, and that it would never happen again.

Frank sat up in his chair, and cleared his voice.

"Mr. Rowen, about what I've been doing."

"That's what I brought you in here to talk to you about," Zale said, his voice low, but firm. "I think you're doing an excellent job. I wanted to tell you that, and, most important, I want to tell you to keep it up, do more of it."

Frank was shocked at what he heard, so much so that he thought his mind was playing tricks on him. He was worried that he had heard wrong, but Zale repeated himself, saying the same thing again.

"Do you know what it is I've been doing?"

Zale brought a slow hand up to his face and rubbed his eyes.

"You're getting the point to these fathers. You're getting them to go back home, and that's what the objective is, and I don't care how you're doing that. All I know is, when I open these files, the right box is checked, and when a phone call is made to those houses, I'm hearing the right information."

"But, Mr. Rowen," Frank said, almost considering telling him the whole truth. Why, he didn't know. Maybe because the man in front of him looked so beaten, and Frank knew that he probably didn't know what he was saying, and if there was any time to come clean about what he had done, this was it. "Mr. Rowen, maybe—"

"Dammit, Frank, I don't care what your method is!" Zale said, exploding for no reason, banging the side of his fist against his desk. He lowered his voice, seeming regretful for the outburst. "It's what we need—now more than ever."

Zale looked up at Frank, and Frank thought that not only did Rowen sound desperate, but he also looked it as well. He looked troubled, as though something had a lock on his brain, and it wouldn't let go, and it was draining whatever strength the man had.

So Frank would help him, because he looked as though he desperately needed help, and when Frank actually thought about it, he liked Rowen, or at least he had no reason to dislike him, and he did believe in him. So Frank would stay after these men, stay on them like the stink on the ass of a two-dollar hooker. He would continue to return the files to the office with the right box checked, and it would be easier now, because he could go to whatever extreme necessary with the permission from the boss to do so. There seemed to be nothing else coming from the tired man, so Frank stood from the chair and was moving toward the door, when he was stopped.

"Why do you think I'm going through all this trouble with this organization?" Zale asked Frank.

Frank thought about the question for a second, then rattled off what for the most part was their mission statement.

"Our goal is to find the fathers of abandoned children and—"

"No, no, no," Zale said, shaking his head. "Why do you think *I* am doing this? Someone just told me that they thought I was doing this for myself. That I was wrongly accusing these men, and that I was taking everything out on them because of something that was bad in my past." Zale paused. "Do you think they're right?"

Frank took a couple of steps closer to Zale's desk. He looked at him, seeing that this man seemed to be questioning everything he devoted his life toward, that he had no idea of what was true or most important in his life.

"Mr. Rowen, I think . . . I know you're doing this for the children," Frank said, with sincerity. "And about that other business. They're wrong. Dead wrong."

A slow, thin smile lengthened across Zale's face, and Frank returned the smile.

That was two weeks ago, and since then, Frank did what he told Zale he would do. He continued to make men do right by their women and children by whatever means necessary.

Frank sucked down the last of his beer, crumpled the can in his fist, and tossed it out the window, along with the other empty cans. He had one can left and considered downing it right there, but he had to go to work, so he slipped it in his glove box. It gave him something to look forward to after work.

Frank drove over to Father Found, and even though he felt as though his brain was wrapped in a thin layer of cotton, he parked his car, he assumed, better than any man could have, buzzed off of cheap beer so early in the morning. He jumped out of his car and was making his way to the door when he saw two black men blocking the entrance. One of them was a huge, hulking man with dark-brown skin. The muscles of his shoulders and arms made his tiny shirt appear like a second skin, and his head was shaved to reflect the morning sun, his eyes covered with dark lenses. The other man, a smaller man, wore dark shades as well, his hair tied back with a rubber band. They sat in the doorway, on the stoop, as if the building was their home.

Frank stopped in front of them, expecting them to clear a path, let him through, but when they didn't move, didn't even acknowledge him, Frank said, "Do you mind getting out of the way? People have to come in and out of here. If you want to shoot the breeze, the bus stop is on the corner."

The man with the ponytail looked up at Frank, tilted his glasses down just a little to expose his hazel eyes, then, with his tongue, rolled the toothpick from one corner of his mouth to the other.

"Was that supposed to be funny?" Mace said, standing, which prompted the big man beside him to stand.

"No, it wasn't," Frank said, not intimidated at all by the two thugs. "I was just telling you, that people have to get by here, and that by you sitting here, it's making that pretty difficult. If you took any offense to that, that's your problem."

"You work here?"

"Yeah."

"Well, I'm waiting here for Zaleford Rowen. I've been looking for him for the past few days. You know where he's at?"

Frank looked both men up and down, and they looked like trouble. The type of trouble that Frank felt he was hired to protect Zale against. Frank searched his memory, trying to remember if he had ever possessed a file with one of these guys' mugs stapled to it, but neither of them looked familiar.

"I'm not his keeper, so I don't know where he's at." Then Frank patted himself down. "And he doesn't seem to be in any of my pockets, so I guess you guys are out of luck. So if you don't mind, I'm going to really have to ask you to move on."

"Have a seat, Kronk," Mace instructed the big man. "I told you that

I'm waiting for Rowen. Now if you got to get through, you can walk your ass on, but until I see my man, we ain't going nowhere, whether you asking or not."

"Well, let me make myself a little more clear," Frank said, looking over his shoulder, and as he did that, his right hand slipped into his jacket pocket, and he slipped on his brass knuckles. Upon first seeing these men, Frank had already sized up the big guy. Frank was sure he could take him. Most guys his size were overconfident, thinking that the size of their body was directly related to their ability to fight. They were oftentimes wrong. The one that Frank had to be cautious of was the smaller one. He looked devious, and dangerous. The type that would fight with a razor blade concealed within the spaces of his fingers. But in the end, Frank was sure he could handle both of them.

"I was asking you to move because I was trying to be polite. But if that doesn't work for you guys, I will haul both of your asses away from this building like they do the trash every Thursday morning."

At that remark, the big man sprang up from the stoop and stood behind Mace, poised to grab Frank and crumple him into a ball like a piece of paper. Mace pushed a hand into Kronk's chest, holding him back.

"And who the hell do you think you are?" Mace said, pulling off his glasses, and stepping right into Frank's face. Then, after a moment, Mace started to smile, and shake his head.

"Oh, hold it," he said, stepping back a little. "I know who the fuck you are. You that white boy that Ro trusts his life with. You the man that supposed to be watching my boy's back. How you doin'? We ain't never met before," Mace said, extending his hand out to Frank.

"And who are you?"

"I'm a close friend of your boss's. My name is Mace. We go back, way back to childhood," Mace said, his hand still floating in the space between the two men. "Now is that enough information, motherfucka, or do you need to see some ID before you shake my hand," Mace said, a smile still on his face, although now a little strained.

Frank extended the fingers of his right hand, letting the brass knuckles slip off into his pocket, then shook Mace's hand.

"I really have been looking for Ro. Do you know where he's been?"

"If the two of you go back so far, shouldn't you have his home address?"

Mace chuckled a little, looking down to the ground. "He doesn't want me coming by his house. Don't ask why. I just want to know that he's all right."

Frank thought the look on this guy's face was sincere enough, and the info that he wanted wouldn't put Zale in jeopardy even if this guy was lying.

"He hasn't been feeling well over the past few days, but I spoke to him yesterday, and he said he's feeling better. He should be in tomorrow. Now if you don't mind moving, I have to get to work."

"Naw, naw. Step out the man's way, Kronk, and go wait over by the car." The big man followed the instructions as obediently as a dog.

Mace stepped closer to Frank, and extended his hand again, which Frank took, more in a hurry to end their conversation than in an attempt to make peace.

"I just want you to know that Ro really trusts you, man. You know how I know that?" Mace asked, still holding Frank's hand, seeming not to have any intention of letting it go till he was finished talking. "Because I told him to get rid of you, damn near begged him. I told him that me and my men could protect him twenty times better than you could. But he said no. For some reason he likes your lily-white ass. But let me tell you something," Mace said, stepping even closer to Frank, still holding a firm grip on his hand. "This man is like a brother to me, he's all I got, and your job is to protect him. If you know what's best for you, don't let nothing happen to him."

"Is that a threat?" Frank said, looking directly into Mace's eyes, through his dark lenses.

"No, that's just me telling you to do your job. That's all." Mace released Frank's hand, then just stood there for a moment, face-to-face with Frank, staring him in the eye, intensifying the warning with the gesture. Mace turned and pimped over to the car, Frank watching him leave. Before Mace got into the car, he spoke the same advice, yelling over the hood of the car at Frank, jabbing at Frank with his pointer finger, his thumb sticking up like he was aiming a gun. "Do your job." Then he and the big man got in the car and sped off.

CHAPTER TWENTY

Martin rolled the sleeping bag up, tied it, and placed it in the corner of the small guest room. His two bags with all his belongings were placed next to it. He was doing the right thing, he told himself, as he turned in a small circle, appreciating the refuge Zale had given him over the last month.

But Martin was ready to go back now, because over the course of time he was staying there, he had spoken to his wife a million times over the phone, and even broke the rules and saw her twice, both times over lunch in a restaurant loaded with people so he wouldn't make a fool of himself, wrap his arms around her, tell her how much he loved her, and take her back before it was time.

He spoke to her over the phone sometimes while he was at work, accepting her phone calls, speaking to her for only fifteen or twenty minutes. Most of the time, they would speak late in the evening. Martin would be sitting patiently by the guest room phone, waiting for her phone call, and when she called, he would allow it to ring a couple of times before picking it up so as not to seem too anxious.

"You could've picked up the phone right away. I know you've been waiting for my call," Debra would say confidently, and all Martin could do was smile. Things like that made him remember how much he missed her. He would lie on the couch and talk to her for hours, arms and legs hanging over the edge like in high school, thinking about what she was wearing, or how great it would be to make love to her at that very moment.

Debra would always ask how the kids were doing, and they would talk about them, share cute little stories, and she would say things like "I can't wait to do that again," or "Maybe we should try to go there," even though Martin made no mention of taking her back, gave her no idea that she would ever see those kids or him ever again. But she spoke as if she had no worry of that, and although her presumptuous attitude should've angered Martin, it reassured him that she indeed wanted them back together as much as he did.

Inspecting the room one last time, Martin looked over at the phone, picked it up off the floor, straightened its cord, putting the slack out of sight behind the couch, and placed the phone back on the end table. Things should be as neat and clean as he found the room.

Now was the time that he would thank Zale and tell him he was leaving. Martin opened the door and walked across the hall to Zale's door, which was cracked slightly open, a dim light escaping through the opening.

Martin rapped lightly on the door with his knuckle. There was no answer, so he knocked again. Still no answer. Martin walked toward the living room, and there he saw Zale, eating the first half of what looked like a peanut butter and jelly sandwich, bending over an open file. The light wasn't nearly as bright as it should've been and that was probably why Zale seemed to be trying to sniff the file instead of reading it.

"I don't know what will happen first, you going blind, or dying from malnutrition, eating peanut butter and jelly for dinner," Martin said playfully, standing just inside the entrance to the living room. "You never quit, do you?"

Zale looked up from the file and smiled, his mouth filled with peanut butter and jelly sandwich.

"Hey, I didn't even hear you standing over there." Then he said, "You know this stuff won't ever wait." Zale gestured down at the folder with the half sandwich.

"Well, I didn't mean to disturb you," Martin said, beginning to turn away, thankful for the excuse not to tell him his news.

"No, no, no," Zale said, closing the file, sliding it to a side. "I need to take a break. Besides there's been something I've been wanting to say to you."

Martin had no idea what that was, but it definitely piqued his interest. He moved in front of a chair, and slowly sat down.

"Well, you probably didn't know it, but this has been a rough time for me. A real rough time. Outside of you, Regina was my only real friend, and when she left, there was a void, a hell of a void."

Zale played with the half sandwich sitting on his paper towel, picked it up as though he was going to take a bite, then dropped it back to the table.

"I'm getting off the subject, and that's probably because I'm not good at stuff like this. What I want to say is that the last month that you've been staying here has really done me a lot of good. Two weeks ago, when I was almost at the end of my rope, I appreciated you being around, just to shoot the shit, or whatever. I was going through a hell of a lot, with Regina, with some personal problems, everything just seemed to be coming down around me."

"You never really filled me in about that," Martin said.

"And I probably never will." Zale smiled. "I guess I just wanted to say that it's nice having you around, partner. And you're welcome to stay as long as you want."

That was the last thing Martin wanted to hear his friend say. He hesitated for a moment, then realized that it would do no good to continue withholding what he had to say.

"Thanks, but I'm leaving tonight."

"Oh," Zale said, sounding surprised and disappointed. "Where you headed?"

Martin stood from his chair, and started to pace the room.

"After two weeks of . . . I've been talking on the . . . it seems like she really . . ." Martin said, nervously rubbing his hands together, trying to get the words out, but not knowing if he could make Zale understand. Then he decided just to come out with the news as best he could.

"I'm going back home. I'm taking Debra back," Martin said.

"You're doing what?" Zale asked, shocked.

"I'm going back to Debra."

"You can't! After what she did to you? After the way she treated you, you can't go back to her!"

"What are you talking about? When I didn't know what to do, I came to you telling you that I wanted her back, and you told me how to do that. You told me about this plan, and it worked, just like you said it would. She missed me, missed the kids, realized that she wasn't appreciating me like she should, and now she wants me back, is practically begging me to come back, just like you said, Zale. It worked, just like you said, and now you're telling me I shouldn't take her back."

Zale slowly stood from the couch, shoved his hands into his pants pockets, and bowed his head.

"It wasn't supposed to work," he said softly.

"What did you say?"

"The plan. It wasn't supposed to work, okay?" Zale said, looking up at Martin. "I mean, come on. You catch your wife cheating on you in some hotel, and what do you do—leave, so she can cheat in your house? Take the kids, so she doesn't have to worry about coming home at a decent hour? Fact is, I thought she was going to take full advantage of you being gone, that she was free. I thought that she would go out there and do more of the same, but just ten times as much, and you would see what she was really about, and you would leave her for good."

"What do you mean, what she's really about."

"Martin, she's not on your side, she never was," Zale said, walking up to Martin.

"Yes, she is, and she always has been." Martin turned his back on him.

"She doesn't support what you're trying to do with Father Found."

"She does. She just does it in her own way."

"You found her soaking wet, oiled up, buck naked, a towel wrapped around her ass, ready to give some man the fucking of his life, and you're telling me that she supports you in a different way. I'll say she does."

Martin stood there for a moment, not saying a word, not appreciating Zale's sarcasm, feeling his partner's heavy presence just behind him. Martin was trying to fight the images that rushed through his head. Flashes of the man's back. Flashes of his wife's legs wrapped around that man's back. Flashes of his face, a look of ownership covering it as he looked down at Martin's wife. Flashes of her face, contorted in a mask of extreme pleasure, her mouth wrenched open, her eyes shut tight, tears being squeezed out of the tiny slits, a testament of the ecstasy her body was experiencing. Martin pushed the images out.

"I forgave her for that," Martin said plainly, stepping away from Zale.

"You did what! How? Why?"

Martin turned and exploded. "How many mothers must my children know before they can get comfortable with just one! Why should they have to suffer? Why should they have to live life without a mother just because of something that I can't forgive! I'm not prepared to do that to them. I'm not going to have them live that way."

"I see," Zale said, skepticism in his voice and all over his face. "You're doing this just for the children, right. That is noble of you, Martin. Very, very—"

"Look at me. I'm a few years from forty years old. I'm average-look-ing at best, and I don't make a lot of money. I don't have a lot to offer." Martin started pacing again. "I'm not going out there to nobody's dance club, walking around, my shirt unbuttoned down to my belly, a huge medallion hanging from my neck, looking like some pimp from some era long gone. I'm not buying any women drinks, knowing they're just looking for a man with benefits. I'm not going to try and convince a woman that I'm the man she should start her life over with. I don't want to start over. I'm happy with what I've got, and although there is a blemish on it, I can get past that, I really can.

"Zale, you don't know how much this woman means to me. A hell of a lot. So much that she could've done a lot more than she did, and I would've still taken her back. I'm actually embarrassed to say how much more. You have to understand, in my eyes, this woman saved my life, my children's lives. She was there when my wife died, and it was as if God sent her down to us to help us through that, as if my first wife herself sent her down, because she knew me, and knew that I wouldn't have made it without help. Zale, I have to take her back, not just be-cause I want to, and make no mistake, I do, but because I have to."

Zale shook his head in frustration. "You're selling yourself short, Martin."

"I need this woman."

"You don't need this woman, from what I'm hearing, any woman would do. Come on, Martin, after all she's done to you, haven't you had enough?"

"There could never be enough. I could never reach that point."

"How can you say that! You're going to let her do what she did to you, let her treat you like shit, and you're just going to take it! Well, let me tell you something. Nothing's going to change. She's going to keep on doing it as long as you allow it, and from what I'm hearing, that's going to be for the rest of your life."

"That's not going to happen," Martin said.

"And why not? Why won't it, Martin?" Zale asked, seeming to Martin more angry than he had a right to be. "Why won't it continue to happen? Because you set her straight. Because you taught her a damn lesson? Did you teach her a lesson, Martin?"

Martin didn't respond, just stood there mute, trying not to let Zale's questioning affect him.

"Did you knock her around a little bit, so she'll know never to do it again, or next time she'll get the full brunt of your anger, your fury, and they'll be racing her off in an ambulance. Did you do that, Martin!"

Martin averted his eyes, couldn't stand to maintain eye contact any longer.

Zale blew out a sigh of frustration, stuffed his hands in his pockets, turned his back, and walked away from Martin, as if in disgust, then stopped and turned to face him again.

"Well, did you at least discuss it? Did you tell her how you felt about it, or did you find out why she did it in the first place?"

"We spoke about it," Martin said, his voice low, feeling somewhat less than a man, in the shadow of his friend. "She told me she didn't know why she did it. She wasn't sure," Martin said, after a long pause.

"Then let me ask you one more question. If she's not sure, if she doesn't know, and you're so eager to take her back, what's to stop her from doing it again?"

On his way home, Martin thought about the last question Zale asked him. He had stood there, looking foolish, not knowing the answer to a question he very well should've known the answer to. But what was worse, he didn't want to know the answer, didn't want to think about it at all. She just wouldn't do it again, she just wouldn't, is all Martin told himself, so the other thoughts, the thoughts Zale was trying to fill his brain with, couldn't enter. He never did answer Zale's question. Just bent down, grabbed his bag, and said, "I'll talk to you in the morning." He didn't look up at his friend before he left. Didn't have the courage, couldn't stand to see that look in Zale's eyes. That look that said, you're making a grave mistake, and if only you had a spine, you'd see that.

■ ■ ■

It was a little after 11:00 P.M. when Martin pulled up in front of his house. He figured that Debra should've been home, and her car was probably in the garage. Martin didn't bother grabbing his bags out of the trunk, because he didn't want to make any more noise than he had to. He wanted to sneak in the house and surprise his wife, see the shock in her eyes when she saw him. Have her run up to him and throw her arms around him, and squeeze him as if she hadn't seen him in twenty years. He had been seeing that image in his head ever since he had left her, anticipating the day that he would return, for he always knew that he would.

Martin tiptoed quietly up the porch stairs, as if there was a way she would be able to hear his heels on the concrete. He wore a huge mischievous grin as he slipped the key into the door and gently turned it. The door opened without a sound. Martin slipped into the house and silently closed the door.

The house was completely quiet, and that led Martin to believe that his wife had to be upstairs in their bedroom, probably sleeping off a long, hard day at work. He mounted the first stair, and as he did, thoughts of sneaking into the room, undressing himself and sliding under the blankets with her, feeling the warmth of her body, brushing up against her soft skin, holding her in his arms, making love to her again, danced around in his head. He took the stairs a bit quicker, still cautious not to make a sound. He didn't want to wake her out of her sleep, at least not yet.

He continued taking the steps in the dark. Four more, three more. He counted them as he climbed, about to burst with anticipation. Two more, and he skipped over the last step, which put him on the second floor, not ten feet from his bedroom door. But as he took his first step in that direction, Martin thought he heard something, something that didn't sound right. He took another step, and realized that it was a voice. But it wasn't his wife's voice. It wasn't a woman's' voice at all, but that of a man.

Martin's body started to fill with anxiety. He didn't know what to do, and he told himself that this couldn't be happening. Not again, not in his own home. He thought about just staying out there. Standing out there in the dark hallway, waiting till it was all over, because he couldn't take seeing his wife with another man again. He would die.

Then he thought about just turning around and leaving just as quietly as he came, never to come back again. Next time they spoke, he would tell her that it just wouldn't work, never telling her why. But the more he thought about it, the more he imagined another man in his house, in his bed, and he told himself that he had to go in there. There was nothing else he could do.

Martin made for the door, taking hard, almost ground-shaking steps across the carpeted hallway, hearing the man's voice louder and louder as he came closer, not understanding what he was saying, but hearing him all the same. Then Martin came upon the door, and with the butt of his hand, struck the door, pushing it open as hard as he could, sending it banging against the back of the wall, and what Martin saw stunned him.

He saw nothing, no one. The bed was made neatly. At the head, the pillows were tucked under the blanket like oversized ravioli, and a throw blanket was folded neatly and placed across the foot. Nothing was disturbed, nothing unusual, and the only thing that caught Martin's eye was the little red light that glowed on the answering machine, as the tape rolled, playing the message.

". . . and again, I apologize for phoning you so late, Dr. Carter, but my wife's contractions are coming closer and closer together. I'm going to try paging you, but if I don't hear from you soon, I'm going to take her in tonight. Goodbye." Then the machine made a series of clicking noises, and the red light went off.

Martin stood just inside the door, his hand still paining him slightly from hitting the door, and the sheet of sweat covering his face from the extreme rage he was feeling a moment ago was beginning to dry. He stood there and started to chuckle. Then he started to laugh, louder and louder. He walked over to the bed, turned his back to it, extended both arms out to his sides, and fell back onto its soft surface.

He laughed for a few more moments, thinking of how angry he had been, and how much of a fool he was for thinking what he thought about his wife. Thinking that she would be in his bed doing . . . Then his laughter stopped abruptly. True, she was not doing anything in his bed, but she sure as hell wasn't home. Martin turned and glanced at the red fluorescent numbers on the clock. And it was going on midnight. What was there to make him think that she wasn't somewhere else doing the things he dared not think about?

Martin reached over to the nightstand and clicked on the lamp. She was at the hospital, that was where she was, Martin told himself. And he would just wait up for her. He would wait up for her, and she would be surprised to see him, like he planned, and everything would be fine.

By 5:00 A.M., Martin had been in and out of sleep, and he had moved to the living room to wait for Debra. He had decided to give up, go on upstairs and get some sleep so he wouldn't be a total waste at work, when he saw the beams of headlights come inside the window and move across the walls. Martin rose from the sofa and raced to the window to look out. It was Debra, and she was pulling into the drive.

All of a sudden, Martin felt like that little puppy dog again. He was so excited that he could barely contain himself, but he forced himself to remember what time it was, how long he had been waiting, and what she could've been doing all that time.

He wanted to greet her at the door, wanted to hug her, and kiss her, but he told himself no. Before he reacted that way to her, he needed some insight into how she felt about seeing him again. She had parked her car in the driveway, so she didn't see his in the garage. She doesn't even know I'm here, Martin thought. He raced back onto the couch, lay across it, and closed his eyes almost all the way, as if he were sleeping, but he allowed just enough space for him to see clearly without Debra knowing that he was awake.

He heard the keys jiggling just outside the door, and Martin crossed his arms over his chest, trying to appear as he normally did when he slept. Then the door opened and he froze, barely able to breathe at the sight of her passing through the dark room. He told himself that she couldn't have seen him, because she went about her normal rituals as she would if no one was there, taking off her shoes, setting her bag down beside the door. Martin continued to watch her through the thin slits of his eyes, as she clicked on the light, and went to the closet to hang up her coat. She closed the door, and when she turned around, she jumped, gasped, and threw her hand over her mouth, her eyes ballooning with shock at the sight of her husband.

Martin just continued to be there, watching her watch him. She cautiously took a step closer to him, looking at him strangely, as if he weren't real. Then she stopped, not three feet in front of him, looking down on him, a single tear spilling from her eye.

Another tear came, and another, then she threw her hands over her mouth and nose, trying to wipe away the tears with the tips of her fingers. She dropped to her knees, just in front of her husband, gently, hesitantly, laying a hand upon his hair.

She placed her tear-wet face on his chest, hugging him around his neck.

"You're back, sweetheart. You're back," she wept.

Martin slowly placed a soft hand on the back of his wife's head.

"That's right, baby. I am."

CHAPTER TWENTY-ONE

Zale passed slowly under the streetlamps that lit the dark street. It was sometime after five in the morning, and he walked down another street he had known to be populated with homeless children and runaways. His hands were pushed down deep in his pockets, his head lowered, his mind a million miles away.

As he continued walking down the street, he came upon people lying on the ground before him, huddled up against buildings for warmth, as a newborn child would grasp for its mother, but he averted his eyes, which was unusual, and walked past them. His mind was no longer on helping *them*, but on getting the fathers that abandoned them. He rationalized this decision by telling himself that his attention would only be diverted from the children for just a little while, and in the end, there would be the same outcome.

Zale's steps were interrupted by a huddled mass shaped like a body covered with rags and blankets. He stepped right up to it, the toes of his shoes stopping on the rags. He should do something, he told himself. He should make some type of attempt to find out who this person was, if it was a child, at least, but he couldn't bring himself to do it. He thought about bending down, shaking this person awake, but Zale's heart wasn't in it, and the most he could do was reach in his pocket, pull out one of his business cards, and toss it toward the body. It floated down, spinning end over end, and landed softly toward one of the humps in the cover.

"Give me a call sometime," Zale said, softly, halfhearted. He stepped over the obstacle as if it were a puddle of dirty water and continued on his way.

It was wrong to have done what he had just done, but he could not help it. It was almost as if he just didn't give a damn anymore, and he told himself long ago that if he ever reached that point, he would surrender. He would give in to the natural scheme of things, let men with no thoughts of the future, or no feeling for responsibility, continue to fill women's wombs with the seeds that would soon grow into unwanted children. Zale told himself if this day came, he would forget about all the children who he knew would experience the pain and torture he went through, and when he passed one on the street, he would turn away, and suppress whatever urge left he had in him to help that child.

And as he distanced himself further away from the body that he had stepped over as if it were a pile made by someone's uncurbed dog, he asked himself, was he approaching that day? Did he really no longer care about helping the children, helping their fathers, and mothers, his community?

Zale stopped and looked back over his shoulder, feeling a pain of sympathy strike his heart, and he realized the answer was quite possibly. And even though he was trying to convince himself otherwise, he also knew what was driving him in this particular direction.

It was what that young white woman told him about himself. She was probably not even three months past graduation, probably hadn't even started paying on her student loans yet, and she was telling him that it was his mother's fault that he was experiencing what he was going through.

She was wrong, sorely wrong, and he thought about going back to that community center, banging on her door, and telling her just where she could shove her fucking Ivy League theories. But, instead, Zale did exactly the opposite of what know-it-all Ms. Eckert probably intended on him doing. Instead of backing off, reevaluating his goals, in light of what was discovered about him, Zale turned up the heat. Zale went after the men with more zeal and rage than ever before. The files of men that he had put aside, considered closed because he could not reach them personally after months and months of trying, he pulled out, and he arranged for arrest warrants to be put out because they had not paid.

The past few speaking engagements Zale had, he thought nothing of the men who sat in front of him, forced to listen to his words. Cared nothing about the harshness of what he had to say to them, and he was harsh. Brutally harsh. Vomiting his rage and hatred out on them during his speeches as if it was the sickness that sat in his belly for so long, festering, tormenting him, making him violently ill to the point where he could no longer hold it in. He degraded them in every way imaginable, calling them every name he could think of, telling them that if they didn't take him seriously, they would see the consequences in the loss of wages in their checks, or wonder why they were being carted off to jail next time they got pulled over for running a stop sign.

He no longer cared even what Martin thought. He had a job to do, and he was going to start doing it. Ms. Eckert felt that how he conducted his business was motivated by personal reasons, well, it wasn't then. But now it was different. Now it was personal!

Zale stepped off the curb, into the street, and a car raced by him, almost hitting him. The wind from the car's speed blew through his clothes, the protruding side-view mirror almost grazing him, yet Zale stood there, a numb look on his face.

The nappy-headed passenger of the run-down car hung his head out the window and shouted, "Watch where you fucking going! Are you crazy!" Then Zale saw the man refocus his eyes, as if he was met with recognition, then he pulled his head back in the car and said something to the driver.

For a moment, Zale was expecting the car to do a wild U-turn, spinning up on two wheels and tearing back down the street after him. This time, instead of the man's head coming out the window, there would be a gun, spraying bullets at Zale, throwing his body up against a building, where he would die, a blood-covered mess. But that didn't happen, the car just sped on down the street, and then Zale continued crossing the street against the flashing DONT WALK light.

The thought of someone killing him entered his mind because the phone calls had started up again. The first one came some three weeks ago. He picked up the phone, said hello, and when no one answered, he hung up the phone, thinking nothing of it. But since then, the same thing had been happening. Phone calls to his job at all hours, and when he picked up the phone, there was just silence for a moment, sometimes breathing, and other times just quick hang-ups. It had brought him to the very edge, had him jumpier than he could remember, looking over his shoulder, fearing for his life, and he once asked himself if he had made the right decision about the recent crackdown. He knew the phone calls were retaliation for some man being squeezed too hard.

Martin had recently burst into his office, and again strongly reiterated that Zale wasn't liked, and that if he continued on his path of berating these fathers, "We will never see another goddamn donation again!"

But Zale just turned a deaf ear to his partner, shook his head, and said, "Un huh," as if what Martin said wasn't of any value to him, and proceeded upon his intended course.

As a result, the few donations that they were receiving did stop, and Martin said nothing, just walked into Zale's office, dropped the big accounting book on his desk, gave Zale a look of disgust, then walked out.

Outside of trying to finance Father Found, Martin was also doing everything he could to stop the bank from taking the building, and he was still waiting to hear from Mr. Kirkland, which seemed to be their last hope. Everything seemed to be falling apart, coming loose at the seams, and there seemed to be nothing Zale could do. He would lose the building, he knew that, and already he had been trying to find ways to run the business from his house.

Zale stopped again, this time not at a busy intersection, but in the middle of the sidewalk, for no apparent reason. His fists still in his pockets, he looked up to the sky, an angst-filled expression crinkling his face. It was ironic, he thought, squinting against the sun peeking over the horizon. The sun was coming out, and it would be a bright, beautiful day, but, for him, it seemed his darkest hour would soon be approaching.

CHAPTER TWENTY-TWO

By the time Zale got to his office, it was well past 8:00 A.M. He came in, took off his jacket, and wearily sat behind his desk. He threw his elbows up on the desk and let his face fall into the palms of his hands. He took a deep breath, exhaled, and realized that he was far too tired to be at work, but told himself that he had to be there. That there was work to be done, and like always, what was in the balance could not afford to wait while he slept precious time away.

Zale sat up straight, feeling a bit better from just the moment of reflection, and reached for the phone. He heard the broken dial tone, informing him he had voice mail. He dialed his service. The computer voice came over the phone. "Please enter your password."

Zale punched in his code.

"You have ten new messages," the computer informed him. "Press one for new messages."

Zale punched the appropriate key and waited.

The first message was a hang-up. "If you would like to erase this message, press seven."

Zale pressed seven.

"Next message."

There was another click. It was another hang-up.

Again, Zale pressed seven and deleted the message.

He waited for his third message. Another hang-up. Zale stabbed the number-seven button again, becoming angry.

"Next message." Hang-up.

"Next message." Hang-up, but this time he pressed the time stamp button.

"Call at three twenty-seven A.M."

Zale pressed the key revealing what time the caller called for the last five messages and they came almost every hour till he walked in his office, not fifteen minutes ago.

He punched the number-seven key again, deleting the last message, and angrily slammed the phone down into its cradle.

This guy was trying to get inside his head, he told himself. He wasn't really trying to speak to him. This man had nothing of importance to say to him, nothing so urgent that he had to call him all hours of the night, because if that were the case, he would've hung up after the third ring when he realized that Zale wasn't in his office, instead of waiting for the fifth ring, just so his hang-up would be recorded. He was doing that on purpose so Zale would know he called, to put something in Zale's mind, to have him jumping at his own shadow on the wall, his own reflection in the mirror. He wanted to make Zale a complete—

Zale jumped back from his desk, startled out of his thought, almost falling to the floor in reaction to the phone ringing. He stared at the phone, his heart beating rapidly, a chill racing through his body. The phone rang again, and Zale snatched the phone off the hook and brought it up to his face.

"This is Zaleford Rowen," he answered, his voice low, suspicious, and full of fear.

There was no answer, but he could detect soft breathing. He listened intently for a moment, his heart pounding so hard in his ears that he could barely hear the caller. He pressed the phone harder against his face in an attempt to make clearer the sounds at the other end.

"This is Zaleford Rowen. You've reached Father Found!" he said, more forcefully, anger starting to find its way into his voice.

Still no answer.

"What the hell do you want! Why are you calling me? Answer me, dammit!"

There was a click. A number of clicks, then the steady dial tone.

"Hello? Hello!" Zale yelled into the phone, then slung the phone across the room, where it crashed against the far wall.

Zale grabbed his jacket, and ran out of his office. He saw Martin speaking to his secretary.

"I'm leaving, and I'll be gone for the day," Zale said quickly, without stopping to even look in the man's face.

Zale flew down the stairs, two and three at a time. Ran to his car, jumped in, and shot out of the gated parking area and into the busy flow of traffic, cutting off a minivan, sending it swerving out of control for a moment.

He wants to get inside my head, the son of a bitch. He wants me to fear him, Zale thought, as he wove in and out of traffic, his shoulders hunched over the wheel, his fists locked around it. He wants to get in my head so I carry around this fear everywhere I go. He wants to hound me, be there every time I turn around, when I wake up in the morning, when I shower before I go to bed. He wants to harass me the way he probably feels I've been harassing him, but that's not going to work, Zale thought. But then realized that it had already worked. The man was already in Zale's head, embedded deeply enough to pull him out of his office, send him flying home so he couldn't accomplish the things he needed to do. But this was just a momentary interruption. Zale would take things into his own hands. He was not going to play the victim again.

When Zale approached his house, he clicked the remote door opener on his garage, sped in, and clicked the remote again, closing the door. He bolted out of his car, flew into his house, and raced into the bedroom. He paused for a moment, then went for the closet, flinging it open and throwing his arm up onto the top shelf, sweeping back and fourth, spilling whatever was on the shelf to the floor behind him. To his shock, it wasn't there. *It wasn't there!* But it was where he last placed it. He knew it. He turned in the pile of mess he made from the closet's shelf, and desperately tried to remember where it was. Zale looked over at the dresser, running over it, gutting it of all its drawers, pulling them out, dropping them to the floor, then ravaging them, tossing underwear, once-folded pairs of slacks and shirts over his shoulder. When he hadn't found what he was looking for, he ran over to the nightstand, yanked out the drawers, and held them upside down, tossing all the contents to the floor, falling to his knees, sifting through the mess, but still to no avail.

He got to his feet, spun around, frozen by indecision, then, for there was no place else to go but backward, he dashed back over to the closet. He jumped, stood on his tippy-toes, and threw his arm back up over the shelf, urgently sweeping back and fourth, hoping that in his desperate need and haste, he had missed it the first time. Then he felt something way in the back. It was pushed back so far that he couldn't see it, and he had to stand on his toes in order to grab it. He groped around blindly for it, got his hand around it, then yanked it down. It was a black case. He took it over to the bed, feeling somewhat relieved, and sat down with it on his lap.

Zale opened the case to reveal a small black .22-caliber handgun. It was the gun he had bought more than two years ago, when he was in the same situation, but he hadn't had to use it since.

He gently placed his hand on it, felt its smooth, cold skin, and somehow, at the same time, began to feel a bit more safe, yet more fearful. He had the gun, and he would use it if it came to that, but it was something that he would hate to do, and would do almost anything to avoid.

Zale pulled the small gun from its mold, loaded it, tossed the case aside, kicked his feet up onto the bed, slid his back against the backboard, and crossed his arms, the gun in his hand, resting on his left elbow.

If the man wanted him, he would be there, Zale told himself. He would be right there waiting for him, and if he chose not to come to his house, then Zale would just have to be ready for him whenever he decided to strike.

"I'm not going to play the victim again," Zale said softly to himself, his body starting to relax, his eyelids starting to fall heavy upon his eyes.

"I'm not going to . . ." Then, against his will, his exhaustion took him.

Zale shot upright in bed, awakened by the sound of movement just outside his window. It was dark now, and he whipped his head around, his hands groping about the bed for the .22. He felt the cold piece of steel, grabbed it up, and held it very close to his heart.

Zale sat there, tense, his heart racing, his mind entertaining all sorts of horrible scenarios. He held the gun tight in his hand, sweat starting to form around the gun's handle in the creases of his palm.

He heard another sound, and it was someone trying the front door again, just like last time. He didn't know what to do. He thought about jumping out of bed, racing to the living room, pulling the door open and shooting the man before he could even get a good look at Zale. Before he knew what hit him, he would be knocked on his ass, bleeding all over the welcome mat. But what if by the time Zale got to the door, the man was already standing in his living room? What if he fired first, and Zale was killed? The possibility held Zale back, frightened in his bed.

He waited, listened, and he heard movement in the bushes outside, moving from the front of the house, along the side where his bedroom was. He was coming to the window, just like the last guy, and Zale wondered if there was a fucking sign tacked to the house reading, "Break in Here." A huge red arrow pointing to his bedroom window.

Zale saw the outline of a man just outside the window. Then he saw the man's form approach the window, cup his hands around his face and try to look in. There was an almost-sheer curtain hanging closed there, so Zale figured he couldn't see in—besides, it was pitch-black in his room—but Zale still feared the man seeing him.

Zale tried to suppress his breathing, which was coming far too rapidly now. He pulled himself into a ball, roped his arms around his knees, the gun still in his hand, trying to decrease the amount of himself that could be detected.

Go away, go away, Zale kept saying in his head, for he thought that he had it within him to shoot this man, but now he realized he might not. All he wanted now was for the man to disappear. If that happened, he would get Rames on the phone and put him out on a blood hunt for this man, so Zale would never be in this position again.

The man tried to look inside the house a moment longer, then stepped back and disappeared through the bushes.

Zale breathed a silent sigh of relief. He was gone, and it was over, and Zale never wanted to experience such fear again. Never. He relaxed himself from the ball he was in and cautiously extended his legs out over the edge of the bed. He was preparing to stand, hoping his legs weren't so weary that he would topple to the floor, when he heard another sound.

It was the back door this time, and it didn't sound as though someone was just trying the door, but trying to break into it. There was a prying sound, like a screwdriver trying to makes its way into the small space between the door and the frame.

Zale scurried back onto the bed, pushing himself into the farthest corner. He will get in, Zale told himself, his entire body starting to coat with nervous sweat. He will get in that door, because it's far too flimsy, and Zale wanted to shoot his damn self, because he had told himself a million times he needed to replace it with something stronger.

Zale heard the lock give, heard the door burst open, heard the outside night noises enter his house along with this strange man. Zale didn't have to worry about this intruder hearing his breathing, because he could no longer breathe. It was as if his heart gave up within his chest, and Zale could feel a tight pain, as though someone had his knee pinned there.

What to do! What to do! His mind raced around the question. His eyes jetted back and forth about the dark room, looking for possibilities.

Go out the window, he told himself, but he was too scared to move. The man would catch him halfway out and shoot him in the back. He was better off where he was; at least he had a chance of defending himself. And at that, he raised the gun in front of him, both hands wrapped tightly around the shaking weapon.

Movement could be heard through the house. He was in the kitchen. Zale heard the bathroom door squeak, then he heard slow, cautious movement to the den. He's looking for me, Zale thought, as he tried to steady the violently shaking gun. He's looking for me, and he's going to find me, because there is no other room to check but this one.

There was extreme silence, and Zale heard soft, careful footsteps approach his room, then they stopped. Zale still had the weapon pointed toward the door, wondering why nothing was happening. What the fuck was going on? It was a long moment that seemed like a lifetime, and Zale could hardly bear it. If you're going to kill me, then come on, you bastard, Zale thought, his finger jittering on the trigger, feeling as if he was only moments from soiling his pants like an infant. Come on in and kill . . .

And before Zale could finish the thought, the figure in the hall stepped into the doorway, and that's all Zale needed to see. He shut his eyes tight, gritted his teeth, and squeezed the trigger. The small gun jerked in his hand, a stream of orange-red fire lit the dark room, and the bullet exploded out of the gun.

"Die, motherfucker," Zale yelled.

Zale heard a body hit the ground, so he reeled off three more rounds in the direction he heard the noise.

"Ro!" he heard someone call. Zale stopped his shooting for just a moment to listen.

"Ro! Put down the fucking gun, motherfucker! It's me!"

And for a moment the voice didn't register, and Zale considered emptying his gun.

"Who in the hell is me?" Zale yelled, his finger still on the trigger.

"Mace, man. It's me, man. Put the fucking gun down!"

"Oh, shit!" Zale tossed the gun aside, jumped off the bed thinking that he may have shot his oldest friend. He rushed over to him, helping him up, then clicking on the light. He looked him up and down, looking for signs of blood.

"Are you all right? Did I hit you?"

Mace just stood there, his mouth agape, body trembling, a look of utter disbelief on his face. He looked as though he was about to speak, but halted, pulling his eyes from Zale, looking at the mess of clothes, tossed drawers, and items from Zale's closet strewn all about the bedroom floor. Then he turned around and saw four bullet holes. One bullet was lodged in the top of the doorframe, three others were buried in various places in the floor. He turned to Zale again, the look on his face full of disbelief, then he spoke—slowly, as if he wanted his question to be fully understood.

"What the fuck is going on with you?"

Zale looked at Mace, feeling almost ashamed at what his friend had witnessed.

"They're after me again, Mace," Zale said, lowering his head. "They're after me."

Mace didn't speak for a moment, looking as if he was thinking, and then he said, "Grab your shit. You're coming with me."

"This doesn't make any sense, Ro. No one knows where the fuck you are, how to get in touch with you, not even your white shadow. I shouldn't have to go busting into your house just to find you."

"You could've knocked," Zale said softly. He looked beaten by all he was going through.

"I did, but you didn't answer."

And it was possible, Zale thought. Maybe he hadn't heard him, or maybe he was just too frightened to answer.

"Ro, who's after you?" Mace said. They were on the roof of a high-rise building, looking out over the city. It was somewhere Mace often went, somewhere that was safe. Somewhere where Zale would not be in danger.

"I don't know. Some pissed-off father again, I guess. He's been calling my office like crazy," Zale said, having a seat on a crate, rubbing his hands over his face.

"So what are you going to do," Mace said, walking over in front of him. "You going to get the white boy to protect you again?"

"That's his job," Zale said spitefully.

"Goddammit, Zale! What is with you? That boy ain't nothing but a glorified rent-a-cop. Let me get my boys. Let me watch your back. I swear on my life that nothing will happen to you."

"I don't need that."

"Why are you putting your life in this man's hands?" Mace said.

"Because I can trust him."

"So you saying that you can't trust me?"

"I'm saying that he has proven himself." And immediately after saying that, he regretted it, because he knew what Mace would say.

Mace shook his head, his face covered with disappointment.

"He's proven himself, because he saved your life. Because he's killed for you, he has proven himself, and you trust him. Well, if that's the case, you should trust me till you fucking die. I don't believe you sat there and said that shit," Mace said, turning and walking back toward the building's ledge. "Have you fucking forgotten what I did for you!" Mace said, turning and yelling back at Zale. "I sacrificed ten years of my life for you!"

"That benefited you as well."

"Did it? How? By getting ten years. I didn't ask you to help me. I didn't even let you in on it, because I wanted you to be clean. I took the fall! I took that fall for you, motherfucker!"

Zale could hear the anger and the sense of betrayal in Mace's voice, and he was sorry for what he said, because he had not forgotten. There was no way he ever could, no way he ever would.

Zale told himself that he wouldn't let it happen, that he wouldn't take the abuse past his sixteenth birthday, but there he sat, on the edge of

Mrs. Connor's bed again, stripped down to nothing but his underpants. She was standing before him, naked, flab oozing over her body, like she was made of wax, and the bright overhead light was melting her.

She was telling Zale to peel off his underpants so they could get down to business, and Zale was scared, as scared as he had ever been of her, for he had never gotten used to her attacks. He was bent over, his arms folded into his chest, trying to hide himself.

"I said, take off the damn panties, little man!" she shouted, and when he wouldn't respond after so many orders, Mrs. Connors slapped him across the side of his head with a heavy hand.

She caught him in his ear, and the pain rang throughout Zale's head as he fell over to his side. But he got back up, shaking off the pain, or at least trying to appear as though he had, and stared her in the eyes.

"I said, take them off!" And she slapped him again. This time, Zale didn't fall, but eyed her with extreme hatred and defiance.

"I'm not doing this no more," Zale said, shocked to hear himself speak these words.

"Oh, you're not, hunh? You're not doing this no more?" Mrs. Connors said, as she walked over to the single chair that sat in the room, pulled the thick leather belt that lay across the back, and lashed out at Zale with it. The leather struck Zale on the shoulder, wrapped around and slapped him across the back. He felt cut, like he had been sliced open with a knife.

The big woman swung again, and Zale tried to grab the belt, actually caught hold of it, but she was too strong, pulling it away, and striking harder next time because of the fight he gave her. She swung over and over again, and Zale had no choice but to recoil in a ball atop the bed, trying to bear the pain of the belt as it burned its shape into the skin it touched.

"You're not going to do this no more! Is that what you said!" Mrs. Connors yelled, sounding as if she could go on forever whipping him.

"You'll do this till I say I don't want you to anymore. You hear me!"

Then, all of a sudden, the bedroom door burst open, slamming into the chair that sat in the corner.

Mrs. Connors spun around, and Zale's attention as well was pulled toward the open door. Who he saw there was Derek, both his hands behind his back, a look on his face that wasn't the look of a fourteen-year-old boy, but the look of a man on the brink of insanity.

"What the hell are you—"

And before the big woman could finish her sentence, Derek came out from behind his back with a huge carving knife. He was midway into his swing before Mrs. Connors could even comprehend what was happening. Her eyes opened so wide they looked as if they were going to explode out of her head, and her mouth formed a word that was never made audible. The huge razor-sharp knife caught her on one side of the neck and sliced cleanly through to the other. A flash of blood gushed out from the wide slit that opened up in her neck, painting Derek's face and shirt red.

Mrs. Connors started gasping, choking, gargling with her own blood as if it were mouthwash. Then she dropped the belt, the buckle clanking against the floor, and she reached for her neck with both hands, wrapping them around it as if trying to close the wound the blood escaped from.

But it was no use, and after another moment of snorting and choking and staggering back and forth, she fell to the floor on her big ass, her legs out in front of her, like a child playing in a sandbox, her back against the bed. Blood ran from her nose, mouth, and a wide, thick trail oozed from her neck, over her breasts, covering her arms and hands, which were still wrapped around her throat. The trail continued over the roundness of her belly, spilling into a wide pool in between her legs.

Zale sat on the bed, not two feet from the bloody corpse, gagging, unable to breathe, unable to make his eyes see, his mind understand what had happened. He jumped from the bed to the floor, stood in front of Mrs. Connors and shook her by the shoulder, as if everything was staged for his birthday. She was dead, and he realized that when the wound in her neck opened up, and he could see the yellowness of the bones that built her spine.

Zale looked back at Derek. He was standing there baptized in blood, the knife still in his hand, an empty expression on his face.

Zale raced over to him, grabbed him by the shoulders, shaking him.

"Why did you do it? Why did you have to kill her!"

The vacant look still in Derek's eyes, he turned to Zale and said, "So we can live."

Zale came out of the deep thought he was in to see Mace still looking out over the lights of the city. Zale walked up behind him, placed a hand on his back and said, "Things were different then. We were different then. Mace, I have to do what I think is right to get through this, and that's to trust Frank. And then, maybe after that, we can try working together."

Mace nodded his head but did not turn to face Zale.

Zale turned and walked away. He stepped into the elevator, looking back at Derek. He had hurt his friend, told him he didn't trust him. Zale had managed to alienate one more person from his life. He took a long look at him, burned his image into his brain, for he knew, after this, he would probably never see Derek again.

CHAPTER TWENTY-THREE

It was 8:05 and Martin Carter sat at his desk, feeling very good about himself, good about his life. He sat there staring at the pictures on his desk. On one side, the picture of his daughters that had been there since his desk was first moved into that office three years ago, and on the other side, the picture of Debra, which he just replaced upon walking into the office this morning. He had taken it down, and shoved it in one of his bottom drawers, way to the back, never wanting to see it again, the day after he found his wife cheating on him. But they were back together now, and Martin thought back to the night he lay awake for her till five in the morning. The night she found him there after he had been gone for three weeks.

She rushed over to him, hugged him, and he hugged her back, and he just paused, just stopped the world around him for that moment and breathed her in, allowed himself to cherish every part of her body that came in contact with his and just appreciate the fact that he could love someone as he loved this woman. But it was five in the morning, and though he feared ruining the moment by hearing information he didn't want to know, he asked her anyway.

"Why are you coming in so late? I've been waiting up for you."

Debra looked shocked by the question, as if being shaken out of a peaceful sleep.

"Oh. One of my patients paged me just as I was about to leave. They delivered tonight. There were difficulties, but the baby was fine." Debra smiled.

"What time did you get the page?" Martin asked.

"Just after midnight." And that was exactly what the man on the recording said he was going to do.

Martin grabbed the framed photo, brought it closer to his face, and couldn't help but smile, remembering the love they just made last night. It was wonderful, especially after he forced himself to stop seeing the man that she was with the night he caught her, to stop feeling as though he was mimicking moves that the man had already done to her. When he kissed her neck, he knew that that man had done the same. When he felt his wife's reaction, Martin knew that that man received the same response.

When Martin caressed her behind, when he spread her legs, and slowly entered her, when he felt her relax, tightening around him, heard her sensual moans, felt her nails digging into his back, he knew that he was not the only one that was familiar with her sounds, her actions. For a long time, Martin thought about this man, and once he stopped for a moment. Still inside his wife, his arms holding him elevated above her. He stopped and just looked down at her. Her eyes were closed, a simple, almost nonexistent smile on her face, and as Martin looked down on her, he wondered if that man was in her mind, as he was in his.

"What," his wife asked, opening her eyes. Martin continued to stare at her a moment longer, the question that was in his mind sitting on the tip of his tongue. He wanted to know the answer, but he suppressed his urge, telling himself that her love was for him now, that the passion she was showing was in response to what he was doing, and no one else.

"Nothing," Martin said, and worked up a smile before she had a chance to question him any further. He told himself that would be the last time he would entertain that thought, ever.

Martin gently placed the frame down on his desk and glanced at his watch. It was 8:20, and there was work he had to do, and plenty of it. He was expecting a call back from Frank. Paging him was the first thing he did when he stepped into his office this morning, and although he knew Frank was probably still in bed, he paged him anyway, quite happy about the fact that he would be waking him up.

But he had not called Martin back yet, and that led Martin to believe that the man had probably rolled over in bed, peeked at the pager, realized that it was Martin and said the hell with it. Martin reached over, dialed the man's pager again, and hung up the phone.

He won't call me back, Martin said to himself. Something obviously got into the man's head and made him think that he was now running shit himself, and had no one to answer to.

Martin pulled over a stack of files, recent files that Frank had returned to Zale over the past few days. He thumbed through the first few of them, noticing that they all had been checked just as he figured. Martin shook his head at the sight.

"They're going on home, hunh, Frank," he said softly, skepticism in his voice.

"Well, we'll just have to see about that. We'll just have to see." Martin turned to the first page of the file, taking note of the name, and then the address, thinking that he could be at this house in less than twenty minutes.

Martin took a left on Ellis Street, passing by a liquor store. A small group of men, holding bottles, congregating around a frail, sick, aging woman in a skintight dress, looked at him oddly as he took the turn.

Martin ignored their stares, paying attention to the addresses of the deteriorating houses that he drove by. Many of them had no address numbers, like they had no windows but plastic stapled and taped to the frames, or no stairs but stacked crates, or no grass but plots of dirt, littered with forty-ounce bottles of malt liquor tossed from passing cars, and broken toys left outside by the many kids that lived in these houses.

Fortunately, the house Martin was looking for did happen to have a number, and he looked down at the open file in his lap and made sure it corresponded correctly. They were a match, and he pulled the car over behind a rusting abandoned car with no hood, doors, or tires.

Martin grabbed the single file, opened his briefcase, and pulled out a photo of Mr. Frank Rames. He slipped it into the file and got out of the car. He walked up to the house and proceeded to climb the porch stairs.

Two bare wires protruded out of a small hole in the doorframe. It was where the doorbell once was, Martin told himself, and instead of striking the live wires together, he banged softly on the door with the side of his fist.

He turned around to see his car, trusting that it would be safe there left alone. It would only be for a few minutes.

He heard the locks being opened behind him, and he quickly turned around to see a woman standing behind the screen door, her hair sticking up all about her head, a nightgown hanging off her body. Food stains covered the space on the gown between her sagging breasts; she had no bra on under.

The house smelled of bacon and eggs, and after a moment, two little nappy-headed children rushed to the door, grabbing either one of their mother's legs, and peered up at Martin.

"Yeah," the woman said, as if she had just been wakened from a sound sleep.

"Are you Mrs. Tilden?" Martin said.

"Yeah, that's me," she said, scratching an itch on her side.

"Is your husband home?" Martin asked.

"Yeah, he in there," the woman responded, to Martin's surprise. It took Martin a moment to speak. Then he asked to see the man.

"He in there sleep. It's early still. I don't think he want to be woke up," she said, the children still playing on her legs. She pushed them away. "And turn off the fire on the stove," she called over her shoulder.

"Well, it's very important that I speak to him. Can you wake him?"

She gave Martin an unsure look.

"Please, I'm from Father Found."

The woman paused a moment, then a smile spread across her face. "You mean Rowen's place?"

"One and the same."

"Oh, okay, okay. I'll go get him. Just a minute," she said, turning, and closing the door in Martin's face.

The man was home, Martin thought, opening the file, staring at the last page. And the box was appropriately checked, he hated to admit.

The door opened again, but this time standing behind the screen was Lemont Tilden. He was a man in his mid- to late thirties, and his hair was braided back in wide braids to the back of his head. He wore a graying, sleeveless T-shirt, and was wiping the sleep out of his eyes. But the first thing that caught Martin's attention was how jacked up his face was. His right eye was purple and red, and it was swollen almost completely shut. The bridge of his nose was cut open, his bottom lip looked like it could've been used to float downstream with, and there were a number of white tapes and bandages covering the other minor scrapes on his face.

"Yeah?" the man simply asked.

"I'm Martin Carter, from Father Found. Can you step out a moment so I can talk to you?"

"What do you want?" Lemont asked, still standing behind the screen door, looking as though he might need it for protection.

"I just want to know how things have been going since you've been home."

Lemont gave Martin a peculiar look. "Why you all care how things been going? I'm home, all right. Ain't that all ya'll really care about."

Martin noticed that there was anger in the words that the man spoke, and that made him curious.

"Can you come out here. Please. So I can talk to you."

Lemont looked over his shoulder, back into the house, then slightly opened the screen door, stuck his head out and looked around a moment before stepping out from behind it onto the porch.

"Now what!" he said, anger and frustration in his voice.

"Mr. Tilden, we care about you and we care about your family. We just want to make sure that everything is going all right."

The man looked at Martin as though he didn't believe a word of it.

"Whatever. I'm here all right. Ya'll didn't have to go and—" Then he stopped midsentence.

"And do what, Mr. Tilden?"

"Nothing."

But Martin knew better.

"Our investigator, Frank Rames, that's who you had contact with; that's who asked you to return home and follow up with us. Is that correct?"

Lemont nodded his head.

Martin brought out the picture of Frank, held it up to Lemont.

"Is this the man?"

"Yeah, that's him."

"When he spoke to you, was he disrespectful in any way? Did you feel like he was rushing you to go back home against your will? Trying to persuade you in any way, or did he go as far as to call you names? Did he do anything that you didn't feel comfortable with?"

Lemont looked down at the photo for a long moment, then looked back up at Martin.

"No. There was nothing disrespectful about how he approached me or spoke to me. Everything was by the book, and when I left him, I felt good about going back home to be with my children." When the man was finished, he looked back at the photo for a brief moment, then said he had to go.

"But I have a few more questions for you, Mr. Tilden."

"I ain't got no more answers," he said, stepping behind the screen door, then closing the big door in Martin's face.

Martin stood there for a moment, just staring at the closed door, trying to assess what just happened, and thought about knocking on the door again but decided not to.

If Martin was to take everything that just happened on surface value alone, he could assume that Frank was doing his job as professionally as he had claimed, and there would be no reason to further investigate all the other files Martin had sitting in the car. But something didn't seem right about Mr. Tilden. The way he looked down at Frank's picture. There was fear in his eyes, if Martin was correct. Mr. Tilden looked scared of the photo. Then there was the answer to Martin's question. The way Tilden answered it sounded as though he was reciting something learned.

No. Hell, no. Martin wasn't convinced, and he wouldn't be until he visited every father he intended to visit today, and heard them, saw their lips with his own eyes, singing Frank's praises.

■ ■ ■

That day, until early evening, Martin visited seven more fathers, catching some of them at home, others on their jobs. He confronted them, telling them who he was, holding Frank's ugly mug shot up in front of them, asking them if this was the man who approached them about returning back home to their children.

They all looked down at the picture, paused for a moment, the same fearful look in their eyes. And when Martin asked if the man was disrespectful, if he was professional, they all answered in favor of Frank. But there was something strange about their answers. They were all almost identically the same. They had the same practiced tone about them, as if they had been told what to say. They all spoke about how they felt good about returning home to their children after leaving Frank, and they all used that one term that no one outside the police force seems to ever use. "By the book. Everything was by the book." Sounded just like some shit Frank would say, and Martin could all but see Frank standing over one of the just-beaten men, telling them that if anyone comes asking about this, tell him it was "by the book."

It didn't take Sherlock Holmes to put this together. It wasn't that hard. And if Martin wasn't able to put it all together by the lame-ass answers that were given to him, there was this huge clue that no one could overlook.

All the men that Martin had seen that morning looked as if they had been in a head-on collision. Some of them had fresh wounds with bandages on them, small splotches of blood seeping through the coverings. Others had aging scars and scabbed-over wounds, patches of purple and black swimming under their skin, bruises that were just about healed and almost undetectable.

After Martin noticed that the third consecutive man looked as if he had been beaten up, he started to ask all of them.

"What happened to your face?" he said, in a by-the-way manner.

"I fell . . . I was jumped . . . Slipped out of the bathtub," or the men responded, "I got into it with my wife." And when the last man that Martin talked to paused, closed his eyes as if he was trying to come up with something, and then said, "I don't know. I just woke up, and my face was messed up," Martin decided there was no more time to play games.

"Did Frank Rames hit you?" Martin asked the man sternly. They were twenty feet or so away from the construction site where the man worked. The man's coworkers climbed a skeleton of a building in the background.

The man glanced over his shoulder, looking as if he was fearful of someone sneaking up on him.

"Did you hear what I said?" Martin asked, reaching over and grabbing the man's shirt. "Did Frank Rames hit you!" He stuck the mug shot in the man's face, let him have a good look at it. And almost as soon as Martin did that, he realized it was a mistake.

The man took a good look at it, and something inside of him seemed to break down. Then he reached up and gently touched one of the small tapes on his face, and winced a little from the pain.

"No!" the man said. "I told you, everything was by the book. Everything was by the book. I told you, he ain't do nothin' to me. He spoke to me, and I felt good about going back. That's all, that's it."

What a wimp, Martin thought, and the expression was all over Martin's face, and he knew the man had no problem reading it.

"You can talk about this. He's not going to—"

"I told you what I had to say. Now I got to get back to work." The man spun on his heel and quickly ran back down to the site.

Martin left the construction site, drove for the next twenty-five minutes, and parked his car in front of his last stop. He looked over at the stack of files sitting in his passenger seat. Seven men, all who had obviously had the hell beaten out of them, and every one of them scared to talk.

"Damn!" Martin grunted, frustrated. "What are you doing to these guys, Frank?"

One thing he did know, Frank was doing a serious job in covering his tracks. Nobody was talking, and Martin was pretty sure that tomorrow, if he were to grab an entirely new stack of files and go out and do the same thing all over again, he would get the same crappy results.

Martin wrapped his palm around his forehead and squeezed, trying to calm himself down. He was tired of running around all day, tired of trying to convince these men to do something to help themselves. It was exhausting, and now he knew why his partner looked the way he did all the time. Zale can keep this side of the business, Martin thought. Give me the numbers any day.

Martin looked down at his watch, and it was approaching 4:00 P.M. He grabbed the last file, opened it up, and thought about saying, To hell with it. This guy was probably scared out of his mind like the others, but Martin told himself that he would leave no stone unturned. He couldn't if he wanted to prove what was really going on.

He grabbed the file and Frank's photo, which was creased and dog-eared from all it had been through that day, and slipped it in the folder.

Martin got out of the car and walked into the building the file said the man worked in. Martin walked toward the back of the building, where he was directed, and was greeted by a secretary. She stood from her desk, an attractive, long-legged woman.

"May I help you, sir?"

"Yes. I need to see . . ." Martin opened the file and glanced at the name. "Peter Mason."

"I'm sorry, sir," the woman said. "He's not in today, and he's expected to be out the rest of the week."

There it goes, Martin thought. The entire day, a complete waste.

"Is he on vacation?" Martin said, fishing.

"No, he's in the hospital," the secretary said, looking saddened.

"What happened to him, if you don't mind me asking."

"He was in a . . . an altercation."

"You gotta tell me where he's at," Martin said, becoming excited.

"Why?"

"Because . . . because. Because we go way back. We went to high school together, and I flew all the way down from LA to see him. Tell me where he is at so I can be there for him," Martin lied, trying to appear as saddened as she was.

She looked at him for a moment with skepticism in her eyes, then, a moment later, she smiled and, grabbing a pad and a pen, bent down and started writing. She tore the page from the pad, walked around the desk and over to Martin, holding the sheet out to him.

"Here's his information. And tell him I hope he feels better," she said, looking as if she was about to start pushing away sentimental tears.

■ ■ ■

Martin stood inside Peter Mason's hospital room. He was looking down on the sleeping man, and, oh, what a sight he was. His face was almost entirely covered in bandages, save for one of his eyes, which was badly bruised, and his mouth, which appeared to be packed tight with gauze. He lay there on top of his sheets in a hospital gown. Both his hands were bandaged up to his elbows, and Martin figured those were defensive wounds. But fortunately there were no tubes or lines or funny monitoring machines charting the man's breathing. He was no doctor, but Martin knew that was a good sign.

Martin glanced up at the TV that was hanging over the bed, softly airing commercials of no interest. Then he quietly pulled a chair up next to the bed and sat down. He shook his head in disgust at the condition the man was in, hating to have to wake him just to ask him some questions.

"Frank, you son of a bitch," he said. Then he gave Mr. Mason a soft nudge.

Surprisingly, the man woke up almost immediately, and slowly turned his head toward Martin.

"Mr. Mason, I'm sorry to bother you. My name is Martin Carter. I'm from Father Found, and I—"

Then Martin noticed the one eye that wasn't covered open with fear, and Mr. Mason started sliding to one side of the bed. "Don't come near me!" he said, barely audible through the gauze that filled the insides of his mouth.

"No, no. Mr. Mason, Mr. Mason," Martin said, reaching for him before he fell off. "I'm not here to hurt you, sir. I just want to ask you some questions." Then Martin pulled out the photo of Frank and held it up.

"Do you recognize this man?"

Mr. Mason looked at the picture for a long moment. Martin could hear him breathing heavily through the bandages over his nose and the gauze in his mouth, and while he was listening, Martin was trying to give the man whatever courage he needed to stand up and say what needed to be said. C'mon, man, c'mon, you can do it, Martin urged silently. Then Mr. Mason spoke.

"Yeah," he groaned around the gauze, still staring at the photo.

"Sir, I have some questions I would like to ask you about him. Do you think that you'd be able to answer them?"

Mr. Mason slowly turned his bandaged face toward Martin, a painfully grave look in his eye.

"Whatever it is you need to know."

CHAPTER TWENTY-FOUR

Frank opened his eyes, for it was all he could do, and the sunlight that sneaked in between the partly raised shades struck his eyes like long thin slivers of glass. He shut them closed again, tightly, trying to think where he was; he knew he was not in his own bed.

He raised his head slowly from the pillow, and it felt as though it would crack in half. The pain was so great, it was like someone shoved a rusty railroad spike into one ear, the tip protruding out the other. He smacked his lips, tasted the stale taste of gin, and cigarettes, and he lifted his hand to wipe saliva from his mouth, feeling the dull pain from sleeping awkwardly throughout his entire body.

Frank looked around the room. It was somewhere he had never been before, but it was all starting to come back to him. He was having a rough night, started drinking in the early evening, and by nine o'clock he was drunk out of his mind. But he continued driving around drinking from a bottle of gin he had just opened.

He pulled up on a curb, yanked a smiling blonde hooker from the street, and they ended up in the motel room he was in now. Remembering that, Frank, as quick as his head would allow him, turned toward the nightstand, where he saw the bottle of gin he had been drinking, only one fourth full now. He looked over to the dresser, and there he saw his wallet sitting folded over. His gun lay next to it.

He eyed the wallet, the thing splitting in two, and floating around a little bit. Frank reached over and grabbed the bottle of gin off the nightstand and downed the last of it.

He winced slightly, but almost immediately he told himself he felt better. It was like the antidote to all his problems. He slowly got out of bed, made it to his wallet, opened it up, and to his surprise, all his money was there—everything, even the money that he should've owed the hooker for the sex.

He bent to the floor, retrieved his pants, and heard a chirping coming from within them. It was his beeper clipped to the belt, and it had been chirping every now and again like that for the past few days. Frank had clicked it to vibrate, because he didn't want to hear it go off every five seconds. He knew who the hell it was—Carter's anxious ass, paging him like there was a blazing fire and Frank was the only man with a bucket of water. Frank plucked the pager from his belt and looked down at the tiny display window, punched a button, and saw that he had twenty-six pages.

"Fuck him," Frank said. "I'm doing my job, and that's all that matters." Frank hadn't checked in in three or four days, he couldn't remember, but he did tell Zale that this was what he had planned on doing. He said that he wanted to devote all his time to his work, and that if he could just grab a huge stack of files and not come into the office, he could work more effectively, and if there was an emergency, he could always be paged. Zale agreed, as Frank knew he would, considering he was so desperate for results at that time. Obviously, Zale hadn't been in to the office either, or Carter's crybaby ass would have spoken to him, found out about the arrangement, and stopped paging him like a madman.

He clicked the pager from vibrate to alarm, then looked over toward the phone and thought about calling Martin, if for no other reason than to tell him to get off his back, but he decided not to. Nothing could be that important for him to page him the way that he had been, and not calling him back was the best way of letting him know that.

Frank's head was splitting, and he knew he would have to take damn near a half bottle of aspirin and drink a shit load of coffee to get rid of the pain. He grabbed his pants, and was about to clip the pager back to his belt when it started beeping.

The noise penetrated his ears like ice-cold knitting needles jabbed into his brain, and it was so painful that he fell from the bed to his knees trying to get to the pager after it jumped from his hand. When he retrieved it, he looked at it just quickly enough to see who it was. Seeing that it was Martin, infuriated, he slung the pager against the motel room wall, where it cracked and shattered into a number of pieces.

"Leave me the fuck alone!" Frank yelled at the broken piece of equipment, his hands squeezing the sides of his aching head.

Half an hour later, Frank drove around the city, a huge cup of coffee between his legs, taking occasional sips from it. He had to get rid of the hangover if he expected to do his job, and he knew it would take this cup of coffee and one more just like it. He would be pissing like a race-horse for the better part of the morning, but he would have his head back. It was how it always went, because it had just about become a routine now. Bash some heads in during the day—doing his part to help the community solve the fatherless problem—get drunk as a cross-eyed skunk at night, then sober up in the morning, just in time for lunch and six or eight more hours of bruising and occasional bloodshed.

Frank told himself that he was enjoying his new life. Whether it was the truth or not, he never really took the time to think about seriously, but it was holding him over.

He was pretty much allowed to do whatever he wanted to, and with the new authority Zale gave him, he was almost happy. He wasn't getting paid much, but what he was doing, beating the crap out of guys that he felt should have the crap beat out of them, was pretty cool, and Frank knew there were definitely a zillion things worse he could be doing. And he wasn't a fool, he didn't intend on this being something he would do for the rest of his life. He would do it for a little while longer, since it provided some form of income, and eventually he would find a better job, a decent woman, get off the sauce, and maybe buy a small house; he had already started putting a few dollars away from each check that he swore he would never touch for drinks or hookers.

It had become his way of life, and since he had nothing else to occupy his time, no hobbies, no steady piece of ass, no family, no shit, he found ways to keep himself busy. Once in while, the thought of the life he once had tried to enter his mind. He would shut his eyes tight and throw his hands over his ears, as if the thought were actually floating around outside trying to find an entrance into his brain through some opening in his head.

He would shake his head like a crazed fool, yelling till the thought went away, because he knew if he entertained that thought, he would start feeling sorry for himself, start crying like a child, and he would realize that what he had now wasn't really a life, but just an excuse to keep on living. He would find himself on his ex-wife's doorstep, begging to be taken back, making a fool out of himself in front of his daughter, and he told himself he would never do that. She can't have that as the last memory of him. He loved them more than anything, but he would never go back. He had a new life now, and that was the end of it.

Frank's bladder was getting tight, and he was surprised, because usually he didn't have to take his first leak until after the first few sips of his second cup. He didn't have time to find a rest room, so he pulled the Impala off the street and drove down an alley. He jumped out of the car, drank the last bit of coffee, tossed the cup to the ground, turned toward the wall, unzipped his fly, pulled himself out, and released the stream of urine.

Frank shook two times, and before he had a chance to straighten himself up, he was tapped on the shoulder. When he spun around, a huge hand was shoved into his throat, and he was slammed into the wall. His head banged against the brick wall. He saw stars for a moment, then shook them, and saw that Mace's huge flunky, Kronk, was holding him by the throat with an arm that resembled a tree trunk.

"Catch you at a bad time, Frank?" Mace said, pulling his dark glasses from his face.

"What do you want?" Frank asked, his voice pinched by the hand across his throat.

"You a hard man to find, Frank. I've been looking for you for the past few days, but you almost invisible. You haven't been going in to work lately, have you?"

"That's none of your damn business," Frank said, struggling to free himself, his penis still hanging from his open fly.

Mace walked right up into Frank's face, slapping his hand against the wall. "That is my damn business," Mace said. "Answer a question for me, Frank. How the fuck are you protecting my boy, Ro, when you ain't even going in to work? Did you know he got fools calling him at all hours of the night. He thinks somebody's after him to take him out again. Did you know that!" Mace said, anger in his voice and in his eyes.

"I knew that," Frank lied. "I was on my way to his—"

"Stop your lying, 'cause I talked to him a few days ago and he don't know where the hell you at!" Mace turned his back on Frank, took a couple of steps, then turned back around.

"You have a small dick, Frank," Mace said, as if their conversation had been about that. "But that's typical for white boys. Only white boys I've seen with big dicks are on those porno flicks, and they all Italian, which means they ain't really white at all, doesn't it, Frank?"

Frank just looked at Mace defiantly, not responding.

"Slide that small, motherfuckin' dick back in your pants, Frank, or does it retract automatically?" Mace said, smiling at the joke he made while Frank pushed himself back into his pants and fastened them.

Mace walked back up to Frank, the smile wiped from his face.

"Now, all jokes aside, let me tell you something. Me and Ro, Mr. Rowen to your punk ass, we go back, way back, and that man means a lot to me, more than your small-minded ass could ever know. I've known him longer than I've known anyone on this earth, and I've done things for that man that I probably wouldn't do for blood, so that gives you an example of how important his well-being is to me. But here's the part, Frank. He's not just important to me, but to all black folks. You might find this hard to understand, but Zaleford Rowen is a great man. I'm sure you heard of Martin Luther King, Jr., Marcus Garvey, and of course ya'll's favorite, Malcolm X. To me, he's like them. He's a man with vision that's trying to help his people better their situation, their lives, and he's putting his own head on the line to do it, which I think is crazy and fucked up, but he don't see it that way. The black race can't afford to lose another great man, because they only come around every thirty or forty years, and, besides that, it would hurt the hell out of me, and you probably don't know this, but it would hurt you, too. But it would hurt you in a different way, like broken bones, severed limbs, and probably a couple of shots to the back of the head, you know what I mean?"

Kronk tightened his grip around Frank's neck for a moment, to drive the point home.

"Now are you getting my point, Mr. Rames?"

Frank looked at the big man holding him pinned to the wall, then looked over at Mace, his hair pulled back in a ponytail like a girl, his elaborate silk clothes draping off of him like some minority version of Liberace, and Frank started to chuckle. And the more he thought about the man's appearance, the more he started to laugh, and the only reason he didn't laugh as hard as he could was because Kronk's big black ass had him by the throat. When Frank was finally able to control his laughter, he turned to Mace.

"Let me tell you something now. I'll do my job because Ro," Frank said the name mockingly, "pays me to do it, and I'll do it because I want to. Not because he means the world to you. I don't care what he means to you, or to the black community. I can give less than a damn. And as far as the two of you go, you're just a couple of low-down, no-good niggers, killing your own people for a couple of dollars, so you can run around here buying fucked-up, ugly clothes like you're wearing. You talk about Marcus Garvey and Dr. King like you're all about the upliftment of your people. What a fucking hypocrite you are.

"And one more thing, if you think that threatening to kill me is going to light a fire under my ass, you're wrong, dead wrong. I don't care about your threats. My life is shit anyway, so if you're bad enough, you can kill me right now, tough guy." Frank looked directly into Mace's eyes, not bluffing, not fearing anything at that moment.

Mace stood back for a moment, then smiled briefly.

"Maybe I chose the wrong tool to motivate you, then. Let's try another. Let me put it this way, if anyone speaks to my boy Ro harshly, let alone harm a hair on his head, I won't kill you, but I'll have my boy Kronk here pay a visit to your ex-wife, Wendy, and your sweet little girl, Bianca. Now how's that?"

Frank lost his mind at the thought that these men would do harm to his family.

"How do you know about my family! Who told you about them!" Frank cried. He started beating at Kronk's arms, and he felt them weakening, until he was hit in the gut with a hard shot from the big man's fist. Frank fell to his knees, coughing, spitting, grabbing his middle.

Mace knelt down in front of him, speaking softly into Frank's face.

"We have our ways of finding things out on the street. But think I'm joking, Frank? I'll kill 'em, because when it comes to my boy, I've killed before. I swear, something, anything happens to him, I'll send my boy, and he'll walk right past you, wave to you on the fucking street on his way to your wife's house to dissect her like a fucking frog, and you won't be able to do shit. Your ass will be flipping the covers on city Dumpsters trying to find out which one of them your family's at the bottom of, you know what I'm saying? You get me, motherfucker?" Mace said, grabbing Frank's face by the cheeks, squeezing, making Frank look him in the eyes. He released Frank's face, wiped his hand off on his pants, as if he had handled something filthy.

The two men walked off, leaving Frank in the alley, still folded over, grabbing his gut. He watched the men walk away, and he thought to pull his gun, fire off a couple of rounds, killing them both, but if he missed, they would surely kill him, and take his family as well, and he couldn't have that.

Frank pulled himself up and stumbled over to his car. What he had to do now, until he could think of something better, was to do his job. Just do what the fuck he was paid to do, and that was to protect Rowen, but it wasn't as simple as that. Somebody was already after Zale, and Frank had to get to Rowen before they did, if they hadn't already found him.

CHAPTER TWENTY-FIVE

Martin stood outside his house, readying himself to go in. It was dark out. He glanced down at his watch; it read 7:45. He had put in a long day at work and still had not accomplished nearly what he had set out to. Most important, he had not found Frank, and that was weighing heavily on his mind. But Martin tried to make it a practice not to drag his problems from work into his home. He would drop all the baggage from the day at the doorstep before going in, so his daughters and his wife wouldn't have to suffer through what he was suffering through. Besides, it wasn't hard to do. By the time he opened the door, saw his little ladies running to greet him, he had always forgotten about all that troubled him anyway.

Martin pulled the key from his pocket, feeling almost unnatural approaching his own door. He had been back for a week now, and he was slowly becoming reaccustomed to his wife, which was taking more time than he thought it would. He wasn't sure why, but there was something inside of him that wouldn't let go of all that happened, and every time he looked at her, he felt a twinge of resentment that he had to mask with a smile, or immediately turn his head away so that she wouldn't feel uncomfortable.

So she wouldn't feel uncomfortable, Martin thought again, shaking his head. I am the one that was cheated on. Since he had been back, since he had brought his daughters home, things had pretty much gone back to the way they had been, almost as if nothing had ever happened. But he did notice that Debra was trying quite hard to be the wife she should've always been. She was more attentive, more understanding of Martin's problems, and more willing to give in to what he wanted. He wasn't really sure how he felt about that, about almost anything anymore. But he told himself that he wanted his wife back, and he had gotten her, so he just decided to let things play themselves out.

Martin opened the door, expecting to see the babysitter shouldering her bag ready to go, his daughters running up behind her, but all was quiet, and the lights in the house were dim.

Martin set down his briefcase and was surprised to see his wife coming out of the kitchen, an apron tied around her thin waist. She walked up to him, a wooden spoon in her hand, and without saying a word, wrapped her arms around him and gave him a kiss on the mouth.

"Hey, sweetheart, how was your day?" she said, taking his jacket from him, hanging it up in the closet.

"Fine," Martin said carefully.

Debra grabbed Martin by the hand, led him into the kitchen, and sat him down at the table. She pulled the cloth napkin off the table, shook it open, and placed it gently in his lap.

"I made you a special dinner," Debra said, smiling. Martin looked over the table, saw the dishes that he had forgotten they had, the silverware Debra had gotten from her mother, and the pair of long white candles twinkling in the center of the table.

He had no idea what all this was about and felt uncomfortable about it for some reason, as if his wife was trying to cushion some tremendous bomb she was about to drop on his head.

"Where are the girls?" Martin said, trying to settle down.

"I put them to bed early so we could be alone," Debra said, pulling the apron from her waist, setting a dish on the table.

"And what is this all about?"

Debra sat down at the table, not across from Martin, but adjacent to him, so close their knees rubbed against each other. Debra covered Martin's hand with her own, still smiling.

"It's because I love you, and I'm happy that things are back the way they were, the way they should be, but it's also because I have some good news." She excitedly squeezed Martin's hand at the end of her sentence.

"Do you know what time it is?" Debra asked, seeming that she was about to explode if she had to withhold her news much longer.

"It's eight o'clock," Martin said.

"And I'm home. Have you noticed that?"

"Yes. How could I not?" Martin said, not sharing the excitement she was experiencing.

"Well, from now on this is going to be the routine. I'm cutting back my hours at the hospital so that I can be home no later than seven o'clock every day." After Debra was finished spilling her news, she looked in her husband's face, seeming as though she was waiting for him to jump from his chair, turn a couple of back flips and a cartwheel, and then give her a big wet one on the mouth, but he did none of that. Martin just sat there, a fork in his hand, thinking over what he had just heard.

"When did you make that decision?" he said, fully aware that he was not reacting to the news the way she wanted him to.

"Is that all you have to say? When did I make that decision? Aren't you happy to hear that?" Debra said, appearing obviously hurt.

"Well, what made you do that? You didn't even talk it over with me."

"Talk it over? What was there to talk over?" Debra said. "How often were you complaining about me coming home late? About me not spending enough time with the girls, not spending enough time with you? So I finally decide to do something about it, knowing that you would just be tickled pink when you heard the news, but instead you tell me that I should've discussed it with you first. You don't want me to be home earlier?" Debra asked, and by the tone of her voice, it sounded as though she really needed Martin to answer that question before she actually knew the answer.

Martin looked at her, and wanted to ask her, Why now? Why all of this now? Why did it have to take him ranting and raving almost every night, her getting caught with another man, just to make her change her hours so that her husband and kids could have her around more? Martin wanted to ask her all this, but he realized that she was really trying to make things better for them. Do what she could to avoid them having arguments, to avoid the resentment they felt for each other, and to avoid whatever it was that sent her into the arms of another man in the first place. So Martin didn't question his wife, just placed a less-than-sincere smile on his face, swallowing whatever ill feelings he had about her and her motivation, and said, "I'm happy that you'll be home earlier. Both myself and the kids will really appreciate it." Then he leaned over the table and gave her a peck on the lips, which seemed to be the cure for whatever his wife was going through at the moment.

After dinner, Debra suggested that the two of them take a shower together, but Martin declined, saying that he would rather shower alone tonight. He had a hard day at work, and he just wanted to stand under the hard stream of water and let it beat down on his neck and back. And as he did that, occasionally lifting his head up so the water could spray in his face, he wondered why he was feeling the way he was. Why had he reacted to the news his wife gave him the way he had and wasn't he happy about it?

Something was bothering him about her, and he just couldn't put his finger on it, and it was driving him crazy. Martin cut the water off, stepped out of the shower, and threw a towel over his head, drying himself off. He stood in the mirror, telling himself that he should be happy, that everything had worked out exactly the way it was supposed to, the way Zale told him it would. His wife came back to him, and not just that, it was as if she was the wife she had never been before. Earlier, at dinner, she catered to his every need. Filled his glass with wine every time it sank to less than half full, poured more gravy onto his rice when she felt he needed it, buttered his roll, and cut his steak. She did everything but dab the corners of his mouth with her napkin and throw him over her shoulder after dinner to burp him. She was trying to make this work with all she had, and doing it with a smile, and supposedly it was all because she loved him, but for some reason, that just didn't sit right with Martin.

Martin slipped on some boxers and a T-shirt and went out to the bedroom, where he found his wife lying across the bed, wearing a purple teddy. When she heard him entering, she rolled up on her side and smoothed her hand across the space on the bed next to her, enticing him to join her.

Martin got into the bed, driven by nothing more than the fatigue he was feeling. He doubled his pillow, placed it behind his back, and sat up in bed, because he felt it would've been rude to fall right off to sleep when he knew that his wife wanted to talk. This had become the routine over the last week.

Debra affectionately slid her hand under her husband's, and intertwined her fingers with his. Debra snuggled up a little closer to Martin, throwing her smooth, bare leg over his hairy one.

"I was just thinking that maybe . . . that you don't have to tell the girls that I'm not their real mother if you don't want to."

"And why wouldn't I do that?" Martin said, turning to look down at her on his arm.

"Because maybe it will be easier for Renee and Rebecca to accept us as a family if they don't know. I mean, I don't see the difference that it would make. We refer to them as my children anyway."

Martin had to turn his eyes away from her. He couldn't believe what he was hearing.

"I'm going to tell them anyway," he said coldly.

"But why? I've cared for them since they were babies. We don't know the effect that something like this would have on them. Why can't we just let them go on thinking that I'm their real mother?"

"Because you aren't!" Martin said bitterly, pushing away from her, looking at her through cold eyes. "It's not just about you, Debra. Have you ever stopped to think that I would want them to know who their real mother was? Are you so full of yourself that you thought that when she died, I just forgot all about her? Did you think that when you came on the scene, my memory was just erased? Debra, let me tell you something. I loved that woman, still love her to this day, and every day

I look down at those little girls of mine, I see my wife in them, and something terrible inside me aches, and I know that only she can make that pain go away, but that'll never happen." Martin lowered his head, regretting his outburst, the words he subjected Debra to, the feelings he let her in on, but he knew they had to come out.

"Debra, my daughters, our daughters, have to know who their real mother is, and it's not because I don't love you as much, but because I love them so much."

Debra didn't say a word, but attempted to place an understanding hand on Martin's shoulder, but when he felt it, he pulled himself farther away, got up from the bed, and walked over and leaned against the dresser, his back toward her. He was angry at her, angry as hell, but not just because she asked him to hold back the truth from his daughters, when at one time she was dying for him to tell them, but also because of the emotions he was feeling, the shit he was going through because of her. It had to do with her cheating, with her betraying him. He was feeling things that he had never felt before, things that he never thought he'd have to deal with, things that he figured he could get over, clear from his mind, but couldn't.

"I'm sorry," he heard Debra saying in a meek voice, but he didn't turn around. "I guess I just really wanted to believe that I was their real mother, and I wanted everything to be perfect this time. I don't want anything to go wrong again."

"How long was your affair with him?" Martin interrupted, turning around to face her.

The question caught his wife by surprise, and he could see it on her face.

"What?"

"I said, how long was your affair with him?"

Debra looked down at her hands, blew out a long sigh, and said, "Three months."

"Three months," Martin repeated, more to himself than to her. "I'm going to figure it was a little longer than that, because you may be trying to save me some pain. Did you use protection?"

Debra looked shocked by his question.

"Well, did you?"

"Why are you asking me these things?"

"Because it concerns my health, and it's something I need to know," Martin said, feeling no pity for her.

"Yes! We used something."

"Every time."

"Yes. Every time."

But Martin wasn't done just yet. There was one more question that he had to ask. This he didn't *have* to know the answer to, for he felt it was childish, and would only satisfy what little ego he had left, but it was something he just really wanted to know.

"Did he make you have an orgasm?" Martin asked.

"What did you say to me?" Debra said, sounding both stunned and angered.

"You heard me. Did he bring you to orgasm?"

Debra got up from the bed, her long hair whipping about her head as she did, and started to make her way out of the room when Martin said, calmly, but with much authority, "Sit down."

At his words, Debra paused for a moment, as if deciding whether or not he really meant it.

"I said, sit down, and answer the question."

Debra did return to the bed, but with plenty of attitude.

"Why are you asking me these questions? Martin, that's over. I thought we were trying to get on with our lives. Why won't you just let it go?"

"I shouldn't have to let anything go!" Martin said, becoming angry. "I shouldn't have to get past shit! If you didn't have your ass out there with some other man, if you hadn't cheated on me, I wouldn't have to ask these questions. I wouldn't have to think about this, suffer through this. But because I have to, I'm entitled to have answers to my questions. And because you did to me what you did, you're obligated to tell me. Now, I'll ask you again."

"No, no," Debra pleaded. "I'll answer you." She paused for a long moment, then said, "No. I never had an orgasm with him."

Martin knew she was lying, and she, too, should've known he knew it.

"I see," Martin said, as though he was working out a problem in his head. "You said you didn't love him, and you said he never made you have an orgasm, but you continued a *sexual* relationship with him for at least three months. Something's not ringing true here. It was one or the other. Either you—"

"All right!" Debra snapped, her eyes bulging with frustration, her body rattling with anger. "I had an orgasm with him, and not just one. A lot. He made me come every fucking time, hard! So hard I wet the damn bedsheets, soaked the fucking mattress, had to flip it over just so we wouldn't both drown in my orgasmic juices. And the shit felt good. Damn good! Okay, Martin? All right? Is that what you needed from me? Is that what you wanted to hear?" Debra shouted at him as he slowly walked toward his side of the bed and slid under the covers.

"No," he said, unaffected by her ranting. "But it was what I expected." He clicked off the lamp and, leaving his wife in the dark, rolled over and went to sleep.

CHAPTER TWENTY-SIX

Overhead, the clouds were a thick, dark carpet, pregnant with rain, threatening to dump their contents all over Chicago, but as Zale looked up, walking hurriedly under them, he knew the rain would not fall. They looked as if they would rip open, explode any moment, but it had been days of them hovering low overhead, and the wait for the rain had been to Zale like the unbearable wait for whoever was stalking him to show his face, make his move.

Zale feared that moment, but he needed it to happen, desperately, because at this point, he was running strictly on paranoia alone, looking over his shoulder every three or four steps, stopping randomly in his tracks, allowing people who were walking behind him to pass so he would know they were not following him.

He had been "on the run" since the night Mace broke into his house. Thankfully, it was only his friend, but he realized that if Mace could get in just because he wanted to talk to Zale, then a man intent on seeing Zale dead would scale mountains to lay his hands on him.

Zale couldn't go back, and he hadn't. For the last two nights, he had been staying in a motel off the highway. A small room, with a large window overlooking the parking lot. Those nights he could barely sleep, for every time a car pulled into the lot, Zale was out of bed, parting the curtains slightly, making sure that it wasn't the man who was looking to kill him. He would wander back to bed, exhausted, but after realizing that his mind would not let him sleep, and that cars would be driving into the parking lot all night long, he decided that it would be best to keep an eye out the window till the sun came up. He didn't want to give anyone the opportunity to stand over him while he was asleep again, because he knew next time the man looking down at him would not be a friend.

As Zale walked down the busy street, he caught glimpses of himself in the storefront windows, and he looked awful. But it was how he knew he looked, for he had given up on his appearance some time ago. He didn't have the time or the energy to worry about things as unimportant as the whiskers dirtying his face, the hair that sprung wildly from his head, or the fact that it looked as if he dug his clothes out of one of the Dumpsters that stood in the alleys.

One thing that did worry him was his health. As he passed another window, one with a mirror in it, he paused just long enough to get a good look at himself, and he could see that he had lost a few more pounds. Three or four, he told himself, as he stuck a thumb into the waist of his trousers and pulled. They pulled freely and effortlessly away from his shrinking midsection, and he accepted the fact that maybe he had lost more than just three pounds.

Zale wanted to eat, but he couldn't get his mind to stop racing long enough to sit down and feed himself, and when he finally did, the small flame that continued to burn in the pit of his stomach, like the pilot on a stove, had turned into a blaze. He feared that if he did manage to get something down, his body would reject it, and he would find himself forced down to all fours, bent over the side of a curb, violently choking up the food, painfully ejecting it from his body. So he didn't eat, more afraid of the pain from eating than the repercussions he faced from not eating. He needed to get his medicine, and suddenly he regretted his lax approach to taking it. If he had been more serious about it, it would've been in his pocket right now, but it was at home in the medicine cabinet where it always sat, where he always avoided it. But there was no way he could go to retrieve it. He could do nothing until he felt safe, and that would only happen when he heard from Frank.

Zale stopped again, like clockwork, and allowed the people who were stepping behind him to pass. He did not shift to one side or move from his path to make getting around him easier. He just stood there and watched suspiciously as they made their way in front of him.

Over the past few days, he had tried paging Frank countless times, but Rames never returned his phone calls. When he called Martin, Martin said that Frank had only been in once in the last week, a few days ago, looking frantic and very desperate.

"He was looking for you, like his life depended on finding you," Martin said. "But when I told him I didn't know where you were, he flew out of here like a madman."

"Have you tried paging him?"

"Tried a hundred times, but he doesn't call back." Martin paused over the phone for a moment. "You have to come in, Zale. There's a lot of shit going down with Rames, and it's something that needs your immediate attention. I found out that—"

"I can't come in. I can't. Not until I get in touch with Rames. I think there's someone after me again, and they could be sitting across the damn street from Father Found for all I know."

"Look," Martin said, sounding desperate. "Just come in. We'll call the police, we'll straighten this out, and we'll handle this business with Frank as well."

"The police won't do a damn thing about me getting hang-ups!" Zale said, looking both ways over his shoulders, feeling paranoid. "They didn't last time, so what will make this any different. Find Rames and tell him to call me on my cell phone."

"But, Zale, you—"

"Martin. Don't say anything else, just find Frank." Zale disconnected the call.

After that, he called his voice mail and was not surprised to find almost twenty hang-ups, and if this man was half as persistent as his phone calls implied, unless something happened soon, Zale knew he would find himself staring down the barrel of yet another gun.

Zale had just started walking again when he was grabbed by the arm. His heart jumped. He spun around, expecting to see a gun in his face, but an elderly man, bent slightly over, a cane in one hand, asked, "Do you have the time?"

Zale just stood there for a moment, his heart still racing, his body still shaking, looking down at the old man. Then he slowly brought his watch into his view, and said, after exhaling, "It's almost five o'clock."

"Thank you," the man said, and released Zale's arm, Zale watching as the old wrinkled hand moved from his sleeve. He was relieved that this was not his stalker, but, nevertheless, this man had been upon him, his hand on him, clutching his arm, his knuckles brushing against Zale's ribs. If this had been the man looking for him, that hand could've just as easily been a knife, one that he could've slid in between Zale's ribs right into his heart, silently, almost effortlessly. In this crowd of people, no one would've known anything till after Zale was stretched out across the pavement, a thick, slow stream of blue-red blood crawling toward the gutter, and the man turning a corner, already a block from where he had killed Zale.

Zale stopped again, looking around, realizing now that he was far too vulnerable, even walking the street. Any one of the people standing around him, walking past him, could be the one after him, and the thought forced Zale slowly off the sidewalk into the doorway of a small store. Paranoia and anxiety were mounting in him now, as he whipped his head left and right, looking into the faces of strangers, any one of which could be the one looking to kill him.

A man pushed at the door, trying to get out of the store, the door bumping Zale in the back, almost giving him a heart attack. Zale pressed himself up against the side of the doorway, looking at the man wide-eyed, his head and face coated with sweat. As the man passed Zale, he clutched his bag tighter, giving him a strange look.

Zale knew at that moment that he couldn't continue like this. He wanted, needed, Frank to protect him, but he couldn't afford to wait for him. He needed to protect himself, just in case the next person that bumped into him was the man that was looking for him.

It was past 10:00 P.M., and after a half hour of sitting in his car a block from his house, Zale drove closer, parking it in front, satisfied that no one was sitting, observing his home the way he was.

Zale made his way into the house, moving very slowly, practically holding his breath, stepping very cautiously, burdened with the thought that his next step might be his last. As he walked through the dark house, clutching his house keys so tightly in his hand that they threatened to draw blood, he felt like a stranger. He felt as if this was someone else's home, as if he had no business there, and was expecting someone to pop out from behind one of the doors and scream for him to get the hell out of there before they called the police on him.

He walked farther into the house, and was relieved to find that everything was how he left it, and it made him believe that no one had been in his house after him, looking for him.

He walked slowly through the dark hallway, the flattened palm of his hand tracing the wall as he made his way to his bedroom. When he stepped into the doorway and looked in, Zale was startled for a moment, seeing the mess that littered his bedroom, not remembering that he had tossed his belongings all about the floor and bed the last time he was here, looking for exactly what he was looking for now.

He stepped into the room, seeing the clothes and other belongings sitting in piles like trash on the ground of a dumping yard. It looked as if this was done by the hands of someone else, by the hands of a man who hated him, because these were possessions of Zale's that he would never treat this way. The way his things were thrown about looked violent. The shirts thrown across the bed and lying out on the floor, the arms stretched out or folded oddly over themselves, looked like torsos—dead, unbreathing torsos, separated from the lower halves of their bodies.

Zale stepped across another pile, saddened by the mess that lay before him, and he realized that even though it was him that had physically torn this place apart, this was done by the hands of another man; the fear that was put on him forced him to do this to his home.

This man had control of Zale. Full control, as if he had strings tied to Zale's arms and legs and was dragging him around like a lifeless marionette.

There was no work being done by him at Father Found, no speeches being made, no fathers being counseled, no women or children being helped. And when someone called the office to speak to him, Zale was sure they were told that he was not available, the same as if he had been gunned down, and was being made up and fitted for a suit for his final viewing. His stalker had won, plain and simple.

Zale saw what he was looking for, bent down and retrieved it from the mess on the floor. He held the gun up, opened it, and remembered that all the bullets had been expended. But he had some more, he thought. He had some more, and he would reload and stick some in his pockets just in case. He would no longer hide. He would no longer be dead to the people who needed him. He had work to do, work that he chose to do, that he felt needed to be done, and no one, no one would stop him from doing that.

When Zale pulled his car in front of the Father Found building, it was after 11:00 P.M., and the clouds had finally opened up, pelting the city with huge, harsh raindrops that hit the roof of Zale's car with enough force to make him wonder whether or not there would be small dents left in their wake.

Zale told himself that he would go into the office tonight, not to get any real work done, but to assess what needed to be done. If nothing else, he needed to make a stand of some sort, to award himself a tiny triumph, a confidence-builder, something that he could build on.

Zale shut the car off, the windshield wipers halting in midmotion in the center of the windshield. He looked out at the building through the rain-blurred glass and tried to motivate himself to go in. He was still scared, but he had the gun in the waist of his pants, and it did give him some strength, some courage, to help him do what he came to do.

He grabbed a newspaper from his back seat, threw it over his head, and jumped out of the car. The rain was falling so hard that it immediately drenched him and turned the newspaper to a limp wet paper cloth draping his head and shoulders.

For a moment, he had trouble sliding the key into the car to lock it, but after a second he managed to lock the door, and when he turned around, his heart skipped a beat, and he questioned his vision because he hadn't heard a sound, but standing in front of him was a huge, dark figure. Zale only had but a moment to comprehend what was going on before he was hit in the gut with a punch forceful enough to send him to one knee.

Zale looked up to try and see who this was, but because of the intense rainwater blurring his vision, he could see nothing but a dark outline, this huge figure silhouetted by a streetlamp that hung high above him.

Zale tried reaching for his gun, but before he could get to it, the man grabbed him by the hair and punched him across the face. Zale fell to all fours, his hands on the rain-wet street, rain soaking through his clothes, falling from his face. He tried for the gun again, but this time he was kicked in the gut. The kick forced all the air out of Zale's body, and he felt that he could not inhale and that he would die before the man even shot him. But the man kicked him again, this time harder, and Zale felt excruciating pain, like something had snapped inside of him, and he flipped over on his back.

Still, he could not see the man who was beating him, but he heard him, breathing hard, grunting something, cursing angrily under his breath.

Zale was hurting, could barely breathe, and when he did, he felt as if he were being cut open with a huge knife. He was on his back, and for some reason, the man backed off just a moment, just long enough for what Zale thought was enough time to reach his gun.

He went for it, not trying to conceal his actions, and even though Zale could not see this man's face, he thought he saw his eyes widen when he saw that Zale was moving for his waist, pulling the weapon from his belt line.

Zale saw the man move quickly, and he knew that he had to level the weapon on him, squeeze off a shot, kill him, or Zale himself might be dead.

He pulled the gun down, and although his hands and arms were shaking uncontrollably, he got the man in his sights had his finger on the trigger, and was prepared to shoot. But just before he could, the man was on him, had kicked the gun out of his hand and sent it flying down the street.

Zale bent and turned his head to follow the path of the gun as it skidded away from him, disappearing under a car. Before he was able to turn back around to face the man, he was grabbed by his coat and slammed against the door of the car.

The man punched Zale in the stomach again, but held tight to him, not letting him fall. Then he reared back and with everything he had, sent a knee into Zale's crotch. Zale's face distorted into an agonizing grimace, his mouth opening, widening, as if he was trying to scream, but no sound was made.

Then the man grabbed Zale by the collar, brought his fist back, and hit Zale with a punch to the chin. Zale was sent flying across the length of the car, but was stopped when his face crashed into the side-view mirror. He felt a huge, deep cut open up under his eye, blood smearing across his face, as it painted the side of the car. He fell to the pavement on his back again. He was just about unconscious, his head spinning, his body dying for oxygen, his organs, stomach, his spleen, feeling as though they had been ripped, torn, but he still kept his eye on the man moving about above him, wondering whether the man was going to beat him to death or if he was going to be more humane and pull out a gun, ending it quickly. At this point, Zale did not care, because he was numb and could feel no more pain, and he had already accepted the fact that he was going to die. What he needed to know was why, and he asked the man that softly, through trembling, swollen, bloodstained lips: "Why are you . . ."

The man paced about over him, the rain still falling in gallons, his body still haloed by the streetlight.

"Because you can't leave me be. I'm trying. I'm trying with all I can to do right by my damn kids. I'm working two jobs and trying to find another, but when you making minimum, you can never work enough. I give them what money I can afford, but I have the fucking courts telling me I need to give them more, and it's because you sent them after me. You telling me that I need to spend more time with them, but how can I do that when I have to work like a damn slave, and I can't move back in because they mama know if that happens, her welfare going to get cut down. I'm doing all I can, and it still ain't enough," he said, sounding sorry for himself, sounding as though he was looking for sympathy from the man that he had just beaten.

"Why didn't you tell me this when I came after you," Zale managed to say, the mere act of talking sending pain throughout his entire body. "I wouldn't have—"

"I don't have to tell you shit!" the man said, stepping nearer to Zale, standing at his feet. "Why should I have to tell you a damn thing? This is my family, my life. I'm just as much of a man as you. Why should I have to okay shit with you? I don't," he said, answering his own question. "You had to be taught a lesson. You can't go around thinking that you have the power to run men's lives. That you can decide how he should deal with his problems, and no one knows better than you, not even himself. So . . . you have to learn your lesson."

Zale didn't say a word, just watched the man. The rain had slowed and just about stopped, and Zale could see the man better now, but he still could not see the features that would tell him who he was. Zale saw the man look up to the sky for a moment, then turn to look over his shoulder, and then slide a hand into his jacket. This was the moment, Zale told himself. This would be the lesson that he was going to get taught, and not even a short moment ago, he was ready— Zale was ready to die, but now that that moment was upon him, he could not accept it.

He tried to move, tried to get up and run, saw his body doing it, his legs working, pulling him up from the ground and running as fast as they could to save him from being gunned down on the street, but his body would not respond.

He thought of begging, thought of giving this man his word that he would never make those mistakes, that he'd stop what he was doing, let Father Found go, and forget about everything. But Zale knew that he would only be lying for that moment to save his life, that he would never stop doing what he was doing, and he would never beg a man for his life, at least not this man.

So there was nothing more to do than to accept what was going to happen, accept it, and be thankful for what he had been able to accomplish.

Zale saw the man pulling his arm out of his jacket and decided that he did not want to see the gun, did not want to look down the barrel. So he closed his eyes and tried to make himself go deaf somehow, to fill his mind with loud thoughts so he would not hear the explosion that would take his life.

He lay there, his eyes closed, counting the seconds in his mind from the time he thought it would take to pull the gun from the man's jacket to the point where he was aiming it at Zale's head and was ready to pull the trigger. And when Zale felt that time had elapsed, when he felt that he was on the verge of dying, he threw his arms over his face, his eyes still closed, and yelled out, "Noooooooooo!"

After what seemed an eternity, Zale realized that he was still alive and had heard no gunshot. He slowly lowered his arms, opened his eyes, and saw the man still standing over him, shaking a match out from a cigarette he had just lit that was hanging from his mouth. There was no gun to be seen.

"Aren't . . . aren't you going to kill me?" Zale asked, shocked by the fact that he was still able to ask the question.

"I ain't going to kill you. I ain't no killer," the man said, taking a drag from the cigarette. "You just needed to learn a lesson, so you'd leave me the fuck alone. So whatever information you got on me, whatever computer you holding me in, or whatever scraps of paper you got Anthony Tyler on, you need to burn, you got that. Or I'll be back for your ass." He flicked the half-smoked cigarette at Zale, and it hit him in the chest and rolled off his stomach onto the ground. "And next time you won't get off as easy."

The man turned and started to walk away, and Zale used all his remaining strength to prop himself up on his elbows and call out to the man.

"Have you been the one calling me?" Zale asked, praying that the man would give him the right answer.

The man turned around, a puzzled look on his face. "Why would I call you. I can't stand you." Then he turned back around and walked off, leaving Zale with the knowledge that he had not come any farther than he had three days ago. There was still someone out there looking for him, and his life was still in danger. Zale looked around, hoping that someone would be passing on the street, but there was no one. So all he could do was settle back onto the ground till morning came and someone would find him, and hope that it wouldn't be his stalker.

CHAPTER TWENTY-SEVEN

Frank slammed on the brakes when he arrived in front of Father Found, sending the Impala screeching and squealing, sliding across the pavement before it came to a hard stop. He bolted out of the car, leaving the door open, not having a second to spare to close it. He had to get upstairs, get to Rowen to find out if it was true.

When Frank had called Father Found that morning, he was checking just to see if Martin had seen or had spoken to Rowen within the last two days, but when Martin's voice came over the phone, Frank didn't even need the man to speak the words in order for him to tell that there was something terribly wrong.

"Where the hell have you been!" Martin yelled into the phone at Frank.

"Have you seen Rowen?" Frank said, paying no attention to Martin's ranting.

"I asked you a goddamn question, Rames!"

"And I asked you one. Have you seen Rowen?"

There was a moment of silence over the phone, and Frank knew that Martin was seething.

"He's here," Martin said, subdued anger in his voice. "But he's injured. And if you were where you were supposed to be, you would've known that."

And that's when everything halted for Frank. He knew he heard what Martin had told him, but he didn't want to believe it. He wanted to ask him how, wanted to ask him when this happened, and how bad Rowen was, but there was no time. There was no time if he had been injured the way Frank thought he had been, almost knew he had been. Frank had to get to the office and find out for himself, talk to the man, see who he had talked to, find out if his family was in danger.

Frank leaped up the old stairs of the Father Found building, out of breath, but continuing to grab the railing and yank himself up the stairs. When he hit the second floor, he ran, flat-out ran as if a wild animal were chasing him.

When he got near Zale's office, he saw Martin. Frank tried to get around him, but Martin stepped in front of him, looking as if he had serious business to conduct with the man.

"Is he in there?" Frank asked hurriedly, frantically.

"You're in a lot of shit, Rames. We need to talk right now. In my office." Martin grabbed Frank by the arm and was about to lead him in the other direction when Frank yanked away from him and said, "I don't care what kind of shit I'm in right now, all right? Is Zale in there!" Frank yelled, pausing between each word of the question so Martin would make no mistake that this was the most important thing in the world to him right now, that lives depended on this, and nothing would stop him from finding out what he needed to know at that moment.

Martin looked at Frank for a moment before answering, and there seemed to be a faint look of concern in his eyes, as if he cared what was going on with Frank, as if Martin wanted to ask him what the matter was, but Frank knew that couldn't have been.

"Yeah, he's in there," Martin said, stepping aside so Frank could pass.

Frank threw open the door of Zale's office, and what he saw both enraged and horrified him. Zale was standing up near his desk, looking down at some paperwork. What Frank could see of his face was scarred and beaten, bruises of purple and black swimming under his puffy, swollen skin. The remainder of his face was covered in small bandages, tapes, and a large bandage under his right eye. Even though he was standing, it looked as though he was barely able to, propping himself up against the desk, balancing himself with a hand placed firmly on its surface. He looked to be in a hell of a lot of pain standing there, and he looked as though he could've been toppled over by a strong wind. Frank ran over to Zale, grabbed him by his collar.

"Tell me that you were in a car accident! That you fell down a damn flight of stairs, that you ran into a door!" Frank said, yelling at the injured man, shaking him, practically begging to be told what he wanted to hear.

Zale didn't say a word, just stood there, a wounded look on his face, allowing himself to be handled by Frank.

"He was attacked," a voice came from behind Frank, and when he turned around, he saw that it was Martin, standing just outside the door.

"He was attacked," Martin said again, looking infuriated, as if he himself had taken the beating. "He was beaten in the street like a damn dog and left for dead." Martin walked into the office, stepping up to Frank. "Where were you, Frank? Where the hell were you?"

Frank didn't know what to say. He turned to Martin, speechless, feeling as if he was being accused of beating Rowen.

"I said, where the hell were you!" Martin said, snatching Frank, pulling him to where their faces were inches away from each other. "If you were where you were supposed to be, doing what the hell you get paid to do, which was protecting that man, none of this would've happened."

"I was doing what I was paid to do! I was working!" Frank said to Martin, sounding unsure of himself, then turning to Zale and repeating himself.

"If you were working, Zale wouldn't be in the condition that he's in. But that's the least of your problems, Rames. There are some things we have to talk about."

"I don't have time to talk about things. I don't have time for any of this," Frank said, pulling away from Martin, then turning to Zale. "I'm sorry about this. I'm really sorry that I wasn't there for you this time, but it'll never happen again. I swear," he said, making his way to the door. "It'll never happen again."

There was no expression on Zale's face, so Frank had no idea what the man was thinking, but Martin, on the other hand, was past infuriated at him, and the man had something on Frank, something that it seemed Martin was sure would take care of him once and for all, but Frank couldn't worry about that now, he thought, as he flew down the stairs, racing out to his car. He reached into the glove box, yanking out everything that stood between him and his cell phone. He grabbed the phone and punched in his wife's work number.

Three rings. Far too many for Frank as he sat anxiously, banging his fist against the door of the car. The phone was picked up.

"Let me speak to Mrs. Rames," he yelled at the unfortunate person that picked up the phone.

"Do you mean Ms. Rodgers?" the person said, correcting Frank on the status of his divorced wife.

"No, I fucking mean Mrs. Rames! Now go, pull her out of class, and get her on this goddamn phone. It's an emergency!"

Again, Frank waited far too long, and when his ex-wife finally picked up the phone, he spoke softly, as calmly as he could, and with the extreme intent of letting her know that she had no choice but to listen to what he said to her.

"Go get Bianca out of school, go home, pack some bags, and drive to your mother's house in Indiana. Don't tell anyone—"

"Frank, what the hell are you talking about? What are you doing calling me?"

"You don't have time to ask questions. You just do what I said. Go get Bianca—"

"You aren't supposed to be calling me, Frank," she argued. "I don't know what you're talking about and—"

"Listen!" Frank said, pulling the phone away from his ear, and shouting as loud as he could into the mouthpiece. "You don't have time to be finding out what I'm talking about! Now I don't know when, but trust me, after a certain person finds out a certain bit of information, I was told that there will be someone sent to find you and our child and kill you both. Do you understand. Now, I don't know if he's serious about this, but I don't want to find out. Do you? Now just go and get the girl and do what the hell I said. Any questions?"

"No!" Wendy said, and with her response, Frank could hear the fear in her voice, and that was a good thing. She needed to be frightened out of her mind, needed to think that if she didn't act fast enough, some huge man the size of a bull would butcher her and her child like a bloody piece of meat. She hung up the phone without saying another word, and now that that was taken care of, Frank knew that he had to try to intercept this man before he had an opportunity to lay hands on his family. When he found him, he would let him know that he had picked the wrong man to fool with.

It didn't take long to find Kronk. Frank knew where he would be, hanging out by the biggest drug house in the city, not three blocks from there, down an empty back alley. Fifteen minutes later, that was where Frank stood, his brass knuckles and fists covered with blood, as he looked down at Kronk's body. The man was not dead, but he was as close as one could get to that point and Frank made sure of that.

He didn't remember how badly he beat him, because during the entire ordeal, it was like Frank had lost consciousness. He just remembered following Kronk's car, then at the right moment, bumping the back of it. Frank remained in his car as the big man got out, looking angry, obviously ready to kick whoever's ass was driving the car that hit him. As Frank studied him approaching the car, he slipped the brass knuckles over his fist and slightly opened the car door.

When Kronk stopped in front of the car door, bent down to look in, and started yelling that the driver should get out, Frank kicked the car door open with all the strength he had, sending the door slamming into Kronk's knees, the window frame crashing into his head. He started to wobble backward, and that was the only opening Frank needed.

He bolted out of the car and immediately started swinging. He swung with a hard uppercut, catching Kronk on the nose as he was falling back, and it busted open, blood squirting out like a squashed tomato. The sight of that blood, the taste of it as some of it splattered across Frank's lips, sent him into a deep, unconscious killing rage.

There was nothing he could really remember after that, but as he looked down at Kronk, he saw that he was pretty bad off. His face was unrecognizable because it was masked with blood. His clothes were shredded and saturated in some places with blood, and Frank didn't know how, but the weird way his legs were lying out across the pavement made it appear as if they were both broken.

Then a snatch of Frank's memory came back, and he remembered dragging the man over to the curb, hanging his lower legs out over the edge, his feet in the street, then kicking down on them, snapping them like toothpicks. Kronk cried out like a baby being branded with a hot steam iron, but Frank kicked him hard in the head, which seemed to do the trick. Then without missing a beat, Frank stomped down on the other leg, and snapped it.

Frank looked down at him now and saw his eyes open some, swimming around in his head a little, and he knelt down next to him, looked into the man's whirling eyes and said in a harsh whisper, "You picked the wrong man's family to come after, motherfucker. Now, I tell you what. If someone finds you before the rats or some old stray dogs pick you apart, you go back and tell that ponytail-wearing fag friend of yours that if he even thinks about coming after my family again, next time I'll come after him. And I'll kill him, I swear."

Frank got in his car and drove off. He stopped at a service station, toting a backpack he had in the trunk in with him. He washed the blood off his brass knuckles, removed his clothes, and washed the blood off his body, all the while thinking about what was going on back at Father Found. Martin was pissed off, very intent on getting Frank in his office. It was because Zale had managed to get himself half killed, Frank was sure. So Martin would shoot off his mouth about how this couldn't happen again, how worthless Frank was. He'd fill the room with a lot of hot air, which he had done in the past, and which Frank has learned to ignore. But bottom line was, they needed Frank just so this same shit wouldn't go down again.

Frank unzipped the backpack, pulled out the clean clothes he always kept for emergency situations like this one, and drove back to work.

When he set foot on the second floor, he was shocked to see that there was no one there. The main room was eerily empty. Neither Martin's nor Zale's secretaries were at their desks, but judging by the half-full mugs of coffee that sat on top of them, the pages of work strewn across them, it appeared to Frank as if they were dismissed quickly, only moments ago.

Frank walked back to Zale's office and knocked softly. The door opened, and Martin stood there holding it, a look on his face expressing the fact that they had been waiting for him for hours.

"Come in," Martin said solemnly, and Frank knew that this was the beginning of the end.

Deny everything, he told himself, because they don't have shit on me anyway.

Zale was sitting behind Martin, still bandaged, looking like a casualty of war, and Martin was leaning against the boss's desk, as if he planned on taking over because of Zale's injuries.

"Sit down, Rames," Martin said.

"I prefer to stand, if you don't mind."

Martin made a beeline for Frank and yelled this time, "Sit down!" Frank stood there for a moment, then took the seat.

Martin paced in front of Frank, back and forth across the office, his hands clasped behind his back. Then, after the third time, he stopped and stood over Frank.

"I never did like you," he said, a sour look on his face. "You're a worthless, low-down, lazy son of a bitch, and I don't know why we even have you as an employee here." Martin gave a look over his shoulder at Zale, who didn't respond in any way.

"Well, I've never liked you either," Frank said defensively.

"I know that," Martin said casually. Then he began pacing again. "Tell me, what is your job description?"

"What?" Frank said.

"Your job description. What is it you are supposed to be doing for us? What do we pay your worthless, lazy ass for?"

Frank was beginning to reach his limit on the insults. "Look, I'm not taking too much more of this shit from you."

"Shut up, and answer the damn question," Martin barked from the other end of the room, his back turned to Frank.

Frank looked over at Zale to get an idea of what was going on, but Zale just averted his eyes, looking down at the desk.

"I'm supposed to locate the men that we select to go after. I'm supposed to inform them that they should come down to our office and speak to Mr. Rowen, or a counselor, if Mr. Rowen is not available. If I can't locate them, I'm supposed to leave them information stating what they should do and my card if they need to contact me with any questions."

"That's what you're supposed to do?" Martin said, standing over Frank, looking down at him as if he were a schoolchild being quizzed. "That's it?"

"Yeah, that's it," Frank said, an edge of bitterness in his voice.

"I see," Martin said, pacing again. "Then why are you beating our clients?"

The question caught Frank entirely off guard, and he couldn't answer for a moment. First he had to understand how Martin found that out, and if he really knew for sure or was just guessing. But Frank knew that there was no way he could know for sure. He beat those men's asses thoroughly, and he knew none of them would have the balls to run to Martin.

"I don't know what you're talking about."

"I said, why the hell are you beating our clients!" Martin yelled, as he marched back toward Frank.

"I don't know what you're talking about," Frank repeated. "I tell them that people want to talk to them here. I give them flyers, I leave my card, that's all I do."

"You don't hit them, beat them, try and physically coerce them into returning home by damn near splitting their heads in half?" Martin said furiously.

"No."

"You don't?"

"No!"

"You lying sack of shit! I don't believe this motherfucker," Martin said, turning to Zale, as if wanting to get his attention. Still Zale had no comment, verbal or otherwise. "You know, I knew you were just about every name in the book," Martin said, "but now I can add liar to the list, because I got you. I got you right where I want you."

Frank sat there in the chair, feeling beads of sweat moisten the collar of his shirt and roll down his back. Martin seemed quite confident, he thought, but Frank would continue to hold his ground.

"Let me ask you one more time, and this is the last time. You never once put a hand on one of our clients in an attempt to get him to go back to his children?"

Frank looked Martin dead in the eyes for a long moment, then said, "No, you son of a bitch."

"Good. Wait right here."

Martin walked out of the office, leaving Frank alone with Zale. He wanted to know what the hell was going on, what did Martin really have on him, but he also wanted to apologize for not being there for his boss. Frank looked sympathetically over at Zale, but Zale's attention was turned down toward the table; his eyes seemed directed to some far-off place.

Frank prepared himself to speak, to say something that would possibly take away some of the pain Zale was feeling, but before he could open his mouth, Martin walked in, stood near the door, holding it.

"You're through," he said to Frank, then five men started into the office, single file, on unsteady feet, as if they were unsure of wanting to be in the same room with their abuser. Five men whom Frank had no problem recognizing, because they were all men that he had beaten down to the ground. Four of the five men had already healed from their beatings, but the fifth man, the last one Frank had dealings with, the banker, still had a couple of bandages on his face. They all looked at Frank with hollow stares, and Frank returned those stares, but with hatred, as if somehow he had been betrayed, as if they had made some sort of pact that wasn't supposed to be broken.

What Frank wanted to do was walk the hell out of there. Tell them that those five men were crazy, and that he had had enough, and wasn't going to tolerate this kind of treatment any longer, but that would've been bullshit, and it wouldn't have made any of this go away.

He didn't know what to say. He looked over at Zale again, and this time Zale didn't look away. He held his stare, practically looked right through him with a deep look of disappointment and disgust.

"So, Frank, you were saying?" Martin said smugly.

"I don't have anything else to say."

"Good, well you can grab your things and get out of here."

"What! What are you talking about!"

"Frank, you sound surprised," Martin said, smiling a bit, seeming to be enjoying what was taking place. "You're fired. You're the hell up out of here. Did you think that you could do what you did and just get a slap on the wrist? No. You're through. Now grab your shit and go."

"That's you talking," Frank said, frantically looking back and forth between Martin and Zale. "I want to hear it from Mr. Rowen. It's not true unless it comes from him."

"I'm your immediate employer, or have you forgotten, and I said, you're fired!"

Frank ignored what Martin said, and turned to Zale, walked over to him.

"I need this job," he pleaded. "Are you firing me?"

Zale didn't answer.

"You need to fire his ass," one of the men said. It was André Hinton, looking ragged as the day Frank beat him. Frank looked over his shoulder sternly, but paid him no mind.

"Are you firing me after what I did for you? After I saved your life," Frank said desperately.

"That doesn't have a damn thing to do with this, Zale. The man has to go and you know it," Martin said.

"That's right. Look what he did to us," another man with a small, cowardly face and a faint voice said. Then André continued for him, saying, "That motherfucker don't deserve to keep shit. He needs his ass whipped to see how it feels."

And that was the last straw for Frank.

"And who's going to do it?" Frank said, spinning, heading for André with intentions to kill. Frank plowed into him, running him into a wall. But before he could deliver a single blow, the other four men were on top of Frank. They were shouting at him, beating him, retaliation for the abuse he had given them.

Martin jumped in. "Stop it! Stop it!" he yelled, pulling the men off Frank. Yanking Frank out of the mob, pulling him out of the office. Zale followed behind them. Martin rushed him toward his office, opening the door and pushing Frank inside.

"If you expect there to be any chance of you keeping this job, you'll stay your ass in here till you're called." Martin slammed the door, then approached Zale.

"The man has to go."

"The man saved my life, Martin. What am I—"

"You're supposed to fire him. That's what you're supposed to do. Who gives a damn about him saving your life."

"I do! I'd be dead right now if it wasn't for him. None of what we have right now would be happening if he hadn't saved my life. So you can almost look at it as though we can thank him for what we have."

Martin placed both hands on Zale's shoulders. "You're looking at this wrong. Do you understand? Your vision is cloudy. We can't thank him for squat. And if you opened your damn eyes, you would see that he's endangering Father Found. He is our employee. He is a representative of this organization as much as you or me, so if this continues, or if word of this gets out, we're done. Do you want that, Zale? Do you want to toss all that you've worked for, all that we've worked for, out the window because you're protecting some drunken loser?"

Zale looked as though he was thinking, but there was still uncertainty in his eyes.

"Zale," Martin said, trying to shake sense into him. "Understand this. We're not on the same page here. He doesn't care about those men, or he wouldn't beat them, and he sure as hell doesn't care about their children, because he's almost taken their fathers away from them by damn near killing them. So if he doesn't care about the children or the fathers, then he doesn't care about Father Found, and if he doesn't care about Father Found, then he don't give a damn about you."

Just as Martin finished, the door opened behind them, and Frank came out into the hallway.

"What are you going to do, Mr. Rowen?" Frank said, an insane look in his eyes.

Zale looked over at Martin. Martin gave him a hard look back, nodding his head, as if to tell him to put the man out of his misery.

"We have to let you go," Zale said, softly, regrettably.

Frank stood in front of the two men, not saying a word, wide-eyed, looking dazed by the news.

"But I need this job," Frank said slowly.

"I'm sorry, but you beat those men. You hurt those men, and we are supposed to be here to help them. How am I supposed to be able to . . ."

And before Zale could finish his sentence, Frank lunged forward at Zale, slamming him into a wall, Frank's forearms in Zale's chest, Zale's collar folded into Frank's fists.

Zale saw Martin preparing to leap on Frank, but he waved him off with a hand.

"You were trying to get those fathers back home, and I got them back home," Frank said. "It doesn't matter how, I got them back home. I was doing my job." He continued ranting while pressing Zale hard up against the wall. "I took files out of here by the damn boatload, and I brought them back here checked off just like you like them. And now you're going to fire me! And then when I was trying to tell you what I was doing, you told me you didn't care what I was doing. You told me to keep on, do whatever it was that I was doing, because I was doing a good job."

"I didn't know that you were harming these men. I wouldn't have stood for it, if I had known," Zale said.

"You're such a fucking hypocrite. You were loving the results, but you didn't like the way I got them, and now you want to get rid of me."

"I don't want to, but I have no choice."

"What do you mean, you have no choice?" Frank said, tightening his grip on Zale. "I saved your life."

Martin took another step closer, but again Zale waved him off with a hand that was not seen by Frank, as if he was afraid that any movement by Martin would send the man into a homicidal frenzy.

"I saved your life. And what about the bastard that just got to you? He beat your ass pretty good, didn't he? But you were lucky. What about the next one? What if the next guy doesn't just want to teach you a lesson, but wants to kill you? What if he wants to shoot you, or knife you, or kill you with his bare hands?" Frank said, his face turning red, spittle flying from his mouth, hitting Zale in the face. "What if he wants to have you by the neck just like this?" and with that, Frank started to bring the ends of Zale's collar together around his neck until he couldn't breathe.

Frank didn't want to do it, but he couldn't control himself. He had been betrayed after all he had given to this man, after he had saved his life. This ungrateful bastard he had up against the wall was, in essence, taking his life, because if Frank lost this job, he would have nowhere else to go. There was nothing lower than this. So Frank continued to squeeze, and when he saw Zale's eyes bug out, and when he felt him struggling, trying to free himself, he just continued to squeeze tighter.

Then he felt Zale's arm go up behind him, waving about, and all of a sudden, he felt hands on him, and he was pulled off Zale and slung into a wall across the hall.

Martin was standing in front of him, his fist before him, looking as if he was ready to attack.

"Are you fucking crazy! Have you lost your mind? Were you trying to kill him? Get the hell out of here before I call the police!"

"I need my job," Frank said, only now realizing exactly what he had done. "I need my job."

"Get out!" Martin yelled again, grabbing him and pushing him in the direction of the stairs.

Zale was still pressed up against the wall, gasping for air.

Frank stopped in front of him. "I'm sorry, Mr. Rowen, but I need my job, and I was only thinking about you. You need me here, because someone is still out there looking for you, and when they find you, they're going to kill you." Frank gave Zale a long, hard look, turned to stare at Martin, who still seemed poised to kill him, then turned and walked away.

CHAPTER TWENTY-EIGHT

After the huge ordeal at the office, Martin was in a foul mood the entire trip home. He was ecstatic over the fact that he had finally gotten Frank, that he had finally proven the man to be what he had known he was all along. But he was disappointed at how Zale was taking it. Martin knew that Zale would've done everything within his power to keep Frank on, and now Martin was sure that Zale felt he had somehow betrayed the man, but that wasn't the only thing that disappointed Martin. Zale was now without protection, and it worried Martin a lot. So much that he suggested that Zale get out of town till this caller stopped phoning, but also just to take a break. To Martin, Zale looked like he was on the verge of a serious breakdown, like he was about to fall apart, and if he didn't get away soon, and try to take his mind off all the bad things that were happening around him, Martin feared that his best friend might regret it.

But it wasn't just the situation with Zale that dampened Martin's mood. Of the five beaten men that stood in his office, now that their situation had come to light, they all wanted to go to the police to press charges against Frank Rames, and Martin wouldn't have had a problem with that if Frank was not connected with the organization. If charges were pressed against Frank, people would not separate him from Father Found. They wouldn't see him as acting alone, but as beating men senseless in order to get them to return to their homes as a practice of Father Found, and Martin couldn't have that because it would surely bury them.

So Martin sat in his office hours after Frank left, and long after he told Zale to go home, and persuaded the men not to go to the police in return for monetary compensation. It was money that Martin didn't have, that the organization didn't have, but he had to do something, and he just told himself that he would find a way to raise it, along with the money he needed to pay the mortgage, because Mr. Kirkland hadn't come through with the grant that Martin was hoping for.

Kirkland gave him some long-winded excuse about forms, policies, and regulations, but Martin paid no attention to what the man was saying, just stared at the wall in front of him, his eyes glazed over, wondering what in the hell would he do now.

He had received another letter from the bank, and they were just moments away from foreclosing on the building, and there wasn't a damn thing Martin could do about it. He had exhausted all his possibilities, and if nothing short of a miracle happened, they'd surely lose it.

When Zale asked Martin how the situation was going, Martin just smiled and simply replied, "Just fine. Nothing to worry about," because he knew news like that would push Zale over the edge.

And on top of all that, Martin was still having doubts and second thoughts about his wife. Feelings that came from nowhere, that seemed to have no meaning or message, feelings that made him angry and resentful of the woman.

So when Martin finally got home, walked in the door, and saw his wife sitting in the living room with his two daughters, the children laughing in Debra's arms, Martin became even more angry.

Debra paused for a moment, asked Martin how his day was and if he wanted her to get him something to eat. Martin barely looked over at her, said, "No, thank you," and hurriedly took the stairs up to their bedroom.

"Is everything all right?" Martin heard Debra say as he climbed the stairs, a frown on his face. Martin didn't even answer. He didn't want to talk to her, because if he had said anything, it probably would've been, "Get your damn hands off my children!"

That's how he was feeling at that moment, as if she didn't deserve to share the joy that one gets from the innocence of children, as if she didn't deserve the unconditional love that they gave. That belonged to him, and it came to her only as a benefit of loving him, and when she decided that she would go fool around with another man, she was not only risking him and his love, but the children and their love, too.

Martin had to control those particular feelings, because he knew that if he separated his wife and his children, although he would be doing it solely to hurt Debra, he would also hurt Renee and Rebecca, and he didn't want to do that.

Martin threw his briefcase on the bed, sat at the edge, and threw his face into his hands. There was too much going on right now at work to have to deal with problems when he got home, and again he blamed that on Debra. At this point, everything was her fault. In the past, if Martin had problems at work, he knew that the moment he entered his house, he could drop all those burdens at the door. This was his refuge, his sanctuary, but now his wife had ruined all of that, by being with another man.

But she would never do it again, she said. She had changed her schedule, been more attentive to the children, and become an all-around better mother and wife, so why did Martin still question her? Why, in the back of his head, did he still wonder if she was sneaking around with that man, or another, for that matter.

He suddenly found himself standing in front of their bedroom closet, strongly considering going in and looking through her pockets, as he had thought of doing when he was first suspicious about her.

Martin slid the doors open, pulled the cord on the light, and stepped to the side of the closet where his clothes hung.

He felt the same urge now as he had then. The only thing that held him back then was the possibility of Debra being innocent, and Martin never being able to face her again after rummaging through her belongings. But now there was no longer that fear, because there was no possibility of her being innocent. She was guilty! Guilty as hell, and Martin had proved that. So Martin stepped closer to her suits and shirts and started to sift through the pockets, outside and inside. He nudged over her shoes with the toe of his just to see if she hid anything in them, and looked through all the compartments, hidden and obvious, of all the empty purses she had sitting on the closet shelf.

Martin really didn't know why he was looking, because even though he had suspicions, he was pretty sure that she was no longer doing anything. But he continued to look, almost hoping to find something, almost hoping that his wife was still seeing this man so he could justify all his crazy feelings, so he could go to her and let her have it, curse her out so bad she'd want to cry, make her feel so bad that she wouldn't feel worthy of being in that house with them. He wanted, needed, to do that, because he realized now that he had forgiven her far too soon, and with far too little suffering, and he was paying for it now.

Martin stepped over to her side of the dresser and pulled open the top drawer. He pushed through the shallow drawer of underwear, lace, silk, and cotton, but there was nothing there.

He went to the next drawer, filled with shirts—nothing. Next drawer, slacks, still nothing. Then he knelt down, pulled open her bottom drawer, and that was filled with a little bit of everything. It was piled high with sweaters, gloves, some purses that Debra no longer carried, a couple of pairs of slippers, and a thin throw blanket.

Martin moved some things around, took some things out, placed them behind him, and when he turned to the drawer to continue looking through it, he was staring down at exactly what he was looking for. It was an envelope. It was lavender, crinkled, and dog-eared, and on it "Sweet Debra" was written in block letters. Definitely handwriting belonging to a man.

Martin stared down at the letter for quite a while, half expecting it to disappear in front of his eyes, but when it didn't, he swallowed hard, and with a trembling hand, reached down and picked it up. He opened the letter. The paper was old and creased, as though it had been read a thousand times, and Martin visualized his wife looking down at this exact piece of paper, grinning from ear to ear at what the man was saying to her. Upon first seeing the envelope there, he immediately assumed that it was a recent letter, one given to her after their affair had been found out. There was no date on the letter, but judging by the condition of the thing, it had to have been at least a few weeks old.

Martin read the letter, stopping at the end of each paragraph, sometimes at the end of certain sentences, feeling as though he wouldn't be able to continue reading, but forcing himself anyway. It was too much for him. This one short letter was too much for him to bear, but then he had to remind himself that this was just one minute fraction of the entire affair. Conversations that his wife and this man had, intimate moments in restaurants, laughing and joking like best friends, and, of course, numerous sessions of lovemaking. If this letter was too much for Martin, he knew if he had insight to any of the above, he would've gone insane and probably killed the both of them.

Martin sprang up from the floor, the letter still in his hand, and went back to the closet. He pulled a suitcase from the shelf, and started filling it with clothes. This was it, what he was looking for, and now that he found it, he realized that he could no longer live with her.

He carried the suitcase to the top of the stairs and set it down. Martin heard his wife and children still downstairs, playing and laughing, but when he descended the stairs, stood in front of them, the crumpled lavender letter in his hand, a look of disgust on his face, the laughing stopped, and Debra, Rebecca, and Renee looked at Martin as if they had never seen him before, as if there was a stranger standing in their house.

Debra started a question, asking him, "What's—" but when she glanced down at his left fist and saw the lavender letter in his hand, she was able to answer her own question.

Martin took steps toward the three of them, and Debra, looking very worried, wrapped her arms around the children, pulling them closer, as if their father intended them harm.

Martin stuck his arm straight out to her, the letter in his hand.

"What is this?"

"It's nothing, Martin. It's nothing."

"Well, if it's nothing, I want you to read it."

Debra looked at her husband as if he was asking her to commit a crime. "I'm not going to read that, Martin. I'm not going to."

"Read it," Martin insisted, jabbing it toward her face.

"No! What about the children?"

And that was just about the worst thing she could've said to Martin.

"What about the children?" he exploded. "You weren't thinking about the children when you had your ass out all night with this man, and didn't come home. You weren't thinking about the children when you knew they were asking about you. When you were doing God knows what, probably on your knees!"

Debra frowned at that one, opening her mouth in shock, but he didn't give a damn.

"So don't give me, what about the children? Read the goddamn letter."

"Daddy?" Rebecca whimpered, and Martin responded with "Be quiet, child, and let the woman read," and stuck the letter in her face again so she could take it.

Debra slowly took the letter from his hand, opened it, then looked up at Martin, regret in her eyes.

"I thought we had gotten past this," she said, her extreme beauty no longer affecting Martin. "I thought you forgave me for this."

Martin didn't say a word, just nodded his head at the letter.

Debra looked down at the letter, and cleared her throat. It did no good, because when she started reading, her voice was still shaky and quivering.

"'Dear, sweet Debra,'" she read. "'I call you that, not just because of how sweet your personality is, but also because of how sweet you taste.'

"No," Debra said, shaking her head, looking away from the letter as if it could cause her to go blind. "I won't read this. Not in front of the girls."

Martin stepped up closer to her. "Read it," he instructed. She shook her head.

"I said, read it!" He was more forceful now, grabbing the hand the letter was in, pushing it up to her face.

"I won't do this, and why would you want me to."

Martin snatched the letter out of her hand, held it up before him. He looked at it as if he feared what was written on the page. He looked at his wife, swallowed hard, then continued where she left off. "'The other night was more than I could've imagined. You're like no woman I've ever met, and the things you do to me are too incredible to put into words.

"'I know you said that you could only see me three nights out of the week, that your husband would probably get suspicious if you were gone any longer. But I don't care about your husband. I must see you, and after I'm done with you, then he can have his turn.'"

As Martin continued reading, he could barely contain himself. Out of the corners of his eyes, he saw both his daughters looking up at him, but he paid them no mind, he couldn't pay them any mind, for his eyes were focused so intently on that letter, and on the visions that played out in his head. He was so angry with her that he wanted to strangle her, wanted to feel it as she took her last breath. Verbal apologies were no good any longer. They were just lies, and from this point on, everything she said would be lies.

"'If you allow me to see you tonight, I will make love to you like I never have before. When you knock on the hotel room door, I'll open it, and yank you inside by your collar, then I'll slam you against the wall the way you like it. I'll rip open your blouse, strip it off you. Yank down your skirt, leave you standing there in your underwear and your heels. Then I'll tie your blouse over your eyes so you can't see, and that's when I'll have my fun. I'll pop open your bra and let your breasts dangle in front of my face, and then I'll come very close to you, so you can feel my warm breath, lick my lips, and then I'll take you in my . . .'"

Martin could read no more. He folded the letter, then looked at Debra. He could see that she was crying.

"I thought you said that it was over. That you had stopped seeing him."

Debra looked up, shock on her face. "I did! That's old. There's nothing going on between us anymore. Why would I do that, Martin? I told you, I love you. I love you and the children. I made a mistake. I wouldn't risk everything I have for that again."

Martin looked at her hard and long, then down at the letter for a moment, then said, relatively calmly, "I don't believe you. I think you're still having an affair. If you did it once, if you didn't care about me, about them then, what makes the difference now."

"I told you. I—"

"No," Martin said, cutting her off, and although he knew she was telling the truth, felt sure the letter was old, and she must have just forgotten to put it out with everything else that came from this man, Martin said, "I'm tired of hearing it. There's nothing more you can say. I can't take the lies anymore, I can't take the questions in my head, and I can't take living with you anymore. I packed a bag upstairs—"

"No, Martin. I don't want you to go again," Debra interrupted.

Martin paused, giving her an odd look. "No, you misunderstand. I'm not going anywhere. The bag is for you. You're the one that's leaving this time."

Debra's mouth opened, and she clutched the children, pulling them closer to her.

"For how long?"

"There should be enough clothes in that suitcase to last you a few days, and then you can call me, and I'll arrange for a time when we're not home . . . so you can come and get the rest of your things." Martin grabbed the hand of either child, and after a bit of their resistance, he pulled them to his side.

"After that, I don't ever want to see you again."

More tears started to stream down Debra's face. She closed her arms around herself and started to rock back and forth on the couch.

"Daddy!" Both Rebecca and Renee cried, trying to pull away from Martin to get back to their mother's side, but he held firmly to them.

Debra looked up at him. She snatched the letter out of his hands, holding the letter open for him to see. "This is old! I'm telling you. I haven't seen that man in a month. I told you I wouldn't do that to you again. Martin, what can I do to prove it to you," she said, smearing tears across her face. "I can call him! I can call him and let you talk to him."

"What would you think I have to say to that man!" Martin said angrily.

"Well, what can I do?"

"Debra, the only thing you can do is walk up those stairs, grab that suitcase, and get out of our lives."

"I'm not going," Debra said, trembling.

"What did you say?"

"I can't. This is my family. I love those girls," she said, reaching out for them. Martin pulled them closer to his sides. "I love you."

And that was the last lie that Martin could take from her. She was trying to save herself, but Martin wouldn't let her, not at his expense, and definitely not at the expense of his daughters.

"No. You're going," he said, grabbing her, forcing her up the stairs against her will.

"Stop it, Martin! Stop it," she screamed, as she fought against him, holding on to the railing, trying to turn around and force her way past him back down the stairs. But Martin was stronger, more determined, and they ended up at the top of the stairs, Martin breathing hard from the struggle.

"Grab the bag."

Debra looked at Martin as if she had no idea of what he was talking about, and if she did, she had no intention of obeying him.

"I said, grab it!" And he yelled so loudly that his wife jumped. Debra reached down for it.

"I'm not seeing him anymore. I wouldn't lie to you."

"Don't you mean, you wouldn't lie to me again?" Martin was done with her lies, plain and simple, there was no changing his mind now, and she must've seen that, for she turned, the bag in her hand, and took the stairs down, her head and shoulders slumping more from her despair than from the weight of the suitcase. Debra could not look at the girls as she descended the stairs. Renee and Rebecca were standing at the foot, their young faces shiny, wet with tears. They were trembling, weeping almost silently, trying to hold in their cries. Debra stopped just in front of the children, turning to face Martin behind her.

"You know that this letter is old, don't you." She spoke low so the children wouldn't hear her. "You know that I'm not still having an affair with that man. I don't want that anymore, and even if I did, I don't have the time. I'm here every day after work. I call you all the time so you know where I am, and you tell me I'm still having an affair. You know that's not true, don't you, Martin. Don't you!"

Martin didn't respond, just nudged her down the last step, just past his daughters. He grabbed their hands, squeezing them as tight as he dared, letting them know that they were not to side with the woman.

"Well, answer me! Say something! Don't you know that I wouldn't do that again!" Debra cried desperately.

Martin looked at her, sympathy on his face. "I don't know anything anymore other than that you have to get out."

"But, Daddy, you can't kick Mommy out. You can't do that!" Renee said. "Where will she go? Where will Mommy go?" And the child tried to free herself from her father's grip, but he held her, pulled her back.

"She's not your mommy!" Martin said spitefully. "She never was."

Debra looked shocked, betrayed at what Martin had said. He knew there was no turning back, and now she knew it, too. Debra dropped her eyes, rested a hand on Renee's head, knelt down, kissed her on the cheek, did the same for Rebecca, then turned and walked out the door.

CHAPTER TWENTY-NINE

Zale lay in bed, a pillow doubled over under his head. Elevating it some helped to keep it from throbbing so much, and there was nothing else he could do to drive away the pain. He had already taken twice as much pain medication as he was prescribed.

But he knew the tightness that he felt around his skull, closing in on his brain like a vise, and the throbbing pain that he felt right between his eyes, wasn't from the beating he had taken, but from the stress that he was feeling, had been feeling since the phone calls began. He had been getting headaches before that, but never this severe, and he knew with everything that was happening now, with Frank getting fired, with the knowledge that the caller was still out there after him, and that he had no one to protect him, the headaches would only get worse.

When Zale went to his doctor to get bandaged up, the graying, distinguished woman didn't look surprised to see that he had been pummeled. She had some X rays taken of his skull and ribs and was relieved to find that he had no fractures, just a couple of badly bruised ribs, which she wrapped.

"Your blood pressure is up, you know that, don't you?" she said to Zale in a conversational tone, as she went about bandaging his face.

"I didn't know that," Zale lied.

"And the last time you took your medication?"

"A couple of days ago."

"And before then?"

Zale didn't answer.

The doctor stopped what she was doing, set down her roll of tape, and looked Zale in the eye.

"What do I have to do to make you understand that I didn't prescribe that medication for the fun of it, Zale. You need it! The type of stress levels that you deal with every day, the long hours you work, the lack of sleep, and the fact that you have hypertension mean you need it. You should be taking that medication every day. You have no choice."

"And if I don't?"

The doctor shook her head, giving Zale an exhausted look. "Then you could die. I've told you this a thousand times. Do you think the answer will change? It won't, Zale. You keep on testing yourself like you're doing, and don't take your medication, you'll be risking your life."

She gave Zale another prescription, and some pills that would relax him, and echoed the advice that Martin had given him, that he needed to take a vacation, a leave of absence. But the doctor wasn't just giving advice. She told him that it was imperative that he leave for a while, that he put everything behind him, stop thinking about work, and go someplace and just clear his mind and sleep.

Ever since he had gotten home today from the office, he had been lying in his bed thinking about that, and he could no longer deny that the idea sounded good. But he was worried about Father Found, worried that already he had missed so much work just running from this man who had been stalking him. He was worried what would happen with the men who wanted to press charges against Frank. And, most important, he was worried about losing the building, and he knew that meant losing the organization altogether.

No matter how much he tried, he couldn't rationalize leaving Martin and Father Found when they seemed to need him the most. He just couldn't leave, spend a month away relaxing, and risk coming back home and having nothing.

But Martin told him that he had everything under control, that he would take care of everything. Zale wasn't sure if he was actually capable of doing it all by himself, but he seemed fairly confident, and Zale wouldn't have taken him on as his partner if he wasn't able to trust him implicitly.

Zale patted the area around his right hand, looking for his gun, and when he felt it he grabbed it and pulled it closer to him. He was still on the run. There was still someone out there after him, and he didn't even feel safe in his own house. He had been lying there in that bed for the last five or six hours, so tired and sleepy that he felt he would pass out from exhaustion soon. But he didn't let his eyes close for fear of someone coming into his home.

He lifted his head slightly, felt the pain that had receded to a faint, occasional throbbing in the back of his skull, and looked down at his torso, which was bandaged tightly with thick white tape. Then he looked at his bedroom, which still resembled a disaster area because attempting to clean it would've caused him far too much pain. He thought about how his life resembled that room: a disaster. And he felt, he knew, that he had no more control over his life, and if things continued on their present course, no more control over Father Found either, and he wouldn't allow that.

He decided, he would go. He would take the much-needed leave of absence, place everything in Martin's control, and disappear for a month, and tell no one but his partner, and maybe . . . Regina. He still thought about her, still wondered sometimes if he had made the right decision by letting her walk out of his life. Many times, he had thought about calling her, but he had always stopped himself, the phone to his ear, before punching in the numbers.

She's better off without me, he would tell himself, knowing that he was just calling to hear her voice, see how she was doing, and maybe tell her he missed her. But that wasn't what she wanted to hear, and Zale knew that. He was sure she wanted a plan for their future. She wanted to hear that he wanted a life with her, marriage, and children, and when he said it, she wanted to know that he was sure about it, to hear his confidence in every word. Zale knew that he was not ready to say those things, so he never called her, and probably never would.

Zale took a moment to put Regina out of his mind, hopefully once and for all, and thought about where he would go. He couldn't believe it, but he was actually starting to get excited by the idea. He had pulled himself up in bed a little, noticing that the pain in his head had all but completely left him, when his phone rang.

It startled him, almost making him bang his head against the head-board of his bed. The first thing he did was look at the clock. It was after midnight, and he only needed one guess to determine who that was calling him.

Zale let the phone ring three more times, staring at it, hoping that it would stop, but it continued to ring.

He would ignore it till it stopped, he told himself, and rolled back over onto his back. But it continued to ring as if it would never stop, and when Zale felt that he couldn't take it any longer, felt the incessant ringing would drive him mad, and reached over to pick up the phone and brought it to his ear, all he heard was a dial tone.

Zale exhaled, tried to control his shaking, and slowly returned the phone to its cradle. But before he could release the phone, it started ringing again. Shocked, Zale yanked his hand from the thing, falling backward on the bed as if the phone had grown razor-sharp teeth and attempted to tear at his hand.

Zale turned his back to the phone, groping for his gun. He turned back around, staring wide-eyed at the phone, pointing the gun at it as if the ringing alone threatened his life. After countless rings, again he could no longer bear it, and he extended a nervous hand toward the phone. He placed his hand on the receiver, felt it pulsate as it rang, the pulses feeling like shocks of electricity storming through his body. He quickly picked the phone up to stop the ringing, to stop the electricity: "Hello?"

He was breathing heavily, as if he had been running for his life, and he tried to quiet himself so the caller wouldn't hear that he was frightened.

"Hello!" Zale said again, after getting no reply, then the caller hung up, and he sat there listening to a dial tone.

Zale slammed the phone down and slowly felt the fear subsiding and the anger increasing. He gently rose from his bed, the gun still held tightly in his hand, wondering what he should do. Then, after a moment's thought, he realized that he should get out of the house. He should get out of the fucking house! And he didn't know why that hadn't occurred him sooner, because if the caller had the phone number to his home, than he surely had the address.

Zale rushed over to the closet, pulled out a shirt, and not daring to set his gun down, slid the gun and his hand through the sleeve of the shirt, slipped his arm through the other sleeve, and looked around the room for his car keys. Then the phone started to ring again.

This time, Zale wasn't going to allow it to ring more than once. He stormed over to the phone, snatched it from the cradle, and yelled into it. "Who the hell is this! Why do you keep calling me! What is it you want? What the fuck do you want? Tell me! Tell me, motherfucker! Tell me!" His chest was heaving up and down, veins protruding from his neck and forehead, and his face had turned a faint shade of red. He stood there, waiting, holding the phone so tightly the muscles in his hand started to ache around it.

"Hello!" he yelled again. "Hello. Say something, mother—"

"Zale," the caller said, and Zale froze. It was a woman's voice, and not even needing to give it a second, Zale recognized the voice. He could not speak.

"Is this Zale Rowen?" the voice asked.

"Yeah," he said, almost more frightened now, knowing who it was, than he had been when he was unaware.

"This is—"

"I know who this is." He paused for a moment, still trying to convince himself that he was actually speaking to the person he was speaking to. "Was it you calling me all this time?"

"Yes."

When Zale heard that, he felt like a fool. Running around, looking over his shoulder, fearing for his life, when there was nothing at all to fear. Nothing.

"Why did you hang up on me? Why didn't you just talk to me?"

"Because I was afraid. Afraid that you were angry at me for never calling you back after I left."

Zale thought about the night so many years ago he lay in his bed and silently watched as the woman he loved gathered her things and walked out of his apartment.

"Cassaundra, I knew you weren't going to call me back. And I'm not angry with you. But why are you calling me now?"

"Because there was . . . there is something that I need to tell you." She paused as if needing to be prompted.

"Well, what is it?"

"Zale, you have a six-year-old daughter."

CHAPTER THIRTY

Much to Martin's dismay, Zale was on a plane out to Washington, D.C., to see Cassaundra and his daughter the very next day.

"You said you were going to go on vacation. You said you were go-ing to stop working, give yourself some time to rest," Martin said, ag-gravation in his voice, when Zale came to the office the next morning.

"This woman says that I have a daughter. What am I supposed to do, Martin?" Zale said, desperately trying to ignore the painful mi-graine he was experiencing at the moment, and had been dealing with ever since he had gotten off the phone with Cassaundra the night be-fore.

"Remember what your doctor said about your high blood pressure, about your stress. What do you think going out there would do to you, after everything you just went through? Zale, you shouldn't go," Mar-tin said, a cautionary tone in his voice.

"Well, what am I supposed to do? Am I supposed to just sit out here knowing that I have a six-year-old daughter that has never seen her father before? Is that supposed to be all right with me? To do that, I would be going against everything that I am working for. I have to go."

Martin looked down at his feet. "Are you sure it's yours?" he said softly.

Zale didn't answer right away, offended by the question, but not knowing exactly why. There was no way that he could know if the child was his. He was simply taking the word of a woman that he once loved, but had abandoned him, and hadn't even had the respect to let him know that he had a child until now.

"I don't know for sure. But if Cassaundra says that she is, I'm going to believe her until I have a reason not to."

Martin just looked up at Zale, shaking his head, but did not com-ment.

"Everything will run smoothly in your hands, I'm sure," Zale said.

"You know it will, like clockwork," Martin said, showing a thin smile of confidence.

Zale stood there in front of his partner. He glanced down at his watch, knowing he had to leave, but needing to say something to his friend first.

"About yesterday, about Frank . . . and . . . you know," Zale said, stumbling over his words. "You were right. You were right all along, and it's not that I didn't trust your judgment but . . ."

Martin stepped near to Zale and rested an assuring hand on his shoulder.

"You don't have to say another word. I know how it is, man. You're the captain, and this is a big-ass ship," Martin said, smiling even wider. "There's a lot to worry about and—"

"And I couldn't have . . . can't do it without you," Zale said, very seriously.

"I told you, you don't have to say that."

Zale reached out and grabbed Martin's shoulders tightly, and looked directly into his eyes. "No, I do have to say it, and you have to understand it! I couldn't have done this without you," Zale said, as if this were his last testament to Martin.

Martin stared at Zale for a moment, matching his seriousness, then nodded his head, and said, "All right. Well, if you want to burden me with all your trust the minute before you leave, that's fine, I guess I can handle it," Martin joked, then said, "You don't have to worry, everything is fine, and it'll be that way when you get back."

Zale didn't have to question that. Just by the look in Martin's eyes, he believed that more than anything in the world right now. He extended a hand out to Martin to bid him goodbye, and when Martin looked down at his hand oddly, as if it was a joke of some kind, he opened his arms wide for a hug.

Zale opened his arms, and the two men embraced. "Don't worry about the child," Martin said, almost in a whisper. "Whatever you decide to do, I'm sure you'll make the right decision."

And as the plane touched down in Washington, that was the dilemma that Zale had been tussling with the entire flight. What was the right decision?

Cassaundra had given Zale her address, after he refused to be picked up from the airport. "I'll just take a cab," he said. "I'm sure you have far better things to do than pick me up from the airport."

When the cab stopped in front of the house that matched the address that Zale had on his piece of paper, Zale reached into his wallet, pulled out the fare, and passed it over the seat to the cabdriver. He lifted his small piece of luggage out of the back seat and got out of the car.

The cab sped off, leaving Zale standing there in front of the house. This is where she lives, Zale thought to himself, as he looked up at the well-kept, average-looking home. This is where she's made her life, and he thought, Would he have been able to give her this if she had stayed with him? And immediately he told himself no.

He stood out there on the sidewalk, his bag in his hand, looking up at that house for far longer than he wanted to. Walking up those stairs, ringing that doorbell, and seeing Cassaundra after six years was something that, now, he wasn't sure he was able to do. He didn't know how he would react, didn't know if, upon seeing her, he would want to embrace her, or shake the woman senseless for never calling him.

She would be beautiful to him, Zale mused. She would be beautiful in that deeper-than-physical way that he had always loved about her, and he would not be able to speak for a while, because he would be so taken. For a moment, he actually started to romanticize the situation, what he would say first, if she would hug him, kiss him, or both, but then realization hit him in the head, bringing him back to the reason he was truly there. This was not a reunion of lost lovers, but a summons of a sort. He was requested to fly down to meet his daughter, and there was nothing romantic about that, especially considering that Zale remembered explicitly telling Cassaundra about his fear of having children.

He walked up the stairs, feeling nothing more now than a need to find out what was actually going on, and rang the doorbell.

Zale glanced down at his watch, more to give him something to do until the door was answered than to find out what time it was.

The door opened, and Zale looked into Cassaundra's face. There she was, smiling, looking just like he knew she would, exactly like she had in the past, like the night she had left him.

She stood there, looking at him through the screen door, and he stared back for a moment. She was as much in awe as he was, then Zale said, "Are we going to talk through the door, or are you going to let me in?"

"Oh! I'm sorry," Cassaundra said, appearing embarrassed, then opened the door for Zale to walk in.

"What happened to your face?"

"What do you mean?"

Cassaundra pointed. "The bruises."

"Oh. Nothing. Goes with the territory, that's all."

"I see," she said, sounding insulted that he wouldn't explain to her the nature of his injuries. "You can put your bag right there," Cassaundra said, pointing down at the space beside the couch. "Have a seat, please."

Zale sat, his knees together, his hands flatly resting on his lap. He looked around a moment. "This is a nice place you have," he said, trying to make conversation, break the ice.

Cassaundra smiled, standing in front of him.

"Would you like something to drink? Are you hungry?"

"Not hungry, just a little thirsty. If you have juice or something, that would be fine," Zale said, looking up at her, feeling as though he had been transported back a number of years.

He watched as she walked toward what had to be the kitchen, and he could not help but notice her shape. She was still fit, not as fit, but still attractive. What little weight she gained was probably because of the child. Our child, Zale thought. "My child," he said, very softly to himself. He was not sure how he felt about that, and told himself he wouldn't give it much thought till he had spoken to her about it.

Zale looked around a little more, and immediately noticed a photo that was sitting on the end table next to him. He grabbed it. It was a little girl standing in a patch of flowers. She was wearing a red dress with a huge white collar, her hair parted down the middle, two braids protruding from either side of her head, and she held a handful of the same flowers she was standing in. She was smiling that same innocent, carefree, ear-to-ear smile that so many children wear and don't appreciate. She appeared to be very happy.

There was no doubt who this was. She looked just like Cassaundra. Zale peered deeper into the picture, studying the young girl's features, trying to find himself in the small face, but was not able to. It was both reassuring and disappointing.

Zale set the picture down, stood up, and walked to the mantel, where he noticed more photos. And there was the little girl again, in almost all of them. Riding on a horse, blowing out the candles of a birthday cake, playing with a huge costumed figure at Disney World. The other pictures were of her and her mother together, and there were a couple with a man. Cassaundra and this man, arm and arm, both smiling wide, like they had won the lottery. Zale had to move one of the frames that crowded the small mantel to eye another photo of Cassaundra and this man kissing, and then there was the picture that Zale had to pick up, hold in his hands, and just let sink in for a moment.

It was this man, whoever he was, and the little girl. The man was bending over from behind the girl, hugging her, kissing her on the cheek, and she was smiling, seemed to be laughing, and squirming about happily, the way a child does when she's being licked in the face by a puppy.

This is supposed to be my daughter, Zale thought, looking down sadly at the picture. But I am not the man that is raising her.

Cassaundra walked back in the room carrying two glasses of apple juice, but halted when she saw Zale with the picture in his hand.

"I see you found a picture of your daughter."

"Have I?" Zale said sarcastically.

Cassaundra set Zale's glass down on a coaster sitting on the coffee table. "Yes, that's Leah."

Zale replaced the picture, sat down, took a sip of his juice, then said, "Who's the man?" It was something that he wasn't sure if he had the right asking, but he had to know just how involved his so-called daughter was with him.

"He's a friend. His name is Carl."

"How much of a friend is he to Leah? Does she call him Carl, Uncle Carl, or Daddy?"

Cassaundra looked at him, shaking her head, not as if shocked by his question, but as if she had expected exactly that from him.

"He's not the topic of our conversation, Zale. He's not the reason why you're up here."

"Then why am I up here?" Zale said, feeling some aggravation. "You say that that little girl is mine. She's six years old. What took you so long to finally give me a call?"

Cassaundra stood up, started rubbing her hands together, and slowly walked over to the mantel. She stood there with her back turned to Zale, and after a moment of silence, she spoke.

"I wasn't going to tell her about you. I hadn't planned on it. Ever. I knew how much you were against children, and I didn't want to burden you with something you didn't want to bother with. That's why I never called you. I had already decided that I would tell her that you were dead, had been killed in an accident of some kind. But a little after her third birthday, she started asking about her father, and knowing how much my father means to me, I couldn't deny her you."

Cassaundra turned to face Zale.

"Especially considering the work you're doing. You're an important man, a great man, and she needs to know that that's her father doing those things. She needs to see you, so she can be proud of you—the way I am."

Zale didn't know what to say. He just sat there, feeling somewhat flattered, staring up at the mother of his child.

"We keep a scrapbook of all the articles done on you. Covers of magazines, photos from the newspaper. Anything that we can stick in there, Leah is cutting and pasting into that scrapbook." Cassaundra walked back across the room, not returning to her chair, but sitting next to Zale.

"I would tell her how busy you are. That you really didn't have time to see her because of all the children you were helping. But, recently, she keeps bringing you up, saying that she wants to see you. Zale, I really didn't want to call you, and I was constantly back and forth. That's why I kept hanging up, because I knew that this wasn't what you wanted, but I couldn't stand another day of looking down into Leah's eyes and having her ask me when would she see her father."

"So you kept her from me."

"Would you rather I had told you when she was born, keep you informed of every major event that was about to take place in her life? Obligate you to witness the sighting of her first tooth, the day she took her first steps, birthday parties, the first day in kindergarten, and the father-and-daughter day that I wasn't able to take her to."

"Then who took her, Uncle Carl?" Zale said spitefully.

"Would you rather I had told you before now, Zale?" Cassaundra asked again, ignoring Zale's remark.

Zale pondered the question, and he couldn't say with total conviction that, indeed, he would've preferred that. Knowing him and all that he was burdened with already, there was no way he could have flown back and forth from Chicago to D.C. to be a father. And some weeks, even calling probably would have been far too much of a responsibility for him.

"No, I wouldn't have preferred it," Zale admitted. "You did the right thing. And I'm supposed to do what now? Now that I'm here, what am I supposed to do?" There was an edge to his voice. "Am I expected to pose for a photo with Carl so you can add to the collection on the mantel, and call it 'Biological Father–Surrogate Father'? Glance up and be able to see the men that fathered your child whenever you want."

Cassaundra was sipping from her juice when the remark was made, and in response to it, she simply lowered her glass, placing it on the table, walked over to Zale, stood in front of him and said, "Get up."

"What?"

"I said, get up!"

Zale stood, not knowing the reason why. Cassaundra grabbed Zale by the arm and hustled him to the door, then opened it for him.

"You're having such a huge problem with this, Zale, then don't do it. If you're bitter because I was trying to help you and not tell you about this child because I thought I knew that you wanted it that way, then I'm sorry. And if you resent the fact that there is another man in my life, a man that loves me, and happens to love Leah, too, well, I'm sorry about that as well. But if you don't think that you can bring yourself to accept those things, grow up long enough to realize that your daughter wants to see you, needs to see you, and get past that inflated ego of yours to know that my daughter only has one father, and that's you, then you can just walk out now, and I'll tell her that you're a man who is still too busy."

He was not the only father. And if there was only one, it sure as hell wasn't him. If he walked past the child on the street, he wouldn't have known she had anything to do with him. He had never seen her before, didn't know the sound of her voice, the feel of her touch, the smell of her hair. He was no father, Zale thought to himself, and what made Cassaundra think she could criticize Zale when it was she who lied to him, and had now dropped this bombshell on him when it was the last thing he needed.

If he were to walk out of there right now, there would've been nothing that he had lost, because there was nothing that he had known, regarding his daughter.

"You're forgetting my bag," Zale said, pointing over to the weekend bag he had packed for the trip.

The remark threw Cassaundra, as he knew it would. She didn't think he could walk out as easily as he was about to. She stood there, looking shocked by what he said. "Well, if you really want it, then go over and get it yourself," she said.

Zale gave Cassaundra a look as if to say "No problem," and nodded his head.

He walked over to his bag, and was bending down to grab it when he heard a voice.

"Mommy," he heard, still bending over. Then he heard the patter of feet coming down the stairs, and Zale still didn't move but remained bent over the bag, afraid of turning around because he knew that the voice he heard belonged to his daughter.

"Mommy, is that Daddy?" Zale heard the small voice ask, and he heard Cassaundra pause a moment and then answer softly, as if not wanting Zale to hear, "Yes, that is."

She looked a lot more like him, Zale thought, as he walked hand in hand with the little girl down the street, frequently looking down at her. It was Cassaundra's suggestion that he take Leah and walk with her down to the park so he could spend some time alone with his daughter.

"It's just down the street, and turn left at the corner. You can't miss it," Cassaundra said, standing out on the porch, pointing them in the direction. Then she gave Zale a confident pat on the back, and whispered in his ear, "You'll do fine."

He wasn't sure about that, because they had been walking for close to ten minutes, the park was in view, and he had not said a single word to the little girl, and although he was starting to feel uncomfortable about it, she seemed to be just fine with the silence, returning his stare every time he looked down at her.

They stepped onto the grounds of the park, still holding hands.

"Do you want to play on the swings?" Zale said, surprised that she didn't take off at the first sight of the things.

"No," Leah said simply.

"How about the slide?"

"No. I always come here. It's boring now."

"Well, how about we just sit down on that bench over there, and just talk a while?"

Leah looked up at him, squinting her eyes against the sun, then nodded her head.

It was quite uncomfortable sitting there next to the young girl who was his daughter, but was also a stranger. Zale didn't know where to start, and he felt that it was his responsibility to say something to her, but not just anything, something fatherly. He felt that she was waiting for a conversation, and if he took any truth from what Cassaundra had told him, she had been waiting for almost all her life.

Zale stole another glance at the girl, and she did look a lot like her mother, but he could actually see himself in her, and that made him proud, but it also saddened him, knowing that this was his child, someone that came from him, and yet she had lived all her life without even knowing him. She had no idea who he really was. Sure, the mother told her that Zale was her father, but the child didn't know that, probably couldn't pick him out of a lineup of just three men, and the only reason she asked her mother if that was her daddy standing in the living room this morning was, Zale was sure, that Cassaundra told Leah that he was coming.

Zale turned to face Leah, and placed his arm around her on the bench. "Can I ask you a question?" he said, using his little person's voice.

"Yes."

Zale scooted a little closer to her, trying to make her feel safe, comfortable, so she wouldn't hesitate to answer his question, because he knew the nature of the question would seem odd to the young girl. "Do you know who I am?"

The little girl looked up at Zale, a perplexed look on her face. It looked to Zale that she was battling with what she had been told and what she knew in her mind. She took a moment, then said with confidence, "You're my daddy." She smiled, but when she saw that her daddy didn't return the smile, it quickly disappeared from her face.

"That's who your mommy told you I was, isn't it?"

Leah nodded her head, looking down at her hands.

Zale scooted off the bench, and came around in front of Leah, squatted down before the girl, and placed his hands on her knees.

"Well, tell me who you think I am. Don't worry about what your mommy told you. Don't think about that. I just want you to look at me, and if you want to, you can think about it a minute, but just look at me, and then tell me who I am."

Zale knew he was setting himself up for a huge disappointment, but he really needed her to answer this question right. All she had to do was repeat herself, but this time say it like she meant it, like she knew it, not like she had rehearsed it all afternoon before coming down the stairs.

Leah was steadily looking him over, at his face, at his tie, his clothes, and Zale knew he was wrong. Wrong to be interrogating this girl like this, and why? Why did he all of a sudden need to know that she knew who he was, when for most of his adult life, he never wanted to have children? Maybe because he didn't want this child to be like all the others he was so used to seeing. Realizing that they have a father only because they know it's impossible for them to be living without one, but not knowing who the hell that man is. Looking at pictures of him, saved by the mother, but not knowing if he gives a damn about the child. Zale didn't want that to be Leah's opinion of him. He needed her to know that her father loved her and cared for her, and the first step toward her understanding that would be to understand, actually, who her father was.

"Well, can you tell me the answer?" he gently prompted her.

The child said nothing.

"Don't worry, just tell me what you think, what you feel, okay?" Zale said, feeling some excitement, looking in her eyes, feeling that she was on the verge of telling him what he wanted to hear. "Who am I?"

"You're . . . you're the man in the pictures in my scrapbook," she said. Then asked, "Am I right?"

"Yes, you're right," Zale said, trying to sustain the phony smile on his face, so as not to disappoint the little girl. And the fact was, she was right. He was nothing but the man in the scrapbook. Nothing but the photos or scraps of paper come to life, with no more significance or worth to her than the yellowing papers his likeness was printed on. Zale was almost sure that her mother made her collect those articles, that Leah would have more interest in cartoon characters, Mickey Mouse and Bugs Bunny, than she would in him. And if she had a choice, she probably would've preferred men like Tiger Woods or Michael Jordan to be her father, because she felt she knew them better. And, in essence, she did. Zale had never shared a single experience with this child, she had never heard the sound of his voice, had never seen his face in real life before now, so he was nothing more than a stranger. There was nothing more he should've expected from this little girl than what he had gotten, and excepting that, he decided to ask the question that he really shouldn't have, but needed to know the answer to.

"If I'm the man in the pictures in your scrapbook, then who is your daddy?" And as Zale expected, it only took her a second to answer that. No deep pondering as she had done for him. A smile widened across her face, and she said, "Carl." And she didn't even have to ask if she got that one right, because she knew it, in her mind and in her heart.

With the answer to that question, the "getting to know you" trip to the park was over. Disappointed and angered by the entire experience, Zale grabbed his daughter by the hand without a word, pulled her off the bench, and took long, quick strides home. Leah in tow, trailing behind, walked as fast as she could to keep up.

When Cassaundra opened the door, Zale pulled Leah into the house behind him.

"We need to talk," he told Cassaundra. "Can you send her upstairs for a little while?"

"What's wrong?" Cassaundra said, obviously sensing that something was wrong by either the tone of Zale's voice or the look on his face.

"We just need to talk. Alone. Please."

Cassaundra sent Leah upstairs to play and told Zale to follow her into the kitchen, where she was starting to prepare dinner.

"Now what's going on?" Cassaundra asked, wiping her hands on a towel.

"How much notice do you need to give up your job?" Zale said, determination in his voice.

"What?"

"I can't leave Father Found, so you and Leah will have to come to Chicago."

Cassaundra threw her head back and laughed out loud. "What are you talking about, come to Chicago? Why would we come to Chicago?"

"Because that child needs a father," Zale said, pointing a straight arm in the direction he believed her room to be.

"She already has a father, and he's sitting right there. That's why I asked you to come down here, so she can meet you."

"And then what?"

"And then, hopefully, you can become a part of her life," Cassaundra said.

"A part, hunh. A very small part. I can't be a proper father to a child from another state. I need her there, where we can spend more time."

"Listen to yourself, Zale. Just stop for a minute and listen to yourself," Cassaundra said, leaning over the table. "Last time I spoke to you, you were almost certain that you didn't want children, you didn't know if you wanted to get married, now you're wanting Leah and me to move to Chicago. Do you even love me anymore?"

Zale didn't respond, just sat there staring at Cassaundra through narrowed eyes, feeling the question was an unfair one.

"Answer me, Zale."

"I can learn to love you again," he said flatly.

Cassaundra laughed a little again, then said, "No, you can't, and you wouldn't want to. Zale, you can be a father from Chicago. There's nothing wrong—"

"There is something wrong with that!" Zale said, raising his voice, standing up from his chair. "You say I'm that child's father. You say that. But if you ask her, Carl is her father. She thinks some man that you're dating is her father, and I'm just some man that she sees on TV occasionally, and pastes in the damn scrapbook you make her keep! There is something wrong with that. A whole hell of a lot wrong with that, and if you can't see it, then maybe there's something wrong with you." Zale slowly lowered himself back to his seat, anger written all over his face.

"Well, what do you suppose I should do?" Cassaundra asked, now a few steps away from the table.

"I don't know, but I'll tell you what I'm not going to do. I'm not going to be some surrogate father or some damn play uncle. You say you asked me to come down here so I can meet my daughter, so she can know her father, so she won't be deprived. Well, that's what I'm trying to do, not deprive her. I want to be a father to my daughter, not halfway, not a little bit, but entirely, the way it should be, and I won't settle for less, I can't. If you want that child upstairs to have a father, her biological father, not some man you met at a bar, it's going to be all or nothing."

"How am I supposed to do that, Zale?"

Zale stood from his chair again. "You can start out by telling Daddy Carl that his services aren't needed anymore, that Leah's real father is here, and whatever you may have told him about me, or whatever he has been thinking, is not true. Tell him that I'm a man that takes care of his responsibilities, so he can go out there, and find a child that was really abandoned by their father. There are plenty of them out there, I should know."

"I'm not going to do that," Cassaundra said with attitude, throwing her hands on her hips. "Carl is a good man, and just because you think that things should go exactly the way you want them to doesn't mean I'm going to just get rid of him. I'm not going to do it, Zale. I'm not going—"

Zale quickly came from around the table, and rushed up on Cassaundra, backing her against the stove.

"You're not. Fine. Then your daughter won't have her father, and you know whose fault it will be, yours. And you don't want that. Trust me, you don't want your child thinking that her mother may have something to do with the fact that she grew up without a father. It'll follow her around for years to come, she'll never forget it, and she'll resent you for it for the rest of her life. I know a little something about that, too." Zale backed off some. "I'd give it some thought. I'll contact you later to find out what you've decided." Then he turned to go, but was met by Leah. She was standing just outside the door, and looked to have been there for some time, for her eyes were saddened, and tears appeared ready to fall. She looked up at her father like a stranger, like a stranger who had no business in her house, and no business speaking to her mother the way he did.

Zale looked down at his daughter for a moment, then called back to Cassaundra. "I'm not going to do this halfway." Then he left.

CHAPTER THIRTY-ONE

When Martin had stopped home from work at noon, two days after telling Debra that he didn't want to see her anymore, he had noticed something different upon walking into the house. He didn't know exactly what it was at first, but he stood in the hallway, turned a circle, looking about the area that he was in, trying to figure it out, when it dawned on him. The big picture that had been hanging in the hallway, over the coatrack, was gone. He told himself that meant only one thing.

Martin walked into the living room and saw that the end table was missing from beside the couch. In the kitchen, the microwave was missing, and upstairs, when he pulled back the doors of the closet and opened the drawers of the dresser, all of Debra's clothes had been removed. Nothing remained but empty space and the bare bottoms of those drawers.

Martin sat on the edge of the bed feeling relieved that she was gone, that she had gotten in, taken her stuff while he wasn't there as he had asked. He didn't want to see her again. He didn't want to see her lugging stuff from the house out to her car, watch her from the bedroom window, because he was afraid that he would've run out there, knocked the things from her hands to the ground and told her that all of this was nonsense, that whatever problems they had, whatever problems he had in his mind, he would work out. He didn't want that to happen, because when those images came back in his head, he knew he would've regretted calling her back, and he would've had to put her out all over again.

The kids were taking it hard, of course, as he knew they would. They kept asking, "Where is Mommy? Where is Mommy?" And all Martin could do was pull them close, kiss them on their heads, and say, "Mommy's not coming back. She had to go, because Mommy and Daddy weren't getting along, and she's not coming back." Martin knew that it wasn't an explanation, knew they still had questions, and knew they felt as if something valuable had been stolen right out from under them, but Martin couldn't tell them the truth, because it would require the whole truth, including the fact that she was not their real mother, and although Martin had blurted out something to that effect during their argument, the kids seemed to have forgotten it, or blocked it out, and Martin felt that they would be better able to handle it after the shock of her leaving had worn off, and they had realized that they could live as a family without her.

Martin grabbed the files and other papers he was looking for, and started back to work. Surprisingly, he had not heard from Zale, so either the situation with Zale and the little girl that was supposed to be his daughter was going all right, or Zale trusted him so much with Father Found that he didn't feel the need to call to get daily checkups.

Martin hoped that was the case, and was glad if it was, because if Zale had called, Martin would've had to lie to him again and tell him that everything was fine, when in fact he was on the verge of having the building taken right out from under him.

No money had come through, he wasn't able to find any anywhere, and the bank had already started foreclosure. And that wasn't the only problem. Two of Frank's victims had been calling constantly, demanding their money, saying they were entitled to it, and that if they didn't get the money they were promised, they wouldn't go to the police but would find attorneys and file suit, or go to the tabloids. They were sure they could get some money from them.

Martin knew that if that happened, Father Found would be destroyed. The tabloids and tabloid television would make a mockery of them, taking whatever respectability they had been able to build over the last three years and turn the entire organization into a joke.

They would make it seem as though Father Found was not truly trying to help families, but had some ulterior motives. They'd make up something, like Father Found was taking kickbacks from the government, or the mob, or that Zale was just some lunatic who had a personal vendetta against fathers who had left their children. That would kill Zale, and if it didn't kill him, it would probably send him right over the top, right off the ledge he'd been balancing himself on, right off into the abyss of insanity. Martin couldn't have that, he just couldn't, especially since Zale had left everything in his hands. He promised everything would be fine when Zale returned, and Martin intended to keep that promise.

Martin opened the door of his office, threw the papers down, and sank into his chair. He tried to think of a way out, tried to think of some businessmen whom he knew that he could borrow from, but he only knew a few, and, of them, none would be willing to invest in an organization such as Father Found. There was no way out, and Martin knew it. He was stumped, and it angered him. He hammered the side of his fist against the surface of the desk, then swiped everything onto the floor with his arms.

They would lose it, he told himself, knowing that at some point he would have to face reality. They would lose Father Found.

"You have a call, Mr. Carter," his secretary's voice said through the fallen intercom.

"Thank you," Martin grunted, and bent down to pick up his phone off the floor, stabbing the button that was flashing.

"This is Carter."

"Carter, where's Mr. Rowen?" It was Frank Rames.

"He's not here, but that's none of your damn business. What do you want?"

"I need to talk to him." Frank sounded desperate.

"I told you he's not here."

"You're lying to me. You don't want to tell me where he is, because you know he didn't want to fire me, and he might give me my job back. He never wanted to fire me. That was you, you son of a bitch!"

"What was that! What was that you called me?" Martin yelled, squeezing the hell out of the phone.

There was a long pause, silence, then Frank said in a soft, frightened tone. "Look, I'm sorry. I'm going through a lot right now, with losing my job and everything. I'm down to my last few dollars and I don't have nothing to do with myself, all right."

Martin turned a deaf ear to Frank's confessions.

"Now, I know we've never got along, but I really need to talk to Rowen," Frank said.

"For the last time, Rames, he's not here. He's out of town to take care of some business. I'll talk to you later." Martin started to hang up the phone, but heard Rames pleading through the receiver.

"What!" Martin said.

"Do me a favor, then. If he calls, tell him to call me, okay?"

"Yeah, whatever."

"Take down this number."

"We have your home number, Rames. Goodbye."

"Look! I'm not at home!" Frank yelled. "I'm not home, and I can't go home till something blows over, all right? So take down this number!"

Martin slid open his desk drawer, pulled out a sheet of paper and a pen, and scribbled down the number Frank gave him. Frank also gave him a room number, and the name of the motel he was staying in. When Martin was done copying the information, he said, "Is that it?"

"Yeah. You going to tell him to call me when he calls?"

"Yeah. I sure will."

"Don't fuck with me. I need for you to tell him," Frank said, the desperate, frightened tone still in his voice.

"I said, I'd tell him." Martin hung up the phone, took the sheet of paper, crumpled it in his fists, then tossed it into the wastebasket beside his desk. "What a loser."

A few hours later, Martin had managed to clean up everything off the floor and replace it back onto his desk, but had not had any ideas on how he was going to solve Father Found's problems. He picked up the phone, intending to call home to tell the babysitter that he would be a little later than usual because he had some things to take care of, when he heard some commotion outside his office.

He heard his secretary's voice yell something, then he heard a man's voice, muffled by the door, but sounding as though it was moving closer. Then all of a sudden, the door busted open, and Mace was standing in the middle of the office, Martin's secretary rushing in behind him, another man, not Mace's usual partner, but just as big, grabbing her by both her arms.

Martin sprang up from his chair and rushed from behind his desk.

"What the hell are you doing!" he said, running over to his secretary, pushing himself in between her and the man and forcing the man off her, pushing him back into a wall. Martin had his forearm buried in the man's neck. He was a huge man. His neck looked the size of one of Martin's thighs, and Martin was surprised that the man didn't pick him up and throw him aside like he'd brush a piece of lint off his shoulder. But Martin kept his arm lodged under his chin, and only turned away from him long enough to ask his secretary if she was all right and question Mace again as to why he was there.

"I came to see Ro, and your little secretary wouldn't let me in." Mace paused for a moment. "Where's Ro? I need to talk to him. And you can get off my man, all right. You ain't doing nothing. He's only letting you hold him like that because I haven't told him to squash your little ass. Now get off him."

Martin turned back and looked into the big man's face. He saw it start to crumple into a scowl, and he felt the man's strength start to fill his body, rumbling like an impending earthquake or volcano about to erupt, and Martin backed off.

"What makes you think you can come in here and handle my employees like that?" Martin said, directing his anger more toward Mace than the large man he had stepped back from.

"He wasn't going to hurt her. I just need to talk to Ro, and she was trying to stop us. If I want to talk to my boy, I'm going to talk to him, and nobody's little secretary is going to stop me, so where is he?"

"He's not here."

"Then where did he go?" Mace said, walking up on Martin.

Martin took a step forward toward Mace to show that he was not intimidated.

"That's none of your business," Martin said smoothly.

Mace spun his back to Martin, and said to his partner, "Get the woman out of here."

Martin heard her squeal, and he turned to see what was happening.

"Don't you hurt her!" he warned the man.

"Should I call the police, Mr. Carter?" she cried as she was being forced out the office.

Mace turned toward Martin, shaking his head. "I would tell her not to do that if I was you."

"No. Everything is fine. Don't call the police. I'll be out in a minute."

The huge man closed the door, leaving the secretary outside, came back in and stood directly to Mace's side, and when Mace stepped forward to Martin, the big man followed, standing not two inches away from Martin's shoulder. The man towered over him, standing at least six foot five, and he appeared to be the width of two and a half men. Martin looked at the wall made of man, felt the warm breath coming from the man's nostrils breathing down on him like a bull about to charge. Martin noticed the man was wearing leather gloves, and he wondered what they were for, because he knew the weather outside was warm.

"What are you planning on doing? You going to beat me to death in here if I don't tell you where Zale is?" Martin said, trying to sound as fearless as possible, even though it took everything he had to stop his voice from quavering.

Mace stepped even closer to Martin. They were face-to-face, as if they were about to kiss. Then Mace smiled and stepped back some, and the big man did the same.

"I wouldn't hurt you, man. C'mon, you my boy's right-hand man, so if I hurt you, I'd be hurting him, told you that. But I do need to know where he is so I can talk to him. It's very important, and I ain't bullshitting about that."

"He's not here. He—"

"Well, where the hell is he?"

"He flew to D.C. He had some business there he had to take care of. He didn't leave an address or a number where he would be, and he hasn't called yet, so I couldn't tell you more than that even if I wanted to."

"Maybe you can help me with something else, then," Mace said.

"No. That's impossible," Martin said, his hand on the doorknob. "I could never help you, because I would never want to."

"I need to know where your pet white boy, Frank Rames, is," Mace said, disregarding Martin's previous comments.

"I thought you were 'the man about the streets.' Why would you need me to tell you where Rames lives? You should know something like that."

"I didn't ask you where he lives. I know that. I asked you where he is, because he ain't where he normally is. The boy is hiding somewhere, and that's what I want you to tell me."

And then it dawned on Martin, why Frank sounded the way he did. Frightened and desperate, as though he was running for his life. If this man was looking for him, Martin was sure that, indeed, his life was in jeopardy.

"I don't know where he is," Martin lied. "But even if I did know, I wouldn't tell you."

"I see," Mace said, rubbing his chin between his thumb and forefinger.

"What do you want him for anyway?"

"Let's just say I need to talk to him."

"Well, I don't know where he is. So if you'd just leave now," Martin said, opening the door.

Mace started toward the door, then said casually, "So, how much more time before the bank takes this old building from you?"

"What did you say?" Martin asked, not believing he had heard correctly.

Mace stopped, smiling again. "You heard me. When is the bank going to take this property back?"

Martin slammed the door shut so no one else could hear about what he thought only he knew. "What are you talking about? Where did you hear that?"

Mace chuckled. "Remember, I am 'the man about the streets.' I make it my business to know shit like that. I know your broke asses are in deep debt, can't afford to pay for this building. I also know there's men you owe money to, and if you can't afford to pay for the damn roof over your head, I know you can't afford to pay them off to keep quiet."

Mace looked around the office a little, stepped over to the window to eye the view. "I don't know. I'll wait till the bank reacquires this, and

I might pick it up as a little project building. I don't know what I'll do with it, but I'm sure I'll think of something. That is, unless . . . you'd like to do a little bargaining," Mace said, leaning on the windowsill.

"What are you talking about?" Martin said, knowing full well what the proposition was.

"You know how far me and Ro go back, don't you, Mr. Carter."

Martin knew.

"And if you don't know this already, the man means the world to me. He's like my only family. I try to help him so many damn times it's pathetic, but he turns me down like a fucking fool, says that he wants no part of what I'm involved in. He don't want dirty money in his organization. That's beautiful," Mace said, chuckling to himself, walking over closer to Martin. "Really moralistic and shit, but it's stupid. If you had the choice to take dirty money to work for a worthy cause that will help the entire community, that would bring fathers back to their children, that would prevent kids from living on the streets, or being abused in fucking foster homes like we were, or not taking the money and being shut the fuck down, and not being able to do shit for no goddamn body, which would you do, Mr. Carter? Which would you do!" Mace said.

"I don't know," Martin said, dumbstruck by what was going on.

"Well, make up your mind," Mace said, releasing Martin, walking away from him. "Because the choice is yours."

"What are you talking about?" Martin said, briskly walking up behind him.

Mace spun around and looked at Martin as though he didn't have the sense of a two-year-old. "I have to spell it out? You tell me where Rames is, and you get not only the money to pay those men off, and the back mortgages you owe the Jews, but I'll give you the money to buy this place. This building will be yours. You will own it. No more worries about owing anybody jack. You can have all that in exchange for one little address." Mace slapped a hand on Martin's shoulder. "What's it going to be, Martin?"

"And all you have to do is talk to him, you say."

A pathetic smile lengthened across Mace's face. "Yeah, that's all we have to do."

And Martin knew he was lying. Knew he was lying before he even asked the question, but he had to hear the lie, hoping that it would make it easier for him to give Frank up. They were going to kill him, and Martin knew that. Something made Martin want to tell Mace to go to hell, because he hated him, hated everything that he was and everything that he stood for, and had no idea why Zale still dealt with the man on whatever level he did.

Martin didn't want to help him, and something told him that later he would regret it, but there was no way out of the bind he was in with Father Found. There was no other way. Martin tried to tell himself that he hated Rames, too, that he cared for Rames just about as much as he cared for Mace, but regardless of that fact, that was still no reason for him to die.

But maybe it was justice. Maybe this was what he had coming to him for beating those men, for subjecting them to his hatred, for inflicting pain on them when they were just lost and had nowhere to turn.

Martin pondered for that moment or two, which seemed like long past forever, knowing that he didn't want Frank's death on his hands, that even though he despised the man, that didn't mean he should die.

"Let me tell you something, Martin," Mace said, as if he were giving valuable advice. "If you don't tell me where he is, the only difference will be is that you won't get the money, and Father Found is done, and so are you, and so is Zale. It probably won't be as soon as I'd like, but I'm going to find Frank, and we'll have our talk. I promise you that. So what's it going to be?"

Martin looked Mace square in the eyes, and he knew that Mace knew he had Martin over a barrel.

Martin turned away from Mace, walked over to his desk, bent down and rummaged through his wastebasket till he found the crumpled paper with Frank's phone number and address on it. He walked back over to Mace, uncrumpling the paper to reveal the information, his head lowered, feeling defeated.

"Here," Martin said.

Mace took the paper, no expression on his face.

"It don't seem like it now, but you making the right decision. You making the right decision for your people," Mace said, slapping Martin on the shoulder again.

I know that. But I just wish Frank could see it the same way, Martin thought, as he watched the two men leave. Half an hour later he punched ＊ 6 9 on his phone. When he heard Frank's voice, Martin spoke.

"Frank, I'm not telling you why, but I'd get out of there now."

Then he hung up.

CHAPTER THIRTY-TWO

Zale walked through the doors of a small, dimly lit bar. He had been walking the streets of Washington for most of the day, and now it was some time after 10:00 P.M. Only a few people filled the place. A couple having a drink at a table, and a man by himself, a few tables down, slumped over, his head resting on top of his stacked forearms. Either he was sleeping or passed out, but the six beer bottles and many shot glasses gathered around him indicated the latter.

Zale approached the bar, noticing another man sitting on a stool at the far end, and had a seat. When the bartender came, Zale ordered a shot of scotch on the rocks, then said, "No, make it a double." He needed a double, and he knew he would be ordering at least two more after that.

He had been pondering what to do about his daughter and Cassaundra all day, and had come up with nothing. There was nothing he could do, because Cassaundra wouldn't allow him to do anything, and that angered Zale. It angered him no end.

One question that he kept asking himself since he left her house was, why did she even tell him about Leah if she intended on tying his hands like she had? She knew that when he found about his daughter he wouldn't be able just to sit back and only see her on holidays, or on her birthday, or whenever he had time to hop a plane to D.C. That wasn't the way to raise a child, and Zale couldn't consider himself a real father doing things that way. And, then, there was the situation with this man Carl, and Zale just knew that he was trying to play father to his child. That he was trying to instill values in Leah that only her real father could, that he was trying to give her the love that was supposed to be given by only Zale. Zale couldn't allow that to continue, but there seemed to be no way around it, and it was driving him mad.

His head had been banging for the better part of the day, and he was thankful that he had thought to pack his medication. He went into his suit jacket pocket and pulled out the bottle. He dumped the one pill that he was supposed to have been taking daily, then dumped another two tablets in his palm, considering how bad he was feeling.

He jiggled the capsules in his hand for a moment, then threw them in his mouth, raised the glass of scotch to his lips, tilted his head back, and washed them down. He grimaced at the strength of the alcohol, but he knew he would feel better soon, if not as a result of the medication, definitely as a result of the liquor.

Two more swallows, and the glass was empty. Zale raised a finger to get the bartender's attention and ordered another double. When he returned with Zale's drink, Zale said, "Go ahead and mix up another. Same thing." Because Zale knew by the time the bartender returned with his third drink, he'd be finished with the second.

Zale sat leaning over the bar, the alcohol already starting to take effect on him, making his head feel light, his senses dull, and his pain not as bothersome. He traced a finger around the rim on his glass and occasionally brought it up to his lips and took a sip. He didn't need anything else to drink, if getting drunk was his objective, because he was already there. But his goal was to forget about what was troubling him, and the two drinks that he had drunk hadn't come close to ridding him of his thoughts, and he felt the third wouldn't do it either.

Zale thought about the work that he did back in Chicago. The way he did that work, the stand he took against fathers leaving their children, how hard he was with them, sometimes brutal. He thought about some of the speeches he had given, and the many names he used to refer to these men. He thought about how he chased them down like dogs, how their problems never concerned him, and how he would take anything and everything he could from them in order to get them to go back to where they belonged.

He remembered so many of those men telling them that there were other circumstances, that they wanted to go back, but the mother didn't want them there. Excuses like: they had been paying, but the mother was trying to get more money than she deserved, or the mother was intentionally keeping the child from her father because she was angry he no longer wanted to be with her.

And now, Zale could remember one man in particular saying that he didn't even know that he had a child. Zale found that extremely funny at the time. So funny that he laughed in the man's face and told him that he would have to come up with a better lie than that. The child was four years old, and he knew that there was no way that a man could have a child, a four-year-old child, living in the same city and not know about it, and if he did, he was one pathetic father.

Over the past three years, Zale had beaten fathers verbally, demeaning them, degrading them, always taking the side of the mothers, sometimes without even hearing their stories. He never gave the fathers the benefit of the doubt, just assumed that they were to blame, and that the last thing they'd want to do was to face the responsibility of raising their own children.

But maybe he was wrong about them, or his approach. Not all of the time, but maybe some of the time. This may be the reason why his organization was failing, why his public image was in the trash, and why no one wanted to donate, help his cause, because they viewed him as a tyrant. He had a little power, it went to his head, and he abused it, abused them, and that was wrong, and everyone saw it, except him. Even his partner saw it, tried to tell him about it, correct him. He could've been right all along, and Zale just couldn't face it.

"I know exactly what I'm doing," Zale remembered saying. "These men are so sensitive because they know that I'm right. If they just go home like they are supposed to, if they just accept their fatherly responsibilities and stop running like cowards, everything would be fine, and it would sure as hell make my job a lot easier."

Now being faced with the exact same problem that at least one of the men he was "trying to help" was facing, he realized that he had been a fool. He wanted to be there for his daughter, and the mother wouldn't let him. He wanted to do the right thing, and to him, it meant more than signing a check for child support each month. It meant more than walking to the mailbox every year and dropping a birthday card to his "daughter." It meant more than having conversations on the telephone long-distance, telling his child how much he missed her and vowing that he would see her as soon as possible. That was not the type of father Zale wanted to be, and it was the reason that he had insisted so strongly on never having children in the first place, because it made finding himself in the exact situation he was in right now a possibility.

Zale lifted the glass of scotch and took another sip, a long one this time, and it hit him like a dull thump on the head.

CHAPTER THIRTY-THREE

It was after midnight but Zale still banged on the door of Cassaundra's house as if his intentions were to break it down. He didn't pause, just continued to bang, occasionally ringing the doorbell. He was drunk, yes, but it wasn't the alcohol making him behave this way, it was the fact that he was being denied his right to be a father, his chance to rid himself of the horror that he relived almost every night and had firmly lodged itself in his brain.

He continued banging till he saw lights come on behind the windows of the house. Then he stopped, banging once more, just because he was mad as hell.

Cassaundra came to the door in a nightgown. Her hair was tossed about her head, and there were both sleep and anger in her eyes.

"What the hell are you doing here, banging on my door like this in the middle of the night!" she whispered harshly.

Zale looked at her for a long, hard moment. He was overcome by emotion, by anger, and didn't know exactly what to say, because he knew it was up to her whether or not he was allowed to raise his child.

"You told me!" was all he was able to come out with.

"What!"

"You told me!" Zale said again, this time jabbing a finger at her, as if he were fingering her out for a terrible crime she had committed.

Cassaundra leaned slightly toward him, taking a whiff. "You've been drinking! I should've figured. Come in here before you wake up the entire neighborhood."

Cassaundra grabbed Zale around the waist and ushered him in.

"You told me!" Zale said again, allowing her to hold most of his weight, for he was exhausted and far too drunk to stand on his own much longer.

"What are you talking about!"

"You told me that I have a child," Zale said, trying to maintain composure, trying to stop himself from breaking down and crying. "You made me a father by telling me that, and now you won't allow me to be one! Why did you tell me? You know how I feel about this. You knew what I would've wanted, and, dammit, you knew that you weren't going to give it to me, so why did you tell me about her?"

"Zale," Cassaundra said, trying to sound caring, but approaching him cautiously, like one would a pet dog that had suddenly gone rabid. "Why don't you sleep it off, and in the morning you can come—"

"I won't sleep it off! There's nothing to sleep off. This is my child I'm talking about!" Zale shouted, stomping his foot down.

"Is there a problem?" a voice asked coming from the top of the stairs. It was a man's voice, and when Zale looked in that direction, he saw Carl.

The man walked down the stairs, tying his robe closed.

"Is everything all right, sweetheart?" Carl said, now standing beside Cassaundra.

"It's fine, Carl. Why don't you go back upstairs to sleep."

Zale looked at the man, shocked to see him there at this hour.

"Is he living here?" Zale said. "He's living under the same roof as my daughter?"

"He stays here sometimes, Zale. That's all."

"Stays here. Sometimes! And how does Leah see all this?"

"She understands," Cassaundra said.

"Understands what? That her mother is fucking some man that's not her father, and that she's not married to. And *sometimes,* when they want to continue fucking, he stays here till the next morning. Is that what she understands?"

"You can't talk to her that way," Carl offered, taking a step toward Zale.

Zale chuckled at Carl's attempt to defend his woman's honor. "And why not, because you won't allow it in her house? Why, because you won't allow anyone to speak that way about your wife, or say such things about your daughter? Really, who are you except some boyfriend, laying up in some woman's house trying to play father."

"Well, I wouldn't have to play father if you were a father."

At that remark, Zale lunged at the man, reaching and grabbing for him, but Cassaundra managed to get in between them before Zale could grab hold of him.

"Stop it! Stop it!" she yelled, and after a moment Zale calmed and backed away.

Carl just stood staring at Zale as if he was ready for anything, and he would prove it if Cassaundra allowed him.

"Zale, you're acting like a goddamn fool! Now we aren't going to discuss this any more tonight. You're far too drunk, and you're not making any sense, and this situation is far too important to discuss with you in this condition."

"I'm not going anywhere till we resolve this," Zale said, feeling worn from the effects of the alcohol.

"Then I'll get you some bedding, and you can sleep on the couch, and we'll talk about it in the morning."

Cassaundra turned to go and get some linen, but Carl stepped in her path.

"That man can't sleep in this house," he said.

Cassaundra took a step back, looked sternly in Carl's eyes, and said, "That man is my child's father, and . . . whose house is this?" She gently pushed him aside, and went to get the bedding.

The next morning, Zale was up early. He had awakened when he heard Carl leave for work. It was 6:00 A.M., and he got up, took a shower, went to the kitchen and sat down and had a bowl of cereal. When he opened the cupboard, he grabbed one of the colorfully decorated boxes. He poured the cereal into his bowl, filling it full of marshmallows and sugar-coated morsels in the shapes of animals and spaceships and things, and he thought to himself, sadly, This is what my daughter eats.

He sat there, spooning the cereal into his mouth from the Bugs Bunny bowl, hoping that he was sitting in what was his daughter's chair. He wanted to know her, feel her as much as he could, because he knew that Cassaundra would not tell him what he wanted to hear, so he had to take as much of his daughter with him as he could.

Last night, after Cassaundra and Carl had gone to sleep, Zale got up from the sofa and crept through the house, over to the stairs. He grabbed hold of the banister and looked up the dark stairway, knowing that up there was where his daughter was. It felt wrong, like he would be violating some form of secrecy, or trespassing on territory that did not belong to him, if he were to climb those stairs and find the room that his daughter slept in, but he had to do it. He wanted to see his daughter sleeping, wanted to see her peacefully dreaming. He could sit there by her side, as if he had just read her a bedtime story and lulled her off to sleep, and, if just for a little while, pretend that that was the way it had always been and always would be.

He climbed the stairs up to the second floor and blindly walked down the hallway, following one of the walls with his hand. When he reached a door, there was no way of telling whether it was his daughter's or Cassaundra's. The last thing he wanted to do was open the door to find the woman that he once loved being used as some sexual toy.

Zale placed his ear up to the door and listened. He heard no sound, so regardless whose room it was, he figured they'd be sleeping, so it wouldn't matter if he entered.

He placed a trembling hand on the doorknob. His hand slid around it at first because of the perspiration on his palm, but the knob turned and the door opened. He stuck his head in, and there he saw his daughter soundly sleeping, her face slightly illuminated by the moonlight coming in through the window. His heart stopped, and it was like looking at an angel. He quickly but quietly stepped into the room and closed the door behind him. He glanced over the room just to get an idea of her surroundings, then he walked to the side of her bed and stared down at her. How beautiful she was—his daughter, and he said it in his head a few times as if he couldn't believe it was true. My daughter. My daughter.

There was a chair beside her bed, and he sat there. This would be the chair that he would've sat in when he read her bedtime stories. He looked over the room again and saw a bookcase. He walked over to it, selected a book, and returned to his chair.

He opened the book, and was about to start reading when, again, he looked over at his daughter. He reached out his hand, slowly moving to touch her, then holding it, hovering just over her cheek. He held his breath, then lowered his palm, and touched her smooth, soft, warm cheek. He held it there for only a moment, realizing that this would be the last time he would ever touch her. He pulled his hand back just as slowly as he extended it, then opened the book again and began reading.

"Once upon a time . . ."

When Cassaundra came downstairs, it was 7:30 A.M. and Zale was fully dressed, sitting on the edge of the sofa, staring out the window, waiting patiently, as if for a bus.

"What are you doing?" Cassaundra said from the stairs. "It looks like you're about to go somewhere."

Zale stood up and turned to look at her. "I am, Cassaundra. There's no reason for me to stay."

A concerned, disappointed look covered Cassaundra's face and she came quickly down the stairs and over to Zale.

"What are you talking about?"

"First, I want to say I'm sorry for last night. I was drunk, and—"

"Forget about last night. What is this about you leaving?" she said, grabbing Zale's arms. "We haven't even talked about Leah."

Zale smiled pathetically and sighed. "Is there really anything else to talk about? You told me that's my child, and I believe you, and I want to be her father. But like I said before, I'm not trying to half do this. I couldn't take seeing her only sometimes. And I couldn't stand to know that when I did, she may be comparing me to some other man who was raising her most of the time."

"She wouldn't do that, Zale."

"Maybe not, but if I thought she was, it wouldn't work. You have to understand, Cassaundra, I have so much to give, just from the fact that I wasn't given to. Being a surrogate father, a part-time father, is not enough for me. It's just not."

"But what about—"

"Don't worry about child support," Zale interrupted. "I'll send you

a check every month for the amount you ask for. I know what my responsibilities are."

"I'm not talking about child support, Zale! I'm talking about our
daughter. I wouldn't have told you about her if I didn't think she
needed you. The money is not the issue. That's not why I had you fly
all the way down here. I just want to know why you won't give to her
what you can. It would be better than nothing, and I think you both
would benefit from it. It sure as hell wouldn't do any harm."

Zale shook his head. "That's where you're wrong. How would it
look for me to do the work I'm doing, say the things I'm saying to
these men out here, try and provide some sort of example to them,
with me having an illegitimate child."

"I don't like that term," Cassaundra said bitterly.

"Well, I don't like it either, but that's how people see it. How am I
supposed to tell men to go back to their children, to return to the
mothers, when that's not where I am? If word got out, and it surely
would, it would do more harm than good. People wouldn't understand, men wouldn't understand, and that's what I'm going to need
from them now, and not just that, but their forgiveness. I've been
wrong about so, so much, and mistreated so many of them. I need to
find a way for them to respect me again, for them to trust me."

"And you're going to do that by lying to them about not having a
daughter?"

Zale had no response for that. She was right. He would be lying, but
this was a case where telling the truth would be far more damaging
than a lie.

"I know you told me about Leah because you figured that what we
could gain from my knowing was more than what we would lose if you
kept it from me. But as selfish as it may sound, I'd rather have nothing
if I can't have it all."

"I don't think you're making the right decision, Zale. Don't you
think you should give it more thought?"

"I thought about it all last night."

"Well, don't you want to at least say goodbye to your daughter?"
Cassaundra said, turning toward the first stair.

"I've already said goodbye in my own way. I'm sure she'll have no problem with me not being here. Carl's a good man," Zale said, only for her benefit. "He has to be if you allow him to be with you." Zale moved toward the door, but stopped short when Cassaundra came up to him.

She looked into his eyes, and he looked into hers, not knowing what to do. It was awkward for him, as he was sure it was for her. He leaned forward, kissed her on the cheek, as if saying goodbye to a stranger after a first date. He struggled to give her a comforting smile, then opened the door, and without looking back, left the house.

As he walked down the street, he noticed that it would be a bright, beautiful, sunny day. He squinted his eyes, not against the sun, but in a failing attempt to keep the tears from rolling down his cheeks.

CHAPTER THIRTY-FOUR

When Zale arrived at the airport, he went into his pocket, pulled out his wallet, and handed the cabdriver a bill. He wasn't sure how large the bill was, and he didn't care, but judging by the way the cabdriver's face lit up when Zale mumbled, "Keep it," it must have been somewhat large.

Zale stepped out of the cab, under a sky that had started to fill with clouds, even though not half an hour ago the sun was shining brilliantly. It was going to rain, and Zale could feel it, the darkness that was all around him, all around everything. For some reason, it was as though his senses were not working right at all. It was like all the noise that should've been heard at an airport he could not hear. The planes that flew overhead like huge metal birds made no sound at all. And of all the taxicabs that jammed the single-lane street that led out of the airport, honking their horns, the cabbies hanging out of their windows yelling obscenities to drivers that cut them off, Zale didn't hear their horns, nor did he hear their barking, just saw their mouths moving, spit flying from their lips, as if he were watching a silent film.

Zale, toting his bag, walked through the crowded airport, bumping into the many people that he passed as if they weren't there. They may as well not have been. He was alone, saw no one, felt no one, was not aware of anyone's existence, and that was how it was since he had left Cassaundra's house. That was the way he wanted it. He continued walking, seeing nothing in front of him but his destination. Gate C3.

He had been alienating people for so long, driving people away from him, when he only had a couple of people near him to begin with. Regina—gone. Not because she had found him cheating, or because they realized that they just didn't get along—in hindsight, he could've dealt with that—but because he drove her away. He did everything to make her go, and when she was telling him how he could hold on to her, he purposely did the exact opposite, because he knew it would get rid of her faster. What was on his fucking mind, he asked himself, as he felt himself bump hard into someone. He heard an angry remark, but it was muffled, barely audible. He paid it no mind and kept walking.

And then there was his daughter. He gave her away as well. There could've been some compromise made, and he knew that, but it was all or nothing, and so he ended up with nothing. It always seemed to be like that. No matter how much he tried to protect himself from losing everything, he always seemed to fail, just like now.

The woman he loved—gone. His daughter—gone, and the organization, Father Found. He had no idea what was going on there, and if things continued on the track they were on when he left, that would be gone too. He would have nothing to show for it after all the work, all the effort, and the good intentions. Not a goddamn thing.

When Zale got to his gate, he walked up to the door where the passengers were boarding.

"Your boarding pass, sir," the flight attendant asked, after Zale had been standing there in front of her, blank-faced, for a long moment.

"Oh," Zale said, snapping out of his trance, and passing her the boarding pass he was holding in his hand.

Zale boarded, threw his bag in the overhead storage compartment, and fell back into his seat. There were a lot of empty seats, including the two on either side of him, and he was thankful for that, even though he probably wouldn't have noticed if there were people sitting beside him or not.

He buckled his seat belt, and almost immediately his eyes started to glaze over and he felt himself falling back into that pit of self-doubt, self-pity, and self-debasement.

When Zale finally reemerged, a flight attendant was standing over him holding a tray.

"Sir, I said, would you like your in-flight meal?"

It took Zale a moment to realize what she was talking about, then, finally, looking somewhat disoriented, he said, "No. No, thank you."

The flight attendant turned and was about to walk away, when she turned back to Zale, a concerned look on her face.

"Sir, is everything all right?"

Zale looked up at her, working a phony smile on his face. "Yeah. Yeah, just fine."

She walked away, and the smile immediately fell off his face. He raised his hand to his forehead to feel if it was warm. It wasn't. He had no temperature, but there was a dull pain in his head, and he knew that before long it would increase in intensity. Zale went into his pocket, took a pill out of his bottle, popped it in his mouth, and swallowed it down, no water. He looked at his watch and saw that he had only been flying for an hour and would have at least another to go before they touched down in Chicago. That was too much time to think about all the mistakes he made, and the sorry-ass situation he was now in. If he started thinking about that again, he would probably turn suicidal and toss himself out of the plane.

He looked through the seat-back pouch that was in front of him for something to keep his attention, but there was nothing but the flight magazine, a couple of empty bags of peanuts, and the flight safety card. But to his right, he found a newspaper, a Chicago newspaper. One of the passengers flying in must've left it.

He pulled the paper out, sat it on his lap, and started thumbing through it looking for the funnies. When he got to where they should've been, he found that they weren't there, and figured that the person who owned this paper needed the same thing from it that he did.

Zale closed the paper, and knowing that there was nothing else he could do to occupy his mind, he reopened the paper to page one. He glanced at the pictures of gory car crashes, the guilty looks of politicians after being caught red-handed in some crime or another, and black people in handcuffs and shackles, an attempt to make the country feel as though they had nothing to fear, because the root of all evil had been captured, and it's printed in the paper to prove it.

Zale continued flipping the pages, reading an occasional outlandish headline or two: "Woman Is Raped by Eleven-Year-Old." "Inner City Fire Kills Twenty-three."

Zale turned the page, having no interest in any of it, until he got to the headline that read: "Ex-Police Detective Slain." And Zale always thought that was a travesty. To die because you devoted your life to helping other people. He started to read the article:

"Yesterday, in a small motel room on the North Side of Chicago, a forty-year-old white male was found dead. He was killed by two .33-caliber handgun rounds to the back of the head, and police are speculating that it may have been a professional hit, perhaps drug- or gang-related. The deceased has been identified as ex-police detective Frank Rames and . . ."

Zale froze. His mouth hung open, his heart stopping, and he couldn't breathe. He stared at the word "and," almost afraid to look back at the name of the victim for fear that his eyes were correct upon its initial reading.

It can't be, Zale thought. It just can't be. The paper was rattling about, for his arms were shaking madly. His fists clutched about the paper as if he were trying to choke the truth out of it.

He forced himself to look back at the name, and, indeed, it was Frank, the man who had saved his life, the man that Zale repaid by firing him, and he was dead, killed like a rabid dog, or a lame horse, like a fucking animal, and why!

Zale couldn't read any more. He had to find out if it was true.

Zale quickly went into his pocket, pulling out his wallet, fumbling through it, and pulling out one of his credit cards.

He jammed the card into the slot to release the air phone that was in the seat back in front of him, swiped the card through the phone, then dialed Martin's phone number.

"Be home, be home," Zale begged, as the phone rang.

"Hello," Martin said.

Zale paused for a moment, still hoping that there had been a mistake, then said, "Tell me it's not true."

"Zale?"

"Martin, tell me it's not true!"

Martin's voice lowered, filled with regret. "About Frank. Yeah, it's true. He's dead."

"Goddammit!" Zale cringed and folded over in his seat as if he had been stabbed in the gut. "Who did it?" he asked desperately.

There was a long pause, then Martin said, "I don't—"

"Who did it!" Zale demanded an answer.

"I don't know, Zale! I don't know. But he's dead. How am I supposed to know who killed him?"

Zale raised back up in his seat. His head was spinning now. "I know. It's just . . . just that that man saved my life, and what did I do? I fired him. I took his job."

"Zale . . ." Martin tried to interrupt.

"Do you know the problems that man had? Do you know all that he was going through? Every day he had to deal with being kicked off the force. He had a drinking problem that he was fighting, and he had recently been divorced, and this was all after losing his only boy in a car accident that he caused because he was drinking. Did you know that, Martin? Did you know all of that?"

"I know." Martin's tone was low. "But what does that have to do with you, and the fact that he's dead? It sounds like you're blaming yourself for his death."

"Do you think that maybe if I hadn't fired him, he would probably still be alive?" Zale asked, as if there was maybe a way to turn back the hands of time.

"Zale, don't do that to yourself. This has nothing to do with you firing him."

"But what if he went out looking for trouble because he was so distraught that—"

"Then that's his fault. Zale, you need to understand something. You didn't kill him, you didn't put the gun to his head and pull the trigger, and you weren't the person that had the power to decide whether he lived or he died. The man that had that power has to live that down. That's not your burden, but his."

"But what if—"

"Stop it, Zale! Stop it!" Martin insisted, raising his voice. "Now, for the last time, it's not your fault! Zale, look at what the man did. He was no angel."

"That man did not deserve to die!" Zale said, and in his mind, he saw Frank, the two slugs burned into the back of his head, dried blood around the wound, matting his hair down to his partially shattered skull. He was lying slumped over a chair in that sleazy motel room. His body limp, his arms dangling to his sides, knuckles hanging just above the bloodstained carpet. It was not how he should've died, Zale thought. Like a dog. Frank was strong, and Zale imagined the man resisted, knew he fought whoever killed him. But he lost, lost his life, and Zale beat himself with the thought that he should've been there to save Frank—to return the favor.

"What did he do so wrong? He was only trying to do what he thought was best, what would help Father Found, and what did he get for that? He had problems, Martin. Like everyone else, he had problems. Like you, like me, and they made him make some mistakes, but he didn't deserve to die because of them! That's not what he deserved!" Zale said, a tear running down his cheek. "That's not what he deserved."

Zale pulled the phone away from his ear and crammed it back into its place in the seat back, but before he hung up, he could hear Martin calling his name.

"Zale! Zale!"

Zale threw his hands over his face, digging his fingers into his skull, wishing that he could . . . that he could . . . there was nothing he could do. He was backed in a corner, and there was nothing he could do to relieve the pain, or lift the guilt, or quiet the chaos he was feeling. There was nothing he could do, and no one he could turn to. There was nothing, nothing but him.

And when he stepped off the plane, walked down the long, narrow corridor, like the passageway to the next life, a darker life, and stood among fellow passengers who were being rushed over to, hugged and kissed, their hands grabbed and pumped vigorously, Zale realized just how alone he truly was.

He stood there, not knowing why, just stood, his carry-on luggage in his hand, waiting as the crowd slowly started to dissipate, the noises of happiness starting to quiet.

He stood there as if lost, not knowing where to go, and frightened by that, so frightened that he could not even will himself to take one step forward. And as he remained standing, looking as calm and as still as one of the columns beside him that held the ceiling of this huge structure off the floor, there was chaos erupting in his head. A montage of images, a steady, relentless barrage of horrid scenes pelting his psyche. But he pushed them away.

Frank's blood-soaked hair. He pushed them away.

His mother lying across the living room floor, looking as if she had died there. But Zale pushed it away.

Mrs. Connors, straddling him, digging her huge mitt of a hand into his throat till he could not breathe, making him see pinpricks of sharp light explode in his head. But Zale closed his eyes, grabbed tight to the handle of his luggage, and pushed the image away.

Derek slit her throat, and the blood shot forward with so much force, it seemed as if she vomited it out of her mouth. But Derek's eyes were lucid, his mind clear, remorseless, even though the woman's blood coated his face.

I killed her so that we can live. And Zale tried to push it away.

The beaten men that lined Martin's office, all appearing so scared, so fearful, and the look in their eyes was questioning. Did they think I ordered such hatred, such abuse on them? Zale wondered at the time.

Push it away.

The children that lay in the streets. Billy who never called him, and an image of the boy's face floated in front of Zale's eyes, but the boy was dead, had been beaten to death, left in an alley, Zale had read that in last week's paper, and I should've never let him go that night, Zale thought.

Please, push it away. Leave my head!

The breaking glass, the way it tore through his skin, as if he had been sprayed with acid. The gun pressed to his head. Then the beating he took. How he saw death before him for the second time, and as he lay on the cold, wet pavement, looked up and saw the stars and wished for God to take him before this man could.

Zale felt himself trembling. Push it away!

The door opened to his apartment, and she left him. Cassaundra left him and she'd never return, and neither would Regina. He wanted to run to her, but he stopped himself. Why?

The names the men called him. The articles that were written about him. The threats that were made against him, and why? Why! He was just trying to help. Help his people. Help the children, but no one could see that. No one! And no one cared, because if they did, he wouldn't have been alone. He wouldn't have been alone, standing in that airport, his face covered with sweat, his body starting to tremble with the intensity to force him to drop his bag.

Something was happening, something descending upon him, and it was an ever-increasing pain, inflaming every receptor in his body, causing thick blood-gorged veins to bulge from his forehead and pulsate in his neck. The lids of his eyes clamped down tight. Zale bit down on his teeth, fighting against the increasing pain he was experiencing, fighting the pain that he knew he had yet to experience fully, all while his brain reviewed the mistakes he had made, every error that contributed to this moment right now. This very moment.

I didn't prescribe this medication for the fun of it. Zale's doctor's voice echoed in his head. And as he stood there, his body rattling, as if fighting large currents of electricity shooting through him, he thought to reach into his pocket. Thought that if he could take a pill, a few, all of them, that all of this would stop. But he knew it was far too late for that now.

It was everything, not just the stress, not just the high blood pressure, the nightmares, the lack of sleep, the low self-opinion, the contempt he felt for his mother, for his father, and all the fathers that had become his father. It wasn't just everything that was forced on him, but it was also what he did to himself, and the image of his daughter, Leah, appeared in his head, and with it came an exquisite pain so extreme, so engulfing, that Zale felt as if his brain was being squeezed in a vise and would soon explode.

Zale grunted, groaned, tried to scream out. *"Arrrgggghhhh!"* His face distorted in a grimace of horrendous agony as he yelled out. Then his body arched forward, his middle jutting out, as if he had been shot in the back. His arms flew out to his sides, his legs snapped under him, sending his body to the floor, where he twisted, spun, writhed in a tremulous mass of flesh and bone, his limbs, his body not his own, wriggling about uncontrollably, slapping the cold tile floor for what seemed an eternity.

And then it stopped.

It stopped as suddenly as it started, and Zale lay there on the shiny floor of the airport, under the bright lights, his bag not two feet from him, his body contorted unnaturally as if he had fallen there from a hundred stories up.

Zale lay there, and all was quiet. He heard nothing, not even his own breathing. Felt nothing, for the pain was gone, everything was gone, couldn't even feel his body on the cold floor, his arm twisted behind his back.

All he could do was see—the bright lights above him, which were starting to blur, and he thought, This is it. This is finally it. And it was ironic, almost funny, and Zale didn't know if his nerves carried the signal to his muscles so all could see, but in his mind he was smiling, it was so ironic.

Of all the shit he had been through, put himself through, and almost got killed twice violently at the hands of others, this was how he would die. The complete irony of this would've been so funny, so very funny, had it not been for his daughter. And again her face entered his mind, but this time there was no pain, just the innocent, angelic face of his child, another child that would go unfathered.

The image became darker and darker, Zale's consciousness slowly slipped, and everything fell away, and there was nothing. Nothing.

Then a moment later, like a flash, a ruckus of people screaming and yelling filled Zale's ears. His eyes spread wide under the bright lights again. Someone was forcing his eyes open, looking into them with a tiny flashlight, and there were countless faces over him—worried, concerned, pity-filled faces. Then Zale could feel his shirt being ripped open, could feel the defibrillator on his chest, could feel his body jerk up off the floor from the shock that riveted through his being.

And Zale thought peacefully, a white haze lowering upon him, the ruckus, the voices of all the people crowded around him, softening to a whisper, then an unrecognizable hum, then silence. And there was the feeling of him smiling again, not on his face, but in his head, as he thought, They're trying to save me. They are trying to save my life. God, I hope they can. And then all went black.

CHAPTER THIRTY-FIVE

Almost six months after Zale's stroke, he stood in a narrow corridor outside a large assembly hall where he was about to speak. It was an arrangement that Zale thought of, and after much hesitation, Martin agreed to it and set it up. This was an opportunity to set the record straight, to clean the slate, to dispel all the rumors in the past, and to verify what little truth was written about him and Father Found in the past. This was Zale's opportunity to tell all the men, all the people, why he acted the way he did, what was truly his motivation, and, most of all, what he intended for the future.

In that corridor with Zale stood Regina. She was looking him over, adjusting his necktie, straightening his collar, and tightening up his general appearance like a nervous mother would do for her child on his first day of school. The engagement ring that Zale gave to her sparkled on her finger as she brought her hand away from his tie.

"You're perfect," Regina said, a proud smile on her face.

"I'm scared."

"You'll do fine. You have nothing to worry about."

"I've given hundreds of these, and never once, even times when I thought my life was in danger, when I was looking into the eyes of men that I thought wanted to kill me, was I scared, but now . . . now I'm shaking," Zale said, swallowing hard.

"It's because now you care," Regina said, placing a hand gently at the back of his neck. "Not that you didn't care before. You did. You cared for the cause, you cared about getting the job done, but now, tonight, you care about how these people will see you. You care about how they will perceive your message, what kind of man they think you are, and should they believe you, whether they will follow your advice, because now you realize that people will be more likely to follow you when they've been asked and they themselves think it's a good idea, as opposed to when they are muscled."

"Is that what I realize?" Zale said, wrapping his arms around Regina's waist.

"Yup."

"And to think, it only took a stroke to bring that to my attention," Zale said sarcastically. "Maybe I ought to have a few more of those."

"Don't you even try it."

The door to the auditorium opened and Martin stuck his head out, and said, "C'mon, they're about to announce you any second now."

Zale acknowledged Martin with a nod of his head. "Well, this is it."

"You'll do fine. And I'll be right out there in the audience cheering you on."

"I'll be looking for you."

Regina kissed Zale on the cheek, then immediately rubbed the imprint of lipstick off with her thumb.

"I love you, Mr. Zaleford Rowen."

"I love you, too," Zale said, then grabbed his cane and started for the door, but stopped, turned around to Regina, and said, "I don't think I'll be needing this anymore," and passed the cane to her.

Zale walked through the door, and up on the stage the announcer was enthusiastically announcing his name.

"And now I would like to present to you founder and president of Father Found, Mr. Zaleford Rowen!"

There was silence. No one said a word and not a single pair of hands joined together to form a clap. With a slight limp Zale slowly walked up the stairs to the stage, amidst a barrage of photo flashes and clicking camera shutters, for the press was there in force, standing all around the sides of the room to get a shot of Father Found's man that almost lost his life. Zale greeted the announcer as they passed each other, then took the podium. When he looked out on the audience, it was much larger than he expected, filled with more than just the men he expected, the fathers he had mistreated, but women as well, mothers of children he had been trying to help. There were senior citizens there, and Zale recognized some influential people from the community, the city, and even the Reverend Jessie Jackson was in attendance. Zale told Martin that this speech would be the important one, told him to try to assemble a decent gathering, but this time he had out-done himself.

Zale looked around and saw Martin sitting in the first row. He looked down at him with a confident smile and nodded his head. Martin returned the smile and the nod. Zale then sought out Regina's face, which he found after only a moment, and she was smiling proudly. Now it was time to speak.

Zale adjusted the microphone, the noise coming through the speaker echoing through the silent room of onlookers. He went into the breast pocket of his suit and brought out his prepared speech, folded in half, placed it on the podium, and said without looking up at the crowd, "You know, I didn't expect that great of a reception, but if I were blind-folded, I would've assumed I was alone in this place. Clapping isn't against the law, you know."

"You don't deserve to be clapped for!" someone shouted from within the crowd, and heads turned, trying to spot the man. Zale lifted his head, and without any effort at all, found the man who had spoken, saw the angry look in his eyes.

"Yeah, I know that," Zale agreed, placing his hands on either side of the podium.

"I was, uh . . . I've had some bad moments, and I can understand why you're mad. Why don't you stand up."

People again turned their heads looking for the man, and Zale looked directly at him, right into his eyes, but the man didn't stand.

"C'mon now. You voiced your opinion and you were right about it, now acknowledge that. Stand up, sir," Zale said, and this time it was more like a demand than a request.

The man slowly stood, looking somewhat defensive.

"What is your name, sir?"

"Raymond Mathews," the man called from the center of the audi-ence.

"And have I had some dealings with you?"

"Yes, yes you have."

And Zale was able to tell just by the man's tone that his experiences with Zale had to have been negative.

"Well, I will start out by telling you that I am sorry. I'm sorry for whatever way I myself or my organization has treated you. If I have demeaned you in any way, made your life more difficult than it would've been without my involvement, I am sincerely sorry. I am."

The man looked up at Zale as if he had no idea what to say, and no idea how to accept the apology.

"You may sit now, sir," Zale said, and the man sat. "And I would like to say that same apology goes to every man, every person, that I have mistreated in the past. For everyone here, and everyone who reads about this in the papers, or sees this on the news, I'm sorry."

Zale lowered his head for a moment, then picked up the speech he had prepared and put it back into his pocket without reading it.

"You know," Zale said, looking back out at the people, "I thought I had . . . no, I did have reason for everything that I did in the past. I had a reason. Many people may know this, but I grew up in the foster-care system. I had not a mother nor a father, and it has affected me, and left me with some very bad memories that I live with till this day, so I know how it feels to grow up without parents, without a father. I know how it feels to think that no one wants me, loves me, or cares if I live or die. Trust me, there is nothing worse in the world than to feel that way when you're a child. So as a child, I told myself that when I grew older, I would do everything in my power to stop other children from feeling that way, to stop them from going through the hell I went through, and that's what I was doing. I was stopping the hell.

"Sure, I could've found a better way. There is always a better way. But I was accomplishing something. It was at the expense of the men I told myself that I was trying to help, but the job was getting done. The funny thing is, it was at my expense as well. I drove myself into the ground, trying to get the job done. I slept half as much as I should've, ate half as much, and worried ten times as much. My life was not my own, but was devoted to the children, and to the fathers who had left them, and somewhere down the line, those men became my enemy. I didn't care what reasons they had for not being with their children, I didn't care what situations they were going through. They needed to get their asses back home, and it got to a point where they needed to go home not because it was best for them, for their children, but because I said so, dammit!" Zale said, banging his fist against the podium.

"I felt I knew what was best for them, for everyone, and my advice would be followed or there would be hell to pay. The world was going to hell on an express elevator, and I was tired of people making up their own minds on how things needed to be done. A leader was needed, and I designated myself that leader. If you liked that, great, things would be a bit easier. But if you didn't, I didn't give a damn. My position wasn't for you to like. It was for you to adhere to, and if you had to suffer, then you just suffered, but you would be returning home, and the job would get done.

"Can I get a glass of water, please," he said to someone standing off-stage, and a moment later, a glass was brought to him. He took a swallow, then set it off to a side.

"I've heard the stories. I've heard them all. Every single excuse for not being a father to a child, and all of them were jokes. All of them, until I received a phone call."

Zale paused for a moment. The room was deathly silent, save for the muffled sound of a low cough. All eyes were on him, and he held them captive. He continued slowly.

"On that phone call, I learned that I have a six-year-old daughter."

Now gasps and remarks were heard within the audience, photo flashes exploded around him.

"That's right, I have a daughter, a daughter that for six years I didn't even know I had. It sounded like a joke to me, like one of the excuses I had been given in the past. I flew down, and I saw my child. I told the mother that we should get back together, marry, for the sake of the child, but she was against it. So here I was, Zaleford Rowen, president of this, founder of that, with an illegitimate child, who I was not being a father to, and would not be allowed to be a father to.

"I had a decision to make. Do you want to know what I decided?"

People from the audience responded, "Yes, yes."

Zale took another sip from his water. "I would abandon that child."

There was an outpouring from the audience, people talking, reporters jotting down notes, more flashes going off. Zale waited till the commotion died some, then continued.

"I had decided that I would have nothing to do with that child. Sure, I would pay the support I owed, but that would be it. One reason being, because I never intended to be a part-time father, the other because I felt that would've been a blemish on my record. I felt that I would have no right to tell fathers what they should do in regards to their children if I were in the same boat. But you know what I realized? I was wrong. I was more than wrong. It was the opposite! The only way I could truly lend some advice of any worth, was if I was in their situation. Your situation. So instead of keeping her a secret, lying to the people I am trying to help in the attempt to seem pure, without flaw, perfect, I am accepting my daughter, not just to appeal to you, but because she needs me, and I need her. I love her.

"I had a stroke recently, and everyone knows it. I thought I was going to die right there on that airport floor, and the person that was most in my mind was my child, Leah. The way I left her, without saying goodbye, the things she probably thought, that I didn't love her, didn't want her, the things I thought when I was a child—I couldn't die like that. I wouldn't die like that. She gave me the will to live, she gave me the will to rehabilitate myself, when I couldn't walk, could barely speak, and couldn't care for myself. I fought, fought like hell, knowing that I had to see that child again, tell her how I truly felt, damn public opinion, to hell with how people viewed me, she needed to know that I was her father, that I loved her, and I always will!

"When the mother of my daughter found out what happened, she was right there at my bedside. And when I was able to talk well enough for us to have a discussion, the first thing I told her was not that I *wanted* to be, but that I was *going* to be, a part of that child's life. Whatever it took. We compromised. And that allowed me to do what I could do, to be in that child's life, even if only some of the time, I would be there. And that can make all the difference in the world. We made arrangements so that my daughter, Leah, will stay with me over the summers, and one of the major holidays of the year." Zale said this looking as though for the first time he truly realized what he had, and what he had almost rejected. He paused, looking over the crowd, holding on firmly to either side of the podium.

"If I had only known what this was like—fatherhood. My life has changed already and I barely even know my daughter," Zale said, smiling more to himself than the people around him, as he envisioned the times he would have with Leah. "But that will change. I will get to know her, and she will get to know me," he said, still the smile on his face. But then it slowly fell from his lips when he came back to the situation he was discussing. He straightened some, his stance more professional.

"There has been a lot of controversy related to the organization, the biggest being the death of Frank Rames. As everyone knows, he was our investigator, and who killed him, no one really knows, and I'm not here to speculate. I'm just going to say that I knew Frank, and I thought he was a good man, but involved in bad situations."

"Didn't Mr. Rames beat and—" a reporter asked from the crowd.

"I have no more comments about Mr. Rames. None. But I will say this. I am not looking to replace him. Father Found will no longer have an investigator, and that is because we will no longer chase men down. It is too much trouble, and it causes too much trouble. We aren't law enforcement, and I realized that I was trying to accomplish too much. If men want to be helped for problems dealing with their family, be it legal, personal, or of any other nature, that's what we'll be here for. We will be more of a resource center for these men as opposed to a form of enforcement or government.

"In closing, I want to say, that today, more than half the black children born will be raised by a single parent, more times than not, that being the mother. Men, those mothers need you. Those children need you. I need you, we need you, we all need each other, because when we walk, it just doesn't affect the father, or the mother, or that child. It affects aaaallllllllll of us," Zale said, raising his voice, whirling his arms around in wide circles to represent the entire population.

"That action, that statement, made of walking out on our children does not stop the day we close the door behind us. We do not carry that hurt, that pain, with us in the suitcases we have at our sides. It is left behind in our children to fester, to grow, to be born in the form of more hate, resentment, and in the example that it is okay for them to leave their children." Zale paused and let what he said reach each person.

"I hurt you men. I apologize for that. But I do not apologize for trying to bring you back to your children. They can't wait any longer. Thank you."

There was silence. No one made any attempt to applaud him, just looked up at him, a suspicion in their eyes as if they were waiting for him to do or say something, exemplifying more of his old character.

Zale was disappointed. There was a lot he had hoped to accomplish with this speech, with his new ideas and approaches, but maybe it was a sign of too little, too late.

He had turned, stepped away from the podium, and started to walk away when he heard a noise. It was the sound of clapping. The sound of a single pair of hands clapping, echoing throughout the large room, bouncing off the walls, and floating over the turned heads of all those people, trying to find out where it was coming from.

Then Zale turned to find out, too, and he looked over the audience, and at the very back of the room, in the very last row, a man stood clapping. It was a man that Zale didn't recognize, hadn't seen before, but then again, he may have. His face may have been stapled inside one of the many files that Zale had dumped while reorganizing. Zale looked at this man, and the man clapped even louder, stuck his fingers in his mouth, and whistled like a fanatic, and after a moment, the clapping was joined by another pair of hands, and it was Martin, standing, smiling. Then another, and Zale looked over and saw that Regina was now standing, tears running down her cheeks, a proud smile on her face. And, gradually, a few people at a time, then more, then the entire auditorium was standing, clapping, as the flashes from the photographers' cameras exploded like fireworks in the sky, as reporters raised their hands, crowding closer to the stage to ask questions, as Zale looked upon all these people experiencing a feeling in his heart he never felt before. They were applauding him.

Contents

Acknowledgments

Many, many thanks to all of you who have been a source of inspiration and support to me throughout my many years experiencing and learning the joys and wonders of good food.

Special fond regards go to the following wonderful people who have been particularly encouraging and supportive during the course of writing this book: my husband, Terry, for his unending love, patience, and passion for good food; my parents, Dolores and Merle Moothart, who have long instilled in me the appreciation of hard work, good judgment, and love of laughter; Ten Speed Press founder, Phil Wood, and publisher, Lorena Jones, for their much appreciated belief in my work; and my terrific editor, Melissa Moore, who has been a great partner and true joy to work with. Thanks also go to the entire editorial and design team at Ten Speed Press for their outstanding work, including my ace copy editor, Jasmine Star; editorial director Aaron Wehner; my initial editor, Amanda Berne; proofreader Jean Blomquist; designers Patrick Barber and Toni Tajima; and creative director Nancy Austin.

And, of course, I must acknowledge my dear cat, "Junior," who has been a constant reminder that the best things in life are simple—plenty of good food, rest, and affection.

Introduction

It's no surprise that there's a resurgence of interest in eating good food. Eating the right type of foods for your own body can make a big positive difference in the way you feel throughout the day, including both during and after exercise. Not only that, the experience of how much more delicious foods truly are when made without unnecessary artificial additives has increased the demand for real food all the more.

This pocket guide is designed as a handy reference book to take along with you whenever and wherever you go grocery shopping. It provides at-a-glance information about what to look for when shopping for nutritious, great-tasting, high-quality foods—in short, good foods.

You'll find out what to look for when reading food labels, definitions of key words and terms commonly used on labels and signage, and how to buy in season. At home, it is an indispensable guide for what to actually do with the food: from how to cook a variety of products and at-a-glance information such as which foods are quickest to prepare to how to store foods for optimum nutrition and food safety.

For more detailed, unique descriptions about a wide variety of good foods from the common to the curious and information on what to do with them, insights on their origins, how they are grown or processed, sustainability considerations, their nutritional attributes and impact on health, and why foods react the way they do within the cooking process, be sure to pick up a copy of *New Good Food: Essential Ingredients for Cooking and Eating Well*, the definitive guide to exploring and enjoying good foods for today's shopper.

Words and Terms to Know

Enriched: Replaces five nutrients lost in grain processing: thiamin, riboflavin, niacin, folic acid, and iron.

Fortified: Food with nutrients added at levels higher than would be found in the original unprocessed food.

Fresh frozen: Food that's been quickly frozen while still fresh. Blanching before freezing is permitted.

Fresh: Food in a raw state—neither frozen nor subjected to any form of thermal processing or preservation. Exceptions include FDA-approved waxes on raw fruits and vegetables, pesticides applied before or after harvest, pasteurization of milk, produce treated with a mild chlorine or acid wash, and irradiation of raw foods not exceeding 1 kilogray (a unit of measure of radiation).

Genetically modified: The manipulation of an organism's genes by eliminating or rearranging specific genes or by introducing genetic elements from one or more other organisms, including across species boundaries.

Gluten-free: A food that neither contains nor is derived from wheat, barley, farro, grano, Kamut, rye, spelt, or triticale, and does not include 20 parts or more per million of gluten.

Imitation: A novel food that resembles and is used as a substitute for a traditional food. Foods must be labeled "imitation" if they contain less protein or a lesser amount of any essential vitamin or mineral than the traditional foods they replace.

Irradiation: A process in which food is exposed to gamma radiation from radioactive materials such as cobalt-60 or cesium-137, or through linear accelerator electron beams, to kill bacteria, insects, or parasites that may be present. However, even after irradiation, careful handling and proper storage and cooking of these foods is still necessary, despite all the marketing of irradiation as a food safety solution. Labeling of irradiated products is not required for all ingredients in a multi-ingredient product. The phrase "treated with irradiation" and the flowerlike irradiation logo have been required on single-ingredient foods for many years, although the term "pasteurization" might be allowed in some instances if other criteria for pasteurization are met. The FDA allows foods that have been irradiated at levels no higher than 1 kilogray (a unit of measurement for radiation) to be labeled as "fresh."

Natural: Minimally processed, with no added colorings or artificial ingredients.

Organic: A labeling term that designates the food or product is certified to have been produced according to certain production and handling standards based on enhancing the health of the soil and harmony of the ecosystem. In the United States, a list of substances allowed or prohibited in organic farming, production, and processing is maintained as part of the national organic standards. Processed products labeled "Made with Organic Ingredients" must contain at least 70% organic ingredients and list up to three of the organic ingredients on the principal labeling panel.

Quickly frozen: Food frozen using a system such as blast freezing, allowing it to quickly freeze to the center of the food with virtually no deterioration.

Trans fats: A type of fatty acid formed when liquid oils are processed into more solid fats, like partially hydrogenated fats, vegetable shortening, and hard margarine, creating a molecular structure that seldom occurs in natural fats. Trans fats have been linked to a long list of health problems, including obesity, infertility, increased risk of cancer and heart disease, and accelerated aging and degenerative changes in tissues. Trans fats are typically found in vegetable shortening, some margarines, and crackers, cookies, snack foods, and other foods made with or fried in partially hydrogenated oils.

Vegan: A diet that contains no meat, seafood, poultry, eggs, dairy products, or products derived from them, including honey and animal fats. Most vegans also avoid other animal products, such as wool and leather.

Vegetarian: A diet that contains no meat, seafood, or poultry. Lacto-vegetarian includes the use of dairy products, and lacto-ovo-vegetarian includes the use of dairy products and eggs.

Label Reading 101

- Choose foods that are minimally processed (and therefore retain most of their original nutrient value) and that don't have added artificial ingredients, preservatives, or hydrogenated fats.

- Buy organically grown whenever possible. It's a good choice for both our environment and our own overall well-being.
- Always opt for products that contain only real food items with recognizable names. The shorter and less complex the ingredients list, the better.
- Ingredients are listed in order of weight, from most weight to least. Trace ingredients are not required to be listed on the ingredients panels if they're considered incidental and have no function or technical effect in the finished product.

Smart Shopping Tips

- Save money by purchasing fruits and vegetables in season.
- Buy grains, flours, pastas, beans, nuts, and seeds in bulk to avoid packaging costs and waste.
- Buy in quantity if you can store larger amounts appropriately.
- Reuse paper sacks or plastic grocery bags each time you shop. Or, better yet, use a cloth tote bag to further help reduce unnecessary production of paper and plastic bags.
- Avoid products that are obviously overpackaged.
- Look for packages made from recycled materials, and try to buy items with packaging that's easy to recycle. Plastic packaging with resin codes #1 PET and #2 HDPE are generally easiest to recycle.

Bulk Buying Tips

- Only buy in bulk if the area looks clean and tidy.
- Bulk bins should look like they are easy to remove and clean.
- Gravity-feed bins that require no handling of scoops are best. When bulk systems rely on customers to use scoops, each bulk bin should have a designated scoop that cannot be used in other foods.
- To prevent young children from touching the food within, the bins should be high up or difficult to open.
- At home, for best flavor retention, food safety, and freshness, transfer bulk items from paper or plastic bags to glass jars or other containers that can be tightly sealed.

Nutrition Facts Labels

Most food and products sold within the United States, and many beverages, are required to provide nutritional information through a specific Nutrition Facts label. Exceptions include food served in restaurants or intended to be consumed on the premises where it was made and food manufactured by small retailers with low-volume sales of food products and few full-time equivalent employees. Also exempt are foods that provide no significant nutrition, such as spices.

Key information found on the Nutrition Facts panel includes serving size, servings per container (except for single-serving containers), and quantities of certain nutrients and substances found within the food: total calories, calories from fat, total fat, saturated fat, trans fat, cholesterol, sodium, total carbohydrates, dietary fiber, sugars, protein, vitamin A, vitamin C, calcium, and iron.

Other nutritional information, such as amounts of potassium, soluble and insoluble fiber, sugar alcohols, monounsaturated fat, polyunsaturated fat, or vitamins and minerals for which Reference Daily Intake levels have been established, may also be voluntarily listed; the percent of vitamin A present as beta-carotene may also appear. Listing of these voluntary nutrients is required, however, if they are added to the food or if the label makes a nutrition claim about them.

WHAT ARE DAILY VALUES?

Daily Values (DVs) were devised to help consumers see whether foods contribute just a little or a lot of particular nutrients. DVs are the recommended daily amounts established for adults and children age four and older of nineteen vitamins and minerals, as well as total fat, saturated fat, cholesterol, total carbohydrate, dietary fiber, sodium, potassium, and protein, based on a daily intake of 2,000 calories—the average amount of calories consumed by most adults and children aged four or older. DVs are calculated based on dietary advice generally consistent with the U.S. Dietary Goals, which are updated by the U.S. Department of Agriculture every five years.

The % Daily Value is based on 100% of the Daily Value for each nutrient.

As a frame of reference, 5% or less of the Daily Value of a nutrient is considered low, while 20% or more of the Daily Value of a nutrient is deemed high. In general, it is best to limit total fat, saturated fat, cholesterol, and sodium, staying below 100% of the DV for each of these per day. In contrast, try to get enough dietary fiber, vitamin A, vitamin C, and calcium, working toward getting 100% of the Daily Value for each of these each day.

Daily Values aren't provided for the following:

- Trans fat, since the recommendation is to keep consumption of trans fats as low as possible.
- Sugars, since the recommendation is to limit the intake of sugars, especially sugars added to food. Although confusing, the total amount listed for sugars on a food label includes both naturally occurring sugars and sugars added to the food.
- Protein, since scientific evidence has shown that inadequate protein consumption isn't a common public health concern in the United States for adults and children over four years old.

Food Labeling Claim Definitions

All food labeling claims are oriented to the reference amount as included in the serving size indicated on the label.

CALORIES

Calorie-free: Contains less than 5 calories.

Low-calorie: Contains 40 calories or less. Prepared/packaged meals and main dishes claiming "low calorie" must have no more than 120 calories or less per 100 grams.

Reduced calorie: Contains at least 25% fewer calories than a food representative of the same type.

Light or Lite: If 50% or more of the calories are from fat, then fat must be reduced by at least 50% per reference amount; if less than 50% of calories are from fat, then fat must be reduced at least 50% or calories need to be reduced at least 1/3 per reference amount.

FAT

Fat-free: Contains less than 0.5 gram of fat.

Low in fat: Contains 3 grams of fat or less per serving. Prepared/packaged meals and main dishes claiming "low in fat" must have 3 grams or less per 100 grams and not more than 30% of calories from fat.

Reduced fat: At least 25% fewer calories than a food representative of the same type.

Lite or Light: If 50% or more of the calories are from fat, then fat must be reduced by at least 50% per reference amount. If less than 50% of calories are from fat, then fat must be reduced at least 50% or calories need to be reduced at least ⅓ per reference amount.

SATURATED FAT

Free of saturated fat: Less than 0.5 gram saturated fat and less than 0.5 gram trans-fatty acids.

Low in saturated fat: 1 gram or less per reference amount and 15% or less calories from saturated fat. Prepared meals and main dishes claiming "low in saturated fat" must be 1 gram or less saturated fat per 100 grams and less than 10% of calories from saturated fat.

Reduced or Less saturated fat: At least 25% less saturated fat than a food representative of the same type.

CHOLESTEROL

Cholesterol-free: Less than 2 mg.

Low in cholesterol: 20 mg or less. Prepared/packaged meals and main dishes must be 20 mg or less per 100 grams.

Reduced or Less cholesterol: At least 25% less cholesterol than a food representative of the same type.

Special considerations: Cholesterol claims are only allowed when the food contains 2 grams or less of saturated fat per reference amount. The amount of total fat must be declared next to cholesterol claims when fat exceeds 13 grams per reference amount and labeled serving. Prepared/packaged meals and main dishes using cholesterol claims are only allowed to use "cholesterol-free" claims per labeled serving size or per 100 grams for "low" and "reduced/

Comparative Nutrient Content Label Claim Definitions

Claim	% of Daily Value (DV) per Reference Amount
"More" "Added" "Extra" "Plus"	Indicates the addition of 10% or more of the Daily Value per reference amount for a specific nutrient or fiber.
"Good Source of" "Contains" "Provides"	Indicates that a meal or main dish product contains a food that contains between 10 and 19% of the Daily Value per reference amount for a specific nutrient or type of dietary fiber. To use the word "contains" or "provides" for nutrients without DVs, the specific amount of the nutrient must be stated.
"High" "Rich in" "Excellent Source of"	Indicates that a meal or main dish product contains a food with 20% of the Daily Value per reference amount for a specific nutrient or type of dietary fiber.

less" claims. The amount of total fat must be declared next to cholesterol claims when fat exceeds 19.5 grams per labeled serving for main dishes or 26 grams for meal products.

SODIUM
Sodium- or Salt-Free: Less than 5 mg.
No salt added and Unsalted: Must list conditions of use and must declare "This is not a sodium free food" if food is "sodium free."
Low in sodium: 140 mg or less. Prepared/packaged meals and main dishes claiming "low in sodium" must be 140 mg or less per 100 grams.
Very low sodium: 35 mg or less per reference amount. Prepared/packaged

Where Used

May only be used in regard to vitamins, minerals, protein, dietary fiber, and potassium.

May be used to describe protein, vitamins, minerals, dietary fiber, or potassium per reference amount. May not be used for total carbohydrate since it has no established Daily Value.

May be used to describe protein, vitamins, minerals, dietary fiber, or potassium per reference amount. May not be used for total carbohydrate since it has no established Daily Value.

Adapted from "A Food Labeling Guide," U.S. Food and Drug Administration, Center for Food Safety and Applied Nutrition (October 2004).

meals and main dishes claiming "very low sodium" must be 35 mg or less per 100 grams.

Reduced or Less sodium: At least 25% less sodium per reference amount than a food representative of the same type which, itself, is not already considered "low sodium."

Lightly salted: 50% less sodium than normally added to reference food, and if not "low sodium," it must be so labeled on information panel.

Light (when used on sodium-reduced products): May be used if food is "low calorie" and "low fat" and sodium is reduced by at least 50%.

Light in sodium: If sodium is reduced by at least 50% per reference amount. On prepared or package meals, "low in sodium" claim must be used instead.

SUGAR

Sugar-free: Less than 0.5 gram of sugars.

Reduced or Less sugar: At least 25% less sugars per reference amount than a food representative of the same type.

No added sugars and Without added sugars: Allowed if no sugar or sugar-containing ingredients are added during processing.

Unsweetened and No added sweeteners: Must be based on fact as applies to the food on which the claim is made.

Fruits, Vegetables, and Juices

Science has corroborated what we instinctively know: eating plenty of fruits and vegetables enhances overall health and well-being. More specifically, it helps reduce the risk of many diseases and disorders that are largely avoidable, including heart disease, stroke, and cancer, as well as age-related eye diseases, such as macular degeneration and cataracts. Both fruits and vegetables are equally essential in the diet, with each making valuable and unique contributions to health that cannot be completely replaced by the other.

The high vitamin, mineral, and fiber content of fruits and vegetables has long been proclaimed to be the reason why they're so nourishing and beneficial. Now, however, compounds called phytonutrients, which were originally thought to provide merely color, texture, flavor, or aromatic qualities, have been recognized for their ability to provide extraordinary health benefits.

Words and Terms to Know

100% juice: Unmodified juice that contains the minimum soluble solids content by weight, as set by the government, for the particular juice in question. Beverages that claim to contain juice must declare the percentage of juice. Those with less than 100% juice must have the word "juice" qualified with a term such as "beverage," "drink," or "cocktail." Juices made from concentrate must be labeled with terms such as "from concentrate" or "reconstituted."

Biodynamic: An agricultural method in which the farm is managed as a self-contained, living organism, integrating soil health and nutrient management not only in conjunction with raising crops and livestock, but also within the context of the subtle rhythms and energies of nature. Somewhat easy to find but not as common as organic, certified biodynamic products will be labeled with the Demeter International logo. As biodynamic standards include those required by organic standards, many biodynamic products will be doubly certified and labeled as organic, too.

Ecologically grown: A catch-all term for what is generally known as biointensive integrated pest management (IPM), produced using methods focused on effectively managing pests and beneficial organisms in an ecological context, such as using other insects and natural predators to rid crops of pests. Although an IPM label will occasionally be used to highlight such products, more often a company or grower cooperative will have their own unique name and standards for their program, along with a specific label. Look for details about the particular requirements of any given label and, for extra assurance that label claims were met, the name or seal of an independent auditing company on the label itself.

Heirloom varieties: A variety that has been known through historical documentation or folk history for at least fifty years. Most are grown through open pollination, which means their seeds are set naturally, often helped by wind, rain, or insects. Unusual names, shapes, and sizes; flavors that range from familiar to complex and unique; and curious colors and mottled facades—all are typical hallmarks of heirloom fruits and vegetables. Typically they will be labeled as "heirloom" to help differentiate them from other types of produce.

Locally or regionally grown: Definitions vary depending on the label used by a farmer, grower cooperative, retailer, or marketing organization. It might indicate how many miles or hours away a farm is, or it could be considered in terms of state or regional production. For specific criteria used to justify the label, look for details on supporting materials or signage. In general, these labels emphasize the importance of supporting producers within a specific area, and the likelihood that fruits and vegetables will be much fresher, and therefore more flavorful and nutritious. Growing methods, including use of agricultural chemicals, will vary with the producer.

Organically grown: A system of production based on fostering and enhancing the health of the soil to produce crops in a way that fosters the health and harmony of the ecosystem, including the people and animals within it. In the United States, a list of substances allowed or prohibited in organic farming, production, and processing is maintained as part of the national organic standards. Certification audits of both domestic and international producers seeking the organic label are conducted by sanctioned or accredited companies qualified to perform rigorous reviews of records and thorough on-site inspections of farms. While use of the USDA organic seal is limited only to producers who are certified, it is not required on their labels.

Pasteurized juice: Normally found as frozen concentrated juice or in non-refrigerated shelf-stable containers, such as juice boxes, bottles, or cans. Pasteurized juice can also be found in the refrigerated sections of stores.

Pesticide-free: Typically, a self-affirmed producer claim simply stating that no synthetic chemical pesticides were used to grow the fruit or vegetable. This does not ensure the produce was organically grown.

Unpasteurized juice: Normally found in the refrigerated sections of stores or at cider mills or farm markets. Unpasteurized juice should have the following warning information on the label or on a nearby sign: "This product has not been pasteurized and therefore may contain harmful bacteria that can cause serious illness in children, the elderly, and persons with weakened immune systems." However, warning labels are not required for fresh-squeezed juices or cider sold by the glass, such as at farm markets, roadside stands, or juice bars, where the juice is made on location and intended to be consumed immediately.

Waxed: Fruit or vegetables coated with a variety of waxes to help prevent moisture loss and reduce wilting and shriveling. Shippers and supermarkets are required to label fresh fruits and vegetables that have been waxed with a sign that says "Coated with food-grade vegetable-, petroleum-, beeswax-, and/or shellac-based wax or resin, to maintain freshness."

Produce Shopping Tips

- Buy only vegetables that are richly colored and crisp or firm, depending on the variety, avoiding any that are limp, spotted, or yellowed.
- Look for unblemished fruit with a light, sweet aroma. Underripe bananas, peaches, plums, nectarines, or apricots can be encouraged to ripen by placing them in a loosely closed paper sack or a ripening bowl made expressly for that purpose.
- When purchasing sprouts, buy only from growers certified to follow stringent food safety standards for growing and handling sprouts, including using only sanitized, uncontaminated seed. The conditions that promote sprouting of the seeds, including temperature and humidity, can increase the potential for growth of pathogens, making raw sprouts a potentially risky choice for children, the elderly, and people with compromised immune systems. Thorough cooking of bean and grain sprouts can help reduce the risks; other sprouts may be too delicate to cook.
- Fresh-cut produce should always be sold refrigerated at 41°F or below.
- When transporting fresh produce, be sure to keep all perishable whole and cut fruits and vegetables cold to maintain both food safety and quality; use a cooler during warmer months and when travel time will be more than 2 hours.
- Upon arriving home, put perishable produce in the refrigerator right away. Discard any leftover cut produce if at room temperature for more than 2 hours.

At-Home Preparation and Storage Tips

- Wash your hands often in hot soapy water, including before and after handling fresh produce.
- Store fruits and vegetables separately, as the ethylene gas produced by some fruits can make certain vegetables taste bitter.
- Remove the outer leaves of leafy greens, such as spinach or lettuce.
- Thoroughly wash or rinse all produce before eating or cooking, including fruits or vegetables that will be peeled, even if they're organically grown. Firm produce should be scrubbed with a vegetable brush.
- Damaged or bruised portions of fruits and vegetables should be cut away and discarded.

- Although prewashed, bagged produce can be used without further washing, it's safest to rinse it thoroughly just prior to use.
- Prevent cross-contamination. Cutting boards, dishes, utensils, and countertops should be washed often with hot soapy water.
- Unless stated otherwise above, store perishable fresh vegetables in a plastic bag in the refrigerator or in the refrigerator crisper at a temperature 40°F or below. Crisper drawers are most effective at maintaining temperature and humidity when they are at least two-thirds full.
- Store fresh basil and cilantro like cut flowers, placing their stems in water at room temperature, changing the water daily, and use within a couple of days. Other herbs should be stored loosely within perforated or partially open plastic bags to provide air flow, inserting a paper towel to absorb excess moisture.
- Refrigerate mushrooms in paper bags, not plastic.
- Potatoes, sweet potatoes, onions, and winter squashes are best stored at cool temperatures (50°F to 60°F). At room temperature (about 70°F), storage time is cut in half.

How Much and How to Choose

At the very least, aim for seven to nine servings of fruits and vegetables per day (five for small children). Given that a serving is relatively small, these minimum amounts are easy to achieve.

One Serving of Fruit
- 1 medium-size piece of whole fruit
- ½ cup of freshly chopped, cooked, or canned fruit (canned in its own juices), including applesauce and fruit cooked in baked goods
- ¾ cup (6 fluid ounces) of 100% fruit juice with no added sugar
- ¼ cup dried fruit

One Serving of Vegetables
- 1 cup of raw leafy vegetables
- ½ cup of chopped raw, cooked, or canned vegetables
- ½ cup of cooked, canned, or frozen legumes (beans or peas)
- ¾ cup (6 fluid ounces) of 100% vegetable juice

Fruit Buying Guide

1 lb. Fruit	Storage
Apples	Fridge: 2 weeks
Apricots	Fridge: when ripe, 2–3 days
Avocado	Fridge: when ripe, 2–3 days
Bananas	Fridge: 2 days (peeled and sliced)*; room temperature: 4–5 days
Blueberries	Fridge: 1 week
Cantaloupe	Fridge: when ripe, 5 days
Cherries, sweet unpitted	Fridge: 2–3 days
Cherries, tart unpitted	Fridge: 2–3 days
Cranberries	Fridge: 1 month
Figs	Fridge: 1–2 days
Grapefruit	Fridge: 1–2 weeks
Grapes	Fridge: 5–7 days
Kiwi	Fridge: when ripe, 1 week
Lemons	Fridge: 1–2 weeks
Limes	Fridge: 5–10 days
Mango	Fridge: when ripe, 3–4 days
Oranges	Fridge: 1–2 weeks
Papaya	Fridge: when ripe, 3 days
Peaches	Fridge: when ripe, 2–3 days
Pears	Fridge: when ripe, 2–4 days
Pineapple	Fridge: 3–4 days
Plums, quartered	Fridge: when ripe, 3–5 days
Raspberries	Fridge: 1–2 days
Strawberries	Fridge: 2–3 days
Watermelon	Fridge: 3–5 days

*When bananas are refrigerated whole, the peel will likely turn black. While the fruit inside is still okay, for visual appeal it's best to peel before refrigerating. Even better—avoid refrigerating entirely by purchasing only what you can reasonably consume and eat them while they are ripe.

Raw Amounts	Processed Yield	Dried Amount**
3 medium	4 cups sliced	2¾ cups
8–12 medium	2½ cups sliced	3½ cups
2–3 medium	3 cups sliced	
3–4 medium	2½ cups sliced; 2 cups mashed	2½ cups whole dried; 5 cups banana chips
3 cups	3 cups whole	2¾ cups
½ medium	3 cups diced	
3¼ cups	3 cups whole, pitted	2½ cups
4 cups	3 cups, whole, pitted	2½ cups
4½ cups	4½ cups whole	3⅔ cups
9 medium	1½ cups	24 medium figs
1 large	2 cups sections	
3 cups	3 cups whole	
3–4 medium	1½ cups slices	
4 medium	⅔ cup juice	
6 medium	½ cup juice	
2 medium	2½ cups sliced	2¼ cups
3 medium	1 cup juice	
1 large	3 cups cubed	2¾ cups
3 medium	2½ cups sliced	2¾ cups
2 large	2½ cups cubes	25 halves
½ medium	2 cups chunks	22 rings
7 medium	2 cups	
3½ cups	3½ cups	
3 cups whole	2¾ cups sliced	
⅛ medium	3 cups diced	

**Note: Check the ingredients list for added sugars before purchasing dried fruit to avoid presweetened dried fruit. Avoid dried fruit preserved with sulfites.

Fresh Vegetable Buying and Cooking Guide

1 lb. Veggie	Storage	Raw Amounts	Processed Yield
Asparagus	Fridge: 2–3 days	22–28 spears	3 cups
Beets	Fridge: 2 weeks	5 medium	3¼ cups diced
Broccoli (flowers and stems)	Fridge: 3–4 days	3 medium stalks	5 cups chopped
Brussels sprouts	Fridge: 3–5 days	24 Brussels sprouts	4½ cups
Cabbage	Fridge: 1 week	½ medium head	6 cups shredded
Carrots	Fridge: 10–14 days	7 medium	3½ cups chopped; 4 cups grated
Cauliflower	Fridge: 4–7 days	1 medium head	4 cups flowerets
Celery	Fridge: 1 week	7–10 stalks	4 cups diced
Corn	Fridge: 1–2 days*	4–5 ears	2–3 cups kernels
Cucumber	Fridge: 1 week	1½ medium	4 cups sliced
Eggplant	Fridge: 3–5 days	1 medium	4–5 cups cubed
Green beans	Fridge: 4–5 days	75–80 beans	4 cups
Green onions	Fridge: 3–5 days	20–25 medium	4½ cups chopped
Greens, kale or collard	Fridge: 4–5 days	12 cups	6–12 cups
Lettuce, red leaf	Fridge: 3–5 days	1½ head	15 cups shredded

1 lb. Veggie	Storage	Raw Amounts	Processed Yield
Lettuce, romaine	Fridge: 5-7 days	⅔ medium head	9 cups shredded
Mushrooms, crimini or white	Fridge: 5–7 days**	22 medium	6 cups sliced
Onions	Cool area: 1–4 weeks	4 medium	2½ cups chopped
Peas, snowpeas/ sugar snap	Fridge: 3–4 days	130 pea pods	7 cups whole
Peppers, all varieties	Fridge: 3–5 days	3 medium	3 cups
Potatoes	Cool area: 1–4 weeks	2–3 medium	3 cups diced
Radishes	Fridge: 1–2 weeks	10 medium	4 cups sliced
Spinach	Fridge: 2–3 days	45 leaves	15 cups
Squash, summer (zucchini, yellow squash)	Fridge: 3–4 days	2 medium	4 cups sliced
Squash, winter (acorn)	Cool area: 1–4 weeks	1 squash	3 cups cubed
Sweet potatoes	Cool area: 2 weeks	3 medium	3 cups cubed
Tomatoes	Room temperature: 2–4 days***	3–4 medium	2½ cups chopped
Turnips	Fridge: 5–7 days	3–4 medium	3½ cups cubed

*Leave corn husks on and refrigerate unwrapped.

**Store in a paper bag.

***Ripen at room temperature; refrigeration not recommended.

Exploring Vegetables

Stroll through a farmers market or the produce aisle of a grocery store and you'll be surrounded by a wide array of beautiful and delicious vegetables, including many varieties beyond those commonly prepared. I hope the following lists of must-try vegetables will encourage you to give a few unfamiliar varieties a try. For a more extensive list of vegetable varieties and flavor profiles, check out *New Good Food: Essential Ingredients for Cooking and Eating Well*.

Leafy Greens at a Glance

Leafy Green	Description
Arugula (also called rocket)	Tender, dark green, jagged leaves; has a somewhat bitter, pungent flavor.
Belgian endive	Looks like a cigar made from pale yellow leaves; has a bitter flavor.
Bok choy	Soft, dark green leaves and long, thick, white stalks; has a sweet, milky flavor.
Baby bok choy	Picked when less mature, it is much more delicate than regular bok choy.
Broccoflower	A green cauliflower with a milder flavor than cauliflower and a hint of green vegetable flavors.
Broccoli raab	Looks more like a type of kale or turnip greens than broccoli; has a bitter flavor with pizzazz.
Broccoli Romanesco	A green-colored cauliflower with beautiful swirled geometric patterns of turrets or cones; has a lighter and nuttier flavor than broccoflower or white varieties of cauliflower.

Leafy Greens and Cruciferous Vegetables

The nutrients in greens are best absorbed when they're served or cooked with oil, particularly olive oil. Beyond the more familiar selection of lettuces, there are many other interesting greens available that are great to add to your repertoire. Arugula, bok choy, Chinese cabbage, collard greens, kale, and mustard greens have dual citizenship in the leafy greens and cruciferous vegetables categories. Although daikon, radishes, rutabagas, and turnips are generally classified as roots, they're cruciferous vegetables, too.

Uses

Use arugula raw in salads and sandwiches, as a substitute for basil in pesto, cooked briefly with other vegetables, or in soups.

Belgian endive's bitter flavor contrasts nicely with milder lettuces in a salad. Braise in vegetable or chicken broth for 5 to 10 minutes.

Best known for its use in stir-fries, bok choy remains crisp even when cooked to a tender stage. Cut the leaves from the stalks and cook the stalks first, stirring in the leaves during the last few minutes of preparation to prevent overcooking. Use raw in salads, cooked in soups, stir-fried, or simply steamed.

Baby bok choy's miniature size provides the opportunity to cook it whole. Use raw in salads, cooked in soups, stir-fried, or simply steamed.

Steam broccoflower whole for a special treat, cooking only until just tender to maintain its pleasant flavor.

Stems of broccoli raab are generally tender enough to eat. Braise or simmer, watching closely to avoid overcooking the leaves.

Steam broccoli Romanesco in chunks or whole until just tender, making sure to avoid overcooking.

Leafy Greens at a Glance, *cont'd*

Leafy Green	Description
Chinese cabbage (also called napa cabbage)	A tall, elongated cabbage with pale green, crinkled leaves and broad-ribbed stalks; has a mild, delicate flavor.
Collard greens	Leathery, gray-green leaves; tastes like a cross between cabbage and kale. For optimum flavor and tenderness, buy in fall or winter and choose a bunch with small to medium leaves.
Dandelion greens	Deeply notched leaves; has a slightly bitter, tangy flavor.
Endive (also called chicory)	Curly, frilly, coarse leaves with dark green edges and pale yellow stems; has a bitter flavor.
Escarole	Broad, coarse, flat leaves; has a slightly bitter flavor.
Kale	Dark bluish green, finely curled, plumelike leaves; has a subtle cabbagelike flavor.
Mâche (also called corn salad and lamb's lettuce)	Small, soft, tender, rounded leaves; has a mild flavor has a faint floral essence.
Mizuna	Long, delicate, dark green leaves with deeply serrated edges; has a pungent, exotic flavor.
Mustard greens	Curly edges, and a somewhat tender but rough texture; has a spicy, peppery, sometimes pungent flavor.
Radicchio	Looks like a small, ruby red cabbage with thick, white-veined leaves; has a slightly bitter flavor.
Savoy cabbage	A tender version of green cabbage with crinkled leaves; has a mild flavor.
Sorrel	Resembles bright green young spinach leaves; has a sour lemony flavor.

Uses

A favorite for stir-fries, its crisp texture also makes it a good choice in salads and soups.

Try collard greens steamed, braised with onions, or sautéed in a fragrant cooking oil and served topped with a finishing salt.

While young leaves can be used in salads, older, larger leaves are best cooked in stews.

Use endive raw in salads for a bitter accent or cook it briefly for a milder flavor.

Use escarole raw in salads or cook it briefly to mellow the bitter flavor.

Braising kale with a little liquid helps tenderize tougher leaves. It's especially good sautéed with olive oil or sesame oil prior to braising.

Use mâche raw in salads and sandwiches.

Mizuna adds a nice accent when mixed with other greens in a salad. It's also good briefly steamed or braised.

Steam, braise, or sauté mustard greens.

Radicchio provides an interesting flavor contrast in salads. It can also be cooked like other cabbages: steamed, braised, or stir-fried.

Use savoy cabbage raw or cooked, as you would regular cabbage.

Use sorrel sparingly in salads, cooked vegetable medleys, and soups.

Fresh Herbs

As a general rule, use three times as much fresh herb as dried. Except for the more hardy herbs, such as rosemary, thyme, and winter savory, fresh herbs should be added only during the last 10 to 15 minutes of cooking—just long enough for them to lose their volatile oils without losing flavor or becoming bitter. Sometimes it's best to add especially tender herbs, such as cilantro and chervil, at the end of the cooking time, when you turn off the heat. On the other hand, when making dips, herb butters, and cheese spreads, fresh herbs should be added several hours before serving to allow the flavor to fully develop.

Edible Flowers

As edible flowers are eaten in such minute amounts, they are nutritionally negligible in terms of standard vitamins and minerals. Nonetheless, they supply a range of beneficial phytonutrients. Eat only flowers known to be nontoxic. Never experiment; always make sure you can identify the flower as safe to eat. When purchasing edible flowers, only buy those grown specifically for consumption. Avoid flowers from florists and, in many cases, even wildflowers. They may be treated with pesticides, herbicides, or fungicides. Even better, grow your own organically.

Since edible flowers are very delicate, wash them by gently immersing them in a bowl of water to remove any dirt and insects, then dry them on a towel. Separate the petals and use them raw in salads, on sandwiches, or as a colorful garnish on pasta, cooked rice and other grains, or any dish you like! Go easy; only a few petals are needed per portion.

Mushrooms

While a few cultivated varieties, such as white button, crimini, portobello, and enoki, can be eaten raw, most wild varieties should be cooked to ensure food safety. Nutrient-wise, mushrooms have long been recognized for their mineral content, especially potassium, copper, and selenium, as well as being a good source of certain B vitamins. More recently, knowledge about their powerful phytonutrient potential has begun to emerge. Some varieties have powerful medicinal or healing functions.

Mushroom Buying, Storage, and Usage Tips

- Choose only whole and dry mushrooms with spongy, firm, plump caps.
- Unlike most other vegetables, mushrooms should be stored in the refrigerator in paper bags rather than plastic.
- Transfer mushrooms purchased in shrink-wrapped or vacuum-sealed containers into a paper bag, with the exception of delicate beech and enoki mushrooms, which can be refrigerated in their original containers, if provided.
- To clean fresh mushrooms, use a damp cloth or soft vegetable brush and only minimal water (to prevent loss of nutrients and a change in texture). Some mushrooms, such as chanterelles and morels, may require brief rinsing in running water to remove dirt embedded within crevices.
- To reconstitute dried mushrooms, cover with hot water and let soak for about 30 minutes. The flavorful soaking liquid is wonderful in soups or sauces; strain it through a paper coffee filter to remove any grit. Much of the flavor of dried mushrooms will be lost to the liquid, but when chopped or sliced, the reconstituted mushrooms provide a chewy texture to dishes.

Mushrooms at a Glance

Mushroom	Description
Beech (also called *hon shimeji*)	This cultivated variety grows in clusters. Each mushroom has a 1- to 2-inch stem and sports a small cap. Brown varieties may be referred to as brown clamshell mushrooms; white types are called alba or white clamshell mushrooms.
Bluefoot	The cultivated variety of blewits. Both varieties are dense-fleshed and whitish, with a blue tint throughout.
Chanterelle*	This beautiful trumpet-shaped, forest mushroom is usually golden in colored, but there are also dramatic black varieties
Crimini* (also called Italian brown mushrooms)	Closely related to the common button mushroom, criminis are similar appearance but brown in color.
Enoki	These creamy white mushrooms have long slender stems and very small round caps.
French horn (also called king trumpet)	This particularly large variety of oyster mushroom is long and conical in shape.
Hedgehog	The cap of this wild orange-gold mushroom has a depression in the middle. Hedgehog mushrooms are characterized by tiny spindles on the underside of the cap.
Maitake (also called hen-of-the-woods)*	Smoky brown in color, maitakes look somewhat like a head of curly lettuce—or feathers.

*Also available dried.

Texture and Flavor	Uses
Somewhat crunchy texture; mild, nutty, and somewhat herbaceous flavor	Individual mushrooms should be separated from the thick base before cooking. They can then be sautéed briefly, stir-fried, braised, or roasted in the oven.
Tender yet firm texture when cooked; deep, earthy flavor	Cook them like any other mushroom—sautéed, roasted, or braised—whether alone or in a dish.
Slightly chewy and dry but meaty; golden varieties have a light, delicate, almost fruity, apricot-like flavor and aroma; black varieties have an earthier flavor	Use quickly after purchase. Sauté or braise and add to pastas, sauces, or soups.
Meatier texture and richer flavor than common button mushrooms	Use them as you would white button mushrooms, raw or cooked.
Crisp, tender texture; mild flavor	Delicious raw in salads or mixed into a stir-fry or other cooked dish just before serving to preserve their exceptional texture.
Thick, meaty texture; flavor similar to porcini but nutty	Delicious sautéed, braised, or roasted.
Reminiscent of chanterelles in both dry texture and wonderful flavor	Can be substituted for chanterelles. Braise, roast, or sauté them, and cover the pan to simmer in their own juices.
Tender but firm when cooked; somewhat earthy and nutty flavor	Cut as you would a cauliflower. Best braised, stewed, or cooked in a sauce, but it can also be roasted.

Mushrooms at a Glance, *cont'd*

Mushroom	Description
Morel*	Morels look like elongated sponges or honey-combs with stems, and can be yellow, brown, or black.
Oyster	Fan-shaped mushrooms that grow on the trunks and limbs of trees. They look like oyster shells.
Pom-pom (also called bear's head or lion's mane)	These mushrooms look like small heads of cauliflower.
Porcini (also called king boletes, or cèpes in France)*	These woodland mushrooms are light brown in color, with very large, flat caps and chunky stems.
Portobello	Dark brown Italian mushrooms with caps ranging from 3 to 8 inches in diameter.
Shiitake*	These tan to dark brown mushrooms have tough, woody stems and broad, umbrella-shaped caps.
Straw	Typically sold dried, canned, or in jars, and only rarely fresh, straw mushrooms have small, tan stems and a conical-shaped cap.
White button	These white mushrooms are the variety commonly sold in supermarkets.
Wood ear*	These mushrooms grow on logs and are indeed shaped like an ear when fresh.

*Also available dried.

Texture and Flavor	Uses
Crisp, chewy texture; deep, earthy, nutty flavor	Use quickly after purchase. Morels are terrific with creamy sauces, pasta, rice dishes, fish, or poultry.
Smooth, velvety texture; delicate, oyster-like flavor	Use quickly after purchase. Lightly sauté and add to sauces, soups, and pasta.
Slightly furry texture; flavor somewhat like lobster or crab	Their delicate flavor is enhanced when baked whole or sliced and sautéed.
Meaty texture; rich nutty, assertive flavor	Grill the caps, or slice them and braise or sauté for adding to sauces or pasta and grain dishes.
Meaty texture; taste similar to criminis, but more flavorful	Exceptional when marinated and grilled or sliced and sautéed.
Meatlike texture; woodsy, almost smoky flavor	Shiitakes add delicious flavor to soups, stews, stir-fries, and pasta dishes. Eat the caps only, and use the tough, woody stems for stock.
Tender texture; delicate, slightly musty, earthy flavor	Use in stir-fries and soups.
Firm texture; silky when cooked; mild flavor	Sautéing, steaming, or baking will enhance their flavor.
Firm yet gelatinous texture; mild and almost flavorless	They add an interesting texture to stir-fries, pasta, and rice dishes.

Roots and Tubers

Potatoes and carrots are the most familiar root vegetables, but many other roots and tubers of all shapes, sizes, and colors deserve equal attention. In general, roasting will provide the most depth and concentration of flavor.

Roots and Tubers at a Glance

Root or Tuber	Description
Burdock	This long, slender root vegetable with an earthy flavor is a perfect complement to sweet-tasting vegetables, such as carrots, winter squash, and onions.
Celery root (also called celeriac)	This tough, knobby root, derived from a different variety of celery than the one raised for its stalks, has a subtle celery flavor.
Daikon	This long, tapered white radish is actually a member of the cabbage family.
Jerusalem artichoke (also called sunchoke)	This small, brown-skinned, sometimes knarled tuber has a unique, sweet, and nutty flavor, not unlike water chestnuts and jicama.
Jicama (HEE-cah-mah)	This light brown root ranges from the size of a potato to a winter squash and is white under its fibrous skin; its texture is crisp, and it's flavor is somewhat sweet and nutty.
Lotus root	This mild-flavored, ivory-fleshed underwater stem of a water lily looks like lengths of sausage. Inside, several tunnels run the length of the root and form an attractive pattern when the root is sliced crosswise.
Parsnips	Parsnips look like white, carrots with a rough surface but have a quite different flavor.

Uses

Scrub burdock but don't peel it, then slice it or shave it with a knife or vegetable peeler. As it can be somewhat tough, simmer 10 minutes before adding other vegetables.

Generally peeled before use, celery root can be cooked like carrots. It can also be grated and used raw as a component or basis for a salad with a creamy dressing.

Used raw, daikon has a hot, spicy flavor great in salads or grated and served as a delicious condiment. When cooked in soups, stews, or alone, daikon becomes surprisingly sweet.

Cook like potatoes—sauté, boil, bake, or simmer in soups. Crunchy when raw, they can also be added to salads or used as a substitute for water chestnuts.

Jicama is very versatile and can be sautéed, boiled, or used raw in salads or for dips. Because the skin is tough, it must be peeled before use. When raw, it has a texture similar to that of an apple and when cooked it is reminiscent of water chestnuts.

Soak lotus root in lemon juice and water after cutting to avoid discoloration. It can be baked, steamed, boiled, or added to soups and vegetable dishes both for flavor and for visual interest.

Usually cooked rather than eaten raw, parsnips' distinctive sweet and nutty flavor complements bean dishes, soups, hearty stews, and curries.

Roots and Tubers at a Glance, *cont'd*

Root or Tuber	Description
Rutabagas	Rutabagas resemble their close cousins, turnips, but have yellow-brown skin and yellow flesh.
Taro	Technically a corm, not a root, taro resembles a hairy potato and is most familiar to people living in Japan, Egypt, Syria, New Zealand, Hawaii, and other islands in the Pacific Ocean.

Squash

Squashes can be divided into two primary categories, summer and winter, denoting the time of year each is at its peak in flavor, the differences in thickness of the skin, the density of the flesh, and the relative water content.

Summer Squash at a Glance

Squash	Description
Chayote	Has a pale green rind, a flavor somewhat similar to cucumber, and a fibrous texture like that of winter squash
Cucumbers, Armenian	Long and coiled, with ridged skin and crisp, pale flesh
Pattypan	Yellow or a very pale green, round, about 2 to 4 inches in diameter, and with scalloped edges
Scallopini	A cross between pattypan and zucchini squash, not surprisingly, scallopinni is shaped like a pattypan but with a dark green color like a classic zucchini

Uses

When eaten raw, rutabagas have a cabbagelike flavor, but when they're cooked, a distinctive nutty, sweet flavor emerges, becoming sweeter the longer they're cooked.

Cook like a potato—bak, steam, boil, or use in soup. It generally can't be eaten raw because of bitter, irritating compounds in the sap. The tough skin should be removed; this is most easily accomplished after cooking.

Uses

Steam or bake or try it stuffed. If peeled, it can be eaten raw in salads or sautéed.

An extra crisp and refreshing cucumber variety; its ridges look striking when sliced.

Smaller pattypans are more tender and are delicious steamed whole. Larger pattypans can be sliced or quartered before steaming, sautéing, or baking.

Prepare them like pattypan squash.

Winter Squash at a Glance

Squash	Description
Acorn	Somewhat stringy, this is one of the mildest and least sweet of all the squash. Its outer skin is ridged, somewhat thick, and typically dark green.
Banana	This very large, pink to orange, banana-shaped squash can grow to immense sizes. Often sold precut into smaller pieces, it has a mildly sweet and fruity flavor.
Blue Hubbard	This blue-gray, thick-skinned squash can be quite large in size. It has a sweet flavor and dry texture.
Buttercup	This squash looks like a dark green globe with a light green crown. With its dry, smooth pulp and very sweet flavor, it's reminiscent of a dry-textured sweet potato.
Butternut	This light brown, bottle-shaped squash has a sweet, fruity flavor.
Delicata	This elongated, thin-skinned squash usually has yellow or beige skin with green stripes, moist flesh, and a very mild, sweet flavor.
Golden nugget	This small, round squash has a very thick, hard orange skin and a sweet, nutty flavor.
Kobocha	This dark green pumpkin-shaped squash is the sweetest of all the squashes and has a delicious smooth and dense pulp.
Red kuri	This medium to large, reddish or golden squash has sweet, golden flesh and a high ratio of seeds.
Spaghetti	This yellow-skinned, oblong squash has a mildly sweet flavor.

Uses

It serves as an excellent backdrop, ready to be accented with other seasonings or a flavorful stuffing. Cut it in half or in wedges and steam, or bake with a splash of oil, a favorite seasoning, and salt or tamari.

It can be steamed or baked.

It is sometimes stuffed with a bread or rice dressing and baked, similarly to a stuffed turkey.

Bake, braise, or steam and season with a splash of oil and tamari.

When cooked, its firm flesh turns creamy, which accounts for its frequent use in soup. It's also a welcome addition to stews and can be baked or steamed.

Best when baked.

Cut it in half before baking or steaming.

Can be baked, braised, or steamed.

Cut in half or into wedges or chunks, and bake or steam.

Can be used as a vegetable substitute for spaghetti: cut in half and bake or steam until tender, then use a fork to separate the fibers into "noodles."

Colors and Peak Seasons for Fruits and Vegetables

The best produce departments will have both the growing method and country of origin clearly displayed for each type of fruit and vegetable. Domestically grown produce purchased during its optimum growing season is always the best buy and more flavorful. Purchase imported produce only when necessary, and be aware that pesticide regulations vary by country.

To experience the diversity of fruits and vegetables and take advantage of the wide range of nutrients they contain, be sure to include selections from all of the color groups each day: green, yellow or orange, red, white or light brown, and blue or purple.

Green

Fruits	Spring	Summer	Fall	Winter
Apples, Granny Smith	x	x	x	x
Avocados	x	x	x	x
Grapes, green (Thompson or Perlette)	x	x	x	x
Honeydew			x	x
Kiwifruit	x	x	x	x
Limes	x	x	x	x
Pears, Anjou	x		x	x
Pears, Comice			x	x
Pears, Packham	x	x		
Vegetables	**Spring**	**Summer**	**Fall**	**Winter**
Artichokes	x		x	
Arugula	x	x	x	x
Asparagus	x			
Beans, green		x		
Beet greens		x	x	

Vegetables	Spring	Summer	Fall	Winter
Bok choy	x	x	x	x
Broccoflower			x	x
Broccoli	x		x	x
Broccoli raab	x		x	x
Broccoli Romanesco			x	x
Brussels sprouts				x
Cabbage, Chinese	x	x	x	x
Cabbage, green	x	x	x	x
Celery	x	x	x	x
Chayote squash	x		x	x
Chives	x	x	x	x
Collard greens	x		x	x
Cucumbers		x		
Dandelion greens	x			
Endive, curly	x			x
Herbs, all fresh	x	x	x	x
Kale			x	x
Leeks	x		x	x
Lettuce, all	x	x	x	x
Mâche	x	x	x	x
Mizuna	x	x	x	x
Mustard greens	x			x
Okra		x		
Onions, green	x	x	x	x
Parsley	x	x	x	x
Peas, fresh	x			
Peas, snowpeas/sugarsnap	x	x		
Peppers, green bell	x	x		

Green, *cont'd*

Vegetables	Spring	Summer	Fall	Winter
Sorrel		x	x	
Spinach	x	x	x	x
Sprouts, alfalfa and sunflower	x	x	x	x
Swiss chard, green		x	x	
Tomatillos	x	x	x	x
Turnip greens	x		x	x
Watercress	x	x	x	x
Zucchini	x	x		

Yellow or Orange

Fruits	Spring	Summer	Fall	Winter
Apricots, dried	x	x	x	x
Apricots, fresh	x	x		
Bananas, red	x	x	x	x
Cantaloupe		x	x	
Carambola (star fruit)		x	x	x
Figs, Calimyrna, dried	x	x	x	x
Figs, Calimyrna, fresh		x		
Grapefruit	x			x
Kumquats	x			x
Lemons	x	x		
Lemons, Meyer			x	x
Mangoes	x	x	x	x
Nectarines	x	x		
Oranges	x		x	x
Papayas	x	x	x	x

Fruits	Spring	Summer	Fall	Winter
Peaches	x	x		
Pears, Bartlett			x	x
Persimmons			x	x
Pineapple	x	x		
Quince			x	x
Tamarind	x	x		
Tangelos				x
Tangerines	x			x
Ugli fruit	x			x
Vegetables	Spring	Summer	Fall	Winter
Carrots	x		x	x
Corn		x	x	
Mushrooms, chanterelle	x	x	x	
Onions, yellow	x	x	x	
Peppers, yellow bell		x	x	
Potatoes, fingerling	x		x	x
Potatoes, Yellow Finn		x	x	
Potatoes, Yukon gold		x	x	
Rutabagas	x		x	x
Summer squash, yellow	x	x		
Sweet potatoes			x	x
Sweet potatoes, Japanese	x		x	x
Tomatoes, yellow		x	x	
Winter squash			x	x
Yams			x	x
Zucchini, golden	x	x		

Red

Fruits	Spring	Summer	Fall	Winter
Apples	x		x	x
Blood oranges	x		x	x
Cherries		x		
Cranberries			x	x
Grapefruit, pink or red	x			x
Grapes, red (Flame, Tokay)	x	x	x	x
Guava, red-fleshed	x			x
Pears, Red Bartlett			x	x
Plums, El Dorado, Laroda		x	x	
Pomegranates			x	x
Raspberries	x	x		
Strawberries	x	x		
Watermelon		x		

Vegetables	Spring	Summer	Fall	Winter
Beets		x	x	
Onions, red	x	x		
Peppers, red bell		x		
Potatoes, red			x	
Radicchio				x
Radishes	x			
Rhubarb	x	x		
Tomatoes		x	x	

White or Light Brown

Fruits	Spring	Summer	Fall	Winter
Bananas	x	x	x	x
Dates, dried	x	x	x	x
Dates, fresh			x	
Figs, brown Turkey	x			x
Lychees		x	x	
Nectarines, white	x	x		
Peaches, Babcock	x	x		
Pears, Bosc	x		x	x
Plaintains	x	x	x	x
Vegetables	**Spring**	**Summer**	**Fall**	**Winter**
Burdock	x	x	x	x
Cauliflower			x	x
Celery root	x		x	x
Corn, white		x	x	
Daikon			x	x
Endive, Belgian	x			x
Fennel bulb	x		x	x
Garlic	x	x	x	x
Ginger	x	x	x	
Jerusalem artichokes			x	x
Jicama	x		x	x
Kohlrabi		x		
Lotus root		x	x	x
Mushrooms, beech	x	x	x	x
Mushrooms, button	x	x	x	x
Mushrooms, crimini	x	x	x	x

White or Light Brown, *cont'd*

Vegetables	Spring	Summer	Fall	Winter
Mushrooms, enoki	x	x	x	x
Mushrooms, portobello	x	x	x	x
Mushrooms, shiitake	x	x	x	x
Onions	x	x	x	
Parsley root				x
Parsnips			x	x
Potatoes, new	x	x		
Potatoes, russet	x		x	x
Shallots	x			
Sprouts, mung bean	x	x	x	x
Taro root	x	x	x	x
Turnips	x		x	x

Blue or Purple

Fruits	Spring	Summer	Fall	Winter
Blackberries		x	x	
Black currants		x		
Blueberries		x	x	
Elderberries		x	x	
Figs, black Mission, dried	x	x	x	x
Figs, black Mission, fresh	x	x	x	
Grapes, purple (Ribier)	x	x	x	x
Passion fruit		x	x	x
Plums		x		
Prunes	x	x	x	x
Raisins	x	x	x	x

Vegetables	Spring	Summer	Fall	Winter
Cabbage, red or purple	x	x	x	x
Carrots, purple	x	x	x	x
Eggplant		x	x	
Mushrooms, black trumpet			x	x
Mushrooms, morel	x			
Potatoes, purple			x	
Salsify, black			x	x

Choosing the Most Nutritious Juices

Here are the most common forms in which juice is sold, listed in descending order of nutrient value:
1. Freshly extracted juice
2. Fresh frozen juice
3. Frozen juice concentrate
4. Reconstituted juice
5. Canned, bottled, or aseptic-packed juice
6. Chilled extracted juice
7. Fruit beverages, drinks, spritzers, and cocktails (contain less than 100% juice and don't count as a serving of fruit)

Grains

Rising interest in the wide variety of grains used in traditional cuisines, in part due to their excellent health benefits, has propelled a whole world of grains from humble fare to trendy and almost exalted status. Formerly obscure varieties, such as quinoa, now commonly appear in recipes in the food section of local newspapers, and they're also frequently featured on menus in restaurants and delis. The real clincher is their extraordinary flavors and pleasing textures. And because several kinds of grains can be cooked in less than half an hour, they can easily be incorporated into a busy lifestyle.

Words and Terms to Know

Bran: The outer covering of the grain, containing the highest concentration of fiber. It is also rich in B vitamins, trace minerals, and potent antioxidants, including lignans.

Endosperm: The largest part of the seed, consisting of starchy carbohydrates, protein, and small amounts of vitamins and minerals, stored as fuel to nourish the sprouted grain during its early growth.

Germ: The life force of the grain, the small part of the seed that sprouts to form a new plant.

Gluten: The water-soluble protein complex found in wheat and several other grains that affects the texture of baked goods and helps give bread the structure to rise. For some people, gluten is indigestible.

Gluten-free: Grains and products that don't include wheat, barley, farro, grano, Kamut, rye, spelt, or triticale. Products may be labeled "gluten-free" if they contain less than 20 parts per million gluten.

Whole grain: Grains or products that contain all of the components naturally present in the seed of a cereal grass plant, including the bran, endosperm, and germ.

Quick-Cooking Grains at a Glance

10 minutes or Less	10 to 15 Minutes	15 to 20 Minutes	20 to 30 Minutes
Couscous, whole wheat and white Rice, kalijira (white) Wheat, farina	Oats, rolled Quinoa Rice, white (basmati, jasmine, long-grain, short-grain)	Buckwheat Bulgur Kamut flakes Rice, Arborio, Bhutanese red, Carnaroli, kalijira brown, parboiled (converted), Vialone Nano Spelt flakes Teff Triticale flakes Wheat, cracked	Amaranth Corn grits, whole Farro, semi-pearled Grano Millet Oats, steel-cut Rice, Camargue red Rye flakes Wheat flakes

Tips for Buying and Storing Whole Grains

- Look for plump, unbroken grains with uniform size and color.
- When buying grains in bulk, make sure the bins are tightly covered and constructed to allow for easy rotation of the bulk goods.
- At home, store all grains in glass jars or rigid plastic containers with good seals.
- Whole grains are best stored at a cool room temperature (below 70°F), and will generally keep for up to 6 months. Refrigeration is ideal.
- Refined grains can be stored at cool room temperature for up to 1 year.

Gluten-Free Grains

- Amaranth
- Corn
- Oats*
- Rice
- Teff

- Buckwheat
- Millet
- Quinoa
- Sorghum
- Wild rice

*Although oats don't contain gluten, in North America they are often listed as being inappropriate for a gluten-free diet, but this is only out of concern that they may be contaminated by wheat during harvest and processing.

Grains That Contain Gluten

- Barley
- Grano
- Rye
- Triticale

- Farro
- Kamut
- Spelt
- Wheat

Grain Cooking Guidelines

Though the amount will vary depending on appetites and what else is being served, 1 cup of uncooked whole grain typically yields enough cooked grain to serve two to four people. All whole grains should be rinsed prior to cooking to remove any dirt and dust. For best results, place the grain in its cooking pot, add approximately twice the amount of cool water, then swish the grain to allow the debris to rise to the top. Carefully pour off most of the water to remove the grit, then repeat the process one or two more times to ensure that all the dirt is washed away. Depending on the type of grain and the cooking method, preparation time can be as little as 10 minutes or as long as several hours. Although refined grains generally cook more quickly than do their whole versions, there are many whole grains that require only minimal cooking time. Cooking on the stovetop in a saucepan using the absorption method is the most familiar way of preparing grains. However, other cooking methods bring out unique qualities, flavors, and textures.

Absorption method: Bring the liquid to a boil in the pot, then add the grain and a pinch of salt. Allow the liquid to return to a boil, then lower the heat, cover, and simmer gently until the grain is tender and the liquid is absorbed. To prevent a sticky texture, avoid stirring or removing the lid during cooking. Let the pot stand undisturbed for 5 to 10 minutes before fluffing with a fork to separate the grains.

Pressure cooker: In addition to reducing cooking time, pressure-cooking also helps retain the distinctiveness of each grain while creating a softer texture and sweeter taste. In general, use ½ cup less water per cup of dry grain than required for the absorption method unless a softer consistency is desired. Add the water, rinsed grain, salt, and any herbs or spices to the pressure cooker and bring to full pressure, then lower the heat to medium-low. Pressure-cooking typically shaves 5 to 10 minutes off the time required to cook grains using the absorption method. At the end of that time, remove the pressure cooker from the heat and let the pressure come down naturally. Allow the grain to rest undisturbed in the unopened pressure cooker for 5 to 10 minutes before fluffing and serving.

Slow cooker: A slow cooker makes it effortless to prepare hot cereal and long-cooking whole grains. All you have to do is add the ingredients—water, grains, salt, and any other seasonings you wish—then plug in the slow cooker, put on the lid, and cook at low heat for about 8 hours. You can also cook grains in a slow cooker overnight, refrigerate them the next morning, and then warm them up that evening for dinner. If you use the high setting, the grains will be ready in half the time—3½ to 4 hours. The amount of water needed depends on the final texture desired. To make pilafs in a slow cooker, only use hearty varieties of whole grains, and use 3½ to 4 cups of water per cup of grain. Parboiled or converted rice and rice varieties specifically used to make risotto are the only kinds of white rice suitable for cooking in a slow cooker. For hot breakfast cereals, the proportion of water to grain is typically 4 to 5 cups of water per cup of grain.

Rice cooker: An automatic rice cooker is specifically designed for steaming rice (and possibly other grains, depending on the model). It shuts off automatically when it senses the water has been absorbed, and it keeps the rice warm until ready to eat.

Baking: Cooking grains in a covered baking dish in the oven is a handy method when all the burners on your stove are in use. To prepare grain for baking, first sauté it in 1 tablespoon of oil or butter per cup of grain, making sure all of the grains are evenly coated with the oil, which enhances the flavor of the grain and helps prevent it from drying out. Then combine the grain, any desired seasonings, and water in a baking dish, using the same amount of water as you would for the stovetop absorption method. Cover tightly with a lid or foil and bake at 350°F until the water is absorbed and the grain is tender. Most grains require longer cooking time when baked than when cooked on the stovetop, usually about one-third longer. For example, white rice will be done in about 30 minutes and brown rice will take about 1 hour.

Rice Varieties and Cooking Instructions

Perhaps the most common staple food worldwide, rice has been cultivated for over eight thousand years. Over the millennia, it's proliferated into a delicious but bewildering array of thousands of varieties. Though only a small percentage are commercially available, interest in ethnic cooking and unusual varieties has brought more types to market recently.

LONG-GRAIN RICE

While the absorption method is the most common way to cook long-grain rice, its firmness allows it to be pressure-cooked if a moist, slightly sticky texture is desired. Thai black sticky rice is an exception. It is best cooked in a special steaming apparatus. Slow-cooking is only suitable for parboiled or converted white rice.

Long-Grain Brown Rice

Absorption method: Use 2¼ cups of water per cup of rice. Combine the water and rice, bring to a boil, then lower the heat, cover, and simmer for 45 minutes. Don't peek until the rice is completely done. Remove from the heat and let stand, covered, for 10 minutes before fluffing.

Pressure cooker: Use 2 cups of water per cup of rice and cook at pressure for 40 to 50 minutes.

Other cooking methods: For variety, cook equal parts of brown rice with barley or with presoaked and drained Kamut, farro, wheat, or spelt, using 2½ cups of water per cup of mixed grains, and proceeding as for the absorption method.

Parboiled or Converted Rice

Absorption method: Use 2 cups of water per cup of rice. Combine the water and rice, bring to a boil, then lower the heat, cover, and simmer for 20 to 25 minutes. Remove from the heat and let stand, covered, for 10 minutes before fluffing.

Other cooking methods: To slow-cook, use 2 cups of water per cup of rice and cook on the high setting for 1½ hours or on low for 2½ hours.

Long-grain white rice (also called polished white rice)

Absorption method: Use 1½ to 1¾ cups of water per cup of rice. Bring the water to a boil, stir in the rice, then lower the heat, cover, and simmer for 15 minutes.

Brown Basmati Rice

Absorption method: Use 2 cups of water per cup of rice. Presoak brown basmati rice in its cooking water for 20 to 30 minutes after rinsing. Bring the rice and its soaking water to a boil, then lower the heat, cover, and simmer for 45 to 50 minutes. Remove from the heat and let stand, covered, for 10 minutes before fluffing. The method and cooking time are the same in a pressure cooker.

White Basmati Rice

Absorption method: Use 1½ cups of water per cup of rice. Presoak and cook white basmati as described for brown basmati, but only simmer for 15 minutes. Remove from the heat and let stand, covered, for 10 minutes before fluffing.

Jasmine Rice

Absorption method: Use 1¾ cups of water per cup of rice. Presoak jasmine rice in its cooking water for 20 to 30 minutes after rinsing. Bring the soaked rice and its water to a boil, then lower the heat, cover, and simmer for 15 minutes. Remove from the heat and let stand, covered, for 15 minutes before fluffing.

Brown Kalijira Rice

Absorption method: Use 2 cups of water per cup of rice. If time permits, presoak the rice in its cooking water for 20 to 30 minutes after rinsing, then bring to a boil. Lower the heat, cover, and simmer for 20 to 25 minutes. Remove from the heat and let stand, covered, for 10 minutes before fluffing.

White Kalijira Rice

Absorption method: Use 1½ cups of water per cup of rice. If time permits, presoak and cook white kalijira rice as described for brown kalijira, but only simmer for 10 minutes. Remove from the heat and let stand, covered, for 10 minutes before fluffing.

Brown Texmati Rice

Absorption method: Use 2 cups of water per cup of rice. Combine the water and rice, bring to a boil, then lower the heat, cover, and simmer or pressure-cook for 50 minutes. Remove from the heat and let stand, covered, for 5 to 10 minutes before fluffing.

White Texmati Rice
Absorption method: Use 1¾ cups of water per cup of rice. Combine the water and rice, bring to a boil, then lower the heat, cover, and simmer for 15 minutes. Remove from the heat and let stand, covered, for 5 to 10 minutes before fluffing.

Thai Black Sticky Rice
Other Cooking Methods: To ensure grains remain separate when cooked and to avoid creating a sticky mass, the best way to prepare Thai black sticky rice is to soak the rice in water for 6 to 12 hours, then drain and steam in a woven bamboo steamer or Thai sticky rice steaming basket over a pot of boiling water until tender, about 45 minutes.

Wild Pecan Rice
Absorption method: Use 1¾ cups of water per cup of rice. Combine the water and rice, bring to a boil, then lower the heat, cover, and simmer for 15 minutes. Remove from the heat and let stand, covered, for 5 to 10 minutes before fluffing.

MEDIUM-GRAIN RICE
The absorption method is the most common way to cook medium-grain rice, but a pressure cooker may also be used. For pressure-cooking, use the same proportion of water to rice, and experiment with the cooking time to determine what amount of time yields the texture you prefer.

Bhutanese Red Rice
Absorption method: Use 1¾ cups of water per cup of rice. Combine the water and rice, bring to a boil, then lower the heat, cover, and simmer for 20 minutes. Remove from the heat and let stand, covered, for 10 minutes before fluffing.

Black Forbidden Rice

Absorption method: Use 1¾ cups of water per cup of rice. Combine the water and rice, bring to a boil, then lower the heat, cover, and simmer for 30 minutes for a chewy texture or for 40 to 45 minutes for a soft texture.

Calrose Rice

Absorption method: Use 1½ cups of water per cup of rice. Combine the water and rice, bring to a boil, then lower the heat, cover, and simmer for 12 to 15 minutes. Remove from the heat and let stand, covered, for 5 to 10 minutes before fluffing.

Camargue Red Rice

Absorption method: Use 2½ cups of water per cup of rice. Combine the water and rice, bring to a boil, then lower the heat, cover, and simmer for 40 minutes. Remove from the heat and let stand, uncovered, for 10 minutes before fluffing.

Italian Risotto Rice

Arborio rice has long, slim, pearly-white grains. Since it contains less amylose starch, it absorbs less liquid than other varieties and cooks up more starchy and sticky.

Baldo rice has long, slim, golden colored grains that have less amylose starch than Carnaroli or Vialone Nano so it cooks up softer, similar to Arborio rice.

Carnaroli rice has the highest amylose content of any risotto rice, making it the top-notch rice to use to make risotto. It absorbs the most liquid while still creating distinct grains and a creamy texture.

Vialone Nano has grains that are rounder and shorter than other risotto rice varieties. Cooking up firmer than Arborio rice, Vialone Nano provides a good amount of starch, creating a creamy but wavy consistency—the mark of a well-made risotto.

Absorption method: Use 4 cups of water per cup of rice. Bring the water to a boil, stir in the rice, then lower the heat and cook uncovered until the rice is firm but tender, about 15 minutes. Drain the rice and spread it on a clean kitchen towel to cool before mixing in salad ingredients and dressing.

Other cooking methods: To make risotto, use 3½ cups of hot stock per cup of rice (do not rinse prior to cooking). Saute ½ cup chopped onion in oil, followed by 1 cup fresh mushrooms or ½ cup dried mushrooms that have been presoaked and softened. Add rice, stirring to coat each kernel with the oil for approximately 3 to 4 minutes. Sprinkle the rice with ½ teaspoon salt (less if using salted stock). Add ½ cup of hot stock, stirring constantly until the liquid is completely absorbed. Repeat until the remaining stock, adding ½ cup at a time. Gradual additions of stock allow the rice to release starch, producing a creamy texture while keeping the kernel al dente. Cooking usually takes about 18 to 20 minutes.

Spanish Paella Rice

Ebro Delta rice, grown in a protected bird sanctuary in northeastern Spain, has larger, more strongly flavored grains than other varieties.

Valencia rice, including the *Ballia, Senia,* and *Bomba* varieties, is grown in the marshy wetlands of the Albufera nature reserve in Valencia, the birthplace of paella and Spain's major rice producing region. Balilla rice absorbs twice its volume in liquid. Bomba absorbs as much as 6 parts liquid to 1 part rice—two to three times more than other varieties.

Calasparra rice, including the Balilla, Sollana, and Bomba varieties, is grown in mountains of Murcia in southeastern Spain and known for its exceptional quality due to cooler weather at high altitude and irrigation with cold mountain water. In general, rice from the Calasparra region has a harder grain and less moisture, which increases the rice's ability to absorb liquid. Calasparra bomba is the rice of choice for paella and tops in quality and flavor.

Absorption method: Use 1¾ cups of water per cup of rice. Combine the water and rice, bring to a boil, then lower the heat, cover, and simmer for 15 to 18 minutes. Remove from the heat and let stand, covered, for 10 to 15 minutes before fluffing.

SHORT-GRAIN RICE

Short-grain rice is often cooked using the absorption method, but there are several techniques and special types of cooking apparatus that can give better results for certain types of short-grain rice. Short-grain brown rice and sweet brown rice can also be pressure-cooked.

Short-Grain Brown Rice

Absorption method: Use 2¼ cups of water per cup of rice. Combine the water and rice, bring to a boil, then lower the heat, cover, and simmer for 50 minutes. Remove from the heat and let stand, covered, for 10 minutes before fluffing the rice.

Pressure cooker: Use 2 cups of water per cup of rice and cook at pressure for 40 to 50 minutes. Experiment with the amount of time to find the texture you most prefer.

Short-Grain White Rice

Absorption method: Use 1¼ cups of water per cup of rice. Combine the water and rice, bring to a boil, then lower the heat, cover, and simmer for 15 minutes. Remove from the heat and let stand, covered, for 10 minutes before fluffing the rice.

Sushi Rice

Absorption method: Before cooking, rinse and drain the rice several times until the rinse water is almost clear, then allow it to drain for 30 to 60 minutes. Combine equal amounts of water and sushi rice, bring to a boil over medium heat, cover, and cook for 1 minute. Then turn down the heat to low and cook for 8 to 10 minutes. Turn down the heat once again, to very low, and cook 10 minutes longer, being sure to keep the cover on at all times during cooking. Remove from the heat and let stand, covered, for 10 minutes before fluffing the rice.

Sticky Rice, or Sweet Rice

Absorption method: Use 1½ cups of water per cup of rice. Combine the water and rice, bring to a boil, then lower the heat, cover, and simmer for 30 minutes for white sticky rice, or 50 minutes for sweet brown rice.

Pressure cooker: Use 1 cup of water per cup of rice and cook at pressure for 45 minutes. A combination of ¼ cup of sweet brown rice and ¾ cup of short-grain brown rice pressure-cooked with 1½ cups of water for 50 minutes makes a delicious cool-weather rice blend.

Other cooking methods: The best way to prepare sticky rice is to first soak it in water for 6 to 12 hours, then drain and steam in a woven bamboo steamer or Thai sticky rice steaming basket over a pot of boiling water until tender, about 30 minutes for white sticky rice, and about 40 to 45 minutes for sweet brown rice.

Wheat Varieties and Cooking Instructions

Wheat is the most commonly cultivated grain worldwide. What we know as wheat today has been hybridized through the years for higher yields, easier harvesting, and specific baking and cooking properties. More ancient forms are still produced, including farro, Kamut, and spelt (described separately).

Whole Wheat Berries
Wheat berries cook more quickly when presoaked for 6 to 12 hours. To retain nutrients, soak the grain in its cooking water, using 3 cups of water per cup of grain.

Absorption method: Bring the wheat berries and their soaking water to a boil. Lower the heat, cover, and simmer until tender, about 1 hour if presoaked or 1½ to 2 hours if not.

Pressure cooker: Use 3 cups of water per cup of wheat berries and cook at pressure for 40 minutes if presoaked or 50 minutes if not.

Slow cooker: Presoaking isn't necessary. Use 4 cups of water per cup of wheat berries and cook on the high setting for 3½ to 4 hours or on low for 8 hours.

Bulgur Wheat
Absorption method: Use 2 cups of water per cup of bulgur. Bring the water to a boil, stir in the bulgur, then lower the heat, cover, and simmer for 20 to 25 minutes. For best results, remove from the heat and let stand, covered, for 10 minutes before serving or using in a recipe.

Other cooking methods: For the soaking method, use 2½ cups of boiling water per cup of bulgur. Pour the boiling water over the bulgur, cover, and let stand for 1 hour. Drain the bulgur in a colander lined with cheesecloth, then squeeze out the excess moisture.

Cracked Wheat

Absorption method: Use 2 cups of water per cup of cracked wheat. Bring the water to a boil, then stir in the cracked wheat, lower the heat, cover, and simmer for 20 minutes. For best texture, remove from the heat and let stand, covered, for 5 minutes before serving or using in a recipe.

Wheat Flakes

Absorption method: Use 3 cups of water per cup of wheat flakes. Bring the water to a boil, stir in the wheat flakes, then lower the heat, cover, and simmer for 15 to 20 minutes.

Couscous, Fregola

Absorption method: Use 3 cups of boiling water per cup of fregola, Stir the fregola into the boiling water, add salt to taste, reduce heat to gentle simmer and cook, uncovered, until fregola is tender, about 10 to 15 minutes. Drain and add butter, oil, or seasonings, as desired.

Other cooking methods: For cooking in soups or stews as a textural addition, use ¾ cup of fregula for about 8 cups of soup, adding it about 15 minutes before the soup is done. Cook at a gentle simmer, partly covered, until the fregola is tender.

Couscous, Israeli

Absorption method: Add Israeli couscous to boiling salted water and cook for 7 to 8 minutes, then drain and rinse briefly under cold water to stop the cooking and remove some of the sticky starch.

Couscous, Lebanese

Absorption method: First soak 2 cups of Lebanese couscous by pouring boiling water over it. Cover and let stand for 45 minutes. Drain the couscous, then cook it in 4 cups of broth for about 30 minutes, until the liquid is absorbed and the couscous is tender.

Other cooking methods: For cooking in soups or stews as a textural addition, use ¼ cup of Lebanese couscous for about 12 cups of soup, adding it about 30 minutes before the soup is done. Then cover the pot and cook until the couscous until tender.

Couscous, Moroccan

Absorption method: Use 1½ cups of boiling water per cup of couscous. Stir the couscous into the boiling water, then cover and remove from the heat. Let stand undisturbed until all the liquid is absorbed, about 5 to 10 minutes. Stir to fluff before serving or using in a recipe.

Other cooking methods: In northern Africa, couscous is traditionally steamed over a hearty meat and vegetable stew in a special two-tiered steaming pot called a *couscousiere*. The couscous is first moistened, then after steaming a bit, it's removed to break up any clumps and then replaced over the stew to steam again. The process takes about 1 hour from start to finish. If you don't have a *couscousiere*, you can improvise with a fine-mesh stainless steel colander that fits snugly into a stockpot, sealing any gaps between the rim of the stockpot and the colander with a damp dishtowel or cheesecloth.

Farina

Absorption method: Use 3 cups of water or milk per cup of farina. Bring the liquid to a boil, then slowly pour in the farina, stirring all the while to prevent clumping. Continue stirring until it returns to a boil, then lower the heat, cover, and simmer for about 10 minutes, stirring occasionally.

Exploring Other Grain Varieties

In the sections below, if instructions aren't given for a particular cooking method, such as pressure-cooking or slow-cooking, that method is either not viable or not recommended for that grain. When presoaking whole grains for quicker cooking, place in the refrigerator if the ambient temperature is warm (above 75° F).

AMARANTH

This ancient Aztec crop is actually harvested from a broad-leaved plant, not a cereal grass. It's extremely nutritious, and its well-rounded amino acid profile makes it almost a complete protein.

Absorption method: To prepare as a side dish, use 2 cups of liquid per cup of amaranth and cook for 15 to 20 minutes. When making a hot breakfast cereal, use 3 to 4 cups of liquid per cup of amaranth and simmer for 20 to 30 minutes. In either case, bring the amaranth and water to a boil, add a pinch of salt per cup of amaranth, then lower the heat, cover, and simmer.

Other cooking methods: To prepare popped amaranth, heat a wok or deep, heavy skillet until very hot. Start with just 1 tablespoon of amaranth and move the seeds constantly with tongs or a heat-resistant spatula until each grain has popped and expanded. Each tablespoon of whole amaranth makes ¼ cup of popped amaranth.

BARLEY

One of the first grains cultivated for food, barley is a great source of beta-glucans, a highly beneficial form of soluble fiber.

Whole Barley

Whole barley cooks more quickly if presoaked for 2 to 6 hours. To retain nutrients, soak the barley in its cooking water, using 3 cups of water per cup of barley.

Absorption method: Use 3 cups of water per cup of barley. Bring the barley and its soaking water to a boil, then lower the heat, cover, and simmer until tender, about 1 hour if presoaked or about 1½ to 2 hours if not.

Pressure cooker: Use 3 cups of water per cup of barley and cook at pressure for 35 minutes if presoaked or 45 minutes if not.

Slow cooker: Presoaking isn't necessary. Use 4 cups of water per cup of barley and cook on the high setting for 3½ to 4 hours or on low for 7 to 8 hours.

Pearled Barley

Absorption method: Use 3 cups of water per cup of pearled barley. Combine the water and barley, bring to a boil, then lower the heat, cover, and simmer until tender. Coarse pearled will take approximately 60 minutes, medium pearled about 50 minutes, and fine pearled about 35 to 40 minutes.

Pressure cooker: For coarse or medium pearled barley, use 2 to 2½ cups of water per cup of barley and cook at pressure for 35 minutes. Don't pressure-cook fine pearled barley, as it's more likely to plug up the pressure vent.

Hull-less Barley

Whole hull-less barley cooks more quickly if presoaked for 2 to 6 hours. To retain nutrients, soak the barley in its cooking water, using 3 cups of water per cup of barley.

Absorption method: Use 3 cups of water per cup of barley. Bring the barley and its soaking water to a boil, then lower the heat, cover, and simmer until tender, about 50 minutes if presoaked or 90 minutes if not.

Pressure cooker: Use 3 cups of water per cup of barley and cook at pressure for 35 minutes if presoaked or 45 minutes if not.

Slow cooker: Presoaking isn't necessary. Use 4 cups of water per cup of barley and cook on the high setting for 3½ to 4 hours or on low for 7 to 8 hours.

Barley Flakes

Absorption method: Use 3 cups of water per cup of barley flakes. Bring the water to a boil, stir in the barley flakes, then lower the heat, cover, and simmer until the water is absorbed, about 25 minutes.

BUCKWHEAT

Despite its name, buckwheat isn't related to wheat, and in fact, it isn't even a true grain, hailing instead from a plant related to rhubarb. Its well-rounded amino acid profile makes it almost a complete protein.

Buckwheat Groats

Absorption method: Use 2 cups of water and a pinch of salt per cup of buckwheat groats. Bring the water to a boil, stir in the buckwheat and salt, then lower the heat, cover, and simmer until tender, about 15 to 20 minutes. For a nuttier flavor, toast the buckwheat groats before cooking, either dry-roasting them or sautéing in butter or oil, stirring constantly for 2 to 3 minutes.

Kasha

Absorption method: Coat 1 cup of kasha with one beaten egg, allowing any excess egg to drain off as you transfer the mixture to a saucepan. Over medium heat, stir the kasha constantly until toasted. The egg coating seals each individual buckwheat groat, preventing the kasha from becoming mushy.

Once the kasha is toasted, add 2 cups of boiling water and a pinch of salt. Lower the heat, cover, and simmer until the water is absorbed, about 15 to 20 minutes.

CORN

Although it's often enjoyed as a fresh vegetable, corn is indeed the product of a cereal grass; and although a variety of forms are grown, all are the same species. It's one of the few grains native to the Western hemisphere.

Hominy (Posole)

Hominy, often labeled as posole in reference to its common use, is a form of dried corn that has been slaked with lime, had its hulls removed, and then been dried again. Dried hominy should be soaked for 6 to 8 hours or overnight before cooking.

Absorption method: Put the dried hominy in a pot and add water to cover. Bring to a boil, then lower the heat, cover, and simmer until tender, about 3 to 4 hours.

Pressure cooker: Put the dried hominy in the pressure cooker and add water to cover. Cook at pressure for 1 hour and then simmer for 1 hour longer.

Slow cooker: Use 6 cups of water per cup of hominy. Cook on the high setting for 1 hour and then on the low setting for 9 to 12 hours.

Hominy and Corn Grits

Absorption method: Use 4 cups of salted water per cup of grits. Bring the water to a boil, then gradually pour in the grits, whisking all the while. Lower the heat, cover, and simmer for 25 to 30 minutes. Quick-cooking grits are very finely ground and will cook in 5 minutes.

Popcorn

Popcorn is a specific variety of corn that has a hard outer protein layer that protects the inner starch layers and a moisture content between 11% and 14%, which makes it especially poppable. Yellow popcorn, with its corny flavor and crunchy, firm texture, pops up the most, expanding up to forty times its original size. White popcorn has a slightly sweet taste, a crisp yet tender texture, and expands up to thirty-five times its original size. Store dried popcorn in a tightly sealed jar or plastic container, preferably in the refrigerator, to retain the moisture inside the kernels. To make popcorn, coat the bottom of a saucepan with oil and place over medium heat. Add ¼ cup popcorn kernels and cover. Once the popping starts, continuosly move the pan from side to side over the burner until most kernels have popped.

FARRO

Also known as emmer, farro is an ancient and unhybridized form of wheat said to have fueled the Roman legions. Because it's lower in gluten than hybridized wheat, many people who are allergic to wheat find they can tolerate farro. Still, anyone with severe allergies or sensitivity to wheat should consult a medical professional before experimenting with farro. Farro's flavor, texture, and thickening properties make it a great addition to soups and stews; it can also be made into a risotto-like dish called farrotto by using 4 to 5 cups of water per cup of farro.

Whole Farro

Whole farro cooks more quickly when presoaked for 6 to 12 hours. To retain nutrients, soak the grain in its cooking water, using 3 cups of water per cup of grain.

Absorption method: Bring the farro and its soaking water to a boil, then lower the heat, cover, and simmer until tender, about 50 to 60 minutes if presoaked, or about 1½ hours if not.

Pressure cooker: Use 3 cups of water per cup of farro and, if time permits, soak for 30 minutes before cooking at pressure for 45 minutes. If not presoaked, cook at pressure for about 50 minutes.

Slow cooker: Presoaking isn't necessary. Use 4 to 5 cups of water per cup of farro and cook on the high setting for 3½ hours or on low for 8 hours.

Semipearled Farro

Absorption method: Cooks in 30 minutes or less with no presoaking. Use 2 cups of water per cup of semipearled farro and cook as you would whole farro.

Cracked Farro

Absorption method: Cooks in about 30 minutes with no presoaking. Use 3 cups of water per cup of cracked farro and cook as you would whole farro.

Other cooking methods: Use it as a hot cereal for breakfast, in pilafs, or in salads, such as tabouli.

GRANO

Grano refers to lightly pearled durum wheat, which has been enjoyed as a grain in parts of Italy for centuries. In fact, the word "grano" means "grain" in Italian.

Absorption method: Use 8 cups of water per cup of grano. Bring the water to a boil, salt it as you would for pasta, then add the grano. After it returns to a boil, lower the heat to medium and cook, stirring frequently, until the grano is tender but still chewy, about 35 minutes. Then, just as with cooking pasta, drain the grano and serve it with a sauce or as an accompaniment.

Other cooking methods: Grano can also be cooked in soups such as minestrone. Use 1 cup of grano for 2 quarts of soup, allowing at least 30 minutes of cooking after the grano is added. For a hot breakfast cereal, use a proportion of 4 cups of water per cup of grano. Bring to a boil, then lower the heat, cover, and, ideally, simmer for about 4 hours so it will become soft and creamy. Alternatively, a delicious, chewy version can be ready within 2 hours.

JOB'S TEARS

Also called *hato mugi* and *adlay*, Job's tears has been cultivated in China for over four thousand years and is used extensively in traditional Chinese medicine. It has a pleasant nutty flavor.

Absorption method: Use 2 cups of water per cup of Job's tears. Bring the water to a boil, stir in the Job's tears, then lower the heat, cover, and simmer until tender, about 50 to 60 minutes.

Pressure cooker: Use 2 cups of water per cup of Job's tears and cook at pressure for 45 minutes.

Slow cooker: Use 4 cups of water per cup of Job's tears and cook on the low setting for 6 to 8 hours.

KAMUT

Said to have originated in Egypt, Kamut is the trademarked name of a variety of durum wheat with kernels two or three times larger than typical wheat kernels. Because it has never been hybridized, it has a different protein profile than modern wheat. Some people who are allergic to wheat find they can tolerate Kamut. Still, anyone with severe allergies or sensitivity to wheat should consult a medical professional before experimenting with Kamut.

Whole Kamut

Whole Kamut cooks more quickly when presoaked for 6 to 12 hours. To retain nutrients, soak the grain in its cooking water, using 3 cups of water per cup of grain.

Absorption method: Use 3 cups of water per cup of Kamut. Bring the Kamut and its soaking water to a boil, then lower the heat, cover, and simmer until the grains are plumped and a few have burst, about 1 hour if presoaked or 1½ to 2 hours if not.

Pressure cooker: Use 3 cups of water per cup of Kamut and cook at pressure for 35 minutes if presoaked or 45 minutes if not.

Slow cooker: Presoaking isn't necessary. Use 4 cups of water per cup of Kamut and cook on the high setting for 3½ to 4 hours or on low for 7 to 8 hours.

Kamut Bulgur

Absorption method: Use 2 cups of water per cup of Kamut bulgur. Bring the water to a boil, stir in the bulgur, then lower the heat, cover, and simmer for 25 minutes. Remove from the heat and let stand, covered, for 10 minutes before serving or using in a recipe.

Kamut Couscous

Absorption method: Use 1½ cups of water or broth per cup of Kamut couscous. Bring the water to a boil, then stir in the couscous, lower the heat, cover, and simmer for 5 minutes. Remove from the heat and let stand, covered, for 5 minutes. Stir to fluff before serving or using in a recipe.

Kamut Flakes

Absorption method: Use 2 cups of water per cup of Kamut flakes. Bring the water to a boil, stir in the Kamut flakes, then lower the heat, cover, and simmer for 15 to 18 minutes.

MILLET

Though usually associated with birdseed in the United States, millet is a sacred grain in China and a staple crop for about one-third of the world's population. It's rich in the amino acid lysine, so it provides higher-quality protein than most grains.

Absorption method: Use 2 cups of water per cup of millet. Combine the water and millet, bring to a boil, then lower the heat, cover, and simmer for 15 minutes. Remove from the heat and let stand, covered, for 20 minutes before fluffing.

Pressure cooker: Use 2 cups of water per cup of millet and cook at pressure for 10 to 15 minutes.

Slow cooker: Use 4 cups of water per cup of millet and cook on the low setting for 6 to 8 hours. For a hot breakfast cereal, consider replacing some of the water with juice, and add some fresh or dried fruit.

OATS

All forms of oats may be considered whole grain, as the only portion removed in processing is the indigestible husk. They're a great source of beta-glucans, a highly beneficial form of soluble fiber. Oats are gluten free, and studies have shown that they don't trigger the symptoms associated with grains that contain gluten. In North America they're often listed as being inappropriate for a gluten-free diet, but this is only out of concern that they may be contaminated by wheat during harvest and processing.

Oat Groats

Absorption method: Use 3 cups of water per cup of oat groats. Combine the water and oats, bring to a boil, then lower the heat, cover, and simmer until tender, about 90 minutes, adding more water if necessary.

Pressure cooker: Use 3 cups of water per cup of oats and cook at pressure for 30 minutes.

Slow cooker: Use 4 cups of water per cup of oats and cook on the low setting for 8 to 12 hours.

Steel-Cut Oats

Also called Scotch oats, Scottish oats, or Irish oats. You can reduce cooking time by soaking the oats in their cooking water overnight, or by toasting them in a pan over medium heat for 3 minutes.

Absorption method: Use 2 to 2½ cups of water per cup of oats. Bring the water to a boil, stir in the oats, then lower the heat, cover, and simmer until tender—about 15 minutes if the oats were presoaked or toasted, and about 30 minutes otherwise.

Slow cooker: Use 4 cups of water per cup of oats and cook on the low setting for 7 to 8 hours.

Rolled Oats

Absorption method: To cook rolled oats in the traditional way, use 2 cups of water per cup of oats. Combine the water and oats, bring to a boil, then lower the heat, partially cover the pot with a lid, and simmer for 10 to 15 minutes. However, some people swear by adding the rolled oats to boiling water, preferring the more chewy, less creamy texture that results.

Slow cooker: Use 2½ cups of water per cup of oats and cook on the low setting for 8 hours.

Quick-Cooking Oatmeal

Absorption method: About half the thickness of oat flakes and smaller. Cook as you would rolled oats, but only simmer for 5 minutes.

Instant Oatmeal

Absorption method: Use ⅓ to ½ cup boiling water per packet of instant oats, which typically contains about ¼ to ⅓ cup thinly cut oat flakes. Just pour the boiling water over the oats and let stand for 1 minute.

Note: Don't substitute instant oatmeal for rolled oats in baked goods. They're too thin and insubstantial and won't produce good results.

Oat Bran

Absorption method: For one serving of hot cereal, slowly pour ⅓ cup of oat bran into 1 cup of boiling water, stirring all the while, then add a pinch of salt if you wish, lower the heat, and simmer for a total of 2 minutes.

Other cooking methods: Oat bran can be added to muffins, hot cereals, breads, casseroles, and soups for its beneficial soluble fiber, as well as its tenderizing and moistening effects.

QUINOA

Although prepared as a grain, quinoa doesn't hail from a cereal grass; rather, it is from a plant related to beets and spinach. It's a nutritional powerhouse and particularly noteworthy for its ideal amino acid profile, making it one of the few plant foods that provides complete protein. Although most commercial quinoa has been prewashed or mechanically processed to remove the bitter-tasting saponins on its seed coat, play it safe and always rinse quinoa thoroughly, until the water runs clear, before cooking.

Absorption method: Use 2 cups of water or broth per cup of quinoa. Combine the quinoa, water, and any seasonings in a pot, bring to a boil, then lower the heat to medium, cover, and cook for 15 minutes.

Other cooking methods: To use quinoa to thicken soup, add a small amount of uncooked quinoa during the last 15 minutes of cooking.

RYE

Rye is a delicious, hearty grain that is primarily grown in the northwestern part of the Eastern hemisphere, which includes the Russian Federation, Belarus, Poland, Germany, and the Nordic countries, where it thrives under cold conditions. Nutritionally, it's noteworthy for containing pentosans, a type of soluble fiber with health benefits similar to those of beta-glucans.

Whole Rye Berries

It's best to presoak rye berries before cooking. To retain nutrients, soak them in their cooking water, using 3 cups of water per cup of rye berries.

Absorption method: Use 3 cups of water per cup of rye berries. Bring the rye berries and their soaking water to a boil, then lower the heat, cover, and simmer until tender, about 60 minutes if presoaked or 1½ to 2 hours if not. With further cooking, the rye berries will split open, making for an even softer, more cereal-like texture.

Pressure cooker: Use 3 cups of water per cup of rye berries and cook for 40 minutes if presoaked or 50 minutes if not.

Slow cooker: Presoaking isn't necessary. Use 4 cups of water per cup of rye berries and cook on the high setting for 3½ to 4 hours or on low for 8 hours.

Rye Grits

Absorption method: Use 3½ cups of water per cup of rye grits. Bring the water to a boil, then gradually pour in the grits, whisking all the while. Lower the heat, cover, and simmer for 35 to 40 minutes.

Rye Flakes

Absorption method: Use 3 cups of water per cup of rye flakes. Bring the water to a boil, stir in the rye flakes, then lower the heat, cover, and simmer for 25 to 30 minutes.

SORGHUM

Sorghum is a gluten-free grain long appreciated as a staple crop in portions of Africa, where traditionally it is fermented to make beer, porridge, and injera bread. To increase its versatility and appeal, neutral-flavored, white sorghum hybrids have been developed with a taste and texture similar cooked untoasted buckwheat, making it an excellent gluten-free grain for cereals, pilafs, and salads.

Absorption method: Use 3 cups of water per cup of sorghum. Combine the sorghum and water, bring to a boil, then lower the heat, cover, and simmer until the water is absorbed and the grains are tender, about 60 minutes.

Pressure cooker: Use 3 cups of water per cup of sorghum and cook at pressure for 45 minutes.

Slow cooker: Use 4 cups of water per cup of sorghum and cook on the high setting for 3½ to 4 hours or on low for 8 hours.

SPELT

A distant cousin of modern varieties of wheat, spelt originated in the Middle East at least six thousand years ago. Although it's higher in protein than conventional wheat and does contain gluten, it has proportionally less gliadin, the component of gluten's protein complex that appears to be most responsible for adverse reactions to gluten. Some people who are sensitive to wheat may find spelt's gluten easier to digest. Nonetheless, anyone with severe allergies or sensitivity to wheat should consult with a medical professional before experimenting with spelt.

Whole Spelt

Whole spelt cooks more quickly when presoaked for 6 to 12 hours. To retain nutrients, soak the grain in its cooking water, using 3 cups of water per cup of grain.

Absorption method: Use 3 cups of water per cup of spelt. Bring the spelt and its soaking water to a boil, then lower the heat, cover, and simmer until tender, about 50 minutes to 1 hour if presoaked or 1½ to 2 hours if not.

Pressure cooker: Use 3 cups of water per cup of spelt and cook at pressure for 40 minutes if presoaked or 50 minutes if not.

Slow cooker: Presoaking isn't necessary. Use 4 cups of water per cup of spelt and cook on the high setting for 3½ to 4 hours or on low for 8 hours.

Spelt Bulgur

Absorption method: Use 2 cups of water or broth per cup of spelt bulgur. Bring the water to a boil, then stir in the bulgur, season with salt and any herbs or spices you like, then lower the heat, cover, and simmer for 25 minutes. Remove from the heat and let stand undisturbed for 10 minutes before serving or using in a recipe.

Spelt Flakes

Absorption method: Use 2 cups of water per cup of spelt flakes. Combine the water and spelt in a pot, bring to a boil, then lower the heat, cover, and simmer for 15 to 18 minutes.

TEFF

An exceedingly tiny grain, teff is only available in whole grain forms because it would be impossible to refine away the bran or germ of each tiny seed. It's the most commonly cultivated grain in Ethiopia and is the principal ingredient in *injera*, the traditional Ethiopian flatbread.

Absorption method: Use 2 cups of water per ½ cup of teff. Bring the water to a boil, stir in the teff, then lower the heat, cover and simmer until all of the liquid is absorbed, about 15 to 20 minutes.

Other cooking methods: To add flavor and texture to familiar grains, include 2 tablespoons of teff when cooking 1 cup of rice, millet, or barley. Uncooked whole teff can also be added to soups and stews, casseroles, and puddings as a thickener and for variety in texture and flavor.

TRITICALE

A hybrid of wheat and rye, triticale combines the nutty flavor and higher yields of wheat with the hardiness and better amino acid balance of rye.

Whole Triticale

Whole triticale cooks more quickly when presoaked for 6 to 12 hours. To retain nutrients, soak the grain in its cooking water, using 3 cups of water per cup of grain.

Absorption method: Use 3 cups of water per cup of triticale. Bring the triticale and its soaking water to a boil, then lower the heat, cover, and simmer until tender, about 50 to 60 minutes if presoaked or 1½ to 2 hours if not.

Pressure cooker: Use 3 cups of water per cup of triticale and cook at pressure for 40 minutes if presoaked or 50 minutes if not.

Slow cooker: Presoaking isn't necessary. Use 4 cups of water per cup of triticale and cook on the high setting for 3½ to 4 hours or on low for 8 hours.

Triticale Flakes

Absorption method: Use 2 cups of water per cup of triticale flakes. Bring the water to a boil, stir in the triticale flakes, then lower the heat, cover, and simmer for 15 to 20 minutes.

WILD RICE

Despite its name, wild rice isn't truly a variety of rice. Its long, dark brown kernels are the seed of an aquatic grass that grows in marshy areas. It has an appealing chewy texture and intriguing flavor that's somewhat nutty, earthy, and reminiscent of green tea.

Absorption method: Use 3 cups of water per cup of wild rice. Bring the water to a boil, stir in the wild rice, then lower the heat, cover, and cook for 50 to 60 minutes, or until the grains begin to split open and become tender but not mushy.

Whole Grain and Specialty Flours

All whole grains can be ground into flour, as can some other foods, but using them in cooking and baking is seldom just a matter of substituting them for wheat flour. Each contributes its own unique flavor and texture. Some have mild flavors, while others are downright assertive. Textures range from silken to sandy. Some have gluten and others don't, which can significantly affect the texture and volume of baked goods, particularly breads that are kneaded. And even within the category of wheat flours, protein content can vary widely, making them perform quite differently in baking. Some types of wheat flour are more appropriate for certain types of baking than others. Understanding the characteristics of each type of flour will not only make experimentation fun and interesting; it will also yield delicious baked goods as a reward for all your efforts.

Words and Terms to Know

Bleaching and maturing agents: Chemicals used to accelerate the aging process for flour or alter baking performance. Qualities affected include whiter color, stronger gluten, and finer texture.

Enriched: The addition of certain nutrients to refined grain products to meet a standard or to restore nutrients lost in processing. Although as many of thirteen nutrients are significantly depleted, only five are required to be added back in: thiamin, riboflavin, niacin, folic acid, and iron.

Hammer-milled: Ground in a mill in which bars swinging on an axle rotate inside a steel cylinder, crushing the grain against the inner surface. A faster way to grind grains, hammer milling also yields a more consistent grade of finely ground flour. However, the speed of the process generates higher temperatures, which can destroy some nutrients within the flour.

Roller-milled: Ground in a machine that features several rollers with different surfaces, ranging from smooth to coarse, set various widths apart. Unlike stone grinding and hammer milling, grinding flour in a roller mill makes it possible to quickly separate the bran and germ from the endosperm and completely control the particle size of the flour through various stages of grinding and sifting.

Stone-ground: The most traditional method of grinding flour. The flour is ground between two flat millstones that rub against each other, slowly crushing the grain and distributing the bran and nutrient-rich germ throughout the flour. Since stone grinding can be just one part of the process, look for products labeled "100% stone-ground."

Flour Varieties and Characteristics at a Glance

Flour	Gluten-Free?	Flavor	Baked Texture
Amaranth	Yes	Spicy, nutty, woody	Moist, fine crumb; smooth crisp crust
Arrowroot	Yes	Neutral	Lightens heavy textures; smooth, crisp crust
Barley	No	Sweet, malty	Moist, cakelike crumb; firm, chewy crust
Buckwheat	Yes	Hearty, earthy	Moist, fine crumb; soft crust

Flour Storage Tips

- Keep flour in moisture-proof packaging, ideally in an airtight plastic or glass container, and at the very least wrapped in a plastic bag.
- Store whole grain flour at cool temperatures: below 70°F, and preferably between 40°F and 60°F (in your refrigerator or even the freezer is great). This will prevent the natural oils in the bran and germ from going rancid. Use within 3 months or up to the use-by date on the package.
- Store refined flour in an airtight container at temperatures up to 75°F. Use within 6 months; refrigerating or freezing will extend shelf life to up to 1 year.

Exploring Whole Grain Flour Varieties

A good starting point for becoming familiar with the characteristics of a wide variety of flours is to experiment by substituting any nonwheat flour for 25% of the whole wheat or wheat flour called for in a recipe. However, if it's necessary to use only gluten-free flour, take some time to learn about the characteristics of various gluten-free flours first, so you'll know how to capitalize on their strengths and compensate for their weaknesses. This will allow you to create gluten-free baked goods with a satisfactory taste, texture, and mouthfeel.

Substitution and Usage Notes

Substitute for up to 25% of the flour called for. May require increased baking time.

Use up to 50% in a wheat-free flour blend. Substitute equally for cornstarch.

Substitute for up to 25% of the flour called for.

Use no more than ⅓ cup per loaf of bread. Substitute for up to 50% of the flour called for in pancakes, muffins, and crepes.

Flour Varieties and Characteristics at a Glance

Flour	Gluten-Free?	Flavor	Baked Texture
Chestnut	Yes	Sweet, nutty	Silky texture
Cornmeal, blue or red	Yes	Sweet, nutlike	Grainy, denser crumb
Cornmeal, white	Yes	Delicate corn flavor	Grainy, slightly dry crumb
Cornmeal, yellow	Yes	Deep, rich corn flavor	Grainy, slightly dry crumb
Garbanzo	Yes	Sweet, rich	Dry, delicate crumb
Garbanzo-fava	Yes	Nutty, somewhat sweet	Moist, tender crumb, with added volume
Gluten flour	No	Tangy	Fine, chewy crumb; crisp, thin crust
Kamut	No	Sweet, rich, buttery	Dense, heavy crumb
Mesquite	Yes	Sweet, with molasses and mocha tones	Dry crumb
Millet	Yes	Mildly sweet to bitter, depending on the age of the flour	Dry, delicate crumb; smooth, thin crust
Montina	Yes	Hearty, nutty	Chewy texture
Oat	Yes*	Sweet	Moist, cakelike crumb; firm crust

*Although oats do not contain gluten, in North America they are often listed as being inappropriate for a gluten-free diet, but this is only out of concern that they may be contaminated by wheat during harvest and processing.

cont'd

Substitution and Usage Notes

Substitute for up to 25% of the flour in yeasted bread recipes and up to 50% of the flour in recipes leavened with baking powder or baking soda.

Can be used interchangeably with other cornmeal varieties, although different colors and flavors may result

Use like blue or red cornmeal.

Use like blue or red cornmeal.

When making breads leavened with yeast or sourdough, combine with wheat or spelt flour and substitute for no more than 25% of the total flour in the recipe. Can also be combined up to 25% with other gluten-free flours and starches to make gluten-free baked goods.

Use no more than 25% garbanzo-fava flour in a flour blend.

Use up to 2 tablespoons of gluten flour per cup of flour in whole grain breads; use up to 4 teaspoons per cup in white breads.

Related to wheat and performs similarly in baking. For best results, keep the dough moist, knead longer, and allow to rest longer.

Use up to 25% mesquite flour in flour blends for muffins, cakes, breads, and cookies, whether with wheat flour or with other gluten-free flours. Sprinkle it on fish, meat, poultry, tofu, or tempeh before cooking for added flavor.

Use up to 50% millet flour in cookies and muffins; limit to ½ to ¾ cup per loaf when making yeasted or sourdough breads, and combine with a high proportion of wheat or spelt flour.

Use up to 20% Montina in a blend with lighter flours.

Use no more than 25% oat flour in breads leavened with yeast or sourdough. Muffins, cakes, cookies, and pancakes can be made with up to 50% oat flour.

Flour Varieties and Characteristics at a Glance

Flour	Gluten-Free?	Flavor	Baked Texture
Potato flour	Yes	Sweet, strong potato flavor	Moist, chewy crumb; soft, dry crust
Potato starch	Yes	Neutral, mild potato flavor	Moist crumb; lightens heavy textures
Quinoa	Yes	Nutty, earthy	Delicate, cakelike crumb
Rice, brown	Yes	Nutty	Dry, fine crumb; soft crust
Rice, sweet	Yes	Sweet	Supple crumb
Rice, white	Yes	Neutral	Dry, fine crumb; soft crust
Rye	No	Tangy	Moist crumb; smooth, hard crust
Sorghum	Yes	Sweet	Fine crumb; crisp crust
Soy	Yes	Pungent, slightly bitter, nutty	Moist, fine crumb; smooth, hard crust
Spelt	No	Sweet, nutty	Moderate crumb; supple crust
Sprouted grain flour	No**	Sweet	Lighter, springy crumb; darker crust
Tapioca	Yes	Slightly sweet	Chewy, springy texture; smooth, crisp crust
Teff	Yes	Sweet, with malty molasses tones	Light, delicate crumb

**Typically contains wheat.

cont'd

Substitution and Usage Notes

Only use a very small amount of potato flour, about 1 teaspoon per cup, in flour mixes, as it has a very strong flavor.

Use up to one-third potato starch in flour blends.

Use no more than 25% quinoa flour when making yeasted or sourdough breads. Use up to 30% quinoa flour in quick breads, cookies, and pancakes.

Use up to 50% rice flour in cookies, flatbreads, and muffins. Minimize crumbling by adding eggs, an egg substitute, or xanthan gum (1½ teaspoons per 2 cups flour) to the recipe.

Use like brown rice flour.

Use like brown rice flour.

Rye flour can yield sticky doughs that don't rise high. Knead gently and for less time. A ratio of one part rye to three parts wheat flour works well.

Use about 25% to 30% sorghum flour in a blend with potato starch and tapioca flour, which will help provide a smoother crust and lighter texture. Add ½ teaspoon xanthan gum per cup of sorghum flour.

Lower oven temperature by 25°F. Use no more than 25% soy flour in quick breads, cookies, and cakes. Use even more sparingly in yeasted breads—no more than 10% of the total flour.

Substitute equally for wheat flour in any recipe. Reduce the recipe's liquids by 25%, then add more liquid only if it seems necessary.

Substitute equally for wheat flour in any recipe. Increase the recipe's liquids or use less flour.

Mix with water before using as a thickener. Can be substituted equally for arrowroot flour. Use up to 33% tapioca flour in flour blends.

Substitute up to 20% teff flour in your favorite recipe, or more if the recipe uses wheat flour. Do not use in yeasted breads.

Flour Varieties and Characteristics at a Glance

Flour	Gluten-Free?	Flavor	Baked Texture
Triticale	No	Nutty, tangy	Dense crumb; semifirm crust
Wheat, durum	No	Sweet, somewhat buttery	Fine, delicate, dense crumb; crunchy crust
Wheat, refined white and all-purpose	No	Sweet to neutral	Fine, tender crumb
Wheat, semolina	No	Sweet, somewhat buttery	Fine, delicate, firm crumb; crunchy crust
Wheat, white whole	No	Sweet, nutty	Coarse, large crumb
Wheat, whole	No	Sweet, nutty, slightly bitter	Coarse, large crumb
Wild rice	Yes	Earthy, nutty	Dry, fine crumb

cont'd

Substitution and Usage Notes

For yeasted breads, use up to 50% triticale flour in combination with wheat flour and let the dough rise once. Substitute for some or most of the wheat flour in quick breads, drop biscuits, cookies, and pancakes.

Especially suited for pasta.

Suitable for all types of baking. Substitute refined white flour for a portion of whole wheat flour within whole grain recipes when a lighter color or texture is desired.

Especially suited for pasta.

Use for bread or as an all-purpose flour

Use less whole wheat flour when substituting for white flour. Initially, try replacing each cup of white flour with about ¾ cup of whole wheat flour, or increase the liquids.

Use up to 25% wild rice flour in flour blends.

Breads

Throughout civilization, bread has provided sustenance and comfort, has symbolized community and sharing, and has even been used as currency. Each country and culture has its own traditional forms and varieties of bread that have been developed over the centuries to complement the local climate, grains, and modes of cooking and baking. Both the skill of the baker and the type of leavening agent used can distinguish one bread from another in terms of optimum flavor, texture, nutrition, and overall digestibility. The way breads are made can also help predict which ones will naturally stay fresh longer.

Words and Terms to Know

Artisan breads: Breads made from scratch with attention to excellence, using time-honored techniques and traditional recipes based on simple ingredients.

Desem: A type of Flemish bread made using a sourdough culture produced from the interaction of organisms and enzymes that naturally occur in wheat flour instead of relying on airborne yeasts and bacteria.

Flatbread: Assorted flat varieties of bread made from dough that's often unleavened. Flatbreads range from thin to a couple of inches high and from crispy to soft depending on the ingredients and baking technique. Almost every culture has its own variation.

French bread: Simple "lean dough" breads that classically hail from France. They contain little or no fat and are typically made from wheat flour, although rye breads (*pain de seigle*) will be found in regions where the grain is grown. The ubiquitous *pain ordinaire* and baguettes are also commonly referred to as French bread.

German bread: Usually dark colored, densely textured bread that is made from whole grain flour with special emphasis on rye, although bread made from wheat is also found in Germany, as well as bread made form varying combinations of both rye and wheat to take advantage of the best both grains have to offer. The addition of seeds, spices, and herbs is a hallmark of German bread baking. A sourdough culture is often used when making rye bread, with or without baking yeast, as its acidity helps modify rye flour's usual sticky, moist texture.

Gluten-free: Specialty breads made without wheat and other grains that contain gluten, a protein that some people can't tolerate.

Handcrafted: Breads formed by hand rather than by machine to avoid overworking the dough and to be more attentive to the condition of the dough during production.

Hearth bread: Technically refers to bread baked directly on the floor of a wood-burning oven or on a hot deck of an oven to create a chewy, crisp crust and, if steam is used, a shiny finish.

Italian bread: Wheat-based loaves made from dough with a high water content for a moist crumb and golden crust. Rather than using sourdough, a *biga* sponge, made by adding a very small amount of yeast to flour and water to create a firm prefermenting agent, is more common, giving the bread a full-bodied flavor with a hint of yeast but without the sourness.

Leavened bread: Breads made using baking yeast, sourdough, or chemical leavening agents (such as baking soda and baking powder) to help the dough rise and provide a lighter texture.

Quick breads: Breads leavened with baking soda, baking powder, and/or eggs, rather than baking yeast or sourdough. Baking soda and baking powder work more quickly than yeast.

Rustic: Made from wet, sticky dough with a high water content dough, resulting in a moist interior with big holes.

Soft breads: Reminiscent of the lighter texture of simple homemade white bread.

Sourdough: Natural leavening resulting from the interaction of bacteria and wild yeasts found naturally in the air with a thick mixture of flour and water. Sometimes labeled "yeast-free."

Reading the Label

What to Look for in Breads

- Whole grain flour
- A simple ingredients list, with little more than flour, water, salt, and a leavening agent
- Preferably 2 to 3 grams of fiber per slice
- Minimal sweeteners; preferably none

Bread and Tortilla Additives to Avoid

- Ammonium chloride
- Artificial colors
- Azodicarbonamide (ADA)
- Bleached flour
- Calcium propionate or sodium propionate
- Calcium stearoyl-2-lactylate and sodium stearoyl-2-lactylate
- Diacetyl tartaric acid esters of mono- and diglycerides (DATEM)
- Fumaric acid
- Hydrogenated fats
- L-cysteine
- Potassium bromate
- Potassium sorbate
- Sorbic acid
- Vegetable shortening

Talking Bread

Baguette (bah-GET): A long, thin bread with a crisp, almost brittle crust and light, airy interior crumb, sometimes referred to as *pain ordinaire* or French bread.

Bâtarde (bah-TARD): Shaped somewhere between a round boule and the long, cylindrical outline of a baguette, with more crumb and less crust than a baguette.

Bialy (bee-AH-lee): A flat, round, savory roll with curved edges, a flour-dusted crust, and an indentation in the middle that is filled with a paste of sautéed chopped onions.

Bolillo (bow-LEE-yoh): Torpedo-shaped rolls with a crusty exterior and a soft interior.

Boule (BOOL): A round loaf shaped like a ball.

Brioche (BREE-ohsh): A light but rich and somewhat sweet-tasting bread made from dough enriched with butter and eggs, traditionally shaped into a fluted round with a small cap.

Challah (HAH-lah): A sweet, rich, light bread with a golden color; often sold in braided form.

Ciabatta (chah-BAH-tah): A fairly flat, relatively shapeless bread with a crunchy, crisp crust dusted with flour and a moist interior crumb with large honeycombed holes.

Croissant (krwah-SAHN): A buttery, yeasted, flaky roll formed into a crescent shape.

Demi-baguette (DEHM-ee bah-GET): A baguette that's half the regular length.

Ficelle (fee-SEHL): A very long, thin bread, about the same length as a baguette but half the weight.

Focaccia (fa-KAH-chee-a): An Italian flatbread similar to a thick pizza crust with a moist interior crumb.

Fougasse (foo-GOSS): A traditional, leavened flatbread from Provence with a moist, dense, chewy interior; shaped to resemble a ladder or tree and baked plain or topped with herbs, nuts, or cheese.

Grissini (gruh-SEE-nee): Thin, crisp Italian-style breadsticks.

Lavash (LAH-vohsh): Also spelled lahvosh; a traditional, thin, large, round, pliable bread also known as Armenian cracker bread.

Naan (NAHN): A round, soft traditional flatbread from India that slightly expands, browns, and blisters when baked briefly at very high temperatures.

Pagnotta (pahg-NAHT-ah): A round, rustic Italian bread that's crusty on the outside and has an open crumb on the inside.

Pain au levain (PAN ah la-VAIN): Bread that's naturally leavened with sourdough; has a thick crust and large, open holes in the interior and a hearty, mildly sour flavor.

Pain de campagne (PAN deh cahm-PAHYN): A country-style French bread typically shaped into a large, round loaf with a chewy, thick crust and an airy, light interior.

Pain paysan (PAN PI-zan): A dark, rustic French bread made from a blend of wheat and rye.

Panettone (pah-neht-TOH-nay): A sweet, golden-colored, airy-textured, cylindrical Italian bread made with candied citrus peel and raisins.

Panini (pah-NEE-nee): A roll or sandwich that's grilled in a weighted press, making the crust crisp and golden brown.

Parisienne (puh-ree-zee-EHN): A broader version of a baguette that's just as long but weighs twice as much.

Petit pain (puh-TEE PAHN): A small French roll.

Pugliese (POOL-yee-ay-say): Traditionally a round, golden-colored bread with a moist interior with small- to medium-sized holes; made partially or entirely with semolina flour.

Schiacciata (sky-ach-CHA-ta): A thin, round or rectangular Tuscan flatbread typically baked with olive oil and other simple toppings.

Stirato (stir-AH-toh): An Italian version of a baguette made with a wet, ciabatta-type dough, with a moist interior and the characteristic holes found in rustic breads.

Wheat-Free Breads

Not all wheat-free breads are gluten-free. If you can't tolerate gluten, see the list of gluten-free grains in the Grains chapter and read bread labels carefully.

If you can't tolerate wheat but some gluten is okay, you may be able to enjoy breads made with some Kamut, Spelt, or rye flour. Consult with a medical professional before experimenting, and start with small amounts.

Injera: This traditional, slightly sour-tasting, spongy-textured Ethiopian flatbread is traditionally made from teff flour, leavened naturally from the wild yeast on the grain itself.

Kamut bread: To be labeled as "Kamut bread," 100% of the flour or grain in the bread must be Kamut. If at least 50% but less than 100% Kamut is used, it can be called "bread with Kamut grain." Breads made with Kamut have a rich, buttery, sweet flavor and an amber color.

Pumpernickel bread: Dense, richly flavored, high in fiber, and moist, all varieties are based on whole grain rye and slowly baked in steam-heated ovens before being vacuum-packed.

Rice bread: Rice flour is a common base for gluten-free breads; however, not all rice bread is gluten free. Rice flour's typical gritty texture is modified by the addition of gums and starches, other gluten-free flours that have complementary characteristics, and sometimes milk or eggs to create a softer crumb.

Rye bread: Most of the rye bread sold in bakeries and grocery stores is considered light rye sandwich-style bread. These mild-tasting, yeast-leavened loaves are made primarily from wheat flour. New York–style rye bread, also known as Jewish rye bread, is made by combining rye and wheat flours and leavening the dough with a sour rye starter and baking yeast; it has a slightly tangy flavor and is baked to have a soft interior texture and a chewy crust, usually sprinkled with caraway seeds. European-style 100% rye bread is made using only organic rye flour, rye sourdough culture, water, and salt—using sourdough as the leavening agent is the key.

Rye crispbread: A brittle flatbread that comes in three basic types—a yeasted version; a sourdough rye crisp commonly produced in Finland and Germany; and a version made without yeast or sourdough, which relies on the incorporation of air into cooled dough.

Spelt bread: Breads made with spelt have a texture similar to wheat-based bread, but their flavor is more nutty and sweet.

Pasta and Noodles

Available in a rainbow of colors and variety of shapes and textures, pasta provides an option to fit any whim and enhance any meal, whether it's topped with a sauce, tossed into soup, or served on the side. Though there are a few exceptions, most varieties fit into two main categories—Italian-inspired pastas and Asian noodles—and many are available both fresh and dried. Within these broad groupings, they can be further distinguished by type of flour used, shape, and whether they have added ingredients for color and flavor. No matter which kind you choose, all pasta is quick and easy to cook, providing the perfect base for a meal in minutes.

Words and Terms to Know

Asian noodles: Wheat-based Asian noodles are softer and more porous than Italian pasta since they're made with a softer variety of wheat. Nonwheat Asian noodles may be made from rice, buckwheat, or a variety of vegetable starches.

Dried pasta: Pasta that is air-dried after manufacture, reducing the moisture content to 12.5%. It can be stored for up to two years at room temperature under normal conditions.

Fresh pasta: Freshly made pasta that hasn't been dried. It must be refrigerated, and its shelf life is generally quite short. Though fresh pasta can be formed into a multitude of shapes, the most common is long, flat ribbons in various widths.

Gluten-free pasta: Made from flours or vegetable starches that are gluten-free, including rice, corn, or bean flour. Wheat-free varieties are also available, but aren't necessarily gluten-free. Read ingredients lists carefully if gluten is an issue.

Gluten-Free Pasta Varieties

- Asian cellophane noodles (made with mung bean starch)
- Bean flour–based pasta
- Buckwheat soba (100% buckwheat only)
- Corn pasta
- Corn-quinoa pasta
- *Harusame* (made with rice, soybean, or potato starch)
- *Kuzukiri* (made with arrowroot starch)
- Rice pasta (including Asian rice noodles and rice sticks)
- *Tang myon* (made with sweet potato starch)

Asian Noodles

Cellophane noodles: Also known as bean thread noodles or glass noodles. Very thin, translucent noodles made from mung bean starch and water. They have a slippery, springy, chewy texture and are virtually tasteless until they absorb flavors from other foods. They shouldn't actually be cooked; rather, soak them in hot but not boiling water just until softened, about 5 to 15 minutes. Loosen and separate the noodles, then rinse and drain before adding them to a dish.

Chinese egg noodles: Made from refined hard wheat flour, eggs, and water. The golden yellow strands of Chinese egg noodles come in various round thicknesses or flat widths. Depending on size, cooking time is 1 to 3 minutes for fresh noodles and 3 to 6 minutes for dried.

Chinese wheat noodles: Round or flat, cream to yellowish beige strands of various thicknesses and widths. Depending on size, cooking time is 2 to 4 minutes for fresh noodles and 4 to 7 minutes for dried. After cooking, rinse the noodles in cold water and drain before using in a recipe.

Harusame: Translucent 5- to 7-inch-long Japanese noodles. They look like cellophane noodles but may be made from rice starch, potato starch, or soybean starch. Prepare as you would cellophane noodles.

Hiyamugi: Japanese noodles made from wheat flour, salt, and water; somewhat wider than somen but thinner than udon. Cook in boiling water for 4 to 6 minutes, just until tender, then rinse in cold water to stop the cooking and remove excess starch.

Kuzukiri: Light-colored, nearly transparent Japanese noodles made from kudzu starch, sometimes with added potato starch. *Kuzukiri* is cooked like regular pasta.

Ramen noodles: The familiar long, thin, extruded noodles, available in traditional and instant form. They're made from wheat flour, water, salt, sometimes eggs, and *kansui*, an alkaline solution made with potassium carbonate or sodium carbonate.

Rice noodles (fresh): Fresh white noodles made from a mixture of rice flour and water and coated with oil to prevent sticking. Briefly soak in hot or boiling water to soften them up and to rinse off the oil.

Rice sticks: Brittle, opaque, white dried noodles made from rice; available in thin, medium, and wide widths. Soak them in hot water for 3 to 15 minutes, depending on the width of the noodles and how they will be further cooked or served. Drain the noodles after soaking, then rinse in cold water to remove excess starch.

Soba: Thin, square-cut, brownish gray Japanese noodles made from buckwheat flour. Cooking time is 1 to 4 minutes for fresh soba or 5 to 7 minutes for dried. Cook just until al dente, drain, and then immediately rinse with cold water to stop the cooking process.

Somen: Very thin, delicate, white, round noodles made from wheat flour, water, and salt. Cook in boiling water for about 2 minutes, just until tender. Drain, rinse in cold water, and drain again before serving.

Tang myon: Also known as *dang myun*. A Korean version of cellophane noodles made with sweet potato starch. Prepare as you would cellophane noodles.

Udon: Thick, delicious noodles made from wheat flour or whole wheat flour, salt, and water; nearly as wide as linguine. Cook fresh udon for 2 to 4 minutes and dried for 5 to 7 minutes. After cooking, drain and rinse with cold water to stop the cooking and remove excess starch.

Pasta and Noodle Storage Guidelines

Dry pasta and noodles	Unopened Package	Opened Package, Tightly Wrapped
Made without eggs	2 years, cool, dry place	1 year, cool, dry place
Made with eggs	2 years, cool, dry place	1–2 months cool, dry place
Leftover cooked pasta	N/A	Up to 3 days in fridge, in freezer up to a month
Fresh pasta	**Refrigerator**	**Freezer**
Fresh pasta	7 days in fridge or check use-by dating on package.	2–3 months*

*Cook without thawing to retain its integrity and texture

Pasta and Noodle Selection Guide

Shape	Examples
Strands: Long cylinders with or without a hollow center	angel hair, bucatini, capellini, spaghetti, vermicelli, cellophane noodles, rice sticks, soba, somen, udon
Ribbons: Flat strips	fettuccine, kluski, lasagna, lasagnette, linguine, mafalda, pappardelle, tagliatelle, trenette, rice sticks, udon
Tubular: Hollow shapes	cannelloni, elbow macaroni, maccheroni, manicotti, mostaccioli, penne, penne rigate, rigatoni, trenne, trenette, ziti
Novelty shapes	conchiglie, farfalle, fusilli, gnocchi, orechiette, radiatore, rotelle, rotini
Tiny soup shapes	alfabeto, ditali, fregola, orzo, stelline
Stuffed pasta	agnolotti, cappelletti, mezzaluna, ravioli, ravioloni, tortellini, tortelloni

How to Use

Italian varieties: Best with finely grated cheese and smooth, not-too-chunky tomato-based sauces that are intended to coat or cling to the pasta. Also good for tossing with olive oil or butter and seasonings.
Asian noodles: Use in soups, salads, and side dishes, or in stir-fries with a sauce, dressing, or light broth.

Italian varieties: Best with pesto, creamy or béchamel sauces, or rich ragout-type sauces. Dried ribbon pasta can stand up to thicker, heavier sauces while fresh versions calls for lighter toppings.
Asian noodles: Use in soups, salads, and side dishes, or in stir-fries with a sauce, dressing, or light broth.

Best with chunky vegetable and meat sauces, or thick cheese sauces that will cling to the pasta and be trapped in the bends and crevices. Match smaller shapes with sauces with more finely chopped ingredients. Also a good choice for casseroles and pasta salads. Larger versions can be stuffed and baked.

Use like tubular pasta.

Use sparingly in soups and stews to thicken and contribute texture, using larger shapes in thick soups and smaller shapes in broth-based soups.

Traditionally, the shape of a given stuffed pasta was based on the filling, but these days anything goes! Serve simply drizzled with oil, butter, or floating in a light broth, perhaps with a dusting of grated Parmesan cheese.

Beans, Peas, Lentils, and Soyfoods

Beans can play a starring role in a meal or be part of the supporting cast in salads, soups, spreads, snacks, casseroles, dips, and wraps. They are also the primary ingredient for making tofu and tempeh. Virtually every culture and cuisine incorporates dried beans, peas, and lentils, often combined with regional grains, pastas, and vegetables in unique combinations. Besides being flavorful and adaptable, beans are a storehouse of nutrition. In addition to being rich in B vitamins, minerals, and phytonutrients, particularly antioxidants, they're a good plant-based source of protein and an excellent source of soluble fiber and resistant starch (another type of dietary fiber).

Words and Terms to Know

Heirloom beans: Varieties of beans known to have been in existence for over fifty years, often originating from a particular region within a country. Heirloom varieties are regaining popularity due to their remarkable flavors, colors, and nutritional attributes. Most heirloom beans will be labeled as such, and their signage or packaging will provide the story behind the bean and its typically unusual, though descriptive name.

Isoflavones: Naturally occurring compounds in plants, most notably in soybeans, that can exert weak estrogen-like effects on the body. Classified as phytoestrogens, isoflavones can bind to estrogen receptors in various tissues, including those related to reproduction. The amount of isoflavones found within soyfoods depends on the level of processing and whether or not the isoflavones are intentionally isolated. As the long-term safety of high supplemental doses of isolated isoflavones is unknown, it is best to get soy isoflavones from cooked, whole soybeans and minimally processed soyfoods, including tofu, tempeh, miso, roasted soybeans, and soymilk.

Soy protein isolate: A highly processed extraction of the protein components from soybeans to create various products that imitate meat or provide a concentrated source of vegetable protein.

Tempeh: A traditional Indonesian soyfood with a tender, chewy texture and mild, mushroomlike flavor. Tempeh is made by culturing cooked, cracked soybeans with the fungus *Rhizopus oligosporus*, in a process similar to making blue cheese. After an incubation period of 18 to 24 hours, the soybeans take on a cakelike form with an off-white color. Small, harmless black spots may appear on the surface as a result of the fermentation process. Tempeh may be made solely from soybeans, or with other grains, sesame seeds, or peanuts. Tempeh must be cooked before eating. It's very versatile and may be baked, grilled, stir-fried, steamed, or added to soups, stews, or sauces.

Tofu: A traditional Asian soyfood made by first grinding and cooking soybeans to make soymilk, then coagulating the soymilk and pressing the curds into blocks. Available in soft, firm, and extra-firm varieties, its custardlike consistency and relatively bland flavor make tofu a very versatile high-protein food ready to be seasoned and baked, stir-fried, grilled, steamed, or added to soups. It is also frequently used to make sandwich spreads and dairy-free dips, dressings, desserts. and smoothies. When frozen and thawed, it has a somewhat meaty texture. A perishable product, tofu is typically found in grocery store dairy or produce sections, sold vacuum-packed or in water-packed plastic containers. Look for use-by dating and avoid any packages that appear bloated. Although some brands of tofu are pasteurized, for best flavor and food safety, tofu should be cooked at least briefly before it is eaten.

Tofu, silken: A type of tofu popular in traditional Japanese cuisine. It is much lighter, softer, and sweeter-tasting than regular tofu. It resembles a custard or thick cream and can be used to make smooth, creamy soups, shakes, dips, dressings, sauces, and desserts.

Beans, Peas, and Lentils Buying Guide

Fresh shell beans: A seasonal produce item, shell beans can be found the produce department or at farmers' markets. Varieties include black-eyed peas, cranberry beans, fava beans, garbanzos, and tongues of fire beans. Prepare and serve them as a tender vegetable. They don't require presoaking, and they cook quickly in boiling water, taking between 15 to 30 minutes depending on the bean and its size. Fresh beans can be stored in a plastic bag in the refrigerator for up to a week.

Dried beans: Virtually every grocery store sells a variety of packaged dry beans, and many sell them in bulk. Specialty grocers and online merchants are a good source for the more unique beans, including heirloom varieties. Select dried beans with smooth surfaces and bright colors. Although dried beans can, in theory, be stored for years, about a year after production they lose moisture and then must be cooked longer. Look for an expiration date on the package and use them within the suggested time frame. Store dry beans in an airtight container in a cool, dry place away from sunlight. Each pound of dry beans is equivalent to about 2½ cups uncooked beans or 5½ cups cooked beans.

Canned beans: It's hard to beat freshly cooked beans, but canned beans come in handy at times. You can use them to whip up a quick, nutritious meal, or give them a whir in the blender with a few other ingredients to make a quick dip for unexpected company. Before you buy, look at both the Nutrition Facts panel and the ingredients label to ensure the brand you choose contains only beans, water, and low amounts of sodium or no added salt. Drain and rinse canned beans before adding them to a recipe. They should be used by the freshness date on the container or within 1 year of purchase. A 15-ounce can is equivalent to approximately 1¾ cups cooked beans.

Reading the Label

Additives to Avoid in Precooked Canned Beans
- Disodium EDTA (color retention agent)
- High-fructose corn syrup
- Sugar

Bean Cooking and Food Safety Tips
- For seasoning, beans may be cooked with chopped onion, garlic, herbs, spices, or kombu.
- Don't add salt, tomatoes, wine, lemon juice, vinegar, or sugars until the end of cooking, as these ingredients can prevent the beans from becoming tender during cooking.
- Cooked beans, including canned beans once they're opened, can be stored up to 5 days in the refrigerator, or up to 6 months in the freezer.
- Kidney beans and lima beans, including their sprouted forms, must be boiled or cooked at boiling temperatures for at least 10 minutes to inactivate naturally occurring toxins that could otherwise cause symptoms similar to food poisoning.

Bean Cooking Guidelines

Boil and simmer: In a large covered pot, combine the beans with fresh water, using 4 cups of water for each cup of beans (less for lentils; see the cooking guidelines below). Bring the beans to a boil, then lower the heat to a simmer to help prevent their skins from bursting during cooking. It's okay if there isn't much water above the beans toward the end of the cooking time, but check periodically to make sure there's enough water to keep the bottom from scorching. The beans are done when they're tender.

Pressure cooker: With a pressure cooker, you can prepare beans in less than one-third the time it would take with the boil and simmer method. Because less water escapes as steam, you only need to add water to a depth of about 1 inch above the surface of the beans before securing the lid. Keep the total amount of beans and water to no more than two-thirds of the pressure cooker's capacity. To prevent the beans from splitting and losing their shape, after bringing the cooker to pressure, turn down the heat and keep the pressure at a low, even level. After the cooking is complete, let the pressure come down naturally.

Baking: Before baking beans, first boil them for 15 to 20 minutes in 4½ cups of water for each cup of beans. Then transfer the beans and their cooking water to a covered baking dish and bake at 350°F for about 3½ hours.

Slow cooker: While slow cookers are good for making soups or stews with beans, manufacturers of these appliances recommend using precooked or canned beans rather than starting with dry beans. If you want to use a slow cooker to cook dry beans, first boil the beans for at least 10 minutes before placing them in the slow cooker. Add water to cover the surface of the beans by about 1 inch, then cook on the high setting (approximately 212°F), until tender, anywhere from 5 to 8 hours.

Quick-Cooking Beans and Bean Products

Ready to Eat	15 to 30 Minutes	30 to 45 Minutes
Canned beans	Black beluga lentils	Lentils (green, brown, Spanish pardina): 45 minutes
Prepared tofu dips, spreads, and salads	Fresh shelled beans	
Seasoned, baked tofu	Red lentils	Pressure-cooking most dry beans if presoaked (including bringing to pressure, approximately 18 minutes of cooking, and letting the pressure come down naturally)
Seasoned tempeh burgers	Tempeh	
	Tofu	

Bean Varieties and Cooking Times at a Glance

Bean	Boil and Simmer	Pressure Cooker
Adzuki	1–1½ hours	15 minutes
Anasazi	1–1½ hours	18 minutes
Appaloosa	1½ hours	18 minutes
Black	1½ hours	15–18 minutes
Black calypso	1½–2 hours	18 minutes
Black-eyed peas	1–1¼ hours	16–18 minutes
Bolita	1½ hours	18 minutes
Cannellini	1½ hours	15–18 minutes
Christmas lima	1½ hours	18 minutes
Cranberry	1–1¼ hours	18 minutes
Fava, peeled and split	30–45 minutes	Not recommended
Fava, whole dried	1½–2 hours	Not recommended
Flageolets	2 hours	15 minutes
French navy	1 hour	15 minutes
Garbanzo, whole dried	3 hours	25–30 minutes
Gigande	2–3 hours	Not recommended
Great Northern	1½ hours	18 minutes
Jacob's cattle	1–1½ hours	15 minutes
Kidney*	1½ hours	18 minutes
Lentils, black beluga (2¼ cups water per cup of lentils)	25–30 minutes	Not recommended
Lentils, brown (2½–3 cups water per cup of lentils)	45–60 minutes	Not recommended

*It's especially important to cook kidney beans thoroughly, boiling them for at least 10 minutes to inactivate a natural toxin that can cause symptoms similar to food poisoning if they're undercooked.

Bean Varieties and Cooking Times at a Glance, *cont'd*

Bean	Boil and Simmer	Pressure Cooker
Lentils, French green (2½ cups water per cup of lentils)	40–45 minutes	Not recommended
Lentils, green (2½ cups water per cup of lentils)	40–45 minutes	Not recommended
Lentils, petite crimson (1¾–2 cups water per cup of lentils)	10–15 minutes	Not recommended
Lentils, petite golden (1¾–2 cups water per cup of lentils)	10–15 minutes	Not recommended
Lentils, Spanish pardina (2½ cups water per cup of lentils)	45–60 minutes	Not recommended
Lentils, split red (1¾ to 2 cups water per cup of lentils)	10–15 minutes	Not recommended
Lima, baby	1 hour	Not recommended
Lima, large	1½ hours	Not recommended
Madeira	1–1¼ hours	18 minutes
Marrow	1½–2 hours	25 minutes
Mung	1 hour	15 minutes
Navy	1½–2 hours	18 minutes
Peas, split	1–1¼ hours	Not recommended
Peas, whole	1–1½ hours	Not recommended
Pigeon peas	1 hour	16 minutes
Pink	1¼–1½ hours	18 minutes

Bean	Boil and Simmer	Pressure Cooker
Pinto	1½ hours	18 minutes
Rattlesnake	1½ hours	16–18 minutes
Red	1½ hours	18 minutes
Rice	1 hour	Not recommended
Scarlet runner	1½ hours	18 minutes
Soldier	1½ hours	18 minutes
Soybeans, black	3 hours	40 minutes
Soybeans, fresh (edamame)	Steam or boil 3–5 minutes	Not recommended
Soybeans, yellow or beige	3 hours	40 minutes
Spanish Tolosana	1½ hours	18 minutes
Steuben yellow-eye	1¼–1½ hours	18 minutes
Swedish brown	1½ hours	18 minutes
Tongues of fire	1½ hours	18 minutes
White emergo	1½ hours	18 minutes

Seven Ways to Aid Digestion of Beans

1. Soak dried beans and discard the soaking water prior to cooking.
2. Cook the beans until tender.
3. Choose beans and bean products that are easier to digest: Anasazi beans, adzuki beans, black-eyed peas, lentils, mung beans, tempeh, and tofu.
4. Eat smaller quantities of beans until your body adjusts.
5. Avoid eating beans cooked with sweeteners.
6. Cook beans with epazote, bay leaf, or cumin.
7. Use a commercial enzyme product containing alpha-galactosidase.

Tofu and Tempeh Selection Guide

Texture	Uses
Tempeh (tender and chewy)	Baked, stir-fried, grilled, pan-fried, broiled, braised, soups, stews. Use as entrée, in sandwiches or wraps, as meat substitute in sauces when crumbled, or serve with pastas or grains
Soft tofu	Nondairy substitute for soft cheeses, such as ricotta and cottage cheese
Firm tofu	Tofu salads, scrambled tofu, and baked recipes
Extra-firm tofu	Stir-fries, sautés, and baked and fried recipes
Silken tofu	Dips, sauces, soups, smoothies, salad dressings

Tofu Buying and Storage Tips

- Check the use-by dating on the package.
- Avoid buying packages of tofu that appear bloated, and never use tofu that has a sour odor or slimy texture—all indicators of spoiled tofu.
- Keep tofu refrigerated at all times. Any unused raw tofu can be kept up to 6 days if stored in water that's drained and replenished daily.
- For extra food safety assurance, tofu that will be used in dips and other no-cook recipes should be boiled for at least 5 minutes.
- Use cooked tofu within 6 days.

Nuts and Seeds

Botanically speaking, only a few of the foods we think of as nuts fit the technical definition of nuts: a dry indehiscent one-seeded fruit with a woody pericarp. Chestnuts, hazelnuts, and acorns are all true nuts. Other culinary nuts, such as almonds and pistachios, fall into the less-than-familiar category of drupes—a type of fruit with fleshy tissues surrounding a pit that holds a seed inside. Yet others are botanically defined as seeds, such as cashews and pine nuts. Of course, most of the foods we think of as seeds are indeed seeds, including sunflower seeds, sesame seeds, pumpkin seeds, and flaxseeds. And, as most of us know, the ubiquitous peanut is actually a legume and grows underground.

Their high protein content is one thing that sets nuts and seeds apart from most plant foods, but even more important is the healthful fats they contain, including heart-healthy monounsaturated fats and the essential fatty acids found in polyunsaturated fat, including linoleic acid (an omega-6 fatty acid) and alpha-linolenic acid (an omega-3 fatty acid). Collectively, these essential fatty acids help maintain the structure of cell membranes, particularly in nerve tissue and the retina, and promote healthy skin. They can also help regulate many vital systems within the body, including the inflammation response, immune function, blood pressure, and blood clotting.

Words and Terms to Know

Blanching: The process of removing the outer skin of nuts like almonds, hazelnuts, and peanuts. While it provides a milder flavor, smoother texture, and lighter color, blanching reduces fiber and significantly lowers the antioxidant value of the nut.

Nut milk: A nondairy milk substitute made by blending ground nuts with water for use as a beverage or in cooking.

Nut or seed butter: A spread made from ground raw or roasted nuts or seeds, with a texture and appearance similar to peanut butter. In general, 2 tablespoons of nut butter is the equivalent of 1 ounce of nuts. Avoid varieties with hydrogenated fats and refrigerate after opening.

Reading the Label

Nut and Nut Butter Additives to Avoid
- Added sugars
- Artificial color
- Artificial flavor
- Disodium guanylate (flavor enhancer)
- Disodium inosinate (flavor enhancer)
- Hydrogenated oil
- Monosodium glutamate (MSG; flavor enhancer)
- Sulfur dioxide (preservative, antioxidant, color retention agent)
- Tertiary butylhydroquinone (TBHQ; antioxidant, preservative)

Nut Butter Storage Tips
- Unopened: 12 months unrefrigerated in cool, dry conditions
- Opened: 2–3 months in the refrigerator

Nuts and Seeds Buying and Storage Guide

Unshelled nuts and seeds should be heavy for their size and free of cracks or holes. Shelled nuts and seeds should look firm and have uniform color inside and out. Avoid any that are shriveled, moldy, or discolored. Buy bulk nuts only from stores that sell them from clean containers in a cool area and rotate their stock frequently. Otherwise, buying packaged nuts may be a better alternative.

Nuts and Seeds at a Glance

Nut	Yield (per pound)	Storage	Protein (grams per oz.)
Almonds, shelled	3 cups	Fridge: 9 months; freezer: 12 months.	6
Brazil nuts	3¼ cups	Fridge: 6 months; freezer: 9 months.	4
Cashews	3¼ cups	Fridge: 6 months; freezer: 9 months.	5
Chestnuts, in shell	2½ cups shelled	Fridge: 3 weeks; freezer: 9 months.	1
Coconut, dried	5¾ cups	Fridge: 6 months; freezer: 6 months.	2
Flaxseeds	2¾ cups	Fridge: 12 months; freezer: 12 months.	5
Hazelnuts	3½ cups	Refrigerate 6 months; freezer: 12 months.	4
Macadamia nuts	3⅓ cups	Fridge: 6 months; freezer: 9 months.	2
Peanuts, in shell	2⅓ cups	Cool, dry place: 2 months; fridge: 9 months.	7

Nuts and Seeds at a Glance, *cont'd*

Nut	Yield (per pound)	Storage	Protein (grams per oz.)
Peanuts, shelled	3 cups	Fridge: 3 months; freezer: 6 months.	7
Pecans, in shell	2 cups	Cool, dry place: 4 months; fridge: 9 months.	2½
Pecans, shelled	4 cups	Fridge: 6 months; freezer: 12 months.	2½
Pine nuts	3 cups	Fridge: 1 month; freezer: 6 months.	4
Pistachios, in shell	3½ to 4 cups	Fridge: 6 months; freezer: 12 months.	6
Pistachios, shelled	2 cups	Fridge: 6 months; freezer: 12 months.	6
Pumpkin seeds, shelled	7 cups	Fridge: 6 months; freezer: 12 months.	7
Sesame seeds, with hull	3 cups	Fridge: 6 months; freezer: 12 months.	5
Sesame seeds, without hull	3½ cups	Fridge: 6 months; freezer: 12 months.	6
Sunflower seeds, shelled	3¼ cups	Fridge: 6 months; freezer: 12 months.	6½
Walnuts, black, in shell	2 cups	Fridge: 12 months; freezer: 12 months.	7
Walnuts, black, shelled	3½ cups	Fridge: 12 months; freezer: 12 months.	7
Walnuts, English, in shell	2 cups	Cool, dry place: 3 months; freezer: 12 months.	4
Walnuts, English, shelled	3½ cups	Fridge: 3 months; freezer: 12 months.	4

Culinary Oils

Just as juice is extracted from whole fruits and vegetables, culinary oils are extracted from nuts, seeds, and oil-rich plants. Olive oil is considered to be one of the first cooking oils, coming into use soon after olive trees were initially cultivated, around 5000 BCE. Although almond, walnut, and flaxseed oils were also produced thousands of years ago, they were most often used for lighting, heating, and medicinal purposes.

The predominant type of fat in a particular oil, whether saturated, mono-unsaturated, or polyunsaturated, is something you can actually easily discern with a glance, based on whether the oil liquid or solid at certain temperatures. While appreciation of the importance of oils and fats in the diet has waxed and waned, these days it's better understood that getting the right kind of fat in one's diet is important for optimum health and well-being. In addition to eating heart-healthy monounsaturated fats, it's critical to achieve a proper balance between omega-3 and omega-6 fatty acids, as this can also help reduce inflammation, as well as risk of heart disease and certain types of cancer.

Words and Terms to Know

Cold pressing: A nonchemical, mechanical process that extracts oil from the source material at temperatures below 122°F. Products labeled "cold-pressed" can be created using various methods—stone pressing, hydraulic pressing, or mechanical pressing—as long as temperatures remain below 122°F. Cold-pressed oils may be filtered naturally to remove any impurities. Extra-virgin and virgin olive oils are the most readily available cold-pressed oils. This process is also used for specialty oils used primarily for their nutritional benefits, such as flaxseed oil, borage oil, and wheat germ oil.

High-oleic oils: Pressed from plants developed through traditional breeding practices to significantly modify the fatty acid profile from being predominantly polyunsaturated to having a high percentage of oleic acid, a monounsaturated omega-9 fatty acid. In addition to being more heart-healthy, high-oleic oils are much more stable against oxidation and have a higher smoke point.

Hydrogenation: A process that artificially transforms liquid polyunsaturated oils into more solid fats, such as margarine and vegetable shortening. Manufacturers like hydrogenated fats because they're cheaper than butter, mimic the consistency and mouthfeel of saturated fats like butter and lard, and have an extended shelf life because they're resistant to oxidation and rancidity. However, these "benefits" are the result of the creation of trans fats, which have been linked to a long list of health problems.

Mechanical pressing: Also known as expeller pressing. This process removes oil by using continuously driven screws to crush the source material into a pulp from which the oil is extracted.

Monounsaturated fat: A form of fatty acids, often dubbed heart-healthy, that can reduce levels of LDL (bad) cholesterol while sparing HDL (good) cholesterol. Monounsaturated fats have a thick consistency when cold but are liquid at room temperatures. Their stability with regard to oxidation is midway between polyunsaturated and saturated fats.

Omega-3 fatty acids: A type of fatty acid found most abundantly in flax-seeds, pumpkin seeds, walnuts, soy oil, and canola oil, as well as many types of seafood. Omega-3s can help reduce the risk of heart disease, cancer, and inflammation within the body. The estimated adequate intake of omega-3 fatty

Culinary Oil Storage Guidelines

Constant refrigeration after opening is the best way to store oils to maintain optimum flavor and nutrition for longer periods of time.

Type	Room Temperature (40°F to 72°F)	Refrigerate
Coconut oil	Up to 2 years	Not required
Flaxseed oil	Always refrigerate	Until use-by date
Monounsaturated oils, refined	Up to 2 months	14–20 months
Monounsaturated oils, unrefined	Up to 2 months	10–14 months
Palm oil	Up to 2 years	Not required
Polyunsaturated oils, refined	Always refrigerate	14–20 months
Polyunsaturated oils, unrefined	Always refrigerate	10–14 months

acids is 1.6 grams per day for men and 1.1 grams per day for women.

Polyunsaturated fat: A type of fat consisting of omega-3 and omega-6 fatty acids, both vital for regulating organ systems within the body. A proper balance between these fatty acids is important for optimum health. Modern diets are generally too high in vegetable oils with high amounts of omega-6s, including corn, cottonseed, safflower, sunflower, and peanut oils, and products made with them. Such an imbalance has been linked to heart attacks, stroke, cancer, arthritis, asthma, and even menstrual cramps and headaches. Polyunsaturated fats are liquid in consistency whether cold or at room temperature. They are also the least stable type of fat, being more vulnerable to oxidation and rancidity, so oils and foods high in polyunsaturated fats must be stored and used appropriately.

Refined: Processed to remove components within the oil to make it more neutral in flavor, less cloudy, and less prone to oxidation (and thus more suitable for high-heat cooking). While many nutrients are removed during refining, the essential fatty acids remain.

Saturated fat: A form of fatty acids generally known to raise LDL (bad) cholesterol. High intake of saturated fats has been linked to increased risk of cardiovascular disease, obesity, and cancers of the colon, prostate, and breast. However, some saturated fats, in particular, lauric, myristic, and palmitic acids, are less problematic. Lauric acid, found in coconut, increases HDL (good) cholesterol even more than it raises LDL (bad) cholesterol. Both myristic and palmitic acid have an overall neutral effect on total cholesterol. Saturated fats are solid when cold and fairly solid at room temperature and are the most stable of all fats, being most resistant to oxidation.

Smoke point: The maximum temperature a fat or oil can be heated to before it starts to smoke, burn, discolor, and become bitter in flavor—all indications that the oil is being damaged by heat. The highly reactive molecules created within the oil as a result are unhealthful, contributing to damage and destruction of cells.

Stone pressing: The traditional method of extracting oil from olives and some seeds, still sometimes used to produce olive oil. Stone pressing generates little heat and protects the olives' natural antioxidants, which help preserve the integrity of the oil.

Trans fat: A type of fatty acid formed in the process of hydrogenation, creating an unnatural molecular structure that's difficult for the body to metabolize. Trans fats have been linked to obesity, infertility, increased risk of cancer and heart disease, and accelerated aging and degenerative changes in tissues.

Unrefined: Minimally processed to retain much of the flavor, aroma, color, and nutrients found in the source material. Since unrefined oils are more sensitive to heat and light, they should never be used for high-heat cooking, and many are suitable only for low- or no-heat applications. Unrefined specialty oils with very low smoke points are best used as a condiment for drizzling on foods.

Virgin olive oil: Olive oil obtained exclusively by mechanical or stone pressing without the use of solvents. Free acidity, or the percentage of free fatty acids, is a rough indication of the quality of the olives and how carefully they were handled from picking through processing. The lower the free acidity, the better overall quality, flavor, and aroma of the oil. Virgin olive oil may have up to 2% free acidity. In contrast, extra-virgin olive oil must contain no more than 0.8% free acidity, with the best versions having as little as 0.1% free acidity.

Culinary Oils at a Glance

Primary fatty acids have been abbreviated as:
M=monounsaturated, S=saturated, P=polyunsaturated.

Uses	Oil Type	Primary Fatty Acids	Smoke Point
High heat: suitable for all purposes, especially frying, stir-frying, high-temperature baking, and other high-heat applications	Avocado (refined)	M	510°F
	Almond (refined)	M	495°F
	Apricot kernel (refined)	M	495°F
	Canola (super high-heat)	M	460°F
	Safflower (very high-oleic)	M	460°F
	Sunflower (high-oleic)	M	460°F
	Corn (refined)	M	450°F
	Palm fruit (refined)	S/M	450°F
	Peanut (refined)	M	450°F
	Soy oil (refined)	P	450°F
	Safflower (high-oleic, refined)	M	445°F
	Sesame (refined)	P/M	445°F
	Hazelnut (refined)	M	430°F
Medium-high heat: sautéing and baking	Canola (refined)	M	425°F
	Grapeseed (refined)	M	425°F
	Walnut (refined)	S	400°F
	Safflower (high-oleic, unrefined)	P	390°F
	Coconut (refined)	P/M	365°F
	Soy (semirefined)	M	360°F

Culinary Oils at a Glance, *cont'd*

Primary fatty acids have been abbreviated as:
M=monounsaturated, S=saturated, P=polyunsaturated.

Uses	Oil Type	Primary Fatty Acids	Smoke Point
Low to medium heat: sautéing and baking at lower, more moderate heat	Peanut (unrefined)	M	350°F
	Sesame (unrefined)	P/M	350°F
	Sesame, toasted (unrefined)	P/M	350°F
	Olive (unrefined)	M	325°F
	Corn (unrefined)	P	320°F
	Soy (unrefined)	P	320°F
	Coconut (unrefined)	P	280°F
No heat: use as condiment or seasoning after cooking, drizzle on bread, or use in salad dressings	Almond (unrefined)	M	225°F
	Flaxseed (unrefined)	M	225°F
	Hazelnut (unrefined)	M	225°F
	Pumpkin seed (unrefined)	M	225°F
	Safflower (unrefined)	M	225°F
	Sunflower (unrefined)	M	225°F
	Walnut (unrefined)	M	225°F

Meat and Poultry

The term "mutualistic" best describes how we should view our connec-tion with farm animals. At its core, this is a specific type of symbiotic relationship in which two very different species reciprocally benefit from their interaction and affiliation with one another. In this case, the mutualistic relationship is between humans and animals raised specifically for their meat or eggs (or dairy products, covered in the next chapter). The farmer's or rancher's commitment is to provide the animals as good a quality of life as possible for the duration of their lives. In turn, consumers who buy meat and eggs raised in this way increase the demand for such products and, therefore, the likelihood that animals will be raised in a more compassionate manner. Because these products have undeniably better flavor and enhanced nutrition as extra incentives, it's a win-win situation for animals and humans alike.

Words and Terms to Know

Bison: The proper name for the American buffalo, which is actually a member of the bovine family and thus related to beef cattle, to differentiate it from the Asian water buffalo and African Cape buffalo, which are both true buffalo.
Conjugated linoleic acid (CLA): A collective term for a variety of very

specific forms of linoleic acid (an essential fatty acid). CLA has positive health benefits similar to but more potent than omega-3 fatty acids, including helping to reduce or inhibit the effects of carcinogens. Meat from grass-fed ruminants, including cattle, sheep, bison, goats, deer, and elk, is high in CLA due to the high proportion of linoleic acid in pasture grasses.

Cured: Refers to meats such as ham, bacon, luncheon meats, and some sausages, which are typically made with sodium nitrate, a synthetic quick-curing agent, in order to maintain their pink or red colors, enhance flavor, and help protect against bacterial growth. U.S. regulations require the addition of sodium ascorbate, a compound closely related to ascorbic acid (vitamin C) to help block the formation of nitrosamines, potent carcinogenic compounds, when cured meat is heated at high temperatures.

Dry-aged beef: Stored for 10 to 28 days at temperatures between 34°F and 36°F and at 85% humidity, a process that allows the beef's natural enzymes to further tenderize the meat by breaking down the connective tissues in the muscle. The evaporation of moisture concentrates the flavors of the meat, making dry-aged beef highly revered, as well as expensive. It is usually found at specialty butchers or gourmet-oriented groceries. In contrast, most beef sold in grocery stores is wet-aged in vacuum-sealed bags for just a couple of days, so it's less tender than dry-aged beef.

Free-range poultry: A labeling term that ideally should designate products from poultry raised with free access to outdoor areas with plenty of vegetation for forage. In the absence of a U.S. Department of Agriculture definition for "free-range," look for information that describes what the retailer or producer means by the term. Beef, sheep, bison, pork, goat, deer, and elk raised primarily on pasture will usually be described as "grass-fed."

Fresh poultry: Whole poultry and cuts that have never been subjected to temperatures below 26°F. While some ice may occasionally be evident on the skin, the poultry is never fully frozen.

Game: A general classification that can include deer, bison, elk, rabbit, pheasant, duck, goose, guinea fowl, quail, and squab. Game meats sold in U.S. supermarkets must be farm raised rather than taken from the wild. Game meats can be raised in any number of ways, from outdoor habitats to confinement in small areas. Added growth hormones are not allowed, but depending on the producer, the animals may receive antibiotics. Flavor, texture, and nutritional value will vary according to how the animal was raised. Game birds can be cooked like their poultry counterparts, while venison and bison meat are best cooked similar to grass-fed beef.

Grass-fed: A labeling term that designates that the ruminant animal consumed only grass and forage during its lifetime, with the exception of milk consumed prior to weaning. Grass-fed animals cannot be fed grain or grain by-products and must have continuous access to pasture during the growing season. Grass-fed meat is leaner and has a stronger and more gamey flavor than meat from grain-fed animals. It varies in texture depending on climate conditions, the varieties of grass and other forage consumed, and the skill of the producer. Special cooking techniques for grass-fed meat will help tenderize it and keep it moist.

Heritage meat: A term used to describe meat from classic breeds of livestock that had commercial viability in the past, with genetics that typically better supported the animal's natural behaviors within a particular climate and area. Examples include Bourbon Red turkeys, Standard American Bronze turkeys, Berkshire pigs, and Gloucestershire Old Spots pigs. Because they haven't been bred to conform to systems of raising animals that are focused on confinement and efficiency, these animals are, for the most part, raised on farms or ranches that allow them to graze and roam on pasture. Heritage breeds may differ from modern breeds in size and conformation (for example, having less breast meat); in addition, the flavor of their meat may be more gamey and its texture somewhat tougher. Use game meat preparation tips for cooking heritage meat.

Irradiation: An FDA-approved method for reducing pathogens such as E. coli and salmonella in fresh and frozen red meat and poultry by exposing it to a particular dose of gamma rays. Irradiation does not make the meat safe to eat raw, nor does it replace safe handling practices, including safe internal cooking temperatures. Irradiated meat can still become contaminated from bacteria after it goes through the irradiation treatment. Federal law requires irradiated foods to be labeled with the statement "treated with irradiation" or "treated by irradiation," along with the international symbol for irradiation—a symbol with a flower within a glowing circle.

Natural: Meat that is minimally processed and free of artificial additives, such as preservatives, artificial colors, and artificial flavors. When used to describe meat, it only applies to meat that has been processed, such as sausages. Natural is not a term that should be used to describe raw meat.

Organic: Meat independently certified as being from animals fed a diet of organically raised foods that aren't genetically engineered. U.S. organic regulations prohibit the use of added hormones and antibiotics; several other countries limit the ban to subtherapeutic antibiotics. To be certified organic, the animals must also have some access to pasture or an outdoor environment. Look for meat from producers that use pasture and foraging areas as the foundation of their production systems rather than an adjunct.

Uncured: Similar to cured meat, but made without synthetic nitrates. Such products are usually smoked, salted, or made with ingredients like celery juice, which impart trace amounts of naturally occurring sodium nitrate. As they require different storage and handling than cured meats, uncured "nonitrate" meat products are usually found in the frozen meat section of grocery stores, or they may be sold thawed in the meat department, in which case they must be sold within a limited time frame.

Tips for Buying Meat with Compassion

- Look for multitiered labeling systems that clearly describe the specific animal welfare measures the producer has used when raising the animal on the farm, during transportation, and throughout final processing.
- Avoid foie gras, the goose liver product that results from force-feeding geese, usually by inserting a tube or funnel down their throats, resulting in a fatty liver enlarged to many times the normal size. Considered a delicacy by some people, the product has been banned by many restaurants, retailers, and towns within the United States due to the inhumane production practices involved. Replace foie gras with pâtés made from other meats or vegetables.
- Be extra vigilant when buying veal. Look for veal raised on pasture or, at the very least, in a group setting with other calves, where they have free access to grain in addition to milk replacement.

Meat and Poultry Buying Guide

Type	Examples	Amount per Person
Boneless cuts	Ground meat, boned roasts and steaks, stew meat, sausage	¼ lb.
	Boneless turkey breast or turkey roast	⅓–½ lb.
Meat with some bone	Rib roasts, unboned steaks, chops	⅓ lb.
	Chicken breast	½ breast
	Chicken, broiler/fryer	¾–1 lb.
	Chicken, roaster	½ lb.
	Chicken drumsticks	2
	Chicken leg quarter	1
	Chicken thighs	2
	Chicken wings	4
	Turkey, fryer/roaster	¾–1 lb.
	Turkey, hen/tom	½–¾ lb.
	Turkey thigh	½–¾ lb.
	Duck/goose	1 lb.
Bony cuts	Ribs, shanks	¾–1 lb.

Meat and Poultry Voluntary Grading for Quality

Grade	Characteristics
Prime (beef, lamb)	Most marbled with fat, tender texture, very flavorful
Choice	Less marbled with fat, tender texture, flavorful
Select	Least marbled with fat, fair tenderness, less flavorful

Meat and Poultry Food Safety Tips

- Keep meat refrigerated. Be sure the time between purchase and home refrigeration is minimal. During hot weather, transport meat from the store or to picnics in an ice chest.
- Prevent cross-contamination. Thoroughly wash your hands, kitchen countertop, utensils, dishes, and cutting boards with soap and hot water before and after contact with raw meat.
- Always marinate meat in the refrigerator. Don't reuse the marinade as a sauce unless it is first brought to a rolling boil.
- Stuff poultry immediately before roasting, not ahead of time, to prevent bacteria from the raw poultry juices inside the cavity from growing within the stuffing. After cooking, remove the stuffing and serve or refrigerate separately.
- Do not allow cooked meat to stand at room temperature for more than 2 hours after cooking, or 1 hour at warm room temperatures. Bacteria thrive at temperatures between 40°F and 140°F, so keep meat either below 40°F or above 140°F, depending on whether the dish is intended to be served hot or cold.

Tips for Cooking Grass-Fed Beef, Venison, and Bison

Grass-fed meat is lower in fat than meat from grain-fed animals. A couple of key cooking hints will help enhance tenderness and its delicious, full flavor:

- Keep cooking temperatures low and don't overcook.
- Use cooking methods that retain moisture and/or add extra liquid.
- Sear before roasting, then cover with a lid or foil while cooking.
- Cook in a slow cooker.
- Braise, stew, or cook in a sauce.
- Marinate before cooking or baste during cooking.

Tips for Cooking Poultry
- Cook game birds as you would other types of poultry.
- Cook poultry with the skin on rather than removing the skin prior to cooking. This will result in more moist and tender meat and still reduce the fat content by about half—leaving not much more than if you removed the skin before cooking.

Buying Hamburger or Ground Beef

Both hamburger and ground beef can be ground from a variety of cuts or from a single beef primal, the area of the cow from which it originates, such as ground chuck, ground sirloin, or ground round. Products labeled as hamburger can contain added fat trimmings from sources other than the primal sources. Added water, phosphates, binders, or extenders are not allowed in meat sold as ground beef or hamburger.

In the United States, the maximum fat content allowed for any meat to be labeled as ground beef or hamburger is 30% (70% lean). Ground beef is typically labeled by its lean-to-fat ratio:
- Extra lean ground beef is labeled as 95% or more lean to 5% fat or less fat by weight.
- Lean ground beef is labeled as 91% or more lean to 9% or less fat by weight.
- Ground round is made from the rear upper leg area of the cow. It's typically 90% lean and 10% fat.
- Ground sirloin is made from the upper hip of the cow. It's typically 85% lean and 15% fat.
- Ground chuck is made from the shoulder area of the cow. It's typically about 80% lean and 20% fat and considered the best choice for making hamburgers although it's quite high in fat.

Raw Meat and Poultry Storage Guidelines

Beef/lamb/pork	Refrigerator (40°F)	Freezer (0°F or lower)
Bacon	7 days	1 month
Chops	3–5 days	4–6 months
Ground	1–2 days	3–4 months
Roasts	3–5 days	4–12 months
Sausage	1–2 days	1–2 months
Steaks	3–5 days	6–12 months
Poultry	Refrigerator (40°F)	Freezer (0°F or lower)
Chicken giblets	1–2 days	3–4 months
Chicken pieces (legs, breasts, etc.)	1–2 days	9 months
Chicken, whole	1–2 days	12 months
Duck, whole	1–2 days	6 months
Goose, whole	1–2 days	6 months
Turkey, pieces (legs, breast, etc.)	1–2 days	6 months
Turkey, whole	1–2 days	12 months

Safe Minimum Internal Cooking Temperatures for Meat and Poultry

Variety	Temperature
Beef, veal, and lamb—steaks, roasts, and chops	145°F (medium-rare; 160°F is medium, and 170°F is well-done)
Ground beef, bison, and lamb*	160°F
Pork, all cuts	160°F
Chicken, whole and parts	165°F

Variety	Temperature
Ground poultry	165°F
Hot dogs and luncheon and deli meats, reheated**	165°F

*Thorough cooking to an internal temperature of 160°F throughout kills E. coli 0157:H7, a virulent and dangerous strain of E. coli that can cause bloody diarrhea in humans and sometimes kidney failure.

**Reheat to destroy any potential *Listeria monocytogenes*, a dangerous bacteria that can grow at refrigerated temperatures.

Cooked Meat and Poultry Storage Guidelines

Variety	Refrigerator (40°F)	Freezer (0°F or lower)
Beef/lamb/pork	3–4 days	2–6 months
Poultry*	3–4 days	4 months
Poultry in gravy/broth*	1–2 days	4 months
Poultry gravy/broth	1–2 days	2–3 months
Ham, fully cooked, whole	7 days	1–2 months
Ham, fully, cooked, sliced	3–4 days	1–2 months
Hot dogs/frankfurters	5–7 days	1–2 months
Luncheon meat	3–5 days	1–2 months
Sausage, fresh, cooked	3–4 days	1–2 months
Sausage, smoked/cooked	5–7 days	1–2 months
Sausage, hard/dry/semidry	21 days	1–2 months

*Remove stuffing from cooked poultry. Refrigerate or freeze the meat and stuffing separately.

Eggs

Eggs are an inexpensive, quick-cooking protein source that is equally versatile as a cooking or baking aid. The best-tasting eggs are from hens raised under conditions that respect their natural behaviors, allowing them to forage extensively outside on natural grasses and insects as well as have free access to protective housing, clean litter, good air quality, and plenty of room to roam.

Words and Terms to Know

Cage-free: Eggs produced by hens that aren't confined to the cramped and crowded wire cages typically used in conventional egg production. Instead, they are allowed to move freely within a chicken house or, better yet, allowed to scratch and peck within a natural outdoor habitat where they can experience direct sunlight and explore their natural environment.

Fertile: Eggs produced by hens who have mated with a rooster and are, therefore, raised in cage-free conditions. The eggs are chilled to a cold temperature shortly after they are laid, which prevents them from developing into chicks.

Omega-3 eggs: Eggs from hens fed a diet supplemented with flaxseeds to enhance the amount of alpha-linolenic acid, an essential omega-3 fatty acid that can help reduce the risk of heart disease, cancer, and inflammation. Hens that are allowed to graze on natural grasses and forage will produce eggs that naturally contain more omega-3 fatty acids than those from hens confined to poultry houses or crowded wire cages.

Pasteurized eggs: Eggs in their shells, liquid eggs, and freeze-dried egg products rapidly heated and held at temperatures high enough to destroy dangerous salmonella bacteria, but low enough to not cook the eggs, coagulate their proteins, or affect color, flavor, nutritional value, or future use. Powdered dried egg whites are also pasteurized due to the process used to make them.

Quality Grading: A voluntary measurement of the interior characteristics of the egg and the condition of the eggshell. Egg packers who want to use the USDA grade shield on their cartons must pay for monitoring services by a USDA grader. Cartons displaying a grade but without the USDA shield indicate monitoring by state agencies.

Ungraded: Eggs packed and self-evaluated by the farmer. They may show characteristics similar to Grade AA or Grade A, depending on the skill and reputation of the producer.

Egg Safety Tips

- Keep fresh eggs in the original carton on the shelf in your refrigerator rather than in special egg compartments found in some refrigerator doors, and use by the sell-by date on the carton.
- Don't wash eggs before storing. A natural protective coating is put on the outside of the egg by the hen after it is laid. All eggs that are USDA graded are washed and sanitized with a special detergent and then coated with mineral oil to reestablish a protective coating.
- Never use cracked or leaking eggs.
- Keep raw and cooked eggs refrigerated at temperatures below 40°F.
- Avoid beverages and foods made with raw, unpasteurized eggs that do not undergo further cooking.
- Refrigerate cooked eggs and egg dishes quickly. Never consume eggs and egg dishes left unrefrigerated for more than 2 hours.
- Cook eggs thoroughly until the white and yolk are firm or egg mixtures

are cooked to 160°F to reduce potential salmonella bacteria than can cause food-borne illness.

Brown vs. White Eggs

The color of the eggshell indicates only that a certain variety of hen laid the egg. Brown and white eggs are equal nutritionally.

Egg Quality and Selection Guide

Egg Quality Grade	Characteristics	Best For
Grade AA (qualities found when less than 10 days old)	Firmly centered yolk; clear, firm, thick white; high overall height; clean, unbroken shell, and practically free from defects.	Poaching, frying, and making soufflés, meringues, and custards.
Grade A (qualities found when up to 30 days old)	Moderately firm yolk; moderately firm white; lower overall height; spreads more readily; clean, unbroken shell; practically free from defects.	Frying, boiling, scrambling, and in general cooking and baking.
Ungraded	May be equivalent to Grade AA or Grade A. Look for clean, unbroken shells and use-by dating.	Depends on quality of the egg.

Egg Sizing

Egg sizing is based on the minimum weight per dozen—*not* the dimensions of the eggs. Most recipes are based on the assumption large eggs will be used. The Egg Size Substitution Guide below provides guidelines for using different sizes.

Egg Size Comparison

Size	Minimum Weight per Dozen
Jumbo	30 ounces
Extra large	27 ounces
Large	24 ounces
Medium	21 ounces
Small	15 ounces

Egg Size Substitution Guide

Large	Jumbo	Extra-Large	Medium	Small
1 egg	1	1	1	1
2 eggs	2	2	2	3
3 eggs	2	3	3	4
4 eggs	3	4	5	5
5 eggs	4	4	6	7
6 eggs	5	5	7	8

Egg and Egg Product Storage Guidelines

Type	Refrigerator (40°F)	Freezer (0°F or lower)
Fresh, whole in shell	3–5 weeks	Do not freeze
Egg yolks	2–4 days	Do not freeze
Egg whites	2–4 days	12 months

Egg and Egg Product Storage Guidelines cont'd

Type	Refrigerator (40°F)	Freezer (0°F or lower)
Hard-cooked eggs*	5–7 days	Do not freeze
Liquid pasteurized eggs, opened	3 days	Do not freeze
Egg substitutes, frozen	3 days after thawing	12 months or until use-by date
Casseroles made with eggs	3–4 days	2–3 months (after baking)
Pies (pumpkin/pecan)	3–4 days	1–2 months (after baking)
Pies (custard/chiffon)	3–4 days	Do not freeze
Quiche	3–4 days	1–2 months (after baking)
Eggnog, commercial	3–5 days	6 months
Eggnog, homemade	2–4 days	Do not freeze

*Note: Eggs that are more than 2 weeks old are best for hard-boiling since they peel more easily.

Egg Cooking Guidelines

Method	Cooking Time
Boiled	7 minutes in boiling water
Fried	2 to 3 minutes on both sides or 4 minutes in a covered pan
Poached	5 minutes in boiling water
Scrambled	Cooked until firm throughout
Meringue-topped pies	15 minutes baked at 350°F
Casseroles containing eggs	Internal temperature at 160°F
Quiche	Internal temperature at 160°F

Dairy Products

Distinctions in taste, consistency, and nutrition among the wide variety of dairy products often come down to the source—the milk from which they were produced and, of course, the animals that supply it. While cow's milk may be the most familiar, whether in the form of milk, cultured dairy products, or cheese, products that use milk from other animals, including goats, sheep, and water buffalo, are also available. In contrast to cow's milk, in which the fat naturally separates out when the unprocessed milk is allowed to set, milk from these other animals contains smaller fat globules, so the fat tends to remain in suspension.

Words and Terms to Know

Acidophilus: Specifically, *Lactobacillus acidophilus*, one of several types of lactic acid bacteria often dubbed friendly bacteria. Friendly bacteria are essential to proper functioning of the immune and digestive systems and help ensure proper digestion and absorption of food and nutrients. Look for the term "live culture"; the live bacteria count in a good-quality yogurt can be in the billions per teaspoon.

Artisanal cheeses: Produced on a small scale, providing more opportunity to produce distinctive, seasonal cheeses that reflect the breed of animal from which the milk is obtained, the plants foraged upon, and the character, passion, and skill of the producer. Enhanced attention to detail means more opportunity to age and ripen cheeses to their full potential, allowing for just the right humidity, temperature, and amount of time to develop the complexity of flavor and aroma to extraordinary levels. Some of these artisans use milk from animals they raise on their own farms, creating cheeses referred to as farmstead or farmhouse cheese.

Bovine somatotropin: Also known as rBGH (recombinant bovine growth hormone) or rBST (recombinant bovine somatotropin). This genetically engineered bovine growth hormone is injected into cows every fourteen days to increase milk production by about 10%. However, cows administered rBST may have reduced pregnancy rates, increased risk for mastitis, enlarged hocks, and disorders of the foot region. To avoid buying milk with rBST, look for organic milk or products stating that no rBST has been administered to the cows. Unfortunately, to avoid being sued by the developer of the drug, all rBST-free claims on labels must include the following accompanying statement: "No significant difference has been shown between milk derived from rBST-treated and non-rBST-treated cows."

Chymosin: Also called recombinant rennet. Not directly from an animal source, this type of rennet is made through a cloning process in which the calf chymosin gene is transferred into a microorganism, which then produces chymosin. Rennet produced in this way functions nearly identically to animal rennet, and unlike microbial enzymes, it can be used to make Cheddar and other hard cheeses. A high percentage of cheeses, especially those made in the United States, Ireland, and Great Britain, are now made with genetically engineered chymosin.

Cultured: A fermentation process initiated by lactic acid–producing bacteria that break down the lactose in milk, resulting in a more flavorful, slightly tart, food. "Friendly bacteria" that are essential to proper functioning of the immune and digestive systems are also introduced during the culturing process.

Homogenization: A process that distributes fat particles evenly throughout milk so the cream doesn't separate. Homogenization is accomplished by spraying milk at high pressure through a small nozzle onto a hard surface to break the fat down into very small particles.

Lactose intolerance: A condition caused by a deficiency in lactase, an enzyme produced in the small intestine that's responsible for digesting lactose (the natural sugar found in milk). Symptoms of lactose intolerance are usually experienced soon after consuming dairy products and include bloating, cramps, flatulence, and nausea.

Microbial enzymes: A term that may be found on cheese labels indicating that, instead of rennet, the enzyme used to make the cheese is derived from microorganisms via a controlled fermentation process. There are debates about whether cheese made with microbial enzymes can match the flavor and aroma of a rennet-based cheese, but their biggest drawback is that they cannot be used to make Cheddar and other hard cheeses.

Pasteurization: A heating process that destroys bacteria that contribute to spoilage or are pathogenic, ensuring the safety of milk within a specified time period. Regulations for pasteurization require that milk be heated to a minimum of 161°F for at least fifteen seconds to kill yeasts, molds, pathogenic microorganisms, and most of the less harmful strains of bacteria. Also called the high-temperature, short-time method (HTST), basic pasteurization provides an extended shelf life of up to twenty days.

Raw milk cheese: Refers to cheese made from unpasteurized milk. This is considered to have a positive effect on the flavor, texture, and overall character of the cheese. U.S. regulations require that cheese made with raw milk, whether imported or domestically produced, must be aged for a minimum of 60 days prior to sale at temperatures not greater than 35°F to ensure food safety and quality.

Rennet: A preparation made from an enzyme extracted from the membrane lining the fourth stomach of a bovine calf. Rennet is used to separate the curds from the whey when making cheese. A hallmark of cheese made with rennet is its firm, dense texture.

Ultra-pasteurization: A method for pasteurizing milk that uses a higher temperature and a shorter time frame. The milk is heated to a minimum of 280°F for at least 2 seconds, although usually for about 5 seconds. Ultra-pasteurization (UP) eliminates more bacteria and microorganisms than regular pasteurization, extending shelf life to 60 to 90 days.

Dairy Products Buying and Storage Guide

Although this chart offers some guidelines on how long various dairy products will keep in the refrigerator, always check the use-by date—even before purchasing.

Type	Storage	Yield
1 lb. butter	Fridge: 1–3 months; freezer: 6–9 months	2 cups
1 lb. cheese, hard	Fridge: 6 months unopened, 3–4 weeks opened; freezer: 6 months, but not recommended	4 cups grated
1 lb. cheese, semifirm	Fridge: 6 weeks sealed and unopened, 3 days opened or freshly grated; freezer: 6 months	5 cups grated
1 lb. cheese, semi-soft	Fridge: 7 days; freezer: 6 months	5 cups shredded
8 oz. cottage cheese	Fridge:1 week; doesn't freeze well	1 cup
8 oz. cream cheese	Fridge: 2 weeks; doesn't freeze well	1 cup
1 lb. ricotta cheese	Fridge: 7 days; doesn't freeze well	2⅛ cups
1 quart fresh milk	Fridge: 7 days; freezer: 3 months	4 cups
1 quart fresh butter-milk	Fridge: 7–14 days; freezer: 3 months	4 cups
1 pint half-and-half	Fridge: 3–4 days; freezer: 4 months	2 cups
½ pint fresh cream	Fridge: 1–4 days; freezer: 4 months	1 cup

Type	Storage	Yield
½ pint ultra-pasteurized cream	Fridge: 2–4 weeks; freezer: 4 months	1 cup
½ pint whipping cream	Fridge: 4 weeks; doesn't freeze well	1 cup un-whipped
½ pint sour cream	Fridge: 1–3 weeks; doesn't freeze well	1 cup
1 quart yogurt	Fridge: 1–2 weeks opened, check use-by dating if un-opened; freezer: 1–2 months	4 cups
1 to 1⅓ cups dry milk	Cool, dry area: 3 months; freezer: 6 months	1 quart reconsti-tuted

Exploring Cheese Varieties

FRESH CHEESE

These high-moisture cheeses are unripened, don't have a rind, and are mild, with a milky flavor.

Varieties included: Chèvre, Cottage Cheese, Cream Cheese, Crème Fraîche, Feta, Fromage Blanc, Kefir Cheese, Mascarpone, Mozzarella, Neufchâtel, Ricotta, Skyr, Yogurt Cheese.

Length of aging: A few days to a few months.

How to store: Keep in the container in which it is purchased and use before the use-by date. Toss if mold develops.

SOFT-RIPENED OR BLOOMY RIND

These high-moisture cheeses with a buttery, rich flavor are surface ripened after being exposed to specific strains of mold that are resident in the ripening room or sprayed on. They're developed under humid conditions, creating the characteristic soft, white, fuzzy or bloomy rind.

Varieties included: Brie, Brillat-Savarin, Camembert, Explorateur, Humboldt Fog, Mt. Tam, Pierre Robert, Saint-André.

Length of aging: Up to 12 weeks.

How to store: Loosely wrap in waxed paper or parchment paper, then light plastic wrap to retain moisture.

SOFT, WASHED RIND

These high-moisture cheeses ripen from the outside in, and the exterior of the cheese is rubbed or washed regularly with a solution of brine, wine, beer, cider, or marc (grape brandy), resulting in a distinctive orange rind and strong, complex flavor.

Varieties included: Chaumes, Chimay, Époisses, Limburger, Livarot, Mont St. Francis, Morbier, Munster (French), Reblochon, Red Hawk, Saint-Nectaire, Taleggio.

Length of aging: Up to 12 weeks.

How to store: Loosely wrap in waxed paper or parchment paper, then light plastic wrap to retain moisture.

BLUE-VEINED

These soft or semisoft cheeses are pierced and inoculated with a type of mold from the genus *Penicillium* during the ripening process, resulting in a bluish-green mold that grows throughout the cheese.

Varieties included: Bleu d'Auvergne, Blue Castello, Buttermilk Blue, Danish Blue, Fourme d'Ambert, Gorgonzola, Maytag Blue, Roquefort, Saga, Shropshire Blue, Stilton, Valdeón.

Length of aging: 4 weeks to 14 months.

How to store: Loosely wrap in waxed or parchment, then light plastic wrap to retain moisture.

SEMISOFT

These cheeses ripen from the inside out and are usually supple to the touch and mild in flavor.

Varieties included: Asiago, Bel Paese, Colby, Edam, Fontina, Gouda, Havarti, Kasseri, Monterey Jack, Muenster (U.S.), Provolone (plain or smoked), Pyrenees, Swiss (baby).

Length of aging: 3 to 12 months.

How to store: Wrap in waxed or parchment paper, then put in a plastic bag, leaving it unsealed, or loosely wrap in plastic to help retain moisture. If mold develops, trim away at least 1 inch around the mold.

SEMIFIRM
These cheeses are ripened from the inside out. Their nutty or fruity flavors develop more complexity with increased aging.
Varieties included: Cheddar, Cheshire, Comté, Double Gloucester, Emmental (French and Swiss), Gruyère, Jarlsberg, Manchego, Pleasant Ridge Reserve.
Length of aging: 3 to 24 months
How to store: Wrap in waxed or parchment paper, folding to seal the edges. If the cheese begins to dry out, loosely cover the paper-wrapped cheese with plastic. If mold develops, trim away at least 1 inch around the mold.

FIRM AND AGED
These dry, low-moisture cheese are ripened from the inside out and have complex flavors with sweet overtones.
Varieties included: Aged Asiago, Aged Gouda, Aged Manchego, Aged Provolone, Grana Padano, Parmesan, Parmigiano-Reggiano, Pecorino Romano, Vella Dry Jack.
Length of aging: 6 months and longer.
How to store: Wrap in plastic or unwaxed parchment paper, leaving the rind exposed to allow it to breathe. If mold develops, trim away at least 1 inch around the mold.

Cultured Dairy Products Guide

Cultured dairy products are flavorful and slightly tart. They contribute beneficial bacteria essential to proper functioning of the immune and digestive systems and help ensure proper digestion and absorption of food and nutrients.
Buttermilk: Traditionally, buttermilk was the watery component extracted during the churning process of making butter. These days, buttermilk's distinctive, tangy flavor is now obtained commercially by incubating skim or low-fat milk with tartar cultures for 12 to 14 hours. Unlike the friendly

bacteria in yogurt, those used to culture buttermilk don't digest lactose during the fermentation process. Despite its name and thick, rich consistency, buttermilk is low in fat.

Crème fraîche: This thick and rich French-style cultured whole cream has a delicious natural flavor blend of tart, sweet, and nutty. Because it's high in fat and low in protein, it can be added to sauces, stews, and soups at any temperature without separating. It whips very well, too, making it a delicious substitute for uncultured whipping cream. Even unwhipped it is heavenly either blended in with cooked or fresh fruit or as a topping. Although higher in fat and slightly thinner, crème fraîche can also be substituted for sour cream in any recipe.

Cultured cream butter: Also called European-style butter, cultured cream butter is made from fresh cream that's been fermented with a live lactic acid bacterial culture before the churning process. The culture provides a more complex and slightly tangy flavor and aroma than found in sweet cream butter. It also reduces the amount of lactose, making it more digestible than regular butter.

Fromage blanc: Slightly tart and smooth in texture, fromage blanc can be used instead of sour cream as a topping on fruit, toast, bagels, granola, and baked potatoes, or it can be blended in with cold foods, such as salad dressings, dips, sandwich spreads, and cold sauces. Fromage blanc can be made with either cultured skim milk or whole milk and thus may range in fat content from 0% to 40%. The very low-fat version will separate during cooking, especially at high temperatures, while those with more fat can be added to hot liquids without curdling.

Greek-style yogurt: Also called strained yogurt, Greek yogurt is made by simply straining much of the natural liquid whey from the yogurt, leaving the creamy milk solids behind. Delicious on its own, it can also be used as a lower-fat substitute for cream cheese, mayonnaise, and sour cream.

Kefir: This cultured milk drink that tastes like a thick, tangy milkshake is made by incubating milk at room temperature with a starter culture consisting of naturally occurring bacteria and yeast along with milk proteins. Some products are highly sweetened. Use as a beverage, with cereal, or as a simple sauce over fruit salads.

Quark: A German-style soft white cheese with a slightly tart taste and smooth, creamy texture. It has more butterfat than yogurt but less than cream cheese. Quark can be substituted for sour cream, cream cheese, ricotta, and cottage cheese. It is an excellent accompaniment to all kinds of fruit and a great topping for baked potatoes and works well as a base for spreads, dips, and desserts.

Yogurt: Made from all kinds of milk—cow's, goat's, sheep's, and water buffalo's milk—all yogurt will be cultured with *Lactobacillus bulgaricus* and *Streptococcus thermophilus* at a minimum. Look for labels indicating that the yogurt contains live cultures. Additional types of lactic acid bacteria, such as *L. acidophilus, L. casei, L. rhamnosus, and Bifidobacteria bifidum*, may also be added to dairy products, both for the unique flavor each contributes and for their additional health benefits.

Tips for Serving Cheese

- Cheeses typically used for grating, such as Parmesan and Romano, are also delicious cut and served as snacks, hors d'oeuvres, or dessert accompanied with fruit and bread or crackers.
- Cheese tastes best when served at room temperature. Allow about 1 hour for the cheese to warm up after removing it from the refrigerator.
- To most enjoy their complex flavors, firmer aged cheeses are best thinly sliced or grated.
- Always freshly grate cheese just before cooking or eating for optimum flavor. Any common grater will do the trick. Cheese rasps—narrow, long graters—are idea for grating cheese especially fine.
- Use a small amount of cheese when cooking or at the table to provide additional depth and complexity of flavor to all kinds of foods.
- There's no rule that dessert needs to be sweet! A cheese plate served with fruit and bread or crackers provides a very satisfying ending to a meal—with or without the wine.

Nondairy Alternatives

Nondairy milks are readily available in an ever-expanding array of varieties. They may be made from soybeans, rice, almonds, oats, or hemp seeds and may be flavored with anything from vanilla or chocolate to carob, coffee, green tea, or strawberries. Never use nondairy milk alternatives as a substitute for infant formula; they don't provide adequate nutrition for infants.

Products in shelf-stable aseptic packaging can be stored without refrigeration up to their use-by date, which is typically a year or more after manufacture. Once opened, refrigerate and use within 7 to 10 days. Fresh or refrigerated products must be kept refrigerated at all times.

Nondairy alternatives to cheeses are available, made like processed cheeses from various nondairy milks. Some also contain a milk-derived protein, calcium caseinate, as an ingredient to help them melt, and thus aren't appropriate for people who are lactose intolerant.

Nondairy Milk at a Glance

Type	Protein	Carbohydrate	Fat	Other Features
Nut milk	Moderate	Low	High	Good source of monounsaturated fats.
Oat milk	Low	High	Moderate	Provides beneficial beta-glucan soluble fiber.
Rice milk	Low	High	Low	Naturally very sweet, and the least nutritious of the alternatives.
Soymilk	High	Moderate to high, depending on added sweeteners	Moderate	Good source of isoflavones. Look for unsweetened or minimally sweetened brands.

Seafood

Seafood consumption has soared recently. Its ease of preparation, versatility, and nutritional attributes account for much of seafood's widespread popularity. It's recommended that healthy adults consume at least two 3-ounce servings of seafood per week, particularly those varieties high in two specific omega-3 fatty acids: eicosapentaenoic acid (EPA) and docosahexaenoic acid (DHA). The human body can synthesize both EPA and DHA, in limited amounts, from alpha-linolenic acid, the plant-based omega-3 fatty acid found in flaxseeds, walnuts, pumpkin seeds, and canola oil. However, the preformed, longer-chain EPA and DHA found in fish, which they derive from their diet of algae, plankton, and other fish, are both a more reliable source and more easily used by our bodies.

Words and Terms to Know

Aquaculture: Raising seafood in ponds, cages, or pens anchored in natural bodies of water or in tanks supplied with filtered and oxygenated water. When purchasing aquaculture products, also known as farm-raised fish, look for those from operations that use no antibiotics, supplemental hormones, or toxic chemicals.

Cold-smoked: Smoked over a variety of hardwoods at temperatures between 60°F and 110°F for 24 hours or more, yielding a moist, tender texture.

EPA and DHA: Abbreviations for eicosapentaenoic acid and docosahexaenoic acid, long-chain polyunsaturated omega-3 fatty acids found in fatty cold-water fish. These longer-chain omega-3 fatty acids, derived from the algae and krill they eat, are more biologically potent and more readily utilized by the body than alpha-linolenic acid. They play a crucial role in normal growth and development, facilitate the growth of brain and nerve cells in the developing fetus and throughout life, help reduce inflammation, and help reduce risk of cardiovascular disease.

Hot-smoked: Smoked over a variety of hardwoods at a minimum internal temperature of 145°F and up to 200°F for a much shorter period of time than in cold smoking. Because hot smoking essentially cooks the fish, its moisture content is reduced, yielding a firmer, drier texture and slightly less rich flavor.

Methylmercury: A more readily absorbed and toxic form of mercury. It often originates in a less toxic form as an air pollutant, but ultimately makes its way into bodies of water, where bacteria convert it into methylmercury. Human health risks depend on not only the methylmercury level in seafood, but also how much is eaten, the person's body weight, and individual variations in the body's ability to handle mercury. Babies in the womb and young children are most vulnerable to mercury, as it can adversely affect development of the brain. The more mercury that gets into a person's body, the longer the exposure time, and the younger the person, the more severe the effects are likely to be. Neither cooking nor trimming of fat can reduce mercury levels within a fish, as it is most concentrated in the muscle tissue of fish rather than in fat or oils.

Marine Stewardship Council (MSC): An independent, global, nonprofit organization that promotes responsible fishing practices by allowing fisheries to use MSC's distinctive blue seal on their labels if they meet MSC standard for sustainable and well-managed fisheries. MSC-labeled seafood can be traced from the label right back to the fishery itself to ensure that only fish from certified fisheries is labeled as such.

Buying and Cooking Live Crustaceans

Lobster and crab are classified as decapods, shellfish that have 10 legs and a hard shell to protect them. While they need to be cooked alive because their meat deteriorates rapidly and can become toxic once they're dead, it is now understood that this class of aquatic animals feels and experiences pain and distress. Accordingly, lobster and crab warrant special attention from capture through cooking to minimize suffering—especially with regard to handling methods and living conditions once removed from the water.

Buying and Cooking Lobster and Crab

Look for lobster and crab that have been transported to market within a couple days after capture and sold within seven days of arrival. Because lobsters are solitary animals, and to help reduce injury, they should be transported in containers that have individual compartments. This set-up should be used in seafood market display tanks, which should contain saltwater maintained at very cold temperatures to emulate conditions that would naturally slow down the decapods' heart rate, metabolism, and neural functioning in the wild. At home, lobster and crab should be refrigerated in their original packing and cooked within 24 hours.

Always stun lobster and crab prior to cooking by placing in the freezer for up to 1 to 2 hours, until the animal becomes dormant, but not frozen. Factor a minimum of 30 minutes per pound and another 5 minutes freezing time per each additional ¼ lb. When ready to cook, immediately plunge the lobster or crab into salted water that is already at a rolling boil.

Other Options for Preparing Lobster and Crab

- Some fish shops have an electronic crustacean stunning machine available in-store. This device stuns and kills the lobster within 5 seconds using a 110-volt shock.
- Raw, frozen, vacuum-packed lobster meat is now available; these products use high pressure processing methods that quickly kill lobsters within a chamber, after which they are immediately packaged and frozen to preserve quality and flavor. Not only is it a better option for the

lobster and more convenient and hassle-free for you, it has much better flavor, texture, and appearance than most meat from lobsters that have been boiled alive. It also opens the opportunity for more cooking options, too, including poaching, sautéing, and roasting.

- Buy precooked, dressed crab; pasteurized crabmeat; or frozen cooked crab.

Seafood Buying Guide

Fish	Amount per Person	Cooking Method
Whole fish	¾–1 lb.	Bake, poach, steam, or grill
Dressed fish (gutted and scaled, with head, fins, and gills removed)	½–¾ lb.	Bake, poach, steam, or grill
Fish steaks (sliced crosswise, with a section of backbone and skin)	⅓–½ lb.	Bake, poach, steam, or grill; stir-fry strips and cubed steaks
Fish fillets (boneless sides of fish)	¼–⅓ lb.	Bake, broil, poach, steam, sauté, grill, or stir-fry
Crustaceans and Shellfish	**Amount per Person**	**Cooking Method**
Clams	Live hard shell: 6–8 medium; live soft shell: 12–20; by weight: ⅔–1 lb.; shucked: ¼ pint	Steam, grill, broil, bake, pan-fry, cook in soups or chowders
Crab	Hard shell: 1 lb.; soft shell: 1–2 whole; crabmeat: ¼ lb.	Hard shell crabs: steam, boil, bake, grill; soft shell crabs: steam, boil, bake, grill, sauté

Crustaceans and Shellfish	Amount per Person	Cooking Method
Lobster	Live: 1 lb.; raw, shelled: ⅓ lb.; cooked, shelled: ¼ lb.	Steam, boil, broil, grill
Mussels in the shell	10–12 mussels; by weight: ½ lb; shucked: ¼ pint	Steam, boil, broil, bake, stew, cook in soups
Oysters	In shell: 6–8; shucked: ¼–⅓ pint	Smoke, boil, bake, fry, roast, stew, steam, broil
Scallops, shucked	Sea scallops: 3–4; bay scallops: 6–12; by weight: ¼–⅓ lb.	Sauté, poach, broil, bake
Shrimp	Raw, with shell: ½ lb.; raw and shelled: ⅓ lb.; cooked and shelled: ¼ lb.	Broil, poach, steam, sauté, boil, stir-fry, or grill

Tips for Choosing Safe Seafood

- Buy seafood only from clean, well-maintained markets.
- Odor within the department should be mildly reminiscent of seaweed; there should not be a strong fishy, sour, or ammonia-like smell.
- Seafood should be refrigerated and properly iced on a thick bed of fresh, not melting, ice.
- Cooked seafood products should be separated from raw.
- Seafood should be free of chemical dips and sulfites used to enhance appearance and color.
- Whole fish should have clear eyes that are convex, not sunken, and the skin should be firm and shiny.
- Fillets should be translucent and light in color, not yellowed or dark. The flesh should be firm and springy when pressed.
- Packages of frozen fish should be tightly sealed with no torn areas, crushed edges, or evidence of freezer burn.

Buying Seafood by Texture and Flavor

Texture	Flavor		
	Mild	Moderate	Robust
Delicate	Flounder Sole Wahoo	Sablefish (black cod)	Herring Mussels Oysters Sardines
Medium-firm	Catfish (farm-raised) Cod Crab Grouper Haddock Hake Hoki Lingcod Lobster Orange roughy Pacific snapper (red) Pollock Scallops Shrimps and prawns Tilapia Walleyed pike White sea bass	Golden trout Patagonian tooth-fish (Chilean sea bass) Rainbow trout Rockfish (ocean perch) Steelhead trout Striped bass Tuna (canned)	Arctic char Bluefish Mackerel Salmon
Firm	Halibut	Mahi mahi Shark Sturgeon	Clams Swordfish Tuna (fresh)

Seafood High in EPA and DHA

Omega-3 fatty acids, known to help reduce overall risk of cardiovascular disease, cancer, and inflammation, are more easily used by our bodies when derived from eating fish that are high in EPA (eicosapentaenoic acid) and DHA (docosahexaenoic acid), such as these:

- Atlantic mackerel
- Mussels
- Salmon
- Anchovy
- Pacific oysters
- Sardines
- Herring
- Sablefish
- Trout

Methylmercury in Fish

The FDA has issued the following Consumer Advisory for pregnant and nursing women, young children, and women who may become pregnant:

- Do not eat fish that contain higher levels of mercury. Larger, long-lived fish have a greater potential to accumulate higher levels of mercury in their bodies.
- Eat up to 12 ounces (2 to 3 average meals) a week of fish and shellfish that are lower in mercury. Young children should limit fish consumption to much smaller portions than considered safe for adults.
- Before eating fish caught in local lakes, rivers, and coastal areas, check whether there are any local advisories related to mercury or harmful levels of PCBs.

Fish with Higher Levels of Mercury

- King mackerel
- Swordfish
- Tuna* (fresh and frozen)
- Shark
- Tilefish

*Canned tuna labeled "chunk light" or "chunk" is typically derived from smaller, younger species of tuna that tend to contain less mercury. Limit consumption of albacore tuna, also labeled "solid white" or "chunk white," which comes from larger, longer-lived species of tuna, to 6 ounces per week.

Fish with Lower Levels of Mercury

- Catfish (farm-raised)
- Crab
- Hake
- Oysters
- Salmon
- Scallops
- Tilapia
- Clams
- Haddock
- Herring
- Pollack (Alaskan)
- Sardines
- Shrimp
- Trout (farm-raised)

Reading the Label

Seafood Additives to Avoid

- Chlorine dips (preservative)
- Sodium and potassium bisulfite (preservative, antioxidant, color retention agent)
- Sodium and potassium metabisulfite (preservative, antioxidant, color retention agent)
- Sodium sulfite (preservative, antioxidant, color retention agent)
- Sulfur dioxide (preservative, antioxidant, color retention agent)

Seafood Cooking Guidelines

As a general estimate of cooking time, plan on about 10 minutes per inch of thickness when baking, poaching, grilling, sautéing, or broiling. Measure the fish at its thickest point and add or subtract 2 minutes for each ¼ inch above or below the nearest inch. The fish is done when it turns opaque and just begins to flake when pierced with a fork in its thickest part. Be careful not to overcook. Keep in mind that fish will continue to cook for a few minutes after being removed from the heat, no matter what cooking method you use. While most fish can be prepared using almost any cooking method, there are a few key exceptions. Grilling is best for medium-firm to firm fish and shouldn't be used for delicate fish. Poaching is best for lean fish.

Baking: Preheat the oven to 425°F to 450°F. Place the fish in an oiled baking dish, skin side down if the skin is present. Brush with oil, then top with fresh or dried herbs, salt or tamari, or your favorite sauce, if desired. Gauge the baking time according to the thickness of the fish.

Broiling: Position an oven rack so the fish will be 3 to 4 inches from the heat and preheat the broiler. Brush both sides of the fish with oil, then lay the fish on a broiling pan. Gauge the broiling time on the thickness of the fish, and turn the fish over halfway through cooking.

Grilling: If you want to grill fish that isn't big or firm enough to be made into steaks, use fillets that have the skin attached to keep them from falling apart while grilling. Diagonal slashes cut ¼ inch deep will help keep the fish from curling and shrinking. Small, whole, scaled and gutted thick-skinned fish can also be used. Fish that weigh no more than 3 pounds should be scored diagonally across the thickest part to permit the heat to penetrate uniformly. To avoid losing natural juices over their long grilling time, large whole fish shouldn't be scored.

Prepare a moderately hot grill—hot enough to sear the surface of the flesh but not so hot that the outside is charred before the fish is cooked through. Place the fish on the grill perpendicular to the grill bars to minimize contact with the grill. Brush with melted butter, oil, or an oily sauce to prevent sticking to the grill. Baste frequently with a pastry brush while cooking to seal in the natural juices. Whole scaled and gutted fish weighing more than 3 pounds require a grill cover and slow cooking over a low fire. Test with a small bamboo or metal skewer in the thickest part of the fish. Any resistance of the flesh means it needs more cooking.

Poaching: In a pan large enough to hold the fish in a single layer, pour in enough vegetable or chicken stock, water, or a combination of dry white wine and water to cover the fish by 1 inch. Bring the liquid to a boil, then add the fish, lower the heat, cover, and cook, basing the cooking time on the thickness of the fish.

Sautéing: Preheat a frying pan over medium-high heat. Cook the fish for 2 to 3 minutes per ½-inch of thickness, and until lightly brown on one side, then turn the fish over and finish cooking on the second side for about the same amount of time, once again until lightly browned.

Steaming: Add about 1 inch of plain or seasoned water to the bottom of a pan in which a steamer can be placed. Bring to a boil, then add the fish, cover, and steam for 6 to 8 minutes per inch of thickness.

Stir-frying: Cut steaks or fillets into thin strips or ½-inch cubes. Shrimp and scallops can stay whole. Preheat a wok over medium-high heat, then add 1 to 2 tablespoons of oil per pound of seafood. Add a small amount of seafood, stir-fry until the fish is opaque and flaky or shrimp or scallops are firm and opaque. Remove the first batch from the wok, then add another batch and stir-fry, continuing in this way until all the seafood is cooked.

Fresh and Cooked Seafood Storage Guidelines

Fish	Refrigerator (40°F)	Freezer (0°F or lower)
Cooked fish, all types	3–4 days	3 months
Canned fish, opened	3–4 days	3 months
Smoked fish	14 days or use-by date	2 months in vacuum package
Fresh lean fillets	1–2 days in original wrapping, best enclosed within a plastic bag and sitting on a layer of ice within a bowl or pan	4–6 months
Fresh fatty fillets	1–2 days in original wrapping, best enclosed within a plastic bag and sitting on a layer of ice within a bowl or pan	2–3 months
Crustaceans and Shellfish	Refrigerator (40°F)	Freezer (0°F or lower)
Cooked shrimp, shellfish, and crustaceans	3–4 days	3 months
Clams, live in shell*	2–3 days in a shallow pan covered with damp cloth	N/A
Clams, shucked	1–2 days in a tightly covered container, immersed in their liquid	3 months
Crab, live	1 day, loosely enclosed in a paper bag	N/A
Crabmeat	2–3 days in tightly sealed container	4 months

Crustaceans and Shellfish	Refrigerator (40°F)	Freezer (0°F or lower)
Lobster, live	1 day, loosely enclosed in a paper bag	N/A
Mussels, live in shell*	2–3 days in a shallow pan covered with a damp cloth	N/A
Mussels, shucked	1–2 days in a tightly covered container, immersed in their liquid	3 months
Oysters, live in shell*	5–7 days with curved side down in a shallow pan covered with damp cloth.	N/A
Oysters, shucked	5–7 days in a tightly covered container, immersed in their liquid	3 months
Scallops, shucked	1–2 days in original wrapping; best enclosed within a plastic bag and sitting on a layer of ice in a bowl or pan	3 months
Shrimp, raw	2–3 days in original wrapping; best enclosed within a plastic bag and sitting on a layer of ice in a bowl or pan	4 months

* Discard any shellfish with cracked shells or whose shells fail to close when tapped.

Seafood Safety Tips

- Keep fish cold on ice when transporting from the market and refrigerate immediately when you arrive home.
- Prevent cross-contamination. Thoroughly wash your hands, kitchen countertop, utensils, dishes, and cutting boards with soap and hot water before and after contact with raw fish and seafood.
- Always marinate seafood in the refrigerator. Do not reuse the marinade as a sauce unless it is first brought to a rolling boil.
- Cook most seafood to an internal temperature of 145°F.
- Do not allow cooked fish to stand at room temperature for more than 2 hours after cooking, or 1 hour at warm room temperatures. Bacteria thrive at temperatures between 45°F and 115°F, so keep seafood either below 40°F or above 140°F, depending on whether the dish is intended to be served hot or cold.
- Thaw frozen fish only in the refrigerator, not at room temperature. Allow about 24 hours for a 1-pound package. To retain more juices and moisture, don't thaw frozen fish completely. If a quick thaw is needed, place the fish in a sealable plastic bag and place in a pan of cold water in the refrigerator. Use thawed frozen fish within 24 hours.

Essential Seasonings

Ask people to describe the primary flavors in food, and they're likely to list four: sweet, salty, sour, and bitter. That a fifth flavor exists may be surprising, but that elusive savory sensation experienced when all the flavor and aroma components come together in a food now has a name: umami (oo-MOM-ee). In fact, umami has been around for a long time. It was first identified in 1908, when research was conducted on kombu, the seaweed that provides the flavor-enhancing properties of dashi, a fundamental broth in Japanese cuisine. The study determined that when the amino acid glutamic acid exists in an unbound form, not linked to other amino acids, it helps provide the subtle taste of umami, which has an ability to expand and round out flavors. Mushrooms, ripe tomatoes, Parmesan cheese, and cured ham all provide umami, as do sea vegetables, soy sauce, and miso. Use any of these ingredients when cooking and a kind of magic begins.

Words and Terms to Know

Gomasio: Also known as sesame salt. This low-sodium alternative to salt is made from ground toasted sesame seeds and sea salt. Use as a condiment on cooked vegetables, grains, and beans.

Herbs: The leaves of low-growing annual or perennial plants that generally grow in temperate climates.

Mirin: A sweet cooking wine made from sweet rice, rice *koji* (a cultured rice product), and water. Avoid varieties that contain sugar and chemical fermenting agents. Mirin can be used in marinades, salad dressings, sauces, and noodle and vegetable dishes, and in overly pungent or salty dishes that need rebalancing.

Miso: A thick, versatile seasoning paste made from cooked soybeans mixed with water and *koji* (cooked grain or soybeans inoculated with a mold that starts the fermentation process). Depending on the type of miso being produced, the aging time may range between two months and three years. Each variety of miso reflects the microorganisms native to the area in which it is made, having a unique flavor and sometimes a unique appearance. Use miso to season sauces, stews, gravies, salad dressings, dips, spreads, and marinades. It can even serve as a stand-in for Parmesan cheese for a new spin on pesto.

Mustard: A condiment that varies in flavor depending on the type of mustard seeds used, whether it includes wine or vinegar, and the particular types of herbs and spices used. Yellow mustard seeds are mild, brown are pungent, and Oriental are sharp in flavor. Most mustards are made from a combination of seeds rather than one variety. Mustards also vary in texture.

Pickled ginger: A condiment made from thinly sliced young, tender ginger roots. The slices are salted, briefly pressed, and then pickled in rice vinegar with shiso leaves. Avoid varieties made with preservatives and artificial color. Serve with sushi, norimaki, and other entrées for flavor and color. It's also delicious as an addition to sandwiches and dips.

Shiso leaf powder: A salty-sour condiment made from the dried purple leaves of the perilla, or beefsteak, plant. (Shiso leaves are also pickled with umeboshi plums.) Use on vegetables, salads, or grains.

Shoyu: Also known as tamari shoyu. Made from soybeans, wheat, water, and sea salt, this naturally produced soy sauce has a rich, savory aroma and a sweeter flavor than tamari. It is best added at the end of cooking or used as a condiment.

Spices: Dried aromatic or pungent seasonings derived from the bark, roots, buds, fruits, berries, or seeds of various plants.

Tamari: Naturally produced, wheat-free soy sauce made from soybeans, water, and sea salt. It has a stronger, deeper flavor than shoyu and is best added to foods while they are cooking.

Umeboshi plums: Made from sour, unripe fruits of the ume tree, which is actually more closely related to an apricot than a plum. The fruits are pickled with sea salt, dried in the sun, and then added to a brine containing dark red shiso leaves, which function as a natural preservative and contribute a natural red dye. Umeboshi plums are sold in whole pickled plum form and also as a convenient paste, with the pits removed. Use in nori rolls and rice balls as well as dips, spreads, salad dressings, sauces, broths, cooked grains, and vegetable dishes. Try the paste spread lightly on cooked corn on the cob instead of butter.

Wasabi: A Japanese horseradish that's less sharp and more aromatic than regular horseradish. High-quality wasabi powder has a dull, greenish color; avoid artificially colored varieties. Mix equal amounts of water with wasabi to form a paste. Cover and let sit for 10 minutes to allow the flavor to develop.

Salt Selection Guide

Finishing salt: Salt produced in open pools with monitored, slow drying and hands-on processing to create broad, irregular, plate-shaped or pyramid-shaped crystals. Fine finishing salts have a crunchy texture that enhances the tasting experience, producing a pleasant burst of flavor on the palate, very unlike the sharp taste of the small solid crystals of common table salt.

Iodized salt: Salt that with added potassium iodide to help ensure people get enough iodine for proper functioning of the thyroid gland, which regulates a wide variety of processes within the body, including growth, development, metabolism, and reproductive function. Iodine deficiency is recognized as the leading preventable cause of brain damage worldwide. A very small amount of dextrose (0.04%) is added to iodized salt to stabilize the potassium iodide and prevent it from breaking down and evaporating.

Kosher salt: Termed "kosher" because it is used to prepare meat according to Jewish dietary guidelines. Continually raking salt brine during evaporation creates coarse, irregular crystals, which tend to cling to meat. Beyond this traditional use, kosher salt works well in recipes that include enough water to allow it to dissolve and disperse. It can also be used as a crunchy topping on meat, fish, pretzels, and breads.

Pickling salt: Specifically developed for pickling applications. It has no iodine, which could discolor pickles, and no anticaking agents, which could settle on the bottom of the jar.

Rock salt: Also known as mined salt. Obtained from inland salt mines, rock salt is used in a wide variety ways: as deicing agent for roads in winter, as salt licks for livestock, as a freezing aid for making homemade ice cream, and, of course, as a seasoning agent. Through an extraction method called room-and-pillar mining, miners blast and drill to remove big chunks of salt, leaving large pillars of salt in place to hold up the roof of the mine. The extracted salt is brought up to the surface, crushed, and screened.

Sea salt: Salt extracted from saltwater. In addition to sodium chloride, unrefined sea salt retains many of the trace minerals found in the sea, although some brands of sea salt are hardly different from typical mined table salt, being harvested and dried on a large scale and refined to remove most minerals, ultimately yielding 99.5% pure sodium chloride. Sea salts may even be evaporated in such a way as to create the same small, dense, cubic crystals found in common table salt, and anticaking agents and iodine are often added. While refined sea salt, like common mined table salt, is fine for general cooking, its flavor is too sharp to function as a finishing salt. At the other end of the spectrum, unrefined salt from unpolluted areas is still traditionally produced in much the same manner as it was centuries ago. During the crystallization stage, the salts in the seawater are encouraged to precipitate using unique techniques that ultimately determine the size, shape, texture, and color of the finished salt.

Table salt: Highly refined salt mined from salt mines or from saltwater. It often contains iodine and additives to make it free-flowing. Compared to sea salt and kosher salt, its flavor is fairly mediocre.

Vinegar Selection Guide

Apple cider vinegar: A tart, apple-flavored vinegar produced from hard apple cider. Use in salad dressings and as a general condiment.

Balsamic vinegar: A dark, dense, syrupy vinegar that is both sweet and slightly tart, the result of a complex aging process that involves transferring the vinegar into increasingly smaller barrels each year. Use in salad dressings and marinades, and as a condiment for fruit, vegetables, and grains.

Fruit vinegar: Light, fresh-flavored vinegars made by infusing the flavor of raspberry, strawberry, or blueberry into white wine vinegar. Use in salad dressings and marinades, and as a condiment for vegetables, fruit salads, and grains.

Herb vinegar: Cider, red wine, or white wine vinegars steeped with herbs. Use on salads.

Malt vinegar: A distinctly flavored vinegar made by fermenting a liquid extract of malted barley. Use in hot and cold vegetable dishes and sautéed potatoes, and, of course, with fish and chips.

Rice vinegar: Also known as rice wine vinegar. Has a slightly sweet, smooth, mellow flavor with about half the sharpness of cider vinegar. Brown rice vinegar has a more full-bodied taste than white rice vinegar. Use in salad dressings and sauces, and as a condiment on fish, vegetables, and grain dishes.

Sherry vinegar: Has a mellow, full-bodied flavor with a sweet aftertaste. Use in dressings for fruit salads and vegetable salads featuring cheeses.

Umeboshi vinegar: A salty, tangy-flavored condiment that isn't a true vinegar but the liquid drawn off of pickled umeboshi plums. Use it in salad dressings, dips, and marinades, or as a condiment on vegetables, beans, and grains.

Wine vinegar: Made from either red or white wine. Red wine vinegar is more pungent and best with strong-flavored greens, meats, cheese dishes, and salads. White wine vinegar has a more delicate flavor and is best with mild-tasting greens.

Cooking with Miso

Miso is high in sodium, so it can be used to replace salt. In general, 1 teaspoon of dark miso is approximately equivalent to 1½ to 2 teaspoons of light miso or about ⅛ teaspoon of salt. A good rule of thumb is to use no more than ½ to 1 teaspoon of dark miso or 1 to 2 teaspoons of light miso per serving. For extra depth of flavor and an interesting interplay of sweet and salty, miso can be used instead of salt when making desserts or it may be added

Miso at a Glance

Light Miso Types	Characteristics
Sweet white miso (shiro miso)	Made from soybeans and rice Sweet, some caramel undertones; creamy texture, white or pale yellow to caramel color
Mellow white miso	Made from soybeans and rice Mildly sweet, subtly tart, smooth texture, medium yellow to light brown color
Chickpea miso	Made from chickpeas and rice Mild and sweet with chickpea flavor undertones, beige color
Dark Miso Types	**Characteristics**
Red miso (aka miso)	Made from soybeans and white rice Salty, savory flavor, thick creamy texture, reddish brown color
Brown rice miso (genmai miso)	Made from soybeans and brown rice Salty, medium/strong savory flavor, thick creamy texture, golden brown color
Barley miso (mugi miso)	Made from soybeans and barley Salty, deep, rich winey flavor, subtle sweetness, thick texture, medium to dark brown color
Soybean miso (hatcho miso)	Made from soybeans Salty, hearty flavor, thick fudge-like texture, very dark reddish brown color

to oatmeal and other hot cereals just before serving, substituting about 1 tablespoon of light miso or 2 teaspoons of dark miso for ¼ teaspoon of salt. For best results, mix miso in a small amount of broth or water and stir it to form a paste before adding it to soups, sauces, or other dishes. Adding it 3 to 4 minutes before serving will activate its beneficial bacteria and enzymes, but to avoid destroying those beneficial components only add miso to foods when their temperature is far below a boil.

How to Use

Dips, spreads, salad dressings, glazes, topping for sweet corn or baked potatoes

Dips, warm-weather soups, spreads, salad dressings, glazes, topping for sweet corn or baked potatoes

Dips, warm-weather soups, spreads, salad dressings, glazes

How to Use

All-purpose variety: use in miso soups, sauces, spreads, marinades, dips, salad dressings

Soups, sauces, spreads, marinades

Soups, sauces, spreads, marinades

Soups, stews, sauces

Sea Vegetables at a Glance

Dried sea vegetables will keep indefinitely in cool, dry, dark conditions. Store cooked sea vegetables for up to 5 days in the refrigerator.

Type	Characteristics	Flavor	Uses
Agar	Off-white translucent bars, flakes, or powder	Neutral	Gelling agent in desserts, vegetable aspics, puddings, and pie fillings
Alaria	Very dark green, almost black leaves	Mild, sweet	Soups, salads, and condiments
Arame	Long, black strands	Mild, sweet	Salads, vegetable side dishes, savory pie and strudel fillings
Dulse	Reddish purple leaves	Tangy, salty	Sandwiches, salads, condiments, and stews
Kelp (Atlantic)	Very dark green leaves	Flavor enhancer	Natural tenderizer and flavor enhancer for beans, soups, stews, and broths
Kombu	Stiff, dark green, broad, flat leaves	Flavor enhancer	Flavor enhancer in beans, soups, stews, broths, vegetable dishes, and condiments

Cooking Guidelines

To gel 2 cups of liquid, use 3 to 4 tablespoons of agar flakes, 2 teaspoons of agar powder, or 1 agar bar. Add to 2 cups of juice, broth, or water. Bring to a boil, lower the heat, and simmer for 10 minutes, stirring to thoroughly dissolve the agar. Transfer the liquid to a heatproof mold and allow it to set. Agar will set at room temperature, but the gelling process is much quicker in the refrigerator, taking only about 45 to 60 minutes.

In soup, use about a 5-inch strip of alaria per quart of liquid. Should be simmered for at least 10 minutes or pressure-cooked for 5 to 6 minutes. In salads, use alaria that has already been cooked or soak it in water or diluted lemon juice for 12 hours.

Rinse and soak arame for about 15 minutes before cooking. Always cook arame before adding it to salads or casseroles.

Briefly rinse dulse or soak it for up to 5 minutes then squeeze out the salty water. When cooking, add dulse about 5 minutes before the dish is done.

Rinse Atlantic kelp quickly under cold running water to remove excess salt. For a light-flavored broth, add a 5-inch piece to 1 quart water, place over medium heat, and remove the kelp just before the water comes to a boil. Atlantic kelp is best simmered for 15 to 20 minutes or pressure-cooked for 5 minutes.

When using as a flavoring agent for a broth or sauce or before adding it to recipes that include a moderate to high amount of liquid, rinse it quickly under cold running water or wipe it with a clean, damp cloth to remove the excess salt. For a light-flavored broth, add a small piece of kombu, about 3 inches long, to 1 quart water, place over medium heat, and remove the kombu just before the water comes to a boil. The longer the kombu remains in the cooking water, the stronger the broth will be.

Sea Vegetables at a Glance, *cont'd*

Type	Characteristics	Flavor	Uses
Laver	Purple to black leaves	Vegetable-like, neutral	Side dishes, condiments, and salads
Nori	Purple to black, paper-thin sheets	Vegetable-like, neutral	Sushi, rice balls, and as a garnish for soups, salads, grains, noodles, and popcorn
Sea palm	dark green ribbon-shaped leaves	Subtly sweet	Salads, soups, and vegetable sautés
Wakame	Dark greenish leaves	Vegetable-like	Miso soups, broths, salads, and stews

Cooking Guidelines

Traditionally, laver is slowly simmered for many hours into a thick, gelatinous puree and then eaten as a side dish. It is also used as the basis for laverbread, a recipe with a four-to-one ratio of laver to finely cut whole oats, which is formed into patties and fried.

To toast nori, hold it a couple of inches above a stove burner. Within seconds, it will change from greenish black to a more vibrant green and become crisp.

Sea palm is generally available only in dried form. For use in salads, soak sea palm in water for 1 hour prior to use. Alternatively, simmer it in water for 5 minutes, then cool and add it to other salad ingredients. For soup, soak it for 10 minutes before proceeding with the recipe.

Minimal soaking and cooking needed. Rinse to remove surface dirt, presoak for 3 to 5 minutes, then squeeze out the excess water. Don't soak it longer, as it will become too slippery. After its tough ribs are trimmed away, wakame can be added to salads or cooked for at least 5 minutes in soups and stews or with veggies. It isn't necessary to presoak instant wakame for use in soups, broths, and stews; just add it to the cooking water. Presoak instant wakame for 2 to 3 minutes before using in salads.

Reading the Label

Condiment and Sauce Additives to Avoid

- Artificial color
- Calcium disodium EDTA (antioxidant, sequestrant)
- Disodium guanylate (flavor enhancer)
- Disodium inosinate (flavor enhancer)
- Potassium sorbate (preservative, antifungal agent)
- Sodium benzoate (preservative, antifungal agent)

Sweeteners

There's no denying that sometimes nothing hits the spot more than something really sweet. Blame it on our genes. Since poisonous plants generally contain bitter alkaloids, scientists speculate this penchant for sweets may have evolved as a protective mechanism to ensure that our early ancestors ate enough high-calorie but nontoxic foods to survive through times of scarcity. However, in these days of plenty, the challenge is to choose sugars wisely and consume them in moderation to maintain a healthy weight. Because sugars contain so few nutrients in relation to their calories, minimizing their intake also helps ensure your diet is comprised of a high percentage of nourishing foods that contribute optimum health and well-being.

Words and Terms to Know

Artificial sweeteners: Synthetic compounds produced through complex chemical processes. Because they have no counterparts in nature, our bodies are ill-equipped to deal with them. They're many magnitudes sweeter than table sugar, so only a tiny amount is needed to sweeten foods, which means they contribute virtually no calories. As such, they are classified as nonnutritive sweeteners. They also don't affect blood sugar levels. Unlike other sugars, artificial sweeteners are devoid of functional properties that contribute flavor, texture, and other attributes to the foods they're combined with. The only thing they deliver is a sweet flavor, although they often have a disagreeable aftertaste. Many of them aren't stable at a wide range of temperatures, which can also contribute to off flavors.

High-fructose corn syrup: Often abbreviated to HFCS. This highly processed nutritive sweetener is created by treating cornstarch with acids and/or enzymes to convert the starch into sugars. HFCS has the same relative sweetness level as refined sugar; however, despite what its name might imply, high-fructose corn syrup requires more insulin for its metabolism than is typically expected with fructose. Food manufacturers like high-fructose corn syrup because it's much less expensive than refined sugar and extends shelf life. It also provides better browning and softer texture in baked goods, and it's easier to blend into beverages. As a result, it makes an appearance in a long list of convenience foods and beverages, contributing to its controversial nature as a sweetener implicated in obesity and other health problems.

Minimally processed natural sweeteners: Tried and true plant-derived sweeteners, including agave nectar, amasake, barley malt syrup, birch syrup, brown rice syrup, cane syrup, date sugar, unaltered 100% fruit juice or juice concentrates, honey, maple syrup and maple sugar, molasses, sorghum syrup, stevia, and the many iterations of natural sugar from sugarcane or sugar beets, including evaporated cane juice: Demerara sugar, muscovado sugar, turbinado sugar, white sugar, brown sugar, and golden syrup. These sweeteners have proven to be exceptional in flavor and extremely effective in cooking and baking, not to mention safe and nontoxic.

Polyols: Also known as sugar alcohols. This class of carbohydrates includes erythritol, hydrogenated starch hydrolysates, isomalt, lactitol, maltitol, mannitol, sorbitol, and xylitol. In comparison to white sugar, polyols can be anywhere from 50% to 90% as sweet. Polyols are especially recognized for certain health-associated characteristics. Because they're metabolized differently than true sugars, they don't raise blood sugar and insulin levels to the same degree. Nor do they promote tooth decay, since they aren't as readily metabolized by bacteria in the mouth. They typically they provide about half the amount of calories as other sugars, depending on the polyol.

Refined sugar: Sweeteners fully processed to remove naturally occurring fiber and nutrients and thereby concentrate the simple sugars.

Unrefined sugar: Sweeteners partially processed to remove naturally occurring fiber and nutrients and thereby concentrate the simple sugars.

Sugar Substitution Guidelines

Here are some handy guidelines for substituting alternative sweeteners for granulated white or brown sugar. For each cup of sugar make the following adjustments to amounts of ingredients.

Type	Substitute per 1 Cup Sugar	Adjustment to Liquids in Recipe	Other Modifications
Agave nectar	¾ cup	Decrease by ⅓ cup	Lower oven by 25°F
Barley malt syrup	1⅓ cups	Decrease by ¼ cup	Add ¼ teaspoon baking soda
Birch syrup	1 cup	Decrease by ¼ cup	None
Brown rice syrup	1–1¼ cups	Decrease by 3 tablespoons	Add ⅛–¼ teaspoon baking soda
Cane syrup	1⅓ cups	Decrease by ⅓ cup	None
Corn syrup	¾ cup	Decrease by 3 tablespoons	None
Date sugar	1 cup	No adjustment needed	Substitute for brown sugar
Fruit juice concentrate	1 cup	Decrease by ⅓ cup	Add ¼ teaspoon baking soda
Fruit juice concentrate (extra-reduced)	½–¾ cup	Decrease by ⅓ cup	Add ¼ teaspoon baking soda; lower oven by 25°F
Honey	½–¾ cup	Decrease by 2–3 tablespoons	Add ¼ teaspoon baking soda

Type	Substitute per 1 Cup Sugar	Adjustment to Liquids in Recipe	Other Modifications
Maple sugar	1 cup	No adjustment needed	None
Maple syrup	¾ cup	Decrease by 2 table-spoons	Add ¼ teaspoon baking soda
Molasses	1⅓ cups	Decrease by ⅓ cup	Add a scant ½ teaspoon baking soda; lower oven by 25°F
Sorghum syrup	1⅓ cups	Decrease by ⅓ cup	None

Refined Natural Specialty Sugars at a Glance

These different varieties of sugar can be substituted one to one for granulated sugar.

Type	Color	Texture	Flavor
Demerara	Light golden brown	Crunchy, slightly sticky	Mild molasses flavor
Evaporated cane juice	Tan or slightly golden	Finely granulated	Subtle taste
Muscovado, dark	Dark brown	Extra-moist, sticky, fine-grained	Toffee flavor
Muscovado, light	Light brown	Moist, fine-grained	Butterscotch flavor
Sucanat	Dark golden brown	Porous granules	Rich molasses flavor
Turbinado	Light golden brown	Medium-sized granules	Mild molasses flavor

Reading the Label

Confection, Topping, and Sweet Snack Additives to Avoid

- Artificial color
- Artificial flavor
- Artificial sweeteners
- Butylated hydroxyanisole (BHA, antioxidant, preservative)
- Butylated hydroxytoluene (BHT, antioxidant, preservative)
- Hydrogenated vegetable oil
- Partially hydrogenated vegetable oil
- Potassium sorbate (preservative, antifungal agent)
- Sodium benzoate (preservative, antifungal agent)
- Sorbic acid (preservative, antifungal agent)
- Sulfur dioxide (preservative, antioxidant, color retention agent)
- Tertiary butylhydroquinone (TBHQ, antioxidant, preservative)
- Vanillin (artificial flavor)

Maple Syrup

Thanks to strict laws in both the United States and Canada, it's easy to distinguish imitation maple products from the real thing. Neither country allows the term "maple syrup" or "maple sugar" to appear on products that aren't pure. Instead, phrases such as "pancake syrup with artificial maple flavor" or "artificial maple flavor sweetener" are required to ensure consumers are not misled. Different grading terms are applied to maple syrups from Canada, Vermont, and the United States at large. Here's a guide to grading terms and qualities:

Maple Syrup Grades at a Glance

Grade	Description
U.S. Grade A Light Amber Vermont Fancy Canadian No. 1 Extra Light	These syrups, made from first sap flows of the season, have a delicate maple flavor and are best for table use.
U.S. Grade A Medium Amber Vermont Grade A Medium Amber Canadian No. 1 Light Grade A	This is the most popular grade for pancakes. Generally made from the mid-season sap run, it has a slightly darker, amber color and a gentle but more pronounced flavor. It's great for table use and good for cooking and baking.
U.S. Grade A Dark Amber Vermont Grade A Dark Amber Canadian No. 1 Medium Grade A	Generally made later in the season, this grade is darkly colored and richly flavored. It's great for table use and good for cooking and baking.
U.S. Grade B Vermont Grade B Canadian No. 2 Amber	Even darker in color and stronger in flavor, this grade is generally the last produced in the season. It's best for cooking and baking and good for table use.

Conversion Charts

U.S. Measure Equivalencies

Teaspoons, Tablespoons, Cups, and Fluid Ounces	
pinch or dash	less than ⅛ teaspoon
1½ teaspoons	½ tablespoon
3 teaspoons	1 tablespoon
1 tablespoon	½ fluid ounce
4 tablespoons	¼ cup or 2 fluid ounces
5⅓ tablespoons	⅓ cup
6 tablespoons	3 fluid ounces
8 tablespoons	½ cup or 4 fluid ounces
12 tablespoons	¾ cup or 6 fluid ounces
16 tablespoons	1 cup or 8 fluid ounces

Cups, Pints, Quarts, Gallons, and Fluid Ounces	
1 cup	½ pint or 8 fluid ounces
2 cups	1 pint or 16 fluid ounces
4 cups	1 quart or 32 fluid ounces
2 quarts	½ gallon
4 quarts	1 gallon
Ounces and Pounds	
2 ounces	⅛ pound
4 ounces	¼ pound
5⅓ ounces	⅓ pound
8 ounces	½ pound
10⅔ ounces	⅔ pound
12 ounces	¾ pound
16 ounces	1 pound

Metric Measure Equivalencies

Milliliters, Liters, and U.S. Volumes	
4.9 milliliters	1 teaspoon
14.8 milliliters	1 tablespoon
236.6 milliliters	1 cup
946.4 milliliters	1 quart
1 deciliter	6⅔ tablespoons
¼ liter	1 cup + 2¼ teaspoons
½ liter	1 pint + 4½ teaspoons
1 liter	1,000 milliliters or 1.06 quarts (1 quart + scant ¼ cup)

Grams, Kilograms, and U.S. Weights	
1 gram	0.0353 ounces
28.35 grams	1 ounce
100 grams	3½ ounces
227 grams	8 ounces or ½ pound
453.59 grams	16 ounces or 1 pound
1 kilogram	1,000 grams or 2.21 pounds (2 pounds + 3¼ ounces)

Metric Conversion Factors

ounces to grams	multiply ounces by 28.35
grams to ounces	multiply grams by 0.035
pounds to grams	multiply pounds by 453.6
ounces to milliliters	multiply ounces by 29.6
cups to liters	multiply cups by 0.24

Oven Temperature Conversions

Farenheit (°F)	Celsius (°C)	Gas Mark
250°	120°	½
275°	140°	1
300°	150°	2
325°	160°	3
350°	180°	4
375°	190°	5
400°	200°	6
425°	220°	7
450°	230°	8
475°	240°	9
500°	260°	10

Index